THE MARGINS

THE COMMONS, BOOK 2

MICHAEL ALAN PECK

DINUHOS ARTS, LLC

*For all the loved ones, friends, classmates, and fellow travelers lost.
Somewhere, past is present.*

It is not down in any map; true places never are.

— Herman Melville

PART I

INTERREGNUM

1

A DRAMA THAT WASN'T THEIRS

Ray-Anne Blair knew the mob-movie rule about keeping your friends close and your enemies closer. She also knew it didn't work for her.

She didn't have any enemies.

She had only one true friend.

And right now, she wasn't even sure about him.

"I don't want to die, Rain," Paul Reid said. "There's just something I have to do."

Ray-Anne waited. Maybe Paul would give something away—some sort of tell that would let her know this was a game he was playing.

Trouble was, Paul meant every word.

So, no. Ray-Anne wasn't sure about Paul at all.

The two of them sat in one of the common rooms at the Stella Grace House, a recovery facility that had a reciprocal agreement with New Beginnings Chicago. Their wicker chairs sported thick cushions with swirling galaxy patterns on them.

Pop Mike had been to see Paul before Ray-Anne and stayed for the few days he was able to get away from New

Beginnings New York. He'd told Ray-Anne that *stella* was Latin for star, and the chairs backed him up.

The stellar chairs didn't do anything to leaven Ray-Anne's mood, however. She kept hooking the cuff of her sweater on a spike of broken wicker, and she was certain that before she left, she'd have a pull in her sleeve and would have to put the garment on death watch.

Death watch.

Was that what Paul was on now?

"Rain—"

"That's the second time you've called me that."

Still nothing to indicate that Paul was messing with her. So why the wrong name? He tried to inch closer so that their knees would touch, but she wouldn't give him that. She folded her legs up under her.

And hooked her sleeve again.

Everything was terrible. Everything.

The kid on the other side of the room—the impossibly skinny one with the hair like a bed of nails—kept whistling the same bit of Vivaldi or Bach while he arranged and rearranged the little plastic Noah's Ark animals surrounding him. He looped like a human sampler, refusing to continue with whatever piece it was but never granting her the mercy of stopping.

"Did you know Hillary Clinton was born here?" Paul said.

Ray-Anne didn't tell him that was another place, but the mistake encouraged her. Maybe she was getting him to open up.

Paul tried to turn his ring—and found for the umpteenth time that he wasn't wearing it. His disappointment gave her a tiny rush of shameful gratification. Did caring about someone become a desire to see them suffer a little just because they let you down?

"Do you think you can get it back?" Paul rubbed his vacant finger, and Ray-Anne's schadenfreude made way for the returning grief of what he had tried to do to himself. "I don't know why they took it. It's not dangerous."

The kid with the thirty-penny hair cycled through the notes again. His consistency was remarkable—the sequence the same every time, as if its source were a sound file and not pursed human lips.

Paul saw her irritation. "Huey," he told the boy. "Silent mode, please."

Silent mode.

Right.

A ringtone.

That was it. A living ringtone.

Maybe the kid learned that little segment from someone's phone. Either way, he cut out the whistling and hummed to himself at a much more bearable volume.

"Mozart," said Paul. "But only that little part of it. I don't think he even knows what he's whistling. I didn't until Pop Mike told me."

Not Bach, then. Pop Mike would have known, certainly. Of all his beloved classical, Amadeus was his favorite.

"The weird thing?" Paul leaned forward to make his point. "I never heard Huey whistle before Pop Mike came here. Never. Not once."

Huey hummed and positioned his animals just so. He had quite a set to play with, and they all looked brand new, not the usual beat-up toys you'd find in a hospital or doctor's office. He looked to be maybe ten years old—too old for plastic animals, probably—but there was something adultlike about how he arranged the figures.

The animals all faced a plastic ark with a hut on top and a boarding ramp from deck to ground. The assortment was an odd sampling of the animal kingdom that exposed the silliness of the Noah story. How had Noah and his wife managed to gather both beavers and gorillas before everything washed out?

The scale, too, was a problem, assuming the menagerie was all one set. The hippos, elephants, and aardvarks were all the same size. And the population wouldn't fit into the ark in any manner that would be livable.

Paul watched Ray-Anne watch Huey. "How did you get in here?"

"What do you mean?"

"Pop Mike was my legal guardian, so he has visitation rights. And after all this, I guess he might be again. But they're not supposed to let anyone else in without asking me."

"You don't want me here?"

"Of course I do."

"I cried. That's why they let me in, Paul. I lost it."

Paul had nothing to say to that. He'd never seen Ray-Anne cry. He probably hadn't thought her capable.

Nor had she.

"You acted like you were upset?"

"I am upset, dumbass."

That stopped him again. She'd never called him names before, either.

"So is Pop. Does that surprise you, too?" Ray-Anne hadn't expected to sound so harsh, but she didn't let it bother her. Pop Mike left them alone for almost a year after launching New Beginnings Chicago because he wanted them to know he trusted them to run things. And now his first visit wasn't to tell them how well they'd done or how proud he was.

No.

He had to come running because Paul decided to get cute with a bunch of pills and a plastic bag.

"We're both a little upset right now," Ray-Anne said. "You should have seen him at Midway. I waited for a half hour after his flight left to make sure he got on."

Cowed, Paul had eyes only for the neutral territory of the ark and animals.

Huey.

There would be no two-by-two for Huey.

For one thing, whoever collected the assortment acquired more than a pair of each creature. There were at least three hippos and five lions. And Huey had carefully laid out a scenario that looked like nothing from the Bible. Noah and his wife weren't trying to get the animals on board. It was more like they were fleeing a flood of beasts intent on devouring them.

The animals were closing in on all sides. Mrs. Noah was halfway up the gangplank, positioned to tell her laggard husband, loitering at the bottom, to speed it up if he hoped to save his hide.

Of course, that was all Ray-Anne's imagining since the plastic figure was posed in a permanent state of standing calm, feet affixed to a base. In fact, it wasn't clear how the missus avoided sliding down the steeply angled gangplank. Maybe Huey had glued her. Noah, just steps ahead of the encroaching horde, also stood stoically on a base of his own.

Still, there was something about the arrangement that suggested a mad struggle for self-preservation. If Ray-Anne side-eyed the scene, there was definitely the sense that Noah was flat-out running for it while his wife told him not to look back, whatever he did.

"I haven't slept in three weeks," said Paul.

Ray-Anne freed her sleeve from the wicker spike again. "That's not possible."

He tipped his head one way and then the other. "I think a

whole lot of things are possible. I'm just not sure I should admit it because I might not want to know what they are."

"You can't stay up for three weeks, Paul. You'd go crazy."

He started to laugh but stopped. There wasn't much funny about that. Because maybe he had.

Edsel, the nurse who'd escorted Ray-Anne in earlier, entered the room to have a look around. A former Northwestern lineman whose imposing size was more than offset by a ready grin, he'd proven to be a soft touch when she broke down while begging to be allowed in. He smiled at Ray-Anne and Paul and ignored Huey altogether.

Ray-Anne couldn't blame him. He probably had to put up with the eternally looping whistle every day.

Paul gave Edsel a nod to assure him everything was okay and waited for him to continue his rounds. "There's always the chance they didn't take it from me to keep me from hurting myself, you know."

"Take what?"

"My mother's—my ring. Last night I had this sort of waking dream. Everybody in here was fighting over it. And I was thinking that's the real reason they don't want me to have it. It's like it's the One Ring or something. And everyone would kill for it."

Huey began whistling again.

"I don't think that's it, though," Paul said. "I mean, it's against the rules for me to have anything personal in here because it's safer that way. Nothing for us to argue over. But it's convenient for them, too. I think they're afraid the ring will help me remember what I need to do."

Ray-Anne wanted to tell him how nuts he sounded. And she would have, but she was hiding some wacky stuff of her own.

Things that should have happened only in dreams but occurred during the day, when she was awake and lucid. Things that were real enough for her to worry she might be hallucinating. Or that something was very wrong with her mind.

She couldn't let anyone know—couldn't land in a facility, like Paul. She couldn't say why that was such a fear, but she did not want anyone cooping her up where she could be examined and have a data file started on her.

Ray-Anne had no concrete basis for that, but it didn't matter. She couldn't allow it. She also couldn't tell Paul what it did to her to be in Stella Grace with him at the moment. Just as she couldn't say why it freaked her out to have him call her Rain. That wasn't her name, obviously.

But it was more than that.

Paul wasn't the only one to say it—or to sound like he did. At least a couple of times a week, when someone said her name quickly or from a distance, the two syllables became one.

Just that morning, seeing Pop Mike off at the airport, she'd been sure he'd called her Rain when saying goodbye. It took the entire train ride back, orange line to red, for her to convince herself he hadn't.

There was plenty of other strangeness, too. But Ray-Anne chose to tell herself it wasn't really there.

"Another thing," said Paul. "It doesn't hurt anymore."

"What doesn't?"

"My ankle. My collarbone. My ribs."

Another source of tension between them—one of so many, really, which made it kind of amazing that they were friends and sometimes seemed to have a shot at being more than that: Paul's injuries and his refusal of any help in dealing with them. He was lucky to be alive, given the violence of the accident he'd survived. Yet he hated when anyone tried to cut him slack or extend him any sympathy at all, never mind suggesting that maybe painkillers might help with the aches and assorted discomforts that still plagued him.

No painkillers for Paul, thank you. He wanted nothing that might cloud his mind.

"How could that be?" Ray-Anne said.

Huey placed two more figurines—a squid and a peacock, both larger than any of the other animals, including the elephants—on the peak of the roof. He had no trouble balancing them.

"I have no idea. But it's the truth. Like I said, I haven't slept. And all the pain is gone. It's like my brain and my body are getting ready for something."

The squid and peacock defied gravity and surveyed the frightful scene below. They were rendered more sharply and painted with more care than the other animals, as if someone at the factory had taken it upon themselves to give the pair the artisanal treatment when a spray-machine job was sufficient for the aardvarks, giraffes, and the rest.

The higher-than-thou duo, one with formidable tentacles and the other boasting a proudly spread tail, stood regal and aloof above it all. They might have been willing to help Noah and Mrs. Noah with a bit of guidance, but not before the terrified humans reached the safety of the ark on their own. The two creatures radiated a reluctance to take sides in a drama that wasn't theirs.

Paul started to say something, but reoriented himself in his chair instead, as if stopping just shy of a grave mistake.

Huey kept on whistling.

Ray-Anne's sweater snagged on the wicker.

"Did somebody really steal George Wickham?"

At first, Ray-Anne had no clue who Paul meant. Then she remembered the African gray parrot that was kidnapped from its locked cage out in front of the Tuxedo Bar, the watering hole next to New Beginnings Chicago. "Last weekend. Pop talked to Elsie, and they don't know who did it. They're hoping for a ransom demand or something, just so they know he's alive."

During his short stay in the City of the Big Shoulders, Pop Mike had formed a surprisingly strong bond with the gray-braided Tuxedo owner, most likely because he and Elsie had similar pasts. They'd both been hippie dreamers who learned to temper their idealism, addressing the world with a nod toward reality and a reluctance to fall into cynicism. Plus, they shared a love of Jane Austen.

Huey continued placing animals around the ark. Even if Noah and his wife made it aboard safely, they'd need plenty of provisions in the hold. The attacking beasts might be patient enough to lay siege. And one could only hope that the peacock and the squid weren't secretly in league with their brethren, intent on driving the humans onto the vessel and into their trap.

"Hey, you know what room they have me in?" When Ray-Anne didn't answer, Paul forged ahead. "Six-six-six. Kind of wild, huh? Why would you have that room in a place like this, with people like this?"

Ray-Anne said nothing. She wanted to return to the only topic that mattered.

Paul shifted position again and tapped his foot on the floor a few times. "I really let him down. Didn't I?"

"You scared the hell out of him. Almost as much as you scared me."

Huey put two tigers and a leopard at the vanguard of a furry force mounting a rear-guard action at the ark's stern. Or maybe it was the bow. It was tough for Ray-Anne to tell which was which. Also, she didn't care.

"I really didn't want to die. I needed to get back."

"To where?"

"I don't know. Or maybe I just can't say. But I think I did something. Something someone really bad was counting on me to do." Paul rubbed his eyes; Ray-Anne suspected it was because he didn't want to look at her before finishing the thought. "And I think you helped me."

"Do what?"

"I don't know." Paul watched Huey as the spike-headed boy contemplated his diorama like it might come to life at any moment and show them the way the ancient story should have played out. "But I have to get out of here. Things are going to move fast."

"What things?"

"I don't know." Huey's whistling loop filled the room, but Paul didn't seem to hear him. "But if I'm stuck here trying to convince them I'm not a danger to myself for even a couple more days, that's not good."

"Are you?"

Paul's reply was equal parts surprise and hurt. "No."

"Are you sure? When you walk out of here, are there more pills and another bag waiting?"

"Look, you have to believe me. You need to back me up so they let me out."

"Because I swear to God, Paul—"

"I said no."

Huey stopped in mid-whistle and adjusted a gorilla.

"How do I know you're telling the truth?"

"I've been in here long enough to see the real problem."

Ray-Anne's sweater caught on the wicker yet again. This time, she was sure she felt a bad pull. "What problem?"

"I'm not going back to wherever I was trying to go. I don't have to."

Huey rebooted his whistling Mozart loop.

Paul continued to ignore him, locking eyes with Ray-Anne. "It's coming to us."

2
TRIPLE J

Jeremy Jameson Johns hated the nickname Triple J. That was why his colleagues in the Perth Amboy office of Manitou Holdings used it on him. Everything at Manitou was about letting the market decide.

The market consisted of an environment where lower-level employees were jammed into tiny spaces like factory-farm hens, pitted against one another to determine who was the most ambitious and able.

There were a few important differences, however.

Factory-farm hens had their beaks trimmed so that they couldn't do any real damage. Manitou would have made fighting spurs mandatory if management thought it would more efficiently identify the winners and losers among the toiling class.

That's where the nicknames came in. Anything that could be used against a colleague in order to expose weakness was fair game. The nickname couldn't be too demeaning or it would invite attention from HR. Were that to happen, the HR operative who dealt with the matter would most likely spank the offending party simply for being ham-fisted enough to force their involvement.

Clear violations of the HR handbook, with its rules against harassment and an overtly hostile environment, were seen as the hallmark of an amateur. Real operators had finesse. They saw the handbook as a friend—a collection of guiding principles for eliminating the competition and avoiding the guardrails.

The nickname did Jeremy one good turn. It helped him stand out in the eyes of Abel Dowd, his office mate.

"This is Triple J," the analyst who introduced Jeremy to Abel said when he marched him into Abel's space. "He's not like us. He's principled."

The "principled" line did him the second good turn. Code for someone who management considered to be lacking in initiative because he allowed ethics and morals to get in the way of building power and capital, it was used to flag employees who were not to be trusted with anything sensitive. In Manitou's case, "sensitive" meant company practices that, if publicly disclosed, would make the firm look bad.

After the analyst left the room, Abel asked Jeremy if he liked being called Triple J. When Jeremy admitted he did not, Abel didn't require a reason—but he never uttered it again.

The principled part of the exchange came into play a few weeks later, when Jeremy was assigned to Abel as a mentee candidate. The assignment was a bad sign disguised as a good one.

On the surface, Manitou management was taking an interest in Jeremy and wanted to help him advance at the company. In reality, nobody at Jeremy's level received mentoring unless they were in danger of being kicked to the curb. Management wanted to make sure the meager investment already made in such a person wouldn't be wasted if there remained a chance of salvaging the arrangement.

Jeremy knew the drill. Abel was told to evaluate Jeremy as keep or cut. If it was keep, Abel would be responsible for his progress from there on out. Abel was considered to be someone who could give Jeremy critical guidance. He was a few bands above Jeremy in the hierarchy, which meant he had a lot more experience at the company. He also was at least ten years older than Jeremy, who at twenty-six was seen as a kid by whichever higher-level execs even knew he existed.

Until Abel set the meeting for their discovery discussion, Jeremy assumed the matter was a waste of time. He would be shown the door, as he had at several previous jobs. Having started his career—such as it was—in editorial work and having been laid off multiple times when the leading minds of various industries realized how little they cared about anything creative, Jeremy was well acquainted with the elimination of the unwanted.

First, they hired you as a contractor rather than a full-timer so that they didn't have to pay benefits. That also made it easier to dump you. In fact, Jeremy thought it strange that they would consider him for a mentor at all when he wasn't demonstrating a fighting spirit or working to destroy his peers. He'd thought for some time that his stint at Manitou would be limited.

Then Abel asked him to get together. And he scheduled the meeting for after work—at Billy Clyde's, a wonderfully tattered dive bar on Ninth Avenue that was far enough from the most-trafficked commuting paths for them to relax without running into too many colleagues—if any.

Jeremy knew that Abel's wanting him to come across the river from the lowly Perth Amboy environs meant one of two things. Either Abel was a jerk who didn't care how much he inconvenienced Jeremy before helping the company jettison him, or Abel was a good guy who might be seriously considering trying to evaluate him.

Abel happily paid for a pitcher. And while he didn't seem to be in a hurry to finish it, Jeremy assumed Abel wanted to keep things informal, letting the flow of the discussion determine whether there'd be a second.

They exchanged personal pleasantries for a while. Then Abel asked his first company-issued question. "Let's say you have a choice of two teams. Team one consists of a couple of A-level employees who are rock stars, and the rest are C-level. Team two is all B-level people. Which would you rather manage?"

Jeremy, who hated such questions, decided to risk brutal honesty, which would either keep the conversation going to a fruitful conclusion or put him on the next bus out of Port Authority and back over the river to his apartment in Jersey City. "What if I don't want to manage anyone? What if I'm a doer, not a manager?"

Abel wasn't thrown at all, which was a good sign. "The question doesn't allow for that. The question assumes you're a manager. Which is it? One or two?"

If Abel was here to find out something about Jeremy, then Jeremy had a right to find out something about Abel. He drained his mug and thunked it down on the table's scarred wood with just enough of a bang to make a statement. "Three," he said. "Death."

Abel took that in stride, too. He waited for Jeremy to continue.

"Those situations only exist in dumb human-resources exercises. And I'd rather die than give it any more thought than that." He grabbed the Billy Clyde's cocktail napkin from under his formerly frosted mug and wiped his mouth.

Abel deliberated, his face a cipher. Then he squinted, as if trying to see through a disguise that Jeremy might be wearing.

Abel wasn't the only one studying him. Porthos, the human-friendly but cat-terrorizing bruiser of a formerly stray tabby taken in by Billy Clyde's staff, lay along the top of the adjacent booth, staring with that combination of scorn and apathy that only members of his species could manage.

"I did a web search on you," said Abel. "Found some stuff, too. One notable item was a blog post that isn't old enough for you to disavow. In it, you called the business side of your old company a bunch of money-lickers."

Jeremy remembered that well. He'd more than once considered deleting it. And he knew better than to try and claim it wasn't his. "I did."

"Care to explain why you chose that term?"

"I couldn't use the word I wanted to because I was hoping the post would go viral, and I was afraid it might get flagged for language. So I swapped out the first two letters after the hyphen."

Abel squinted again—for quite a bit longer this time, coming to what was clearly a meaningful decision.

He ordered another pitcher.

3

THE DIASPORAS BEGAN ANEW

Almost all of the vet-a-lings made poutine out of whatever meal was served in the evenings. Stella Grace's old-timers considered being included in the group, whose name was a combination of veteran and ding-a-ling, an honor because it meant you could hack it. And you could only be officially honored with the distinction by others who'd already made the cut.

Of course, they weren't really old-timers. Anyone who'd been at the facility more than a year was included. Time and longevity were valued differently at Stella Grace, where one was seen as possessing a valued skill if he or she could remain twelve months without being cured and discharged or transferred to a facility for the truly bad cases.

It wasn't really poutine, either, according to the guy who'd assigned the nickname to the dinner mess the patients smashed together. The former Stella Grace orderly, known to lore only as Ollie Quebec, used the term to describe what resulted from the patient practice of mixing whatever was served in an effort to mask or improve each individual offering's sub-par flavor. Even on nights when nothing tasted like much, it was an attempt to bless the combined ingredients with any flavor at all—the hope being to luck into something that was greater than the sum of its parts.

Paul wasn't at the poutine-making stage yet. Maybe it was his long years of knowing that any food that didn't make you sick was better than no food at all. Or the fear that insulting the food gods by debasing their gifts might earn you a lesson.

Most likely, it was that Paul had looked up poutine and thought the official dish made sense: a blend of fries, bacon, mushrooms, cheese curds, and gravy—or some variation thereof. The Stella Grace take on it, which might be a mash-up of brussels sprouts, cauliflower, canned corn, and pork?

No.

No, thank you.

Huey Dusek wasn't there yet, either. Huey Dusek never would be. Paul had yet to see the kid eat. For some reason, the staff never made him come to the table, as they did with the other patients. You sat down, and you made a good show of cleaning your plate. Because everyone knew what it meant if you didn't, and poutine or no poutine was a much more comfortable way of taking in nutrients than being strapped into a bed with an IV or an NG tube. Yet somehow, Huey was allowed to eat or not eat according to his own schedule, according to whim.

That was one of Huey's superpowers—remaining beneath notice. The staff left him to his own devices, and the other patients didn't want to deal with him, either.

At first, Paul had felt bad for the kid and tried to get him to interact with others or, barring that, to convince others to pay some attention to him. Paul knew what it was to be odd man out, and it worried him that Huey spent so much time alone.

It didn't take long for Paul to see he was wasting his time. Huey wasn't interested in being socialized, while the other patients—and even the staff members—didn't seem to grasp the concept of interacting with him. So Paul let it be, which was a familiar tactic. When all else failed, it was hard to argue against letting something innocuous stay the course.

After dinner, Paul found Huey in the Libra Room, which was one of the many smaller sitting, reading, or game rooms scattered around the floor—all named after constellations, all interchangeably suitable for the activities assigned to them. It was just a matter of what someone on staff had carefully chosen to place in a given space: a bookcase of aged hardbacks and dog-eared paperbacks with a few crack-screen e-readers in one, a scarred assortment of Trivial Pursuit, Yahtzee, Monopoly, and Scrabble in another, all with intermingled game pieces and dice.

Despite the rooms' assigned purposes, books and games migrated through each, dropped cards and playing pieces gone AWOL marking their journeys. Every Sunday night, a grumpy staff member had to tidy up and put everything back where it belonged. Come Monday, the diasporas began anew.

Huey had replaced the room's chess-table pieces with animals from the ark and had stopped, mid-game, to gaze out the window at the swaying trees in the hospital's yard.

"Hey," Paul said, dropping into the opponent's chair. It slid unexpectedly, and he nearly smacked it into the table, which would have wreaked havoc on the board. He was fairly certain Huey would have been able to put everything back from memory, but he had no desire to prove it.

Huey acknowledged neither Paul's presence nor the close call.

Paul picked up a seal, jumped an alligator with it, and removed the outmaneuvered reptile from the board.

Huey watched the trees.

Paul slid the seal to the opposite side of the board.

"King me."

When Huey did nothing, Paul launched into a seal bark and clapped his hands like flippers.

Huey showed no emotion, but he put the two animals back where they'd been. "Wrong game."

"I know. Are you Fischer or Kasparov in this one?"

"They never played each other."

That, Paul hadn't known. Pop Mike had more than once tried to teach him chess and its history, stressing that the game and its emphasis on thinking several moves ahead had a lot to say about living life overall. Paul never really took to it. He'd tossed out the only two players he remembered.

The ark sat on a nearby windowsill, its remaining creatures out on deck, placed as if they all were watching the game's progress. On top of the ark's hut, the squid and the peacock watched from their higher vantage point.

Something about that was disquieting. He was glad he hadn't knocked them off. Yet he also wasn't sure they could be unseated. "How come the peacock and the squid are always up in the nosebleed seats?"

"That's the closest I can get to what they really are. There's no way to make the others a part of them."

Sometimes it was best to let Huey's answers stand on their own.

Outside, clouds blowing across the setting sun made a here-and-gone-and-here-again light show of the branch shadows on the east wall of the room. With the ebb and flow, Huey's eyes were alternately cast in darkness and given the appearance of being lit from within.

"She looks much better without the spider." Huey studied the board.

It took Paul a second to understand he hadn't meant one of the animals on the board. "Who?"

"Rain."

So Huey had picked up on the mutation of Ray-Anne's name that got under her skin so. Paul had been certain Huey never listened. "The spider?"

"It didn't fit with anything else on her arms."

Now Paul was confused. If Huey was talking about Ray-Anne, she hadn't had a bracelet or any jewelry on at all. All she wore was a watch. And arms? She'd been wearing long sleeves, so Huey hadn't been able to see them. Even if he had, she didn't have any ink on them. "I'm sorry, Huey—what about her arms?"

Huey shrugged.

Paul reached over to move one of the animals. He wanted to see if Huey would react again. When Huey didn't, Paul jumped a tortoise with a monkey.

As soon as Paul took the tortoise from the board, Huey put it back. "She'll forgive you," Huey said.

"Ray-Anne? For what?"

"You forgave her. She'll forgive you." Huey turned back to the window. After that, nothing Paul did to the board could get a rise out of him.

A few hours later, after Paul had brushed his teeth, he stopped by the Libra Room again to see if Huey was still there. The boy was gone, but he'd replaced all of the animals Paul had moved.

Only now the situation was more dire. Noah and his wife were making a lonely stand on one side of the board, a wave of creatures attacking from the other in orderly fashion, each on its own square, like real pieces.

The humans were badly outnumbered.

And while Paul had never been much good at chess, he remembered enough to recognize one thing: a lion had Noah in checkmate.

4
YET HERE SHE WAS

Audra Farrelly wasn't supposed to be here. She'd done herself in. Because she'd had to.

And she'd taken enough attacking Ravagers down in flames with her to launch her name into the halls of legend. It was a second death of sorts and one that had been a rarity before the ascent of Brill—the first demise taking her from The Living World, the next removing her from The Commons.

A novelty at the time. That was before many of her Envoy colleagues joined her in the practice, most of them having less say in the matter than she had. According to the rules they'd all thought were in play, it wasn't supposed to happen.

She certainly shouldn't have come back again. Yet here she was.

Just when she'd gotten used to the sort of in-between, sporadic ghost state she'd attained in order to provide Porter with counsel during Paul Reid's Journey, here she was. With all the familiar aches and pains a solid state entailed.

The problem was that she had no information whatsoever as to the location or nature of *here*. She'd gotten used to that, too, The Commons being a fickle place that called upon its servants, denizens, and operatives at odd hours and for odder reasons in the best of times, never mind after an eternity-long ordeal from which it had only recently been rescued and begun healing.

So sitting in what she guessed was some sort of corporate interview room—with sterile white walls, a table and two chairs, and faintly buzzing fluorescent lights above—was less of a surprise than it might earlier have been. Even the Ouija board had ceased to be a puzzling presence a few hours after she'd begun receiving messages on it from an unknown presence. And that had probably been a grand total of four or five days before, in L.W. time. Not that it mattered in The Commons, where if it were required, one could forego sleeping, eating, drinking, and all bodily functions just because the realm itself needed you working on something.

Audra tried not to ask too many questions. Which was an odd rule to follow when the only other thing in the room with her was an occult toy designed for providing answers.

All she knew was that there must have been a time when she wasn't in the interview room. But then she was. There must have been a time when the board hadn't been in there with her. But she couldn't recall. It just was.

While Audra knew very little about the being with which she communicated, she knew two very important things and suspected another. She had a very strong feeling it was a fellow fire entity. Furthermore, she knew for sure that it was very, very powerful—probably the strongest thing she'd ever encountered in The Commons, and she'd come upon true strength in her time.

She knew it wanted something from her. Something simple but important.

And as a bonus fact, she knew that everything about this

being and the current situation scared her nearly to a third death.

I don't wish to frighten you. The words were spelled out letter by letter as the game's planchette moved so quickly and with such force that Audra felt as if her arms would be yanked off her at the shoulders. Again, whoever or whatever was moving it was strong beyond her understanding while, she suspected, trying to be as gentle as possible. She didn't know where she was, but she knew that the amount of influence and sheer will required to get the board in with her and communicate to such a degree put her own abilities to shame. It put a planet's worth of Audras to shame.

It didn't wish to frighten her.

Too late.

This didn't feel like The Commons trying to influence or flat-out command her. Everything was different: color, taste, feeling, smell—you name it. But it was every bit as strong.

They'd been going back and forth on this one topic the entire time, the mystery fire entity revealing as little as possible and Audra trying to figure out what was going on. After all that time and effort, all she really knew was that the entity moving the planchette under her fingers was strong. It held back a tremendous amount of heat, which was saying something, given her own abilities. And it only needed one thing.

Audra believed that it didn't mean to scare her. But that changed nothing. It only needed one word from her, and it seemed to know she'd already reached her decision after the lengthy and exhausting conversation had yielded so little. It all came down to her strong belief that she wouldn't be going anywhere without reaching a decision on the matter at hand. And if The Commons had acquiesced enough to this being's will to allow it to communicate with her, that was most likely a big clue as to what her answer should be.

No reason to prolong it. If she was right, she'd find out. If she was wrong, she'd discover that, too. But she doubted she'd be around long enough to understand why.

A third death. Was such a thing possible when she wasn't sure she'd ever had a third or even a second life?

Audra removed her hands from the planchette and rubbed them together. It felt like a small bit of preparation to calm her for whatever would come next. She took a breath and let it out.

Try again. This time felt like it had more purpose to it. And it really was such a small thing to do.

"Yes," she said.

The planchette gave a little jump on the board. Had the room suddenly gotten warmer? It hopped again, impatient for her follow-through. She'd said what she'd said, and while she supposed she could still change her mind, there was nothing telling her to consider doing so.

Audra gently placed her fingers back on the planchette.

At first, nothing happened. Then it slid slowly to the letter *Y*. It lingered there, somehow managing to both remain in place and communicate a startling amount of power and strength. Nothing in the known universe had ever sat still with so much force and presence. It was as if it were waiting for her to acclimate to her decision and its response.

The letter *E*. Now the power built upon that of the previous letter.

Audra was puzzled as to the source of the planchette's trembling. It was her own hands.

The letter *S*. The force was now trebled, the presence of the whole word somehow more than the sum of its parts, especially since the fire entity had spelled it out rather than choosing the "yes" option at the top of the board.

Audra was just beginning to wonder what came next when she, the room around her, and whatever world lay beyond, erupted into flames.

5
A LONG, SLOW DECLINE

Jonas Porter had tried to convince himself it would work. Brill was gone. The Commons was already repairing itself. There was a huge backlog of Journeys to be conducted. And for every lost soul needing guidance, it seemed there was a corresponding Envoy or Envoy wannabe ready to use whatever ability he or she had to see that soul through to Journey's End. Moreover, there were just as many former bureaucrats or bureaucrat aspirants who wanted to run the machine rather than serve as one of its cogs.

That's where the problems started, as they did with any organization. Those who'd been in positions of authority before fleeing for their lives during the bloodiest part of Brill's reign saw no reason why they shouldn't return to running things now. Porter's eternity of showing up to work just to keep Corps HQ from being eaten by the disuse protocol meant little to them. Thanks for your service, Jonas.

Which they were able to do because Porter, despite being the hero of the hour after guiding Paul Reid to a new day for The Commons, was happy to be sidelined as the man in charge. Mostly, he wanted to be outmaneuvered so that he could return to his true calling: Journeys.

Porter's desire to lead went no further than overseeing a two-person team—him and a Journeyman. Two people, facing whatever The Commons could throw at them, with the standard heartbreaks, horrors, and heroism that brought them to a successful end, whatever the subsequent destination might be.

Porter remained nominally in charge but didn't want to be. Even The Commons itself seemed to agree with him. The table he and Charlene Moseley covered with spreadsheet and graph printouts was still in the director's office he'd commandeered many years before, though the office was now half its earlier size. The message was clear to Porter: the powers-that-be that were even higher than the self-appointed bureaucracy bigwigs saw his place in the hierarchy as smaller than it once had been.

Such was the artfulness of The Commons' workings that anyone who hadn't spent many years in its service would never know it had once been different. Ancient plaster walls had shifted to shrink the room without any sign of work being done. The woodwork was clad in the same multi-layered armor of paint. The space was less spacious. The window offered a more limited view of the world outside—and it had never offered much of one to begin with.

"It's not a pretty picture," Charlene said, shaking her Etch A Sketch with a little more vigor than was necessary until it went from showing a stunningly rendered three-dimensional graph to a simple-but-elegant table. Porter had to hand it to The Commons and its sense of nostalgia: it delighted in giving them tools, like his Newton and Charlene's current device, that looked like the originals but operated at a level far beyond what was originally imagined.

"It isn't," Porter said, flipping from the printout of the graph to the printout of the table. He tried not to let Charlene see that by humoring him in his old-school preference of paper over pixels, she'd rendered him nearly helpless because fitting the data to paper required digits so tiny his reading glasses were useless.

But Porter didn't need to read the numbers themselves to understand that The Commons, its Envoys, and its bureaucrats had a big problem on their hands. If the analytics were correct—and while Porter and his colleagues had initially blamed the systems they'd inherited from Brill for what had to be faulty reporting, the new systems came up with the same ones—they were looking at a mysterious leak of massive proportions. Simply put, the system was seeing a lot fewer new Journeymen and a great deal less Essence coming in. Nobody knew where any of it was going or why.

Even worse, only Porter and his few allies recognized the problem. Everyone else either didn't want to talk about it or hoped it would fix itself.

The Commons was capable of righting itself once it decided to, just as the steam-abacus tracking of Porter's early career had given way to the mag-card apparatus that had done its duty better than anyone expected.

Thus, when Brill's old system began to show the slowing arrival of new Journeymen and the never-before-seen shortfall of Essence throughout The Commons, everyone just assumed it was a minor glitch.

Porter, Charlene, and June Medill believed that the Brill-era measurements might actually be right. Fewer dead were coming into The Commons. Some of the Essence that was already there was leaving. The big question was, where was it all going?

June Medill. The thought of her always distracted him. Was there any better statement of Porter's new position within the Envoy hierarchy than having that little attack dog of a woman reporting to him? That wasn't an easy question to answer.

For one thing, June Medill didn't technically report to anyone. Porter and Charlene—who was the official head of active Envoy operations after Porter's move to a higher and mostly-for-show title—never ordered June to do anything. They pointed out a challenge, and June determined her own way of addressing it.

That said, the woman was loyal as could be. She didn't see her trimming, carving, and warping of assignments as insubordination. She viewed it as fulfilling the request Porter and Charlene should have made to begin with.

And the pit-bull part of her was indispensable when she sank her teeth into an antagonist.

They were their own little entity. And with rare exception, the bureaucrats were too busy to notice that Porter and Charlene, with the effective-but-abrasive assistance of June, were pretty much able to do whatever they wanted. The problem with rare exceptions, though, was that they were still exceptions.

"They're never going to believe us," Charlene said. "They haven't yet. Why would they now? She gave the Etch A Sketch an aggressive shake to see if it would generate a new visualization to further bolster their case. But it redrew the same graph, which, while beautifully rendered to the point of looking like something you could reach into the screen and pull out, told its big-picture story in the simplest way: a steadily rising line plateaued for a time, then eased into a long, slow decline.

Porter held his century-of-service paperweight up to the sunlight beaming through the thick glass of his window, which, while smaller than it had been, still managed to capture its share of the afternoon rays. He sometimes was able to convince himself that the light was the rays of the same sunbeam that called the Shrine of the Lost home, come to visit and remind him he was still vital to the cause. But that was a foolish sentiment. Just as the hologram in the paperweight would only ever be a close approximation of him no matter how many different ways he tried tipping it, his value to the Corps would be minimal as long as he was a warrior without a war. Or an Envoy without a Journeyman.

When someone rapped on the doorjamb, the characteristic insistence of it told Porter who it was without him looking.

"Good afternoon, Ms. Medill," Porter said, shifting to his most officious tone. June lapped up anything that nodded at corporate culture, and it was the least he could do to make her happy. "What do you have for us?"

It wasn't enough this time. "Nothing good, I'm afraid, Mr. Porter." June's tone was a mix of concern and sadness, which was a damned sight better than the full-on fear Porter and Charlene had worked to ease out of her after her abuse at the hands of Brill's regime. She handed over a sheaf of printouts. Unlike Charlene, who sullied her hands with paper only to suit Porter, June was a print devotee. Not only that, but she was masterful with print preferences, so the font was readily legible to Porter's old eyes.

June now had Charlene's attention, too.

"I completed several rounds of verification before bothering you with this, but I'm confident in what I'm about to say." She shuffled through her copy of the report, flipped to the last page, and then went back to the front. She looked anything but confident.

"It's all right, June," Charlene said, aware that even if June had moved past her old terror of delivering disappointing news to management, she was struggling to do so now.

"Tell us, and we'll tackle it as a team," Porter said.

June licked her lips. "Well, I pulled the transit report. And I hadn't done that in some time—and I want to apologize for that—though it was still within the required interval."

"Apologize?" said Charlene.

June shuffled nervously in place. "From the pattern I'm seeing, I don't think it would have changed anything had I gotten this in front of you earlier, but part of me wonders if that's only the case because I desperately need it to be." More shuffling. "What I'm trying to tell you, sir"—now she glanced Charlene's way, despite herself—"is that there are quite a few Railwaymen and Highwaymen who can't be accounted for. Quite a few, sir."

"Quite a few?" said Porter.

"Quite a few."

"Okay." Porter placed his paperweight on the desk softly so as not to startle June or cause her to misinterpret the move as a fit of pique. "They sometimes go dark on us, but they always come back online. How many?"

"Half."

If Charlene had been holding the paperweight, she might have dropped it. "Half?" Most of her earlier softness was gone.

"Fifty percent," June said. "I checked and verified."

Porter nodded, thinking.

"Where's Po?"

"I was about to ask that very thing, sir. That very thing." June shuffled her papers again, flipped to a page in the middle of the bunch and handed it to Charlene. "If he's reachable, may we ask him what he knows about demons?"

"Demons."

"Yes, sir." June checked her print-out, as if hoping it would change so she wouldn't have to say anymore about this. "Day-trading demons." She handed the print-out to Porter. "Who cheat."

6

THE FIRST FLASHES OF THE DELUGE

It was true that Paul hadn't slept in three weeks. But that didn't mean he hadn't been dreaming.

Most of his long nights in Stella Grace were spent following the same routine, the regularity of which was a comfort to him. Paul had spent much of his life with no control over his time. So when he had a chance to create a faithful cycle that could be repeated or not, depending on what he felt like doing, he seized it. That routine became the rule, the practice a daily affirmation that he really did have some say-so in how he lived.

Paul's nightly life in the dark—or as much dark as there was in a group facility—started out with him lying in bed until he was confident his fellow patients' sleeping meds had kicked in. Then the strangeness could begin.

Not everyone was on knockout pills, so he avoided other nocturnal nomads if he could. Not because he didn't like anyone else, but because he chose to use his insomnia for exploring himself and the world he was in—which felt, increasingly, quite different from the world he'd been born in.

The idea was to sit and try to feel his way into learning

more about what this odd new place was. Conversation, or even the presence of someone else, interfered with that.

Paul wasn't on any sleeping medication, but it wouldn't have mattered if he had been. When he'd first arrived—after what they called his attempt at suicide and he called trying to right an unnamed wrong—they dosed him nightly.

To no effect.

He'd just get up and hit his usual nighttime places to occupy his mind. The reading room was first, followed by the game room and then the various group rooms, starting with the smallest and moving to the largest as he tried to find the right atmosphere for any given night.

Paul favored the reading room—not only for the books, but for the vibe. It was the energy from the volumes. From the people who'd sat in there, absorbed in story and information. Whatever it was, Paul often found himself pulling something out of a case at random and opening to whatever page happenstance chose for him. He'd then fall into a phrase, a paragraph, or an entire piece that comforted him or provided some insight into his current situation.

One long night, he grabbed a coverless copy of *Moby Dick* and chanced upon a line that said true places are not on any map. That gave him something to think about until sunrise. Paul believed he'd been to at least one true place in his life, but he couldn't remember where.

Another time, in the game room, he'd watched an owl in a tree for hours.

It watched him back.

The entire time.

On this night, Paul spotted Huey in the smaller TV room with his ark buttoned up by his side, its animals safely stowed and awaiting the first flashes of the deluge. The television was off, but Huey stared at the screen, eyes half-lidded, as if whatever he saw there was the most tedious of reruns.

Paul had never seen Huey watch anything. He only ever came into a room with a TV when it was off.

He moved on before Huey spotted him. Or maybe Huey knew he was there but wasn't in the mood for company, either. Other than Paul, Huey didn't seem to want anyone but his animals around him.

And the love and regard with which he treated them was contagious. Nobody but Paul ever messed with the ark or its creatures. They never moved them around or futzed with them in any way, which was an unheard-of sign of respect, considering the ark wasn't Huey's personal property, as far as Paul knew.

A few hours later, Paul lay face-up on his bed, watching a house centipede cut a halting zigzag across the ceiling, its waving legs a field of wind-blown wheat. Other patients squashed the poor things when they could reach them. Paul wouldn't end a life lightly, particularly after one of the orderlies told him the centipedes hunted bad bugs and, provided nobody killed them, could live for years.

The bigger the centipede crushed, the longer the streak cut short. You could take that upon yourself if you chose, but you had to understand and own the deed.

Understand and own the deed. Not a bad standard to live by.

Which brought Paul to the most interesting part of his nights. The current part.

Paul watched the centipede through closed lids. He wasn't sleeping. He could hear everything around him, from the rare passing of a midnight driver to somebody's far-off dog barking before it was shut up.

Whenever he first went into this state, it was as if his lids were a pair of lenses showing him things he couldn't see when his eyes were open. Open, the centipede was not there. Closed, it crept across the expanse.

That was the case with other things as well.

There was the time Huey came into the room and flopped down on the second bed, which was unoccupied because Paul's former roommate had signed himself out. Paul, who at the time still believed sleep was a necessity and was struggling to get some, rolled over and opened his eyes to find the bed empty. But when he closed them again, there was Huey, elbows up and out, his head on a pillow of fingers as he, too, studied the ceiling.

Paul wanted to ask Huey if he saw the dark-of-night ceiling shows that nobody else ever mentioned. Like the army men from the toy room who marched in and conducted upside-down maneuvers for an hour or two after midnight. Or the spawning salmon from the labels on the cans in the kitchen. Or Huey's own ark animals, who spent a couple of hours one night playing a game of capture-the-flag on the wall.

But Paul hadn't been able to ask. That was the other thing about the eyelid dreams. After the first few blinks, when he was able to verify that what was seen through closed lids was invisible to open eyes, Paul found himself unable to move, unable to speak. And while part of him knew he should be panicking at his helplessness, a stronger and more experienced part—the battle-ready Paul—managed that fear and allowed him to ride the visions out, giving him the calm necessary to observe and listen.

That was the favor of helplessness: removing choice, it gifted you the freedom to think and learn. Paul only needed to pack away his fear of the centipede dropping onto his face and stinging the hell out of him. He had to ignore the girl who wandered in one night to stand and look down at him—the girl he'd never seen at Stella Grace.

Tonight's round of there-but-not-there was tactile rather than visual. At first.

Paul's ring itched—a maddening encirclement of screaming-to-be-scratched that started off warm and grew to be hot, hotter, and then blistering. How something could itch and hurt so much was beyond him. The how of it wasn't important. He just needed it to stop.

Finally, after what felt like a good hour but probably wasn't, the pain retreated back into his finger, as if the loop were tightening, pulling itself down beneath the skin's surface and into the bone before departing altogether, leaving only the faint metallic weight of the unseen ring in its place.

The ring he wasn't wearing because it was taken from him when he arrived at Stella Grace.

The ring he wanted Ray-Anne to try to find for him.

Paul didn't know how long he lay there on his back. He still couldn't move. Usually, the spells broke only with the first light of day. But somebody else in the room had no such problem.

Whoever it was managed to come in without making any noise whatsoever. There was only the sense of movement by his head, at the bedside night table. He felt it but couldn't hear a thing.

The person checked to see if they'd woken him up. The barest glimpse at the edge of his vision was all he needed to identify the interloper.

For an instant, the spikes of Huey's hair came into view as the boy placed something on the table.

Paul initially thought Huey had slipped up and revealed himself without meaning to.

But Huey was aware that he had—and didn't care. It was if he knew Paul was unable to do anything.

Paul should have been afraid.

He wasn't.

Huey was strange, but no more so than Paul or anyone else in the building. And Paul had never gotten any kind of bad feeling from him.

Still, it was a relief when Paul, without hearing Huey depart, had the sense he was once again alone in the room.

Then it was only a matter of waiting until he could move again.

7

A ROVING SHERIFF OF SORTS

Whenever Po visited Mrs. Blesmol, he hoped to be told nothing of import. The monk was the only one she'd allow in her den, nestled deep in the tunnels beneath the Dharma Rangers' missile silos.

The hippie soldiers and Envoys required regular check-ins with her in order to keep tabs on the changes—or lack thereof—happening underground. With The Commons reverting to its normal operations, the fear was that the silo complex and its tunnels might be reabsorbed into the bones of the world, to be used for some other purpose. If that happened, the Dharma hippie soldiers, nearly all of whom were bona fides, might find themselves finally called to complete their Journeys. Bona fides, unlike mythicals, were not created by anyone's imagination. They were people who'd passed from The Living World, and sooner or later the revived system would pull them into its rightful process.

Few of them were looking forward to the experience.

Thus, Po ventured down into what the Dharmas referred to as the D-cubed tunnels—for deepest, darkest, and diciest—to partake in pleasant conversation. He didn't mind the uneventful nature of the small talk, mostly because it meant he and the Dharmas had nothing to worry about in terms of reabsorption or heavy activity among the beetle-rats, which Mrs. Blesmol told him were formally known as muridines.

Every few months, Po met the kindly old lady, who was a human-sized mole-rat. Sitting in the packed-down burrow that served as Mrs. Blesmol's living room, the two of them chatted over tea. Po enjoyed his time with Mrs. Blesmol because it was quiet and routine, and he suspected she knew that. Which was why she would talk only to him and not some put-upon soldier who couldn't wait to get away from her and back up to civilization.

The conversation started the way it usually did, with Mrs. Blesmol asking about Po's job and missions and Po sharing whatever detail the rules allowed, which wasn't much. He was a roving sheriff of sorts, assigned to locate and deal with errant mythicals, some of whom were nuisances and others who were violent and dangerous. Once he found them, he convinced them to change their ways and habits, if possible. If that wasn't an option, he did whatever was necessary to bring them in and turn them over to the Dharmas, who had converted part of their tunnel complex into a prison and rehabilitation facility.

When the mythical in question was convinced to behave in a manner that fit with the return of The Commons to its original mission, they were released. If they couldn't be convinced, the prison was able to hold just about any type of problematic being for as long as needed.

Often, that wasn't very long. As part of its return to form, The Commons appeared to be reabsorbing the most recalcitrant of mythicals. It was difficult to predict which ones or when, but quite often an occupied cell turned up empty. Nobody and nothing escaped the facility. The Commons simply took them back, and as far as anyone knew, they were never heard from again.

The deepest unexplored tunnels could be the perfect hiding spots for some of the worst mythicals, which was where Mrs. Blesmol came in. A hunched old creature with poor eyesight and waves of wrinkles hidden beneath the handmade house dresses and shawls she favored, Mrs. Blesmol was tapped into what was happening underground. Po never tried to find out where she got her information, and she never asked for payment.

Po's company was enough for Mrs. Blesmol. And strangely, despite her very poor eyesight, she never had a problem understanding his signing. The Envoys provided Po with a translating device so that he could communicate with those who didn't sign, but it had a bit too much personality to unleash on the mannerly Mrs. Blesmol. And it was a comfort to use sign since those who were fluent in it were a rare find.

The routine, too, was comforting. Po would ask Mrs. Blesmol about her children, which gave her the chance to grouse about how seldom they came to visit since their father —her husband—had gone wandering. She would offer up the same stories from when they were babies that she always shared. Finally, she'd let him go on his way with whatever information she had about miscreants hiding in the tunnels or, more commonly, her reassurances that nothing of import was going on.

It was an arrangement that served them both. Po knew Mrs. Blesmol's information was accurate and comprehensive. He also suspected that while she wanted him to believe his visits helped keep the muridines away, the situation was in fact reversed, and she kept the creatures from bothering him when he ventured down to see her.

Po also understood that Mrs. Blesmol was lonely—and for

good reason. He was almost certain her husband was dead and would never return from wherever it was he'd gone. Sadder still, he thought her children might be, too. But she'd never, ever share that with him or explain what had happened to her family. So he visited for information—and to do a good turn for a soul who had no one else.

"You're not leaving until you've tried the blackberry." Mrs. Blesmol poured yet another cup of strong assam from her beloved antique samovar. She insisted he honor her ritual of taking a bite of one of her fresh-baked Russian tea cookies and keeping it in his mouth as he sipped the tea. It was one bite, one sip until he'd sampled all of the cookies several times and was so elevated from the caffeine and sugar that he might've been able to levitate back to the surface. The blackberry was delicious. All of them were.

Po made sure the pleasure showed on his face as he let the sweetness dissolve in a mouthful of tea before swallowing.

Mrs. Blesmol appeared to be satisfied, which was good enough for him. Then it was time for more serious matters, if she had any to discuss. "What do you hear of that poor, precious baby?" she said.

The situation in question was worrisome. A nine-year-old from the hippie soldiers' complex, a girl named Mira, had been missing for more than a week. She'd sneaked out on her own to gather morels in the woods as a surprise for her mother and hadn't been seen since.

Po signed that the search continued.

"My neighbors haven't said anything." Mrs. Blesmol put her empty teacup down and made no move to fill it again. She turned a cookie over and over in her hand.

The mention of her neighbors was enough to set Po's skin to tingling with the expectation of new pincer bites. As Mrs. Blesmol's cookie turned, he wondered if perhaps her thoughts had moved on to her own missing loved ones. He sipped his tea.

"I don't have as many neighbors as I once had, you know. That's one of the more concerning things I need to pass on. They aren't consistent in their answers, either. Some claim large groups of them have moved elsewhere, though they can't say where or why. Others tell me to be careful, that there's something cold and bad down here that hunts them. Normally, I'd dismiss such talk as the fear of small and simple creatures. But now and then, I think I feel something, too."

Po signed and pressed for more detail. He even ate more cookies than he wanted just to keep her talking.

But when the tea was exhausted and the cookies finally gone, Mrs. Blesmol grew quiet. The visit was over.

On the way out, Po walked the old train tracks of the tunnel more carefully than usual. He wasn't one to spook easily, especially since he felt comfortable that Mrs. Blesmol had instructed the muridines, along with whatever other creatures she might consider her neighbors, to leave him alone.

Yet he could not rid himself of the feeling that there was someone or something else down here with him—something that watched and tracked him. No matter how many times he turned quickly to see if he might surprise a watcher behind him, there was no one. But the feeling didn't fade until he made his way to the stairway Paul Reid had built to the surface, The Commons having absorbed the collapsed tunnel roof and piles of Sisu from the train ride he and his friends took so many eons before.

Long after Po no longer felt observed and pursued, he still could not shake the impression it left. Whoever or whatever had been watching and tracking was no stranger, but he firmly believed he wouldn't know who it was until they chose to reveal themselves.

8

I'M YOURS

"Jonas."
When the speaker of his Newton crackled with Audra's barely audible voice, the word spoken was more static than name. The signal was weak.
Or Audra was.
Or both.

From the first time Audra had called upon Porter to help with the long plan to defeat Brill, his contact with her had been spotty. She'd provided whatever guidance she could while The Commons rebuilt itself but hadn't attempted to appear to him since their conversation at Austen's Night Lights and Brill's subsequent fall. He didn't push. He was grateful to have whatever contact he could, and usually that meant via the Newton.

The other quality of Audra's voice was a constant, sadly: it carried with it a burden of pain. That was there even in her cheerier moods. But the distortion of the current connection rendered it worse than usual—and more immediate.

He pulled the unit from his coat pocket. The Newton, which he'd denigrated when it was assigned to him, had proven to be an indispensable source of information once he'd launched himself into helping The Commons rebuild. Audra must have known it would be when she talked him into rescuing it after Paul tossed it into the reeds, just as she always seemed to understand when Porter was alone and able to talk.

"Audra?"

Her reply came via text, which was not a good sign. He'd heard from her less frequently of late, which he'd taken to mean she didn't believe she was needed. Only now did it occur to him that she'd gone dark because she wasn't able to reach out. *Jonas*, the screen said.

"I'm here." Porter resisted the urge to ask her how she was; he feared he already knew.

I don't know connection time or which details are allowed through. Sticking to basics.

That made sense. Wherever she was, The Commons enforced its rules and strictures—many of which were very fluid—and harshly so at times. If she overreached and told him too much, the connection might be cut out for no stated reason. That was simply the way of things.

You?

"I'm fine." Porter knew Audra wasn't asking as a formality. She needed to ensure he was in a place where he could give her message the attention it needed because there was no guarantee the Newton would save it for playback later. Strictures once again. Attention must be paid.

I've had close contact with a fire entity I thought I could handle. I was wrong.

No wonder Audra's signal wasn't strong. A fire entity could mean anything from a living flame or a sentient meteorite to something of a more biblical flavor—an incarnation of the burning bush or even Lucifer himself. There had been several versions of each spotted in The Commons over the years, all spawned by a different take on classic religious texts or even heavy-metal songs devoted to one or the other.

"Are you all right?"

The answer was a while in coming. *Wrestling pain down. You know me.*

Yes, he did. Audra was a fire entity herself, though Porter hadn't known until she'd taken herself and a host of Brill's Ravagers down in flames. She'd never told him the details of that day, had never spelled out how she'd found her way back or even what such a return meant.

Death wasn't required to provide clarity. The Commons and its Essence made their own decisions and felt no need to brief the likes of Jonas Porter or his contemporaries about the particulars. Audra had an ability with both fire and heat, and —ever since she surpassed her limits fighting Brill's forces—a terrible sensitivity to both as well.

It got too close. I got hurt. I wanted to warn you should it contact you or yours. Even if it's not openly hostile, it can still do a great deal of damage.

"Thank you," Porter said. He was grateful. With The Commons in its current state of flux, all warnings were appreciated because some very bad beings and things were bound to be shaken loose. "Is there any way I can help you?"

That reply was long in coming, too. *Be careful.* Another gap. *I'm yours.*

That would be it for now—and maybe for some time, then. That last phrase was their standard sign-off. Were they to share their exchanges with anyone else—and they didn't—the expression might easily be mistaken for one of affection. While they did care about one another, it was shorthand for the letters that had helped lay Brill low after being delivered to Paul inside his ring: IMUURS. The letters themselves were too powerful for everyday use. To use them casually could mean diluting them so that they wouldn't serve when needed. Or one might inadvertently raise forces one couldn't control in a moment of carelessness.

Thus, the coinage was employed because it was safer and because it reminded them that they each belonged to the mission of the other. The two of them were linked because everything he and Audra faced in The Commons ultimately was.

The dead and their Essence were going missing, along with the Railwaymen and Highwaymen. Some day-trading demons were involved, as was something that very well might set it all to burning. And though it was difficult to imagine how those disparate parts might fit together, Porter had been around long enough to believe that they almost certainly did.

"I'm yours, Audra." He knew she could no longer hear him.

And the phrase sounded more dangerous than it had only a moment before.

∽

THE COMMONS HAD RECLAIMED EVEN MORE of the Dewdrop Inn since Po's last visit. It hadn't ever recovered from the battle and the ensuing storm Paul Reid called down upon it in his now-legendary defeat of Brill's Ravagers. Only the swimming pool and its long-abandoned office were left, the motel and the surrounding complex having reverted back to the original landscape some time before.

Po couldn't say how long it had taken. The tunnel and staircase Paul created in a time that seemed so long before provided an easy route to where he needed to be whenever Porter asked him to check up on the area.

He made his way up and out of the pool and continued on

to his destination as quickly as possible. To tarry meant to remember—and Po tried not to do that, though he all too often failed.

Goodbye, friend.

Without warning, Ken had given himself to the greater good of The Commons just a stone's throw from this spot by the pool.

Without warning. Po couldn't blame him. If the mummy had told him of his intent, Po would have tried to stop him, and that would most certainly have spelled disaster for them and for The Commons.

Ken had carried out his plan, and now Po was without his friend.

All things came at a cost. He understood. But as he fulfilled his duties to the Envoy Corps and to Porter, he used the busy days and nights to hide the fact that in many ways, he remained among the glass and gravel of the parking lot, tears flowing even now.

No, Po couldn't harbor any resentment for his friend, who'd done what he'd believed was right to contribute to something far larger than all of them. Yet to Po, nothing was larger than his friend—and the blame for that loss lay at his own feet.

He'd failed to defeat the Shade before the mummy sacrificed himself. He never saw it coming.

A true friend would have known.

A true friend would have made a difference.

This was a place of sadness and loss, and Po was glad for its return to the surrounding landscape. When the pool eventually collapsed in on itself, as he hoped it would, then the stairway would be sealed, and he'd never have reason to come here again.

But now he checked the pool office—a small cinder-block

structure with a pass-through counter, a desk, a chair, and a few stools—in order to rule out a possibility. He should have known what he would find because of the type of place the Dew Drop Inn was. Grief made its home here, and there was more of that waiting for him.

There were signs of a campfire behind the pool office. Inside the office lay a torn-open child-size backpack in pink camouflage. Near it lay a shiny red barrette with a hand-painted "M" and a flood of tiny jewels glued to it.

Mira. The girl had been here. As had others, judging by the rotting food remains and other leavings.

A child's clothing lay on the floor, arranged in the shape of a small girl. It indicated that Mira hadn't left on her own. Po thought he knew who'd done this. And if he was right, the Dharmas could call off their search.

He returned to the site of the fire for a closer look and, poking around in the ashes with a stick, found the telltale molted outer skin, confirming his fears. The little girl's Essence was potent, and her killer had increased in size as a result of absorbing it.

Po pulled out his Envoy-issued Tamagotchi, which hung on a necklace beneath his robe, and peered into its screen. The creature within, which alternated between primitive pixels and a very lifelike three-dimensional depiction, called itself Joel and nearly always presented itself as some form of living sandwich.

Appearing as a cheeseburger, Joel playfully stuck his pickle tongue out before spying the molted tissue hanging from the stick. He adopted a more sober demeanor, morphing into a pixelated blob. Then he conjured up a 1930s-era telex unit, sent a message, and paused until he received a response.

Po let Joel drop to a hanging position outside his robe so he could see what Po saw.

"Is that what I think it is?" It was Porter's voice coming from the unit's tiny speaker. Joel had connected to the gray man so that he could review the situation himself.

Po didn't answer.

"Parix," Porter said. "Is there any sign of the girl?" The weight of his tone indicated what his words did not—if Parix was involved, there was almost no point in asking the question.

Po dropped the stick and the molted skin into the ashes of the fire and turned the Tamagotchi unit so that he was looking into Joel's eyes. But again, he didn't answer.

A longer stretch of silence.

"I'll tell them," Porter said.

There was nothing left but the communication of details. Po signed what he'd found, including how he'd discovered the girl's clothing. Neither of them needed to spell it out: the clothes were all that was left of poor little Mira. Po told Porter he'd bring the clothes back with him so that her family could have them. Or he could continue to track Parix.

"No, that's far too much of a risk right now," Porter said. "If you discover anything more about his whereabouts, we'll certainly use it when we're ready to deal with him. For now, wrap the clothes up and leave them for recovery. I'll send someone. I need you to look into something else for me."

9

THE ANIMALS OF THE MONTH

The room lightened with the dawn. Paul was finally able to roll over in the bed and see what Huey had been up to.

There on the night table sat Huey's prized peacock. In front of it, as if the bird were making an offering, was Paul's ring.

Marlys, the nurse with the smoker's voice and hack, made the rounds to wake everyone up, her coughing announcing her approach and giving Paul enough time to pretend to be asleep, as he would have been if his meds had done their duty. She stopped in the hallway to wheeze for a moment before looking in on him. "Up and at 'em, Reid—breakfast in thirty."

Paul feigned grogginess. "Okay." He hoped his was the voice of someone who'd just been in the middle of a dream. He hoped even harder that she wouldn't notice the ring next to his bed.

Marlys continued to the next room, her fading wheeze the measure of her departure.

Paul scooped up the ring before another passing orderly or nurse could spot it, then rolled to face the window and cupped it to his chest so nobody could see it. A closer inspection verified that it was indeed his.

Unus Pro Omnibus. Omnes Pro Uno. IMUURS. As nonsensical as ever. Paul had no idea why his mother had had the ring inscribed with all that, but he knew the one thing it did mean: the ring was his. And it had returned to him.

Paul got out of bed and stuck the ring in the jeans he planned to wear that day. After breakfast, he'd see if he could catch Huey alone in one of the rooms and find out how and why he'd done Paul this not-so-little favor.

In the shower, Paul realized he'd left the peacock out on the night table. It wasn't a big deal, but it was probably better if nobody spotted it in Paul's room. He didn't want anyone knowing that Huey had paid him a late-night visit.

After he dried off, he wrapped his towel around his waist and came out into the bedroom to discover that there was no need after all.

The peacock had left after doing its job.

～

AS USUAL, Huey wasn't at breakfast. Paul wolfed down his powdered eggs in a hurry so that he could go find the boy and talk to him before it was time for the first round of group therapy. All too often, getting through breakfast in a hurry was a challenge, as every day they finished up their session with a question to answer for the next one, and patients would try to find out what responses others had planned so that they could come up with something insightful and unique.

Today, luck was with Paul. While a few people interrogated one another to see if they could trick anyone into revealing anything, everybody left Paul alone. He wasn't sure that was a good thing—being too much of a loner drew unwanted attention from counselors who considered socially isolating to be a worrisome sign—but today, it was just fine by him.

He made his way to the game room. The door was closed, which was odd, because that was a no-no. Other than when they were using the bathroom or showering, patients weren't supposed to hide themselves away.

Paul opened the door to find Huey sitting in his favorite chair. The animals were once again arrayed in mid-game on the chess board, the peacock and squid watching them from atop the roof of the ark's hut. Huey gave Paul the ghost of a smile when he came in and went back to studying the board. It was almost as if he'd been waiting for him.

Paul shut the door quietly. "We have to make this fast. If we leave that closed, we'll get them all suspicious—and I don't want them finding the ring."

Huey kept his attention on the animals.

"Okay. How'd you get it?"

"Aren't you going to put it on?" Huey reached over to move a monkey forward.

"Why, so they can just take it again?"

Huey didn't answer.

Paul was about to ask again how Huey had executed his little heist when the sound of someone trying the door stopped him. Trying. It hadn't been locked when Paul came in.

Huey half-turned to Paul with the same echo of a grin.

Whoever was outside inserted a key into the lock.

Huey went back to contemplating the arrangement on the board.

Edsel stepped in as if he'd expected to find something untoward occurring. "Dammit," he said to himself, ignoring Huey and Paul.

"Morning, Edsel," Paul said with more enthusiasm than he

felt, hoping some preemptive friendliness might head off a lecture about locking the doors.

Edsel ignored that, too.

Marlys's hack heralded her arrival. She raised an eyebrow at Edsel, who shook his head. "He was in his room," she said. "I woke him up."

"And he wasn't at breakfast?"

Now she shook her head.

Neither of them appeared to see the two boys in the room.

Huey continued to watch Paul. "Aren't you going to put it on?"

Paul attempted to glare him into shutting up.

Neither of the nurses reacted. They had yet to acknowledge the boys' presence.

"What the hell?" Paul said.

Huey nodded toward Edsel's keys, which jingled while Edsel and Marlys tried to puzzle the situation out.

The nurses didn't know Paul and Huey were there. And Paul had entered a locked room without a key. So who else couldn't see them? And what other locked doors might Paul be able to open?

Huey looked at the board with its arrangement of animals, glanced at the nurses, and gave Paul a full-on smile. He was having a ball.

Marlys chewed her lip, thinking, and noticed the board. "Where'd that come from?"

Edsel followed her gaze. "Dunno." He apparently hadn't seen the board or its animals until Marlys pointed them out.

She picked up one of the gorillas. "There's no way he just walked out of here," she said. "Let's do a sweep. I'm betting we find him passed out in somebody's room. It seemed like he hadn't shaken off his meds when I did the wake-up pass." She studied the plastic figure. "You know, my brother had a complete set of these. The ark, too. Dad used to take us to the gas station, and you could buy the animal of the month if you filled up. We made him get gas at the Noah's ark station even if the prices there were higher. And that was during the gas crisis. Man, we loved these things."

Marlys's cough had disappeared for the moment. The way she held the gorilla and looked at it, Paul couldn't help but wonder where her brother was now.

Huey still had eyes only for Paul. It didn't bother the boy that someone was handling his beloved critters. "I'll say goodbye now, Paul." Neither Edsel nor Marlys heard him. "Take care of yourself. He's coming. And so are they."

"Who?"

Huey didn't answer. Instead, he watched Marlys as she put the gorilla down and picked up one of the lions.

"He had the whole set," she said. "I was the only one he let play with it. But only when he was there to watch me."

"Shouldn't we keep looking?" said Edsel.

"Yeah." She plucked the two figures off the hut roof and gave them a once-over.

"Weird."

"What?"

"Whoever kept this whole set together put these two in with them."

Edsel gave her a blank look.

"There wasn't a peacock," Marlys explained. "And there definitely wasn't a squid."

∼

LATER, Paul tested his apparent invisibility by walking right past several nurses and up to their station door without any of them noticing. Just to be safe, he waited until they were all otherwise occupied with one thing or another before entering. He was certain the door was locked, but he once again had no need of a key. Nor did he need one to enter the storage room and reclaim the wallet, keys, and other stuff they'd taken from him when he'd been admitted.

It was as if he were a ghost.

But weirder.

After he'd gathered the rest of his things and was about to leave, Paul returned to the station to see if he might be able to access one of their computers and delete his file so that there wouldn't be any trace of the disappearing kid in their system. He moved fast. Once Edsel and Marlys spread the word, all of the nurses would look for him and realize he wasn't in the building. Then they'd raise the official alarm.

As it turned out, that wasn't a problem. Edsel and Marlys passed by and were discussing a toilet that wouldn't stop flushing. They were no longer talking about Paul. They weren't looking for him.

He waited until one of the doctors stepped away from the keyboard and found that once again he'd gotten lucky. She hadn't locked her screen, and the system the hospital used wasn't all that different from the one at New Beginnings.

Paul was able to navigate fairly easily once he got used to the slight differences. Which led to a series of puzzling things for him to chew on when he went back to look for Huey, hoping to say goodbye for real.

Huey was nowhere to be found.

And as Paul easily made his way through the different layers of security and let himself out without anyone saying a word, he wondered for the second time in only a few hours what the hell was going on.

His entire time at Stella Grace, Paul had never succeeded in getting anyone else to talk to Huey or even acknowledge his presence. Why hadn't he considered the reason for that before now?

But that wasn't even what wigged him out the most as he shut the front door to the building and made his way down the street, greeting the shockingly blue sky and its bigger-than-big cottony clouds for the first time in what seemed like months. The scariest part was what his search of the hospital's system had revealed.

The database contained no sign of a boy named Huey Dusek.

Huey had never been there, as far as the hospital was concerned.

It also contained no sign of anyone named Paul Reid.

10

THE NEST

Annie hunted for Zach by moonlight. Turning on any artificial light in the house would wake Bobby. And when her ex-husband was aroused in a manner he hadn't chosen, his next move wasn't a yawn—it was rage.

So she made her way through the rooms by the full glow of Selene, thanked whichever spirits chose to make the night sky clear and bright, and moved as fast as she could in her bare feet. Her son was only two but was frightfully good at getting around.

She'd been pulled from a sound sleep by the certainty that something in the house was wrong. Something in addition to what she already suspected. Something to do with Zach.

A careful, quiet check of his crib revealed its vacancy.

The good news was that their ranch-style house had no stairs for her son to fall down. The bad was that it was easier for him to sneak outside, his success announced by the white of the moon washing across the laundry-room floor. That light was granted free entry by the back door, which stood fully open.

"No, no," Annie said in a low voice before chastising herself for breaking the silence.

Her son's laughter, which echoed strangely through the night air of the backyard, further disrupted the quiet.

Again.

Louder this time.

How was that possible? Zach never laughed. He never responded to anything. All thoughts of Bobby and his temper went sideways.

Annie knocked the screen door open with the heel of her palm and was out the door and down the concrete steps of the back stoop in one fluid motion.

Zach's next laugh told her where he was—the other side of the bushes, in the neighbor's yard.

She ran across the grass and pushed through the arborvitae that Bobby refused to cut back because, he said, privacy was more important than neatness. His priorities gave her a few good scratches to take with her. A thin-to-the-point-of-dissolving ancient concert tee and underwear made for lousy shrub-battling gear.

Across the neighbor's backyard, against the back fence, Zach rolled on the ground, giggling. The sound, though completely new to Annie, should have pleased her.

It did not.

She slowed, not wanting to descend on him in frightened-mother mode.

Annie approached Zach casually, now grateful that the neighbors were gone on vacation for a couple of weeks. It wouldn't do to have them spying her out the window in little more than her undies while her kid chortled his way around their property in the middle of the night.

As she drew closer, she saw it. Movement in the air around

him. On his pajamas. His face, his arms, his hands. She ran to him, biting down hard on the scream.

Bugs.

Giant bugs everywhere.

Flying around him in a cloud, crawling all over him as more buzzed from a hole in the ground. The first fiery contact of one bouncing off her thigh almost made her cry out. The burning started out bad and grew worse.

Another hit her neck. Maybe it was the same one.

Her arm. Her ear.

Hornets.

She grunted through the next scream fighting to make itself heard and reached for her son, who remained covered in the thumb-sized insects. They weren't attacking him.

Annie was another matter.

The hornets pouring from the hole to defend their home went straight for her, diving and stinging. Hot needles on her face, arms, legs, feet, hands.

She reached out to clear them off of Zach, which only made things worse for her. One flew at her eye, and she recoiled as it got her just under the eyebrow. She closed her mouth as another headed for it. Her lip erupted in pain.

Annie began shrieking despite herself. She fell to the ground, her stung eye already swelling closed. The assault continued as the angry buzzing filled her ears. She began desperately rolling, crushing a few of the hornets beneath her. They popped as she dispatched them.

Each little victory was anything but. Most of the assailants managed to get a sting in before dying.

Annie was on fire. It dawned on her that she might die right here, followed by her son, should the furious bugs decide to turn on him next.

Zach must have realized what was happening—that the hornets on her didn't mean the same thing as the hornets on him. His laughter stopped. And so did the buzzing and stinging.

The pain was gone, as was the swelling of Annie's eye.

The fire was replaced by the tickle of the fluffy, cool something that served as a layer between her and the ground.

Annie, disbelieving, rolled over and sat up.

Zach stood a few feet away, watching her.

The entire lawn was a solid bed of dandelions. And not just a normal infestation, where a carefully cared-for expanse might erupt into a polka-dot scrim of bright invaders.

There was no grass to be seen. Instead, the moonlight illuminated a solid blanket of dandelions—layer upon layer. Annie's hand sunk in past her wrist.

Zach's feet were utterly obscured.

She looked around to see that they were surrounded in yellow. The back fence was now a wall of furry butter buttons. So were the arborvitae bushes separating this yard from theirs. The wood and shrubbery were completely enveloped in flowers, as if the dandelions had joined forces and decided they would now be a creeper vine.

Annie looked back toward the neighbors' house to see that whatever force propelled the dandelions into their takeover had shown no discretion or mercy there, either. The entire structure was smothered in highlighter yellow—the back deck, the rear wall, the windows and door, the roof of the house and its chimney. How to explain this?

The hornets were gone. The hole from which they'd emerged could no longer be seen through the yellow. It was as if the waves of anger and venom had been magically turned to flowers, along with her swelling and pain.

Annie got to her feet, still waiting for the previous moments' agony to return. How could she trust that such a miracle was real? She wiped tears from her cheeks and cradled Zach's face in her fingers.

Her little boy was fine. He hadn't been stung once, hadn't been in any danger. Moreover, he never took his eyes from hers, which was a rarity.

She knew then that it was true. The hornets. The pain. They'd been transformed into the bed of dandelions surrounding the two of them.

"Honey," Annie said to her son. "What did you do?"

Her own voice woke her from the dream. Annie was in her own bed, Bobby beside her, his heavy breathing and wet exhalations a relief and a confirmation that he was deeply sleeping.

Her mumbling hadn't woken him up. Thank God.

Annie pulled the comforter and sheets back in carefully timed increments, checking and rechecking each time that Bobby was still safely slumbering, his precious rest undisturbed. Sometimes, if she had to pee during the night, she just held it rather than risk his wrath.

Her stealth game was on tonight. She crept out of bed in her waffle henley, long underwear, and socks—a tee and underwear were fine for a dreamtime summer night, but San Francisco in the cool spring was another matter.

The fog obscuring the streetlamp outside confirmed that she really was where she thought she was. The Inner Richmond in its familiar state—wrapped in an Arthurian England shroud of mist. As if any confirmation were needed, a foghorn from out in the bay echoed up and over the tree-lined hills of the Presidio.

Annie left the bedroom and closed the door behind her with kitten-like silence. Or that of a ninja. A ninja was the more reassuring imagery, since she'd need one to defend her if she woke Bobby up.

Half-sliding, half-tiptoeing down the hall, she expertly

avoided the creakier parts of the parquet flooring. She couldn't shake the dream. Often, she'd wake up to find that whatever she remembered of a given night's imagery fell quickly out of her head, but not this. Part of her said that it was because this dream had been different. This dream had been at least partly true. It had happened to her, happened to Zach. He'd been a toddler in the dream, as if it were calling up an event from their shared past. And the part that hadn't happened to them was still real. The transformation of threat and pain into beauty. It had just happened to someone else. Someone she'd known at one time. Or something like that.

That was crazy. But it didn't mean it wasn't solid in its own way.

When she got to Zach's bedroom door, it was partially open, as always. She opened it further, sliding in with sock-clad furtiveness to avoid waking her son.

Good luck with that. Zach was on his back in his bed, his fingers interlaced behind his head on the pillow. He was the seven-year-old he was supposed to be, not the toddler from the dream. And he was completely awake, watching her as she entered his space.

It was almost like he knew what she'd dreamt, knew she'd be coming to check on him. Just as she couldn't say for sure which, if any parts of her dream were real—or, at least, were related to things that had happened—Annie couldn't definitively prove what she knew was the case all the same.

Her son had been waiting for her.

11

THE CC DAMSELS

"Just because you don't believe it doesn't mean it's not happening," Val said with more umbrage than she'd probably intended—and definitely more than Ray-Anne wanted to hear. "It's like climate change."

Val's stated full name was Vailala Madness. She insisted that Ray-Anne and everyone else use that rather than her birth name, which was Nora Dugard, as Ray-Anne discovered when Val showed her ID in order to volunteer. Ray-Anne was happy to call Val whatever she wanted because Val was indispensable to New Beginnings Chicago.

Val oversaw their computer, network, and other assorted tech needs. She was a whiz with all things digital. When she found out Paul and Ray-Anne were short on help after setting up in the city, she hit her contact list and brought in a full complement of hardworking young women, all nearly as gadget-savvy as she was. They were also all devoted to New Beginnings, as many had their own past difficulties and could relate to the people helped by the operation.

In return, Ray-Anne put up with Val's eccentricities, superstitions, and reading of patterns and portents into things when none were warranted or existed. Val carried both moonwort and mugwort on her person. She could tell you what each was for and where to buy them cheap, and she'd do that whether you asked or not.

Ray-Anne tried not to worry about what it could mean for New Beginnings' donations and reputation should it ever get out that Val's assumed name was her camgirl moniker—and that all of the volunteers she'd brought in were members of the group she founded, The CC Damsels. And that all of the Damsels were able to devote so much time and energy to helping at New Beginnings because they made their own schedules due to their line of work.

The Damsels—or the CCs, shorthand for "Cargo Cult"—were an assortment of ladies who financed their education and creative side projects via burlesque and cam sessions that were more mission of mercy than anything naughty. The Damsels launched their enterprise assuming naughtiness would be the order of the day. But each of them found that their higher-paying customers were lonely one-percenters who just wanted someone neutral and trustworthy to talk to.

They were social workers for rich men—and some women—who were unable to demonstrate vulnerability or softness in their real lives. So the rich paid handsomely for a virtual sympathetic ear.

All the Damsels were offbeat. All were gorgeous in whatever way the client wanted them to be. And aside from the inevitable flakes who fell into the mix but chose not to stick around or were culled by Val before they could cause any real trouble, all were sharp and loyal.

Val saved the Chicago operation from failing before it began. She and her people were as caring as anyone Ray-Anne had ever seen when dealing with new arrivals and residents. They were wonders with the young girls who showed up needing help, especially when dealing with abuse. And they were able to reach the boys who otherwise might have wandered off.

New Beginnings Chicago was such a success that when Pop Mike visited, he never said a word about the unusually large quotient of volunteers who looked like they'd stepped out of the pages of an alternative-apparel catalog or moonlighted as convention-booth girls down at McCormick Place—which many of the Damsels did.

Of course, Pop Mike and everyone else were so despondent over Paul's suicide attempt that such things weren't top of mind. But Ray-Anne was fairly certain he was happy to trust her and avoid asking questions that didn't need to be asked.

It also helped that the Damsels allowed Ray-Anne to call them by their birth names so that Pop Mike, who reviewed the staff files of who did what, didn't wonder why no one he met had any paperwork on them. Even Val answered to "Nora" without complaint—and returned to Val-hood as soon as Pop Mike was gone.

Val deserved more than the scant attention Ray-Anne paid to her concerns. But Ray-Anne couldn't stop thinking about what Paul said.

Something was coming to them. What could he have meant? And based on some of the weird things Ray-Anne herself had noticed lately, what if he wasn't crazy?

"You need to see this, Ray-Anne."

Ray-Anne was reconciling the New Beginnings checkbook, which she insisted on doing on paper as well as via the web interface because she knew Paul couldn't stick to a budget.

Val slid her laptop over. It, like Ray-Anne's, had been donated in a batch from a finance site that had refreshed its entire inventory. On the screen, the cloud-based spreadsheet app had generated a beautifully rendered graph.

Beautiful except for the lines, which were all headed downhill.

"What is this?"

"Occupancy. Beds, meals. We're losing people."

Ray-Anne pulled the machine closer. "They're leaving?"

"No more than usual. It's not that more people are taking off. It's that they're not coming in to begin with."

Ray-Anne studied the graph—as if staring at it long enough would compel it to explain itself—and traced the downslope with her finger. "Why?"

Val grabbed a screen wipe and made use of it. She forgave Ray-Anne for smudging the display; she wasn't so generous to anyone else. "I don't know, but it's freaking me out. I told you about the girls who stopped showing up to dance at The Skinner Box." She chewed her lip. "It just sets me off. I mean, yeah—it's the flaky girls. The ones who often disappear for a while. But now they've stopped showing up at all. As in, never again without a word." She went over the screen several times with the wipe—more than was necessary, by Ray-Anne's standards. "Laugh if you want."

"I don't."

"Good. Because, I don't know—what if they're all going somewhere? The Skinner Box girls and the people who aren't finding their way here?"

"Where would they go, Val?"

Val offered up the ghost of a smile when she heard her preferred name. She still hadn't recovered from Ray-Anne having to call her Nora during Pop Mike's stay.

Ray-Anne didn't know why Val's real name bothered her so much. But she could imagine many good reasons, based on her own experiences, and could understand why any one of them would need to remain buried.

Val's slight grin faded. "No clue. I'm just putting it out there."

Ray-Anne said nothing. She didn't know, either. But given what Paul had said, maybe he did. And according to him, it was now headed their way.

She looked again at Val's declining graph. It was steep enough to make a good sliding board for the Y-axis digits if they ever decided on a little playground fun break.

But the numbers probably understood enough of what Ray-Anne and Val knew to avoid trying something so foolish.

You never went over the edge.

Because there was no guarantee you'd find your way back.

12

LIGHTNING FLOWERS

The Lichtenbergs woke Paul up.
He didn't remember lying down, hadn't intended to sleep. Yet there he was, curled up on his side on the very bench he'd thought would carry him out of the world like a magic carpet with a bonus view of Lake Michigan.

Lichtenberg. He hadn't heard of that phenomenon, either. Not until one of the kids from New Beginnings New York, who'd gotten into an NYU summer art program, came back and convinced Pop Mike to let her photograph the kids and staff for a project.

Pop Mike agreed because he thought he'd be able to use the pictures in the revamped donation brochures he was working on. But the girl didn't tell him she was shooting infrared, which resulted in a top grade and a gallery showing for her—and photos that were way too eerie for Pop Mike's brochures. In the end, it took some doing just to convince him to allow a link to her online gallery from the New Beginnings website.

Pop Mike was proud of her, especially when her exhibition

was celebrated in both local and national media. But the shots freaked him out. And the ones of Paul disturbed him most of all.

Paul and Ray-Anne shrugged them off in order to help convince him that the poor girl hadn't intended to ambush New Beginnings or trick Pop Mike. She was heartbroken, in fact, because all of her success meant little if Pop Mike was mad at her.

But the truth was that Paul and Ray-Anne found the photos to be more unsettling than anyone. They just didn't blame her for it. And they didn't want to upset anybody further.

Paul never understood the technical details of the girl's setup, but it had something to do with her having modified her digital camera on her own to stop it from blocking infrared rays. Her pictures were beautiful.

Her other pictures.

The shots of Paul, while cool, were bizarre.

She found him painting an exterior wall on a hot summer day and convinced him to let her shoot with his shirt off. Paul hated the way he looked—all ribs, ropey muscles, and white skin. But she insisted he looked great.

When they reviewed what she captured, Paul at first thought the camera had somehow seen through his skin to his veins and arteries. There he was, painting. With what appeared to be patterns of glowing blood vessels spreading up and over his back and shoulder blades, like branches. Or cancer. And multiple tendrils extending across his shoulders and down his arms.

It took a couple of web searches before he found the closest thing: Lichtenberg figures, also known as lightning flowers. They were the fractal patterns that showed up on the skin of some people who'd been struck by lightning and were, according to various theories, the path of capillaries that burst when the electricity flowed through them. Under normal conditions, you couldn't see them on Paul's skin at all.

"Wow," the girl said when she saw them. "You've got some serious juice flowing through you."

She managed to convince him to let her use the shots, even though they made him uncomfortable. She did the same with Ray-Anne, who, in another odd occurrence, didn't fully show up in any of the pictures taken of her. She was but a mere suggestion or a shadow of herself in the images, like those supposedly taken of Bigfoot or the Loch Ness Monster.

Fanciful.

Not real.

Ray-Anne was no happier with her shots than Paul was with his.

And Pop Mike didn't like any of them.

They were the most popular of the gallery showing's offerings, particularly when word got out that Paul was the guy some charitably called the Bus Boy. It was a wonder that Pop Mike didn't turn against the project then and there, but the girl was so over the moon with her success—and understandably so—that he let it ride.

The showing was extended twice. When the girl made a small killing selling prints on the web and donated part of her take to New Beginnings, Pop Mike was slightly mollified—just so long as Paul and Ray-Anne decided they could live with it.

Now here Paul was on the bench, where they'd found him before he'd been able to send himself to wherever he was supposed to go. He knew why Ray-Anne thought it was so nuts. But his reasons weren't just strong feelings. They were something he knew. Yet if anyone expected him to explain it, they'd be waiting a long time.

It was just there. Like the burning of the lightning flowers.

Half itching, half heat.

And it was strong enough that it woke him from the first sleep he'd had in three weeks.

Paul sat up on the bench.

The sun was just rising, though a mix of clouds and lake fog blunted it. Rubbing his arms and shoulders did nothing to alleviate the burning of the Lichtenbergs. He pulled up his sleeve to check his forearm and saw nothing.

Paul scratched anyway. It didn't help. He wondered what would happen if the same jogger who'd found him with the bag over his head were to come along now and spy him squirming like someone had pranked him with itching powder during the night.

Night.

Sunrise.

How long had he been on the bench? He'd left Stella Grace in the morning and wandered to Foster Beach as a planned detour on the way back to New Beginnings, where he intended to tell Ray-Anne and everyone else there that he'd been given a pass to leave the facility. Maybe he'd even stop in to say hello and then return to Stella Grace and finish his stint the official way so he could get back to his life.

But Paul knew that wouldn't happen—not with the thing that was coming at them.

The thing he didn't need to go to anymore, as he'd told Ray-Anne.

He couldn't say for certain what it was, but he knew it was as real as the dog he watched sprinting up and down the dog-friendly part of the beach, sand flying as it ran.

Which was when he remembered that the dog-friendly area had been closed due to rising lake levels.

And realized there wasn't anyone with the dog.

And that the itching and burning of the lightning flowers

had stopped.

The dog, a big gray poodle, continued its sandy circuit, mouth agape, running on an open throttle. Dogs did that, frantically exploring as if they hadn't been there the day before and the day before that.

This was different, though. It was like the big, happy pooch had been let out to run in the open after months or years of being penned up. Paul wondered where the owner was.

A moment later, the dog saw him watching and stopped dead, sand shooting from under his paws in one final arc as he skidded to a halt. He took a few steps back, hopping from side to side as he studied Paul with his head turned one way, then the other.

Paul stood and walked over to the closest part of the enclosure.

The dog trotted up to the fence to give Paul a sniff. It wasn't a poodle after all. It was built a bit too thickly, and the added bulk was muscle. A labradoodle, maybe. Paul took a risk and reached over the fence to pull the dog closer and check his tag, which jingled against the barrier's steel.

Angus. Angus the labradoodle.

Paul let go before the dog could feel threatened. "Where's your owner, Angus?"

Angus snorted once and took off running across the enclosure again, headed for the gate on the other side. His escape would be a failure; both gates of the dog-lock were closed.

Paul turned to scan for the dog's owner, who surely couldn't be far.

Nothing.

When he turned back, there was no sign of Angus, either.

The enclosure was empty, and when Paul checked, both gates were solidly latched.

13
TINGLE

In the morning, Bobby pouted into his coffee.

Annie didn't need him to speak his mind. He thought she hadn't put enough sugar in it, even though she'd stirred in packet after packet until it was the caffeinated glucose soup he preferred.

Her knee tingled. *Bobby was a patient, kind man.* Nevertheless, she didn't want to give him any excuse for a mood he'd take out on her or, worse, on Zach.

Another tingle from her knee. *Bobby didn't have a temper.*

This morning, Bobby was actually on the better end of his anger spectrum. He merely glowered silently at his phone instead of blaming her or riding Zach for some perceived infraction.

If Annie made the hard-boiled eggs in a batch on a Sunday so that they'd have them right away in the morning, they didn't reheat right. If she made fresh ones, they took too long. Cereal was mushy, and the low-carb diet he adopted ruled that out anyway. She wasn't dumb enough to bring up all the sugar he dumped into his coffee. Why set him off?

His clothes needed to be put out for him, yet he never liked what she chose.

Why couldn't she shower at night so she could boil fresh eggs for him and make the bacon that was never done quite right while he got ready in the morning?

It was too quiet without the radio on.

Why was the radio tuned to music?

Why news?

Caring for a special-needs seven-year-old was nothing compared to handling an ex-husband who, after making a decent case for rekindling their relationship almost as soon as she and Zach got off the bus from New York, turned petty, impatient, and mean. And that was when he shared any emotions with them at all.

Zach, consistent as ever, opened the bottle of prescription pills Bobby kept on the kitchen table and shook two crimson caplets out into the cap. Then he peeled his egg carefully and proceeded to stare into the randomly arranged shell fragments like a tasseographer using whatever materials were at hand.

Bobby held his hand out. His eyes never left his phone.

Zach grabbed the bottle cap and dumped the caplets onto Bobby's palm.

Bobby, with a victorious smirk, popped the pills into his mouth and washed them down with a swallow of sugary coffee goop. He didn't thank his son. He didn't acknowledge him.

Bobby would have treated an obedient dog better. And this would be his only interaction with Zach all day, assuming Zach didn't do anything to set him off. "Did you hit the knee?" he asked Annie, sucking down another dose of goop while swiping at his phone. He didn't look at her or her knee. And the fact that he called it *the* knee rather than *her* knee told

Annie all she needed to know about the flavor of his concern. The surgery had been expensive, and he wanted to know that the investment was being looked after.

"I'll do it at the office."

"Do it here. Before you go."

"First thing when I get in. I promise."

Bobby swiped at his phone. He usually didn't like taking his pills without her also dosing her knee. He let it slide this time.

When Bobby left for work, and Annie took Zach to school before heading to the office, it provided a break from the tension. It was never long enough.

It had gotten so that whenever the trolley poles on the 33 bus popped off the overhead wires rounding the corner of Golden Gate Park, stopping the commute cold, Annie hoped the driver would struggle to hook them back up. Any delay getting to work and seeing Bobby again was a welcome mercy.

At Ambit Academy, which was tucked into the side of the hill next to the UC San Francisco campus, Annie would invent excuse after excuse to dawdle. Even Zach would finally lose patience and want her to leave. Her presence interfered with whatever rhythm he and his Autistic Spectrum Disorder companions maintained between themselves.

That is, if Zach was even ASD. Annie had her doubts, and the older he got, the more those doubts grew. On the spectrum, they said. She suspected her son wasn't on any spectrum they'd ever recognize.

They covered the blocks from the bus to the school too fast. "Good morning favorite mother 'n' son!" Maddy Tartarin called from her driver's-side window, rolling up to the Ambit drop-off curb as Annie was pulling the school's front door open for Zach.

"Morning," Annie tried to infuse the word with an enthusiasm she didn't feel.

Maddy remained still, framed by the widow, her toothy display frozen. Clearly, she was waiting for Annie to notice something. She gave her head a shake that was subtle by her standards, fanning out her hair. In the back seat, placed as if she were being chauffeur-driven, her daughter Addy watched all involved. Her eyes met Zach's without expression—their usual exchange, though Annie often suspected there was a level of communication she simply missed.

As much as Annie couldn't stand Maddy, Zach and Addy shared a mutual affection. Which was good because Annie wanted Zach to have friends but terrible in that it gave Maddy an opening to crowbar her way into their lives.

"How was your weekend?" Annie said, attempting to sound like someone who cared about the answer.

Maddy's grin fell. "You don't see it?"

Annie forced herself to smile. It felt like she'd bared her teeth in threat. "I'm sorry. See what?"

Addy got out of the car and stood beside Zach. The two of them watched their mothers without looking like they saw anything, which was their way.

Maddy shook her hair again.

Now Annie caught on. The woman's formerly chestnut-brown shoulder-length tresses were now a deep burgundy.

"You like?" said Maddy.

"Yes!" Annie nailed the desired tone of excitement properly this time. "It's really cute, Maddy."

"I started out wanting to go you." Maddy reached out to lift a length of Annie's red hair with a finger and then released it. "Or your son because it's remarkable how his is a perfect match for yours. But we just kept getting darker."

"Wow." Annie turned to look for Zach, hoping for a way

out of the conversation before Maddy tried to pin her down on her social calendar—it was usually something that involved volunteering with Silicon Valley money ladies—but her son and Addy had made a break for it.

"They went in," Maddy said, smiling at what Annie imagined she saw as her chance to put something on the schedule.

An SUV behind Maddy's car honked, holding it a little longer than necessary.

Maddy acted as if she hadn't heard. Her grimace held. "It would have been fine if we'd stopped at your shade of red. I mean, since you don't look anywhere close to your age."

"Thank you. That's very kind of you to say." Annie wasn't sure how else to respond. What was her age supposed to look like? Was there a visual standard for upper thirties?

"And Zach. He doesn't look his, either. Still waiting for that one to grow!"

Now Annie truly didn't know how to respond. She never did in the face of a hollowly benign sentiment masking the real view that her son wasn't quite right compared with the others. Such prejudices persisted even in a community whose members should know better.

Maddy's severe grin stood its ground as the SUV behind her honked again. "What are you up to next Sunday?"

14

A GUN ALWAYS KNOWS ITS TRUE LOVE

Exiting the garage on her motorcycle, Ray-Anne glanced at the still-empty cage outside the Tuxedo Bar. George Wickham the parrot was still gone. When the place was open for business in the warm weather, Elsie kept him outside in his cage, accompanied only by the hand-carved sign made by a regular that warned, simply: "No. He bites."

Which he did, if you were dumb enough to offer your finger for sacrifice. Yet someone had whisked him away from behind the locked cage door.

Ray-Anne hadn't spoken to Elsie about it, but Pop Mike said she was beside herself over the fate of the ornery old bird. "In these times, there's a place for a sharp beak and a cutting attitude," Pop Mike had said. "And we need people who understand that, so keep an eye on Elsie and make sure they don't steal her next." He was kidding. Probably.

She headed for Lake Shore Drive. A sharp beak. She could use one herself.

Too many things were in an in-between state. It set her on edge.

When she trusted an assortment of women she'd only recently met more than the guy she'd moved to Chicago with in order to launch a new operation, things were out of alignment. She didn't know how to make them right. She wasn't even sure how to define the problem. And that made it worse.

Ray-Anne shot up the Foster Avenue on-ramp and into the flow of traffic on the Drive. Her almost-too-powerful horse was a Y2K Superbike, given to New Beginnings by the mother of some rich kid whose dad wanted his son to have the most speed money could buy. The kid's mom decided she'd rather see her son live long enough to apply to college.

So the bike was part of the New Beginnings stable. It was used exclusively by Ray-Anne, who did courier and messenger work on it, paying New Beginnings a fee for its use and donating most of her income to the house.

She goosed the bike, shooting the gap between a Range Rover and a Tesla, all three of them ignoring the posted forty-mile-an-hour speed limit. That was the practice for everyone on the Drive, which was treated like a superhighway even though it wasn't one.

Ray-Anne was in front of the luxury SUV and then beyond, passing the Tesla, before the driver of either car understood what was happening. Pushing past the bike's physical limitations was surreal—something that shouldn't have been allowed to occur. Yet it happened. Ray-Anne chose not to question how she was able to do such things.

Lake Michigan and its beaches passed in a blur to her left, the water blue as a Caribbean destination on days like today. To the right, the high-rises of Chicago were but a smear, a visual testament to her speed and reflexes.

Ray-Anne didn't know whether she was racing toward or away from something. Both, probably. And while she was able to choose and exploit gaps between fast-moving cars, she sensed she'd fallen into a larger in-between state of existence over which she had no control.

Something was coming, according to Paul. And something had happened already. Something they'd done. Only nothing had.

It didn't matter that many mornings, she woke up feeling like she'd been a part of something big. A wedding. A birth. A death. A victory. A defeat. Something. But by the time she was fully awake, she'd forget whatever it was, assuming she'd known at all.

Two questions—both big, both obvious.

What had happened?

And what was coming?

Ray-Anne pushed the bike harder, the other vehicles no more than video-game pixelations now. She had no answers. So she went faster.

Taking the Drive to Wicker Park was going out of the way. But it gave Ray-Anne a chance to open up the bike and thread the traffic needle with as tight a set of maneuvers as physics would allow. More, maybe. The point was to clear her head. And when she was pushing those limits, with the cyclists on the Lakefront Trail mere colored flashes on her left and the boats of Belmont Harbor little more than that, it was as if she'd achieved a state between states—opened a view into a world beyond.

That sensation was stronger lately, no matter how she tried to pretend it wasn't. It was as if she were picking up strength and skill from somewhere else, letting it bleed into her. Which was crazy. And which left her wondering whether she had any right to challenge Paul on his nutty statements. Not for the first time, she understood that she was closer to his way of seeing things than she cared to admit.

By the time Ray-Anne dumped out on Division and

slowed down to normal traffic speed, she reached a state of detente with what she was about to do. She'd stick with the plan to visit Paul at Stella Grace. The fact that she was going there by a route that took her miles south and west before heading back up to the hospital didn't make her a hypocrite for criticizing Paul even though she herself was veering from the straight and narrow. Not at all. He'd tried to leave everyone who loved him behind, and that was a sacred promise broken.

Paul claimed he hadn't intended to die—that it was just a means to an end, the point being to get to the other place. She could take him at his word. But what difference would motives have made when she and Pop Mike were visiting his grave?

She started back in with the physics-defying maneuvers before catching herself. That was how much what Paul nearly did to himself messed with her—planting himself on a bench with a nice view of the lake just north of Foster Beach, pills already at work.

If a midnight jogger hadn't spotted Paul from the trail and noticed the curious way he slumped. If he hadn't been an off-duty fireman who knew what to do.

Ray-Anne had weird inner workings of her own. But at least she planned on sticking around to see things through.

When she rolled up on Pawn King, she was relieved to see that though nearly all the merchandise in the window was different from the day before, the only item she cared about was still in the same spot. She'd lost count of the times she'd stopped by the pawn shop, with its strange neon sign cycling through its two namesake chess pieces—red for the pawn, blue for the king. She didn't know why she kept returning. She'd come upon the shop while looking for a birthday gift for Elsie, who collected antique hip flasks and displayed them behind the bar at the Tux.

And there it had been.

Ray-Anne had never made it into the Pawn King to inquire about flasks. When she saw what was in the window, there among the tarnished brass instruments, the obsolete medical implements, and the antique badminton set, she was afraid to enter. No idea why. She'd been afraid every day since, though she kept coming back to check and make sure it was still safely behind the glass.

Today was different.

Today she went in.

"I'm sorry," said the Pawn King, who wore a baseball cap with a crown on it, when she asked him for a price. "I don't know what you mean."

Had a plague of madness hit Chicago, like one of those antibiotic-resistant superbugs? "In the window. Right by the big sax."

The Pawn King unlocked the gate to the window case and pulled it open with a tortured-steel cry that was both squeal and rasp. The two of them winced at the assault. Then he slid the curtain aside to reveal the window merchandise from the back of the display.

It wasn't there.

"I'm not sure what you think you saw, miss." The Pawn King was a patient grandpa explaining to a little girl that she couldn't have seen a unicorn, no matter how urgent her need to believe. "I couldn't sell one of those if I wanted to. I'm not licensed. And it's illegal to sell replicas in the city. What's a pretty young lady need with that, anyway?"

Ray-Anne scanned the case. She knew what she'd seen out there on the sidewalk—and had seen almost every day.

The Pawn King let the curtain fall back into place, closed the gate, and locked it again. Mercifully, going the other way, the screech was muted. Perhaps the case was embarrassed for her. "Maybe the light just hit one of those horns in a funny way," the Pawn King said, as if a patronizing tone was the balm Ray-Anne needed. "Or maybe it's hiding until the person it's waiting for comes along. You know what they say. A gun always knows its true love."

The man was trying to be kind in his own way. But Ray-Anne knew what she'd seen.

"I do need to clean the window." Seeing Ray-Anne to the door, the Pawn King pulled it open and held it for her. He was so eager to get her outside that he grazed his foot, ringing the sleigh bells hanging from the push bar. "Heck, as filthy as that glass is, a trombone could look like anything." He tried for a smile of understanding. "Even a shotgun."

15

THE WORK OF CLAWS

After two weeks of paperwork, Jeremy began commuting from Jersey City to his new home in the Times Square office. He shared a space with Abel that was small but evenly divided.

No longer was Jeremy in the open-office layout of Perth Amboy, where even a mindless job such as opening reply envelopes for a Manitou retirement-investing subsidiary was nearly impossible to do amid the text alerts, ringtones, and reality-TV play-by-play of Jeremy's colleagues. No longer was he robo-scheduled, which kept contractors like him from planning any aspect of their lives because they might have a shift scheduled with twelve-hour notice—and have it canceled with four.

Best of all, Jeremy traded mail-sorting duties in a hellish subsidiary for a new set of responsibilities in one of Manitou's nerve centers—the data-analysis and reporting unit. Here, Abel promised, Jeremy would learn to put the storytelling skills no longer valued in the editorial field to use earning a more stable living and, assuming he got along with everyone, gain a bit more job security. Or as much as one could in the corporate world.

So far, so good. Abel pulled the data and put together the appropriate visualizations while Jeremy watched him do it so that he could eventually handle that part. Then they discussed the financial-performance story to be told based on the day's headlines and the information flow from the field and the Manitou clients.

Then Jeremy made a tale of it. It was a process that was already working smoothly.

Except, that is, for Jeremy's fear that he was losing his sanity—and his deeper terror that Abel or someone who hadn't taken Abel's liking to him would find out.

It had already been a worry when he'd worked in Perth Amboy. At first, he thought crazy people were using the prepaid response envelopes included with the marketing materials for the company's various investment schemes as a way to get their message out into the world. And that was true in some cases.

People stuck everything from dirty pictures and deeply personal poetry to religious pamphlets and little comic books into the envelopes and sent them back. Some even wrote long message-in-a-bottle letters about their lives, hoping someone might answer.

There was the guy who thought a Japanese soldier who didn't know World War II was over was living under the canopy of his neighbor's overgrown hedge. And the lady who was certain that the raccoons going through her garbage at night were informing on her, though she wasn't sure who they worked for.

All of that had been a balance of funny and sad. One of the only things the Perth Amboy mail-sorting people bonded over, in fact, was seeing who could come up with the nuttiest stuff.

Then came the letter, stuck inside one of the standard reply envelopes, directed to Jeremy. It was from an old woman asking his assistance in reaching a dead brother whose Piper Cub had gone down in a storm he'd been told not to fly in. She'd known Jeremy's full name.

That was followed by the fear-of-God comic that would have been just like the others frequently sent in were it not for the main character, whose lack of faith doomed him to eternal torment.

He was named Jeremy. And he looked like Jeremy.

Jeremy didn't enter those into the competition for wackiest mail. He never showed them to anyone. He just chalked them up to a combination of weird coincidence and a lack of judgement brought on by robo-scheduling and a near-constant sleep deficit.

But sleep brought with it the dreams, which cycled through patterns of awfulness. He was strung up in a web with countless other people—cocooned, eyes and mouth sewn shut—while unseen things scuttled over him. He was buried in a desert with only his face above the sand, scarcely able to breathe without inhaling grit. He could hear the cries of others being attacked nearby and the work of claws through the grains. He was defenseless. And he was next.

The dreams continued even after he'd started the new gig with Abel and established a healthier pattern of working hours that allowed him to get enough sleep. And the waking lunacy followed him to Manhattan, where it actually managed to get worse.

His commute included a walk from Port Authority to the office, on Broadway between Forty-Fourth and Forty-Fifth. Jeremy was familiar with what the area used to be. Bartenders and others in the neighborhood who'd known it decades before tried to tell him there was no way he could understand how much it had changed, how bad it had been. All of the glitzy theaters, both movie and stage, were porn houses for years. He could not have negotiated the route from bus to desk without staining his brain with the sights, smells, and effluent of the street.

Jeremy agreed with them. He couldn't imagine it. What he didn't tell them was that he didn't need to. Because while he usually saw the same bustling family-friendly environs they did, that wasn't always the case.

There was the morning he walked past a body with a sheet over it lying face-up on Forty-Second. He'd stumbled upon a film shoot, he figured, and all it would have taken was a jolt of Colin Clive's lightning for it to sit up and be on its way, like Boris Karloff with his neck electrodes.

It wasn't a prop or promotional gag, he saw when he got closer. It was a real body. And when he made his way around it, he couldn't help but look back.

What had appeared to be a solid figure under the sheet wasn't anything of the sort. It was a writhing mass of something bad. Something that flicked and struck the underside of the sheet, like snakes, or hopped up in little lumps, like frogs. It took Jeremy hours to pull himself together. Abel asked him if anything was wrong more than once, and he said no each time.

There was the evening a guy staggered across his path on Forty-Fourth, drunk or high, and took a header into a pile of garbage bags. Jeremy was the only one to stop. He'd had plenty of experience with New Yorkers' ability to ignore anything or anyone, but not even the tourists noticed the guy.

The man lay where he fell, face-up, cushioned by restaurant leavings and other assorted filth. His eyes were wide open, his mouth agape, and Jeremy had no doubt he was dead.

Nobody else saw him. It wasn't just that they didn't want to. He wasn't there to them.

Taking a closer look made it worse. The corpse was that of the father of a kid he'd gone to high school with. That, or it was his twin. But it was him. Even though the man had died of a heart attack a decade earlier.

All of that would have been bad enough without the craziness that made its way into the Manitou offices, where it threatened the job he was so damned grateful to have. A week or two after the garbage-bag incident, he got out of an elevator with one of the other analysts he'd trained with and grabbed the handle of the frosted-glass door to hold it open for her.

The handle grabbed him back.

Somehow, he kept up his bit of cheery conversation with her even though what had been steel was now a warm human hand squeezing his knuckles in a firm grip.

"Why, thank you." The other analyst gave Jeremy a bit of a flirty smile for his gentlemanly ways while he labored to avoid shrieking like a madman.

Right as he was going to try making the door let go, it released him. It wasn't a hand at all. It was the same metal handle it had always been.

So, yeah. Crazy.

Now, coming up on nine in the morning, things were reaching the breaking point. The madness had found its way into his and Abel's office, where it surely meant to torment him until he gave himself away, and Abel was forced to admit he was mentoring a head case.

They'd established an effective routine to start their days. Abel's visualization software pulled in the previous day's performance numbers and threw together some rough sketches before they even arrived. Once the two of them got in, Abel cleaned the data up enough to tell Jeremy if any of the things he was about to highlight in his write-up were off and needed to be checked again.

For a few weeks, it had gone very well.

Until the piercing screams started.

The first one came when Abel was off grabbing them coffee: a field-whistle-high shriek. It was almost enough to make Jeremy flee the room. Initially, he thought it was a smoke alarm, but when he poked his head out into the hallway, people were chatting and going about their normal routines. He was the only one to hear it.

The next time it happened, he was able to pretend it hadn't. It wouldn't do to have anyone walk past just as he bit through his own tongue.

An hour later, the third scream came with a more disturbing quality. It was a human voice—that of a woman in pain. Abel, who'd just finished off round two of the caffeine, had to have heard Jeremy's intake of breath, but Jeremy kept his back to him as if nothing unusual had occurred.

Jeremy chanced a look up at the wall, where the noise had originated. He had to keep it together yet again when he saw what looked like a veiny skin graft applied to the wallpaper. A tiny pair of lips, slightly parted, occupied the thing's center, and its surface rose and fell with its breathing.

"What's up?" said Abel.

"Nothing, why?"

Abel had noticed Jeremy gaping at the thing on the wall, and he, too, was looking up at it. "You can see that?"

Jeremy decided against playing dumb. "Can you?"

"If I choose. But normally, I don't want to. Neither does anyone else. It's not even supposed to be there. It's not yelling at you, is it?"

"Not now. Only when it feels like scaring the crap out of me."

Abel watched the thing. "It's a focusite. They feed by robbing you of your concentration. It's not good that it's doing it to you." He studied Jeremy. "We'll take care of it. I'll talk to Mr. Truitt."

16

BATTEN-DOWN TIME

The walk back to New Beginnings was supposed to clear Paul's head. Instead, it was as surreal as his exit from Stella Grace and his long sleep on the bench.

While Paul was on his unplanned vacation, Chicago had turned into something out of a post-apocalyptic movie. There were no people on the streets. He hadn't been surprised by that at first, given the hour, but it started to get weird as time passed and the city didn't show up.

No cars, cabs, or buses.

No open coffee shops.

No humans.

Paul half-expected to see Charlton Heston pull up in a red convertible to machine-gun a shadowy figure in a window.

This was what Pop Mike called batten-down time. When things go wonky, as they most definitely were now, you sealed your hatches. You made sure everything was tight, and you prepared to do whatever was necessary to make it through the storm without taking on water. The old man loved his metaphor, but he was right.

When Paul put it all together: the nurses unable to see him

and Huey, their disappearance from the system—assuming Huey had ever been in it at all—his lost day and night and now this dystopic vision of Chicago, it required him to wire himself pretty tight in order to hold it together.

Was post-apocalyptic the accurate way to describe it? There weren't any skeletons, garbage, or zombies. Not that Paul was complaining about the missing undead.

Everything looked to be normal until little details began jumping out at him. Like the fact that there weren't nearly as many cars parked on the street as there should have been. And all of the ones he saw were booted. Every one.

Nobody drove past.

The 92 bus didn't show up along Foster, and no one waited at any of the stops.

Only when he walked under the red-line tracks did he realize he hadn't heard an L train go by.

Batten it down.

Batten it down, and let Ray-Anne explain once he got to New Beginnings.

If he let a little of the bad stuff in, the seal would be broken —the game lost.

As Paul headed for Sheridan Road, the sun hadn't made much progress in its rise. The fog had lifted, but the clouds overhead remained the same banded spread of coral and violet that had been at his back when he left the beach. And the angle of the light hadn't changed. It was as if the sun had decided to go on break while climbing.

Batten down.

Paul rounded the corner onto Sheridan, a couple blocks north of New Beginnings.

Angus the labradoodle was headed straight for him, racing across the squares of sidewalk with the same verve he'd displayed on the sand. The dog pulled up short when he saw

Paul, then did his sideways hop of appraisal, panting for all he was worth.

Well, at least somebody was trying to add some life to the catatonic morning. And the pooch wouldn't get hit by a car before his owner got ahold of him, given the complete lack of moving vehicles—and vehicles that were incapable of moving. The sole car on the current block sported a big yellow boot, too.

"Come here, boy." Paul's spoken words were a greater disturbance to the eerie quiet of the morning than he'd intended them to be.

Angus sat down and panted at him. The sound of that, too, was louder than it should have been in the strange stillness—and it carried farther than Paul would have expected.

Paul slapped his thigh a couple times. The whack of palm on fabric echoed off the street.

The dog hitched back and forth, enjoying the game. Then he barked and took off back the way he'd come until he was but a capering blip in the weird light of the weird morning.

The battening discipline held up as Paul drew closer to New Beginnings and heard the dog barking again. It held steady when he saw what Angus was all excited about.

In front of the Tuxedo Bar, George Wickham the parrot sat in his cage, gazing down at the labradoodle with equal parts imperiousness and disdain.

Clueless, Angus yapped and rose up to dance on his hind legs.

Tall as Angus was when he stood, the big dog was nevertheless unable to get near the parrot's safely enclosed observation post. And the pole was sturdy enough that when he knocked it with his forepaws, the cage remained motionless.

Elsie was no dummy. Passing mutt after passing mutt had made a play for the bird over the years, along with more than a few feral cats. The perch was practically light-pole thick, and the sturdy screening beneath the bars ensured that George Wickham was safe from bird-napping attempts and climbing assaults, too. And he knew it.

Paul shushed the dog. Angus shut up, but he maintained enough of a distance to keep Paul from grabbing his collar. Little victories.

The Tux was closed and dark, given the early hour. So what was the parrot doing here by himself? Elsie never left him out when she wasn't nearby to keep an eye on him, and she certainly wouldn't have done so after he'd already inexplicably disappeared once. Yet the Tux stood silent and bereft of humanity, the bird an abandoned sentry harassed by passing pooches.

Paul looked to New Beginnings, and his hatches began to take on water.

New Beginnings, too, was dark and dead.

A former nursing home with nearly 200 rooms, New Beginnings Chicago was never without lights or people. It had been built in 1919 as a luxury hotel, and everything from its imposing presence to its architecture, which Pop Mike said was Renaissance Revival, demanded life and light. As Pop Mike said of their operations, they'd go dark when they were no longer needed. And while that was the dream, it would never be the reality.

It looked to be the reality now.

No lights.

No sound.

Even worse, when Paul tried the front door, he found it was unlocked, exposing the entire facility to the world at large. And while the mission of New Beginnings was to help the less fortunate members of that world, it was certainly key to its survival to monitor their comings and goings.

Where was Ray-Anne? Where were the various staff members and volunteers? Who was checking residents in and out?

Paul held the front door open, too overcome with growing worry to go all the way inside.

Angus took that as an invitation to explore. He galloped into the building, through the foyer, and into one of the dark hallways, nails skittering and dog tag jingling in the unseen depths.

Maybe it was just a power failure, and Ray-Anne and whoever was on duty had gone to check the breaker board without realizing the door was unlocked. Which made no sense. The door defaulted to being locked.

From somewhere in the darkness, Angus barked again.

It wasn't the playful noise of an excited dog with a new space to explore. It was something real. Something he'd confronted.

The barking was cut short after an open-throated cry of real pain.

Paul's Lichtenbergs began itching again in earnest. He made his way past the empty front desk and headed into the dark to find the dog.

Now came the static-current feeling up the back of the neck.

What had happened to the happy dog in an empty and near-dark building that should have been anything but empty and near-dark?

The answer came, fast and brutal.

Halfway down the hall, a large, viscous puddle on the floor reflected some of the weak light from the newly installed emergency beacons and the exit sign at the hallway's end, like a waiting water trap. On top of everything else going on, there was a leak to deal with.

As Paul drew closer, preparing to step gingerly through the puddle, it moved.

That wasn't possible.

Yet it did.

And moved again.

And rose up in front of him.

Before Paul could react, a vertical slit appeared in the now upright puddle. Something shot out of the resulting gap in the dim light, straight at him. It caught him in the throat. With the impact came a wave of pain—and a despair that washed over him.

Violation.

Trespass.

Theft.

Something was being taken from Paul that might never be returned.

Paul understood Angus's cries.

Then the blackness was complete.

17
KNEE-DEEP IN DO-OVER

Annie's assigned tasks were easy, and that wasn't good. She relished a challenge when diving into data—a multistepped approach to answering questions and measuring performance calling for queries only a data jock with a puzzle fetish could write, run, and improve. The work at Manitou was anything but.

Nobody at Manitou wrote queries or worked with raw data. Rather, the geniuses who paid for her chair and desk, the on-site barista and artisanal-coffee bar, and all the rest had hooked piles and piles of venture-capital money with a different approach—virtual reality. Annie spent her days with her head inside a surprisingly light VR rig—a setup that was both auditory and visual and, if she wasn't careful, would have her believing that what it presented was the real world.

The real world of the Manitou offices took up the whole of a former merchandise mart on Market, between Ninth and Tenth. The space was enclosed within walls so thick that even when the rig wasn't on, Annie might as well have journeyed to another realm. Often, especially working nights, it felt like she'd done just that.

The revolution launched by the Manitou founders was turning data management into what was essentially a three-dimensional video game. Annie didn't work with numbers; she manipulated objects in an immersive environment nearly convincing enough to make her lose herself.

The work consisted of navigating digital warehouses, retail spaces, and any other representation allowing her to shelve objects where they were supposed to go, retrieve others from places they weren't supposed to be, and answer questions or tidy up when necessary. If the data that needed cleaning was particularly dirty, she might find herself facing more of an archeological dig than a packed storage space. But for the most part, the job remained a daily routine: pick things up, get information from them; put them back where it made more sense, if needed.

Glean. Clean. Organize.

Annie didn't love it. It was a living.

Her knee tingled. *Annie was lucky to have the job. She got free coffee, food, and snacks, and she never had to leave the building during the day.*

In fact, leaving was frowned upon if it meant a drop in efficiency.

Another tingle. *Which was all right, of course. What was more critical than efficiency?*

Still, Annie tried to brighten up her surroundings, which in her case, didn't mean plastering her cubicle walls with photos and such. She had one shot of Zach on her desk, a favorite where he looked as if he was about to smile—or maybe just giving it hard consideration.

Sometimes, deep in the data, Annie enjoyed a strange anomaly of the VR goggles: she swore she saw Zach's face from the photo looking down at her as she toiled. And when she got lucky, he really did look happy.

By the time one of the Manitou nurses showed up to hit Annie's knee—Bobby's expression, not hers—Annie was almost halfway through a massive book warehouse. Sitting in the chair through the morning hours had stiffened up the old injury pretty thoroughly. She'd just completed a comic-book section of the storage area, and working the lower shelves of the steel racks in the VR world had her knee throbbing. It was almost as if she'd been doing the physical work—slipping issues out of their protective bags to assess their health, re-bagging them, separating random piles into stacks organized by title—for real.

"Hello, Annie." The nurse, Hannah, spoke in a low but distinctive voice. All of the on-premises health people knew to approach the data techs in as sedate a manner as possible in order to avoid jarring them while they worked. Even in a virtual realm, a startled jock knocking over a carefully arranged stack or stacks could mean a lot of do-over work or an even bigger mess than they'd started with.

That took time. Time was money. And Manitou was very, very careful with its money.

Annie stepped back from the *Mausoleum of Madness* issues she was reorganizing, tapped out of the environment, and removed her headgear. Though the setup was wireless, she moved as if she were surrounded by fragile cables. More than one tech had dropped or jostled their setup, only to find when stepping back in that they were knee-deep in do-over. Or as some called it, doo-doo-over

Hannah, one of the more recent additions to the Health & Wellness team, stood enough of a distance away to signal respect for Annie's space, enthusiasm and injector at the ready.

Annie had a bit of a soft spot for the kid. Hannah was young enough that the newness of what she did provided her with a real reason to come in every day.

"Good morning, Hannah." Annie rotated her chair to face the nurse and rolled up her pant leg to expose the tiny port just below her knee.

"Good morning, Annie." Hannah was pleased to be recognized. "Mr. Brucker requested I stop by for your intake, just in case you didn't get a chance to do it before you left home this morning.

Bobby was Mr. Brucker. Annie was Annie.

The thing was, if Annie was even a little late for her intake, as it was officially called, the knee would start to bother her. So it made no sense for her to be sloppy about keeping up with her meds when left to her own devices—especially since the obscenely expensive experimental implant, which Manitou had paid for entirely, gave her the gift of a pain-free life and a fully functional knee so long as she kept up with the schedule. Yet sloppy she was.

Hannah broke the seal on the injector and knelt by Annie to swab the knee port.

On her best day, Annie couldn't drop to the floor that smoothly, never mind rise to her feet again. But after a dose, she could get a lot closer to it than she'd ever been able to since being wounded. And that was surely worth something.

"Ready?"

"As ever." Annie always said that.

And she never was.

The stubby injector slid easily into the port. Then came the part Annie dreaded. The implant twitched like a living thing, an addict presented with the fix it had been longing for, and felt like it was drawing the dose in. She'd been told time and again it was her imagination, that the device was inert.

Still, Annie swore the thing swelled with both liquid and relief following an intake.

Not that she didn't do that herself. Any discomfort she was feeling in her long-suffering joint faded almost immediately. Which once again left her wondering why she so often delayed taking her medicine.

The knee tingled. *Annie really needed to show more gratitude for these treatments, which were pre-tax and subsidized by Manitou.*

She thanked Hannah for her assistance. The nurse once again appeared to take no small amount of joy from hearing Annie say her name.

Hannah pulled the cartridge from the injector, accidentally flinging a stray drop or two from it as she pushed it into the disposal unit she wore on a belt holster. "Sorry." She dabbed the errant medicine off of Annie's desk with a sterile wipe.

As Annie once again donned her headgear to return to her comic books, she realized what the problem was, if you could call it that. It was the garish shade of the stuff being sucked into her, a hue not to be found anywhere in any of the makeup, clothing, or jewelry she wore—though, admittedly, her collection of those things was modest. That was, if not all of it, then a good part of it.

Pink was never one of her favorite colors.

18

REALITY'S USUAL SET OF RULES

Ray-Anne wanted to make amends. She felt like a bit of a hypocrite, treating Paul like the one with all the problems when she'd just demonstrated some challenges of her own.

She stopped by the Stella Grace office to ask about the ring. She was pretty certain they wouldn't allow Paul to have it back until he'd proven he was fit to walk out the door. And then they'd insist on giving it directly to him. But she wanted to be able to say she tried.

The staff member in the administration office was mystified. He'd recently catalogued everything being held because state law required it. They weren't holding any rings, much less one from somebody's mother.

Ray-Anne almost asked him if he knew the Pawn King.

"What was the patient name again?" The man typed like he just wanted to put the matter behind him.

It also bugged Ray-Anne that he remained standing. It was dismissive, like he couldn't be bothered to take the time to sit and concentrate on her request. "Paul Reid."

The admin sat. He typed furiously, frowned, and attacked

the keyboard anew, shifting into humor-the-nutty-girl mode. Maybe he did know the Pawn King. "I'm sorry," he said. "There's nobody by that name here."

"What?" Now came that floaty feeling, like Ray-Anne had just side-shifted her cycle in between two fast-moving cars and should have been squished, but was operating outside reality's usual set of rules.

The admin went from Pawn King patronizing mode to a flat-eyed look of assessment, which was a whole lot more worrisome. "There's no Paul Reid here," he said calmly. "Nor has one ever been admitted." The assessment was no more comfortable as its duration lengthened.

"What about Huey?"

The admin watched Ray-Anne. He'd probably never heard of Huey, either. And if he asked, she didn't even know the whistler's last name. "Listen," he said with a forced softening. "Why don't you have a seat? I'll have someone come out to talk."

A rattle of steel behind her. A delivery man fought to get a cart filled with supply boxes through the front door.

"Excuse me," the admin told the man. "That has to go to the dock around back."

"I always bring them in here." Shoving and yanking, the delivery man wrestled the cart over the threshold.

"Listen," the admin said.

The delivery man didn't. He rotated the cart and pushed it into the room.

The admin went out the door behind his desk, reappeared in the room, and planted himself in the delivery man's path. "It's not my rule."

Ray-Anne headed for the elevators. Luckily, one was waiting, though she thought she'd crack her teeth from clenching while she waited for the doors to close.

Upstairs, she checked the common room where they'd endured Huey's looping. There was no sign of Paul, and the surrounding halls and rooms were eerily silent except for the sound of someone coughing nearby.

She made a quick circuit of the floor, hoping to spot Paul or, barring that, maybe catch some of Huey's Mozart to prove to herself that she wasn't losing it.

Nothing.

No Paul.

No Huey.

Ray-Anne was searching so hard that she didn't realize she'd come upon the cougher until she nearly collided with her. It was a nurse.

"May I help you?" the cougher said.

"I hope so." Ray-Anne dropped into the same bright, cooperative act she used on city officials and donors. "I'm looking for Paul Reid."

She was prepared to have the nurse ask her for some ID so that she could prove she had a right to see Paul but not for the same confusion she'd prompted downstairs. "I'm sorry." The nurse endured another coughing fit before composing herself again. "We don't have anyone by that name on this floor."

"What about Huey? Hair like this?" She held her fingers up in a rooster comb. "Whistles? Whistles a lot?"

The nurse shook her head as she stifled another round.

"Are you new?"

"I've been here fifteen years."

Ray-Anne knew she was pushing her luck when she asked if maybe she could see room six-sixty-six, where her friend Paul was staying.

"No—I'm sorry, miss."

"Would it help if I said please very nicely?"

Another short coughing jag. "I'm afraid not. We don't have

a room six-sixty-six. Not since the '70s. I think it was all those devil movies." She put down another coughing rebellion and scanned Ray-Anne with the same assessment as the admin.

The phone at the station down the hall rang. Another staff member answered. Listening, her eyes settled on Ray-Anne.

Ray-Anne thanked the nurse and headed for the stairs.

The nurse looked as if she might not be inclined to let her skate away. Another coughing jag struck.

Ray-Anne took the steps two at a time.

19

THE RUBBISH GLADIATOR

"You suckers. You patsies. You victims. You fools." The Rubbish Gladiator was in fine form as Abel and Jeremy approached him on the way to pick up their first-of-the-morning caffeine. He expertly speared flattened coffee cups and their corresponding cardboard rings, cigarette butts, crumpled napkins, and assorted societal detritus cast down by office grunts, executives, and other midtown commuters.

The Rubbish Gladiator had a rolling trash can he used both as a receptacle for his vanquished litter foes and as a shield positioned between himself and any passerby who got too close. Because the sidewalks were packed, that was pretty much everyone in sight, so the Rubbish Gladiator was in constant motion. Fred to the rolling can's Ginger, he avoided contact and stabbed his trash targets in a fluid ballet of eco-mindfulness and misanthropy.

Jeremy initially assumed the Gladiator worked for a neighborhood business co-op. Over time, he came to realize that what he'd thought to be an official uniform was actually a ratty security-guard outfit that was probably a dumpster find.

And the logo on the Gladiator's ball cap was that of a local moving service.

And, of course, there was the ranting.

"You have the power," the Gladiator said to the passing businesspeople. "And you just give it over to them."

They ignored him, favoring their smartphone screens and leaving it to the Gladiator's grace to ensure a lack of collisions.

Rangy and in his forties or fifties but probably older, the Gladiator was part scruffy warrior and part doomsayer. Outrage completed him. "They're conning you," he told a passing lawyer type, leaning in. "They'll turn your sons into battle meat and your daughters into whores." He didn't appear to be bothered when she paid him no mind. "And then." He laughed. "And then."

He returned to his rhythmic mantra. He always did, repeating it in a rhythm to all of Times Square and beyond—and to nobody at all. "You suckers. You patsies. You victims. You fools."

The man was disturbed, and Abel, like everyone else, pretended not to see him. Yet there was a gravity about him that left one wondering if maybe he had a point. Jeremy wanted to stop and see what else he might come out with.

Abel, however, was single-minded about his morning caffeine on any given day. On the random days when he decided that the office brew, good as it was, would not do the job, and only the sugary espresso concoction available a few blocks away would measure up, he was an irresistible force.

At Zip 'n' Sip, the line was out the door, which only convinced Abel he was right to have come. If not, then how come everybody else was there, too?

Once inside, Jeremy was surprised to see a windup mechanical pigeon wandering the floor, ambling between the feet of those queued up for their morning jolt juice, robotically gifted at evasive maneuvers. Periodically, it stopped and cooed, at which point sparks filled its eyes and fanned out from under its tail. Yet just as everyone outside had done with the Rubbish Gladiator, the crowd in here ignored the little bird.

"Annoying, but cool—sort of," Jeremy said, scanning the room for whoever was selling the toy. That was the way of these things in New York: whenever you spotted a little gadget on the sidewalk, the street vendor hawking it was usually a few feet away.

Not at the moment, though. The bird wandered on its own, dodging disaster time and again as the shuffling customers advanced in line.

"What is?" Abel perused the chalkboard's line-up of hand-crafted liquid speed, which was lovingly spelled out in every color available in the owner's box of chalk. He followed Jeremy's gaze, but his eyes slid right over the robot pigeon.

"The drawing," Jeremy said once he realized Abel, like those on the street who missed so many of the crazy things Jeremy saw during his commute, didn't see the bird. He nodded to the chalkboard, where a cartoon boxer with a cappuccino for a body exhorted the customers to man up and take him on. "Do they hire somebody to draw those?"

Abel shrugged. He had eyes only for the offerings.

Jeremy watched the crowd proceed toward the counter as the pigeon let out with the sparks again. None of them noticed it.

"That screaming thing on the wall," Jeremy said as Abel paid for their drinks with the company card, stirring his concoction with a straw. "What the hell is that? Is it real?"

"As real as anything else. If you see it and hear it, that is. Which you do. And which is why you need to be careful." It was clear Abel didn't want to have the conversation within earshot of others.

Outside, the Rubbish Gladiator repeated his rant about battle meat and intimate servitude. As Jeremy and Abel drew closer to him, he launched into his standby rhyme: "You suckers. You patsies."

Abel once again joined the passing crowd in ignoring him.

No. As was the case with the mechanical bird, Abel simply couldn't see or hear the man.

But Jeremy could.

~

MR. TRUITT'S office was smaller than Jeremy thought it would be. Granted, he'd had only a few minutes to imagine it because he never knew he'd be sitting here at all. But when he and Abel got back, caffeine-and-sugar bombs in hand, a waiting email asked Abel to bring Jeremy over.

Jeremy had assumed Mr. Truitt—everyone knew his first name was Gerald, but nobody was foolish enough to use it—wasn't aware of his existence. Now he and Abel sat at the man's modest-yet-elegant antique desk, which was made of an indeterminate dark wood and was large enough for work without being vulgar.

The same went for the office it occupied. Mr. Truitt, the second-in-command at Manitou, could have claimed a corner spot if he'd wanted one. But he was the kind of executive who sought the middle ground between a display of his stature and a setting humble enough to encourage underlings to relax and open up.

The word was that Mr. Truitt had once reported to a self-aggrandizing type with a monstrous desk and office and had learned the hard way that imperious management didn't work. Nobody knew where or who that had been, but rumor had it that whatever took down his boss had nearly drawn him in as well—a sinking ocean liner pulling a lifeboat down with it. That was the story, anyway. Jeremy certainly wasn't about to ask for confirmation.

Mr. Truitt sat and stared at Jeremy.

Jeremy assumed it was a test of sorts. So even though it went against his nature, he held the man's gaze far longer than he otherwise might have.

Until a shrill scream from the wall startled him into looking away. It was followed by another at a slightly higher pitch.

Truitt grinned in amusement and turned to look up at the two focusites, on the wall over his shoulder, almost all the way up at the ceiling. After a moment of what might have been silent communication with him, they faded away.

"Those two don't trust you, Mr. Johns." Mr. Truitt let that hang between them long enough for everyone to recognize who was in control of the room. "However, Mr. Dowd here assures me that you're unprincipled."

Jeremy didn't know how to react.

"That's code," Abel told Jeremy, his voice a bit higher than usual. He, too, was nervous. "It's a compliment. Like a mobster saying you're a friend of ours." He laughed.

Mr. Truitt didn't join him. Nor did Jeremy.

Truitt studied Jeremy again, his fingers drumming on his desk. "Well," he said. "That you're sitting here at all should tell you whose counsel I favor."

"Thank you, Mr. Truitt."

"Save your gratitude until you understand what you're in for. And do keep up."

Abel forced a chuckle, as did Jeremy. It seemed the wisest choice.

Jeremy wasn't sure how much to celebrate having this man's attention. It wasn't lost on him that Mr. Truitt mentioned the focusites in the same tone a man might use to discuss the Yankees or the Lexington subway line. The reality of them was simply a given—and he didn't disapprove of them in any way.

Mr. Truitt turned to the data visualizations spanning his three large monitors. He hit a combination on his keyboard, and the intricate graphs, their lines and bars pulsing like heartbeats, were projected on his office wall as the lights dimmed. "Now," he said. "Illuminate my morning, Mr. Dowd. What news from our friend?"

"Apalala has hit the one-hundred-and-twenty-day mark, which is another record," Abel said. "I don't think anyone's questioning its stability anymore."

"Excellent, because I've personally assured Mr. Callibeau that we shan't see any more instances of late reporting. It's all real-time from here. Which means that you've personally assured him as well, Mr. Dowd. And you, Mr. Johns."

"Understood, sir," Abel said.

"Good. But Mr. Johns has no earthly idea what we're talking about." He gestured with his hand, and the graphs took on a three-dimensional aspect. Only then did Jeremy understand that there were no monitors. The data visualizations hung in the air on their own, entities all to themselves. "If you are among the unprincipled, Mr. Johns—and you are—it's safe for me to relate the basics and leave it up to you to enlighten yourself further."

"Yes, sir."

Mr. Truitt paused to stare at him. Maybe "sir" wasn't a term to be employed here. "Forget much of what you may have learned at other companies," Mr. Truitt said. "They are play-acting, trading in currencies and trifles that are but representations of real meaning. We deal in the ultimate commodity—Essence."

The next pause was clearly intended to prompt Jeremy to ask the question everyone knew would follow. "Essence?"

"Essence. If I explain too much about what it is, you'll think me mad, and that will render the rest of this conversation pointless. Thus, I'll leave you to come to it on your own, with the able assistance—pun intended—of Mr. Dowd."

In the near darkness, Mr. Truitt's hands moved in a quick gesture. The graphs moved aside, revealing other visualizations. One looked like a medical readout, the other like an oscilloscope from an old sci-fi series. Jeremy hadn't heard any keys being tapped. Manitou must have given Mr. Truitt some impressive tech. "Now," he said. "Mr. Dowd."

"The algorithm has been learning for some time," Abel said. "It recalibrates in milliseconds rather than seconds now and is able to redistribute any concentrations well before they happen. As of this morning, it appears that the AI has reached the point of what they're calling virtual sentience."

"Interpret for Mr. Johns, please."

"It's making its own decisions like a living thing. And honestly, sir, nobody can say what it's doing. Not anymore. It's too far ahead of us, and it moves too fast."

"Tell Mr. Johns that's not worrisome, Mr. Dowd."

"It's not a worry."

Mr. Truitt hadn't really intended for Abel to reassure Jeremy. He was telling Abel to give him a guarantee.

"Again, Mr. Johns," said Mr. Truitt, "the short version. I was fortunate enough to learn a very painful and expensive lesson in Essence management in my previous situation. I deem it fortunate despite the very real agony and cost involved because the man who paid the true price for the strategy-gone-wrong was not me. I suffered, but I survived. He did not.

And now you, Mr. Dowd, Mr. Callibeau, and all of Manitou may benefit from what my former employer perished to prove: greed burns."

With another gesture, one of the graphs became a pie chart, and the monitor zoomed in on it. At least, that's what Jeremy told himself happened. It looked like the screen grew at Mr. Truitt's silent command—but that wasn't possible. Was it? Then again, sometimes the walls screamed at him, and robot pigeons roamed around coffee-shop floors.

Mr. Truitt moved his finger, and an arrow indicated the dominant part of the pie, which was nearly all of it except for a small sliver. "Under the old model, favored by my former employer"—Jeremy noted that he never used the word superior—"it was a winner-take-all scenario with the aim of gathering as much as possible. That was a fatal error. Controlling that much Essence was not sustainable over the long run, though I'll give him this—he was able to do so for a very, very long time."

With another gesture, the chart divided itself into many slices. Now the arrow pointed to one that was only a little larger than the next-most dominant slice.

"That was fine for him but not for us." Mr. Truitt left the enlarged pie chart hanging in the near-dark. "You can gather all the Essence you want, but if you allow it to concentrate for too long, it builds adjacency. You'll never manage it, never control it." He reached across his desk to grab a pitcher. The water flowed and the ice cubes clinked. There had been no such pitcher or glass on the man's desk before the lights went out. "That's the key to everything. Control. It remembers what it was. It wants to go where it thinks it should. And the longer you allow it to concentrate, with too much stored together for too long, it builds in willfulness—builds in adjacency. Management is the key."

"How do we manage it, sir?" Jeremy wasn't sure if asking another question would add to the impression he'd made or work against it, but it seemed a reasonable risk.

Mr. Truitt took a long sip, cubes colliding with one another. "A good question. Really, Mr. Dowd—well done bringing this young man into the discussion." More clinking.

Jeremy struggled to figure out if he was being mocked.

"The notion of focusing on control as much as quantity was Mr. Callibeau's innovation, not mine, Mr. Johns, which is why we report to him and not the other way around. You cannot win by greed alone. And honestly? Control is a more subtle art than crudely acquiring and holding." The ice cubes bounced off the glass and one another as he took another long draw, and Jeremy wondered if the pitcher contained only water. "It involves monitoring adjacency and concentration. And fission." He drained the glass and set it down. "That's where Apalala comes in."

20

THE STILLNESS OF THE TERRITORY

Po connected with a gandy dancer a number of miles away from the Dew Drop Inn. Porter had arranged for him to meet up with the dancer, which was a sentient-robot form of the old railroad handcars laborers used to repair and align tracks. In The Commons, the tracks nearly always maintained themselves. However, the maintenance cars, powered by collected ambient Essence, served as inspectors verifying that the tracks hadn't gone rogue combined with a short-haul delivery service of supplies or people when the load or destination didn't justify using an engine or an entire train.

Po was relieved that this one didn't want to communicate. Given what he'd discovered at the Dew Drop, he was in no mood for small talk. He knew who had taken the child, and he could not help but feel responsible.

Parix. An Essence leech. That distinction put the creature in the same class as Mr. Brill's Shade, but he was something else entirely.

The Shade had been an extension of Mr. Brill—a powerful and destructive creature but one that required guidance lest it perform as a mindless golem. Parix, on the other hand, was cruel and intelligent. The younger and more innocent the Essence taken, the more he enjoyed it. The more suffering induced in the victim, the greater the amount of Essence claimed.

Enforcement of whatever law existed was only a portion of Po's official duties. Porter and Charlene preferred to leave that work to the Vigils, the elite police force that Brill forcibly conscripted into the Ravagers but that had begun to be restored along with the rest of The Commons. Po understood the logic of that, but logic was not the whole of his calculation.

An Essence leech took Ken. Now another had taken a child. If Po had been allowed to make the pursuit of Parix a priority, perhaps that child would still be where she was supposed to be—finding her place in the hippie-warrior community of the Dharma Rangers, laughing and discovering.

Po had no illusions about his chances against Parix, whose strength rivaled that of Brill's Shade. Alone, Po was no match for him. But he dearly would have loved to have taken his shot or, barring that, to have led a team of Envoys or Vigils to find the leech and stop the atrocities.

The monk shifted position on the shipping crate he'd chosen as his perch, watching The Commons slide by as the gandy dancer made good time. They covered long stretches of uncommitted territory, either barren flats that had reset to that state while waiting to transform into something else for an assigned Journey or lush prairie that appeared to be uniform but could have masked all sorts of conflict playing out in its grasses or beneath its surface.

The stillness of the territory they passed was all illusion. The Commons was ever-changing in small, subtle ways when it wasn't reshaping itself to meet the demands of a given assignment. Essence and fascinating doings lay dormant in even the most featureless parts.

Doings just waiting to be prompted or discovered by a young girl such as Mira. Doings that would now have to be uncovered by another child. Or not at all.

Po watched the lazily swaying grass pass, as if he was on a sailboat and the vast stretches of prairie were a pleasantly calm sea. He was going to visit the demon day traders at Porter's request. But missions had a way of folding back in upon those who accepted them, and if he was meant to pursue Parix, he would find himself doing so at some point.

But he dreamt of doing so as soon as possible.

∼

THE GANDY DANCER dropped Po where the tracks crossed a multi-lane road leading into an office park. Po would walk from here. He hadn't been told where the gandy dancer was headed, but he saw the tops of what looked like container cranes in the distance and picked up the smell of salt air when the breeze shifted.

He hopped off the velocipede, patted its deck as a thank you, and began walking toward the park. The gandy dancer pulled away.

The demon day traders had obviously prospered in their business, which in its earliest days was not in any way acquainted with the principles of legality or ethical behavior. That was why Po was acquainted with them. The cycle of their relationship was fairly consistent.

The demons had tapped into a dark-side Essence exchange during Brill's time—a black market for that which made up the universe. Initially, they'd posed as legitimate businesspeople and specialized in fleecing those foolish enough to invest with them. It had been the usual scheme of making up for one customer's losses with the gains of another and then moving on when enough of their marks—or Mr. Brill—caught on.

After a time, the demons learned enough to drop the more fraudulent parts of their practice. There was no need to cheat investors when legal trading yielded better margins and didn't periodically require shutting down their operations and skipping town.

After Paul Reid defeated Mr. Brill, the demons remained in business, even though the gradual return of the real system prevented them from trading Essence. Somehow they continued to make markets and profit from trades. It wasn't clear what was being traded or who their partners were. Yet Po was certain they weren't doing any real harm, whatever they were up to, since the Envoys' systems would have alerted him to it. So he simply paid them a visit now and then to remind them to behave themselves—which they did, somewhat—and let them keep operating in return for providing him with whatever useful information they might come across.

Po had heard various versions of their origin, but the most plausible and entertaining held that they were former putti who'd decided to devote themselves to trading and commerce outside of their official duties. Caught by whichever deity they were supposed to have been serving, they were altered to resemble what that deity said was their true nature. Thus, the formerly pink-cheeked, adorable toddlers were now leathery-winged, standard demons with reptilian features and nasty dispositions.

They were naturals in the market, though. Even when they weren't manipulating trades or taking advantage of insider tips and were forced to rely on instinct and legitimately obtained information, they were formidable.

The last time Po visited, the demons had been operating a boiler-room operation above a convenience mart that never seemed to be open. Now, as he approached the address Porter had given him, it was clear they'd moved up to more posh real estate.

Where the only grass evident in their old location had been clumps of scraggly weeds fighting their way through cracks in the mart's decaying parking lot, this building boasted an emerald-green landscaped lawn. And while that may not have meant an actual landscaper maintained it, it indicated that The Commons cared enough to keep the grass healthy and cropped short for the tenants here.

The steps leading up to the building's front entrance were chalk-white concrete—pristine, with no faults in evidence apart from the straight, neat grooves that were meant to be there. The stainless-steel railing gleamed in the sunlight.

There'd been no signals or alarms to prompt Po's visit, so the demons' apparent success was probably due to the more respectable side of their trading. Probably.

Po was not here to confront them about any wrongdoing. But no one had told the demons that.

At the glass double-doors, he pushed the sole buzzer, which was for a company called Azazel Partners. He heard nothing, but he assumed the mechanism was working. His suspicion proved correct when a blue light began to glow on a small camera above the door. He was being observed.

Nothing happened, which wasn't a shock. The demons were never happy to see him. The last time he'd stopped by, he'd forced them to divest themselves of interests in both an arms manufacturer and a make-up distributor because the two firms were causing Essence bound for more noble purposes to be drawn into the wrong streams. Those streams threatened to affect at least a handful of Journeys in ways that were not beneficial to anyone but the demons.

After a few minutes, the door clicked loudly. It opened for Po before he could push it.

He stepped into the entryway and was promptly attacked from above. A stout, shirtless demon dropped from the ceiling, intending to stun Po with his mass.

Po was ready for him. He fell to his right, rolling, and came up in battle mode.

As expected, the attacker was G-man, a mid-level trader in the organization and a self-styled warrior and protector of the trading operations. It was all Po could do not to laugh at the compact, barrel-shaped demon, who was bare-chested but wore creased suit pants and perfectly shined shoes. He hadn't expected to punch it out with anyone today. "You're going down, baldy," G-man cried. Wings flapping, he launched himself at Po, who caught the demon and redirected him face-first into a set of padded waiting-room chairs.

G-man always greeted him like this.

Po had no wish to hurt him unless he had to.

The demon flipped the chair with his momentum and tumbled past it, taking out a large potted plant. Soil and planter shards coated him. He cursed, stood, and dusted himself off. "That was a lady palm," he said. "Three hundred when it was half that size. Porter's getting that bill."

Flapping again, G-man vaulted the overturned chair. He came straight at Po once more, fist cocked.

Po stopped him with a kick to the chest, their combined forces meeting in a jolt to his solar plexus—or whatever passed for one in a demon.

The effect was the same. G-man fell out of the air and met the floor with his face.

Po stood over him.

The demon had no more left. He emitted a high-pitched whistle, struggling to draw his next breath.

Po allowed him time to recover.

An inner door across the front room opened.

"Son of a bitch." A demon named J.P. filled the doorway in a tailored pin-striped double-breasted suit. He regarded the demolished plant with a look of concern, then spotted his fallen partner. "Sorry, Po." He walked over to inspect the downed plant. "G-man didn't tell anyone who was here. He knew we'd try to stop him."

Po nodded. Only his attacker and an innocent palm had suffered.

J.P. spent a futile few seconds trying to right the plant but soon gave up. It tumbled back into dirt and ruin.

On the ground, G-man managed to roll over. His whistles had become a concerto of inhalations and groans.

When the demon appeared ready, Po reached down to offer him a hand and helped him up.

"Want a tour?" J.P. said.

21

APALALA

"Nobody's ever seen Callibeau," Abel told Jeremy when they were well into their burgers and past their first round at Billy Clyde's. "I haven't, and I don't know anyone who has."

Jeremy considered the implications of that as Porthos the cat issued a rare meow from atop the booth wall near Abel's head. Clearly, the two of them were Porthos's only hope for a snack because they were the only customers who ever ate anything. And while the same sound from any other feline might have been a request for a taste, from Porthos it was more of a demand for tribute. The big guy had eyes only for the ground beef that wasn't coming his way.

There were several people at the bar watching golf on a massive relic of a tube TV hanging from the ceiling. And the few others scattered around the surrounding booths were strictly drinks-only.

Why were Abel and Jeremy the only ones who ordered food? Were cats a code violation? Why did Billy Clyde's need a cat? And without those answers, why did they dare to eat here?

"Did you hear me?"

"Yeah. Just trying to process all this." And Jeremy was, by parking it in the back of his skull to let his subconscious worry away at it. The world had gotten very strange, and he didn't know what bothered him more—that everyone around him seemed to accept it, or that he did, too.

Porthos the cat stopped watching Jeremy's burger and turned his attention to a spot on the ceiling. A focusite protruded from the many layers of paint on the filthy pressed tin. Porthos wasn't perturbed by it. The cat turned his attention back to the target at hand—Jeremy's beef—as if a mouth up above were nothing out of the ordinary. Maybe cats were used to such things because they saw them all the time.

"Anyway." Abel washed down a massive mouthful of burger with a healthy draw of beer. "The story is that Callibeau is the real power, but he brought Truitt in for hands-on management."

Jeremy didn't mention it, but he strongly suspected that referring to Mr. Truitt by his last name was a bad idea. Somehow, the respect implied by using the man's title—even in thought, and certainly when speaking—felt like a safer way to go. "Where does Apalala come in?"

"Artificial intelligence. AI-guided oversight of the Essence, which means the people working for Callibeau and Manitou can't get too close to that Essence and gain any influence over it through adjacency. It's not likely that would happen, but you never know. We're working within a hacked system, so there are no guarantees. Apalala is basically a living algorithm. It's always learning, always reinventing itself. It monitors the Essence, its adjacency, and its concentration. And when the time is right, it'll frack it."

"There'll never be a right time," said a woman at the bar who was close enough to listen in on them—and had been.

"Right doesn't enter into it." She swiveled on her stool to face them. "Only wrong."

Abel wasn't quick enough to hide his reaction. He wasn't happy to see this woman.

Jeremy had noticed her around the Manitou halls. She set off all his alarm bells, too, albeit at a reasonably low level. He'd worked in enough offices to know who to avoid getting cornered by. This woman, with her always-messy do and her sweaters matted with pet hair, was that rule personified.

"Hello, Mallory." Abel's greeting had a back-against-the-wall quality to it. "Jeremy, have you met Mallory?"

"We've seen each other," Mallory said before Jeremy could answer. She drained her cocktail and placed the empty glass on the bar, all the while eyeballing Jeremy. "You're new." Before Jeremy could confirm that, she stood and approached their booth, stopping to look down at Abel and box him in.

Porthos gave her the same stare he'd given the focusite. Then it was back to the burgers.

"Mallory works in internal communications," Abel said. "She's our best copy editor."

"I'm your only copy editor. Not that it matters, since no one gives me anything to edit." As Abel was about to respond, she leveled a finger at him and stopped him cold. There was a certain gravity to her; she even had Porthos's attention again. "You haven't gotten me on his calendar." Her finger remained aimed like a gun. "That thing is up to something. You know it. I know it. And Mr. Callibeau needs to know it."

"He already does, Mallory." Abel regained some of his composure. "Apalala was created on his orders. And it's supposed to be up to something. It's doing what he wants."

"Get me on his calendar."

"I can't." Abel put his burger down and leaned back, taking his beer with him. "I keep telling you, you have the wrong guy.

I'm Abel Dowd. You need to talk to Anne Bladow. Abladow in the email directory. Get it? I'm Abel Dowd. She's abladow. We're not the same person."

"It's up to something." Mallory lowered her finger and stuck her hand in her pocket like a gunfighter holstering a shootin' iron.

Up above, the focusite shrieked.

Of the three of them, Mallory was the only one who didn't look up at it.

Even Porthos looked.

"Shut up," Mallory said.

Abel frowned.

"Not you. It." She'd heard it, too, then. She shouldered her purse. "I'm going."

Abel nodded.

"It's up to something," Mallory told him again. "You'll find that out. Get me on the calendar."

"Abladow."

Mallory turned back to the bar and took most of a stack of bills off of it, leaving a few for a tip. Then she exited without another word.

Porthos watched her go.

"That woman," Abel said, refilling his mug from their pitcher and taking another long pull, "wigs me right the hell out." He reached for his burger. "But whenever I worry I'm truly losing it, she serves as proof I could be a lot worse."

Porthos continued to stare after Mallory. And he kept watching for a long time, even after it was certain she wouldn't return.

22

THERE IS NO I IN SCALDED

G-man insisted on accompanying Po and J.P. while the latter led the monk through the offices. As often happened, Po regretted how hard he'd kicked him. G-man was probably a few hundred years younger than his colleagues, which made him the equivalent of a teenager. He was given to foolish acts.

But G-man had teeth and claws he was willing to employ if a fight lasted long enough. And while Po doubted the demon bore him any true malice beyond testing his mettle, G-man could easily have done him real harm. No apologies would help the resulting wounds or broken bones heal any more easily or any less painfully. So Po kept him in line, even if his heart wasn't in it.

J.P., for his part, seemed to have forgotten the matter as soon as it was over. Except for the plant, perhaps.

But G-man's progress from pained gasping to labored wheezing as he walked with them convinced Po to take it easier on the young demon the next time. Which was exactly what he'd told himself the time before and the time before that.

Po suspected that G-man actually looked up to him, which was why he was so committed to besting him. Pride and competition drove the demons, which explained why J.P. beamed as he showed Po around. Even if he might inadvertently incriminate himself or reveal too much about the operations to an official representative of the Envoys, he couldn't help it.

It was a big improvement over their past setups. The trading operations took up three entire floors—the top one devoted to the partner demons' personal accounts and the two below housing a brokerage operation for those willing to pay the demons a percentage of their gains to do their trading for them. Whatever the demons were up to, they'd found a way to prosper.

J.P. was one of the elders of the group. It showed in the way he moved slowly and with care. He kept his withered wings, long since grown vestigial with age, folded. Yet there was a bounce in his step as he walked them past cubicles of cold-caller and data-analyst succubi, mandragoras, and imps.

"We need three different headset sizes," he told Po. "We break them up into teams that compete against one another to keep productivity up, and the winners get slow-roasted by the losers. You wouldn't believe how much they love that, though the imps prefer a good lava soak. Either way, it's all about motivation and teamwork. Everybody wins, or nobody does. There is no *I* in *scalded*."

J.P. was proudest when introducing Effie, his daughter, who topped her bracket month after month and was the youngest team leader at Azazel.

Unlike her father, who was as keg-shaped as his contemporaries, Effie was serpentine, sporting a whip-like body with slender limbs and functional feathered wings instead of the rawhide-like ones of her father and his friends. She said nothing when introduced, smiling shyly at Po and studying him through the thick lenses of her large spectacles.

"My girl." J.P.'s wide grin showed his crocodilian teeth off to good effect. "My girl."

If demons were capable of blushing through their scales, Effie would have. But she surprised Po by signing that it was nice to meet him. Sign was a rarity. Aside from Mrs. Blesmol and the Envoys who accommodated the Journeymen who required it, Po encountered few who understood sign, let alone anyone who could answer in kind. He smiled, and the young demon showed her fangs before her shyness regained control.

"You keep up the good fight, hon," her father told her. "Onward, upward."

When they reached J.P.'s office and were seated—Po with tea, the demon with a stone stein of thick liquid that bubbled with something writhing in the concoction's heat—J.P. leaned back in his luxurious leather chair. "So what's to say? Life is good."

Po checked the necklace from which Joel hung to make sure the Tamagotchi faced J.P. On the tiny screen, Joel presented himself in the form of a large-eyed living flame. Watching Po sign, Joel interpreted in a gravelly voice with a thick Brooklyn accent he said he'd borrowed from an early-cable comedy about a former mob lawyer.

"And how's business?" Joel said for Po.

"Good. Nothing to report, which is also good. You know us, Po. We fly low. That means behaving ourselves." He organized his features into an expression that was purely amicable—he was a being of pure cooperation, as far as he was concerned.

Po said nothing.

"The boss ain't buying it," Joel said, though Po hadn't signed anything. "You know that, right?"

J.P. knew it, but he also understood that Po didn't have any specific suspicions to investigate.

Po signed. "See, the boss and I didn't come here to dig into anything you and yours might have going on," Joel said to the demon. "Not this time. But we've had word of a certain fire-based entity and its activities—activities which are proving to be quite worrisome to us."

"Is that exactly how he's wording it?" J.P. studied Po's hands.

The Tamagotchi didn't answer. He never tried to hide his embellishments. He also never altered the spirit of anything Po said, and he resented any implication that he might.

Po didn't mind, so long as his points were made.

"How worrisome?" said J.P.

"It has done grievous injury to one of ours, and we do not like that—we do not like that at all," Joel said after Po signed in response. "So we would very much appreciate it if you, in your business dealings, would keep your ears to the flames and let us know if you hear of any such creature."

"You hardly need to ask. Whatever assistance we may provide, we are more than glad to provide it." J.P. showed his teeth again. Now it was only an approximation of a smile, as if he couldn't manage to pull a pleasant expression out of whatever he was thinking. He was hiding something.

Joel's digital gaze went from J.P. to Po. He'd picked up on it, too.

Even subterfuge was useful, in this case. Knowing that the demons were trying to sit on information meant that Po could have the Envoys or even a Vigils intelligence team look into their doings. That would not have been Po's first choice, but if J.P. declined to be fully transparent with him, Po was willing to escalate.

Joel's expression spoke for him. The Tamagotchi would relay the request to the higher-ups as soon as Po authorized it.

Po stood. He'd give the matter more thought before asking anyone to spy on the demons, because to do so risked irrevocably altering the dynamic of their relationship. But the weight with which Porter had asked him to talk to J.P. left no doubt. The Envoy intended to find whoever or whatever had hurt Audra and determine what that meant for The Commons.

They were interrupted by a baby-like squalling from the indoor tree in the corner. The plant, coated in slimy gelatin that hung from it in long ropes of goo, was tall enough to brush the ceiling and had tendrils extended into the tiles above to support itself. One of its bulbs had split open, revealing the face of a toothy, frog-like infant that gave awful voice to its hunger.

J.P. stood, pulled a bottle of something dark crimson from a nearby cabinet and inserted the nipple into the frog-baby's mouth. It began to suck as J.P. murmured softly to it. The bottle whimpered in pain.

Po left the demon's office without saying anything more and shut the door behind him.

J.P. understood that Po expected to hear from him if anything useful came his way.

On the way out, Po nodded a goodbye to Effie. The snake demon watched him pass with a directness that was a far cry from the timidity she'd displayed in front of her father.

∽

THE ROUTE back to the railroad tracks, which Po planned to shadow until the next gandy dancer came along, led past a picnic table and a stand of thick trees.

The Margins

"Boss, you feel that?" said Joel in a low voice, muffled by the fabric of Po's robe.

Po did. He was being watched by what felt like a familiar presence. There was no clear reason why he knew that, but he did. And there was no explanation for how quickly that sensation dissipated when he turned to see if he might catch whoever was studying him.

There was no one. Nothing.

"Weird," said Joel.

It was. But Po stopped walking anyway just as he was about to pass through the trees ahead. Trees were perfectly willing to part with information if one listened carefully and with a free mind. What they had to tell wasn't always easily understood, but whatever came through was frequently useful.

The first tree.

Po gazed into its heights. Someone or something was up there. He waited for whoever it was to understand that he would not be ambushed. It was most likely G-man positioning himself for a rematch. Po promised himself he'd exercise better restraint this round.

A rustling disturbed the leaves' peace on the windless day. Effie slithered down out of the branches, encircling the tree's trunk until she dropped silently to the ground. "I wanted to make sure my dad wasn't walking you out." She waited for Po to indicate that he believed her. "They didn't tell you, did they?"

Po didn't answer.

Effie sighed. "They're afraid." She glanced around to reassure herself that they really were alone. "I mean, they're afraid of you, too, but they're way more scared of it. And you need to know—you and the Envoys."

When they returned to the front door of the Azazel building, Effie punched a combination into the keypad by the entrance and opened the door. She went into the entryway first and looked upward, glaring.

G-man muttered an indistinct curse and dropped to the floor in front of them, looking sheepish. He started to try to explain himself but wilted under Effie's hard stare.

Po gave him a sympathetic pat on the shoulder as they passed.

23

TWO CHECKED BOXES

Porter's influence in the Envoy Corps had dropped. Two checked boxes on the form explaining why his request was rejected made that clear. One said, "Priority." The other, "Resources." As in, the first was judged to be low, so the second would not be made available to him. No matter that a child had been murdered by a known killer whom the Commons authorities hadn't seen fit to deal with. Nor that more would disappear if nothing were done.

The Dharma Rangers, the formal name adopted by the hippie soldiers, were on their own. That was the way of the new leadership. Allies were supported in word, not deed. Those who'd had no hand in defeating Brill favored inaction, which was seen as safer even though it was what had allowed Brill to amass power in the first place.

Not if Porter had anything to say about it. Which he did.

As did the Dharmas. And if Porter wasn't able to convince his higher-ups that they should deal with this situation before it got worse, the hippie soldiers would take matters into their own hands.

"Tell them we will act," Nicolette said when Porter

informed her of Po's discovery at the Dew Drop Inn. Had she meant they'd act if the Envoys or Vigils did not, or were they going to move on their own no matter what?

Porter knew not to ask that question, especially of Nicolette. She was not the type to grieve and leave the bloody work to others. That was the mistake made by many who went up against her, Liam, and D.W. While an attacker studied the best way to take on the two redoubtable-looking men, Nicolette got off a round or, in close quarters, pulled a knife and used it. She was deadly when riled.

Tell them we will act. Nicolette was riled now. So Porter had only a short window of time in which to show the Dharmas that he and the greater organization could protect them. And his new bosses would not make that an easy task.

One good thing about the desk duty the new order assigned him was that those at the top weren't aware of his capabilities and had no interest in them. That left him on his own to practice and explore.

With The Commons returning to itself, Porter's powers had recovered from the rule of Brill. Abilities were available to him that hadn't been there during Paul's Journey.

For one, he was able to practice jumping about the newly growing realm and establish waypoints, which involved familiarizing himself with a given location enough to transport himself there quickly. Some were easily used because he'd repeatedly returned to them until he'd established adjacency. Others were accessible because they were natural roundhouses, like the Shrine of the Lost, though they weren't as powerful. In some cases, Porter took a risk by jumping to them without established adjacency first. With a touch of bad luck, he could end up in the wrong place or in the right place at the wrong time. Like a normally safe house that happened to be engulfed in flames when he arrived in the living room, for instance.

Other adjacency came from friends and those he'd gone into battle with. As with location adjacency, which required him to visit periodically in order to keep it alive, personal adjacency only lasted as long as the relationship. As long as a given friendship continued, he could jump to that person when conditions were right. When conditions were less than optimal? Hello, risk.

Thus it was that Porter had options when stonewalled by his nominal leadership. He wanted a trusted Envoy sent, backed by a team of Vigils or, barring that, at least a couple of them. He'd been given nothing. But they hadn't said he couldn't look into poor Mira's death himself. Had they done so, he'd have ignored them.

There were two tricks involved. The first was to jump when the traces of Po's Essence—left behind by his visit and charged more than usual due to how upset he was upon discovering the crime—were still connected through Porter's friendship with the monk. The second was not telling anyone where he was going. He'd be there and back before his nominal superiors knew he'd ever left.

The minor downside was that the distance involved might well exhaust him upon arrival, but that wasn't a big cause for concern. It was a recon visit. It wasn't like Porter would be heading into a battle.

∽

The minor downside wasn't so minor. The jump to the remains of the Dew Drop Inn took more out of Porter than he'd bargained for. He arrived right at the spot of Po's grief. The monk had folded the unfortunate girl's clothes and wrapped them in an old Inn tote bag. Because of that, his residual Essence had been left behind next to the ashes of the fire he'd shown Porter via their link.

The problem was that in those ashes was the molted skin of Parix, the girl's murderer and Porter's quarry. Any shed elements from a leech continued to absorb Essence from whoever and whatever it could for some time. Such was Parix's power that little of Po's Essence remained, requiring Porter to expend more of his energy locating his destination. Once Porter got there, the molted skin sapped some of his vital energy, too.

That was, unfortunately, the new reality of The Commons in the post-Brill era. The Envoys and the others under the umbrella of the Commons authority were rebuilding along with The Commons itself. But with Brill's defeat came a sizable power void, and into that had stepped a whole range of mythicals—good, bad, and aggressively in-between. The best of them offered the nobility of Po and the late Ken. The worst were like Parix—malevolent and exceedingly dangerous.

After recovering for a spell, Porter took a look at the old pool office to see if Po had missed anything. He hadn't. Here were the leavings of an independent little girl who, because she hadn't been afraid to explore her world, had made an easy victim.

Parix's flavor of savagery was the nastiest: he enjoyed what he did. He should have been a priority.

But the Dharmas, while mostly bona fides, weren't officially on Journeys and thus didn't count toward anyone's numbers. So the higher-ups allowed this to happen. Heads would shake. Regrets would be expressed. And nothing would be done.

Parix should have been a priority.

Outside, Porter examined the bag with Mira's clothing,

The Margins

which also contained her torn backpack and her bejeweled barrette. The bright pinks of the pack's camouflage pattern and the cheap-but-charming jewels affixed to it were that of a child who'd wanted the world to know she was in it. She'd announced herself with her expression of beauty. Wasn't that what so many wanted—to be seen and noted?

Seen and noted.

That was all Parix and his kind needed in order to harm and kill.

Parix should have been a priority.

Porter's outrage at the loss of the child was nearly a physical thing. He'd leave Essence of his own here, certainly.

No longer the last of the Envoys, Porter had a new mission here in The Commons. The powers-that-be didn't consider the threat of Parix and other bad mythicals to be worth their time.

So Porter would take the matters on. As would Po and anyone else he could enlist to help him.

Porter carefully tucked Mira's clothing and belongings back into the tote bag. The rasp of them sliding into the nylon almost masked a barely audible hiss that came from behind him, in the ashes of the fire pit.

Porter turned to see the ashes shift. The pile was higher now, as if something had concealed itself beneath them.

The ashes hissed again, further reshaping themselves. When they began to whisper, Porter jumped back and raised his staff.

Too late.

A pair of tube-like appendages sprung up from the ashes faster than Porter would have thought possible and bit into both sides of his neck, going for blood.

Parix should have been a priority.

∾

"Ms. Moseley."

At first, Charlene thought somebody had snuck into her office to mess with her. That's how long it had been since the last time the talking View-Master alerted her to anything. She'd forgotten what its voice sounded like.

She looked around her cluttered office. Most of the mess was a disorganized cypher to Charlene because she'd inherited the space and, being an all-digital gal, had never bothered to look through any of it. She had no idea where the thing was hiding.

"Ms. Moseley." There. It was peeking out from behind the multi-runged holder filled with manila folders she'd never so much as glanced at. "Situation critical, Ms. Moseley. Mr. Porter is under attack."

That made no sense. Charlene grabbed the unit, which was finicky on its best days, and peered into its eye pieces. For the umpteenth time, she struggled to shake the feeling she was raising a plastic face—and a mocking one, at that—to her own for a smooch. She had no desire to kiss the little wiseass, which was more hassle than help most of the time.

Porter had been in his office an hour before. Who could be attacking him? The unit either had it wrong or was playing games with her—yet again—because it was tired of being ignored. Of course, she'd have been willing to pay more attention to it if it put more care into doing its job.

Charlene waited with the unit held to her eyes. It had nothing to show her but near-darkness at first. Then, slowly, an image began to chunk in and fill the viewing area with fuzzy yellow and sky-blue blocks that gradually sharpened into a discernible hand-colored photo. It was an old travel postcard that appeared to have been torn up and taped back together with a few of its pieces missing. On it, a smiling family posed on chaise lounges by what looked to be a motel pool. The caption said they were "about to make a splash" wherever they were staying. Unfortunately, one of the missing pieces contained the name of the place.

"Ms. Moseley, Mr. Porter has gone off-line. Mr. Porter is under attack and has gone off-line." It didn't help that the news was delivered in the same featureless tone the toy used to discuss the bears of Yellowstone and the Teapot Dome scandal.

Charlene held the device at arm's length and examined it as if it were a child she suspected of lying to her. From time to time, she longed to see into its mind to gauge its intent.

Only it didn't have a mind.

View-Master in hand, Charlene got up and hurried into the hall, nearly taking out June Medill in the process.

Two doors down, Porter wasn't in his office. The lights were off, which meant the motion detector hadn't picked up any movement in the room for some time.

"Where's Mr. Porter?" said June, who'd recovered and caught up.

"Ms. Moseley," the device said yet again. "Situation critical."

24

AN ACT OF UNPARALLELED FOOLISHNESS

The angry whine of the wire reader's dot-matrix printer woke Audra from her painkiller-infused sleep. She rolled over. Movement came more easily as her burns healed. That was to be expected for a being of fire. But it didn't make it any less painful.

Once again, the clock was no help—more ghost-in-the-machine code than legible digits. The Commons wasn't ready for her to know what time it was. And there were no guarantees it ever would be. Information had come on a need-to-know basis for a while now, and it seemed Audra wasn't due much of it. Not yet.

Time and fact went from predictable and known to warped and meaningless in The Commons. It was as changeable as the weather. What Audra had worked out thus far was this: she had much to contribute, but not for a bit. She'd remain in her current quarters with the capabilities and details provided to her until it was time for her to play her role.

It was a waiting game. It often was, in a place where one's

days were not numbered the way they had been in The Living World.

In the efficiency's bathroom, Audra splashed water on her face and studied her dripping visage in the mirror. The seams and scars documented two truths: Audra was a fire entity who knew what it was to be taken by the flame herself, and she'd had long experience with waiting.

Out on the little wooden desk provided to her until such time as The Commons saw fit to enlarge or otherwise improve her environment, the irritating cries of the printer settled into a shrill repetition. Audra ignored it. The dispatches were never anything but routine notifications from Envoys in the field or updates on mundane administrative tasks. And the perfect repetition of the printer's whiny pattern could well have meant that the system was wasting copious amounts of ribbon and paper with gibberish or was otherwise misbehaving again.

Audra carefully patted her face dry. Thank goodness for soft towels, especially since The Commons wasn't known for reliably providing such items. Better yet, the drying wasn't nearly as uncomfortable as it had been even a few days past. The burns really were healing.

The printer's squeals continued. If it were allowed to keep going, the pile of sprocket-holed paper would be gone, along with much of the black ribbon's capacity. The Commons could always make as much as was necessary, but Essence was Essence, and Audra had always been one to close the icebox door promptly and tightly and turn off all lights before leaving a room.

She tugged at the string of the overhead landlord halo, then pressed and held the button on the front of the printer to take it offline. It didn't change anything. The same lines were spat onto the pages again and again. She flipped the power switch to off, but the printing continued. Finally, she gave in and began gathering the long accordion of connected pages.

Every line was the same. "Situation critical: Envoy Jonas Porter under attack. Status: unknown." Over and over and over. Once she'd absorbed the message, the printer stopped.

Audra grabbed her purse and began digging through it.

∽

"The staff is quite the prize—second only to you, Envoy."

The accent sounded Czech, but concentrating on that took an enormous amount of effort as awareness returned. The first cough brought him back.

Porter's mouth was filled with dust, and he wasn't able to do anything about it. He was face-down on the ground with someone on his back, holding him there, forcing his face into —ashes, he recalled, not dust. And if that someone so chose, they could grind him into the fire pit hard enough to stop his breathing.

The situation came into sharper focus. The Czech accent rang slightly false, as if the person using it had only recently acquired it and wasn't accustomed to it. Because they weren't, Porter recalled as the attacker on his back shook him. They were speaking with an acquired voice—a stolen voice.

"And the sleeper awakens." The speaker was Parix.

Porter felt himself being rolled over. The weight was on his chest now, and he was pinned down firmly. Not that it was necessary to confine him. He was completely drained. Even thinking strained him to his limit, and moving anything but his eyes was out of the question. The ashes made his eyes water, and it was a struggle to blink the resulting mixture away. Each movement of his lids was a demonstration of how much muck the human eye could store.

The Margins

His vision began to return to him—and he almost wished it hadn't.

Parix. The Essence leech had taken Porter like a rookie, concealing himself in the ashes at some point after Porter's arrival.

No Envoy had ever laid eyes on Parix and survived to report anything about him. For so deadly a creature, his file was remarkably slim.

Parix was a large jumble of joined tentacles without a body proper. It seemed he might not even be visibly detected were it not for the ashes coating him at the moment, which lent him a surface and an outline. The tentacles ranged in thickness from that of a child's wrist to that of an adult's thigh, and each ended in a lamprey-like cavity lined by row after row of sharp, conical teeth.

Porter's neck burned and throbbed on both sides. Those teeth explained his weakness.

"The sleeper awakens further." The leech was amused for now. The voice came from one of his tentacles. Two others were poised above him, looking down, acting as eyes or some other form of sensor.

A grim situation, this.

"I suppose I should extend my gratitude to you for saving me the trouble of tracking you down," Porter said. "I hadn't heard that generosity was a key attribute of yours."

The tooth-lined tube regarded him for a moment. "Is this how the vaunted Envoy Jonas Porter addresses one whose latest harvest is but one child among many? With humor? I know you value young life too dearly to make light of its loss."

Porter forced a laugh that sounded more genuine the longer he kept it going. Desperation motivated one to excellence. "We misunderstand each other. I'm no longer the vaunted Envoy. Would they have sent me out after you alone if

I were? They don't value me enough to provide backup." His vision a bit clearer with every blink, he hazarded a quick glance around and saw that he'd gotten lucky—his only hope lay a few feet away to his left. He looked right past it, lest he alert the leech as to his intent.

"Or," Parix said, considering the situation as the awful toothy maw drew closer to Porter's face, "you were foolish enough to pursue me alone, rusty from inaction and addled with age."

Porter laughed again. Faking it came more easily this time. Mid-guffaw, he did the unthinkable, which was the only reason he got away with it. Gambling that Parix didn't realize how much he'd recovered, he slowly brought one hand up. With the other, he pulled the sleeve of his coat down over his fingers and moved to wipe his eyes.

Perplexed by how funny Porter seemed to find the situation, Parix relaxed and let him.

Which was what Porter had been hoping for. He curled his fingers into a fist, gripping the fabric of his coat around his fingers and knuckles to form as much of a protective layer as he could, and rammed his covered hand right into the mouth of the creature's tentacle.

Parix responded with a muffled choke and bit down in reflex, which only made it worse for him.

Porter wedged his fist in. His hand and wrist flared with pain in multiple places as teeth pierced his sleeve and the skin beneath. They bit deeper as Parix tried to pull away and free himself, choking all the while.

Porter waited until the tentacle mouth gagged. He pulled his hand and forearm out. When he felt some of the weight leave his chest as the mythical struggled to recover its breath, he punched what looked like one of the seeing tentacles, which rewarded him with a cry of pain. Then he twisted to his left, reaching for what he'd felt.

There. His fingers closed upon the heel of his staff. He pulled it to him as Parix coughed and hacked, furious.

The leech compensated. Any of his tentacles could alternately function as mouth, eye, or limb. Accordingly, another one rose up to take over the seeing duties from its injured sibling while a second swung around to fasten onto Porter's neck again with a slap and a flare of pain as sharp teeth bit into skin.

A black void washed over Porter as his Essence left him. But he got lucky again. When he raised his staff to smack Parix with whatever strength he could muster, he inadvertently ambushed another tentacle targeting his neck's other side.

Parix was too strong and too fast for his own good. The staff went right down the throat of the moving tentacle and jammed hard into its inside wall. Porter felt several inner teeth tear loose with the impact. More than one of the other tentacles yelped or squawked.

Adjacency. As the staff bit into the soft inner wall of Parix's tentacle, Porter was flooded with conflicting information and sensations.

The first was the nearness of Paul, which Porter took to be either an illusion or a memory rising to the surface of his consciousness as some of the Essence Parix had just stolen returned to him. Paul was far off in The Living World but was near somehow. Not possible.

Wriggling lights appeared, fish-like, at the edges of Porter's vision. He'd soon be out again. Yet he couldn't shake the very strong sense that Paul Reid, who was among the living, was somehow accessible to him. And that, like Porter, he was in trouble.

The adjacency revealed further detail. Parix had attacked Paul, too—and recently. In The L.W.

Again, that was not possible since Parix was in The Commons. But there it was.

Before Porter could consider the matter further, he was awash in fire—an all-encompassing flame hotter than any he'd ever encountered. And behind it, the pain and fear of one known to him. Beloved to him.

Audra.

None of this made sense. And still the connection was there—a thread linking everything Porter was picking up on: Paul in a vulnerable state, Parix, Audra, and a frighteningly potent fire entity—most likely the one that had nearly killed Audra.

"I am no longer amused or interested, Envoy." Parix's pained voice issued forth from the tentacle stretching above. "We will have an end to this."

Porter agreed. And he knew that such an end, if he were to prompt it rather than Parix, would only come through an act of unparalleled foolishness. The pain in his neck grew sharper as Parix fed.

Porter had no choice. And in times when choice was lacking, impossible things—baldly stupid and thus unexpected—were wholly doable.

Resisting the urge to succumb to the black fog, Porter gripped his staff more tightly and turned it within Parix's tentacle gullet. His effort was rewarded with another grunt of pain from the leech. Then he devoted himself to one last bout of concentration.

∾

"Ms. Moseley! Ms. Moseley! Potential breach imminent!"

The Margins

Potential breach imminent? What did that mean?

Porter, whom Charlene would have counted on for guidance in the current situation, had been attacked and was now off-line. She wouldn't even allow herself to consider the ramifications of that. He'd up and left. Now it was on her to figure out what a potential breach meant. Breach of what?

Charlene looked into the View-Master's eye pieces again. It was attempting to fill in the missing postcard piece with the motel's name, but the result thus far was more Rorschach test than legible alphabet characters. Whatever data source was causing it to flip out was distant and potentially unreliable. That explained why the panic wasn't spreading to the rest of the system.

Or not. Only The Commons knew its reasons for what it did.

"We can invoke the all-hands protocol," said June Medill.

Charlene hadn't even heard the woman enter her office. She hadn't knocked, which was extremely unlike June Medill.

The View-Master physically shook with alarm.

"Not yet."

"Why not?"

"Let's give Porter a chance." Charlene didn't want the higher-ups to know Porter had gone out on his own. She'd have to rely on the integrity of the systems The Commons had brought back online in recent months. If this breach was as much of a threat as the View-Master said, the powers-that-be would receive an alert no matter what she did.

"Where is Mr. Porter?"

Charlene checked the View-Master again. Now the letters were about as clear as the most difficult rows of an eye chart—as seen by someone with myopia. But it was enough to jog her memory. The line about making a splash was a reference to more than just the pictured swimming pool. "The old Dew Drop Inn," she said.

"Where Paul Reid destroyed those Ravagers? What's he doing there?"

"I have no idea."

"Ms. Moseley! Breach initiated!"

Charlene did the only effective thing she could for the moment. She closed the door.

June Medill looked surprised. It was probably the first time she'd ever had someone shut a door with her on the same side of it.

Not for the first time, Charlene found herself wondering if prayer worked in The Commons.

25

HER COLORFUL HISTORY OF TRAUMA

"I can't lie to you." Annie's chair faced away from the therapist. It was hard not to question whether he remained behind her from one moment to the next.

"I'm glad to hear that."

Annie had no idea what the man looked like, but his presence and voice comforted her. She couldn't come up with his name or anything else about him. She couldn't even recall why she'd chosen him to talk to. She felt there must be a level of trust based on her history with him. She just couldn't remember any of it.

"You'd know if I lied."

He said nothing.

"That's a yes?"

He still said nothing.

That should have been a concern, as should the other details of the shadowy room. For one, it was much larger than typical therapists' offices. Annie had plenty of experience with those, thanks to her colorful history of trauma. For another, the only light came from the green glow of mysterious plastic-wrapped machines that filled the room's periphery. That glow, in turn, revealed the presence of even more units, which lay dormant.

They sat in a dead space.

Yet Annie felt at ease here, with this man.

"Why would you lie after everything you've already told me?" he said.

"Because there has to be a point where you'll report what I'm telling you if it gets bad enough."

More silence from him.

But not from the rest of the room. Small things skittered behind the machines now and then. Annie periodically heard the faint squeak of something outside the open window, which breathed summer air and the smell of grass into the space.

It was pitch-dark out there. So the green glow and the therapist's voice were all she had to keep her company.

"How's Bobby?"

"I don't want to talk about him." Annie shifted position. It was difficult to make herself comfortable.

"Why not?"

"You'll judge."

"Will I?"

"Won't you?"

"What would it tell you if I did?"

"Only what I already know. I shouldn't have gone back with him."

Still more silence.

"I don't want to tell you what he's like. What he does. I'm afraid you'll think I'm a bad mother to keep my child under his roof."

"Is it a home?"

She chewed on that. "No."

"Why did you go back with him?"

"He had a job for me. No Bobby, no Manitou. No Manitou, no help with my pain—and no money. No money, no food. I have a son." She'd done it again—described Zach as her son rather than theirs.

In past sessions, the therapist had pointed that out. He didn't now. Maybe he knew there was no need.

A longer, repeating squeak from outside in the dark, as if someone were wheeling a tiny cart. Or running on a hamster wheel.

Nails—or claws?—skittered across the floor. Annie resisted the urge to pull her feet up onto her chair. She didn't want the therapist to see that. "I keep dreaming about Zach being in danger." She stopped, weighing whether to continue. "There's just so much there that seems more real than the life I live when I'm awake. The reef. The monsters in the water. I don't know what they are, but they're—"

"Bad?"

"Really bad. And they want my son." She considered again whether to continue. She trusted this nameless man. But did she *trust* him? Well enough. "I think it happened. All of it. For real."

The therapist let that hang in the dark. Sometimes Annie wanted to yell at him for leaving her in doubt when she'd taken a risk with such an admission.

"Do you?" he said.

The screens under the plastic covers glowed just a little bit brighter.

"Yes. The hornets, too. And things I haven't shared with you."

"Why haven't you shared them with me?"

"Because I don't know what they are. They're behind the reef—out of reach." She laughed.

"What's funny?"

"I'm afraid to tell you."

"On top of everything else you've already shared."

Oh, what the hell. "Liberace." She chuckled again while he waited. "I don't know why that's funny. But it is."

"You know that's not really what I said to you, right?"

"I know." Annie didn't, actually. When had he said something like that? Outside, the squeaking sounds multiplied. If they were wheels of some sort, there were more than one of them moving now. A lot more. "And I know it's not really funny."

The therapist left that to the soft green light and the darkness beyond.

The green glow grew brighter still as the volume of the squeaking wheels increased. Now Annie could make out a table across the room. A table or a desk. On it was some sort of device she couldn't quite see, even in the brighter glow. A toy Martian or robot of some sort, with an outsized rectangular head and stick legs. Or maybe it was something else entirely. It was too dark. She didn't know enough. And she didn't trust what she knew, assuming she knew it at all.

"Why can't you tell me what any of this means?" Annie said. "How do I protect Zach?" It hit home. "That's the secret, isn't it? Nobody can know too much of it. No one person. Not too big a piece or it puts everything at risk. Right?"

"No." Despite the therapist's denial, the squeaking grew. Did that mean Annie was on the right track? "We know almost nothing this time. We're not certain who the players are. I don't think The Commons even knows. Not all of it. But we did what they wanted. We didn't know that at the time. But we know now."

That last part came out tinged with a bit of fear. The squeaking grew, as did the sounds of tiny feet and claws behind the glowing screens.

"Did what?" Annie said. "What did they want? What's The Commons?"

"You already know what The Commons is. And you don't know what we don't know."

"What don't you know?"

"Who they are."

"The ones who we helped." Now she was doing it. Touching a part of the conversation that shouldn't make sense to her but did somehow.

More silence. Annie could almost hear the man weighing whether he was going to tell her or not. "Bobby." He paused again. "If I can ever help you, I will. Trust me. If it comes to that, and I can, I will."

Annie believed him. Trusting the therapist felt familiar to her, though she didn't know why.

The squeaking stopped at the same time the screens all went black, throwing the room into complete darkness.

"Things are going to move fast," the therapist said.

The surprise pain of hard fingers on Annie's shoulder pulled her right out of the room.

26

THE FLOATING DISAPPOINTMENT

Mr. Truitt preferred the iron-fist-in-a-velvet-glove approach. He also hated clichés about as much as he hated anything in this and every other world, so he let Jeremy and Abel know he'd appreciate it if they never told anyone he'd employed that expression.

Jeremy was impressed. By not stating an explicit threat, Mr. Truitt took a velvet-glove approach to the problem of having the velvet-glove expression tied to him. It also covered any other thing he told them. It was a nifty trick.

It also worked. Jeremy would tell no one outside their triangle anything Mr. Truitt said. Not just because so much of it was unreal. Jeremy accepted that his reality had changed. But he also understood that Mr. Truitt meant what he said.

Mr. Truitt was the old-school gunfighter who knew that his opponents were best kept in line if he never actually shot anyone. They just needed to see that he was wearing his pistols.

The three of them sat in Mr. Truitt's office with the lights out again, bathed in the neon wash from his graphs. The visualizations hung in the air in front of them as objects unto themselves—no monitor needed.

Yes, some serious tech was available here at Manitou.

That or something else.

Jeremy didn't puzzle over what was behind the wizardry. He thought of the displays as screens rather than try to figure out what they really might be because they had bigger problems. And by they, he meant Abel—and, through Abel, him.

Abel was undergoing the velvet-glove treatment as Mr. Truitt let the floating graphs continue to ask the question he'd mouthed only once—and very quietly at that. That had been an uncomfortably long time before. Now he sat and let Abel sweat.

No matter what type of graph they chose to express the latest standings, the picture was the same.

The bars were shorter.

The denominators were lower.

Worse still, it looked like a trend. There was somehow less Essence in the world.

"Mr. Truitt," Abel said. "I'll answer your question with a question, and then I'll do my damnedest to provide only answers after that. Do you think Apalala might have something to do with this?"

"No."

Abel visibly relaxed. Had the answer been the affirmative, things would have gotten pretty hairy for both of them. Apalala was their baby. If the program were to be found responsible for the floating disappointment in front of them, they'd find out how quick Mr. Truitt—and Mr. Callibeau, for the head of Manitou surely was aware of what was happening —would be to shift to the iron fist.

"From all I've seen, Mr. Dowd, this drop began well before

the introduction of Apalala, and it's been accelerating at a steady pace. I think your algorithm is doing what it's supposed to be doing. However, it's allocating and reallocating a diminishing account balance—or balances, really—and I want to know why."

"How frank might I be here, Mr. Truitt?"

"I care little about protocol or courtesy here, Mr. Dowd. Do not be politic. Be incisive and correct."

"I was thinking that maybe *why* isn't the question to start with. I'd go with *what*, *where*, and *how*. In that order."

"Go on."

"This was discovered when, last night?"

"Yes."

"For the *what* of it, then, has anyone taken a look at the quality scores and how they've changed over time? Which Essence is disappearing? Is it the same across the board?"

Mr. Truitt snapped his fingers in approval.

Jeremy resumed breathing. He hadn't realized he'd stopped.

With a gesture from Mr. Truitt, the graphs shrank and floated up and away, a new one taking their place. A rainbow of lines rose slightly from left to right, though they flattened out as their rate of increase apparently slowed. And crossing them, from upper left to bottom right, a gray line gradually tumbled through the standings. At the far right of the graph, the most recent rankings continued the decline like a stone falling star. "Bravo, Mr. Dowd," Mr. Truitt said—and he meant it.

"It's not the moths," said Abel. "It's the dee-dees."

"It is. They are our *what*, Mr. Dowd. Now find our *why*."

When Abel spoke again, his voice had tightened. It was one thing to define the questions. It was quite another to come up with answers. "I'm on it. Has Mr. Callibeau been told?"

Mr. Truitt let out a sigh. "Mr. Callibeau doesn't need to be told. Mr. Callibeau knows everything as soon as it occurs."

The lights came up.

Jeremy took one look at Abel's expression and wished they'd remained in the dark.

A shrill tone sounded in the office—not nearly as alarming or irritating as the screams of the focusites but not far off, either. Jeremy managed not to jump.

Abel didn't look as if he'd heard the alert, but that probably wasn't a good sign. He was so deep into his own fears that the piercing sound, somewhere between an air-raid alert and a cry of pain, couldn't touch him.

"When it pains, it roars." Mr. Truitt waved his fingers to bring up a message that appeared in the air and quickly swiveled toward him so that only he could read it. "Whoever came up with that saying should be punished. I'll make a note to do just that."

Abel scarcely moved.

Mr. Truitt let out another sigh when he finished reading. "Well, Mr. Dowd, you'll be disappointed to know that your own difficulties will not win the day. Someone's managed to top you."

Abel said nothing.

"What's happening?" Jeremy said to kill the silence.

The message in front of Mr. Truitt dissipated as he waved it away. "It seems one Mallory Chiklis has filled a server room with smoke. When questioned, Ms. Chiklis explained she was performing an exorcism." He brought another screen up. Once again, it was visible only to him. "It was one of the Apalala server rooms, Mr. Dowd."

The mention of Apalala pulled Abel out of his fear freeze. He waited to see if Mr. Truitt might offer any details on the consequences that were sure to be forthcoming.

"Much to do. Much to rue, Mr. Dowd." Mr. Truitt laced his fingers behind his head and leaned back in his chair to stare at the ceiling. The report in front of him faded. "Much to do. Much to rue."

27

THE ABYSS GAZES BACK

Upstairs in J.P.'s office, Po once again made sure Joel was facing the demon boss, but he let Effie interpret for him. He suspected that hearing Po's side from his own daughter might help keep J.P. off-balance and, if Po were fortunate, slightly more honest.

As it turned out, there was no need for Po to say anything. Effie's unyielding glare did all the work.

"We tapped into a heavy hitter—a huge mover," J.P. said. "We were thrilled because we saw the chance to gain a fat client or, even better, a shot at taking on a partner who could carry us into the big leagues with him." He gave his daughter a smile. "Or her."

Effie didn't return it.

"Then—and I hate to admit this, really, but I will, to make sure we're out in the open with one another—we got scared."

Po let his silence ask the question.

"Yes, us. Scared." J.P. glanced at Effie again.

"Daddy." Effie's tone gave no quarter. "You weren't afraid until I told you to be."

"Maybe, maybe. That could be true. But in the end, I did

the right thing, didn't I? I recognized that I should listen to you, and we didn't pursue it."

Effie stretched her wings in frustration and folded them again. A loose feather dropped off and floated down in a zigzag pattern toward J.P.'s desk.

No one watched it.

"Okay." J.P. slapped the surface of the desk. "May I be frank with you? So you know you can trust us?"

"My superior assumed you would do that from the start," Joel said.

Po did his best not to hear any sarcasm in the use of the word "superior" while J.P. looked to his daughter for support.

She drew herself into a tight corkscrew and leaned forward, face on hands and elbows on coils.

"We were going to report it. Honest, we were." He was speaking as much to her as he was to Po and Joel.

"Report what?" said Joel and Effie simultaneously, before Po could finish signing the same question. "Daddy," Effie added.

"This will sound crazy, all right? That's another reason we were slow to tell you. We didn't want you losing any respect for us as a source." He waited for a response.

All three of them left him hanging.

"The heavy hitter wasn't what scared us. We knew to tread carefully, of course, but it takes more than that to spook us. He held up an index finger to accentuate his point. "We put no small amount of effort into tracing his whereabouts to verify he was for real. That's when we got jumpy. You're not going to believe where he was. You ready?"

"Daddy." Effie's patience was wearing even thinner.

"The Living World. The. Living. World." J.P. slapped the papers in front of him with each word. "Now, we are required by law—or, at least, by you, which is more important—to report it. And we did not because the next piece silenced us altogether." He reached into his desk for a half-smoked cigar and made to light it until he caught the expressions on the faces of his audience. He squinted at Joel to verify that even the Tamagotchi wasn't buying his act and jammed it into the corner of his mouth, unlit. "We're fire beings. And as such, we know when there are other fire beings involved." He considered what he was going to say next, flicked the lighter to life and began to lean into the flame with the cigar.

"Daddy."

J.P. stared into the flame, but didn't touch the cigar with it. "The market he made wasn't in The Commons. It was in The Living World. That alone should have sent me running to you guys, not only because it's required but because anything able to pierce the barrier between The Commons and The L.W. should have rung all the bells. Which it would have. But we like to know what we're dealing with, especially before we pass the word on." The flame flared for so long that no one but a fire entity would have been able to hold onto the lighter. "So we were really surprised when we discovered that another fire entity had been watching this heavy hitter, too. Then we saw that we were seriously outgunned. This fire entity was way bigger than us, bigger than the heavy hitter, bigger than anyone we'd dealt with before. The situation was too hot." He clicked the lighter closed.

Joel coughed for effect. He didn't want to let J.P. off the hook.

"We thought that would be it," J.P. said. "We hoped it would. And I mean really hoped. But the heavy hitter—the big mover—was somehow aware of us and was interested in doing business. So he reached out. Which meant this ancient fire entity, if it was watching, might know about us, too. You know, gaze long into the abyss, and the abyss gazes back and such. And maybe, if it was so interested in the heavy hitter, it's in the biz as well—and would see us as competitors. Or potential forced partners with no say in the terms of the deal. So we moved. Far, far away and into this space. Changed all of our contact info, our domain, our website, phone number, company name—the works."

Po signed.

"And you still didn't report it," Effie said for him.

J.P. flicked the lighter to life again, but now he stared off into space instead of into the flame, as if his native fire had grown too dangerous even for him. "No. I didn't. I definitely did not. At all, ever."

"Why not? You haven't told me that part, Daddy. They could shut us down for good."

"They could, sweetie. They sure as hell could." J.P. didn't mean Po, the Envoy Corps, or the Vigils.

Po signed.

Joel waited for Effie to interpret. When she didn't, the Tamagotchi stepped in. "Who could shut you down, J.P.?"

J.P. stared at the flame for another long stretch. "We checked and rechecked, and every time we did, the market the heavy hitter was trading in showed up as being in The Living World. We were going to report it. But—"

"That would be bad for business," Joel said.

"It would be bad for continuing to exist. Our gal who checks that for us, the best tracker we have? She tried a tracer on the ancient fire entity before any of us knew she was planning to do it. When it came back, she didn't try again, believe me. She didn't want to tell us what she'd done, but she knew that if it sensed her and she didn't warn us, that might be it for everybody." He closed the lighter again. "Here's why I didn't report it, Po. The real reason. And it's why we're going to move again, and we're probably going to shut down for a while, whether our clients like it or not. That tracer came back and told us where the ancient fire entity was." He set the lighter down on the desk.

The silence that held while J.P. chewed his lip and considered what he was about to reveal surprised even Po, who more than anyone else in the room appreciated the power of saying nothing.

"The Pines. The ancient fire entity is in The Pines."

28

THE GIANT SWITCHBOARD

The grip on Annie's shoulder hurt too much to be part of the VR simulation—and that was the intent.

"Wherever you are, it's not where you can do what you should be doing—which is why you're not doing it." Bobby's voice was as clear as it would have been if Annie hadn't been wearing the VR gear. That was odd. He loosened his hold after a moment, which was long enough to deliver the unspoken part of his message.

She pulled the helmet off, noting that it felt lighter than normal, and met his gaze in the mirror she'd affixed to the corner of her monitor. She'd told herself it was there to prevent anyone from startling her, but maybe it was time to admit she'd had only one person in mind. "I'm on the number," she said, and it was true. She was right on track to meet her data-management quota for the day.

"I can see the numbers. That's not what I wanted to talk about."

Annie rubbed her shoulder until she saw in the mirror that Bobby had noticed.

Her knee tingled. *He didn't really mean to hurt her; he was just a little too enthusiastic sometimes.*

"What's up?" she said.

"I wanted to tell you—could you turn around, please?"

Annie had been waiting for him to ask.

Another tingle. *It wasn't that she was resisting him. He didn't deserve that. He merely forgot his manners sometimes. Didn't everyone?*

She swiveled her chair to face him.

"I want to tell you something." Bobby conjured his most sincere face.

Tingle. *Not necessary. He always spoke from the heart.*

"I don't have much practice at being a father." Bobby swallowed and stuck his hand in his pocket. A muffled jingle followed as he began fidgeting with some coins. "Okay, I don't have any practice. But I plan to fix that."

The coins were usually a tell. But of what?

His struggle to make himself vulnerable to her. He was a good man, but honesty was a sign of weakness in his professional world. This was difficult. He needed empathy, not suspicion.

"I want a better relationship with Zach." It came out as the release of something long pent up. "I need that. We need that. He's a good boy."

"He is." Annie didn't know what else to say, but she wanted him to see she was supporting him.

Tingle. *She was grateful to Bobby for making this effort. It was hard for him. And if he said it, he meant it.*

"We're a great combo."

Tingle. "Yes. We are." It felt like she was sincere. It really did.

"Good. That's good." Bobby gave her a sheepish smile. "Well, I won't keep you from the numbers. That's what we're here for."

"Yes." Annie turned to pick up her VR helmet as one of the interns—the pretty one who never seemed to be without a man trying to talk to her—passed by with a covered cup of coffee from downstairs. Right before Annie lowered the rig back over her head, she spotted Bobby in the mirror as he gave the girl a quick wink and turned to watch her walk away.

Tingle. *Bobby. Always taking an interest in the new talent.*

∽

LATER THAT AFTERNOON, Annie enjoyed a lucky find that was sure to earn her a few points with Bobby and management. Or a little less grief the next time she fell shy of her numbers because she did the job right rather than fast.

The task for the latter half of the day involved a setting that was one of Annie's least favorites—the giant switchboard. She didn't know who chose that metaphor for data routing and storage, but an armory-sized facility containing array after array of vintage cord switchboards straight out of a Norman Rockwell painting was a punishable offense, to her mind. It made for lonely duty since each data jock experienced it as the sole occupant of the entire facility. She assumed the aim was to make it easier for them to focus.

It didn't. The isolation made for lonely work, which was no surprise. And the voices that were an integral part of the simulation were downright eerie. When a call came in, Annie was told through a Ma Bell-era headset who the caller wanted to connect to. The callers came off as real—too real. They were only chunks of data, but each call sounded like it was coming from an actual human. Some couldn't wait to connect with the person they were seeking; others did nothing to conceal their dread. Still others laughed their way through their request, while a few—the most disturbing ones—could scarcely stop crying long enough to get all of the digits out.

It was slow work, much more ponderous than, for instance, the robot-warehouse model, which called for the direction of quietly efficient machines as they went about their business. And it managed to be creepier than even the nanotech ant mounds, where the little buggers were so lifelike that Annie felt as if they'd turn and carry her off to be devoured by the queen.

Things got worse as the work progressed. First, there were the no-answer calls that somehow defeated the fail-safes. The way it was supposed to work was that a voice would call from a known number. Annie would ask which number they wished to connect to, ring it, wait for an answer, and then complete the connection. The data went where it was supposed to go, and she was on to the next.

Only now, callers told her the numbers they wanted to connect to, but when she rang, there was no answer. Yet the calls went through when she plugged the cord into the requested jack. A connection to no one.

When she looked around the facility, she saw a first for the current simulation: a handful of boards were already completely plugged in, though no one manned them.

It could have been the scenario shifting, of course, which happened all the time. A warehouse that had human workers in a pick-and-pack operation was replaced by automatons the next time she pulled that duty. The time after that, the machines were newer, faster, and quieter.

It could have been, but it didn't feel like it.

Normally, the huge switching facility was vacant and dark except for the lights over Annie's own board. Normally, all other boards were completely empty, their plugs sitting at attention in perfect rows, waiting to be deployed by the next operator to come on shift.

However, as Annie worked, more and more of the dark boards were plugged in each time she turned to check them. The first time around, it might have been just a few plugs. Then the entire board. Then multiple boards.

She shouldn't have cared. The system worked in its strange and wondrous ways, and nobody—Bobby especially—was interested in her opinion of the arrangement. The smart play was to go head-down until she hit her numbers.

Smart until the unexpected up its game and boards began disappearing altogether, fully plugged in one moment, gone the next—panels blank, plugs missing. That wasn't right, and she was obligated to report it to cover herself.

Tingle. *No, not to cover herself. To continue the efficient operation of a necessary project. It was about collaboration.*

Annie connected to the red jack for internal communications. The voice of the woman who answered was even more disturbing than the too-real fake voices she'd been working with. This was the voice of fear. Nerves. Annie wondered what this woman thought would happen to her for relaying a message about a problem to the proper parties. Then again, this was an immense company with all sorts of characters in charge who were much like Bobby but turned up to eleven. Annie tried to picture having to tell such a boss about an issue. She'd be scared, too.

Annie's knee tingled as she finished explaining the plugged-in and disappearing boards. By the time she went back to work, she knew she'd done the right thing and was reenergized by having had the opportunity to contribute to the constant improvement of the effort.

Team Manitou: won for all; all for won.

Another tingle. *Go, team.*

29

TRUE BOUNDARIES

It was no illusion. Paul was within reach, impossible though that was. Even through the approaching void of unconsciousness, Porter could feel him.

It was a strange combination of strength and weakness. Paul's abilities were there. They were buried within him due to his having returned to The Living World, but he was a Nistar still. His ability to transfer Essence from one being and form to another remained, locked away within the laws governing The L.W.

Yet Paul was unaware of Porter's connection; he didn't even appear to be conscious. Parix had attacked both of them, boosting the adjacency that already existed between them and granting them access to one another.

That should not have been the case. The barrier between The Commons and The Living World was inviolable, as were the barriers between all worlds. Existence itself would be forfeit were that ever to change.

Still, it had changed—in a fundamental way. Paul was of the living, and Porter was able to reach him all the same.

Paul had survived whatever Parix had done to him, but

Porter had no doubt the mythical planned no such outcome for the Envoy. The leech was putting a full effort into taking every bit of Essence Porter possessed. He wanted him gone. And if Porter wanted to avoid that fate, he'd have to act very soon.

Porter had seldom tested the true boundaries of his jumping ability—not in distance, volume, or number of connections. Stronger when younger, he'd only survived to an advanced age by refusing to flirt with his limits. Now it was his only option.

The details of what Porter was about to try weren't clear to him. He was under attack, in pain, exhausted, his very life force being sapped as fast as Parix could claim it. Instinct was all he had left. Were he to give up now, the leech would win.

There would be more Miras.

More victimization.

More grief.

Porter reached out.

Parix, sensing the change, drew harder from the living well of Porter's Essence.

Paul was unable to answer.

Porter gave his staff another twist, causing Parix just enough pain to weaken his assault momentarily. Porter's concentration began to establish a hold. He'd never done anything like this before; he was transporting the reality of The Commons itself to Paul in an attempt to restore some of Paul's Nistar ability in The Living World.

No response.

Porter pushed harder, willing his need to Paul in The L.W. Even if Paul were asleep, his innate power might be able to do what was necessary. And it was such a desperate attempt that if it worked, Parix wouldn't see it coming.

If it worked.

Porter sent Paul his potential, and he pushed Paul to answer in kind. In theory, the results would wallop Parix with sufficient Essence to hurt or even incapacitate him. Porter needed only an instant or two to jump himself away.

The dangerous part, of course—and it was hazardous to the point of absurdity—was that Porter was breaching the barrier to The Living World. It could be argued that his being able to contact Paul and use his powers meant Porter had already pierced the barrier, but this was like finding a faucet dripping, opening the spigot fully, and then telling yourself there was no difference.

There was also the small matter of Porter's inability to form a clear idea of a destination. Anything was better than staying put and being killed by Parix, but it was a roll of the dice. He could put himself deep inside solid rock or thirty feet below the surface of a lake.

Sometimes a dumb decision was the correct one.

Then again, only the survivors were around to say so.

Porter pushed.

Parix pulled.

The Envoy's Essence continued to bleed out of him.

∽

THE DEVICE THE Commons had given to Audra was an electronic Halloween novelty called a Speaky Shrieky, and it was a far cry from the battered flip phone she'd always used to communicate with Porter. After Brill's fall, change became the order of the day. So now she had to deal with a primitive screen meant to cycle through a variety of movie-monster faces while its accompanying speaker offered up an assortment of ear-splitting screams.

One couldn't say The Commons lacked a sense of humor.

Sitting on the edge of her bed, Audra fiddled with the unit's brightness and volume knobs, which, apart from the power switch, were the only controls it had. Usually, they functioned in whatever way was needed in order to communicate with Porter or whomever else she was able to contact. But now all she accomplished was a subtle shift in the lazy waves of brightness lapping across the screen and a change in the low hum coming from the unit's speaker.

Pain flared where Audra had been burned in her encounter with the fire entity. It was so sharp that she nearly dropped the Speaky Shrieky, but the sensation gradually faded to low-level discomfort. It was a warning. The creature that had hurt her was seeking to reestablish contact or, at least, was near enough to do so if it wished.

What came next overwhelmed even the reminder of her injuries. The focus of Porter's effort. It hurt because there was a distinct wrongness to it. He'd somehow defeated age-old layers of protection and safeguards that weren't ever meant to be toyed with, attempting the forbidden at an incalculable cost to himself.

Here was the Envoy. And right with him was a power she knew too well—a power so vast that she couldn't get a read on its limits.

Here, too, was an Essence leech on the verge of achieving her friend's destruction. And all she could do was observe and endure.

"Jonas," Audra said through the veil of her own suffering. "What are you doing?"

The only answer was an increase in heat as the all-powerful flame drew nearer.

∼

PORTER FEARED he was assisting Parix in his murderous effort rather than doing anything to help himself. He struggled to maintain the connection with Paul while also trying to will the incapacitated Nistar into understanding what Porter needed from him. Porter sent Paul the unreality of The Commons and asked for enough Essence in return, pulled from wherever Paul could safely find it, to break Parix's hold long enough for Porter to jump.

That assumed Porter didn't pass out or perish first.

The breakthrough came in increments, not all of them welcome.

Paul finally received the delivered reality and plea and, whether he consciously understood it or not, began feeding Essence through to Porter. This furthered the rule-breaking. One didn't pierce barriers, and one certainly didn't steal Essence from The Living World, where it was likely being enjoyed by something that was alive.

Something.

Porter couldn't say where it was coming from.

Could Paul?

Audra was somewhere in the mix as well—so faint she could scarcely be detected, but there. If she understood what Porter was up to, she couldn't have been happy about it. The way Porter saw it, self-preservation was a legitimate excuse.

With Parix's bite and theft came a bond between Porter and the leech, whether the two of them wanted it or not. So the Envoy sensed the leech's surprise when the available Essence increased exponentially. From parts unknown.

There was a momentary pulse of fear as Parix tried to ascertain what, exactly, was happening. But the mythical accepted the increased flow.

Greed. Just what Porter had hoped for. It would always be a weakness.

The next moment brought what no one could have anticipated.

Porter had asked for Essence.

Porter got his wish.

It started with Paul and Audra—and ended with flame.

The bidirectional jump of Commons reality to The Living World and the Essence Paul sent back should not have worked. The barrier should have blocked it, and the sheer power and volume of the exchange should have knocked Porter out, if not killed him.

Yet the barrier was permeable. Something was off.

A great, unknown power was on Porter's side. He was able to resist Parix's onslaught and deliver what the leech sought.

What Parix sought.

And then some.

The Essence coming through Porter to Parix shifted in nature. Essence didn't have a temperature. It was metaphysical, not physical, and couldn't possess such a measurable property. Yet what flowed through Porter was a sudden heat beyond what he could withstand. More than that.

It became the equivalent of pure flame.

Fire.

And again, Audra and Paul remained a part of it until they weren't, until they were supplanted, usurped, subsumed. Something else joined the exchange and either Audra and Paul were lost in the flow, or the unnamed something overwhelmed the process and dropped them from it.

It hurt.

Porter's very existence felt as if it had been set alight. And that passed into Parix who, as Porter had hoped, had to choose between letting go and suffering great harm.

But Parix couldn't have broken contact if he'd wanted to. And oh, did he want to.

Porter's unwanted bond with the monster confirmed that a moment before the leech sounded his version of a scream.

What flowed now wasn't fire, technically.

But it burned.

How it burned.

The only reason it didn't initially harm Porter, it seemed, was that he'd merely completed the circuit and served as the conduit rather than the recipient. It would destroy him, given a little more time, but he didn't intend to stick around.

Porter had a split second to jump and save himself while Parix suffered.

The leech couldn't let go of him because Parix was overwhelmed, incapacitated while taking in more than he could handle. But he was weak enough for Porter to kill the connection from his side of it.

Essence flowed through Porter, unbearable but empowering just the same. Black fog was not the danger now; conflagration was.

Porter did the only thing he could.

He twisted his staff and jumped blind.

∽

THE SPEAKY SHRIEKY, true to its name, let out a wail of terror that yanked Audra back into a waking state. Her burns ached. So did her mind. The unit lay on the ground, where she must have dropped it. Moving gingerly, lest she lose her balance, she leaned over to pick it up.

There was nothing to see on the screen, which no longer offered any light. But the pure darkness there, a black presence that was a thing of its own, told the tale.

Adjacency. Audra connected to the fire entity via its attack on her, and it used that to reach Porter and the leech attacking him. It maintained contact as Porter made his jump, fueled by far more Essence than he'd asked for.

She knew where the fire entity was now. She knew why it had done what it did to her.

"Jonas," Audra whispered to herself after sitting with her new awareness long enough to understand that it was no illusion. "Oh, no, Jonas."

Much had changed. Had been changing. Audra just hadn't been aware. But with her new awareness came the terrible understanding that more would change very soon. She didn't necessarily want that knowledge, but nobody had ever given her a choice in such matters.

The fading pain of the burns was replaced by stark perception. Audra knew where Porter had gone. She wasn't the praying type, but she offered one up now.

Things were going to move fast.

30

THE FALL-DOWN GAME

The sha-kunk lady didn't ask Zach for his money. Again. She forgot every day now, which meant Zach no longer heard her cash-register drawer go *sha-kunk* when she closed it.

It didn't matter; Zach's mother and I'm-Bobby had already paid the school for the lunch Zach assembled from the food-line counter. Giving the kids at Ambit Academy things to do such as paying for lunch that was already paid for was supposed to teach them something. Zach took the lunch-food items rather than having them handed to him because what-would-you-like lady and what'll-it-be-today man no longer asked him either of those things.

Sometimes, Maddy's daughter chose them for him. Which was all right because she could see Zach and knew what he liked. Sometimes Zach thought Maddy's daughter knew it better than he did.

Other than Maddy's daughter, most of Ambit Academy didn't see Zach anymore. Which was all right because that was the planned result, as Mrs. Good Morning Class liked to say.

Mrs. Good Morning Class usually saw Zach, too, but only because she was reminded he was supposed to be there when she took roll call. On the days Zach's name vanished from Mrs. Good Morning Class's list, she didn't see him until Maddy's daughter got upset about Zach's disappearance and told Mrs. Good Morning Class that she needed to call on him. At that point, Mrs. Good Morning Class checked her list again, got confused, and apologized to Zach and Maddy's daughter for missing Zach's name somehow. That's how she put it—missed it somehow.

There was no somehow to Zach. That was the way it worked more and more at Ambit and in his world in general.

Because of The Margins. Which was because of The Commons. Which affected everything and would affect it more because things were going to move fast. Zach understood that, even if he didn't yet know just what The Margins were.

Moving fast was one of the reasons Zach never used people's names. Not the names he was told to use. Things changed, and the person with a given name became someone else, and maybe the name didn't fit anymore. So it made more sense to call them what they were to Zach, or to other people, or to other things.

Zach's mother. Maddy's daughter and Addy's mom, which was how that lady always described herself to Zach when she, for some reason, thought Zach had forgotten who she was. I'm Addy's mom.

Maddy's daughter, who saw Zach better than even Zach's mother could—which wasn't Zach's mother's fault because she tried very hard—looked like she'd been slapped whenever Addy's mom did that. Zach was glad Addy's mom didn't do it much anymore because he didn't like seeing Maddy's daughter upset. Maddy's daughter also got upset when Addy's mom called Zach small. Which was not all right.

Then there was I'm-Bobby. Zach would never call him Zach's father, even though he understood that Zach's mother couldn't have brought Zach into The Living World without him. But I'm-Bobby, when introduced to Zach, used a dark voice to tell Zach's mother that he was not Dad or Daddy to Zach.

"Not *father*," he said when Zach's mother introduced them. "I'm Bobby." Then he'd turned to Zach with the hard look he wore all the time now. "I'm *Bobby*."

Zach played along because it was easier. He never called I'm-Bobby anything out loud anyway. I'm-Bobby didn't want to hear much from Zach. Which was all right because Zach didn't want to tell him anything.

Back in the-room-kids-wanted-it-to-be—which was called that because Mrs. Good Morning Class had told them over and over that the room was not a classroom but was instead whatever they wanted it to be—Maddy's daughter insisted on playing the fall-down game.

The fall-down game was all right. Zach didn't understand why anyone would want to make something collapse when everything did if you waited long enough. But the game was simple. Maddy's daughter built a tower of wooden blocks. Then they took turns pulling a block out until the tower fell down. Whoever made it fall was bad.

The routine was always the same. Maddy's daughter would grow frustrated with Zach, but eventually it all worked out. They removed their pieces until a lot of them were gone. Then Zach would look at his rolly-phone until Maddy's daughter got bored and glanced around the room to see what other kids were doing. When she did, Zach would sneak a piece back in to make the tower safer. He didn't like tearing it down. He wanted to help it stand. He also didn't like to win anything if it meant Maddy's daughter lost.

After a while, Maddy's daughter would notice that the tower was staying up too long, so Zach would pull a key piece and bring it tumbling down, giving her the win. If someone had to destroy a thing, at least it didn't have to be Maddy's daughter. She would figure out what he was doing one day; Zach hoped that day wouldn't come soon.

Zach called his phone the rolly-phone instead of a smart phone because it wasn't always smart. It did, however, roll whenever he moved his thumbs across it and made the little square pictures go side-to-side and up-and-down.

I'm-Bobby didn't want Zach to have the rolly-phone because I'm-Bobby didn't want Zach to have anything. Which was not all right. But Zach's mother said he could have it because it didn't have a plan.

Zach's mother was wrong. The rolly-phone definitely had a plan, and it told him what was supposed to happen if he asked the right questions. Most of the time, it didn't tell him a lot. Sometimes it pretended he hadn't asked a question at all.

"Go." Normally, Maddy's daughter respected the fact that Zach never talked. She'd say things without speaking, the way he did. But when she was mad or wanted him to do something he wasn't doing or wasn't doing fast enough, she used her words. Now she wouldn't look away until he moved.

Zach gently pulled out a block that wouldn't harm the tower with its removal.

Maddy's daughter did the same.

Zach focused on the rolly-phone until she looked away again. When she did, he replaced a block. A barn appeared on the rolly-phone, which meant Zach had a message.

He had a message because he'd sent out a question. Which didn't mean he had an answer.

When Maddy's daughter looked to see if Zach had gone yet, he removed a harmless block and watched her as she studied the tower. He did that long enough for her to think he was paying attention to the game and then rolled the rolly-phone again until he got to the barn. The barn was a place for kids smaller than Zach, which was why nobody—not I'm-Bobby, not Zach's mother, not Mrs. Good Morning Class—paid any attention to it. Which was all right.

Zach zoomed until he was inside the barn. He went to the middle. He climbed up a ladder, and then he climbed another ladder. Then he moved in reverse and, finally, to the side. A rooster crowed. Zach liked the rooster, but he liked the pig more, the cow more than that, and the duck the best. All of them meant that Zach had done the moves right and that the app would let him see his message.

It wasn't the rolly-phone's job to have a plan. But it had one for him anyway, just as there had been one the last time it was needed. And the phone was connected. It was just that nobody else knew it was. Which was all right.

"Go," Maddy's daughter said. She wasn't happy. Zach hadn't realized how long he'd kept her waiting while rolling the phone.

If Maddy's daughter got really not happy with him, she'd knock the tower down. When it wasn't even her turn. Then she'd avoid him the rest of the day. Maybe the next day, too, if he made her mad enough to cry.

Which was not all right. He liked Maddy's daughter. A lot more than he liked Addy's mom.

Zach plucked a block from the tower. It wavered convincingly.

Not convincingly enough for Maddy's daughter, whose face went tight. She knew Zach wasn't trying to win. She'd also know if he was too obvious about losing on purpose.

At the moment, none of that was as important as the waiting message. Zach stood up.

Maddy's daughter's face went from shout to question.

Zach held up one finger, then six. As he walked away, Maddy's daughter giggled. She did that every time he highlighted the sixteenth letter of the alphabet. He didn't know why she thought it was funny when he was only telling her where he was going, but he was happy when she did.

In the bathroom, Zach locked the door. There was but one toilet, which meant they were supposed to use the lock in case they forgot to flip the outside sign to red or in case somebody thought it would be funny to open the door and let everyone in the-room-kids-wanted-it-to-be laugh at them as they sixteenth-lettered or worse.

Zach rolled into the barn app again, went through the hay loft and did a fast triple-tap. That allowed him to jump through the air to the silo ladder, climb it, and open up the silo hatch.

If Zach hadn't done the inside-middle-up-up-reverse-side movements correctly, he wouldn't have been able to make the jump. He'd have ended up in the mud with the pigs. And he knew it wasn't just mud. Which was not all right. Though it would have made Maddy's daughter laugh if he'd told her about it.

Zach didn't fall. Because this was all only for him. And Maddy's daughter wouldn't have been able to see or hear any of it, even if he'd tried to show her.

Even though nobody could see his messages, he checked them in the bathroom anyway, just in case. That was how important it was.

Zach reached into the dried corn that filled the silo all the way to the hatch. He never put anything more than his arm in because that would be very dangerous. He'd been told that over and over again. It was just an app in a rolly-phone—but not really.

When Zach reached into the dried corn, it was as if he were lying on the silo roof for real. He felt the sun on his back, smelled the corn dust. He had to be careful not to breathe too much of it in. And he had to hang on. If he fell in, he might never come out. Not without help. And maybe not even then. Just as if it were real life. Which was another conversation. "That's another conversation" was something else Mrs. Good Morning Class said a lot.

He dug in up to his elbow and felt around. The corn shifted as something made its way to him through it. When he could feel the edge of the envelope, he grabbed it. Pulling his arm back out wasn't easy. The corn wanted him to stay. It was tougher each time.

Maybe the corn was hungry.

Maybe Zach shouldn't think about that.

Zach closed the hatch and pocketed the envelope. Then he took a deep breath and jumped back into the hay loft. He could only open the envelope in the barn, and he couldn't take it outside.

The message wasn't an answer. Zach had guessed it wouldn't be but had to try anyway. He'd asked the barn—as he always did, by mouthing the words silently—to tell him what The Margins was. He only knew the name, that it was connected to The Commons, and that it was also connected to —well, everything.

When Zach opened the envelope, it talked. "Margins!" it said, much happier than it should have been since it wasn't telling him anything. He opened the envelope wider to see if it would say anything else. "Margins!" it said again.

Zach recognized the voice. He knew it could tell him more if it wanted to, but it wasn't time for that yet.

When Zach came out of the bathroom, he found that Maddy's daughter had knocked the tower over and left the scattered blocks for him to clean up. That was all right. He had something more important to think about.

The envelope had definitely been empty. So how did the little farmer hide in it?

31

MULTIPLE ANOMALIES

"Po," said June Medill.

That one syllable tipped the scales for Charlene. June Medill could be irritating beyond words, but she wasn't afraid to make a decision and was useful when an opinion was needed. Charlene weighed the suggestion. "Why?"

"He's one of our best and has the strongest adjacency to Mr. Porter of anyone active and capable of helping. And he's already in the field." June Medill licked her lips. The nervous tic broadcast just how much she wanted to present a strong case. "Also, sending anyone else means word gets out that Mr. Porter violated protocol by leaving without updating his status in the system. Po is one of us. If he can, he'll have Mr. Porter back here before anyone knows he's gone."

It was interesting that when she drew the circle, June Medill included herself inside it along with Porter, Po, and those who'd been involved in Brill's downfall to one degree or another. Another point toward taking the woman more seriously and, perhaps, trusting her. Certainly, there was an advantage to her being underestimated since nobody would think of her as an insider.

The thought made Charlene feel a little guilty, but there was no denying the truth of it. "And what if he doesn't?" she countered. "What if Po can't find him or can't help?"

"Then we go all-hands. And a reprimand or demotion will be the least of Mr. Porter's worries."

Charlene thought Porter was nuts when he volunteered to take June Medill under his wing after the Envoy Corps began rebuilding in earnest. The woman was seen as damaged goods. She was tainted by her association with Brill, despite playing a critical role in warning Annie Brucker to flee at a key moment and saving the anti-Brill effort from shutting down before it started.

Yet Porter saw something in her. Now Charlene understood that she needed to listen to Porter more often. "Can you do it using outside channels so the message isn't intercepted or logged?"

June Medill's eyes lit up like the worst kid on the team with a long-desired shot on goal.

Yes, Charlene needed to heed Porter more often—provided she ever got the chance again.

∽

"Ms. Moseley. There are multiple anomalies across the steam lines."

The View-Master snapped Charlene out of a two-hour failure to get routine throughput analysis done because she couldn't stop thinking about Porter, his whereabouts, and his welfare. "Details."

"Ms. Moseley. Reports indicate a complete periphery failure of steam-line insulation."

"Meaning what?"

"Initiating visuals."

The View-Master took over Charlene's computer monitor. A map of the area around Envoy HQ and its surrounding buildings replaced her graphs and spreadsheets. An overlay of the steam-pipe systems feeding Essence to HQ rolled across the screen.

Periphery was right. All of the main trunks sported animated orange rings radiating outward, indicating precisely where the overheat failures were occurring.

"Surveillance camera view."

"None available."

"Why?"

"All cameras are off-line."

"Does Engineering know?"

"They do."

On the screen, the animated rings turned red. The insulation and cooling systems had recently morphed according to some whim of The Commons, though Engineering had a pretty good guess as to why. For as long as they'd remained practically dormant due to Brill's rule and Envoy HQ lying nearly fallow—thank you again, Jonas Porter, for keeping the lights on—the network of steam mains under the buildings and the wider neighborhood were swathed in asbestos. Theory held that with Brill's defeat and the slow return of The Commons to its age-old duties, the realm had some catching up to do. New arrivals from The Living World meant an influx of knowledge, which included, among other things, the fact that asbestos was dangerous. So The Commons altered the pipes.

What nobody was prepared for—and this was but one example of the bizarre surprises awaiting those expected to operate within the altered environment—was what replaced the insulation. In fact, the apprentice engineer who'd taken it upon herself to cut into the new pipes just to see what was going on faced universal derision when she filed her report.

After breaking through with her cutter, she was rewarded with a generous spray of liquid to the face. A nutritious liquid with a familiar flavor.

The new insulation was, as far as anyone could tell, composed of a sealed layer of breakfast cereal and milk. Further investigation revealed that The Commons was trying out different cereal types to see which it preferred. It started with O-Wow oat rings, then Square Deal frosted shredded wheat. More recently, the milk came out in colors befitting insulation that was either Shortcake Break, Blue Bombers, CitruNami, or Cocoa Completes.

It wasn't much odder than other things The Commons came up with, and it paid to remember that the realm merely echoed what originated with humanity and Mother Nature. Most absurdity began with people.

All in all, a system built on cereal and milk wasn't nearly so funny as those who didn't understand the ramifications thought it was. Engineering didn't get how the hell it worked, which meant they couldn't fix it if anything went wrong. If those steam mains overheated, as they were wont to do, those who got a kick out of it would quickly discover how vital the system was to Envoy HQ and the ability of The Commons to fulfill its main mission of mounting and overseeing Journeys. Never mind that it was uncounted years behind in that mission, so any delay was a big, big problem.

The animated disturbance icons turned an even deeper crimson. A moment later, they flared—and everything went dark. Charlene's monitor and all the lights died as she felt more than heard a collective groan emanate from the walls, ceiling, and floor of her office. Now her space was lit only by the natural light spilling in from the windows.

"Ms. Moseley. The system is under attack." The calm tone of the View-Master was an unnerving contrast to its warning. Charlene had deactivated its emotional component. It would report a nuclear strike just as impartially as it would announce the first day of spring.

"Details."

"Ms. Moseley. All systems are off-line due to a steam-main failure along the entire periphery. Rerouting has commenced."

Out in the hallway, someone said something about staying away from the windows and entrances. June Medill relayed the message as she hurried down the hall, shouting, warning all occupants to prepare for security measures. What was happening?

The auxiliary system kicked in. Mini-LED floodlights in vintage wire cages lit up the hallways and offices.

Out in the halls, heavy gates dropped or closed, some with a sliding impact, others with the deep boom of a vault being slammed. An old L.W. sitcom featured that as a gimmick in its intro and outro, but Charlene couldn't come up with it, nor could she fathom why she was thinking of that when she needed her brain for more pressing matters.

Her monitor came back to life. Then the *sshhh-THOOMP* of steel security blinds sealing off her window scared the bejesus out of her. On screen, the entire sector of the map area surrounding Envoy HQ and its nearby buildings was black. No more overheating there. The steam mains were out of commission altogether.

"Ms. Moseley."

Before the View-Master could continue, June Medill appeared in the doorway, the squat little woman's expression pale but admirably controlled. "Charlene." The formal "Ms. Moseley" was gone, the gravity of the situation having done away with June's usually unassailable etiquette. "We have multiple breaches."

"Ms. Moseley," the View-Master repeated. "We are under attack."

June Medill nodded an affirmative.

From down the hallway, faint enough to be a long sprint away, came multiple loud thumps followed by a cry of pain.

"Ms. Moseley," said the View-Master again. "Casualties reported—severity unknown, quantity in flux."

The view on Charlene's monitor shifted. Internal security cameras remained off-line, but external views kicked in, one by one. A black tank silently made its way down the street toward Envoy HQ. The outside cameras had no microphones. Soon, another view showed another tank, this one trailed by a black troop carrier.

"Ravagers?"

June Medill gave a grave nod. If anyone would know, it'd be June. She'd been beaten unconscious in her first encounter with the shock troops after arriving in The Commons aboard Paul Reid's bus.

"That's not possible." Charlene wasn't sure if she was arguing with June or the security cameras. "They went when Brill did. And since when do they have tanks?"

Internal-camera audio returned from somewhere in the building. They still weren't relaying locations. From the monitor's speakers came another cry of pain that was then smothered.

"Ms. Moseley," said the View-Master. "Casualties continue to mount."

Envoy HQ was not designed to be defended from within. Its systems went into siege mode and sealed everything off, trusting outside forces to come to their aid when called. As far as Charlene knew, said forces consisted only of the Vigils, and there wasn't much warmth between them and the Envoy Corps these days. Never mind that the Vigils' numbers hadn't yet rebounded to those of an effective law-enforcement operation, and they might be dealing with any number of problems at the moment.

Still. Ravagers? In tanks? Charlene dug into her bottom drawer for her M11 and her bayonet and hung both on her belt, thanking her innate paranoia for winning out every time she'd worried it might be crazy for a bureaucrat to keep a pistol and knife at hand.

They were under attack. By Ravagers. And, given that this was The Commons, who knew what else? "June, I'm taking a look around. Lock the door behind me, and don't open it for anyone you don't know."

"The protocol is tap code."

Charlene had forgotten and tried to hide it. "Yes. I-N, right?"

"Two-four, three-three."

"Right. Tap code for in."

Charlene turned the doorknob as quietly as she could. No use letting whoever or whatever awaited know she was about to make herself a juicy target.

"Charlene?" June Medill paused to absorb the situation. She had no combat training whatsoever, and soon she'd be in duck-and-cover mode. "Should I send out a system-wide alert?"

"System-wide plus allies. If everyone else is getting hit, too, we're on our own. But if not, let's get some help in here. We're not good at this. We're a big turtle that hides in its shell and waits for the cavalry."

The hall outside was lit only by the center row of emergency LEDs running along the ceiling. The office door locked behind Charlene as soon as she closed it. Maybe she should have left June the knife, at least. She'd be defenseless if something came through that unfortified doorway. Then again, the idea of giving June Medill a weapon of any kind seemed like a danger all its own—mostly to June.

Not that Charlene was a force to be reckoned with. She'd had only basic training with both the pistol and the knife and had never had to use either in a combat situation. Truth was, she was no fan of guns in a noncombat situation—or even in one such as her current predicament. Anyone who didn't train regularly in real-world scenarios was likely to put a bullet in someone they shouldn't.

Given that, Charlene moved carefully down the hall with her hand on her knife. She didn't want to have to use it or the M11 under any circumstances, but it helped to know both were there.

At open office doors, she peeked in to see if anyone was inside. All were empty. At closed doors, she tried the tap code but got no response. Either those offices were empty, too, or their occupants hadn't remembered the protocol, either.

A loud pop and creak from further ahead. There was nothing down that way but closed office doors and a sealed set of medieval-style wooden gates banded in iron. Even in providing security, Envoy HQ—and behind it, The Commons—retained its sense of fun. The problem was that the demise it failed to prevent might be just as novel in its gruesomeness.

Charlene drew closer to the gates, tap-coding each door she passed.

Another creak and pop. From the wood itself. Something pushing against the other side? Those gates were nearly a foot thick.

Charlene pulled her knife from its sheath and twisted the

knob at the end of its handle. Two tiny LEDs in the knife's guard threw some more light on the scene. Her colleagues with any combat experience had laughed like hell when she found a rubber-banded collection of cookie-box tops in her drawer and sent them in for what was dubbed a special-forces knife. They'd laughed even harder when it arrived because no knife worth anything in battle had lights in it. Charlene had the last laugh now.

Another thump.

Charlene stepped back.

The wood groaned like a living thing. The doors actually flexed, then flattened again.

She waited a few moments and crept forward, betting that the doors would hold. Something glistened in the LED light—a jelly-like substance oozing from where the doors joined one another and where they met the floor. They were supposed to provide a water-tight seal. What could put that kind of pressure on them? Or was that the seal melting?

The goo on the floor grew thicker as more of it squeezed underneath.

Charlene aimed the knife light at it.

Its surface began to shimmer in rainbow waves, like sunlight hitting oil on water.

She found herself drawn to it. Her inner alarms went off but were soon silenced.

The colors changed patterns, as if they spoke a language all their own. The goo was friendly. It wanted to help. Blue gave way to red. Then the two joined in extravagant purple. A wash of yellow. Red again. Orange joined the dance. Pulsing. Glowing. It had a music to it. It beckoned to her.

Charlene drew even closer as the door continued to weep jelly, adding to the living art on the floor. Another step.

The colors extended beyond her, embraced the soles of

her boots and caressed their way up and over the laces. All the while, the colors continued to sing their visual aria.

She'd been suckered.

Without warning, the goo solidified and tightened around Charlene's feet and lower legs. Then it pulled back and yanked those feet right out from under her.

She fell backward, doing her best to roll with the impact.

The goo wouldn't let her.

She whacked her head hard on the floor and saw fireworks. It knocked the appreciation of the colors right out of her—along with some of her consciousness.

Luckily, she wasn't out cold. Charlene lay on her back in the goo, aware of a burning sensation in her hands, neck, and anywhere the jelly made contact with flesh. Nothing severe. Yet. Through the postimpact cloud in her head, she had a vision of an old horror movie with a rolling blob containing corpses of people and animals being digested.

Another loud thump on the doors, followed by the further protest of the wood and iron.

Charlene tried to sit up, but the goo held her flat on her back.

Tendrils of the shiny jelly worked their way up the sides of the gates. The hinges were flush with the wall so that the seal would be stronger and harder to tamper with, but that didn't appear to stop the goo from having its way. Steam began to rise from wherever it coated the wood and steel.

Burning. More burning.

The jelly began to shimmer again.

Charlene no longer felt the pain. The colors were shutting down her senses, but that didn't matter. The goo was her friend.

"Stand back from the doors!" A muffled male voice from the other side. "I'm hitting it in five! Four! Three!"

Charlene tried to tell this guy that she wasn't standing at all. And she certainly wasn't far enough from the door for him to safely hit anything.

But the colors. Everything was fine.

"Two! One!" A loud crack of energy.

It nearly fried her. She was plugged into something. Sizzling, followed by a scream that was there and not there at the same time.

The jelly ruptured and spattered like water thrown onto hot oil.

And Charlene was lying in it.

Another scream. A different one.

The jelly.

And her.

The current coursed through Charlene for what seemed like a month or two, then shut down abruptly.

So did she.

32

HIS OWN WEIRD LITTLE WORLD

"At some point, he has to get tired of dealing with all the misdeliveries and start putting things in the right boxes," Zach's mother said. "I mean, he has to—right?"

Zach's mother and Zach had just finished clearing the dining-room table after a late-evening dessert, and she was carrying out her nightly ritual of checking the mailbox hours after they'd gotten home. She never remembered to do that until well after dark.

I'm-Bobby never cared about checking the mail at all. It was as if he knew nobody would ever send them anything worth looking at.

In the living room, I'm-Bobby slouched on the sofa, maintaining a line-of-sight to where Zach sat. I'm-Bobby didn't answer Zach's mother's question. He was using his hard look on Zach while Zach focused on the rolly-phone. He didn't think Zach noticed him watching.

"I mean, don't you think?"

I'm-Bobby still didn't answer. He was not happy with Zach having the rolly-phone. He had not been happy about that since Zach's mother was given it by someone at work who, she said, got it from something called a vendor and wasn't allowed to keep it because of policy.

At first, Zach thought I'm-Bobby wanted the rolly-phone for himself. But I'm-Bobby already had a much more expensive one. With a plan. The kind of plan Zach's mother was talking about.

To I'm-Bobby, Zach having any phone at all was not all right. But I'm-Bobby didn't say why.

"Wait, this is for me." Zach's mother tore open a plastic envelope and peeked inside, then pulled out a piece of paper and gave it a quick scan. "Vitamin samples." She shook her head. "Why do they want everyone to take more and more vitamins?" She didn't have long to ponder the question. The kettle she'd left to boil on the kitchen stove began a low whistle which rapidly increased in urgency and volume.

I'm-Bobby's stare was heavy, like hands trying to pull Zach down to the floor, trapping him there and making him disappear from the lives of I'm-Bobby and Zach's mother.

Zach made his way over to where Zach's mother stood with the puffy vitamin envelope, rolling the phone screen all the while. That was the trick—use I'm-Bobby's anger over the phone to cover up what Zach was really doing. He'd once seen a magician on TV who explained how to do what he did. He called it misdirection. People didn't think Zach would know a word like that, but he did. And it was easy to make people like that believe something about Zach to hide what he didn't want them to see.

The whistle rose in pitch. Zach's mother dropped the puffy envelope with the vitamin samples onto the side table and went into the kitchen to turn the kettle off.

Zach grabbed the vitamin envelope and followed her into the kitchen. While Zach's mother filled her mug with hot water and yo-yoed her teabag in it, he took a look inside the envelope at the vitamin samples. They weren't right, but that wouldn't be a problem. Zach waited for her to put the kettle back on the stove and then offered her the envelope.

It took Zach's mother a moment to realize what he was doing. "Oh, thank you, honey." She took it from him. "I know just the place for these." She stepped on the trash can's foot pedal, raising the lid, and dropped the envelope in. Which was all right.

When Zach's mother turned around to get her half-and-half from the refrigerator, he caught the trash can lid before it closed fully and quietly fished the envelope back out. She began pulling leftovers out to get at the creamer—which was, according to her, always in the back, no matter what. He stuck the envelope up under his shirt. He hoped there was nothing nasty on it. Like gravy. Or fat. Or soup. He slipped out of the kitchen and headed for his bedroom.

I'm-Bobby picked up where he'd left off, watching him from the sofa, suspicious. Zach kept his hands in his pockets and sucked his stomach in so that I'm-Bobby wouldn't see the secret he carried.

"That phone is bad for his thing," I'm-Bobby told Zach's mother as Zach rounded the hallway corner, hurrying now that he was out of I'm-Bobby's sight. "It's not connected to anything. It encourages him to stay in his own weird little world."

Once in his bedroom, Zach silently closed the door. In case Zach's mother came to see what he was up to, he moved fast, pulling the stolen vitamin envelope from beneath his shirt and checking it quickly. It hadn't picked up anything from the garbage, so he hid it deep in his sweater drawer, which was not going to be opened for a while, given the weather they were having.

He changed into his pajamas so that Zach's mother and I'm-Bobby wouldn't wonder what he'd been up to and went back out into the living room. I'm-Bobby sat with the universal remote in hand, aimed at the entertainment center like a gun. Zach liked the universal remote's name, though it worried him somewhat to have such a thing in I'm-Bobby's hand. He knew it didn't make any sense, but sometimes he feared it would give I'm-Bobby control of the universe.

"This doesn't have monsters or anything else we wouldn't want a small boy to see, correct?" Zach's mother sat down on the sofa a small distance from I'm-Bobby, then seemed to remember what she was supposed to do and scooted over closer to him.

Zach settled in on her other side.

I'm-Bobby didn't answer. But when he turned on the TV and hit "play," Zach's breath came up short.

There was the thing he couldn't watch, no matter how much time passed.

On the screen, Captain Hook hung from a rock outcropping above the snapping jaws of his nemesis the ticking crocodile. Terrified and screaming, he was swallowed by it over and over, each time managing to free himself as he cried for help and swam for his life.

I'm-Bobby chuckled.

"Bobby!"

Zach jumped up and dashed down the hall for the safety of his bedroom as Zach's mother laid into I'm-Bobby.

"I didn't know the DVD was in there." I'm-Bobby's voice was fainter with the distance Zach put between them. "He must've been watching it."

Down the hall, Zach stopped, leaned against the wall in the dark and inhaled deeply, the way he'd been shown.

"He was watching something that scares the hell out of him?" Zach's mother couldn't hide her anger, which was rare.

"Well, why does it scare him, anyway?" I'm-Bobby said. "Kids a lot younger than him love that movie."

The following silence meant Zach's mother was giving I'm-Bobby her own version of the hard stare. But not hard enough, Zach knew. I'm-Bobby and those I'm-Bobby worked with kept her too weak for that.

"Face it. Your son isn't getting any better."

"Our son." Zach's mother sounded hurt now, her anger already gone. The shots in her knee saw to that.

Zach went into his room and shut the door again. He had work to do. He had to ask the vitamins he'd stolen for a favor. Not the vitamins themselves, but their Essence. It wasn't something he was normally able to do, but with things beginning to move, and the crossing-over that had begun, it might work if he asked nicely enough and, as they said on TV, made his case. Maybe.

It wasn't the vitamins that needed to be convinced. It was something else. Something he didn't understand. But he didn't need to. It only needed to understand him and what he wanted.

But Zach couldn't ask until he calmed down. And that would take a while. He lay down on his bed and stared up at the light from the streetlamp spilling across the ceiling.

In the cone of yellowish white, Hook's shadow fled across the water.

The crocodile's shadow was right on his heels, snapping and snapping and snapping.

33

DYNAMITE 8

Right before bed, Annie and Bobby argued about the Dynamite 8 again. Which, of course, set her knee to tingling like mad. But she wouldn't give in. She'd decided to stand her ground on whatever small things she could, and this was one of them.

The Dynamite 8 solved a real problem. They shouldn't have disagreed about it, but that didn't stop Bobby from doing his damndest. The intersection by their place lay along a route that commuters crossing the Golden Gate used as an end run around rush-hour traffic. That caused more volume than the light on the corner could handle, especially since some genius engineer decided to make the light's cycle short. As in way too.

Early weekday mornings meant nonstop horns. And even before the horns started, the delivery truck at the nearby Wake and Bake pâtisserie arrived. Loud braking and back-up beeping ensued as the driver found just the right place to stop before putting on the blinkers. After that treat came the clanking of the carts being wheeled into the bakery proper.

Complaining improved things for a few days, but there were always new truck drivers on the Wake and Bake route.

And nothing would ever cure commuters of their honking addiction. So white noise was the answer.

Annie and Bobby made do with a fan for a while, but that pushed the air around the room in a way that made it tough to sleep and raised dust, no matter where they aimed the thing.

The outlook improved a couple of weeks into a new Ambit self-reliance experiment that called for Zach to be dropped increasing distances from home so he could get comfortable with walking on his own. The program had already caused some tension. Annie thought it was a great idea to teach Zach independence. But Bobby, of all people, feared he'd be grabbed off the street. By whom, he wouldn't say.

"There are people who do that." It almost sounded like Bobby knew those people.

"The drivers follow at a distance without him knowing," Annie fired back. "They wouldn't let anything happen."

"They can't protect him." Bobby ended the discussion there and wouldn't talk about it again.

Annie persisted. She waited until after Bobby had taken his red pills, when they seemed to have their maximum calming effect, to press the matter. Enough of that, and he finally relented.

It worked out well, too—except for the Dynamite 8, which was mostly weird, not bad.

One day, Zach arrived home from school with a perfectly preserved '70s-era eight-track player in hand. The driver who tailed him swore up and down she'd kept an eye on him the whole time, and he hadn't picked it up anywhere or interacted with anyone.

Nevertheless, Annie, who came home from work early on walking days in order to be there to greet Zach, was shocked to see him toting the Dynamite 8. It was a cherry-red number which, they discovered when they Googled it, was a color the good folks at Panasonic termed explosion red. It was fitting, given that the gadget strongly resembled a detonator.

It did cause some minor blowups. Zach wouldn't give them any indication as to where he'd gotten it. Annie walked the route, which had no vintage shops along it, to see if maybe a street vendor had lost it. She unearthed nothing illuminating. After a time, they just came to accept that either Zach would let them know in time, or they would never find out.

Beyond its mysterious acquisition, Zach spent a lot of time listening to the tape that was in the player when he brought it home. The problem with that wasn't that it was too loud or that they didn't like the music. Not at all.

The tape was blank. All it did was hiss. And if Zach turned the volume up enough, it emitted an impressively loud hiss, too—far louder than anything a small portable player should have been able to produce.

Bobby tried to take it away, but Zach would have none of that. He held on as hard as his little hands allowed. Finally, after the red pills kicked in, calming Bobby as much as Bobby could be calmed, he let Zach keep it.

Over time, even Annie began to wonder if maybe Zach was spending too much time with the hiss. But he began leaving the player in Bobby and Annie's bedroom before he went to bed at night, turning it on and leaving the volume up. Nothing they said or did could make him take it back, and Annie wouldn't let Bobby throw it out.

Then they discovered that the hiss was much more effective than the hum of the fan for traffic blocking. Even the Wake and Bake truck couldn't get the better of it. The Dynamite 8 stayed.

Not that Bobby ever learned to like it. The device clicked when switching tracks. Annie got used to that, but Bobby never did. Still, even he had to admit that they slept better.

And Zach was ever-vigilant about making sure they went to bed with it on, refusing to go to his room unless it was in place and playing.

Now Bobby watched her over the lip of his cup of water, washing the red pills down with a couple of hearty swallows. That part of the nightly ritual complete, he pulled her knee injector from the drawer.

"Babe, can I skip tonight? Please?" Annie let an extra note of pleading bleed into her tone. "If this thing gets to tingling, I'll be up half the night."

His look hardened. He glanced ever so briefly toward where the Dynamite 8 sat hissing away on the dresser. The message was clear—dose the knee, or Zach's wishes would go unfulfilled. And Zach would know. He always did somehow. That would provide Bobby with yet another way to upset him.

More than three hours later—Annie knew exactly how long it took because she kept checking the clock—the tingling of the knee subsided. After that, she finally felt herself drifting off.

In the dream, she climbed a long, steep outdoor staircase of painted concrete. The steps carried her up between charming bungalows and Craftsman-influenced houses visible through the short fences topping the walls on either side. She sensed that Zach was with her and moved slowly so he could keep up, but every time she checked, he wasn't there.

The evening air was warm-going-cool and pleasant, and she periodically caught the breath of night-blooming jasmine. She passed under canopies of vines, and shaggy, untrimmed palm trees stood right and left, like sentries.

She checked again. Still no Zach, but Annie continued to feel his presence and maintained a pace she thought would be comfortable for him. For her part, the steep grade should have tired her out, yet she ascended with ease.

Further up, a midnight-black cat on its way down approached. It looked right through her, as if she were a wraith, but Annie knew that even before she became aware of its presence, it was aware of hers.

The cat stopped and sat on a step. She drew closer, and it deigned to acknowledge her, calmly watching her climb while it licked its paw.

Annie held out a fist for the cat to sniff. It stared at her with a level of disdain only a feline could attain and ignored the gesture. Then it continued on its way down as if she'd never been there at all.

Annie had to admire the cat's style. It knew how to play the game.

At the top of the stairs, Annie turned to look out over the neighborhood. The hills were rife with houses on streets that switchbacked their way upward. Other staircases were evident, but only after she'd looked long enough to spot them. In the distance, over the rooftops of the homes closest to her, a section of some sort of man-made lake or reservoir was visible.

The steps were empty. Zach would not be coming.

A breeze carried faraway voices to her. Indistinct, they were tangled in several conversations at once. The knowledge came to her the way it often did in dreams—not there at all, then a certain understanding.

There was no breeze. It was only the sound of one—an all-encompassing hiss that delivered the hint of thoughts spoken.

Abruptly, the breezeless hissing stopped with a jarring click before continuing once again. If that hadn't been enough to awaken her, the crack of the Dynamite 8 hitting the floor would have done the job.

Annie opened her eyes to see a furious Bobby standing over the now-dead player, waiting for it to exhibit some sign of life so he could ensure he hadn't just stunned it. He lashed out with a kick, then cursed when the resulting pain reminded him that bare feet were no match for a hard-plastic machine, not even a deceased one.

Annie shut her eyes and pretended to be asleep before Bobby could notice that she wasn't.

He climbed back into bed. After a time, his breathing dropped into the rhythm of solid slumber. Even at rest, he sounded angry.

Annie lay awake in the dark—the cat, stairway, and hissing voices gone.

She forbade herself to question who, exactly, she was in bed with.

She was afraid the knee might tell her.

34

THE BOY YOU APPEAR TO BE

He dreamt of walking in a desert. A man gripped his elbow and spoke softly to him. The man was close, but his voice came from a distance. It was difficult to hear him.

In the way dreams go, what he knew as truth shifted. It changed because it was no longer true—or because he'd been wrong about it all along.

The man was trying to steer him toward water. Only it wasn't water. It was merely the way he needed to go.

He was thirsty—so thirsty that he couldn't swallow. The dream was a white oven.

When the man held his staff out and asked him to take hold of it, he did. When the man sent him another world to fill all of his senses, the sights, sounds, tastes—and, yes, memories—flowed with such speed and force that he wasn't able to take note of them or recognize any single part. Nor was he able to understand how he sent back what returned through him.

Fire.

Enough to render him naught but cinders of past deeds committed by a passed young man.

But that wasn't what happened.

He did what was asked of him, though he had no feel for how. Nor did he believe he was capable of such an act or worthy of such power.

No.

That wasn't true.

He'd done it before.

Deep down inside him, on the other side of the wall.

Paul knew who he was.

It was only a matter of time before he'd remember.

∼

"That was a feat," someone said. A heavy accent. Not one Paul could name, though it was the same one the plumber who fixed New Beginnings' never-ending pipe and drain issues spoke with. "I would ask how you managed it, but I don't believe it was you. It was the Envoy. And something else. Something I don't intend to meet again without a great deal of assistance at my side."

Paul awoke to a deep-seated exhaustion.

Desolation.

Regret.

Heartsickness.

As if he'd suffered the loss of something which would never be restored.

Something had moved through Paul. Taken most of him with it.

Turning his head toward the voice was a project. Paul's skull made the move before the halo of pain around it rushed to catch up.

His ear rolled into wetness. He was lying in shallow water and what felt like mud.

In near-complete darkness.

The only light source was a rectangle of amber at the top of a set of wooden steps a few yards to his left, and spilling down those steps was what appeared to be a mass of thick tentacles, one of which was held up straight, its tooth-rimmed opening facing him.

Paul tried to raise himself up on one elbow, but succeeded only in sinking his arm deeper into the muck. So he settled for raising his head out of the water.

The tentacles actually laughed at him.

Paul's neck burned. With a little more effort, he was able to raise his hand to what felt like a ring of small wounds spanning his throat and chest—the kind of thing a tentacle with teeth could inflict.

It hurt too much to be a dream.

Paul wanted to go back to the gray man with the staff. At least he didn't bite. And he was on Paul's side.

Paul wasn't sure how he knew that, but he did. And more about the gray man lay behind a wall in the dark, just out of reach.

"Do you know whose it was? The heat?" The sides of the standing tentacle undulated whenever its thickly accented voice issued forth. "Or are you merely the boy you appear to be? I suspect the latter. You have power, but you've forgotten it. Which is best. Still, you don't have that kind of power, that kind of strength."

That kind of power.

Sad but true.

It wasn't his and never had been. It flowed through him. That was all, but it was enough. And the knowledge that he didn't own it made him strong.

It was the reason the power chose him.

Paul couldn't say how he knew any of that, either, but he did—just as he knew that the power was responsible for the lightning flowers on his arms.

The Lichtenbergs. Their itch was gone.

Paul ran his fingers along the length of his forearm. He couldn't see anything, but the lightning flowers were no longer there.

As his memories and power reasserted themselves, as the knowledge of the gray man showed hints of itself behind the wall, they'd faded into him.

Become part of him.

He was the conduit for power once more—and would be as long as it wanted him to be.

Paul's returning consciousness brought something else with it that was no gift: a stink that was practically corporeal—a funk of stagnant water and something rotting that he wanted to know nothing more about, given that he was lying in it.

"Nasty, I know," the tentacles said. "I have no love of it either, though there are fools a-plenty who assume I'd choose to dwell in a place such as this. 'Parix is a thing of the sea,' they say—'a thing of the swamp.'"

Parix was its name, then.

Parix let out a dismissive sound. "And sometimes I inform them of their error as the last of their lives slide out of them."

"What is this place?" Paul wanted to keep Parix occupied. Having him employ the tentacle mouth for talking was far preferable to its other demonstrated use.

"They kept the charges here. But the charges are gone. Now this place returns to its true nature."

Charges.

Paul felt as if he should know what that meant, but the

meaning was hidden behind the same barrier concealing the gray man and his staff.

The mass of tentacles undulated down the stairs and entered the watery muck without a sound. Paul lost track of it until Parix rose up from the swamp right next to him. Several tentacles struck a vertical pose before curving back down toward Paul, examining him.

"You know you're not my preference?" one of the tentacle mouths said. "Too many years. I prefer mine on the larval side. As do they."

The mystery of who "they" were would have to wait. Paul lay perfectly still as the tentacles swayed in the air over him, as if trying to decide their next move.

"Whatever happens to you," Parix said, "it is just a balancing of accounts for 'fixing' The Commons. Because of you, we mythicals are hunted like game."

"What did I do?"

"What was expected of you—which you will do again." Parix hovered over Paul in anticipation, weaving lazy patterns in the fetid air of the dank space.

Paul found it increasingly difficult to breathe.

"You do not know, do you? What was expected of you."

Paul saw no point in answering. Whatever was coming was coming, and he'd need all his strength to live through it.

"Here," Parix said, the word fading into his approximation of a laugh. "I'll educate you."

This time, Paul saw the strike coming in the dim light spilling down the stairway.

Not that it did him any good.

The tentacle got him lower on the chest this time, and he sank into the black swamp once more.

The Speaky Shrieky woke Audra with a moan. It sounded like the device was in a state of deep discomfort but meant it had something to show her. Thank goodness it had stopped its trademark screaming.

For now.

That wouldn't last.

While Audra slept, the space around her had been hard at work. An efficiency no longer, it was now a bedroom adjacent to an office area. And she wasn't free-floating, location-wise, anymore. She was definitely somewhere, though she wouldn't know precisely where until it was the proper time.

Audra sat up and waited for the toy's screen to give her an indication of what she needed to know.

No image appeared.

This wasn't something she'd be shown after all. But it was something nonetheless.

The Speaky Shrieky was part of a larger network—a device far more capable than its collectible-shop appearance and comic bent would indicate. It was a connector.

Audra went into the bathroom and splashed water on her face.

Still the apartment had no windows. Still its outside surroundings were kept from her. But they were there.

In the newly created office, a large L-shaped desk held a '90s-era desktop minitower with a bulky monitor and clunky wired keyboard. Audra did not scoff. She knew The Commons, and she knew appearances were deceiving—usually very much so.

She sat down to boot the machine. It was up and connected immediately. Nostalgia was a useful veneer, but speed and efficiency were everything.

During her nap, an anomaly had been added to a list that already included Porter's impossible jump—and it was major.

Audra did a print-to-screen with the file, and all of the text flowed bottom-to-top in a blur, too fast to read. It took her a moment to remember the ancient DOS commands. She got it properly paginated and scrolled back up to the top.

A Nistar. And not a new one.

Dared she hope?

What followed was a full page of details too arcane to be of any use. Then a section on Porter.

Oh, Jonas. How to help him?

Next came what she was looking for.

The Nistar.

Disconnected in The Living World, but closer than she'd have thought.

Only random details bled through at first. A suicide attempt intended to set things in motion. Good God. What if he'd succeeded? He hadn't, but much was in play now.

The Nistar, still unnamed, remained at risk.

Audra might be able to do something about that, however small.

Then came the name. Audra leaned back in her chair. More knowledge would arrive, but for now, this would do.

The next big piece was in play.

He desperately needed help, but Paul Reid had returned to the board.

35

AN OBLIVION QUEST

"An exorcism?"

Abel, lost in thought, shook his head after a few seconds. "Sage. I don't know how, but she found the right intake duct for one of the Apalala rooms and was burning a bundle of sage below it. She said Apalala is a demon, or a monster, or some ridiculous thing, and that Manitou is possessed by it."

"She's lucky the sprinklers didn't go off."

"They wouldn't. Those rooms have a sentient fire-suppression system. It evaluated the threat and let the tech team know what was going on. And she's not lucky, believe me. She got caught."

Jeremy let that one lie. He didn't want to dig into what Mallory's punishment might be, especially if it would get Abel thinking too much about his own predicament if he didn't come up with better answers for Mr. Truitt. Jeremy had thought that if he kept Abel talking, it would help his colleague unwind and think clearly. Jeremy had never seen a challenge met squarely by anyone too freaked out for rational thought.

The lunchtime crowd at Billy Clyde's was anything but a crowd. The hard drinkers wouldn't get started until later in the afternoon, and nobody came for the food. The few patrons who were there let them have their space, and even Porthos steered clear of them. Which was saying something since Abel's burger sat untouched as he downed beer after beer like he was in a contest.

Porthos was a cat—with cat's instincts. Abel probably smelled like desperation, and since he was too large to kill and eat, he was best avoided in case his loser-in-the-making funk brought failure down on the heads of those near him.

"Do you know that for a moment there, I thought I had a shot at answering those questions?" Abel's gaze was unfocused as he stared through the table. "I even believed I could pull this out to the point of hauling us up in the organization. Really shine."

"Why can't you? Why can't we?"

Abel blinked several times and let out a bitter laugh. "We might if we had the time. But you heard him. Callibeau knows everything as soon as it happens. How patient do you think he'll be?" He took a long gulp from his mug. "What was that Truitt said? Much to do? Much to rue? What the hell does that even mean?"

Jeremy watched Abel tip the mug back again. This wasn't beer at lunch. This was an oblivion quest. Could he signal the bartender to cut them off without Abel catching on? Jeremy needed this job. "How do we know Callibeau's that bad? So he knows. It looks like he pretty much gives Mr. Truitt free rein."

Abel muttered something.

"What?"

"You don't know how it works." Another long pull off the mug. "If we fall through the file, you don't know what happens."

"What file?"

"It's an expression. In the catalog business, they keep a file of customers. Those who order a lot are sent every catalog as it's printed. Those who taper off and order less get catalogs less frequently because it's not worth the postage if they're not buying. The less you buy, the fewer catalogs you see. At the point where you stop buying anything, no catalogs for you. You've fallen through the file."

Jeremy nodded as Abel took another long swallow. The situation was more worrisome than he'd thought.

"We do not—" Abel paused to tilt his head at his burger as if noticing it for the first time. He pushed it to the side.

Across the bar, Porthos the cat looked over when he heard the plate slide across the table and weighed the situation. Nope. The beef was tainted with terror and loss. He rolled over and faced away from them, flicking disdain their way with his tail.

"We do not want to fall through the file. You don't understand how easy it is to do that." His mug empty, Abel refilled it.

Jeremy, still on his first pour, took a token sip. "Then tell me." He reached out to lay his hand on Abel's forearm, stopping him from taking another gulp. No information would come from someone too blotto to speak. He looked around to make sure nobody was close enough to hear them.

The only patron within hearing range was curled up against the window a couple of booths away, softly snoring off a daytime bender. The guy looked like he didn't have a cent to his name, but he must have gotten his load on here at Billy Clyde's. Why else would they let him sleep there?

"Let's start with what you were saying in there," said Jeremy. "What's a moth?"

Abel looked around, too. He thought so little of the

passed-out guy that he ignored him. "Convince me you're ready to hear it."

Whatever was going on had scared the crap out of Abel. It was eating him up. He wasn't really seeking justification to share the burden with Jeremy. He wanted permission.

"Who else knows what you're about to tell me?" Jeremy said.

"The big picture? I'm the only one at my level, and that's because Truitt gets frustrated with Callibeau, Manitou, and the big boys. He shouldn't have told me as much as I know."

"So you're carrying this all by yourself. There's nobody else you can unload on."

Abel took a long pull from his beer. Jeremy let him. "No."

"No one."

"No one. Everybody else who knows is at the main office up on Sixth, where Truitt started."

"There isn't anyone you can talk to there?"

Abel shot Jeremy a look of disbelief. "Remind me to tell you about the main office on Sixth sometime—the stories Truitt's told me. We should get down on our knees and thank whoever's responsible that we don't work there. We don't *ever* want to work there."

Jeremy took a real sip from his mug. "So if it's that big and that bad, you don't have to tell me everything. In fact, I don't want to know. I don't want to end up on your side of the table, looking like you."

"Thanks."

"Sorry." Another real sip. "Look, let me help you. Give me only what I need to know to say what I think of it. I can tell you if I honestly think it's not your fault. Or maybe what your options are if it is."

"It doesn't work like that." Abel swallowed and blinked.

Then his face twisted up. "It doesn't work like that! You don't know!"

A woman at the bar glanced over her shoulder at Abel but decided he wasn't more interesting than the soccer match on the muted TV in the corner.

The drunk against the window coughed a few times and shifted positions.

Jeremy held his hand up for another time-out, which Abel took. When the drunk began quietly snoring again, Jeremy nodded at Abel to continue.

"What do you think of what you've seen since taking this job?" Abel said. "You think you're crazy?"

For whatever reason, Jeremy didn't. "No. I don't."

"I don't think I am, either. I know I'm not. But the world I thought we were living in doesn't exist. In fact, it's not just one world."

"The multiverse."

"I don't know what that is." Abel took another pull, and Jeremy decided that now was not the time to do anything to make him decide against spilling some of the truth. "I'll lay out the basics. If you don't believe you're crazy now, you'll think I am after I'm finished. But the next time you see the focusites on the wall, screaming at you, you'll know that whatever insanity I've got, it's contagious. Okay?"

Jeremy nodded and took another drink of his own beer. He felt the need for its protective blanket of foam. He topped his mug off.

"We talked about Essence already, right? Let's call it the energy of all living things. Anything that dies passes into the next world, an afterlife, and they take that Essence—that energy—with them. And let's say there were people there who figured out a way to capture that Essence for themselves, even if it meant capturing the people who it was part of."

Jeremy forgot to keep the doubt off his face.

"Just let me go through this, all right?" Abel said. "Then you can walk out the door if you like. But I'll warn you, the way this works is that the knowledge itself is a form of Essence. Once you learn enough about something, you may find yourself learning more because it wants you to know. It doesn't happen to everybody, but it happens. Are you cool with that?"

Jeremy took a sip. "Yes." And he was. At least, he thought he was.

"So this is what Mr. Truitt was talking about. Let's say someone on the other side, who he worked for, had control of everything coming into this afterlife. Someone with ridiculous powers and all sorts of superhero-type stuff that I truly don't understand—because that sort of thing is real in that world. And then some other people on the other side took that guy down and freed everything up. You with me?"

Jeremy nodded.

"This is where adjacency comes in. This Essence likes relationships—things that are close to other things. If A is related to B and you can't get to B directly, you might be able to get to it through A or at least keep an eye on it. That's adjacency. Make sense?"

"Yup." Jeremy would need more beer.

"So let's say there were people here in our world who were waiting for Mr. Truitt's boss to be taken down in the afterlife."

"Why?"

Abel took a mouthful and actually swished it around his mouth, as if whichever cheek the larger share of it ended up in would determine whether or not he continued. He swallowed. "The whole challenge on the other side is managing the freed-up Essence of the dead. It's too much to handle, ultimately, and it tends to have a mind of its own. So if you concentrate too much of it in one place in an attempt to be all-powerful, like Mr. Truitt's boss did, you have a hell of a time keeping it from rebelling against you. It wants to leave. It's not supposed to stay put. On this side, in The Living World, the Essence is contained in all living things, and it's at its most potent in people. So let's say if you can control the people, you control the vessels holding this stuff. And it won't concentrate in this world to cause problems. And let's say it's not sentient because it's locked up in the living."

Now Jeremy found himself swishing his beer as he thought that through. Maybe the craziness was contagious after all. "You keep saying 'let's say.' "

"Bear with me—it's my own stupid version of playing it safe." He took advantage of the second it took Jeremy to nod yet again to help himself to more suds. "So let's say this is the problem the people on this side had. The Living World, this world, is where there's potent, living Essence that's easier to manage. But the kinds of superpowers, for lack of a better term, that you'd need to do that only exist in the afterlife, which is separated from The Living World by an unbreakable wall. It's as strong as anything in the universe because it's the fundamental stuff of the universe. The worlds cannot come together, or they're all at risk. So you're screwed. The Essence you can control is on one side, but the powers and abilities you need to claim it are on the other. And there's no way to break through."

"Got it."

"So when the people in the afterlife took out Mr. Truitt's boss, it required so much force that it blew a hole in the wall, which is just what Callibeau and Manitou thought it would do. Several holes. They didn't have to be huge. All Callibeau and Truitt need to do is to be able to access the powers available on the other side and then use them to control the Essence on this side. Nice, huh?"

Jeremy went blank as he contemplated that. These were people willing to mess with the fabric of the universe. Or, at least, to exploit something going wrong.

Abel didn't acknowledge Jeremy's distress. "So that's where Mr. Truitt comes in. Adjacency. The holes are blown, and he was connected to the boss who had the power to manipulate and manage Essence. The people here bring him through to this side, and with him, they can access that power. They're golden." Another long pull. "Or they were until the Essence started going away, which is what's showing up in those graphs of Mr. Truitt's. Who knows where it's going?"

"Could it be leaking through the holes between here and the afterlife?"

Abel shook his head. "It can't. That's one thing they checked out to make sure they wouldn't lose the living Essence on this side. Living Essence can't go to the afterlife without its vessel dying first. Not even with the holes. It's not even easy for Essence to come backwards from the afterlife to here. It might not be possible. So they're looking for other answers. Which is why I need to be able to answer some of those questions Mr. Truitt was asking. Apalala is a program. All Apalala does is reallocate Essence. For the time being. It doesn't move it or do anything it's not supposed to do. So Apalala isn't getting rid of the Essence, and it's not us." Another pull from the mug. "God, please let them believe it's not us."

Jeremy only half-heard that part. He was too busy working through the basic model as Abel had presented it. When he did, the horror of it became real.

"So they're using people's life-force."

Abel hesitated, then took another pull. "Yeah."

"Well." Jeremy took a pull to equal Abel's. "What happens to the people they're using?"

Abel drained his beer. Clearly, this part didn't sit well with him. He looked at the pitcher. It was empty. He stood, pitcher in hand. "I'm not comfortable telling you about that right now."

"Why not?"

"Because I'm a part of it." He bounced the empty pitcher in the palm of his hand, started to walk away from the table, and stopped, his back to Jeremy. He said something low and unintelligible.

"Sorry?"

"I said . . ." Abel bounced the pitcher again, smacking it into his palm harder this time. "That because of me, now you are, too." Then he went to the bar for another pitcher.

Jeremy watched Abel pass the sleeping drunk in the booth. He never looked at him.

Just like the pigeon. Just like the Rubbish Gladiator.

A tiny jolt of nervous energy made its way up Jeremy's spine.

Abel couldn't see the drunk.

36

OJOS DE DIOS

"Look, Val—just call me if he shows up, okay?"

"Who?"

Ray-Anne loved Val as much as she loved anyone at New Beginnings. But she wanted to scream that combo of bewilderment and concern right the hell off her face. "Paul."

Val processed the name. "Right. Yes."

Ray-Anne was reasonably confident the girl wasn't just saying what Ray-Anne wanted to hear. It wasn't an easy call. "Okay."

Val smiled, relieved.

At the door, Ray-Anne turned to see Val back at the computer already, as if the conversation hadn't occurred. "You have my number handy?"

"Sorry?"

"My cell. You have my cell number."

"Absolutely. Why?"

The in-between floaty feeling again. "If Paul comes here. You'll call me."

Puzzlement again. Honest, not suspicious. Val licked her lips, the question about to emerge.

"Jesus Christ, Val." Several of the New Beginnings kids looked up. Ray-Anne didn't talk like that to anyone. Not with that tone. And certainly not Val.

Val's confusion vanished. She didn't have to take that from anyone. She knew it, and so did Ray-Anne.

"I'm sorry," Ray-Anne said.

They went through it again.

∼

Ray-Anne went to the bench. Not because she thought Paul would be there; because she needed to cross it off the search list. She believed him when he said he hadn't really wanted to die—and that he no longer needed to go where he'd intended. But as things got weirder, she still wanted to put that possibility out of her mind.

Regardless, she was disappointed to find the bench empty, but only because it would have been such a relief to find Paul safe and sound. Otherwise, she didn't want to think of him ever again visiting the place where he'd nearly gone out of her life.

It was hard to look at the bench. He'd tried to do it here. This was his platform: an assembly of wooden slats and curved steel with so many peeling layers of different-colored paint that the effect was one of slow, piebald death.

Here, Paul sat down to quit the world. And the bench served as a willing accomplice. Just because objects were inanimate didn't mean they weren't culpable.

She hit the streets and ran the bike as fast as she could without attracting any attention from the gendarmes, as Pop Mike was fond of calling them. The Chicago cops generally let her slide once she mentioned New Beginnings, but she didn't want to deplete that line of credit.

On a whim, she dropped down into Wicker Park again, headed for the park itself. She found herself a spot, did her usual short-term security routine on the bike, and headed in on the Damen Avenue side of the park.

Seasonal transients called the park home in the warm weather. They annoyed the locals, hit a few shows, and enjoyed their chosen lifestyle for as long as they could carry it off. The travelers were like any other group. There were the great, the terrible, and everyone in between.

Ray-Anne and Paul knew and trusted several of the good ones, who often tipped them off when some of the younger and newer travelers were in need of New Beginnings outreach. Sometimes those in trouble accepted the help to get home, provided that home existed. Other times, New Beginnings became that home for a while.

Grease, an elder diplomat of the younger set, greeted Ray-Anne. The girl sat on the ground among her worldly belongings, her back against the fountain. She bisected a fresh bit of graffiti on the wall that read, "Too fast for you to catch." Next to Grease, a scruffy puppy of indeterminate breed—something between Jack Russell and vampire bat—lay flat on his back, legs splayed as Grease scratched his little belly. At nineteen or twenty, Grease was actually a near-college-grad who'd fled school and her family for—well, for no reason she was about to tell Ray-Anne or Paul. And they hadn't asked. "Where's the boy?" Grease said when it became apparent Paul wasn't trailing Ray-Anne.

"That's what I was going to ask you."

"If I had the answer, wouldn't I keep him for myself?" That was part of Grease's shtick with Ray-Anne. She delighted in pretending she wanted to steal Paul away, no matter how many times Ray-Anne or Paul insisted there was nothing between the two of them.

"Has Broward seen him, you think?"

"I wouldn't know. I haven't seen Broward."

Ray-Anne let the silence ask what would've been an awkward question.

"Broward is back frolicking amongst the sun bunnies of his native peninsula, and he is breaking the hearts of Delts and Kappas wherever he sets foot." Grease's bravado faded, and her face darkened. She stopped scratching the puppy's belly. "I hope." The little dog flipped over and began gnawing on Grease's hand. She winced at the kiss of the needle teeth.

"Really?"

"Really. Broward's gone, Ray-Anne. Not a word. He always lets me know when he's gonna leave, where he's going, and when he'll be back. Always." The puppy pushed its luck and tried to chew its way up Grease's arm. She replied with a light cuff to the snout. The pooch accepted the challenge. "And he's not the only one. This is Leslie's pup. She's ghosting us, too."

Ray-Anne considered the possibility raised by Broward and Leslie going missing at the same time.

"No," Grease said, guessing the direction of Ray-Anne's thinking. "They wouldn't. They don't even like each other. And not in a hate-makes-horny way, either." Leslie's puppy gave Grease's thumb a nip. "Ow."

Ray-Anne recalled Val pointing out the dropping arrivals at New Beginnings and the unsettling absences of various Skinner Box girls who'd missed their shifts.

"I can't find Paul," she said.

"I can't find Broward."

The puppy stopped fussing and watched the two of them.

∾

RAY-ANNE SAT ASTRIDE HER CYCLE, at a loss for where to look next. Yet look she would. She put the bike in gear, checked for traffic over her shoulder, and eased out onto Damen.

A bike messenger blazed past, trailing an assortment of kite-like God's-eyes and dream catchers from a pair of rear panniers. It was a close enough shave that one of the wood-and-knit creations whomped Ray-Anne in the helmet—hard, with a lot more heft than it should have had. She very nearly spilled.

That cyclist hadn't been in the bike lane when she'd looked. She was certain of it. And he or she didn't slow down in the slightest to see if Ray-Anne was okay.

Ray-Anne was a supporter of her nonmotorized cousins, but way too many of them were rude and ignored traffic laws. Nevertheless, now was not the time to chase this one down to dispense verbal justice, no matter how richly deserved it might have been.

She got moving again. Up ahead, the messenger sat at a red light. The God's-eyes and dream catchers floated and bobbed, spread out in the air like a peacock tail. The cyclist wore a tall top hat, coal-colored curls spilling out from under it. A long scarf striped with red, yellow, and black graced the biker's neck, its ends also drifting in the air above.

To hell with it. Ray-Anne could catch this jerk, deliver her spiel about how two-wheelers needed to stick together, and decide where to look next for Paul without losing any time. She gunned the bike and shot up Damen. It wasn't much more than a block. She'd be on the messenger with time left on the red, drop an attitude payload, and be on her way.

She passed under a CTA bridge, a loud blue-line train drowning out the rev of her engine as she rode way too fast.

The messenger turned and looked right at her through the

God's-eyes and dream catchers. It was a guy. And she could've sworn she saw him laugh.

A piece of her mind. Indeed.

Rather than wait for the green and risk getting caught, the messenger pulled the bike up onto the triangle between the straight-ahead and right-turn lanes, rode over it, and took off down Milwaukee. His acceleration was uncanny. One moment, he was standing on the pedals, and the next he was burning along on his bike, colorful adornments waving in the wind like arts-and-crafts mockery.

Ray-Anne caught the right-turn lane as the light turned green. Her bob-and-weave abilities remained on their game, and she was on Milwaukee before the walk signal lit.

The cyclist was already several blocks ahead, halfway to Ashland.

That was not possible.

Nor was the way the top hat stayed in place, no matter how fast the bike went.

It wasn't just that the messenger had gotten so far ahead in the couple of seconds it took Ray-Anne to safely make the sharp turn down onto Milwaukee. It was also that the fantail craft items remained afloat—and had hit her helmet way too hard for a project straight out of art hour at a Park District day camp.

The God's-eyes and dream catchers weren't kites. They weren't supposed to fly in the wind. And they weren't balloons, either, so they shouldn't have remained aloft when there wasn't any breeze. Yet they floated along with the scarf, which also defied the laws of physics.

Tossing aside her rule about avoiding attention from the fellas and ladies in blue, Ray-Anne made Milwaukee Avenue a blur and gained some ground on the bike.

But not as much as she should have.

Approaching the red at Ashland, the messenger used the bike's profile to his advantage, squeezing between cars in the straight-ahead and right-turn lanes to maintain some of the lead on Ray-Anne, who couldn't do the same on her cycle. He made the right onto Ashland well before the light turned green.

By the time Ray-Anne was able to follow, the messenger—God's-eyes and dream catchers greeting everyone in his wake—was already at Division.

Again. Impossible.

He turned around to smile at Ray-Anne. It was enough to make her suspect she was being led into something. But who concocted a scheme that counted on a bicycle maintaining a lead on a motorcycle?

A cyclist who could take and hold such a lead, that's who.

Ray-Anne punched it hard. She took the turn onto Division as fast as she could after first making sure she wasn't about to mow down any families out for a stroll.

The messenger was even farther ahead.

Ray-Anne continued to push a lot harder than she should have, given the street. Traffic was traffic. Without doing something really stupid, she couldn't catch the messenger, who had the advantage of a bike lane and no obstacles to contend with.

She lost ground.

Within a short distance, Ray-Anne lost the messenger altogether. The bike was nowhere to be seen.

Dammit.

Ray-Anne cruised a few blocks more of Division at legal speed, the needle on her own inner tachometer slowly falling back to a sane zone as she wrestled her frustration down. What, exactly, had that been about? A surprisingly hard knock on the helmet, some rude behavior from a cyclist in a city chock-full of them, and she'd completely forgotten about Paul and the conversation she'd just had with a justifiably worried Grease. She'd taken off in the name of verbal street justice.

Stupid.

A couple of blocks later, at a stop sign, another surprise popped up in a day that seemed to have plenty in store for her. She found herself in front of the Pawn King building, having almost passed it without realizing.

The shop was gone. The building sat vacant, its neon sign dead, a retail-space-for-rent sign affixed to the inside of the display-case window—the now-empty display case, judging by what she could see from the street.

Ray-Anne double-parked and dismounted, taking her time in approaching because she was reluctant to confirm what she already knew.

The case was empty. Stranger still, the for-rent sign looked to have been there for some time. Along its bottom, which was sealed to the glass with tape made gooey and brown by the combo of sun and dust, were the carcasses of many flies. Long-dead ones. Too many and too old for them to have been there only since Ray-Anne's last visit.

The already bizarre day got much more so when Ray-Anne looked down at the bottom of the case again. There, atop its holster, lay the shotgun she'd stopped so many times to admire.

It hadn't been there when she'd first walked up to the building.

It was now.

She raised a hand and spread her fingers to touch the glass, hoping to confirm what she was seeing with a second sense.

The window wasn't there. Nor was the rental sign, the tape, or the dead flies.

They had been, though. Hadn't they?

Ray-Anne's hands moved with a will of their own. They gently placed themselves on the gun as if it were a holy relic, precious beyond measure, in danger of shattering at her touch—a patient in need of a healing caress.

It felt right. She lifted the gun with care, like something revered. It was much lighter than it should have been. So much lighter.

Ray-Anne carefully laid the gun back down in the window case and reached for its holster. The leather was the same temperature as her own skin—as if it were alive, an extension of herself. Without any further thought, she strapped the holster across her back and tightened it.

She didn't pause for even a moment to figure out how to do such a thing. She just knew.

She picked the shotgun up again and, in one fluid motion, dropped it over her shoulder and into the holster. It hit bottom and settled in like her offspring. Or an old friend and partner.

Which it was.

Only then did Ray-Anne think to look up and down the street to see if anyone was there to witness her theft of a deadly weapon.

Nobody. The traffic was gone.

More knowledge there for the taking when it had not been just a moment earlier: Ray-Anne would return to New Beginnings with the gun on her back, and nobody would say a thing. And she wouldn't see the bike messenger on the way.

The cyclist had already led her where she was supposed to go—so that she'd find what she was meant to find.

Ray-Anne didn't know whether to cry or sing. It was the beginning of what would feel like a long trip home.

Or not.

Maybe home was on its way to her.

37

NOT ALL RIGHT

At the breakfast table, Zach used what Mrs. Good Morning Class called his hidden strength to hide his nervousness from I'm-Bobby. Zach had already asked his hidden strength, which was the tough center Mrs. Good Morning Class said he and all of the other kids at Ambit had been born with, to give him the courage to sneak down into the kitchen the night before, while Zach's mother and I'm-Bobby slept.

It came through for him, and he did what needed doing quietly, without waking I'm-Bobby, which would have been not all right. Not all right at all.

Now Zach fought to hide how scared he was when I'm-Bobby reached for his bottle of red pills. The vitamins had been blue, not red. And they'd been a different shape. Zach asked them to change to look like I'm-Bobby's pills, and they had. But that didn't mean they'd stay that way or that I'm-Bobby wouldn't sense something wrong with them.

I'm-Bobby wasn't paying much attention to Zach or his pills. He was too busy scowling at his phone—which he did every morning—either because he didn't like the email he'd gotten from someone at work or because he didn't like whatever news he was reading.

I'm-Bobby scowled a lot. He did it again as Zach tipped two of the pills into his hand. Zach was glad I'm-Bobby was distracted. Otherwise, he would have seen Zach's hand shaking. And that would have been not all right. At all.

"Didn't we just have one of these parent-teacher things?" I'm-Bobby shook the pills in his loosely clenched fist like game dice as he thumbed his way through his email.

"Three months ago, yes." Zach's mother held the plate she was washing up to the light that spilled through the window and examined it for bacon grease. If I'm-Bobby put the dishes away later and found any signs that Zach's mother hadn't cleaned a plate perfectly, he'd wash it himself and make her watch as he did it "right." Sometimes he'd drop the plate by accident, though Zach and Zach's mother knew there was nothing accidental about it.

"Well, if it's called parent-teacher, that means just one parent, right?"

Zach's mother put the plate into the dish drain a bit harder than necessary and turned around to fix I'm-Bobby with an angry stare.

"Okay. Just kidding." I'm-Bobby winked at Zach and swallowed his pills, which, mercifully, retained their new form and color.

When other people winked like that, it was an attempt to bond with someone. Zach knew better. Whenever I'm-Bobby succeeded in annoying Zach's mother or hurting her in any way, I'm-Bobby always made sure Zach was aware of the victory.

Zach didn't let I'm-Bobby see how angry he was that I'm-

Bobby had hurt Zach's mother. And Zach certainly didn't let I'm-Bobby see Zach's relief when I'm-Bobby finished washing down his red pills with the last of his grapefruit juice. He knew better. For once again, he'd seen what was hiding behind I'm-Bobby's eyes.

The fake red pills I'm-Bobby was taking were going to cause problems for Zach and Zach's mother, and Zach could only hope it was worth it. I'm-Bobby's red pills, like the pinkies Zach's mother had taken in The Commons, were designed to alter the person taking them. But where stopping the pink pills had made Zach's mother a better person—the person she truly was—doing the same with Bobby's red pills would reveal who he was, too. And that was the scary part.

Bobby without his medication was scary. And that's what Zach's mother needed to see and remember.

Zach had substituted the changed vitamin samples for Bobby's red pills, which went down the toilet the night before. Zach's mother needed to see the real I'm-Bobby. Or enough of the real I'm-Bobby to understand what she needed to do. What she needed to do would have to happen before all of the real I'm-Bobby came back. Before he was his true dangerous self.

Zach's mother already knew that. But she needed to be reminded.

The little farmer in the barn in the rolly-phone said so. And while the farmer could really make Zach mad sometimes, he almost always told the truth.

The truth was that I'm-Bobby was not all right.

∽

IN THE CAR, I'm-Bobby complained because Zach's mother hadn't been able to find her ID badge, which would have caused real problems for her at work. By the time she found it, she and Zach had missed the bus and needed to get a ride from I'm-Bobby, who really didn't like to go to Ambit.

He said it was because "that woman" always seemed to be there whenever he did, and she always insisted on talking to him. I'm-Bobby couldn't stand "that woman." The woman was Addy's mom.

"Well, I like that we can go to school and then to work together." Zach's mother watched I'm-Bobby with more warmth in her eyes than Zach had seen in some time. As awful as I'm-Bobby was to Zach's mother, she still managed to find that kind of feeling for him, even if it was for a very short time.

I'm-Bobby cursed and held the horn for a long time when some kids were slow to get on the school bus a few cars ahead of him.

Zach's mother's warmth turned to sadness, as if there were a new reality she saw coming. Or one that was already there—and maybe had been for a while.

When the red flashers on the school bus stopped and traffic got going again, I'm-Bobby hit the gas. He didn't show any sign that he'd let Zach's mother's small moment of tenderness in.

Zach knew where that tenderness came from for Zach's mother and, despite the other things he knew, he hoped she'd remember having it. She would want to know she'd said something nice to I'm-Bobby while she still had the chance.

Her waking self didn't know it yet, but things were going to move fast.

∽

Putting Zach to bed, Zach's mother leaned over to sing low so I'm-Bobby wouldn't hear her. I'm-Bobby didn't like her singing. And he especially didn't like it when Zach's mother did it while tucking Zach in since, he said, it made Zach soft. "And he's plenty soft already," I'm-Bobby always added. There was nothing soft about the way he said it.

Zach's mother had a stable of songs she cycled through—one a night. "There's a Hole in My Bucket" and "Oh! Susanna" were favorites. So were "Marianne" and "Cindy." Tonight, Zach's mother sang "Bye Bye Blackbird" because she didn't know how sad that song made Zach, and he didn't want her to know. It was a song about leaving. Zach had already done enough of that, and he suspected he might not be finished with traveling alone.

Still, he usually let Zach's mother make it to the end, so it surprised both of them when he found himself reaching out to gently lay his fingertips on Zach's mother's knee. Her bad knee. Right on the spot where the hole was. Where the needle went in.

Zach's mother stopped singing and looked down at Zach's hand. Then she laid her own hand on top of his, her touch light. She squeezed. "Your father loves you, Zach. He just doesn't know how to say it." She relaxed her grip again. "Or show it."

Was it the knee? Touching it made her think of I'm-Bobby and allowed her to lie. Zach decided it was the knee.

They sat like that without saying anything for a short time. Zach could hear her breathing, as if she were fighting to move something heavy. Then Zach's mother kissed him and told him she loved him.

Before she left and closed the bedroom door behind her, Zach's mother made sure to turn the light on in his closet and leave the door ajar. She assumed that he, like most other kids his age, was afraid of what might go on in there in the dark.

In that, she was right. Zach had faced his share of monsters on the other side of doors. He hoped to never have to face any again.

But as was the case with the traveling, such comfort was not his destiny.

38

WHORES AND BATTLE MEAT

Outside, after what would have counted as a few days' worth of lunch hours and a few happy hours' worth of pitchers, Jeremy helped Abel down the block. He'd planned to help him into a cab, but he couldn't do that to a cabbie. So the new plan was to take the cab with him and try to warn the driver if Abel was about to be sick. Jeremy didn't know if he'd be able to wrestle him out to the curb in time—or even get him to lean out the door—before things got messy. He prayed he wouldn't have to find out.

Their progress was slow because Abel kept stopping to stare at a guy pushing a mop bucket around one of the adult-video places. He mumbled something Jeremy couldn't understand.

"What?" Jeremy wasn't sure this was something he really wanted to hear.

"Tell him I'm sorry."

"Who?"

Abel nodded toward the mop-bucket guy, who waited while a man in a suit exited one the store's booths and then disappeared inside, mop at the ready. "The moth."

"The moth?"

Abel nodded again and stumbled against Jeremy, who struggled to hold him up. How much did a mug of beer weigh? How about a dozen?

A few passersby spared a glance for the lurching combo of Jeremy and Abel, which was quite generous for New Yorkers. Nobody offered to help, of course. Jeremy couldn't blame them, given that everything about the two of them suggested that whatever they'd been drinking would be on the sidewalk for all to inspect at any moment. He needed to get Abel into a cab before a cop noticed and decided an intervention was required.

"They don't take tickets!"

Wonderful. Now the Rubbish Gladiator was on the scene. Though to be fair, he was patrolling his own territory. Jeremy and Abel were the interlopers.

"They obey no schedule!"

As usual, no one paid the Rubbish Gladiator any mind. If the fast-walking commuters could have, they'd have happily walked through him and his trash can. But physical laws were in play, and they knew it. Plus, he had that spear.

Jeremy guided Abel in the direction of the nearest avenue, hoping they'd have a wider array of cabs from which to choose. As they made their way toward the Rubbish Gladiator, he deposited two squashed coffee cups into his can and leaned on his spear, watching them approach. Jeremy prepared himself to be harangued for public drunkenness and whatever other sins the man might decide they'd committed. He imagined that given the time, the Rubbish Gladiator was capable of a wide variety of grievances. And the man certainly looked to have a free schedule.

Abel perked up, as if sensing he was being judged, but his

eyes swept right past the Rubbish Gladiator. His knees quit on him again, and Jeremy nearly let him fall.

"Did he tell you?" The Rubbish Gladiator sized Jeremy up as Jeremy wrestled Abel into a forward zigzag motion again. "He told you, didn't he?"

"Tell me what?"

The Rubbish Gladiator nodded, answering his own question. Whatever he was thinking, he'd been right as far as he was concerned. "He told you," he said. "He did." Then he turned his attention back to the task at hand. "No tickets!" he yelled at a passing girl who was too engrossed in thumbing the screen of her phone to react. "No schedules!"

Jeremy moved on. He'd begun sweating heavily. Supporting dead weight was a lot of work, and he didn't even want to think about the long odds he faced convincing a cabbie to allow the clearly demolished Abel into his back seat, vomit fee or no vomit fee.

"No tickets! No schedules!" the Rubbish Gladiator continued as Jeremy battled gravity and inertia to get Abel to the corner. The man's voice began to fade as he rolled his can away. "You suckers! You patsies! You victims! You fools!" He'd returned to his standard mantra. "Whores and battle meat! Battle meat and whores!"

Jeremy was more sure now than he'd been last time. It wouldn't have mattered if Abel had been stone sober. He wouldn't have seen the Rubbish Gladiator or heard a thing he'd said. Just like all of the people passing by. Only Jeremy knew he was there.

"Hey!" Something about the distant cry made Jeremy stop and turn. With half a block between them, the Rubbish Gladiator once again zeroed in on Jeremy and Abel. "He told you!"

"Yes!" Several people spared another New York glance for

the drunken maniac who carried his incapacitated pal while screaming at ghosts. "He did!"

That pacified the Rubbish Gladiator. He turned away and continued rolling along, spearing something on the sidewalk with deadly accuracy and vigor. Then it was back to calling people patsies, victims, and fools.

Abel mumbled something else, and Jeremy hoped with all the hope in him that it didn't have anything to do with being sick. Otherwise, neither of them would make it home by midnight.

"What?"

"Tell him I apologize."

"Who?" Had Jeremy been wrong about the Rubbish Gladiator? Had Abel been aware of him?

"The bucket moth." Abel nearly fell yet again, and Jeremy caught him and stood him upright. Crazy as it seemed at the moment, there was a note of real grief in his voice. "Tell the bucket moth I'm sorry."

"He knows." Jeremy got Abel moving again, sure as he did so that the man with the mop knew no such thing. He set his sights on the corner, which was approaching far too slowly. He refused to think about whether Abel was really sorry or not. And he certainly didn't want to find out what Abel might be sorry for.

Abel laughed and shook his head, as if he knew Jeremy was lying just to comfort him. Then he muttered again.

"I'm sorry, Abel. I didn't get that, either. Let's just walk, okay?"

Abel stumbled forward the best he could, Jeremy doing most of the work. "I said what about the mom? And the kid? Do they know?"

"Absolutely. You bet they do."

"She doesn't." Abel was barely intelligible. "He might."

Jeremy didn't try to get Abel to explain who the mom and the kid were or what they were supposed to forgive Abel for. He was pouring sweat, and when they finally reached the corner, it was a struggle to hail a cab and support Abel at the same time. It was such a struggle, in fact, that he thought nothing more about what Abel might have done to some unnamed mom and her son.

39

THE SLEEPING THINGS OF THE WORLD

Everything was different. Yet everything was returning to its rightful state. Ray-Anne held these opposing thoughts in balance, accepting each as truth. She wasn't surprised by her ability to do so. She had a long history of finding equilibrium in ambiguity.

Like the shotgun. She scarcely felt its weight on her back, but it helped influence the handling of the bike all the same. She commanded the machine with more authority. The cycle hadn't ever been too heavy for her, but now it responded to her moves as if the mass—not the weight—of the gun in its holster were its own navigation device.

It felt right.

Right meant cornering faster than she should have been able to, the wheels and asphalt joined as if magnetized. And right meant achieving ridiculous speeds on surface streets knowing there was no one who would get in her way.

Because there wasn't anyone.

Traffic was nonexistent, as were pedestrians and parked cars. The occasional vehicle sat in a parking lane like those rusty, flat-tired bicycles left to rot at L stations, forlorn and abandoned. There weren't many of the orphaned vehicles, but all were booted. Some looked as if someone had been living in them.

It was the sleeping things of the world that caught Ray-Anne's eye, mostly because those, along with a combined feeling of somnolence, state-shifting, and a coming wakefulness, were dominant now. Words couldn't express it. She couldn't hope to know why this was happening.

But she could hope to find out. She suspected she would.

And she feared she wouldn't like the answer.

Paul.

Where was Paul?

Lake Shore Drive was empty, which was bizarre. Ray-Anne opened the bike up. The lake, in one of its startlingly blue-green phases, passed by in a ribbon under a gray sky blobbed with cloud cover.

As Ray-Anne approached North Avenue Beach, she glanced over at the ship-themed bar with the name she could never remember. She looked again. Then slowed.

Even from a distance, it was clear that the bar was no longer the fake cruise ship it had been. It was now some sort of antique submarine, painted in gray and done up as if it had smashed its way up through the soil and concrete next to the path, with large chunks of asphalt jutting into the air or laying up against the sub's side.

Adjacent to the sub, a splash of red and yellow on the Lakefront Trail was a bright contrast to the dull stone shades of the undersea vessel. Two medium-sized parachutes, attached to the back of a bike on a kickstand, floated at an angle to their host, as if the parked cycle were moving along at a decent clip. There was no wind. A few feet away from the bike stood its rider, facing away from Ray-Anne. What was it about physics-defying cyclists today?

Ray-Anne did the unthinkable for a ride on the Drive: she slowed to a dead stop and looked behind her. On any normal day, she'd have been rear-ended and crushed already. But there was nothing coming. Just in case, she pulled over and put her blinkers on.

The cyclist studied the sub. It wasn't the same rider Ray-Anne had chased earlier. This one had no hat or scarf, and a long mane of blue hair hung down her back.

The cyclist turned to see Ray-Anne watching, gave her a grin, and strode over to her bike. Then she hooked the kickstand up with one foot, threw her leg over the seat and got going in one fluid motion. As had been the case with the curly-haired cyclist down on Division, she came out of the blocks absurdly fast.

Ray-Anne did the same. With a quick glance over her shoulder to ensure nothing was about to splatter her, she revved the cycle and was up to speed in no time, working the gears via reflex.

It made no difference. On the empty bike path, the cyclist enjoyed even more freedom than her God's-eye-loving compadre had. As fast as Ray-Anne was, the bicycle was faster. She shouldn't have been, of course. But shouldn't didn't seem to matter much as the cycle and its trailing parachutes shrank in the distance, leaving Ray-Anne in the dust by the time she'd passed Belmont Harbor.

How could that be? Ray-Anne ran down the list again. Parachutes floating in windless conditions when the bike was standing still, a bike that could outrun a motorcycle. Especially, she noted with wounded pride, *her* motorcycle.

Sense and logic were on holiday. Ray-Anne suspected that changing rules would be the norm from here on out.

And some very big changes at that.

∽

Exiting at Lawrence, Ray-Anne considered how the pieces of the picture indicated a landscape-wide change in the things around her. The impossibly fast messengers. The missing people and cars. The disappearing pawn shop and the window with the shotgun calling to her like a siren.

Normal was on hiatus. And it didn't bother her a bit.

So far.

Ray-Anne pulled up in front of New Beginnings, which boasted an expanse of curb that was practically all parking space. Another first.

Heading in, she spotted George Wickham preening in his fortress of a cage. The parrot rocked backwards and forwards a few times before settling in to watch her.

The Tux itself was dark and empty. During normal business hours.

Muffled barking from above was especially loud in the heavy silence. Up in a New Beginnings second-floor window, a big gray poodle-looking dog stood up against the reinforced glass, paw pads flattened as he either greeted her or was attempting to scare her off. It was tough to tell with some dogs.

It was even tougher to know what this dog was doing in New Beginnings. As much as she and Paul loved animals, pets weren't allowed. They already had enough on their hands.

A thin arm wrapped itself around the dog's chest and pulled him away from the window with some urgency. Somebody didn't want anyone to know they were up there. Too late.

Under George Wickham's watchful eye, Ray-Anne walked to the building. The front door was unlocked. Not good.

Clearly, Paul hadn't come back here. He never would have allowed that.

Inside, it was almost too dark to see, and the lights wouldn't turn on. Ray-Anne didn't have long to worry about it, however, before the scrabbling of nails on the hard tile floor announced the arrival of the pooch from upstairs.

Ray-Anne pulled the shotgun over her shoulder, pumped a round into the chamber, and drew down on the ill-defined lump of the quickly approaching dog, trying to gauge its intent. She had a little extra time due to the pronounced limp that slowed the dog's progress. He favored his right-rear leg.

"Don't shoot! Don't shoot!" A tall, skinny young girl with a shaved head tumbled into the lobby, all limbs and joints. "He's friendly! Don't shoot him!"

The girl stopped and stared at the shotgun, which Ray-Anne pointed dead-square at the kid's heart as the dog skidded to a stop just a few feet away, panting and wagging its tail as if this all were just a game. "Ray-Anne?" The girl's question was a mix of surprise and residual fear, but the voice was familiar.

"Lexi?"

The girl nodded and knelt to wrap the dog in her slight arms. She'd been the one pulling him away from the window upstairs. "You're not gonna blow us away or anything. Right?" The dog barked—he was worked up, not angry. Lexi shushed him.

Ray-Anne was still aiming the gun at Lexi and had more pressure on the trigger than she should have. Where did that come from? She willed herself to drop it over her shoulder and into its holster. "When did you come back? Where is everybody?"

"Angus."

"What?"

Lexi scratched the dog's fluffy head, and he attempted to wriggle out of her grasp. "His name's Angus. That's what his tag says. He knocked me over when I got here."

"Where is everyone?" Ray-Anne recalled that Lexi was thought to have some sort of attention-deficit thing but hadn't stuck around long enough for an evaluation.

Lexi shrugged. "It was just Angus when I got here. At first, he wouldn't let me near him. Then he wouldn't stay still long enough for me to read his name. I think somebody hurt him." With the shotgun out of sight, she let Angus go.

He approached Ray-Anne with caution, rear leg suspended in the air, and sniffed at her feet.

Ray-Anne extended a fist and let him smell it. "You haven't seen Paul? Or anyone else?"

Lexi came closer, most likely to save the dog should Ray-Anne get trigger-happy again. She shook her head. "But when I do, I'll tell him I'm sorry for skipping out on you guys."

That was one quirk Ray-Anne recalled now. Lexi sent messages indirectly by explaining what she'd say to someone else. That was her way of apologizing to Ray-Anne for disappearing. "Where'd you go? Are you all right?"

The girl shrugged again, which was understandable. Not many at New Beginnings could say whether they were okay or not. "I went back to Joliet, but nobody was there. It creeped me. I mean really creeped me. No buses showed up, and there wasn't anybody to hitch with. So I had to walk." She pulled off a sneaker and sock, wincing, and showed Ray-Anne the ball of her foot, which was more broken blisters than skin.

"We'll go to the nurse's office and get that cleaned up."

Lexi pursed her lips and nodded, blinking back tears. Her trip had been no small thing. "I had to sleep in the forest preserve." She left it at that.

Angus the dog bumped his head against Ray-Anne's fist.

She scratched behind his ears, and the last of his defensiveness dropped. The poor thing. Being standoffish didn't appear to come easy to him.

"When I got here, this one guy tried to talk to me outside. He was going to follow me in when I opened the door, but Angus ran out and bit him." She laid her hand on her thigh, near her groin. "I mean really bit him. The guy didn't even yell, but he left. Then he was out there again, looking at the parrot. When Angus started barking, he limped away."

Ray-Anne scratched more enthusiastically. "Good boy."

The dog leaned into her. He had more heft than she would have thought.

"Oh." Lexi pulled something out of her pocket and clicked it. The penlight cut away some of the dark with its harsh beam. "I found this in the bus station. Man, did it save me."

Angus turned toward the whiteness of the pen's illumination but made sure not to pull away from Ray-Anne's fingers.

Ray-Anne took the offered penlight from Lexi, gave Angus one last pat and walked over to the admissions counter, sweeping the light across it. "No note from anyone?"

"No."

Over on the far side of the countertop, the glint of the penlight on cellophane revealed an old friend Ray-Anne hadn't seen since her arrival at New Beginnings in New York. Standing on its end in the middle of the counter, sentry-like, was an unopened box of Sisu.

Ray-Anne had looked for Sisu off and on since arriving in Chicago—though not that hard. The truth was, she viewed the candy the way she viewed exercise: it was something she did to maintain discipline, but she couldn't say she enjoyed it. Still, in a world gone off-kilter and strange, she was happy to have something she could count on. She peeled the wrapping off, opened the box, and offered one of the flat disks to Lexi.

The girl sniffed it and, while dubious, popped it into her mouth. A second later, she carefully removed it again with thumb and forefinger, like it might go off. She dropped it on the floor for Angus, who, like any dog, wanted a taste of whatever humans were putting into their mouths.

The candy didn't last much longer in his than it had in Lexi's.

Ray-Anne took one for herself while Lexi offered a sheepish, apologetic look. The familiar, challenging licorice flavor filled her mouth, and Ray-Anne began to feel a bit lightheaded.

At first, she thought she'd gone too long without eating, but it wasn't so much a sensation of weakness as it was a fundamental shift in perspective, as if someone had reached inside her head and turned her mind 180 degrees. She reached out to steady herself on the counter.

The vertigo wasn't just physical—it was worse. It was as if the connection between her head and the world around her had rebooted and loaded an updated operating system.

Luckily, Lexi was busying herself with the dog, slapping her thighs and shuffling sideways to get him going. And get going he did, nails sliding on the tile as he panted happily.

The spell lifted as quickly as it had taken hold. The world returned to her with, in some profound way, more focus than it had previously had.

"Rain, is that your bike out there?"

"Yeah." Ray-Anne wasn't quite ready to let go of the counter, but her situation continued to improve as various neural pathways came back online. "Wait. What did you call me?"

"Sweet." Lexi pushed through the front door and went outside, Angus on her heels. The girl and the dog limped with the same rhythm, as if they'd coordinated their routine. "No more walking for us," Lexi said before the door closed and cut off whatever she might have told the dog next.

It took another minute or two for Ray-Anne to recover fully. Only then did she realize it hadn't occurred to her to spit the Sisu out even though the strange wave of unreality had kicked off when she'd put it in her mouth. And it was probably just as weird that she happily pocketed the box so that she could finish it. It may have been dosed with something—okay, she didn't really think that—but it was an old friend. She headed for the door, stepping more cautiously than she had before.

Outside, Lexi stood by the motorcycle.

Angus sat at attention a short distance shy of it, his tail dusting the sidewalk. It looked as if part of him wanted to go to Lexi, but someone or something more authoritative than the girl wanted him to stay put. He wouldn't budge, no matter how Lexi slapped her thighs.

Finally, she gave up. "When did you get this, Rain? It is audaciously peak."

Ray-Anne stopped next to Angus, the question of Lexi's new name for her dropping down the list of her momentary priorities. She hadn't gotten the cycle that Lexi was admiring, though it was a truly unique and beautiful machine.

The motorcycle Rain parked in the spot had been replaced.

Lexi's demeanor grew more sober. "Rain?"

Rain looked at the girl. Because Rain was her name. Ray-Anne was just what was hung around her neck at birth.

"When did you start packing?"

Rain drew her shotgun in one fluid move and cradled it. It was like breathing. "That's not really the question." She gave the gun a visual once-over before dropping it back over her shoulder and into its holster again. "Why did I ever stop?"

From his perch in front of the Tux, George Wickham the parrot let out a series of squawks and chirp-like noises. Ray-Anne had never heard the bird make any noise whatsoever.

It took a moment for it to register.

The parrot was chuckling.

40

THE SAME STAIRWAY AND THE SAME PALM TREES

When Zach woke up in the middle of the night, the closet door was closed. No light spilled out between the bottom of the door and the carpet. The light was off.

Zach's mother would not have done that. I'm-Bobby might have, but Zach would have heard him if he'd come in, and he never did anyway.

Zach shifted onto his side to watch the door, trying his hardest not to make any noise. Maybe if whoever or whatever was in the closet thought he was still asleep, it would leave him alone.

There was something in there. The closet floorboards creaked and popped with its weight as it brushed against the other side of the door.

Something big. Heavy.

In the quiet of the dark bedroom, Zach could hear breathing. Fast out followed by a stuttering pattern of fast ins. Then fast in followed by a series of fast outs. Again.

Crying. Something was crying.

Scared. Or in pain.

That was different. That was not scary. Something needed help.

Zach swung his legs over the side of the bed and lowered his bare feet onto the carpet. Then he shifted his weight onto them as slowly as he could, making sure that the floorboards underneath wouldn't creak the way they had in the closet, giving him away. He'd done this before, and he knew the spot. He managed utter silence.

He'd practiced moving around the room silently in case he ever needed to move without I'm-Bobby hearing him, and now Zach was glad he had. He made it to the closet without a sound.

At the door, Zach was sure of what he heard. Crying. Something frightened.

It threatened to be a shared emotion, so Zach didn't give himself time to think about how afraid he should be. When there wasn't room to be scared, bravery was all that was left.

Zach reached out, grabbed the knob of the closet door and turned it quick and hard so it wouldn't squeak or click. Once that was done, he pulled the door open—slowly enough that whatever was inside couldn't knock it open and use it against him but not so fast that he would scare it even more.

The crying and breathing stopped. There was nothing there. The closet was empty. And maybe there had never been anything in there to begin with.

Zach reached for the overhead pull-string.

"No," said a small voice from the back of the closet. "Please. No light."

Zach dropped the string and took a step backward. He stared into the inky dark of the closet, trying to see who was speaking to him. Now he was really thrown. It still felt as if whatever had been in the space had left. Zach had no sense that what he'd heard and sensed when the door was closed was still there.

Yet a voice had spoken to him—the voice of something tiny and weak, something barely there. On the other hand, whatever had been there just moments before had been anything but small. He waited for whatever it was to decide what to do next.

"You know, don't you?" The voice remained frail.

Zach nodded.

"I'm not fooling you, am I?"

Zach shook his head.

There was a moment of silence as the thing came to a decision. "May I stay?" Now the voice was much deeper—the sound of something huge and powerful, though it worked to keep the volume down.

Zach suspected that for the voice to hide its power—masking its true might—was no easy task. Oddly, he wasn't frightened at all. Maybe he should have been, but he had a lot of experience with voices coming from strange things and places. And he trusted that experience when it told him that the voice in the closet didn't mean him or Zach's mother any harm.

He didn't care about what it might want to do to I'm-Bobby.

So he nodded again. Yes. The voice could stay.

Some of the fear was gone from the voice the next time it spoke. "Thank you." It let out a long breath, as if it had been holding it all this time.

Zach went back to his bed and sat down, watching the empty space of the closet. Now came the steady, deep breathing of the very big thing as it shifted, the weight of its presence returning. The floorboards creaked again, and the hangers with Zach's pants and shirts on them jingled as the very big thing brushed against them.

Zach couldn't help but think of dogs he'd seen making circles in their beds before lying down. So he lay down, too.

Soon the breathing in the closet began to slow. Whatever it was, the very big thing was tired.

Zach's own breathing slowed to match the breathing of the very big thing. Just before he fell asleep, he thought he heard the voice in the closet thank him again.

He also heard the very big thing tell him its name. Aidan.

When Zach woke up later, it was still dark. The closet door was closed again, and the light was out.

∽

IN THE DARK, Annie listened to the noises of the night. Bobby's breathing was wet and jagged. He shifted as he slept, occasionally kicking her, his manner at rest a simulacrum of his waking mind.

The large tabletop fan he'd picked up to replace the white noise of the destroyed Dynamite 8 provided a humming backdrop. As they had done with previous fans, they experimented with positioning so that it didn't blow things off the dresser or skip air off the walls and ceiling into their faces, keeping them up.

They'd only sort of gotten it, which was the case every time they'd tried previously, but they decided to live with it.

Well, Bobby decided.

When Zach first spotted the pieces of the Dynamite 8 in the trash can, he frowned. Then Bobby brought the fan home, and Zach hadn't done anything more to mourn the eight-track player's passing.

There in the dark, Annie understood why Zach saw the

fan as a suitable substitute, as much as he'd loved the Dynamite 8. The fan didn't really sound like a fan. Not to her.

Unaccountably, it produced the same hiss the tape player had—a hiss that, when she allowed herself to listen, sounded like it carried soft voices whispering through the air. It was crazy, but that's what she heard—the same voices she could have sworn came from the tape player.

When she slept, Annie dreamt of the same stairway and the same palm trees.

PART II

INTERSECTION

41

DROOG COSPLAY

"Charlene?"

Someone was talking to her. Deep in the mists of slumber, Charlene reviewed the possibilities. Annie? Could be. Her old Army buddy. They'd called each other that even when they'd still worn the uniform, in anticipation of enjoying veteran status together.

That wouldn't happen for them.

"Charlene, are you able to hear me?"

They'd taken the wrong road at the wrong time. A boom road. That's how Charlene had thought of it once she'd been able to think again.

It hadn't happened when they'd reunited in the office, either. In the Brill days. Because there were much bigger things to worry about then.

Now there was a distance between them yet again. Charlene and her friend were in different worlds.

The voice wasn't Annie's.

She tried to open her eyes but couldn't. Something was wrapped around them, taped into place. It felt like she was in a bed, and someone had taken her clothing off. Which made it comforting that the voice was female. She hurt in assorted places—neck, arm, leg, back—and when she moved a little, she could tell that those spots, too, had been bandaged. "Beatrice?"

"Welcome back, dear. How are you feeling?"

"In pain."

"Where?" Beatrice sighed. "That's a foolish question, I know."

"My eyes are the worst."

"That's what I was just working on. A moment, please."

Hands across her face, over her eyes, fingertips a whisper on her forehead. Then the flow of something. Something good.

The pain in Charlene's eyes faded, then vanished. "Wow."

"Thank you." Beatrice was flattered—and too modest about all the good she did.

"Thank *you*." Charlene remembered the hallway now—the burning goo, the doorway, the voice warning her before she went out. "How bad is it?"

"Not as bad as it was. I've been working while you've been out. Let's call it the equivalent of a month overall. Even longer for your eyes, which is what I've been concentrating on."

Beatrice was the nurse and healer at Envoy HQ. A mythical—and such a mythical at that. She'd been some sort of religious character in a role-playing game, able to lay hands to heal wounds and fight disease. Now a pleasant-looking granny lady in a nurse's uniform, she was one of the most indispensable people fighting the good fight. She always expressed progress in units of time. A month out meant that she'd healed Charlene to where she'd be after convalescing for that amount of time—even if only a few hours had passed in real time.

"What happened?"

"You were attacked by some sort of acid blob, from what we've been able to surmise. It looks like there are Ravagers outside and some mythicals working with them inside. You were burned. Then Harris was able to zap the blob enough to make it fall back. But he didn't know it had a hold of you." She sighed. "It's highly conductive, apparently."

Harris. One of the Envoys-in-training. He looked like your average high schooler, maybe a college freshman. But he was quite literally a dynamo, able to generate lightning-level electricity. He was getting better at controlling it but had a ways to go. Charlene was lucky she hadn't been killed. "What burned me?"

"Mainly the giant Jell-O mold." Beatrice leaned close to Charlene's ear. "The kid got you some, too, and his jolt sent some of the acid jelly into your eyes, but I haven't told him that," she said in a low voice. "He's on the other side of the curtain and can hear us. He's been torturing himself over this."

Charlene nodded her understanding and felt Beatrice pat her on the hand.

"Okay, then. I'm going to try to take the dressing off your eyes. They'll still be sensitive. May I?"

"Why not?" Charlene could come up with several important reasons, but she needed to get back into the fray.

The fingers on her face again. Beatrice had an incredible touch. Gently and slowly, the healer pulled the tape and bandages away from Charlene's eyes. "Don't rush it," she said. "Try to open them when you're ready."

"What's the gunk?"

"That's a conductor for my healing. I charge it with my ability, and it dispenses it and keeps you recovering while I'm not here. It's best to go slow with eyes. Hang on." She gently wiped some of the jelly away.

Charlene tried parting her lids a bit, squinting against even the dim light that greeted her. Sensitivity, but no pain. She blinked with care, and the picture of Beatrice leaning over her became clearer.

"Okay, close again."

Charlene closed, and Beatrice wiped some more of the jelly away.

"Open, please."

This time, it was easier. The picture of Beatrice came into focus immediately, though Charlene still had to fight against the light.

"They'll be touchy for a bit. I had to push a little harder than I normally would, so they're over-tuned, in a sense. That'll go away."

Charlene was tucked into a cot in one of the infirmary's bed bays, a curtain maintaining her privacy. As she'd suspected, she was in her bra and underwear, and her arm and leg were wrapped in dressings. Another one was taped across her stomach, and it felt like there was a big one on her back.

"We scared up some replacement clothes for you." Beatrice indicated a matching set of white pants, socks, and a shirt folded on a nearby chair. "Yours were a lost cause."

"I'll look like I'm doing droog cosplay."

"Cook's whites were all we could find."

"I'm sorry—they'll do fine." Now the other woman was perfectly in focus. "Thank you, Beatrice. Really. You're a treasure."

Beatrice looked away. Her place was where The Commons needed her to be and nothing more, she told anyone who tried to praise her. "Get dressed when you're ready," she said, standing and pulling the curtain aside just enough to get through. "You've got people out here who are worried about you." She stepped out and closed the curtain.

Charlene sat up. Given the size of her dressings, she should have been in a lot more pain than she was. And she wasn't nearly as groggy as she probably would have been without Beatrice's help, considering the wallop she'd undoubtedly absorbed. Harris was capable of serious voltage.

Standing took time, and getting dressed was a challenge all its own. But Charlene managed to get the whites and socks on in a reasonable amount of time, and she was relieved to see that while her boots bore the scars of her encounter with the acid blob, they were still intact enough to wear. She donned them and stood, checking herself out. She'd been right about the droog outfit. All she needed was a bowler.

Beyond the curtain, Beatrice and three others awaited her in varying states of worry. Harris, the skinny young generator, looked as if he expected a suspension at minimum. He could hardly face her.

Next to him was the silver-haired and silver-bearded Reinhard, a former Vigil who was himself an Envoy trainee after switching services because he felt he was too old to fight at the level needed to be an effective policeman and soldier. Which said something either about Reinhard's standards or the standards of his old outfit, because the man remained quite formidable. Due to his experience, he was informally considered to be a level above the other trainees, and Charlene had no doubt that part of Harris's sheepish attitude came from having been told precisely what he'd done wrong by Reinhard and how much and how long it would take to make up for it. Harris was one of the more powerful trainees, so Reinhard rode him extra hard.

Completing the trio was Koko, another trainee who'd successfully completed her Journey in the post-Brill time and was given the choice of continuing to her destination or staying on as an Envoy. She'd decided to remain. Koko wasn't much of a talker, but she had a remarkable ability to affect the speed of things, slowing even the fastest-moving object to a near-standstill when given the chance to concentrate. She was sharp, patient, and even-keeled. Of all of the trainees, Charlene and Porter agreed, Koko was among the best. Given the chance, she'd be one for the books.

"How is being upright?" Beatrice asked Charlene. "I think I got to you soon enough to avoid the aftereffects common to electrical trauma."

Harris winced.

Reinhard put a hand on the boy's shoulder.

"I'm all right." Charlene goosed her tone to sound more chipper than she felt. She gave poor Harris what she hoped was a reassuring smile. "And I'm a lot better than I would have been if it weren't for you, Harris. I understand thanks is in order."

With that, Harris appeared to let himself breathe again. He glanced at Reinhard, who gave him a quick nod. Charlene knew the Reinhard type. He'd read you the riot act. Then he'd build you back up and move on, expecting you to do likewise —but with a lesson under your belt.

Charlene walked to the boy and extended her left hand. The right one, while not bandaged, felt as if it'd been microwaved.

Still nervous, Harris raised his right hand, dropped it, and gently shook Charlene's hand with his left. "Koko did as much as I did," he said. "I mean, in a good way, not the hurting part. She slowed the blob down so that it couldn't take out the door and get to you." He held onto her hand. "I'm sorry, ma'am. It didn't occur to me that you were in contact with it when I cut loose. I thought I gave enough warning. I didn't even know it was you." He glanced at Reinhard again.

"You did well, Harris," Charlene said. "And it's Charlene or Char, please. For all of you. We've got too much to do to bother with formality. And I thank all of you for your contributions. We'll be needing more of those."

"Yes," said June Medill from the doorway. "And sooner than you think."

42

AS WELL WE ALL SHOULD BE

At the railroad tracks, Effie kept Po company while he waited for the next gandy dancer. Partly, he suspected, it was because she was fond of him. That was just fine. He had a good feeling about her, and she was a positive influence on her father, who needed one.

When she began asking questions, Po understood at least part of the reason she'd elected to sit with him. She wanted to know about The Pines, and her father wasn't about to tell her.

At first, it was just a game of willpower. Po took Joel out and placed the Tamagotchi on the bench beside him. Effie would ask, Po would shake his head, and Joel would needlessly interpret Po's refusal.

"Why not?"

"He does not wish to," said Joel.

"That's not a reason."

"He does not wish to."

It was surprising how long such a thing could go on.

"I'm not a little girl," Effie pointed out. "And we both know that with me on your side, my father is a lot more cooperative."

"He does not wish to."

"A *lot* more cooperative."

It was surprising how long such a thing could go on.

Finally, Po relented. Effie was right on several counts, and there was no harm in telling her the facts of the universe—or those that were generally accepted to be true. He signed.

"You got paper? Something to write with?" Joel said.

The demon produced a felt-tip pen and a beat-up spiral mini-notebook from her purse. "You're lucky I have either. I'm a digital girl."

Po flipped through the notebook until he found an open page. He drew a circle and wrote the word "Ingress" inside it. Around that, he drew another circle and shaded the area around his initial circle, like a moat. He labeled the resulting dark ring "The Pines." Directly below, he drew a larger circle bumping up against The Pines and labeled it "The Living World." Then he drew a similar circle to the right, touching both The Living World and The Pines, and tagged it as "The Commons." He began to sign.

"See if you can keep up, sweetie," Joel said.

Po stopped and frowned at the Tamagotchi.

Effie smiled, acknowledging Joel's unbidden embellishments to what Po was trying to tell her.

Po continued signing again.

"Everybody in the know—anyone who matters, anyway—agrees that Ingress is the source of everything. Different faiths"—it came out as "fates" when Joel said it—"have different names for the concept, and they don't all agree that it's the starting point for everything. Sometimes it's seen as a place where, say, Adam and Eve or Ask and Embla or other first people hung out. But for the sake of this discussion, we'll agree that this is where everything started, okay?"

"All right," said Effie. She was torn between interest in the topic and trying not to laugh at Joel's shtick, which was what Porter called it when the Tamagotchi spoke at length.

"Now, Ingress being the source of everything means just that—everything," Joel said as Po kept signing. "It creates the virtuous and the wicked, and it's a place of power. I mean, power like you wouldn't believe. Power for good, power for bad—and I do mean bad—which is where The Pines comes in."

Po traced a path with his finger from Ingress, through the surrounding ring of The Pines, and into The Living World.

"Think of The Pines as a filter between Ingress and other worlds. You ever seen an air filter on a car that's been driven rough?" When Effie shook her head at his attempt to be helpful, Joel was silent for a moment. "Never mind, then."

The young demon gave him a sympathetic stroke with the tip of her tail.

Po regarded Joel and looked at Effie long enough to reinforce that much of what was being said was shaded by Joel's word choices. He drew multiple circles the same size as those he'd drawn for The Living World and The Commons until they formed a ring around The Pines and Ingress, like a daisy with round petals. He didn't label any of these.

"Theory"—"teary," as Joel pronounced it—"holds that there are infinite worlds beyond the ones we're aware of."

Po drew more blank circles bordering the rounded petals to indicate that the pattern went on and on.

"Such is the universe, all of it starting with Ingress."

Po traced a path from Ingress to The Living World again.

"There are forces dark and powerful filtered out by The Pines before they can make it into The Living World," Joel said. "They've been there a long time—since the beginning of Creation, some of them. They are pissed, and they're always looking for a way out."

Po tapped The Pines with his finger.

"They can't get out because The Pines are impregnable." Joel paused. "Seriously? Impregnable? You can't just say there's no way through them except for mortals?"

Po continued, ignoring Joel's scolding.

"Whatever's in The Pines is stuck but good, and I cannot tell you how grateful you should be for that. What's there—and there's a lot of it—is very, very old; very, very big; and very, very, *very* bad."

"What about these walls?" Effie pointed to where The Living World bumped up against The Commons and where The Commons touched The Pines.

"What gets through is only what's supposed to get through," Joel said for Po. "Mainly, it's traffic from The L.W. to The Commons and then some from The Commons back into The L.W. But all other movement out of The Commons is to parts unknown."

Po tapped all of the blank circles for emphasis.

"When the system's working, that traffic comes from completed Journeys."

"So it's important that the barriers hold up?"

"Oh, sweetie," said Joel. "It's the whole game. You know the line about good fences and good neighbors?"

"No."

"You do now."

Effie considered Po's drawing. "And Dad is so frightened because whatever he was tracking is in this Pines realm."

Po nodded.

"As well he should be," said Joel. "As should we all."

∽

Later, after it became clear that the gandy dancer would be some time in coming, Effie had to return to the office or risk her father's ire—both for being away from work and for spending too much time with Po. While J.P. may not have seen Po as an enemy, specifically, he was not regarded as any kind of friend to the demons' enterprise, either.

After dark, it became noticeably cooler. Po welcomed the opportunity to sit and consider what J.P.'s story might mean. It simply wasn't possible to make contact with The Pines. He'd never heard of anyone doing such a thing. To accept even the possibility would be to bring the most foundational protections and structures of the universe into question. What dwelled in The Pines—one couldn't say *lived* and have it apply to everything there—was not meant to be inflicted upon any outside realm. That was widely known.

Unfortunately for Po, Joel wasn't able to raise Porter or anyone else. He, too, might as well have had an impermeable barrier around him. He settled into a meditative state, shutting out all external influence and bearing witness to the stillness of his own mind. Po was not always able to wrestle down his lack of patience. That, like his quickness to anger, made for a never-ending struggle.

The night stars and Po were one when he achieved this state, his consciousness reaching out to the pinpoints of light. Something out there was off, but he couldn't get a fix on what it might be. He fell into what peace he could find and observed.

Later in the night, when all was black, and dawn hadn't yet made its way around to the sky above, Po was pulled from this state.

He was being watched.

It was now an increasingly familiar presence—the one Po

had felt before finding Effie in the tree. The one from the tunnels.

For a moment, Po tried to pretend he was not aware of it, but whatever or whoever it was knew he sensed it.

"Incoming mail, boss," said Joel from the bench beside him.

With that, the presence watching Po withdrew—and did so without delay. Within an instant of Joel speaking up, the feeling of being observed ceased.

"It doesn't sound good," Joel said. "It's about Porter."

43

FROM THE FROZEN TO THE DAMNED

Hot.
Cold.
Wet.
Hurt.

Porter had no sense of sight or hearing.

No.

Waking up brought his brain back online.

He brought his hand to his face until his palm touched his nose, then wriggled his fingers. He saw nothing, but there was, at least, the illusion of movement. He still had the ability to see.

It was just ridiculously dark.

He put his hand to the ground. It slapped what felt like damp, sandy soil with a covering of wet leaves and twigs.

At least there was no Parix attacking him.

Which didn't mean the leech wasn't somewhere nearby, watching Porter's slow revival, waiting to jump him again. Porter had gone all-out with his abilities, fueled by those of Paul and something else—something unnamed but most definitely there. It was entirely possible he'd brought Parix along with him.

Porter continued to recover from the shock of the jump—the biggest and most reckless of any he'd ever attempted. His mind cataloged the information available to it. He was on his back in the dark. On wet soil. And wherever he was, it smelled like forest—damp wood, rotting leaves. Yet there were no sounds of life. No insects, no furtive movements in the underbrush. This place was dead or slumbering.

He was on his back, and he was not dry. Either it had rained recently, or where he'd landed was always damp. It felt like the latter.

He was also periodically struck by waves of stinging pain traveling over his skin like visitations of some energy current. It enjoyed a brief tour of him before returning to the wet floor of the forest, gleefully tormenting him all the while.

No, not a current.

Fire.

It was a burning or, at least, the echo of a burn, as if he'd pulled his hand away from a flame in time to avoid anything worse than minor damage. His other arm was under him, twisted and without feeling. He freed it and used his better arm to hold it straight up over him. Within a few moments, the burning sensations that had romped over the rest of him announced themselves on the formerly numb limb, too.

When he was able, Porter flexed the fingers of that arm, then bent it and straightened it a few times until it felt reasonably okay again. He felt in his coat pocket for the Newton.

Thank heaven for tiny triumphs. It was there, and its screen felt intact. If it had cracked, it might or might not have healed itself.

He powered the device on, and it brought him to the traditional Newton screen, which was rare. Normally, it only looked and behaved like a real Newton according to its own whims and those of The Commons. This was worrisome. It often indicated a weakened connection to the part of The Commons Essence with which Porter and the other Envoys interacted. There were worse possibilities, too, but he chose not to dwell on those.

Porter turned up the screen's backlight. The wan green glow of it was barely able to make a dent in the blackness of the forest. He could see the skin of the hand holding the device, his sleeve, and little more.

Rolling onto his side, he checked the ground. He was lying amid a carpet of dead leaves, and that was all he could tell. The glow didn't even manage to make it a foot into the black shroud. It was as if the darkness were an entity of its own, working to smother any light Porter might introduce—as if it didn't want him to understand where he might be.

Porter raised himself up to the point of leaning on his arm. Within the weak glow of the Newton, it was all leaves and rot. No Parix to be found. Of course, if the mythical were around, Porter had just announced his presence to him and any entity hostile or otherwise with his glowing screen. But it couldn't be helped.

Ignoring the continuing visitations of the burning pain, which, thankfully, were becoming fewer and farther between, Porter got to his feet. The darkness clung to him. He held the Newton aloft, as if another foot of altitude might throw the light farther.

It didn't. But far, far into the darkness, a pinpoint of light appeared like a response. Something, seeing the Newton, had roused itself.

Porter promptly turned the backlight off.

The faraway light didn't follow suit. If anything, it

appeared to grow larger after a time. Just a tad brighter. It was coming for him. Slowly, maybe—but coming.

Porter turned the light on again, held the Newton close, and scratched a quick message across it: "Hey, Rube!" A distress call.

He assumed the note wouldn't be sent or received for some time—if at all—but if the opportunity arose, it might let his colleagues know of his predicament while he was otherwise trying to stay upright and alive. He turned the backlight off again.

A shift in the damp air brushed his face—no benign wind, that, but rather the passing of something so massive that it might have been moving miles away. It brought with it a suspicion Porter preferred not to entertain.

Yes, his current location was a mystery, and it might not be the best place to have ended up. But it couldn't be *that*.

He commenced waiting for the light and whoever or whatever was holding it to arrive, mentally gearing up for the conversation or confrontation to come. It needed to be the former, as Porter had nothing left for even a small jump, never mind a fight. If he was to survive here against any other neutral-to-hostile entity, it would be by talking him, her, or it into refraining from any attacks.

As he dropped the Newton into his pocket, what at first sounded like the mere rub of plastic on fabric became just the hint of a voice mentioning something that sounded like "God." He pulled it out again. There were no other sounds from it. And he couldn't afford any unexpected utterances when dealing with whatever was headed his way, so he powered the Newton down and pocketed it. When it was in full Commons mode, there wasn't any real true way to turn it off, but in another troubling sign that he'd well and truly jumped farther than he'd meant to, the device went dead and cold, as requested.

Porter briefly considered leaving the path, which, assuming the light headed for him was traveling that same line, probably meant moving at a ninety-degree angle from the growing dot. But just as it was often a mistake not to stay put and wait for rescue when lost, wandering in the dark could easily mean stumbling into something far more dangerous than whatever was on its way to him. Or he could simply step off a cliff.

The coming light managed to make its way toward Porter both too slowly and too quickly. The sense that he'd brought himself to an ill-advised destination continued to grow, if only because the darkness seemed to sponge up his fears and feed them back to him. The chill and the feeling of being both hemmed in by thick trees unseen and exposed in the open had its way with him.

Cold.

Wet.

And, as much as he tried to resist it, afraid.

The light had been the size of a pinprick, a cigarette burn, and then a bullet wound. Now it grew to the size of a fist.

With it came dread.

Trepidation.

The hairs on the back of Porter's neck laddered up to attention.

Porter had reviewed whatever Commons-recorded files were available on the operative players in the takedown of Mr. Brill in order to glean all he could of its timeline and how it happened. The Commons being The Commons, those files took the form of everything from zines and videos to bubblegum comics and primitively taped poetry-slam and blues accounts.

They shifted form.

They disappeared.

Sometimes they reappeared, and sometimes they were gone forever.

But what stuck with him was something he never wanted to see repeated—the suffering of a Journeyman or other traveler stuck without the help of an Envoy.

Annie Brucker and her son, Zach. The former had what amounted to the suggestion of a guide when helped along wherever possible by Charlene and even June Medill. The latter, a small child with talents and challenges of his own, was actively tricked and misled in a ruse that was necessary but cruelly dishonest.

There was Annie, pursued by flames and an unseen something in the dark reek of a decaying basement. There was Zach, handed down a moldering stairway by the young victims of the same faceless threat in hard pursuit of him. Both made it through, facing down their terrors and outstripping them because they hadn't any other choice.

The files were documented heroism. Porter felt that deeply when taking them in.

But this was something altogether different. He'd Envoyed Journeys uncounted, as he'd told Paul Reid. Crossed terrain ranging from the frozen to the damned. Yet while he'd been at risk in some of those times, his stakes were never anything compared to those he'd guided.

Whatever occurred, he returned to the job.

The Journeymen, however, were to be sentenced one way or another—and their travels and doings decided that fate starting with the very first moments, even when it wasn't quite fair because they knew nothing at the beginning. And they had no choice but to trust their new friend Jonas Porter, who for all they knew was no friend at all.

This was the first time Porter himself could say he knew how they felt. He'd jumped to parts unknown, and something was headed straight for him. It made for what the more corporate-minded of the Envoy ranks would refer to as a great opportunity to get some learning.

But first he'd have to survive it.

With the coming light, more of his surroundings were revealed to him. By the time it reached the size of a landmine, say, or a small artillery shell, it managed to show Porter the trees on either side of where he stood without revealing anything about what was moving toward him. For all he knew, it was a toddler with a lantern on a bike. Or an elephant-sized angler fish, adapted to land and ready to chomp him in two.

Now Porter could see he was standing on a narrow path through a thick forest that presented a near-wall on either side and a solid canopy overhead. It wasn't so much that someone had made the trail as it was that the trees parted in order to clear the way for him to walk to his fate—or to deliver it to him via the light, which grew ever nearer.

Making matters even more confusing was the fact that the path was more of a curved trench with him in the bowl of it. To either side rose walls of roots, detritus and mud, as if he were standing in the ancient travel route of a great serpent.

It looked like what he could see around and above were old-growth trunks and branches. However, it refused to remain a clear image for long. Maybe it was the shadows, but none of it would stay still.

What at first certainly appeared to be ancient woods took on a different character when viewed from the edge of Porter's vision. No longer were they plants, but a mass of tangled, writhing worms.

Then viscera, recoiling and twisting as if their host were under assault.

Bones, like tightly packed ribs, in catacombs filled with plague dead from long ago.

The claustrophobic alleyways of packed-in ghettos only recently emptied of terrorized inhabitants, the trucked-away victims' tears and sickness still palpable in the black damp.

The devastated moonscape of a bombed-out Dresden—or someplace much like it.

People had died here.

Life had been extinguished.

And worse.

Because, as Porter knew well, there was always much, much worse.

Whatever held the approaching light shifted states, too. Like the brush of the massive presence felt earlier, it now seemed that something undefinably huge, a thing without limits, bore the lamp before it. As it drew near, Porter thought it might simply continue through him, wiping his existence and that of the surrounding area away without a thought for what it had done.

Porter had dealt with very bad players in his time, as had his colleagues. He'd long before mastered the skills and mental discipline required to hold instinctive panic at bay in order to do his job.

He wasn't sure he'd be able to do that now.

What drew near was threat and hostility due to its very existence, not its attitude.

It was enmity without end.

Old.

And it took notice of Porter in the same way Porter might note an inchworm hanging from a thread—with a reflexive visual observation at most and a violent dispatch if the tiny thing got in the way.

The light drew near enough for Porter to see that it came

from what appeared to be an ordinary lantern. But he couldn't shake the feeling that it hadn't had any specific form only moments before.

Likewise, as the person holding it began to take shape in the gloom of Porter's perception, it appeared to be trying on various options in order to give the impression it wished. Whatever was about to step forward so that Porter could see it, it was much, much larger than him. Even if were to appear before him as the smallest of children, Porter would be dwarfed by its presence.

The floating lantern drew within a half-dozen yards or so and stopped. It took another few moments before Porter could make out any details of the slight young man holding it. And before those details solidified, Porter had the final impression of something much larger and bestial—and of a memory very painful to him.

"Hello," said the slight young man, who wore a business-casual combination of collared button-down shirt, khakis, and a phone earpiece that blinked blue. On his feet were penny loafers entirely unsuited for the forest terrain. He regarded Porter, unblinking, through a pair of rimless glasses.

Porter found himself unable to answer. His mind's eye still beheld the persona this being had rejected right before settling on its current countenance. He found himself working his way through basic-training mind-calming exercises—the ones taught to rookie Envoys to prepare them for impossible-to-anticipate aspects of the Journeys they'd be facing.

"I'm sorry," the young man said, and his tone indicated that he meant it. "It's just so very rare that I have to present to anyone new to me, and sometimes I grab at a form that's meaningful but not desired. My earlier choice was—"

"John." Porter had recovered enough to speak. "Jack to

some but John if you didn't know him." He allowed himself one deep breath. "My son."

His son.

It was as if Jack had been there and left him again. Though Porter knew that wasn't really the case.

"I'm sorry," the young man said again. "I've settled on my true form."

Porter knew that, too, wasn't really the case. At best, it was but one of this being's true forms.

"You know where you are, Jonas Porter."

"Porter will do, please. And I don't know at all where I am. I've had only a vague suspicion, and I haven't allowed myself to entertain the possibility as being anything more than that because—and I hope you understand—to be in the suspected place is not possible for a being of my limited power. Even if it were, I hesitate to consider how short my stay would be."

The young man nodded, and that assent gave Porter the hope that maybe he'd last at least a minute or two longer in this place. "We've had one other that I know of."

One other. A piece of Envoy lore. And a name Porter didn't want to conjure up because to do so might mean he'd influence his companion to deliver him to a similar fate.

An Envoy. Long ago.

It was all theoretical because nothing was known of what had happened. One detail made its way into his consciousness —a photo of the Envoy in question appearing out of nowhere on an office refrigerator. It was his official portrait, smiling, but with tears flowing down his cheeks and a look of real terror in his eyes. It was said to have burst into flame that couldn't be extinguished until it burned itself out. Porter never knew the truth of the tale, but one of the HQ fridges did indeed have a black scar on its door which had been painted over, and not very well.

"You are here," the young man said. "Call me Apalala. Please."

"Very well, Apalala."

"I'm glad I found you first," Apalala said. "And as much as it may sound like pure jest, I hope you believe me when I say this. Welcome to The Pines."

44

SOMETHING OF YOURSELF

He dreamt of walking in a park. A girl gripped his elbow and spoke softly to him. The girl was close, but her voice came from a distance. It was difficult to hear her.

In the way dreams go, what he knew as truth shifted. It changed because it was no longer true—or because he'd been wrong about it all along.

Paul turned to look behind them. For but a blink of time, he saw the boys who'd done what they'd done laid out across the grass and turf of the ball field, unmoving. But they weren't there.

"Don't look," said the girl.

She was beautiful.

The shining light of her.

Her green eyes.

Then he looked down at her hands, which were sticky and red. Spatters on her sleeves. When blood got out in a fight, there was more than you'd think, and it landed where it wanted to. People didn't know that.

The sound of a chain dropping into the grass in which they stood.

He checked.

There was nothing there.

"Don't look," she repeated. Then she reached up to ruffle his hair, breaking into a big grin as those green eyes shone. She was amused that he was taller than she was now.

When she finished, he reached up to check his hair, but it was clean. None of the blood had wiped off on him.

She took a step back, hands on hips, and continued to smile as she watched him, waiting to see what he'd do next.

There was no blood on her now. And her clothes were intact.

It all came back.

Paul wasn't sure he could hold it all. It felt too full, too big for him.

"How are you, Martha?" he said when he was ready. "Are you okay? They told me you wouldn't talk to me."

Martha's smile left her. "I wanted to. But I couldn't. Do you understand?"

Paul flexed his fingers. Sticky.

Looked at them.

Red and tacky with it.

The combo bike lock and chain, in the grass at his feet, red and sticky, too.

And worse.

That was the truth of it—of that day in the park.

"I wanted to, too," Paul told her. He caught Martha looking at his hands and at the bloody chain in the grass. He knew she was going to tell him not to look again, but that's not what she said.

What Martha said next was drowned out by the loud chop of blades in the air.

A helicopter.

Paul felt the beat of it, but didn't look to see where it was.

It wasn't there.

He turned to check the ball field again, and the chopper noise ceased its rhythm. The bludgeoned boys had all been tagged and bagged, unseen now in their black cocoons.

"We have to get you away from here."

"How are you?" Paul said, as if he hadn't heard her.

Martha's smile wasn't coming back. Paul knew that, too. "I'm all right," she said.

Paul feared she was lying, but he was glad that he didn't know for certain. "How did you get here?"

"Do you want me here?"

Paul didn't have to answer.

"That's how."

Paul turned to the ball field again. Now there was a black covered military truck in the middle of the diamond, on the pitcher's mound. The bagged bullies were gone. Had they been put into the back of the truck?

"Paul." Now the voice, farther away than it had been just a moment before, wasn't Martha's at all. The voice was one that went right into him, filled him to the point of bursting with it.

It wasn't Martha anymore.

Long red hair—hair as familiar as the voice, hair that had led him into a fight. A big one. Though he couldn't remember when or where.

The truck was gone, the diamond empty.

Paul hurried after the woman.

The red hair was gone. She was Martha again.

When Paul caught up to her, Martha looked troubled.

"What?"

"I'm not in charge here," Martha said and continued walking.

What did that mean? Was he in charge? Or was it just that she had no control over the way things were going?

Paul's ring finger began to itch, though it was bare. He stopped walking. The itch grew until it felt like a current was running through him in a path encircling his finger.

Martha stopped too, her concern gone. She waited for him to say or do something.

He had forgotten.

Somehow, he had forgotten, despite how important it had been back at Stella Grace.

Paul reached into his pocket for the ring and slipped it onto his finger.

Now Martha broke into her broad grin again, but there was a tinge of sadness in the green of her eyes. That had never been there before, no matter what kind of a scrap she might have found herself in.

What had Martha been through? Where were they going, together or separately?

"Martha."

"This isn't fair, Paul. Not that I have any say in it. But it's not."

"What isn't?"

Martha reached out to brush her fingers against his cheek, as if to prove to herself there was something real of Paul there. He imagined it was something a big sister would have done. Martha was the closest he'd ever had to that. Her hand moved to his shoulder, and she gave him a gentle squeeze. "Promise."

"What."

"Promise me you'll keep something of yourself. For you. Just a small part. That's the only way to make it out the other side of all this. Don't give them everything."

"Okay."

"Promise?"

"Yes."

Martha let go of Paul and took a step back, giving him what he knew was one last assessment. The sadness returned. "It was a special thing to see you, Paul." She looked down at the park grass, her smile faltering. When she looked back up at him, it had recovered somewhat. "A seriously special thing." She reached up to once more give him the barest of strokes on his cheek, then started to walk away.

Something told him to turn to the ball field again.

His mother was there, in the center of it, watching him. Red hair. The face from the photo, but older somehow, though it didn't appear to have changed on the surface.

And, like Martha, she was sadder, too.

Paul turned to tell Martha to wait.

Martha was gone.

He looked back to the field.

His mother was nowhere to be found.

45

THE HAPPIEST DISCIPLINARY NOTE

"Before they took out the cameras, I marked them here, here, here, here, here, and here," said FinePoint. His finger indicated several dots on a transparency map of Envoy HQ projected by an ancient elementary-school overhead onto a pulldown screen.

HQ and The Commons in general loved vintage tech. Much of the place ran on it. And FinePoint, a mythical who came into existence as an animated pen that popped up to offer help to users of a '90s-era word-processing program and was widely considered to be one of the most annoying avatars ever created, was a master of it. So much so that when he was found wandering the server room not long after the facility had begun to repair itself, he was pressed into service.

FinePoint spent all of his time in human form—a character option included in the program he was created for—but retained the same irritating qualities he had as a talking pen. He popped up constantly, tried to help when he wasn't needed, and never seemed to hear those who didn't want him around.

There was no doubt that he was essential to the upkeep of

HQ, though. Things just worked better when he was on the job.

He was a vital support person who was terrible out in the field—and knew it. In situations such as the one they were currently in, he was the guy you wanted around. He knew the building; he was a whiz with improvised fixes to keep things stumbling along if they weren't able to run smoothly.

The news FinePoint shared now was not good.

"That's a lot of heres," Charlene said. "Is there anywhere they aren't?"

Around the big conference table, various noises of agreement were voiced in the darkness. A dozen Envoy trainees and support people had crowded into the room, which was lit only by FinePoint's projector.

FinePoint was silent. The failure of his usual talkative nature said much about the invasion of his beloved facility. Aside from the sealed central compound that included the infirmary, the conference room they currently sat in, and the offices directly around Charlene's and Porter's, all of HQ could be overrun by the enemy. And they weren't even sure who the enemy was.

"I'm sorry," FinePoint said, finally. "Our systems are spotty at best with all outside Essence cut off downstairs. I was only able to mark the areas taken over by the outsiders when I could see them. With the cameras out, I'm blind."

"What about the audio we heard before?"

"That cut out, too."

Which would explain the silent View-Master on the table in front of Charlene. They were unable to see or hear anything going on in the rest of the building. Now they were all worried sick about who was down.

"And outside?"

FinePoint laid another transparency over the first,

expanding the map to include the streets around HQ, which took up an entire city block with its multiple-story granite structure. It was as thick and formidable as a fortress, but in reality it was never constructed to serve as one. The internal security barriers and other schemes intended to keep attackers out had been a Commons retrofit.

The streets were all filled with near-solid lines of black marks.

"Tanks." Charlene forgot to hide her dismay. "There's such a thing as Ravager tanks?"

"We're lucky they seem to be happy keeping us locked up in here," FinePoint said. "As much as The Commons has fortified this place, it wouldn't withstand a full-on military assault."

"So the question is why. And inside, it's who. Who's wandering our halls and attacking us?"

"Mythicals," June Medill said.

The silence that followed was particularly uncomfortable. Beatrice and FinePoint were mythicals. As were plenty of others working with them. Anti-mythical sentiments weren't the problem they had been in the past, but they could reappear if the screams heard over the internal speakers were the handiwork of bad mythicals.

"Yes," FinePoint said. "That's what that acidic blob was. And I say *was* without knowing if Harris got all of it. I'm not sure he did." The tightness in FinePoint's voice was an uncomfortable reminder that he had a long acquaintance with rejection and bad will. One of his biggest fears was that it would happen to him again.

Charlene couldn't easily tell him that it wouldn't. "Well, we'll know who and why if we can get our systems online," she said. "Any chance of that?"

The Margins

"I only just figured out what took them down," FinePoint said. "Right now, I have no idea how to bring them back up."

That prompted some muttering from the dark of the room. "What did it?"

FinePoint removed the maps and slapped a photographic transparency down on the projector's glass. The image wasn't particularly sharp, but it showed what appeared to be a little plastic man in some sort of construction gear uncoiling wire as he backed away from an Essence main down in an access tunnel.

"And that is?"

"Bear with me." FinePoint picked up the transparency and the unfiltered square of light on the screen had Charlene squinting again. Her eyes were still sensitive. She was relieved when he laid another photo down. Now there was a gaping hole blown in the Essence main. Clover-green milk gushed from the break and onto the floor.

"Those little men did that?" Harris said from the other end of the table. Charlene had him in the briefing to reinforce that she wasn't mad at him for zapping her. To his credit, he'd pushed back. He wanted to join Reinhard and Koko in patrolling the halls.

"Cereal prizes," FinePoint replied. "They're plastic cereal prizes. Sappers and engineers who are little demolition experts. And the security system down there doesn't see them as a threat because our mains are insulated with cereal and milk. So every time a main heals itself, the sappers come in and blow it again. The overheat takes out the mains, and there goes our power."

"Cereal prizes," Charlene said. The whole situation was so absurd, even by Commons standards, that she couldn't think of anything else to add.

FinePoint snickered.

Charlene was reminded of just how many computer users had searched for ways to shut him off over the years. "What are our casualty estimates?" She knew the question would kill the laughing jag.

She was right.

"We don't know."

Charlene let that sink in. They'd heard what they'd heard, of course—and it had been bad.

"Where's Mr. Porter?" The question came from somewhere back in the darkness; Charlene couldn't say exactly who'd asked it. A bit of murmuring followed.

"We don't know that, either," Charlene said. "He's not in-house."

The darkness erupted with discussion.

"Hey!" June Medill yelled in her June Medill voice. She repeated it until the room quieted down.

"Porter is in the field, attending to a classified matter." Charlene waited as the quieting din faded to silence. "He didn't file a destination—which is a breach of protocol, I know. When he's back safe and sound, that will be the happiest disciplinary note I'll ever write."

Some chuckling in the shadows. At least there was still room for that.

"He's pretty much incommunicado, wherever he is," Charlene continued. "But we've sent word, and I see no reason why we shouldn't hear from him."

A loud crunch and thump from the other side of the closed conference-room doors cut off all conversation.

Harris and Charlene jumped up and were headed for the doors when they blew off their hinges with a loud crack.

Reinhard was hurled inward by something outside. The former Vigil rolled into his landing and came up onto his feet. He saw himself as too old, but he was the only one who thought that at the moment. Something had used him as a projectile to blow two solid doors open, and he was already up and ready to wade in, Harris at his back.

A massive man-shaped pile of rocks stepped into the doorway from the hall, holding Koko aloft by the throat with one hand.

She tried to speak, but the huge stone man squeezed, choking her words off.

One meaningful look from the rock creature stopped Harris and Reinhard's advance. They understood what was at stake.

Reinhard's ability was to make a weapon of just about anything, but he hadn't found a useful object at hand. And after zapping Charlene, Harris wasn't in any hurry to put Koko at risk.

"Say goodbye to the lady here," the rock man said in a rough, low voice. "And then get ready to—"

Those in the room never found out what the rock man had planned. Koko's power to affect the speed of events kicked in as hard as she could make it happen, thus saving herself.

Everything stopped.

46

THE RIPPING

The gandy dancer didn't arrive until the sun was high in the sky and Effie had returned to talk to Po some more.

He had to apologize for not carrying his end of the conversation, as he was too worried.

Joel did his best to chat with the demon, but once Effie realized it wasn't coming from Po himself, she left, dejected.

Po regretted hurting her feelings. It was yet another time when Ken was dearly missed. The mummy would have known how to make Effie feel wanted. He'd have sent her on her way with the glow of being appreciated.

But Ken was gone.

Porter was missing.

And now, on a different gandy dancer than the one that brought him out this way, Po felt very alone in the world.

"It's the rare passenger who pitches in," said the thick-mustached dancer driver from the other side of the handcar pump he and Po worked furiously. The reason for the dancer's tardiness was apparent as soon as it showed up. Unlike the earlier model Po had ridden out on, this one was a true handcar, powered only by the coveralls-wearing old gentleman aboard it. Once they got going, it took some convincing—mostly insults and, finally, threats from Joel—for the driver to put his pride aside and allow Po to help pump so that they could make better time.

Compounding Po's distress was Joel's inability to raise anyone for an update. Not Porter, who'd gone silent, thus sending Po hurtling back to his friend's last known location. And not Envoy Headquarters, which was an even worse sign.

Envoy HQ simply did not go silent.

Po tried to translate worry and urgency into effort. Between his steady, rhythmic strokes and those of the dancer driver, who seemed eager to step up and meet the challenge of a worthy pump partner, the little railcar began to approach the speeds reached by the unmanned car that had carried Po to the office park.

"Incoming," Joel said.

Reluctantly, Po let the progress go back to a one-man show and pulled the Tamagotchi out. He turned his back to the dancer driver and settled down, cross-legged, placing Joel on the bed of the car in front of him. They switched to sign-only mode now—the exchange might include sensitive information—and Po hunched over to block the dancer driver's view of Joel's screen just in case.

Don't get excited, Joel signed. *It's Effie, not HQ.*

Any word from—

No. Still nothing.

Po contained his disappointment. He didn't want Joel communicating it to Effie after he'd already been less than enthusiastic about seeing her that morning.

She says it's important, and she has to hurry so her dad doesn't realize she's getting in touch with you.

Po signed an enthusiastic greeting and asked Effie to continue.

Effie responded with the qualifier that though she knew she could trust Po, she needed him to reassure her that her father would never know the source of the following information.

Po agreed.

Things went badly here after you left. I was worried Dad would be upset with me for coming down to see if you were still there, but he had a lot more to think about than that.

Po had to ask her to continue.

We're almost completely wiped out. I've never seen Dad cry before. Well, tears of rage, but still. He kept yelling about how we've been burned out, including the clean stuff, and that's what seems to hurt him most. Whatever came after us even took the legitimate holdings.

You've been robbed?

Worse. They didn't take anything. They destroyed it all. It's ashes. All of it. That's a representation of what happened, of course, since it's just Essence that's moved on. But whatever did it manifested as fire.

Fire.

Yes. Hot enough that it even damaged other companies' holdings because of the adjacency. So on top of our losses, Dad has to deal with trying to make it right with a bunch of other trading interests. They're convinced this is all because of shady things he was doing that made the wrong people or creatures mad. They are not happy.

I'm sorry. Please send my regrets to your father.

Maybe in a while. G-man keeps telling him it's no coincidence that it happened right after you were here looking around. And Dad's not arguing with him for once. I don't have the capital to take your side, either.

The dancer driver coughed.

Po turned to look at the man.

Ashen, he was sweating heavily. He was doing his best to keep up a brisk pace while powering the car alone, but the days when he was capable of that, if ever he had been, were well in the past.

Po hunched forward again to block Joel's screen from the man's view, though it didn't appear that snooping was a priority for the driver at the moment. *My apologies, Effie. I must go. Thank you for letting me know.*

You're welcome. You can make it up to me in a way to be named later. Does your order let you date? Don't answer now. I should get back to Dad before he guesses what I'm doing anyway. Though I doubt he will. He's too busy yelling about the burning and the ripping.

The ripping? As in rip-off?

No, ripping. Tearing. That's the weird thing here. Whatever wasn't burned was shredded. All that was left was burnt or torn-up leavings.

He doesn't have any suspicions as to who might have done this —or is he just not telling you?

I don't think he knows. That's what makes it so terrible. He just keeps saying that all they have to go on are burnt spots and claw marks.

Claw marks. Who had J.P. and the other demons gotten on the wrong side of?

Claw marks, Joel signed for Effie. *Big ones. Really big ones. As in, T. rex big. In fact, I was thinking—uh-oh. Gotta go, Po.*

Po thanked her and signed another farewell, but he wasn't sure Effie got it.

Joel confirmed she hadn't; she'd cut the connection abruptly. "Daddy's back," he said.

The dancer driver coughed again. It was a pale facsimile of the last.

Po tucked Joel back into his robe and stood to help the driver pump.

The driver slumped to the ground, signaling Po with a forefinger that he needed only a moment to rest.

Po took over with renewed vigor, trying to make up for the lack of the driver's help. When the man began snoring, it was clear he'd be powering them the rest of the way to the Dew Drop Inn.

∾

AT THE RUINS of the inn, Po found the tote bag he'd left Mira's clothing and belongings in dropped carelessly into the ashes of the fire pit. It looked to have been kicked around and partly wrapped in shed skin.

Po didn't have anything near Porter's feel for adjacency, but his senses were more finely attuned than those of many in The Commons. Right now, they screamed of Parix.

Porter.

Despite the danger of coming into contact with Parix's skin and losing Essence to it, Po was overcome by concern for his friend. There was something else in the pit.

"You need to stop, please, boss," said Joel from beneath Po's robe.

Po reached for the bag.

"I'm begging you here, boss. If you don't feel what I feel, then that worries me even more."

Po stopped and pulled the Tamagotchi out into the open.

"Seriously," Joel said. "You aren't picking up on that?"

Po signed that Parix's leavings were nothing to trifle with, true, but he could handle them.

"Yeah, the skin's one thing. But I'm not talking about the skin. You don't feel it? What's behind it? Or around it, maybe?"

Po calmed himself and let his senses take over.

Yes.

Another threat in the pit. One he couldn't identify.

"There's not much left of it, but that's a gateway," Joel said. "One of Mr. Porter's. So ask yourself, what happened to stop him from closing it behind him? Have you ever known him to leave one of those things sitting around for someone to fall into?"

Po began to step forward again.

"Stop!" said Joel.

If Po could follow Porter, he could help him.

"Not another step, boss! I'm begging here!"

Joel's tone had the intended effect. Po halted.

"There's no coming back from the other side of that. Not for Mr. Porter. And certainly not for us. I am telling you that where he is? It's not a place he can handle. And if he can't handle it, there's no way your fists and feet and my tiny-little-sandwich-on-a-screen act can."

Po signed, asking Joel if he knew for sure where Porter was.

"I do. And I'm not saying it out loud while there's even a wisp of that gateway still there. I won't even do it after it's gone. Let's walk for a while, and I'll tell you."

Po stared at the fire pit and the little girl's bag. He was abandoning both his friend and her.

"Boss, please."

Finally, Po turned and walked away, each step heavy with guilt. He continued into a nearby woods and out the other side.

On Joel's insistence, he found a stream to cross. The Tamagotchi wanted water between the two of them and the gateway. Even then he insisted Po keep walking.

When Po finally stopped, Joel felt just safe enough to tell him where Porter had gone.

But only just.

After that, Po didn't question Joel's fears. He wanted to cry for his friend the Envoy.

It was that same knowledge that helped him withstand the Tamagotchi's further pleading when he hurried back to the Dew Drop Inn and the ashen remains of the gateway.

47

THE ACCRETION OF NAMES

There were three sub-basement buttons on the elevator panel that had never been there before. Abel said it was because he had clearance and because he wanted to go to them. When he'd told Jeremy where they were going, Jeremy assumed they'd use a secret way down. It hadn't dawned on him that extra buttons would appear when needed.

He'd forgotten where he worked. Manitou. An investment operation without peer. An alpha organization among alpha organizations, as Mr. Truitt had told them more than once.

Manitou could do anything.

The elevator descended for so long it was comical. But there wasn't anything funny about what Abel was taking Jeremy to see.

"There used to be thirteen sub-basements," Abel explained. "But Mr. Callibeau, Mr. Truitt, and the Manitou powers-that-be got nervous about keeping too much here. Control and whatnot. So now it's just these three floors, and two of them are empty. The going theory is that the other two will just fade out one day, and there will only be one button left."

"How far underground are we going?"

The elevator stopped, settled, and seemed to sigh with either sadness or relief. The doors opened onto a typical office-basement hallway of LED overhead lighting, painted cinder block, and nothing else.

"Who said we're underground?" said Abel.

Jeremy let him lead.

The hallway was long, empty, and featureless. Jeremy hadn't heard the elevator doors close. He looked back to reassure himself that it was waiting for them.

There was only an expanse of hallway behind them.

"It'll be there when we leave." Abel began walking, and Jeremy hurried to catch up. "If it's not, we'll have much bigger problems to worry about."

"That's comforting."

"No, it's not."

Abel's statement about not being underground confirmed the gut feeling Jeremy had as they walked. He'd been in deep sub-basements before, and they all shared a heaviness to them, as if the primal senses appreciated how much of the planet was pressing down from above, warning of potential entombment. There was no sense of that.

Jeremy tried to convince himself the place wasn't so scary because of that. He did not succeed. They continued on.

When Jeremy was about to ask Abel how far the walk would be, the overhead lights went out, plunging them into complete darkness. It was the kind of dark things move in, even though it's impossible to see, because the mind comes up with stuff like that just to be cruel. Or maybe it was only Jeremy's mind that did that. He'd never risked asking anyone else because he didn't want to find out he was alone.

The Margins

"Happens all the time down here," said Abel. "Aim for my voice and keep moving."

Jeremy couldn't. The fear that he'd fall or walk into something was too strong.

The lights flickered back on, but they were different now. A long line of lightbulbs hung overhead, not all of them working.

Instead of an office sub-basement hallway, they were in what appeared to be an old mine tunnel with earthen walls. Jeremy stood between the rails of an underground train track, the train nowhere in sight, thankfully.

Farther up in the dankness, Abel walked on, increasing the distance between them. He nonchalantly stepped from wooden tie to wooden tie as if this were the tunnel they'd been in all along.

The old lightbulbs began flickering more severely, with bouts of dark loss in between the little victories of light. Those victories were too short. Finally, the bulbs fell into defeat.

Before Jeremy was enshrouded in blackness again, he saw movement in the earthen wall a few feet behind Abel. It looked like someone or something had stepped out into the tunnel from a side opening, but in the blackness, he couldn't be sure.

Right next to him in the dark, something skipped along the floor of the tunnel, like a piece of glass on tile. It clicked off the wall and struck Jeremy lightly on the toe of his shoe. That didn't sound like an earthen tunnel.

When the lights came back on, Jeremy stood in the plain basement hallway again. Abel was even farther ahead—still walking, not looking back at him.

A marble lay on the floor a couple of feet from Jeremy's shoe.

"It's yours," a child's voice said from behind him.

Jeremy turned around. A small boy stood there. He looked to be about six or seven, with filthy, tangled hair that hadn't seen a comb, shampoo, or a pair of scissors in eons. His dirty, ratty clothes were not on speaking terms with soap. He wore no shoes.

"Pick it up," the boy said.

Jeremy looked up the hallway. Abel was nowhere to be seen.

"It's yours," the kid said again. "It's not real, but it is. Pick it up. Before your friend comes back."

Where was Abel? Why hadn't he warned Jeremy about this? What was this kid doing down here? "Who are you?"

"I'm where you're going," said the kid. "I'm not really there. But my body is. Same with my brother, but I haven't seen him in a while. Do you think you'll see him?"

Jeremy could only shrug. He didn't have one concrete thought at the moment. And he feared he might never again, the way things were going.

"If you do, tell my brother to look for me. That's as much for him as it is for me. He gets scared. Tell Mom and Dad I love them. And not to worry about me. Now pick it up. Hurry."

Jeremy knew it couldn't be a good idea, but there was something about the kid that made him want to help. He picked up the marble—a cat's-eye of blue, green, and white.

The kid nodded at Jeremy's pocket.

Jeremy pocketed the marble.

"Do not show your friend."

"Do you need help?"

The kid smiled in a way that only a much older adult should ever smile—sad, resigned to something Jeremy could only guess at. "Yes. But so do you." With that, he turned and ran off down the hallway in the direction of the elevator that was no longer there. He called for someone once and then again, but Jeremy couldn't make out the name he was shouting.

"Hey." Abel stood behind Jeremy now. He'd come back to look for him. "Were you trying to tell me something?"

Abel hadn't heard or seen the kid. "Yeah. I was asking you how far we had to go."

"As far as we have to. Come on. And don't do that."

"What?"

"Don't get separated from me. Seriously. Don't."

Jeremy weighed telling Abel about the marble. The kid had told him not to, but how was he to know whether to trust that or not? When they started walking, he casually dropped his hand into his pocket.

The marble wasn't there. Jeremy checked for a hole in the cloth, but that wasn't the problem. It was just gone. He tried to take comfort in the fact that its absence settled the question of whether he should tell Abel about it or not. He was just as successful as he'd been telling himself the hallway wasn't terrifying.

They walked.

Jeremy was reminded of pulling all-nighters in school, going without sleep and using coffee as a crutch. After a while, you were dying to lie down and wide awake at the same time. It was as if someone were robbing him of his strength and feeding him someone else's.

It felt all wrong.

There was no doubt about that.

This place, what it was doing to him, their presence here. Not cool. He was sorry they'd come, and he didn't want to stay.

"You freaking out yet?" Abel's manner was far too casual.

"Kind of." The feeling of being drained continued. "Yes."

"Yes, as in kind of—or yes, you're sure of it?"

Their footsteps made no noise. Jeremy stamped his foot.

The sound came to him as if it were traveling a great distance to do so—and only under protest. "Yes."

"Exactly." Abel puffed out his cheeks and then let the air burst from his mouth in a forceful sigh.

On they walked.

There was no way the hallway could be so long.

Yet it was.

Until it wasn't.

Abel stopped and extended his arm to halt Jeremy's progress, too. Just like that, they'd arrived at a massive steel bank-vault door—round and boasting a formidable three-bar hinge mechanism. "First time I came here, I nearly broke my nose walking into this damned thing."

The conflicting sensations of exhaustion and jumpiness grew more pronounced. Abel, too, appeared to feel it, taking the kind of deep breath one uses to stay awake while shifting his weight from one foot to the other, antsy. "Just wait until I open it."

Jeremy saw no mechanism for doing that. The huge door had no wheels or handles of any kind, never mind a keyhole or dial for entering a combination.

Abel was studying him.

"What?"

"I'll say this out loud. It's more for you than it is for me, but it's for me, too. You're not going to try and tell anyone I showed you this."

"No."

"I say *try* because I doubt you'd actually be able to do it. But the effort would give us away for sure. It'd be bad—really bad—for us. Worse for you, but bad for me, too."

"They don't know we're down here?"

"I don't know. I certainly didn't tell them. And I've never seen anything to show that they monitor my visits, so maybe they're not aware I brought you with me. Or maybe they are, but it won't be a problem unless you try to say something and show them you're a risk." He waited, watching Jeremy.

"I said I wouldn't."

Abel left it at that. "Abel Dowd," he told the door. "Welfare and wellness inspection." The door remained closed, no part of it moving or reacting to Abel's voice. "Three weeks, two days since the last." Still no effect. He laid a hand against part of the giant hinge for a second. "Come on, it's me."

The door liquified, dropping to the floor in a mass of thick, red goop that coated Abel's hand and splashed up to coat the two of them in crimson. Then the smell hit.

Blood.

Jeremy's stomach bucked. Abel hadn't warned him of anything like this.

A moment later, the red was gone. From the knees down, they were soaked in what felt like water, their shoes drenched in the flash flood that spread out into the hallway behind them, coating the floor in an inch of liquid.

Abel, to Jeremy's disgust, touched his fingers to his lips and tasted them. "Salt," he said. "Blood, then tears. They're mad at me."

The liquid went away. Jeremy and Abel were once again as dry as they'd been when they arrived. "I'm sorry," Abel told the blank space where the vault door had been. "Please accept my sincerest apology."

The space, which to Jeremy's eyes was a dark void into which he couldn't see, like a closet with a burned-out bulb, shifted. It shimmered in the air like black mist, gradually turning smokier and then solidifying. Within a half-minute or so, it had become something akin to obsidian gelatin with some sort of netting embedded in it.

"Click," said Abel.

As if the gelatin had heard, it lit up from within.

Jeremy immediately wished it hadn't. The wall of gelatin wasn't black, and it wasn't a wall. What filled the vault to its entrance, floor to ceiling, was a solid gelatinous tissue that was the rose pink of diluted blood. What he'd taken to be netting across the surface was a network of finger-thick blood vessels.

Within the jelly-like tissue floated unclothed human bodies, connected by the blood vessels, as far in as he could see. They were suspended in various orientations—some head-up, others feet-up, most of them at different angles. Some looked as if they'd gone to sleep in fetal positions, while others appeared to be frozen in a physical struggle to free themselves.

"Wait for it," said Abel.

Jeremy had no time to ask Abel what he was waiting for. The voices began visiting. The voices and the names. Some whispered, some spoke calmly, as if telling a teacher they were present. Others shouted—some in rage, some in fear—as if defiantly arguing that they existed or giving in to the suspicion that they might well not.

Robert. Cameron. Melissa. Devorah. Mall-Micha-ura-John-ily-Kim-becca-ric-ward-vin-ita-Miguel-rue-vid-llary-Tom-Merri-bert-cent-ian.

It all blended together in Jeremy's head. At the same time, each voice, name, and person managed to maintain a separate presence.

Out of the accretion of names came a question Jeremy couldn't hear but understood. Someone was asking about their child. Their son. The kid Jeremy had seen in the hall. He started to say what the kid had asked him to—to tell them he loved them and not to worry—but as soon as he began, he was thanked. Then those voices were gone, replaced by more names.

Bever-rold-ara-chell-Mi-arry-rol-ent-oss-ren.

The names continued to roll through him, their pieces overlapping one another. It was like they were reaching into him and setting hooks—some of them worse than hooks. Fingers.

Jeremy was being invited into the organism, beckoned to join those within. And it made perfect sense. He took a step toward the space where the vault door had been. He didn't mean to raise his hand, but the next thing he knew, he was reaching out, as if for an embrace. He took another step.

Abel grabbed him by his collar, pulling him back hard.

The vault door was restored.

Abel had saved Jeremy from going face-first into the shiny steel. He let go of Jeremy once it was clear Jeremy had come back to himself.

Jeremy backed away from the vault door and found himself leaning against the opposite wall, head nestled into the crook of his arm. He was drained.

"They'll do that," said Abel. "They want company. That's who's taking your strength from you while giving you some of theirs."

Jeremy, cradling his head, tried to nod. "They," he said. "Those are..."

"Charges," Abel said. "Their Essence is running part of this facility, with other parts going to other Manitou locations. Mr. Callibeau and Mr. Truitt don't like to concentrate them or the Essence source too much—or at all, really. It takes a lot more than this group to power the whole building, of course, but the Essence is pulled in from multiple locations that are spread out, so the charges don't build up too much adjacency. The fact that they almost pulled you in tells you what can happen if you get too many of them together in one spot and let a big group bond well enough to work together. Nobody's sure they even know they're doing it."

Jeremy leaned against the wall until he no longer heard the names. He put his hand on his thigh to make sure he still had legs and was still standing on them. There in his pocket was the marble, a solid nugget against the skin.

On the way back to the elevator, the hallway didn't seem nearly so long as it had been on the way to the charges. Jeremy checked his pocket when he didn't think Abel was looking.

The marble was gone again. And while Jeremy told himself it had been there, the truth was that he didn't know for sure—and probably never would.

48

OLD BONES, OLD GROANS

The door to the apartment didn't exist until the Speaky Shrieky told Audra to leave. With its appearance, Audra had reached a point of reckoning. She'd known the overall rules when she and Jeanne made their decisions and set in motion the long, hard fall of Mr. Brill. They'd been difficult choices, though it was others who'd faced the awful danger in order to free The Commons.

The effort had involved the powers of The Commons itself, which played a hand in the way things were laid out but needed the conscious efforts of Audra and others to make requests.

That was the way of The Commons. One asked. One did not direct.

There were debts to pay. Audra dropped the Speaky Shrieky into her bag and threw the strap over her shoulder.

The door had a New York-style multi-bar deadbolt Audra had only seen in a few places in The Living World. Here in The Margins, she'd bet they were a lot more popular since the people and beings one would want to shut out were countless. Four metal rods extended from the center of the door, where the lever was, to four steel rings fastened to the doorframe. It was like a mini-bank-vault. Only it guarded life.

It took two hands for Audra to move that lever, and even then she had to push to the point of aching before the mechanism withdrew the rods from their metal sleeves. They did so with piercing complaint.

Old bones, old groans. Audra had no idea who'd coined the phrase, but it had to have been someone with experience.

The old metal-clad door opened after requiring more of a tug than seemed fair, given what it took to open the deadbolt. But nobody'd ever said the afterlife was just.

The hallway outside was lit with the harsh white neon of bare industrial tubes hanging from the ceiling. Old tubes, old ceiling, old floor tiles. The air smelled like dust. And something worse.

When Audra stepped out, the door closed itself behind her, as she'd suspected it would. She knew what she had to do now. Move matters forward. Pay off some of her debt.

The hallway walls were cinder block with several layers of slush-gray paint. The space was brightly lit but still managed to be terrifying.

The dark was scary. Everyone knew that. But anyone who didn't understand that a sunny day could be filled with dread had not lived a full life.

Audra immediately spotted the trash-chute cover on the wall further down the hall. That was a common trait among meaningful objects in both The Margins and The Commons when presented to those drawn into duty. If they were within line of sight, one couldn't see anything else.

She walked toward the chute. A dried ficus leaf lay beneath the sign warning residents not to put camphor balls, naphthalene, or a whole host of other forbidden objects and materials into the chute. Audra turned around and went back to her apartment door, which opened easily.

When she'd retrieved what she sought and stepped back out into the hallway, she heard the deadbolt bars rasp into place of their own accord. She wouldn't be allowed back in until she'd completed her task.

Now the light seemed just a little more harsh.

A debt to pay.

Audra rounded the hallway corner and felt the presence—no, presences—muffled by the thick stairway fire door in front of her. She knew which obligation would now be settled. It was behind the red steel of the portal, with its small square window and its thick wired glass.

The thumb-button on the door handle depressed with hardly a push, and the door started opening before she'd put much effort into it.

The stairway wanted Audra to enter. Of course it did.

When she stepped into the stairs and let the door shut behind her, Audra was at first surprised to see that the lights in there—the same facility lighting from the hallway—were already on. She'd thought these challenges only came to life when called upon in order to preserve Essence. But again, the stairway was eager to settle the score.

Old bones. She couldn't say she was up to this, leaning on the railing more heavily than she'd have liked. She didn't want the powers in this place to sense her weakness.

That made her feel ashamed. A little boy had succeeded here without any ability or knowledge when the place hadn't wanted him to. Who, then, was she to feel sorry for herself?

So down Audra went, against the grain of stiffness and years.

As she descended, the lights flickered with excitement.

The stairway was blessed with a do-over and had no intention of losing two in a row.

She stopped, and the lights went out.

Complete and absolute blackness ruled the stairway. Audra saw nothing, and the railing was her lifeline.

When she continued down, slow and careful, she soon sensed the presence of the lost children who had helped Zach Brucker—and who were now there to help her.

Sensing became feeling as they tried to take her hand and guide her down the dark steps, their urgency palpable. They were desperate to ensure no one else would join their ranks.

They'd saved Zach. They'd save Audra.

She thanked them for their offer of help and refused it as gently as she could.

Their resulting distress was evident.

A few hard-fought landings down, she heard a stairway door open and close far above after she'd softly pushed the small hands away for the umpteenth time.

They tried to pick her up against her will.

"I must do this myself." Audra moderated her tone but not her volume. She didn't care if the being now descending the many steps above could hear her. In fact, she hoped it did. She wanted it to know it faced a different set of rules now. "Please allow me that."

The children did so for two or three more landings before the wet slap of the pursuer above broke their discipline and they were grabbing at her again.

"Please," Audra said. "No."

The unseen children obeyed.

But Audra knew that if she were to stumble even a little, they'd raise her aloft and have her on her way down with all the speed they could muster. She'd never stop them once they'd started. So she grabbed the railing even harder until she realized she'd heated it without meaning to. She chuckled despite the pain her ability caused when it reached her injuries. And she nearly apologized to the children. That more than anything may have been what caused them to allow her to proceed on her own.

When the burning old lady tells you to let go, you let go.

The progress was slow. Audra, accompanied by the fiery complaints of her burns and the ache of hips, knees, and thighs, could go no faster. If anything, she was losing speed.

To their credit, the unseen children didn't lay a hand on her. But their panic never subsided.

The wet slaps of the pursuer above didn't help. She understood its game as it increased its pace with as much noise as it could generate. It wanted to frighten its potential victim as well as terrorize the children, who were all previous captures. When Audra didn't give it the satisfaction of quickening her own descent—mainly because she couldn't—she hoped it was disappointed.

Finally, the pain and difficulty made Audra's choice for her. Wrapping an arm around the railing for support, she slowly lowered herself to a sitting position on the stairs and listened to the heavy, wet approach of the being above.

The children freaked out. Now there were many small hands on her, trying to draw her downward.

"Shhhhh," Audra said to calm them, though they were silent. "You must allow me to do this."

The children acquiesced, but it took some time. It seemed that some were more stubborn about helping her than others were.

Audra sat in the dark and rested, listening to the steps of the pursuer, which had slowed its own pace. She suspected it didn't want to catch her too quickly. It sought to savor every moment of the game.

She didn't know how much time went by. A place such as the staircase ate time or refused it entry altogether. The rules did not apply.

Audra could sense the fear and confusion of the gathered children, who filled the staircase below. She waited until the pursuer in the stairway above had drawn to within what sounded like a few landings and stopped. It, too, was probably trying to figure out exactly what kind of prey she was. Why didn't she play the game?

Feeling a bit rested, Audra grabbed the railing above her with both hands and started to pull herself up. Now multiple small, cold hands helped her. She let them, but resisted when they tried to ease her downward. Instead, she climbed the few steps back up to the closest landing and felt her way to the wall, leaning back against it. Then she waited again.

After a short time, the pursuer was nearly upon her. It was on the landing above, watching.

The children retreated to the next landing down. As much as they wanted to help her, they had to preserve themselves.

The pursuer drew a bit closer, coming down in complete silence now. She wasn't scared, so it didn't bother to make noise. It sent a host of tiny somethings down the stairs to confront her.

Audra said nothing and didn't move.

The tiny somethings stopped, and she heard no more of them. Again, why bother if it wasn't having an effect?

The smell of something rotting reached her. If it couldn't scare her, the entity up there wanted to make Audra as uncomfortable as possible.

In actuality, Audra was terrified. She was aware of how stairways such as this worked, and she knew how unspeakably dangerous they were. She'd thrown the pursuer off by breaking from the known pattern of the victim, which made it curious.

That could change at any time—and would. For now, keeping up the illusion of fearlessness was paramount.

"I see you," Audra said to the blackness above. "Even in the dark. And I pity you. You could change, but you won't. There is still a chance. You can be forgiven, you know."

No reply. But the stench continued unabated. And she could feel the presence—massive, heavy, wet, and dark earth filled with squirming entities—come closer. It made no sound as it slowly came down the stairs until it loomed over her.

"You've exceeded your purpose, dear." Audra's tone was that of a teacher. It was reckless, but her long experience told her that only the completely unexpected stood a chance of seeing her through this. Just so long as it didn't hear the beating of her heart in every breath. "You were to present an obstacle to these children. You were never meant to keep them for yourself."

Still nothing.

Audra recalled a tale told by one of her Journeymen—an outdoorsman who'd surprised a grizzly and her cub. The mother attacked, tearing into him with tooth and claw. But in the middle of it, after she'd pinned him down, and he was staring up at the bear through his own blood, she stopped. She looked into his eyes, studying him, and he looked back. It was a coming to terms. He had no idea how long it lasted, but she resumed ripping at him again in short order. He'd only escaped by dumb luck, thrashing his way loose and throwing himself down a bluff. But he never forgot the exchange. It was as if they'd paused to agree on the rules.

This was what Audra pictured now—the big predator examining its victim, whether it had eyes or was using senses she couldn't even imagine. Anything could happen from here if she failed to act.

"I'm freeing them," Audra told the darkness. "All of them. You've no right to keep them. You never have."

After a moment, a wet slap brought the pursuer even closer, practically upon her.

Before she could stop herself, Audra threw her arms up, her hands radiating a wave of heat outward. Her burns flared in pain, but she scarcely noticed. And despite the fact that she'd directed the heat forward, she could smell the sleeves of the shirt she wore heating up. She knew how this went. If she lost control, she'd set her own clothes alight.

The pursuer stopped. This, too, was new to it.

Audra knew the heat wouldn't keep it back. Not by itself. She'd only surprised it. "I am," she said. "Freeing them." But she heard the doubt in her own voice, and she was sure the pursuer would, too.

It didn't help that the locket on the thin chain around her neck was getting hotter and hotter. That and the smell of her sleeves were signs that the pursuer had her rattled. The heat was emanating from her in places uncontrolled. It was getting away from her. Which was what had happened with the Ravagers, in the end. The final one taken down by Audra's fight then had been Audra herself.

Audra didn't normally wear a watch or jewelry of any kind for just that reason. Which was why she'd had to go back to her apartment for the necklace and its Celtic tree-of-life locket once she realized the task and destination in front of her.

The locket.

The tree of life.

Knowledge. Yes, yes, yes. She did have plenty, even if it wasn't exactly what she needed. Then again, who was to say it wasn't?

The smell of the pursuer enveloped her as it moved down to just within touching distance. That wasn't due to any hesitation on its part. It was toying with her.

In the background, the desperate whispers of the unseen children grew louder, but that was all. Much as they wanted to save her, the captives were helpless. They wouldn't even come within reach.

Audra forced a smirk.

Feign strength, gain strength.

The stench grew stronger. The pursuer was not impressed. Invisible in the dark, it was peering into her face, looking and hoping for signs of terror.

Audra would never give it that satisfaction, come what may. She hooked a finger under the chain around her neck and pulled gently until the locket was pinched between forefinger and thumb, holding it out in front of her.

As she'd hoped, the smell faded a bit and the presence drew back.

"I do know you," Audra said. "And I have that knowing here."

The whispering of the children died down to nothing. They hadn't expected this, either.

"Shall I show you, dear? Are you really so stubborn? Or will we all agree to behave?" The heat continued coming off of her in waves. Her injuries cried out. But Audra betrayed nothing of that.

The pursuer withdrew further.

Audra dropped the locket back under her shirt.

The pursuer immediately began to inch closer again.

"If you force me to take it out one more time, I won't put it away until you're suffering or dispatched altogether," she said, thankful that she'd succeeded in keeping the tremor from her voice. This was a bluff. Maybe what the locket contained could harm the pursuer, but Audra had no idea if that was the case.

The pursuer didn't, either. But it knew power—and respected it. The presence retreated even farther this time.

"I'll let them know you cooperated," Audra said. That, too, was a lie. But she might have to come back this way, a possibility she'd rather not think about at the moment. All those stairs.

Audra pushed herself away from the wall, grabbed the railing once more, and continued her downward progress. When she got to the landing below, she felt herself supported by the children. Surrounded. The fight-or-flight adrenaline faded, and her relief threatened to take her to her knees, but the children held her up.

Would she ever be able to make them appreciate what they were doing for her? Had they allowed her to collapse, the pursuer would have been on her within a breath or two.

Exhausted from the fear, stress, and stairs, Audra gave herself over to the children, who descended the steps with her lifted over her heads. They cradled her in gratitude. She'd made them a promise. They'd received it, and now they had hope for the first time in years uncounted.

This was the debt. She knew that the way The Commons —and by extension The Margins, which drew much of its Essence from the same place now—saw its version of justice was that because her decisions and Jeanne's decisions had placed Zach and his mother in danger and caused them to suffer, Audra and Jeanne had to settle accounts by facing comparable peril. There was no official voice or body to tell her that, but such things were canon to Envoys and those who'd been a part of the structures long enough.

The Commons committed sins of its own, and the lost children were but one example. Most had been taken as a

The Margins

result of failed Journeys, as far as anyone knew, while others may have been mythicals or even part of The Commons infrastructure.

Such was the cruel calculus of the place to which she'd devoted herself: succeed, and you move on; fail, and you don't. And whatever anguish might befall you in your defeat, the system that created your Journey and your trials would not seek to deliver relief unto you.

Audra would change that in whatever small way she could. She'd promised without understanding how she might do it but was certain that she would. If she understood anything about The Commons, The Margins, and the larger setup, it was that she was needed. And her service, given freely for more years than she'd admit to, would now come at a small price. Depending on the strong and the righteous meant preparing for the eventuality that they'd bring both to bear on you when warranted.

Audra lost track of time in the darkness. The pursuer, with its stench and foreboding, was left far above. Maybe it had begun its own long climb to whatever empty doom it called home.

Sometimes it felt as if there were no longer hands bearing her ever-downward, but currents of air or waves of shifting sand. The children had no life of their own and thus no warmth. Yet there was a vitality and a thankfulness that could not be denied.

Finally, the descent stopped, and Audra was gently set on her feet. The small hands remained as she tested her legs. When it was clear she would be able to stand, the hands withdrew, but she felt the children standing near, ready to catch her should she falter.

The darkness succumbed to a dim gray. Audra turned to

see a door, identical to the one far above, with the same square window.

Outside, the sun rose over a wide dirt-and-gravel trail extending across an expanse of tall prairie grass. In the distance was the profile of a small town. Within a short time, faster than the pace of a normal sunrise, the gray light became ever more yellow until it was that of morning.

Surely, it wasn't so simple.

Audra shuffled over to the door and depressed the thumb-button over the handle. It opened as easily as its companion far above.

The breeze, which picked up the aroma of dewy grass just beginning to warm in the morning sun, washed into the space at the bottom of the stairwell. Another sign that the pursuer had well and truly retreated.

Audra felt more than heard the collective sigh of the unseen children. The daylight did nothing to reveal them, but they were there. "For you," she said, indicating the door and the wonder of the landscape beyond.

There was only silence.

Knowing the risk that the door might close behind her and end her mission then and there, Audra stepped through the doorway and into the sunshine, then turned back to the children. She held her arms up, took a deep breath, and let it out, smiling.

Nothing.

Audra reentered the space, the packed-in children clearing a path for her. At the back, the sunlight revealed another flight of steps going further down into blackness.

The basement. Her destination.

Perhaps Audra needed to continue on her way. Maybe the children had to recognize their freedom without any prodding from her. She made her way over to the top of the dark landing, her strength returning in fits and starts.

The pursuer was well and truly gone. There would probably be no punishment in store for it since it was, in the end, merely doing its job despite the fact that it wasn't supposed to have kept these poor children forever. But it would have to start over, as they all did one way or another.

Audra drew her necklace up and toyed with the tree locket for a moment, watching the doorway to see if there was any indication that a few of the children might be venturing out.

There was no sign of that.

"Well." Audra fought to keep the disappointment from her voice. "Well."

Leaning on the railing for support, she began to climb down into the dark. And if the children hadn't yet decided to accept her gift to them, at least none of them tried to accompany her on this leg of the trip.

49

THE ODDLY METALLIC TASTE

He would not have survived the forest without Apalala. Porter had been on countless Journeys and assessed the odds more than enough times to know when a challenge was insurmountable, an opponent too formidable to even consider fighting.

As they followed the forest path in a tunnel of trees, Porter knew they were being watched. He also knew enough not to look to either side or ask Apalala who might be studying them in their passing. In such a place as The Pines, to pay heed to a presence might well be all the invitation it needed to make itself known.

If this was indeed The Pines.

It couldn't be, despite Apalala's claim to the contrary.

But if it was, Porter had no idea what that meant for him or how much longer he might continue to exist in his current form with his mind intact.

One didn't worry about surviving The Pines because one didn't go to The Pines.

Not anyone who was currently or had ever been human.

Not anyone mythical.

Not any being that was anything less than god- or devil-level.

That was why The Pines existed—to keep such power from ever making its way into The Living World, The Commons, or any of the unknown worlds where those with abilities ranging from minor to reasonably impressive dwelt.

If one accepted the structure taught to any rookie Envoy, all realms were represented by a circle. Whether they were actually round or not was besides the point. The idea was to represent them.

Ingress, at the center of the seedhead, was where everything came from. The Pines was the filter ring around it, trapping all entities too malevolent or too powerful to be allowed into the other realms. The travel went only in one direction. Ingress was the creation point, and everything flowed outward.

Nothing and no one went from the non-center realms back into The Pines or Ingress. It was impossible.

But Porter was here. He had to concede he was surrounded by power beyond his understanding.

His teeth hurt. He couldn't ignore the oddly metallic taste in his mouth, as if he were breathing blood.

As far as blood went, he had the feeling that one sneeze might set his nose to trickling at any moment. Along with other choice orifices.

Wherever he'd landed, it wasn't a place for him or anyone like him. With every step across the rotting carpet of the forest floor, he felt as if he might be pulled apart. And he'd already made the mistake of walking too close to Apalala, drawn in by the blinking blue of the young man's earpiece, only to feel that the azure glow of it was famished and about to pull him in the rest of the way.

He had to use all of his will to slow his pace, allowing

Apalala to increase his lead to the point where Porter was threatened no longer. Then he had to speed up again so he wouldn't be at the mercy of the awful scrutinizers hiding among the trees.

"Don't do that again." Apalala's tone was that of one so used to being obeyed that there was no need to be firm.

"I won't, believe me." Porter needed no such command. Apalala was his protector, no matter the skinny-businessman affect he projected.

"You're going to ask me how I came to be here," Apalala said. "Don't. And don't ask me why you shouldn't."

Porter said nothing. He didn't want to admit he'd been about to ask that very thing.

They continued along the path, the light cast by Apalala's lantern showing Porter more than he wanted to see of the dense wood on either side, yet less than such a lantern should have revealed. The trees denied the light access.

Periodically, Porter swore there was a presence keeping pace behind him. Whatever it was didn't breathe as it walked. And there was no guarantee it was walking, really, for he heard no footsteps other than his own.

Silence. Why did only silence accompany Porter's footsteps? He couldn't hear Apalala's steps in the dried leaves and other assorted forest scraps, either.

With that thought, the non-breath on his neck had a faster, identifiable rhythm to it. Whatever was keeping pace with Porter was laughing at him now.

"You can't hear me walking because I'm not here," Apalala said, though Porter was certain he'd kept his thoughts to himself. "And anything traveling any path but its own will soon find itself no longer able to walk at all."

The laughing stopped. The non-breath was gone, as was

the presence—banished by the sound of the young man's voice, unremarkable though it was.

But that was just it. Beneath the veneer of a mortal-sounding voice, it had a much greater weight to it, no matter what Porter's ears told him. So did its threat.

Porter's curiosity got the best of him, particularly since any information might mean the difference between survival and its alternative. "Apologies if I misheard you, Apalala, but did you say you're not here?"

"Not entirely. Not in one place. Not in another. That's why you've come."

"I didn't choose to be here. So it's certainly a surprise to me, if not to you."

Apalala continued without answering. Porter took that as confirmation that he wasn't surprised.

The being that had been following and then not following Porter didn't come back.

They walked on. Porter didn't know for how long. He couldn't feel time passing the way he had both in The Commons or in his Living World lifetime because with every step, he doubted that he'd ever had a life.

Porter couldn't stay in this place.

Apalala stopped and faced right, holding his lantern out to peer into the curtain of trees. He squinted, shook his head, scowled, and squinted once more. He pursed his lips and blew a puff of air, as if to extinguish a candle or remove dust from a window.

The night receded into the trees. Porter couldn't see it happen because the darkness was constant, but he felt something retreat from Apalala the way a spider might in the face of a sudden gust.

Apalala stepped forward and pulled a set of keys from his pocket with a small canister dangling from them. The keys didn't jingle or make any sound whatsoever. He aimed the canister and depressed the trigger button on top of it. There was no hiss, no visible stream, yet a dot of flowing neon yellow appeared in the air and became a line as Apalala appeared to spray-paint nothing with nothing. He traced a square in the air and put a dot in the center of it, whereupon he inserted one of the keys into that dot and turned it.

From the darkness ahead came the rustling of something very large moving.

Apalala held the lantern out ahead of him again. There was now a path through the trees where there'd been nothing but dense growth before.

He removed his key from the air. The glowing square and keyhole faded into nothing. The young man headed down the newly cleared path.

Porter lagged behind to search for any sign that the glowing box had been there. The return of the breath on the back of his neck spurred him onward.

They walked. Once again, Porter couldn't tell if there was no passage of time or if it was just that he couldn't sense it.

Apalala stopped.

Because Porter couldn't hear the young man's steps, he nearly barreled into him.

Apalala blew into the air ahead again, and Porter felt the darkness back away once more. Now the lantern arm revealed a massive, thick bush with hanging branches so close together it looked like a domed hut made from vines. It was about the size of a backyard gazebo.

Apalala got down on one knee and used the invisible paint directly on the lower part of the vines' surface. He painted an upright rectangle about the size of a shoebox, grasped the vine at the edge of it, and pulled. It opened like a small hinged door. He reached into the void, extracted a fire extinguisher, and placed it at his feet. Then he sprayed another upright rectangle, which soon became a full-sized set of double doors bisected by a vertical line. He painted a small dot to the right of it. "Step back and shield your eyes." He blew on the door, and the vines flared into bright flame. Apalala used the fire extinguisher to douse them after a few moments.

Porter was able to look again when the flames were gone. There was no smoke. Nor did the vines show any sign of being burned. But in place of Apalala's split rectangle stood a set of elevator doors.

The young man touched a finger to the dot he'd painted and was answered by a hum from deep within the vine structure. After a short delay, the doors opened on an LED-lit elevator car. Apalala waved Porter inward.

Porter stepped into the elevator without a word and was relieved when Apalala joined him, the doors closing behind them.

Whether this was The Pines or not, it was no place to wander unheralded.

50

NONE OF I

He dreamt of walking in the snow. A woman gripped his elbow and spoke softly to him. The woman was close, but her voice came from a distance. It was impossible to hear her, though Paul knew she was trying very hard to get through to him.

In the way dreams go, what he knew as truth shifted. It changed because it was no longer true—or because he'd been wrong about it all along.

Paul was blindfolded. He must have been, though he couldn't feel anything around his eyes. The woman led him onward, his feet crunching through the frozen surface of the snow and into its depths with every step. He might have lost his balance and fallen, but the woman's grip and the steadiness of her words kept him upright, even if he couldn't hear her.

Yet he knew the voice was not that of a stranger. He so badly wanted to believe it really was her.

Onward they walked. And while Paul understood that it was very cold out—the hard kind of cold that sometimes comes after the snow has finished falling—he didn't feel it as long as she guided him.

They stopped.

Paul raised a hand to clear his vision, but the woman—or someone with her, possibly—gently stopped him and lowered his hand back to his side.

Other than the rasp of Paul's breathing, all was silence. He felt a slight breeze, but it, too, made no sound.

The woman let go of his arm, but remained beside him. She wouldn't leave him, whatever happened.

And something was going to happen. It was already happening.

"There was an old woman, as I've heard tell," said a man somewhere in front of him. Paul didn't know the voice. "She went to market, her eggs to sell."

The ring on Paul's finger began to burn. And he felt a corresponding warmth from the woman who'd guided him. It was very slight, but it was there.

"She went to market all on a market day. And she fell asleep on the King's highway." Paul may not have known the man, but as he continued reciting the rhyme, it became clear that the ring did, just as it knew who the woman next to him was. It was clear, too, that the ring wasn't ready to let Paul know her identity. Not yet.

"When the little old woman first did wake, she began to shiver, and she began to shake," said the man. "She began to wonder, and she began to cry, 'Lord, a mercy on me. This can't be I!'"

The cold made itself known, despite the continued burning of Paul's ring.

The ring was giving him something, though he had no sense of what. And with its gift came the loss of the ability to ignore the harsh weather. The chill began to seep through coat and clothing, and he suppressed a shiver.

"'If it be I, as I hope it be, I've a little dog at home, and he'll know me,'" the man said. Though the rhyme was childish, the man's tone was one of import.

Forsake not the silly, Pop Mike often told Paul and the others. It's a cloak for the sacred.

"'If it be I, he'll wag his little tail. And if it not be I, he will bark and wail.' Home went the woman, all in the dark. Up got the little dog, and he began to bark." The man paused. Paul thought he could sense a silent exchange between the man and the woman beside him. Someone coughed nearby. Others were here as well? "He began to bark, so she began to cry. 'Lord-a-mercy on me! This is none of I!'" Then the man fell silent again.

Paul's ring grew hotter. It was as if the whole of it were singing a tune he couldn't hear but was aware of all the same. And while he didn't know what the words were or even their language, part of him heard.

And understood.

The woman he knew and yet wasn't allowed to know stirred. She wanted to tell him something—something easily understood. But the rules here would not permit it. "Hark, hark, the dogs do bark. The beggars are coming to town," she said instead. "Some in jags, some in rags, and some in velvet gown."

The ring grew hotter still. Paul wasn't able to say anything.

Now the frustration he felt coming from the woman was almost a physical wave. But she, too, wasn't able to change any of this. "A little boy went into a barn and lay down on some hay," she said. "An owl came out and flew about." Her voice dropped to a murmur. "And the little boy ran away."

Everything spun—slow at first, then faster.

Paul took a step back in an attempt to remain upright but wasn't successful. He fell backward into the snow.

Neither the man nor the woman tried to help him.

∽

THE HEAT of the ring woke Paul up.

This time, it was no dream, though the situation was decidedly nightmarish. The ring was almost unbearably hot, yet the pain remained on the surface. There was also biting cold, the two sensations competing with each other.

Knowledge from the ring flowed into him along with that heat.

Memories.

His memories.

The bus and beyond—and what occurred while he lay in the hospital bed, the focal point of tubes, flowers, cards, and blinking lights.

A dream and not a dream.

The details blew past too quickly for Paul to identify any one and dwell on it, but there'd be time for that. They would stay with him now.

For now. And possibly forever.

Paul couldn't move. He was locked in ice.

Miles deep.

Leagues wide.

Around him in depth and thickness to the point of measurement being meaningless.

It. Hurt.

The sharp teeth of it.

The ring had the knowledge and the heat. But that didn't serve to protect him from the ice that held him prisoner.

A cold that would harm him.

That would end him.

Forever and ever and ever.

Paul did not want to give himself over to it. But such resistance also offered no meaning. The cold already had him.

That was why Ray-Anne had done what she'd done. With the man he'd fought. Had forgotten. Was now recalling.

A betrayal that couldn't be a betrayal because she hadn't yet known him. Hadn't yet joined him by the lights on the hill.

Oh, God, did it hurt.

Cold.

This was what she'd escaped from.

Not this. But yes, this.

It hurt.

Anything to not be in this.

Violation. Trespass. Theft.

Of her.

Of him.

Hurt.

And the knowledge of the ring burned on. Its flame continued its work.

Paul thought he had forgiven Ray-Anne for the betrayal and the pain when it was made known to him what she'd done. Her bargain. With the man.

Anything to not be here. To not do this.

He hadn't understood what forgiveness was.

He did now.

Ray-Anne.

Whatever you had to do to escape this was fair.

Ray-Anne.

The name twisted within. Woke something. Something he'd forgotten.

Now he understood what she'd felt when she heard what

he'd tried to do to himself. When she saw him after the attempt.

Stupid. He was so stupid.

Ray-Anne.

Rain.

Not Ray-Anne.

Rain, though that wasn't how he knew her.

And not how she knew herself.

Though she might if ever Paul emerged from this.

Which he wouldn't.

Which he might.

It hurt.

Rain.

That was what would see him through this.

Rain and the blue Night Lights.

It was the cerulean flames Paul beckoned to, to the girl he saw in them, as the cold took him.

Violation. Trespass. Theft.

Of Rain.

Of Paul.

The cold won.

51

IF YOU SEE THEM, SEND THEM HOME

Audra began to lose her resolve on the fifth landing down.

Too dark.

Too far.

Too hard.

Two flights up, she'd been certain the basement was the destination. Now she began to doubt there was a destination at all. She couldn't see a thing, which was a favorite trick of Commons obstacles.

Sensory deprivation. One or all.

Venturing into the unknown with almost no way to guess what was coming.

What's your level of resolve?

Do you really want this when you don't know what it is?

Old bones. She'd been a fool to think she was equal to this task. This was for the young. Jeanne should be here. Or Jonas, even. Audra and Jonas were both of indeterminate age, she because it was nobody's business and he because it didn't matter enough to him to keep track of such a thing.

Audra descended stairs like the old lady she was, while

Jonas, though decidedly slower than he'd been in his relative youth, remained willing to dive into a fray, making up for stiffness of movement and loss of speed with guile and the kind of judgement gained only by long experience.

She was not the one to take this on.

The next flight continued in much the same manner. The one after that stalled about halfway down.

It was a process of leaning on the railing, feeling for the next step and the one after that, then grabbing the ornamental ball at the turnaround to start down the next flight.

Until she stopped.

Audra told herself it was only to rest, but her fear had gotten the best of her. She hung onto the railing, her heartbeat keeping time with her short, shallow breathing.

Did she know there would be a next step after the one she was on? If anything, she was certain she'd meet only empty air and an endless drop.

She knew how these things worked. You tested. You felt for the solid surface below. You worked your hands down the railing and hung on, just to be safe.

But once you commit, and the trap has you, the safety fades. Then it's only a question of whether you ever actually reach the bottom.

She couldn't move.

Which was unacceptable.

Jonas needed her. She knew where he was.

So many needed her, and yet here was where she'd abandon them to their fates. Above, dark pursuit ensured she hadn't lost her nerve; she'd been forced to go on. Here, there was no such prodding. She'd stay put and tire, too exhausted to continue or to find her way back up.

The old lady's humming made its way up to her, along with the familiar wail of a tea kettle at full boil. It was faint at first, to the point where the two sounds were one—a relaxed and content woman somehow shrieking with a steaming need for attention.

But as Audra let the noises in and decided they were welcome, they separated and grew more substantial. After a moment, they were joined by the aroma of something wonderful baking—sweet and filled with care.

Audra gave herself a moment to take in the full healing of the sounds and the smells. Her death grip on the railing relaxed until it was a safe, firm hold. The fear abated as someone—the humming woman, she assumed—attended to the kettle's need. The cry of it settled down into silence and then, remarkably, Audra could hear the gurgle and hiss of boiling water being poured.

Someone was steeping tea, making a home down here homier.

The fear retreated in the same way the pursuer above had been set back on its heels by Audra's false bravado. But there was nothing false about this. The woman, perhaps without knowing, had helped her.

No, not a woman. It came to Audra along with the knowledge that the ritual of the tea and the tune, which she couldn't quite place, were not meant for her. They were a beacon calling to others—others long gone. That it gave Audra strength was a happy accident, but one that pleased the mythical behind it.

"If you see them, send them home, sister," said the kindly voice of the old one below. Below—yet Audra also knew that even when she completed her downward journey, it wouldn't take her to that voice, with its tea and its baking. "Tell them, please. The monk does his best, but only your own make for proper company from time to time."

Audra took heart from the presence and the comfort of a

home kept warm for loved ones. The mention of the monk was all the explanation she needed for why this particular presence was able to give her aid. God bless adjacency.

"I'll do that," Audra said aloud. "If I see them, I will." With another couple of deep breaths, she was ready to start anew. "And I thank you."

"I'm trying, sister," the mythical responded. Her presence had begun to fade to near nothingness already. "I am trying."

With that to help carry her in the same way the presence of the caught children had—only closer, stronger—Audra descended farther into the dark once again. She didn't even feel for the next step. She knew each time that it would be there.

Long after she'd lost the loving scent of tea cookies and the sad warmth of a mother's yearning for her lost children, Audra leaned on the supporting strength to help her all the way down to the subterranean space that held her goal.

The basement.

For Annie Brucker, in one of her moments of greatest challenge, a lightless underground space had been a place of threat, a realm to be escaped as quickly as an exit could be found. Annie was told she was not alone, and indeed she had not been.

None of that was so for the dark space that greeted Audra once she descended the last flight of stairs. They were the steps to any unfinished basement in any suburban-American home. The steps taken calmly by a child who, having been fearful of the unknown, came to understand that not all darkness hid threats. Because the dark knew what the light would have revealed, had it been present—there simply was no danger. In this basement, there was naught but footfalls.

At first.

Then there was something. The very thing Audra had

made it all this way for, though she hadn't known until she'd arrived. A thing of potency—of force already known to be great but now seen to be even greater than she'd realized.

That was the thing about strength. It wasn't possible to know it truly until it demonstrated its potency.

Audra made her way down a basement hallway that was, like the stairs she'd descended, completely dark.

As she approached her destination, however, that destination provided—if not light, then its own ability to be discerned. Such was its way. In order to perform its duties, if duties they were and not desires to be satisfied, it had to be seen.

At the end of the hallway was the door to the furnace room. When Audra reached it, she was able to sense it clearly.

The door opened easily, as if it were helping her. Inside was the large steel cabinet that served as the destination for the trash chute she'd been drawn to on her floor so far above. Thankfully, the chute had no offending odor to it.

On the adjacent wall was what she sought: the furnace. It was a great brick beast that didn't fit with the rest of the building. It was something from a more ancient time. Nothing had to make sense to anything but the Essence of The Commons or The Margins.

Audra tried the door to the furnace. It was shut tight. The door had a handle, but it didn't move in the least.

She took a step back, composing herself. "I have braved hazards to stand here before you," she said. "I have been challenged—and defeated—by greater danger over the time of my service. I have suffered, and I continue to suffer. I cannot force you to do my bidding, but I have earned the right to ask. And even you may not withstand the consequences of your refusal. Thus."

Audra tried the door again. It opened itself once she touched it.

Now her ability to see was complete. And here was what she'd come for.

The source of the dried leaf she'd found in the hall when she'd first set out. The little door set into the bark in the interior of the furnace, where there shouldn't have been such a thing—and hadn't been until very recently.

Unable to escape the feeling that it had to bode well, despite her difficulties in getting there, Audra smiled to herself.

Then she reached for the door in The Dinuhos Tree.

52

AN OUTSIDER IN ANY GIVEN SPACE

Evil was done here—plenty dark and plenty of it. The malice and trauma took up residence in the floors and walls, the vibrations of past deeds assaulting Porter whenever he wasn't actively blocking them. And given how toxic and exhausting it was to be in The Pines already, it was a fight just to dull the sharpness of the intrusion.

Much like The Commons, The Pines felt no obligation to make sense. After Porter and Apalala entered through the doorway created in the bush, they'd descended into what looked to have been an underground prison of some sort.

Apalala led Porter down numerous corridors ranging from mid-twentieth century American penitentiaries to medieval dungeon hallways of slick stone, fragrant slime, and water oozing its way up from cracks and seams where the floor had settled. Sometimes the areas they walked through were well lit. At other times, Porter was forced to navigate by the blue light from Apalala's earpiece because the lantern was gone. Porter hadn't noticed Apalala getting rid of it, and he thought it better not to ask. Such beings had their reasons for what they did.

For his part, Apalala was familiar enough with the layout to move confidently in the dark. Either that or the man could see in it. If he was a man. Which he was not.

There was the sense of something much larger moving through the corridors ahead of Porter. It was a feel to the air, a sense of limited space. Just as one might stop without knowing why when blindfolded, only to peek and spy a wall just inches away, Porter had the distinct impression of something massive leading the way.

While Apalala continued to walk with silent footsteps, Porter periodically picked up the rasp of something scraping the ceiling—something as hard as the stone. There was also the clicking of something sharp on the floor as Apalala moved, faint as it was.

Here and not here, Apalala had said. That wasn't the only contradiction. He was slight of build and immense at the same time.

Such thoughts and calculations helped Porter distract himself from what he saw when they passed through well-lit areas.

Saw and felt.

What he picked up on layered onto and into the walls themselves was chiefly made up of screams, pain, sobbing, and panic.

This had been a place of torture. Several of the cells they passed contained stray leavings of it: an altered antique phone, its crank and wires ready to come to life when duty called once more; modified chairs with carefully measured pieces of lumber, rope, and stacks of bricks; a long wooden board, a towel, and empty jugs.

Then there were the other-worldly methods, which Porter was happy to be mystified about.

In one room, which had its door removed, a water cooler

tank contained some sort of viscous soup with a dozen or so eyeballs floating in it. As Porter and Apalala passed, one of the eyeballs turned and spotted them. It lunged at the wall of the bottle, pupil opening like a mouth to reveal rows of suckers as it fastened itself to the inside of the glass. The other eyeballs followed suit.

Porter couldn't help but jump, though there was a distance between him and the creatures. Next to the tank was a chair with handcuffs hanging from its arms.

The subsequent room was worse. As they passed its open door, the sawed-off end of a baseball bat, its narrower end wrapped in tape, rolled out toward them, as if someone unseen had kicked it.

It stopped at Porter's feet. The bat had rows of screw-heads protruding from its upper end. Someone had scrawled "Silencer" on it in marker. It was mottled with pink, suspicious-looking matter and, in a few places, what could easily be hair.

"Keep walking," Apalala said.

The inside of the room had been painted white at some point, but the walls were coated in dark-brown spattering. And Porter swore he heard the ragged breathing of someone in pain.

"Keep walking," Apalala repeated, this time in a tone that would tolerate no disagreement.

Porter obeyed. That was the only word for it. Every helping urge he had told him to see if there was anyone who might be saved, but every survival instinct told him to do exactly what the young man said lest he himself end up passing some time with the hungry eyeballs or the studded club.

Down the corridor, Porter's foot sent a small plastic something skittering across the floor. It caromed off the base of the wall and came to rest face up.

"Leave it," Apalala warned, still walking.

Too late.

Porter glanced down and couldn't unsee what he saw. He stopped to pick it up.

It was an Envoy ID badge. On it was a photo of Carl Levy with Carl's name and signature next to it.

Carl.

Affable, unflappable Carl, who had been able to affect people's moods at will.

Carl.

One of far too many who'd gone missing in the days of the Brill purges.

The card cried out to him. Had Carl suffered here? How could that be?

"It's not real," Apalala said, his pace never slackening. "Not all of it. The facility is reading you and trying to weaken you using what you care about. The anguish you're reading in the structure is merely a reflection of events that may have occurred elsewhere and to others. All of this presents itself based on what you're capable of understanding—and what hurts."

Much like The Commons. Porter should have known right away, given the many Journeys he'd led through environments custom-formed for each Journeyman's experience. He pocketed the badge anyway and hurried to catch up to Apalala.

"Was he a friend of yours?"

"A colleague. We never learned what became of him."

"Now you have." Apalala didn't break stride. "What was presented to you was based on the real card. And his fate."

"But you said—"

"Not all of it."

They were in an Alcatraz-era corridor. The air had a dank

smell and feel to it—a dimension to the surroundings that was new.

The building—or whatever it was they were making their way through—had taken energy from Porter's reaction to seeing Carl's card and Apalala's confirmation. He didn't want to give it any more to work with. The inside of his mouth still tasted somewhat of coppery blood. And the air smelled of an electrical fire's ozone.

When had he last eaten or slept? The Pines was no place for him, Porter thought for the umpteenth time.

"That's why we're doing this." Apalala didn't look at Porter. "We need to get you out of here."

They passed through a section with several burned-out fluorescents overhead. As they continued down the hallway, the lit ones became increasingly rare. Then they were in darkness again.

Porter heard Apalala scraping against the drop ceiling overhead. At one point, it sounded as if a fixture was torn loose when they passed under it, the clang of metal and the cracking of the glass on the floor much closer than Porter would have liked. It almost crowned him.

Yet Apalala said nothing, so Porter didn't, either.

Porter held his staff out ahead of him in the dark to ensure that Apalala wouldn't let him walk face-first into whatever might be ahead. The staff felt much lighter than usual, as if it weren't capable of serving as a focal point for Porter's abilities. Or maybe Porter had no abilities.

Regardless, caution was best in the blackness. No need for a broken nose in addition to being stranded in the filter of Creation along with entities of malice unmeasured.

"Oh, they know their measure," Apalala said. "It's just not a scale you would comprehend."

"Nor would I trouble you to try to explain it to me." Porter wondered at his own tone. He needed to remember that the young man—or the young man he saw when they were in the light—was almost definitely all that stood between him and a round or two with the studded bat.

"I don't fathom all of this myself," Apalala said from the dark up ahead. "Those who do are not anyone I would want to hear from."

On they walked. A few times in the dark, Apalala turned right or left without telling Porter he was doing so. Yet Porter knew to follow; the being's presence had its own gravity.

When Apalala stopped, Porter once again nearly stumbled into him. His staff came into contact with something hard, which Porter told himself was the man's heel. But it felt as if he'd jammed the stick against a boulder, and it was a good thing he'd been proceeding with care or he might easily have given himself a good jab to the ribs.

Apalala didn't apologize. Instead, he began tracing with his canister, as he had above, at the surface. The line of paint glowed green in the darkness as he outlined the perfect rectangle of a door. He then painted a knob, which he obscured from view with his hand as he grabbed it. A hand, Porter couldn't help but notice, which was a great deal larger than the one Apalala had sported in the full light.

The restrictive clunk of a locked door followed. Second and third attempts yielded the same result. Then came a mildly exasperated sigh followed by the groan of steel under stress until it surrendered with a metallic pop. Apalala opened the door, and the flat fluorescent light from within had Porter squinting again.

Rubbing alcohol. Antiseptic. Old smells of an old infirmary.

It made sense since, by all appearances, the facility hadn't had a need for healing skills in some time. That hadn't been part of its mission. Or if it had, they were meant to preserve victims for even more abuse.

They entered the infirmary, and the door slammed shut behind them with a note of pique. The facility was probably none too happy about Apalala breaking its lock. A moment later, though, the sound of the lock falling into place indicated it either hadn't been broken after all or had repaired itself.

The infirmary was designed in an open layout—wheeled gurneys separated by curtains, which were all pulled back and neatly fastened to the walls. The sheets on the gurneys had not a crease in them. They were spotless and appeared to have been freshly made. In addition, the tubes in the ceiling lights were all working perfectly.

It was an odd contradiction. The place had the feel of having been long abandoned; no one had entered the space in a very long time. Yet it was perfectly kept. The room had an eagerness to it. It wanted to heal in a building that had no use for such abilities. The infirmary wouldn't concede its circumstances. Porter almost wished he had a cut or some similarly insignificant injury he could disinfect and bandage in order to make the room feel useful.

"It'll be useful enough in a moment." Apalala led Porter to a high, narrow transfer cabinet set on a wheeled base. A segmented roll-up door stretched from top to bottom.

Porter waited for Apalala to break the door's lock, but the slight man merely inspected it as if there were nothing more for him to do.

"Why did you come here?" Apalala continued to study the door as he spoke.

"I don't know."

"Guess."

Porter mulled that over. "I didn't intend to."

"I would think not. A move from The Commons to here is

a step backward—and a remarkably foolish one at that. I would have said it was impossible, but obviously it is not. Now please answer my question."

Porter thought some more. "We're seldom able to choose our place of battle, if ever. And when it doesn't come to us, we journey to it. Even when we haven't opted to do so."

Apalala nodded, apparently satisfied. "You understand that by all rights you should have lost your mind by now. You're not supposed to be able to endure this place."

It wasn't clear to Porter whether the place in question was this facility or The Pines in general, but it didn't much matter. "I'll not lie to you and say it's easy, Apalala. I can't rid myself of the taste of metal and blood, and my breathing passages all feel like I've been using drain cleaner for a nasal spray."

"Yet you survive."

"I do."

Apalala looked the locked door over for another moment or two. "Why do you suppose you're able to be here? Is it your traveling ability? Does that grant you an innate immunity?"

Porter considered the matter. To him, it wasn't so much a talent for inhabiting a space as it was a knack for leaving the last one and a willingness to move to the next. Truth be told, he hadn't ever asked himself that question. "I think," he said, "that when you don't accept your current world, abandoning it isn't nearly as distressing as it is for those who do."

"Meaning?"

"That one of the few advantages of being an outsider in any given space is the ease with which one can move on to the next."

Apalala gave a slight nod. He might have had something to add. Instead, he continued to squint at the cabinet's roll-up door. He raised an eyebrow in question.

The door answered with a click and rose just a hair.

Apalala turned to Porter with an air of expectation.

Porter stepped forward and grasped the door handle.

Something huge swatted him. His last thought was that the train's engineer should've given him a warning honk.

∼

Porter awoke to an acute feeling of nausea and the suspicion that someone had split his skull like a seasoned log. He lay on his back on one of the gurneys. He vaguely remembered hitting them hard enough to upend more than one, yet nothing appeared to have been disturbed.

Apalala stood by the cabinet, watching him.

Porter initiated an attempt to sit up. The resulting slosh told him his right hand was submerged in a gelatinous goo of some sort. "Are you trying to make me wet myself on top of everything else?"

Apalala cocked his head in the same curious manner that preceded Porter's trip to oblivion.

"I guess you never went to camp." Porter remained in place, gathering his strength. "That's all right. Neither did I."

Apalala's expression indicated no additional understanding.

Porter withdrew his hand from the goo and was surprised to find that it was dry. He tried again to force himself upright; his stomach and head refused to cooperate. He waited for them to reconsider and tried again. It took him two more attempts. Once he succeeded, he saw his staff resting on the gurney beside him.

Apalala continued to watch, betraying nothing.

After a few moments, Porter's nausea subsided. The pain in his head withdrew to a hangover-level throb. "Was I concussed?"

"Along with your fractured jaw. You also suffered three cracked ribs and a ruptured eardrum."

Porter worked his chin back and forth carefully. There was only a slight stiffness, and his ears and ribs didn't bother him at all. "Should I thank you for putting me to bed after you got me smacked into nothingness?"

"I did not put you anywhere."

Porter continued to confirm that his face was, in fact, in one piece.

"This is a place of healing," Apalala said. "It welcomed the opportunity to practice its art after so long."

Porter grabbed his staff, leaning into it as he rose from the gurney and tested his feet. As always, he was awfully glad to have the stick with him.

"I was standing too close to you when you tried the door," Apalala said. "The safeguard that injured you was intended for me."

"Apology accepted." Porter took some of his weight off of the staff.

"The door realized its error in time to soften the blow. What it would have delivered to me would have erased you from existence."

Porter stood up straight, looked up at the ceiling, and slowly worked his head around in a circle. The lights doubled on him but soon resumed their rightful single state. "What now?"

When Apalala didn't answer, Porter looked at him again.

The young man indicated the cabinet with a glance.

"Come on now," Porter said.

"I will maintain a safe distance."

Porter eyed the cabinet. He was reminded of the times he'd bent down to hug his childhood dog, Boss Tweed, at the same time the monster mutt jumped up to give him a kiss. The collision of skulls left him dancing in pain while Tweed wagged his tail in apology, ears hanging low, begging for forgiveness. It wasn't visible to the eye, but the cabinet's air was somehow one of remorse.

Porter approached it, staff at the ready, though he was quite certain he and his stick were no match for a piece of furniture that had down-regulated its strength and still knocked him into a state worthy of extended-stay convalescence. "Why am I here?"

Apalala cocked his head again.

"Here," I mean. "With you and this cabinet."

"Because you do not wish to be."

"This is my way out."

It had been a question. Apalala again said nothing, but Porter took his silence for confirmation.

Porter rolled his staff between his palms. Already, the throbbing in his head had faded to a tolerable level, and his stomach no longer felt like that of a mother-to-be in the throes of morning sickness. He breathed deep and made his way over to the cabinet.

Apalala increased his distance.

Porter held his staff at the ready. He grasped the door handle with a reflexive flinch. There was no kick in the face this time.

Still, the door didn't budge.

He tried again.

It wouldn't.

"Looks like your doors have picked up some bad habits from their brethren in The Commons. Ours do this, too."

"There is an understanding," Apalala said.

It took Porter a second to recognize that the young man was addressing the cabinet, not him.

Porter tried the door again. It slid up easily, as if counterweighted.

Inside, several shelves of medical supplies greeted them—rolls of gauze, a few clipped bandages for sprains, various tubes and bottles in a variety of colors and sizes, a pair of scissors curved like a bent finger, and more. Porter looked to Apalala.

"Again."

"Sorry?"

"Close it. Then open it again."

Porter pulled the cabinet door down. Its lock clicked into place.

"There is an understanding," Apalala repeated.

The lock clicked.

Porter pulled the door up. This time, it was even easier.

The sight of tree bark—living wood—greeted him. The shelves of the cabinet and everything they'd held were gone. In place of all of that, taking up all of the interior, was a tree trunk with a familiar closed door set into it.

Impossible.

Porter looked behind the cabinet. There was just empty space and then the wall of the room. Underneath was more of the same, as the cabinet sat on a set of large wheels.

Nevertheless, there was a tree in the cabinet.

The Dinuhos Tree.

53

FOR EMPTY ROOMS COULD CARRY NEWS

"Don't try to fight it," Abel told Jeremy after they'd grabbed a table at Billy Clyde's.

Jeremy stared at a baby focusite that had taken up residence overheard, as if the little bastards' leaders had sent the rookie out to see if he might be able to shake Jeremy up and get him in trouble with the boss now that he'd seen something of import. "I'm not," he said. He was lying.

The jumpy part of the contradictory feeling he'd had at the vault had left him. Now only exhaustion remained. Likewise, though he no longer heard the names being spoken, his head remained heavy with the weight of them, as if they'd taken up permanent residence in his memory and were testing the tolerances of his skull.

Abel filled two mugs from their pitcher and pushed Jeremy's over to him.

Jeremy didn't even want to look at the beer. He was afraid that anything he sent down to his stomach would come back up at double-speed.

Abel didn't drink from his, either. Maybe he didn't want a repeat of the last visit, when Jeremy had to babysit him. Or maybe whatever he wanted to talk about called for relative sobriety.

"Who are they?" Jeremy felt more than heard a whispered giggle in his head. He already knew who they were. They'd all told him.

"The charges we just reviewed are, to put it as elegantly as I can, the dearly departed."

"They're dead."

"Yes."

Michael. Mallory. Robert. Devorah. Those had been their names. Those and so many more. They'd wanted Jeremy to know they were there. Having him know meant everything to them. "They didn't seem all that dead to me."

"That's the problem. I can explain it to you using a rather goofy analogy. But first, I want you to not hate me for what I tell you. I require it. I can't worry about you judging me."

Jeremy saw that Abel was serious. "Okay. No judgment."

"It may not seem like a big deal, but it is. Just like trying to tell somebody would be. It's all about avoiding anything that would flag you or me."

"Okay." Jeremy tried to keep a small spark of annoyance from showing. He didn't understand the sudden mistrust coming his way when he'd thought he and Abel enjoyed a pretty solid bond.

Abel watched him for a few long seconds. It didn't help Jeremy's irritation quotient any. "In the meeting, you heard me mention dee-dees. That stands for dearly departeds."

"Dead people."

"Yes."

"As sources of Essence."

"Yeah."

"And that's what you're measuring. People as sources of Essence."

"You know, there used to be an old wives' tale that you could hide risky conversations by framing everything as a question since their scanners wouldn't pick up on you passing information along that way. It's not true, of course. It never was. So I won't embarrass myself by making everything an interrogative." Abel looked around the empty bar. The bartender was someone they hadn't seen before, and even Porthos was keeping his distance.

Abel was going to tell him whatever he wanted to tell him, but he was going to do it his own way. "People," he said quietly, for empty rooms could carry news farther than populated spaces might. "As sources of Essence. But let's call them dee-dees, please, so I can make it through this. That's the foundation of all atrocities—the belief that those you're victimizing aren't people."

Jeremy took a small sip from his mug to fortify himself against what was to come. He strongly suspected he'd need it.

"Let's say we rate the quality of those things. At the bottom are your basic moths. They are, for lack of a more forgiving term, the dregs of society. The down-on-their-luck. The forgotten. They shed ambient Essence just by virtue of not mattering. Nobody cares about them, so they give up Essence through despair and desperation. In a society such as ours, they don't matter. They aren't of consequence, and it costs them. The less human they're seen as being, the more Essence they shed."

Jeremy opened his mouth to comment, but found he had nothing to say.

"Yup," said Abel. "Tell me about it. By the time they die, they don't have nearly as much Essence in them because they've given up so much of it. Given it up because they've given up—on themselves. Because everyone else gave up on them."

The poor and the lonely. The forgotten. Even their very life energy was substandard. Jeremy didn't know whether to cry or rage.

Abel, seeing that, sighed and nodded. "Then there are those who are known as the dearly departed, the dee-dees, or sometimes the double-Ds." He waited for Jeremy's response. "I know. I didn't come up with it. But making a joke of it is what allows those in power to do stuff like this. Or to make their underlings do it. Again, those are the dearly departed. Dearly is a part of that because someone cared about them. Those are the ones we want. You saw some of them downstairs. Dead people." Now Abel took a sip of his beer.

Jeremy sincerely hoped this wouldn't be a repeat of last time. He really didn't feel like carrying Abel again, and he wanted this to be a conversation of clear explanation.

"Here comes the awkward analogy," Abel said. "Let's say I'm standing on one of those transporters."

"What, like a beam-me-up transporter? That kind?"

"Yes."

The look on Jeremy's face must've given his feelings away. "Again, I know," Abel said. "I've been on your side of the table."

Jeremy gazed into his beer, wondering if it might make this conversation easier after all.

Abel ran his finger around the rim of his mug. "So yes, the beam-me-up kind. You know how when the transporter's energized, the person turns into shimmering light before they disappear? That light is what we're made up of. It's Essence. Life energy. And when we die, we leave our bodies behind and become pure Essence. That can be captured. But if you keep too much of it around, you run into adjacency problems because it's connected to Essence from other dead people as well as the living through their past lives and history. It's even worse when it's in charge form. That's why we've only got the one floor downstairs when we used to have more. Management's very skittish about concentrating storage."

"Why is it on this side?"

Abel smiled and took a larger sip, as if celebrating. "I knew you were smart enough to pick up on that. I knew I wasn't making a mistake. What's your thinking in asking that? How do you mean?"

Jeremy found himself sipping again. "The dee-dee Essence. And the charges. You said this Mr. Brill stored charges on the other side."

"The Commons."

Now Jeremy was confused. Was that yet another grade of charge?

"That's the name of the place on the other side," Abel explained. "The Commons. And we're in The Living World. Or The L.W."

Jeremy digested that. "Okay, The Commons. So Mr. Brill stored his charges there, but since he was brought down, everything's flowing normally, correct? So why are there charges here on this side?"

"Nobody knows."

"Nobody?"

"Nobody I know of. Mr. Truitt doesn't get it, and he says Mr. Callibeau doesn't, either. And I believe him."

"So how—"

"There aren't supposed to be any charges anymore," Abel said. "That was Brill's creation as a way to store the Essence in a form he could use, and it was a mistake. And they're definitely not supposed to be on this side. But they're being created somehow."

Jeremy took a long draw of his beer. "So, you're telling me—"

"That there's stuff going on here that nobody understands. They thought they did. Let's go back to the transporter. What's supposed to happen is that the Essence, like the shimmering light in the transporter, travels through the barrier in its purest form. On the other side, in The Commons, the Essence becomes a person again. And they go on a Journey—they're presented with a challenge to overcome—to determine what becomes of them and their Essence. That's how it's supposed to work. And it did until Brill began capturing that Essence—those people—in The Commons and imprisoning them, storing them in charge form."

"But he couldn't sustain it."

"He did for a long time, but he wouldn't have been able to forever, no. And then he was overthrown. Which is what Manitou was waiting for."

Jeremy took another long draw and kept it in his mouth, as if savoring it when he was really just trying to think all of this through. It was unbelievable, of course, and he shouldn't have bought into it. Yet he did. "Why were they waiting for that?"

Abel sighed and gave Jeremy a world-weary half-smile. "This is where Callibeau's evil genius comes in. He guessed that any battle to overthrow Brill would be big enough to punch holes in the barrier between here and The Commons, and he was right. Through those holes—those gaps—we can access some of the Essence-manipulating abilities in The Commons and pull them through to control the Essence here. We can stop the energy, the Essence, from being transported through the barrier to The Commons. We can capture it and use it here. But there are developments nobody foresaw, the charges on our side being one of the biggest. Some people think the process that created them in The Commons is being pulled through to here inadvertently, and that's why it's happening. Either way, a charge on our side is like the dead person never becoming that light or energy at all. They just lay down on the transporter, go to sleep, and never release the Essence. Maybe not sleep. Maybe more like a coma. Whatever it is, we can't get to their Essence if they remain in charge form." He took a pull from his mug. "Then there's the Essence that's disappearing altogether, which is a separate mystery." He took another. "Anyway. Manitou is trying to address those developments."

"How?"

"That's the part you're not going to like."

"I already don't like it," Jeremy said.

Abel gave him a knowing shrug in response to that. Apparently, he didn't like it, either. "Uselings."

Jeremy said nothing. He didn't like even the sound of that name, and he wasn't sure he wanted to know what, exactly, they were.

"We have to manage the Essence that's supposed to cross over to The Commons so we can keep it on this side, so we can control it, and so that it doesn't do to us what it did to Brill. Same with the charges. We can't have them get too concentrated, either." He took another pull. "So we recruit people who are told as little as they need to know to do the data management that keeps the Essence in check so that we don't go the way of Brill."

"I thought Apalala did that."

"It does. But it needs help. And the uselings keep things under control so Apalala can work with the Essence."

Now it was Jeremy's turn for an extended pull. "Then who are the uselings?"

"The dead who don't want to die."

"Come again?" Another pull for Jeremy.

"We recruit some of the dee-dees—a portion of the dearly departed who don't want to stay dead—and let them remain sentient so they can work for us. It's just a matter of finding the ones who are willing to do the job in exchange for not dying."

"And what's the job?"

"Making sure the dee-dee Essence doesn't cross over—that it doesn't regain awareness or figure out what's happening to it so it doesn't misbehave."

"That's awful."

"For who?"

"Everyone. They're betraying their fellow humanity."

Abel drank again. "Maybe. But I'm not dead, so I don't know what I'd be willing to do to avoid it if I had the choice. And neither do you."

Jeremy considered what he'd just been told. "They're kapos."

"English, please."

"The prisoners who guarded the other prisoners in concentration camps. The Nazis depended on them to keep things running."

Abel said nothing. He didn't have to.

Jeremy stared into his mostly empty mug. The froth there had nothing to tell him. "So what's that make us?"

"I didn't know what the job was before I took it. You didn't, either."

"So? Does that really make us better than them?"

Another long pull for Abel, who kept the beer in his mouth for some time before swallowing, as if the liquid were the truth he didn't want to let in. "That." He took a breath and let it out. "That is a question I ask myself every damned day. And now you will, too."

54

MIND THE GAP

Opening the furnace door was the easy part. Whether Audra would be able to do what was needed next had been decided a long time ago. But it was also being decided right now. It wasn't anything she pretended to understand.

Jonas pretended to, but the metaphysics were beyond both of them.

What it all boiled down to was this: as far as anyone knew, The Dinuhos Tree was about to be asked to do something it had never done before. Nor did anyone know if the Tree was even capable of it. On top of that, it already knew what Audra needed and had already decided whether it would agree to it.

She was wasting time thinking about it.

Audra stepped back to where she'd been when she convinced the furnace to open and adopted the same confident stance. It was confidence she didn't feel. But sometimes bluffing had to do until real courage emerged. "I have something to ask of you," she said to the door in the Tree. "I know you know what it is. But I am requesting an exchange beyond any I know of you granting up until now."

Which the Tree knew.

On with it already, girl.

Audra pulled the necklace and locket out into the air and held it forward, letting it dangle between her fingers with just enough slack to swing back and forth a few times before it stopped of its own accord. If she and everyone else she'd toiled with were correct now—and they'd been oh, so wrong in their most recent major efforts—what was contained in the hanging bit of jewelry was enough.

If they were wrong, it all ended here. Or began to end. The timing and sequencing wouldn't matter.

"I offer this," Audra told the door in the Tree. "The knowledge of all we've accomplished. Of all of our failings. Of the price we've all paid. And the price paid by those who were never given a choice."

The Tree's door didn't open on its own.

Audra hadn't really expected it to. She pulled on the little brass handle—a hanging ring set into the wood. The door didn't give at all, and she didn't try very hard. It wouldn't do to offend the Tree.

"With this, I offer the service and sacrifice of, among others, myself, Paul Reid, Ann Elizabeth Thomas Brucker, Zachary Robert Brucker, Ray-Anne Blair, the monk Po, the noble undead Khentimentiu, and Jonas Porter. I offer our triumphs, our failings, our kindness, our cruelty, our probity, our misdeeds. I put before you, with this vessel, our inducement and motive—virtuous and dishonorable alike. And I ask you to give it its due."

Audra tried the door again. It still would not move.

She unclasped the necklace, took it off, and fastened it into a loop again. The last thing she needed was to have the locket fall off the chain. Then she let out a sigh. "Look." She dropped the formal tone. "This is everything. This is all. And it isn't anything new to you. It's proof that we know enough about what we're doing and what we're sacrificing to make an informed effort at saving our worlds and worlds unknown. If that's not enough, we're trying to save you, as well, so is it too much to ask that you pitch in on your own behalf? You haven't lasted this long by ignoring when you have skin in the game."

She tried the door again. Still nothing.

The locket spun slowly on its chain, and she noticed for the first time that it was far from pristine. Rather, it bore tiny scratches and pock marks appropriate to its age and the things it had seen and absorbed. It had taken on some of her own qualities—the damage she felt and wore front and center.

"If you want me to offer up my future and my hopes for a return to the life of old, I can't do that," Audra said. No matter how much her voice wanted to break, she'd be damned if she'd let it. "We both know that's no longer on the table—no longer mine."

Audra lowered the necklace, letting it dangle at her side now. "And if you expect me to offer you anyone's future but mine, you already know I wouldn't do that even if I could. Who would you want me to betray? Jeanne Reid is well beyond me now, as you know. Jonas Porter has always been my friend. He's given more than I could ever take from him. Besides, if I even suspect it's him you want me to hurt, I'll burn you until I'm nothing but ash and smoke."

Threats now. Audra was down to laughable threats. She raised the necklace and held it out again. This time, there was no swing or twist to it at all. "Now open and do your part, damn you. Or be prepared to accept your foolishness as a mark and a stigma for whatever little-deserved time you'll have left."

She pulled the little ring handle again. The door in the Tree opened easily.

As Audra stepped back to consider her victory, she did her best not to let the Tree see the shakes as they tried to have their way with her. Let it never be said an old lady couldn't bluff with the best of them when push came to shove.

Her confidence lasted until the Speaky Shrieky let out one of its signature screeches, splintering the silence of the furnace room and conjuring for Audra the urge to rocket up to the ceiling and hang there, fingers embedded in the fabric of the building like a cartoon coyote. She wouldn't have blamed the Dinuhos and the furnace had they decided to shut their doors again and save themselves right then and there. Mercifully, they appeared to be made of hardier stuff.

She reached into her bag to check the Speaky Shrieky's screen. The message there explained why the infuriating little unit had gone full-on ear-splitter: "Hey, Rube!"

A distress call.

From The Pines.

Things were no longer *going* to move fast. They'd already started, no matter how disjointed and difficult to track.

Despite the nature of Porter's missive—it was a cry for help, after all—Audra was encouraged. That his Newton would be able to reach her Speaky Shrieky from a realm so thoroughly locked up and blocked off since Creation itself meant that she was about to ask the Tree for the possible. She hadn't any assurance of that until now.

It was also absolutely terrifying. A sign that all of existence was indeed facing the peril for which she and forces unknown had been called into action. But any blessing that wasn't mixed was not to be relied upon.

Other matters were completely reliable. Porter's message contained far more than the two words he'd sent, even if he wasn't aware of it—which he wasn't. What it contained, exactly, was not for her to say. That would be picked up by the

Essence of The Margins and The Commons. And it would be stored, sent along, or acted upon according to the shifting dictates and rules of combining realms currently under pressures and stresses mighty enough to crush them.

Likewise, anything she sent to Porter would do the same, provided it made it through at all. It would be a message from her and a message to and from beings unknown. Those meant to receive it would do so, she hoped. And all she had was hope.

Audra hit reply and carefully considered what to thumb in next. When communicating between dimensions, an economy of verbiage was paramount. After several misfires, she settled on three words.

Mind the gap.

She sent the message on its way. And though she wasn't the prayer type, she said one to herself all the same to boost the chances that it would get there on time and be understood.

That done, Audra placed the Speaky Shrieky into the Tree. As she'd hoped, it fit without any problems, despite the fact that the door was way too small to accommodate the unit. The key was to look away, sparing herself the inevitable dizziness prompted by seeing something that shouldn't be permitted to occur.

With the unit safely inside, Audra shut the little door. She had no clue whether or not the Tree would take her offering for keeps. She needed the stupid thing. But if it was not to be hers anymore, there was at least one benefit.

She wouldn't have to listen to its screaming.

∽

The Margins

PORTER HAD LOST track of how long he'd been staring at the door, Apalala silently watching him in turn, by the time the Newton announced a reply to his message with a rare tactic. There wasn't a vibration, a sound, or any such thing. Instead, Porter suddenly found himself with an urgent longing to look at the device.

It was a welcome diversion. The damned door in the damned Tree refused to open.

He'd tried a gentle pull. Then one with some muscle behind it. Both efforts came to naught.

Apalala observed. Porter couldn't help but think of a documentary crocodile baking itself in the sun, doing its utmost to convince nearby prey that the inaction was authentic—that it was perfectly safe to step just a foot closer to see what might be found among the river grasses.

A reptile. What was it about the unassuming young man that suggested one?

Porter was considering doing something truly stupid—bringing his staff and abilities into play to see if he could jump the Dinuhos's resistance to opening away—when he was overcome with the need to check the Newton. Good thing, too, since any attempt to force the Tree wouldn't have worked, and the happiest outcome for Porter would have been if the Dinuhos ignored the insult.

Porter angled the screen away from Apalala without, he hoped, letting on that he wished to keep the message from him.

Mind which gap? The meaning of Audra's reply wasn't clear, which was probably fine because it would reveal itself in time.

He hoped.

Giving Apalala a reassuring smile and nod for no reason

he could think of, Porter reached out to the door with the Newton and softly knocked on it.

It opened on its own.

Porter looked into the deceptively small compartment in the Tree, its rough interior lit by a twisted-wire bulb you'd find in a hobby shop or the neighborhood Little Free Library. He placed the Newton inside and closed the door, giving Apalala the most nonchalant wait-and-see expression he could muster.

The young man's expression remained unreadable.

∽

Audra hadn't expected her offering to work, and the Tree did not disappoint.

When she opened the door to the Dinuhos after waiting a few respectful moments, the Speaky Shrieky remained within. The good news was that it was in the same condition and position it had been when she'd closed the door. Stories abounded of a displeased Dinuhos refusing an offering with prejudice in various ways. An item flipped upside-down meant minor irritation, as did finding nothing given in return after the door was opened again. An offering fouled or destroyed was a sign that you should take it back—and you might want to think long and hard about trying the Tree's patience ever again.

These things didn't happen often. But they did happen. Even worse, you couldn't be certain that what you received from the Tree was what you thought it was.

A flipped item or an empty Tree interior could be just what it appeared to be. Or you could return home with a piece of awful luck, an invisible rider, or worse.

The Dinuhos, like so much in The Commons and its

neighboring realms, appeared to be a silent, simple thing to try. It was anything but.

The Commons didn't kid. Nor did the Dinuhos. And here in The Margins, the stakes were higher.

Audra took the necklace and tree-of-life locket off again. She'd known all along that this was what was required of her, but again, there were subtle rules and traditions to these things. Offering the Tree something too quickly or lightly might mean your trade was devalued because it came too easily to you.

The locket did not come easily. Audra cupped it in her palms and warmed it. As she did so, she allowed her memories to glide through her mind's eye.

Her many, many Journeys with those she'd guided, both the successful and the failed.

Her final battle with Brill's minions and her decision to push herself far beyond what they—and she—could withstand.

Her own Journeys, the details of which were a mixture of events and consequences known to The Commons at large as well as sacrifice and suffering she'd never told a soul about.

Her friendship with Jonas Porter and colleagues long gone who'd deserved far better than they'd gotten.

Her gratitude at being given another chance.

Her sorrow over the choices she'd made in achieving Brill's downfall and helping to seal the fates of those involved—some known to her or to them, some yet to be revealed, some never to be understood.

Her final gift, placed into the locket with the life-giving warmth she bequeathed to it. A secret one would think didn't need to be kept secret. But Audra had kept it deep within her.

When all was said and done, when the curtains were

drawn on what was to come, that one truth would remain, placed into the locket.

Audra's truth was this—no matter what the future held, she'd gladly do it all over again.

~

PORTER WAS STILL TRYING to figure out what Apalala might be up to when the Dinuhos delivered Audra's message in exchange for his own offering. He absorbed the information in the two lines of text as if a multivolume encyclopedia had been dropped on his head, volume by volume. Everything made both more and less sense at once.

We speak to one another and ourselves in so much more than words. The living and the non-living do the same, and the universe converses both with other realms and with itself in lights and darks, movement and rest, song and cacophony.

Thus, Porter grasped the fact he was only getting a small part of Audra's message, and Audra herself knew neither the whole meaning of what she'd sent nor the details in their entirety. That was The Commons speaking through her.

She knew it. And she counted on Porter to likewise understand his part.

The simple version? They'd all do the best they could and hope they were doing the right thing. Even though that was exactly what had caused them to make what Porter now saw as a mistake of cataclysmic proportions.

He felt hot. Apalala's steady gaze wasn't helping. In fact, a crazy part of him suspected that it wasn't just the rush of shame as he began to appreciate the magnitude of what he, Audra, Paul, and the others had wrought. The young man brought his own heat.

Nonsense.

Porter was simply losing it.

And why wouldn't he, given what he now understood—and what the parts of the message that were beyond him might convey?

In defeating Mr. Brill, in doing the right thing, they had done exactly the wrong thing. That was why Porter had been inadvertently able to jump to The Pines. Why he'd been able to touch Paul and draw upon his raw Nistar power. Why Parix had been able to get to Paul, too.

They'd played right into the hands of the patient ones, who'd waited eons for Brill's downfall. More important than Brill taking a fall, in fact, were the battle that would do him in and the necessary forces brought into play.

They'd made worlds collide.

Overlap.

Intersect.

Worlds whose divisions were the basis for the entirety of existence itself. So righteous in their victory and so certain of the justness of their acts.

Their hearts had been in the right place, of course. Brill had to go. Absolutely.

So maybe Porter could take solace in that as life, death, and all things in between came to an end.

55

FOR REASONS UNKNOWN BY FORCES UNKNOWN

First Lexi found an old-school pager.

Then Angus the dog ran away.

The three of them had been staying in the powerless and deserted New Beginnings Chicago for what Rain estimated was a few days. It was estimated because Rain's phone had no juice.

Lexi's did, for some reason, though its charge indicator showed that it shouldn't have worked. But even though it could be turned on, it wouldn't do anything other than show the usual icons for apps that didn't work and display a time that didn't change. It was forever stuck at three thirty-three in the morning.

Rain, who was now comfortable with that name, spent much of her time on her new cycle, looking for Paul in a mostly deserted Chicago—though there were more and more people every time she went out. Who the people were, she had no idea. And nobody wanted to talk. Mostly, they were furtive and scared, as any reasonable person might be in a place that looked so much like home—but wasn't.

Rain focused on Paul. She couldn't find him. Which would

have driven her nuts if she hadn't had all the other craziness to distract her.

She was two people, Rain and Ray-Anne. Furthermore, her sense of being Ray-Anne, the person she'd been for a couple of years now, was fading as the identity of Rain reclaimed its rightful place.

It was something she couldn't puzzle out consciously, much like she'd never asked Lexi to stop calling her Ray-Anne and start calling her Rain. It had just happened. And it continued to do so as she worked her way through the box of Sisu she'd found and let mile after mile roll away under the cycle. With each licorice-flavored disk dissolved in her mouth and with each fruitless ride spent searching, the shift happened faster.

The layers of Ray-Anne fell away like a protective coating that was no longer operative in order for her to be who she really was—and needed to be. She'd been Ray-Anne because that was who was placed in her head for reasons unknown by forces unknown. Now she was becoming Rain again.

Every answer raised more questions. Some might be answered by distance clocked on the cycle or by the time she finished the Sisu.

Where were she and Lexi?

If she wasn't really Ray-Anne—or if, more accurately, Ray-Anne wasn't the whole of her—then who was Rain?

Who was Paul?

She could only hope that understanding would come with time.

For now, she'd settle for knowing why her new cycle was so damned fast.

Why it seemed to be electric but didn't ever need charging.

How it seemed to know what she planned to do on it

almost before she herself did, leaning into turns without her consciously guiding it.

Why it felt as if it were breathing beneath her, more a living partner than a machine.

Who had it belonged to before her? While it ran perfectly, the dings and scrapes on it told her she wasn't its first owner.

All in time.

And as this information awoke within her, as the circuitry of the memories returned to life, sometimes it was all she could do not to lose it again.

Rain had thought she was living in the real world. But it hadn't been her reality, though it was indeed The Living World.

Now she wasn't completely sure where she was.

Yet.

All in time.

"Who's going to feed George Wickham?" Lexi toyed with the decades-old dead pager she'd pulled from one of the desk drawers in the New Beginnings office. She and Rain were sitting in front of the building in two of the rolling chairs they'd liberated from a conference room.

Angus, lying on the sidewalk nearby, kept watch.

Something was coming. They both knew that.

It was a feeling they shared, like the knowledge that it wouldn't rain anytime soon, that it wouldn't get dark or particularly bright out, and that the rare person crossing the street a block or two away probably wouldn't talk to them until that person had sorted out where they were and what they were doing.

It was like a collective agreement had settled into everyone's heads. They all seemed to be fine with waiting to see what would happen. And for now, there was no reason to seek out the company of others if those others weren't seeking them out in turn. That just felt like the flow of things.

Except for the creeper who'd bothered Lexi. During one of their sitting times out front, he showed up at the corner, no definite purpose to his stance, as if sizing up whether he had an opportunity for whatever it was he had in mind.

Rain was pretty certain of what he had in mind. She knew those men well.

Neither Rain nor Lexi noticed the guy there until Angus sat up and growled.

The man was taking tentative steps toward them but stopped dead when he spotted Angus.

The big dog stood up and growled again.

Rain casually pulled her shotgun out and laid it across her thighs.

The creeper made himself scarce.

Rain's memory hadn't returned entirely, but here was something she'd learned about herself by observing her own thoughts and actions. Had the man made it necessary, she'd have shot him without hesitation.

The revelation should have been cause for concern. It wasn't. It was who she was, and it was better to know that.

Otherwise, at the moment, Rain was more concerned about George Wickham the parrot because she wanted to keep Lexi calm. "I don't think we need to feed him."

Lexi mulled that over and took a sip of the black tea they'd made inside.

That they were able to make tea at all was just another indication of the halfway state of the Chicago they found themselves in, where the sun neither blazed fully nor set. The tea was hot because the gas oven and range in the kitchen worked, enabling them to boil water. It was black because there was no cream in the empty, lifeless fridge.

So it went.

Lexi took a sip and swallowed, making a face. She still hadn't adjusted to tea without cream. "Why don't we need to feed him?"

"Are you hungry?"

"No."

"Neither am I. And I don't need this tea, physically. I'm not tired. I'm not thirsty. What about you?"

"I like tea."

That would have to do. Lexi grimaced while drinking the black tea but claimed to like it. She didn't come at things directly. But Rain suspected she thought she did.

Lexi took another sip of her tea and flipped the cover of the pager up and down like it was a therapy doll she was supposed to take her anger out on.

Rain understood the frustration. She felt like something was supposed to happen, but that knowledge made the waiting in this limbo version of Chicago even more frustrating.

Limbo. That felt like something close to the truth—but not quite.

It wasn't purgatory. But it was close, like a limbo had infected the city she'd been living in.

The idea was crazy, but Rain wasn't. She didn't question her own sanity. It all felt real, like sitting through a movie unspooling out of order in her own head—or maybe in an order that was safer for her.

But she wasn't dreaming.

She was waking up.

"If you keep banging that thing around, you're going to break it," she told Lexi.

The girl stopped bullying the dead pager.

Rain sighed. "What the hell am I saying? You can't break it if it doesn't work."

"It hasn't been charged in forever, I'll bet. If the power comes back, and we charge it, maybe it'll turn on." Lexi flipped the cover open more carefully and tried the power button for the umpteenth time. The pager remained among the deceased. "You try." She held the pager out to Rain with what was either enthusiasm or defiance. With Lexi, it was difficult to tell one from the other. Most of the time, she was enthusiastically defiant.

Rain watched the corner where the creep had been and pretended not to notice Lexi offering the pager.

"Please?" Lexi was two parts self-sufficient rebel and one part child in need. And while Rain was not mommy material, she was a sucker for the kid's practiced whine.

Rain knew deprivation all too well. She hated to see it in certain people, and Lexi was one. She reached out without looking; Lexi put the pager in her hand. This would be quick. She thumbed the power switch and was already handing the unit back when it came to life.

Lexi beamed with triumph. "Ha! See if anyone sent you anything."

"It's ancient, Lex. If there's anything in it, it's a message from twenty years ago."

"Yeah, but wouldn't it be cool if it was a twenty-year-old message to you?"

Rain decided to humor her. She'd be taking her back into New Beginnings and locking the front door in a bit, and she wanted to build up some good will in order to make the case for going inside.

That was part of her continuing effort at establishing discipline in a place that didn't encourage it. She made Lexi keep a night-and-day routine, though their current reality was subject to neither of those things. They went into separate bedrooms to lie down, Angus going with Lexi.

Rain never quite slept. The best she could manage was to keep her eyes closed for a while.

Lexi insisted that she slept, but Rain was fairly sure the girl said that because she thought it would make Rain happy.

Happy.

The idea of such a thing was stranger than their lives here.

The pager wasn't hard to figure out. It was old enough that it couldn't help but be simple due to its limited functionality. With a second or two of tinkering, Rain accessed its inbox. "See?" She held the screen out to Lexi to show her there weren't any messages in it.

"Give it a second."

"Lex, nobody's going to—"

The sound of a Jeep horn beeping was followed by the voice of a happy little man shouting, "Mail call!" Did an ancient pager really have the tech to do sound files?

"Told you!" Lexi bounced with the thrill of being right two times in a row. "Open it! Maybe it's from somebody who can tell us what's going on or what we should do!"

"It's probably about a meeting that happened in the twentieth century."

"You don't know. Maybe it's from somebody who wants to meet us!" Lexi was up and out of the chair, grabbing for the pager.

Rain let her take it. The pager went dead again. "See? It doesn't even work."

"It does for you." Lexi pressed the pager back into Rain's hand, and sure enough, it revived. She scanned the screen before letting the device go entirely. "Read it. Come on. You can already see who it's from. Maybe it's important. Who's Charlene?"

56

A MORNING OF FIRSTS

No matter how much the tingling of the knee told her Bobby hadn't meant to do it, Annie's fingers said otherwise. She carefully probed her cheek and jaw to check the swelling when Bobby made left turns and looked away from her.

It hurt to press on it. She feared the makeup she'd hurriedly slapped on before they'd gotten in the car to go to Ambit and the office succeeded only in making the injury look more gruesome.

The phone again. Bobby didn't want Zach to have the phone. She couldn't understand why it was such a big deal.

But everything was, no matter how many meds Bobby popped. The more the pills failed, the more he took and the more irritable he became. But he'd never gone after Zach before.

This was a morning of firsts. Though it certainly wasn't the first time he'd come for her.

Zach fooled those who didn't know him—and Bobby knew nothing about his son. Bobby was surprised at how hard

Zach fought back when Bobby tried to grab the phone from him.

Initially, it was just Bobby being mean. But once Zach succeeded in keeping the phone away, it was a battle. Zach ran, and that was another thing that was surprising about him. He was a lot faster than he looked. He just didn't bother with speed unless something mattered to him.

The phone mattered.

Bobby caught nothing but air when Zach dodged. Zach headed for the dining room to take advantage of the circular table, keeping it between the two of them, which only made Bobby more furious.

Finally, Bobby grabbed the edge of the table and pushed with both hands. Zach would have been crushed against the windowsill if he hadn't been quick. As it was, the edge smacked against the painted wood hard enough to gouge it as table and sill traded bits of color.

The vicious gambit worked. Bobby trapped Zach when the boy dove under the table. Bobby hauled him out by the belt and went for the phone again. Zach jammed it into his back pocket, all defiance, and Bobby raised a hand.

Annie waded in and took the hit. It was a harder blow, she told herself, than it would have been had he aimed it at their son.

It ended there.

Zach kept the phone. Bobby put the table back, showing far more concern for the damage he'd done to the furniture than he did for Annie, who went first to the kitchen for ice and then to the bathroom for foundation and concealer.

In the car, she lowered her visor, pretending the morning sun was bothering her. At the next left, she chanced a long look in the visor mirror. What had been an angry red in the bathroom was now swelling. As she'd feared, her eye was closed up a bit—enough for someone who looked twice to notice. She'd have to stay at her cubicle as much as possible, hoping nobody would figure out what Bobby had done.

Again.

Her knee tingled. *Bobby had gotten angry, yes—but he'd only tried to discipline Zach, and she'd gotten in the way.*

It felt better to think that. Then the pain generated by another brush of her fingertips forced her to admit the truth.

Until another tingle from her knee brought forgiveness again.

Annie needed to raise the visor before Bobby suspected she was checking herself out. When she'd spent a couple minutes trying to cover up the damage before they'd left home, he'd gotten mad.

Tingle. *No. He was just upset with himself for what he'd done, and by examining his handiwork, she was rubbing his face in it.* His *face.*

She raised the visor, inadvertently swiveling it, and its mirror gave her a view of Zach in the back seat. What she saw there stopped her. Not even the knee was equal to the challenge.

Zach stared at the back of Bobby's head with an unblinking anger she'd never seen in him before. There was nothing childish about it. It was the cold, calculating judgment of a seasoned warrior—one communicating a silent promise of punishment to come.

When he noticed her watching him, Zach met her gaze in the mirror.

And held it. Which wasn't something he did.

Annie suspected that more firsts were on the way.

She wondered what Zach's would be.

Then she wondered about hers.

∽

Bobby walked into the office building ahead of Annie, hurrying to grab an elevator. He nearly let the doors close before she was able to get on. It was as if by leaving her behind, he'd separate himself from any suspicions about who'd whacked her in the face.

Tingle. *No. He's conscientious and wanted to get to work.*

After Bobby hurried off to start his day without so much as a glance back at her, Annie went to the women's room to check herself again. Two younger data jocks talking about a date gone wrong stopped chatting when they saw her and exited without another word. So much for the foundation and concealer.

At the water cooler, it was the same thing. An analyst digging in the fridge stopped searching and walked away empty-handed as soon as he got a gander at her. When she said good morning, his reply was little more than a mumble, as if speaking any louder might implicate him in whatever crime had been perpetrated.

Annie had nursed a slight worry on the way in that somebody might make an anonymous call to HR on her behalf. Those initial encounters banished that fear.

Fortunately, the VR headgear would hide her face from view for much of the day. Plus she'd get ahead in her numbers. She did, however, suffer momentarily when she donned the helmet carelessly and let it brush the swollen side of her face.

By lunch, she'd fallen into the rhythm of connecting call after call. But the last one she grabbed before stopping to eat was not a data avatar at all. It was one William Belden from the Standards & Practices division, which was responsible for Manitou's data security. Strangely, it was a live call rather than voicemail or a text-to-speech email. Calls were a rarity with these guys.

Belden wanted to personally thank her for reporting the disappearing switchboards the last time she was immersed in this scenario. It was a "non-minor anomaly," he informed her, non-minor being S&P's way of saying somebody had either screwed up or was caught doing something they weren't supposed to be doing.

Which meant that the live call made a bit more sense. They were very grateful for her conscientiousness and devotion to the Manitou mission, he said, and she should know that her call had saved the organization no small amount of loss of integrity and, potentially, closed a worrisome breach.

Annie didn't celebrate Belden sharing all this with her. S&P never did such things, which told her that they might be wondering how much she really knew about whatever they'd uncovered. She herself might now be under suspicion.

It didn't help when she scraped the VR rig against her bad cheek again while taking it off. And she couldn't help but wonder who might have gotten into trouble because of her, even though the tingle of her knee insisted she'd done the right thing.

She had.

Hadn't she?

57

ALL THIS SILENCE AND ABSENCE

With another sleepless night under her belt, Rain was handed a plan. After all the time spent sitting in chairs and guarding the sidewalk, she knew what to do next.

Rain had been paged.

Told what to do.

And she'd answered.

It would have felt better to know who was giving her the marching orders. Whoever it was claimed to be an Envoy and said Porter, a man she was only beginning to remember, was a friend of hers. Had this happened in what Rain had thought was the real world just a couple of months earlier, Ray-Anne would have written it off as craziness.

But now Ray-Anne was Rain, and everything else was bonkers, so it fit right in.

Nobody ever said this would be easy, whatever this was. But so far, she'd gotten a gun, the skill to manage it, restored memories, and an eerily fast cycle with a mind of its own. So she'd play along.

Rain popped a Sisu into her mouth and hoped that as she

continued to depend on the candy for her memory restoration, whatever came back would support her decision to obey for now.

She knocked on Lexi's door and found that Lexi, too, had only played at trying to sleep. "Pack up your stuff," Rain told her.

"Where are we going?"

"Out. I'll be back in a minute. Be ready."

Outside, zombie Chicago was once again gray, listless light. It reminded Rain of the artificial dusk right before the downpour hits, but in this case there was no sense of an impending storm.

Or maybe the storm had already arrived.

She'd expected to see Angus outside standing guard. He hadn't been up in Lexi's room or patrolling the hallways. Most of the dog's routine involved staying with Lexi or making sure no one got in to bother Lexi. He was all about the kid, but he wasn't anywhere to be found.

Rain made her way over to the Tuxedo Bar and George Wickham's cage. Part of her worried that she'd find it empty, killing her new mission before she'd even started. But even if that were the case, nothing would put her back in a chair on the sidewalk, doing zero.

There the parrot perched, looking for all the world as if he'd been stuffed. George Wickham wasn't often the most animated beast, but when Rain peered in at him, he ignored her with the practiced disdain of an A-list celeb.

The always-locked door to the cage opened easily. Still no response from George Wickham. But this was what she'd been asked to do. She extended a hand as a perch, hoping the bird would discover the joy of cooperation. She had a lot to do, and this was just the first part of it.

He gave her hand a glance and stayed put.

"Come on, Georgie." Rain hoped she'd chosen a parrot-friendly tone. She'd never really dealt with George Wickham before—the sharp beak and talons weren't much of a draw—so she didn't blame him for not trusting her. And he didn't even know about the plan to tuck him inside her jacket for a loud, terrifying motorcycle ride.

George Wickham wasn't having it.

Rain wasn't about to make a grab for him. Again—talons and beak.

A sneeze from behind her, a distance away. Rain turned to spot the creepy guy, emboldened without the attention of Angus or the shotgun, standing down the block from the New Beginnings front entrance.

That was all the opportunity George Wickham needed. With a loud bout of flapping, he burst from the cage and was free before Rain could even think to overcome her fear of being bitten or clawed.

Dammit.

The bird made for one of the spindly trees in front of the Tux. He perched on a branch high enough for Rain to abandon any hope of reaching him.

"Oh, God, George. Seriously?" The tree was too fragile to climb, and Rain assumed the parrot would very much enjoy waiting for her to make the attempt before flapping away once she got within striking distance. Shooting him down was out of the question, of course, though it was looking more and more appealing. "George."

The bird tilted his head to have a look at her, as if she might just be the dumbest thing he'd seen since the world went mad. Then he took off and flew up over New Beginnings. Within a few seconds, he was a mere speck against the gray clouds.

"Crap." Rain closed the door to the cage in what was probably her most pointless move since walking outside. Then she headed for the creep at a fast walk just to see what he'd do.

The creep followed George Wickham's example and fled once it was clear she was coming for him.

The front door to the building flew open, and a distraught Lexi covered the distance to Rain in a panicky instant. "Angus is gone!"

∽

IT TOOK some doing to convince Lexi to put on her backpack and get on the back of the cycle.

"What are you gonna do, shoot me?" the girl had said over and over as Rain tried to convince her Angus would be fine on his own. Finally, Rain's frustration and despair must have been plain enough to see. Lexi shut up and marched outside to stand by the bike.

Now, speeding down Ashland, Rain was forced to semi-obey the law because other vehicles were on the road. It wouldn't do to smear her and Lexi all over the asphalt before the adventure even started, and figuring out why cars had started to reappear would have to wait for another day.

Lexi was a bit more agreeable after Rain told her they were headed to Wicker Park to see Grease and whatever members of her roving camp were with her and that maybe they'd help search for Angus. Lexi had always looked up to Grease, though she'd never have admitted such a thing. And that get-along spirit turned to full-blown euphoria when Rain parked the cycle, and they made their way to Grease's part of the park.

"Boy!" Lexi broke into a run. Sure enough, there was the big labradoodle, interrupting his roughhousing with Leslie's bat-dog puppy to meet Lexi halfway. Lexi and Angus happily collided and collapsed into a hugging, kissing, yipping mound of girl-pup joy.

Rain was happy to see the reunion.

It might help what was coming next go more smoothly.

"How long's he been here?" Rain asked Grease.

Cozied up to a bit of red-and-orange graffiti that said, "Rhyme doesn't pay," Grease had moved all of five feet from the spot against the fountain where Rain had last seen her. "Time and I are no longer on speaking terms," she said. "Probably not that long, I guess. He's been keeping that bitey little thing off me when he hasn't been pacing around like he's waiting for something. Something like you. You think he knew you were coming?"

Rain watched Angus and Lexi settle into a mind-meld, hugged out, heads touching as they basked in each other's rediscovered presence. "Not me. Her."

"Then there's the other guy." Grease pointed up at a nearby lamp post. George Wickham perched on its finial, studiously ignoring the two of them. "You know him?"

The bird rocked from side to side, as if unable to contain his glee at having pulled off his little surprise. But he wouldn't look at them.

"I might have said 'yes' a day ago. But I don't think I do, no."

The catching up took only a few minutes. Grease still hadn't heard from Broward. Or Leslie. The latter was of consequence because there was no way Leslie would have up and left the pooch for such a length of time. "She doesn't care about anyone, but she loves her fur-babies," Grease said.

"So you're the official dog-sitter."

"Apparently. Which is fine because I like the little jerk." Grease looked over to where Lexi, Angus, and Leslie's little dog were squaring off in some sort of staring contest. "But I'll say it—all this silence and absence is making me nervous. And not just a little, either."

"Well, absence is why I'm here."

Grease waited for her to explain.

Lexi had no such patience. She rose, fists at her side, eyes narrowing. "No."

"I don't have a choice, Lex. I won't be that long. I'll come back for you."

"You don't know that. Admit it. You don't."

Rain had to concede the point.

Lexi went into full-on squint mode.

Angus broke off from from his staring battle with the little dog and came over to stand beside Lexi.

"I'm coming with you," Lexi said.

"No, you're not."

"Try and stop me."

"You need to stay here with Grease. And Angus." Rain eyed the dog. Truth be told, she didn't know that he wouldn't try to follow her himself. He wasn't just any dog. "And George Wickham." She glanced at the parrot up above. That was a long shot. And she suspected he wasn't just any parrot. Was anything just anything? Was anyone?

Silence.

Grease stood, walked over to Lexi and put a hand on her shoulder.

Lexi shook it off. She continued to glare at Rain, who calmly returned the stare until Lexi had a moment to think it through. Something changed in the kid's eyes, and her air went from anger to resignation. She crouched by Angus and gave the big labradoodle a hug. "Everybody leaves," she told the dog.

"It won't be long." Rain was less than convincing.

"Everybody leaves." Lexi walked over to where Grease had been sitting and plopped down against the fountain. She didn't say goodbye.

Angus ambled over to lie down beside her. He didn't say goodbye, either.

58

THE DESTINY ROUND

Jeremy and Abel blew through what they'd come to know as the destiny round. It was the choice between continuing to drink, taking out a loan against your next day's well-being, or stopping and dealing with an annoying hangover at worst. To order another was a commitment. It wouldn't be the last, and you'd pay for it in more ways than one.

Already, Jeremy couldn't recall who'd been the one to forge ahead and get it from the bar. Maybe it was just too difficult to determine which pitcher was the decider.

Jeremy's judgment was off. Probably because he was heaving it up and watching it spin down into the city sewers in the sole stall of the none-too-fresh Billy Clyde's men's room. After he finished and struggled to his feet, blinking the tears from his eyes, he wasn't sure which restroom he'd run into. So it was a small comfort to spot the urinal on the wall on his way out.

Back at the booth, his seat had been usurped by Porthos, and Jeremy wasn't confident enough in his relationship with the brute to risk trying to move him. He'd seen Porthos's claws when the cat stretched, and they were intimidating. He also didn't know how the regulars or the bartender might react to him manhandling the house pet.

It might be fine.

It might not.

Jeremy liked Billy Clyde's, for all its questionable cleanliness and camped-out drunks. He didn't want to take a chance on being banned—or even admonished, really. But he did need to sit.

The soccer-watching woman from their previous adventures saved him on her way back from the women's room. Seeing Jeremy's predicament, she scooped Porthos up and deposited him on a table a few booths away before reclaiming her own spot at the bar.

Another match on TV. Somehow, this woman always seemed to find soccer to watch, no matter the time of day or night. Maybe there was always a ball being kicked around somewhere in the world, and one needed only to know which channel to land on. Either way, he was grateful, and he demonstrated said gratitude by pouring himself into the spot the cat had kept warm for him.

Jeremy waited for Abel to mock him for being gone so long or ask if he was all right.

Instead, Abel peered into his half-full mug. He and his beer had reached a state of detente for the nonce. "Do you ever wonder what the hell it is they stare at?" he said without looking up from his suds.

"Who?"

"Cats."

In his new spot, Porthos had settled in as if being there had been his idea all along. He was now intently gazing at the drunk in the booth, who was sleeping sitting up and had no idea he was being observed. It was for the best. Porthos's stare was so unsettling as to do his species proud. Still, it wasn't clear how Abel knew what the cat was up to; he hadn't so much as glanced in that direction since the soccer fan rescued Jeremy.

Abel couldn't see the drunk. He thought Porthos was staring into space.

Jeremy didn't say anything. With the newfound illusion of sobriety brought about by donating his share of the pitchers to the bar's plumbing, he was hoping Abel would slow down and let him keep it that way.

He also wanted Abel to stay lucid enough to pass along whatever other information he might want to divulge. Already he'd probably told Jeremy more than he should have about where the Manitou leadership wanted to store charges in The Living World so that adjacency wouldn't be a risk.

They'd been drinking too much.

Abel had been talking too much.

It was an interesting setup once you removed all empathy concerns. Foreclosed houses in far-flung unfinished suburbs were being put to use, with Manitou telling investors they were buying up the distressed properties in order to flip them. That was proving to be unreliable and unwieldy, however, so there was a new scheme involving stack upon stack of shipping containers in storage facilities being actively acquired by Manitou interests. That's as far as Abel got before Jeremy had jumped up to inspect the Billy Clyde's porcelain.

"We can tell ourselves we're better all we want." Abel dipped an index finger into his mug and began stirring his beer with it.

"Better than what?"

"The uselings. They're worse than I've told you. The best ones—or the most useful ones—manage those they have some adjacency with. Friends or family, if that connection exists. Or someone a little more distant but still related, like somebody they've been told they might know by a social-network algorithm. So they're not just betraying the rest of humanity to stay alive—if we can say they're really living. They're doing it to people they have something in common with."

Jeremy had nothing to say to that. He was trying to make sure he wouldn't have to make another trip to the bathroom. And he wasn't sure if the nausea was due to the ill-advised alcohol intake or the curse Abel had put on him with his revelation.

"You believe me. About all this." Now Abel was watching him.

Jeremy did believe him. Already, he'd taken in so many small mysteries, between the focusites and all of the people and things that only he seemed to be able to see. So he was comfortable with the idea that there might be much larger ones. He would have been shocked if there hadn't been.

"Belief. That's the key. To everything." Abel held his beer finger up and examined it from different angles in the weak light of the bar, as if he'd taken a reading of something only he could measure. "The big lie. Bad people have always relied on the big lie to get away with bad things."

Jeremy took a deep breath. He held it until he was reasonably confident he wouldn't be sick again—in the next few minutes. "What's the big lie?"

"Whatever you want it to be. But it's best if you have scapegoats. Somebody to blame. You get everybody mad at them. You work their fears. It's all the scapegoats' fault. And there are so many ways they're betraying you and hurting you. You lie so much that they believe you. Because who would ever be capable of lying that much? You're the only one who can save them from the scapegoats. From the enemies. And you make them so crazy with rage and fear that they can't see you're the one they should be afraid of."

"Who are the scapegoats here?"

Abel sipped his beer, made a face, and poured some more from the pitcher. He tried it again. No face this time. "I don't know. Truitt, Callibeau, and the rest of the leadership don't trust me with that." With enough beer in him, Abel dropped his bosses' formal titles. "Or they haven't decided. There are always choices. Just look at race, gender, sexual orientation, religion. Humans never run out of options for who to kick."

Jeremy looked over at Porthos, who'd learned all he could from the sleeping drunk. The cat was now watching someone at the bar but was fighting to stay awake. "What's the big lie meant to cover up?"

Abel held his next sip in his mouth again, savoring it before answering. "The next step."

"Which is?"

"Stopping the Essence from being wayward or rebelling. Fission. Fracking. It was the next module in the works for the Apalala framework, which is why Mallory Chiklis tried to exorcise it, even if she didn't know the details and just got a bad feeling from it."

Jeremy knew he didn't want to hear the answer to his next question. But there wasn't anything else to say. So he asked Abel what fracking entailed.

As he'd hoped, Abel was not quick with his answer. But being slow didn't prevent him from giving it.

And once he had, Jeremy's decision to start drinking again was an easy one.

59

THE SHAPE OF A FINGER OR TWO

Annie was wide awake at an unknown time, staring at the ceiling. She couldn't bring herself to look at the clock and confirm the lateness of the hour. But she knew the soreness in her jaw had kept her up for a long time now. She couldn't remember who said the innocent sleep while the guilty don't. But she knew they had it wrong. Bobby's snoring was proof.

If he'd noticed her chewing on the other side of her mouth at dinner, he didn't say anything. No more than he acknowledged the plum-colored cloudiness where he'd made contact. Annie leaned into the mirror as he stood brushing his teeth. She could almost make out the shape of a finger or two in the discoloration. Yet Bobby rinsed, washed his face, and crawled into bed as if it were just another night. When she finished, turned out the light, and crawled in next to him, all that greeted her was the buzz of his slumber.

He slept. How?

Tingle. *And what about her? Was she so weak that she couldn't take responsibility for her part in what happened?*

Annie turned her attention away from that. It was past midnight, she suspected, and the light patterns on the ceiling were creatures of their own making. Regret ruled while shame romped. But had the lights pulsed, or was it merely her blinking? The white-noise fan sounded remarkably like the dearly departed Dynamite 8. Remarkably like it.

Responsibility. There was a thing.

Manitou, with its insistence on ruling its employees' lives, was the source of Bobby's pills. Strangely, she'd always been perfectly comfortable not knowing what those meds did for or to him. But before they'd gone to bed, when he thought she was engrossed in checking his recent contribution to her complexion, she saw him pop a good half-dozen. He knew they weren't doing what they were supposed to—and the bloom on her face was a sign of their failure.

Who was Bobby without the pills? Manitou knew. And Annie, watching the ceiling critters migrate from wall to wall with the passing headlights of a car below, did, too.

Zach's eyes in the visor mirror in the car.

Her boy.

Zach.

Tingle. *Their boy.*

Annie slipped out of bed. She was getting very good at slipping. Move, listen for Bobby's sleep breathing, repeat. It would have been easy were it not such a high-stakes effort.

Even her barefoot steps in the hallway seemed too loud to her, though they couldn't possibly be heard over the fan. Which really did sound like the Dynamite 8.

The little slats of light that usually came in through the blinds on Zach's bedroom windows were absent from their nighttime haunt on the hallway wall. His door was closed.

Annie turned the doorknob with practiced stealth,

thankful Bobby had been too busy with whatever game he'd been engrossed in last weekend to notice her lubing the hinges on the doors. Her eyes had to adjust to the heavier shadows of Zach's room before she could make much out. Normally, the balance between light and dark in the bedrooms was fairly uniform. The same slivers that made it into her bedroom due to the angle of the streetlights made it into Zach's.

But not now.

Zach's closet door was open, which was a no-no. That had not been the case when she'd left the room earlier in the night. She was sure of that. And there was no way he would have opened it without the light on in there.

Curiouser and curiouser.

Annie crossed Zach's bedroom and closed the door to the closet. Was it just her imagination that the room appeared to brighten as she did so? She wanted it to be when she heard something shift inside the closet and felt that movement travel along the floor.

Something big.

She stood for several long moments, hand on the knob of the closet door, trying to make herself open it again. If Zach woke up and saw her hesitating, she'd doom any chance she'd ever have to convince him there was nothing to fear in there. Especially when Bobby took so much delight in casually dropping ideas about what might live in Zach's closet whenever he thought the boy might be listening.

She willed herself to open the door and wanted to laugh. There was nothing there. There never had been.

Had there?

Annie chanced a look around the room. Was the room now as dark as it had been when she'd come in? She closed the closet door again. Was the room now brighter?

This was nuts.

She crept over to Zach's bed. He was wide awake, staring intently up at her. She tried to tell herself that the hard intensity of his gaze couldn't be the same as it had been in the car. He couldn't maintain it that long. It was just a trick of the low light and her overactive imagination acting up again.

Zach closed his eyes when she bent down to give him a kiss on the forehead. But when she straightened up, his gaze returned in all its ferocity.

Not for her. For his father.

No tingle. The knee didn't have anything to say about that.

Annie snuck back into her bedroom and climbed back into bed. She felt sleep coming on as the fan's hiss once again reminded her of the Dynamite 8. She was dreaming, she thought, the blades' impelled air bringing whispering voices into the room once again.

Annie was reminded of a nasty fight she'd had with Bobby some time before—one in which he'd been so mean she'd made herself forget it. It may have had to do with Zach. It may have had to do with work. Not that either of those things was required in order for Bobby to turn to his dark side.

He said he'd read that female vets were five times more likely than male vets to hurt or kill themselves. He'd given her a cold smile, adding that maybe things would work out for them after all.

What did Manitou know about a husband who'd say that, and what were the things the pills no longer kept him from doing to her and her son?

No answering tingle from the knee.

Soon enough, Annie drifted off for real.

The stairway, the sunshine, and the shade of the palm fronds awaited as she burrowed beneath a blanket of darkness in the night.

She hoped she'd see the cats. She could do with beings who expressed their disdain with only a look—or the withholding of one.

60
WHEN NOBLE INTENTIONS DESERT ONE SO YOUNG

I'm-Bobby was not all right. Zach had made him worse by stealing his pills and giving him fake ones.

Now Zach's mother was not all right. I'm-Bobby had hurt her instead of Zach, when hurting Zach was what he'd meant to do.

Zach didn't get angry often. It was new to him, and he didn't know how to control it.

That scared him. Because uncontrolled anger was what people like I'm-Bobby did, not people like Zach.

It was wrong to steal I'm-Bobby's pills. Now Zach's mother was hurt—and could be hurt again. Which made him angry at I'm-Bobby.

And angry at whoever left him the message in the rolly-phone silo. It turned out to be dangerous for him and for Zach's mother.

After Zach's mother left his room, Zach wanted to go after her. He wanted to make her feel better and to tell her how sorry he was for what I'm-Bobby had done. But he didn't. He was afraid he might have gone with her to her room to do whatever he could to hurt I'm-Bobby while he slept.

It wouldn't have worked anyway. Zach's mother would have stopped him.

Or I'm-Bobby. Then Zach's mother might have been hurt even more.

Maybe it would have worked too well. Which was worse?

"You know the answer to that." Aidan was back. Zach hadn't noticed the closet door opening or the room growing darker. The floorboards in the closet creaked with Aidan's mass. His voice rumbled with more presence than it had when Zach first met him. And every time Aidan left and came back, it seemed as if the wood complained harder and his speech contained more power.

Zach didn't know where Aidan went. But he did know he should let Zach's mother know about him. Things that lived in the closet were never good. Not according to any story Zach had ever heard.

But Zach had decided to prioritize, which was what Mrs. Good Morning Class was always trying to get him to do. Mrs. Good Morning Class would be very happy to know Zach was prioritizing if ever he were to tell her about it. She'd give him one of the big smiles she always wanted him and the others at Ambit to give to her. "Big smiles, everybody!" Then she'd make her disappointed clicking noise if his own smile didn't appear. And it wouldn't.

Zach didn't deserve any big smiles. He'd done something that got Zach's mother hurt. And Zach's mother didn't even know.

The silo message in the rolly-phone had told him to look out for the vitamins in the mail. It told him to switch the pills for the vitamins. But it hadn't told him what the switch would do to I'm-Bobby.

Anger.

Zach was afraid of it when it was sent his way and when it

came from him. But maybe he shouldn't have been. Maybe Zach's anger was what he and Zach's mother needed.

"One day in the future, perhaps," Aidan said. "Not even in the distant future. For now, however, I ask you to trust me. I will see to this." The floorboards creaked as whatever Aidan was shifted again.

Zach now understood that while Aidan put on a weak voice when they first met so that he wouldn't scare Zach, he wasn't so weak at the time. He was weakened, and that wasn't the same thing. Aidan had only needed a place to hide until he'd recovered from whatever happened to him. From the burning-leaf smell that had hurt him. Zach let him stay, and now that smell was gone.

"Yes," Aidan said. "And I will not forget what you've done for me."

But Aidan also approved of the silo message's plan to switch Bobby's pills. "What happened to your mother was not the intent of the plan." His voice made the metal drawer pulls on Zach's dresser ring ever so slightly. Zach didn't know how it was that no one else ever seemed to hear Aidan when his voice could do things like that. But they didn't. "As you know, I would not ever allow such a thing to go on for long. Which is why I will never be far. From you."

Zach knew that wasn't completely true. It was bending the truth, as Zach's mother accused I'm-Bobby of doing before her knee told her not to think that.

No.

Not her knee.

What was in her knee.

To say it was her knee would be bending the truth.

Anyway, Zach knew Aidan traveled very, very far from him. He'd been doing that since the first time he promised he wouldn't. It was just that he could return to Zach very quickly.

"Yes," said Aidan. "I will be here. And I will care for whatever requires my care."

As angry as Zach was, he was worried about what Aidan meant by care. Zach didn't like I'm-Bobby. I'm-Bobby was not all right. But Zach didn't want to see I'm-Bobby badly hurt or killed, either.

"I wouldn't," Aidan said. "They'd only insert another into your lives."

Aidan had said that before. He never said who *they* were. And he never said he wouldn't hurt or kill I'm-Bobby because it was wrong to do that to people. He only said it wouldn't help them.

"True," Aidan said softly, and the ringing of the drawer pulls made it sound as if his rumbling voice had a little bit of a laugh to it. "I have noticed, though, that you merely wish him to not be hurt *badly*. How tragic it is when noble intentions desert one so young." The drawer pulls stopped their ringing, but the laughter of them lingered.

"Never far." With that, the closet floorboards sighed as they were relieved of their burden. The closet door eased closed in perfect silence, and the room allowed the light from the streetlamps in again.

Never far. Zach believed that only as much as he needed to in order to fall back asleep.

He would have told Aidan he believed it all the way.

But Aidan would know Zach was bending the truth.

61

NOTHING IS TRULY YOURS

He dreamt of walking in a garden. No one gripped his elbow or spoke to him. There was no voice. There was nothing.

In the way dreams go, what he knew as truth was absent. It left because it was never true—or because he had no right to it.

Paul had no claim to the truth because he'd done a great wrong, had believed a lie—and had told one long ago. He'd fought so hard for what he'd seen as right, only to perpetuate corruption. And even if he hadn't known at the time, he should have questioned more before deciding his actions were the answer.

That *he* was the answer.

That was why Paul was here.

Here was not the garden in which he found himself, beautiful as it was—its identical bonsai trees arranged in a way that perfectly inhabited both the space they occupied and the space between them.

Relief. Like a drawing using negatives.

Absence of awareness trumped the presence of it in Paul's

case, which was what allowed them to use him. To use all of them.

Relief. There would be none for him—or anyone.

Because of Paul.

Because of what Paul did.

For a long while, he didn't take more than a few steps into the garden, which was bounded by walls of gray stone and carpeted with crushed white rock bordered by clay bricks. At first, the bricks appeared to be randomly placed, but looking away from them at an angle revealed that they'd been placed with intent.

He just couldn't determine what it was.

Paul's fellow travelers in the garden were evasive, furtive. When he looked directly at them, they were but shadows. But when he gave his attention to the trees, there the others were.

The trees, for their part, were not merely identical. They were the same tree—in different locations, yet in the same place. And no matter which tree he thought he was approaching, he continued to walk in the same direction. No matter where he turned, he walked the length of the garden.

Likewise, the other garden-goers at the edges of his vision appeared to be going their own way, too—each in a random direction.

Yet they walked a path parallel to his. He knew what he had in common with them. But to accept it would doom him.

As he approached the garden's opposite end, the air around him grew hotter. The feeling was the same as what he'd experienced when unleashing the energies that ultimately served the ends of an unknown enemy.

Those who'd used him.

Shamed him.

The heat washed over and through him—poisoned air and light, an ill will turned too bright. This was all perception rather than reality, a memory of something that had happened long before. But with the heat came awareness.

Knowledge.

As the heat intensified, the others walking in the garden dissipated, becoming translucent. To his horror, Paul could see through their skin to their bones.

As one, they cried out.

As one, they raised hands and arms to shield themselves. It was useless.

They were skeletal.

Burnt black.

Eyeless.

Then ash.

And one lone voice—a child's—screamed in words Paul shouldn't have been able to understand but did.

An airplane.

When Paul fruitlessly held his hands up to block the assault of the heat and white light, he saw his own bones within them.

Paul knew what the garden was. Who and what it held. It had happened. Long ago and not to him, but it had.

To the others.

The light he couldn't take. The heat he would not be able to withstand.

No.

Paul had done this before and had not been undone. He would not now, either.

Not so the others. They fell around him, some struggling to hold themselves together, all failing.

Paul felt the tears dry on his cheeks as quickly as they fell. He registered his own cries, though he hadn't until then been aware he was shouting.

His ring—his mother's ring—held in front of his face with

his pointless hands, grew hot upon his finger, as it had at times before. It was as if it melted into him, though it appeared to float freely on the mist of his flesh.

Fear and pain without.

Fear and pain within.

He'd done this.

They'd done this.

How could they have committed such an act, and with such determination and sense of purpose?

Paul cried out. And when his cry died, so did the heat and light.

With it went the others in the garden, their still or writhing forms fading along with the unbearable embrace of a sun too close.

All was peace in the garden now, its pain and people gone.

The bonsai, too, were gone. Except for one at the end of the garden—the end he understood he now must approach.

Paul studied his hands, which were corporeal once more. They were unharmed. So was he, the ring on his finger as it always had been.

But something had changed. Understanding filled Paul when there'd been but flashes of it before. Of his situation and of those who'd only moments before been there with him.

Their deaths were not his, but he shared their current state.

Charges.

Those in the garden with him were charges from decades before, the victims of a great act of anger and violence intended to end a time of anger and violence. A black and egregious paradox that was not his, but with which he had shared history because of where he was born and what he'd done in The Commons.

Often those who thought themselves noble were ignoble as could be.

Such was Paul.

The garden of the wronged had been filled with charges, and now there was only one.

Paul.

For that's what he had in common with them in the strongest sense. Where they were stored, he didn't and couldn't know. Just as he didn't know where he himself was. Theirs had been a state of fire, his of ice.

Paul was in the garden and not in the garden. He was frozen somewhere, his Essence to be exploited.

The others were dead.

He was not.

But that wouldn't save him if he couldn't free himself.

Save himself.

And by doing so, save others—those he'd wronged with his actions and those he hadn't.

Twisting his ring—an old, nervous habit that sometimes managed to serve him well—Paul walked toward the one tree left. The other trees were this tree. The other charges were Paul.

If he stayed where he was, he'd never be able to help them move on to be at peace. And many more among the living would be at risk as well.

His steps were nearly silent, but the slight sound they did make was one of dust.

Dust and ash.

Paul stopped a short distance from the tree. Respect for the miniature tree, which had a mass and power of its own despite its size, kept him from stepping any closer to it. A beautiful presence, it had a shape eerily like the crime it had witnessed and survived.

Paul struggled to say something adequate. But when he opened his mouth to speak, he was stopped by a silent, gentle guidance.

No.

The word was not spoken, not heard in Paul's head. It was simply there.

And now he knew what he needed to tell the presence in front of him.

"I'm sorry," he said.

If the tree heard, it gave no sign. But Paul thought he sensed the dust and ash around him shift of its own accord. And that shifting was like a nod.

Turn.

At the opposite end of the garden, where there'd been nothing, stood another miniature tree. One Paul knew.

It stood unencumbered by the tourist walkway that had led up to it when last he'd seen it. A bonsai.

Paul remembered standing before it without understanding how such a memory could be real. It existed in isolation, without bookend events around it.

He'd stood before this tree but couldn't connect it with anything else. Yet he knew it had played an important part in other events.

The Dinuhos. That's what the tree was called.

Paul turned back to the survivor tree to tell it goodbye. He wanted to show it the proper respect.

It was no longer there.

This was no longer the same garden.

Paul turned back again. All that was there was The Dinuhos Tree. Even the crushed rocks and the paths bordered by the bricks had departed.

No, not the same garden at all.

Paul started walking. As he drew closer, the Dinuhos grew

The Margins

larger in a way that made him dizzy. And as he drew closer still, he saw why.

The Tree was growing.

As Paul closed the distance, a steeply arched bridge appeared over a moat surrounding the Tree. A moon bridge.

The moon bridge was steep enough that it had steps built into it, and Paul had to grab one of its railings to climb up and over. The Tree grew with every step Paul took. By the time he set foot on the other side, the Dinuhos had reached its full size.

There was a door in the trunk, so perfectly fitted that it was like a natural part of the Tree. In the place where a tiny doorknob should have been was a knotted silk cord that did not appear so much to be threaded through the door as much as it was an outgrowth of it.

Paul gave the cord the gentlest of tugs. He couldn't shake the feeling that he might hurt the Tree if he put any effort into it.

The door didn't move.

Of course. In his memory of the previous encounter with the Dinuhos, a cheesy tourist sign in front of it spelled out a process of leaving something and getting something.

He needed something to offer. But what?

As usual, Paul's wallet only had a couple of dollars in it. He sheepishly pulled the money out and was almost embarrassed to give the cord another tug to see if the Tree would accept it.

He wasn't surprised when the door was just as difficult to open as it had been before.

Paul checked his pockets. His flip phone.

He almost laughed at anyone wanting that, never mind a sentient, all-powerful tree. But it was his only other option. He opened it up and turned it on. "It works fine," he said. "And it's the only phone I've ever owned, so it's worth a lot to me."

He tried the door. No good.

"It means a lot to New Beginnings. I use it all the time." He almost couldn't finish that sentence, stupid as he felt. He hit the power to turn it off again, but found it was already shut down. There was his answer, then.

Paul had nothing else to try. He twisted his ring, thinking. Once. Twice.

The door in the Dinuhos opened of its own accord, its motion as unhurried and smooth as a resting butterfly's wing.

It took the growing warmth of the band around Paul's finger for him to acknowledge to himself what the Tree wanted.

His mother's ring.

No.

Paul said it to himself and then out loud.

The door didn't move.

"I'm sorry," he said. "I can't." Before he realized he was doing it, Paul pushed the door closed.

The door opened again with the same steady, lazy motion as it had before—a tulip petal greeting the sun.

The ring grew hot, to the point where it hurt.

This was a dream, Paul reminded himself, though it certainly didn't feel like one. How could there be enough heat to cause him pain? He was frozen in ice. When he'd woken up to find himself encased in it, unable to move, he'd known it was real. He was in charge state, though still alive.

He hoped.

The hot ring had hurt then because he'd actually been awake. But it hurt nearly as much now, in a dream.

If it was a dream.

It was.

Paul knew that, just as he knew the name of the Dinuhos. He was dreaming, but it was more real than any other he'd had, even more real than walking with the man and with Martha.

It hurt.

Not as much as it had in the ice, but still.

It hurt.

Instinctively, Paul pulled the ring from his finger, and it was immediately cool to the touch. It wanted to be away from him.

Paul's ring. The only thing he had left that had been Jeanne's.

The photo was precious, but that was merely an image. The ring had been on her—a part of her.

He looked inside it and read the words there, his hazily returned memories holding them within the misty recall of how they'd gotten there.

He remembered a marble.

A piece of glass.

He couldn't quite come up with the details on either of those things, but they'd been involved in the creation of the words.

All the time Paul had been at New Beginnings and Stella Grace, he'd forgotten. He'd assumed Jeanne had had the inscriptions engraved there and hadn't understood why, even after looking up the Latin.

Unus pro omnibus, omnes pro uno.

IMUURS.

One for all, all for one.

I am you. You are us.

Paul held the ring to his lips and closed his eyes, hoping for help from somewhere—from anyone—to guide him in this decision.

The piece of glass.

The marble.

Offerings.

One offers what one must.

"Mom," he said. He placed the ring inside the little chamber in the side of the Tree and closed the door again.

This time it stayed closed.

Recalling how the exchange worked, Paul waited a bit and gave the knotted cord a soft pull.

The door stayed shut.

Okay, he told himself. It wasn't meant to be an instantaneous trade.

He waited and tried again.

The door held fast.

Another moment and another attempt.

The same result.

Would the Dinuhos steal his ring from him? Or had someone else received it without giving anything in return?

What had he just done?

Paul tried to twist his ring. Of course, it wasn't there.

The heat and pain had been real. Was this a dream? Had he just been tricked into giving up the most precious thing he owned?

He didn't remember everything yet—many of his memories remained blurry or moved in fits and starts, like people seen through a glass-block wall—but he knew he needed that ring.

And he wanted it even more than he needed it.

It was his mother's.

His mother.

Paul tried the door again.

Nothing.

Now he didn't care if The Dinuhos Tree felt pain; he yanked the cord.

Still nothing.

He'd been duped. Fooled.

When he was on the street, and even when he'd been a resident of New Beginnings, such a thing would have marked him as prey. Maybe not bottom-rung, but someone to be targeted more readily than he would have before being exposed.

Naïve.

A punk.

Angrier now, Paul gave the cord another hard yank—hard enough that he lost his grip on it. His temper got the best of him. He pulled the cord as hard as he could several times. Now he hoped it hurt the damned Tree. On the last pull, he lost his grip again.

Paul took a few steps back and came into contact with the edge of the moon bridge. "Are you kidding me?" he said to the Dinuhos. He repeated the question, but with an additional word thrown in. Seriously? Now he was cursing a supernatural entity of unknown power—unknown other than the fact that it had a lot of it.

Before he knew what he was doing, Paul walked quickly over to the Dinuhos and smacked the door hard with the heel of his palm.

It hurt him more than the Tree, but he did it again.

And again.

Again, and again, and again.

The door in the Tree flew open, and the Dinuhos hit back. It was like someone had stiff-armed him. More like ten someones.

He went flying and ended up on his back on the bridge, the wind knocked out of him.

Again, it hurt.

And again, it didn't feel like a dream.

It should have kept him down. Hell, it should have snapped his spine. But the pain only increased his fury.

Paul was back up on his feet in an instant. Where that came from, he didn't know. Nor did he know the origin of the heat in his chest or why what should have been a real ache in his back became a near-unbearable thrum of energy crying to be set free.

There was no thought. Paul thrust his hands forward and felt a shockwave leave him, from the whole of him.

The barest question began to form in his mind. What was he doing? But he swatted that doubt away just as the force of him slammed into the Tree.

Paul didn't know how he was doing it, but he hit the Tree with a serious jolt that only rose in intensity as he leaned into it.

When the branches began swaying, Paul thought he'd begun to make his point, but the Dinuhos didn't so much as lose a leaf. Instead, the door opened wider, as if welcoming his attack.

Which only made Paul madder.

Somehow, he managed to direct even more force at the Tree. It had stolen from him. He knew it wasn't a rational thing to do in this situation, and as he gathered himself and went at the Tree again, he was aware that this had to be a dream because he wouldn't have reacted like this in real life—whatever that was—and wouldn't have done anything this stupid.

But the branches of The Dinuhos Tree merely continued to undulate, as if kissed by a breeze.

Paul hit it harder still. He broke out in a cold sweat, the force flowing through him from somewhere unknown but directed by him, given purpose. It was his to use so long as he used it with humility and with an understanding of the right and wrong of it.

He was attacking a tree. A sacred Tree honored and respected by all in The Commons.

This was right?

The door remained open, and Paul began to understand this, too.

Yes.

It was right.

This was his offering, together with his ring. Whatever it was he was meant to receive in return, it required something at this level from him.

Within moments, Paul was beyond intensifying his attack. He had lost control of what was coming through him, and he remembered the last time he'd done this, when he defeated the man at the heart of his last struggle.

Brill.

Mr. Brill.

And while he and Rain had thought they'd accomplished something good, it had not been so.

Dupe.

Fool.

Victim.

Whoever had done Paul wrong was going to be punished.

He pushed even harder, and it began to feel as if the river flowing through him was tearing at its own banks. Striking a new path. Plowing through a bend to form a newly straight route.

And still he leaned into it.

And still the river flowed through him.

The banks gave way within.

Sucker.

Patsy.

With one last rush through Paul and from him, the energy and the heat went cold.

The door in the Dinuhos shut.

Then the back of Paul's head met something hard behind him.

The moon bridge.

62

THE PLACE BETWEEN THEM

Porter assumed that offering his Newton to the Dinuhos was the right choice when the air in front of the Tree's open doorway began to shimmer. The chamber in the wood was heating up. Serious energies were being brought to bear, and The Dinuhos Tree was at the heart of it.

The offering had been his willingness to let the Dinuhos take the Newton if it wanted, and the Tree considered his sincerity sacrifice enough. Now, with the Newton sitting in what was rapidly becoming an oven, it might be destroyed if Porter didn't risk offending the Tree and reclaiming it.

Before he could doubt his reasoning, Porter made a grab for the Newton. He just as quickly withdrew his hand, shaking it in pain. "Are you able to get to it?" he asked Apalala.

"I think not," the young man said, but he stepped forward anyway.

The door snapped shut in an instant.

Apalala looked to Porter for guidance.

"He acts in my stead," Porter told the Tree. "I grant him full agency."

Now Apalala was able to open the door. A wave of fierce heat emerged. It was a wonder the Newton hadn't melted already, but that was probably a testament to its hidden strengths. Apalala reached in and grabbed it but wasn't able to pull it back out. "As I expected," he said.

Porter laid his hand on Apalala's arm. The heat was so intense, he had to pull away immediately. It wasn't at all clear how much was coming from the Dinuhos and how much from Apalala himself.

The brief contact between Porter and Apalala was enough for the Dinuhos to allow the Newton to be reclaimed. Apalala put it on top of the cabinet to cool.

The door remained open. The business at hand was not finished, though Porter had no idea what to do next.

Waves of heat continued to emanate from within the chamber. Heat—and something else.

Sounds.

Voices Porter could pick up as long as he didn't try to listen to them. Too faint for words, but there. He looked to Apalala.

"I have nothing to offer," the young man said.

Porter believed him. This was not Apalala's responsibility. His part was unclear beyond escorting Porter in a realm where he wouldn't have survived an hour otherwise. Who knew if he had any role to play beyond that?

An offering.

A sacrifice.

What forms might those things take? And what did Porter have to give up that would be meaningful?

Nothing.

No thing.

Which is what he did indeed have to offer.

More than one, in fact.

Porter dug into his pocket for Carl's ID badge. He was

unable to place it in the Dinuhos. Once again, the energies at play within it were far too much for him. He handed the card to Apalala.

The young man hesitated. It occurred to Porter that there was probably a very good reason the Dinuhos and Apalala were reluctant to interact—and he should probably have a thorough understanding of that before proceeding. Nonetheless, he nodded his encouragement to Apalala, who took the badge and placed it within the Dinuhos.

Carl's badge.

To Porter, it was seeing a debt called in from long ago, when he'd made decisions based on expediency rather than what was right. Envoys such as Carl Levy had been the ones to pay the price. Not for the choices of Porter alone, but that hardly mattered.

When Carl went missing during the time of Brill, Porter and the others in positions of authority made the mission of keeping the Journeys going the priority. Carl was an old hand, as were others who'd disappeared.

Porter knew Carl needed help. He tried to make the case that the most experienced of the Envoy Corps should be split off to locate him and the others who'd vanished. But word came down that the Brill issue would be worked out levels above, and Porter chose to respect the chain of command.

He had abandoned Carl and the other Envoys who were taken by Brill. He could hide behind protocol if he wanted, but that didn't change a thing.

By the time he cleared his docket and went looking, there was nothing to find. Carl was gone. So were the others.

When he returned to Envoy Headquarters to find the operations there depleted, too, he had no choice but to remain to stave off the disuse protocol and keep the facility open.

It was all a convenient excuse for his failure. And whether

this place was exploiting his guilt to hurt him, as Apalala said, or was revealing Carl's true fate to him didn't make much difference.

Carl had been a gentle man whose reason for being was the mission. He'd never failed to make things better for those in trouble.

No one had come running when he needed help.

If the Dinuhos would accept it, that was as good an offering as anything else Porter might have had to give. His guilt. His responsibility. His sorrow over what he hadn't done for Carl and the many Carls of the Envoy Corps.

Porter was willing to do whatever was required to balance the scales. The foolish act of jumping without a known destination had brought him here. If the Dinuhos, or The Commons, or whatever forces they acted in concert with wished it, he would do so again. Send him to his punishment or send him wherever he might do the most good. Porter would place himself in the hands of that power.

The Dinuhos's door began to grow. It stretched itself beyond the bounds of the cabinet. Perhaps that was just how Porter's senses and perception represented what was happening, but the waves of heat reaching out to embrace him firmly were no illusion. It was the touch of something preparing to take him onward.

Porter snatched the Newton from where Apalala had left it atop the cabinet. Fortunately, it had cooled enough for him to handle it, though the sense of warped reality that came with the energies enveloping him made it a real struggle to hang onto the device long enough to pocket it.

The Dinuhos had accepted Porter's offering. Acknowledging his debt to Carl and the others like him was not enough to repay it. Porter would have to settle that up another day, but the Dinuhos saw it as a fare of sorts. That and Porter's foolish willingness to place himself in its care.

What happened next would never be clear to him.

When Porter turned to thank Apalala for his help, the young man was no longer there.

Nor was the room itself.

Perhaps the Dinuhos and its doings blanked it out. Or maybe the room was no longer necessary.

Porter had no more time to think. He was being drawn into the Dinuhos. He held his staff tight against his chest, giving it a fast, tight turn as he did so. Over the course of his long career, he'd never have risked focusing his ability to jump without knowing his destination, yet here he was doing it for the second time.

Something behind him. A massive presence had taken the place of Apalala—or maybe it was Apalala.

It rushed past Porter, glancing off him with such force that his conscious mind was nearly knocked clear out of his head. He had a brief moment to wonder what might have happened had such a being directed its might squarely at him before the reality of the shift hit home.

This world was a strange place.

All the worlds were.

So was the space between them.

63

THE PRODUCT OF A DAMAGED MIND

"I won't say it, boss," Joel offered right after Po used the stick to cast Parix's skin aside and just before he attempted to step through the remnants of Porter's gateway. "I won't say it, but if you take me with you, we are not the friends I thought we were."

Technically speaking, then, Po and Joel's stated friendship remained, because neither of them went anywhere. When Po tried the degraded portal, his world turned inside out, and he woke up flat on his back in the fire pit after an indeterminate amount of time had passed.

Joel was frozen in place on his screen, and Po was forced to reboot him before he returned to his old self and could then spend the next five minutes lecturing Po on how lucky they both were that his misguided effort had failed miserably.

When Joel was again unable to raise Envoy HQ or anyone else, Po tried the only other thing he could think of.

"I'm not sure whose side you think you're on, but it isn't yours or mine," Joel told him a while later.

Po ignored him and continued stirring the water and ashes with a stick. It had taken him countless trips to the stream with the empty coffee can he'd found in the ruins of the Dew Drop Inn to fill the shallow fire pit with an adequate amount. It didn't make the chore any easier with Joel listing all of the ways the effort was foolhardy, dangerous, and the product of a damaged mind.

Po considered turning the Tamagotchi off for a while, but even Joel's companionship was better than none at all. Also, the chiding distracted him from how many trips he'd had to make.

"I know what you're trying to do, and I also know it's not going to work," Joel said. "You know it, too. I usually feel sorry for you at times like this, and I humor you while you screw up, but I think I'd do you a bigger favor by convincing you to stop. We can put our heads together and figure out something better."

Po finished stirring the ashes and water and looked into the puddle's surface. The resulting murky water presented a distorted vision of the sky and clouds above. He sat down, preparing to meditate, and signed to the Tamagotchi, presenting Joel with a choice.

Joel could join him in meditation and help in the quest for guidance. Or Po could drop him in the puddle so that he could explore what the water had to show them from the bottom up. Joel went with the former.

After a time, Joel pulled Po from his inner exploration. "Uh, boss?"

Po took a moment to bring himself back. Though Joel had probably refrained from meditating, at least he'd remained quiet.

Even if Joel hadn't joined him in an altered state, it seemed that someone or something else had. At one point while Po journeyed inward in his quest for a message from outside, he felt the familiar presence of whoever or whatever had been watching him while he waited for the gandy dancer. He didn't let on that he'd sensed this presence, hoping it might reveal itself, but it pulled away again.

Joel waited for Po to catch on to his reason for disturbing him.

There.

In the surface of the puddle, reflected in the floating ash as a presence of its own.

The Dinuhos Tree.

"You see it, too, right?"

As Joel spoke, the sun pierced the clouds above, revealing the Tree in perfect clarity, the little door in its trunk easily seen now.

An offering.

What was the Tree looking for from Po? What would it offer in return?

This was a development of note, for the last time Po saw the Dinuhos—with Rain, Ken, Paul, and Porter—he hadn't approached it. The only other time he ever encountered the Tree, he'd done the same. It was his belief that the Dinuhos had no interest in Po or any other mythical. The Tree was an inhabitant of the Journey—another way for a Journeyman to walk the given path.

Not now.

Now it was here for him.

"Hey. Hey! Don't screw around!" Joel shouted as Po held him out over the Tree's door in the water. "I tried! I meditated! Is it my fault I suck at it? I've got a lot on my mind!" When Po didn't move him any closer to the water, he fell into a hopeful silence but broke it when Po lowered him a little more. "Okay, okay. I didn't try. Happy? I didn't even try!"

No reaction from the Dinuhos.

Po hadn't expected one, and he was not at all prepared to

make an offering of Joel. He'd wanted to see if the Tree would respond. He withdrew the Tamagotchi.

"Wow. Wow, boss. I'll thank you now and yell at you later once I've pulled myself together," said Joel. "And don't you get all judgy on me for losing it, either. I'd love to see you try to maintain that tough-nut-to-crack routine of yours in such a position. Yes, indeed—I would love to see it."

Po dropped Joel into his pocket to muffle whatever else he had to say. The Tamagotchi clacked against something else down in there.

Po knew what his offering would have to be—and knew it without any sign from the Dinuhos.

Was he truly ready to part with it? No. That was why it was needed—because something precious had to be risked.

Po withdrew the offering from his pocket and held it out over the water. For a long, worrisome moment, nothing happened. Then came the click of the door in the Dinuhos unlatching, the sound tempered by the water.

"Boss," Joel said, all humor and rebellion gone. "Boss, no."

Po lowered his offering to the water's surface as the image of the Dinuhos in the water became perfectly clear. The open door beckoned, growing larger as Po's hand was just about to touch it.

"Boss. Boss, wait!"

The Tamagotchi's urgency came too late. Fast as he was, Po was unable to pull back before the open door of the Dinuhos claimed him.

Even if he had been able, the rush of the familiar but unnamed presence approaching quickly, overwhelming him as he entered the Tree's void, would have prevented any retreat.

Po was pulled into the Dinuhos.

The oncoming mystery presence was pulled in with him.

That was Po's final understanding before he transitioned to another plane, another world. The presence that had trailed and watched sought to accompany him through the door.

The Dinuhos allowed it.

It closed the watery portal behind Po, and he left The Commons.

64

YOU COUNTED YOURSELF LUCKY

Audra was exhausted. The only thing that kept her climbing up out of the basement was the entirely made-up hope that perhaps The Commons would see fit to have an elevator waiting when she reached the first floor. There was no chance of making it back up to her apartment on her own—none whatsoever.

Everything had gone the way she'd wanted. The Dinuhos had taken her locket, its door refusing to open again after Audra placed her offering within it. She'd waited, knowing the situation wasn't going to change but hoping all the same. Then she'd accepted what she'd already known to be true: nothing remains yours because nothing ever is.

As was the case with the awesome abilities granted to Paul Reid.

As was the state of Porter's powers and hers—all of it borrowed.

Life, too.

You cared for these things as best you could. And when it was time, you gave them up with grace and moved on. If you had any say in the timing of it, you counted yourself lucky.

Audra was not so lucky when she finally reached the top of the basement stairs and half-staggered into the first-floor hallway. There'd been as many steps on the way up as there had been on the descent, but it certainly seemed like more. And there was no mercy offered as a reward for her good work.

She had only the energy to note that everything looked the same as it had. There was no gift of an elevator awaiting her.

Such was the way of The Commons.

Such was the way of all.

Sliding sideways along the wall, Audra let it support her as she closed her eyes and waited for her breath to finish the climb and catch up with her. She wouldn't let herself ease down any lower. Nor was she foolish enough to sit, knowing she'd never find her way to her feet again.

She allowed her eyes to close briefly—and became increasingly aware of the change that had visited the hallway since she'd left, which seemed like a good week before.

At some point, it had rained. The air making its way through the still-open door brought with it the smell of damp earth warmed by the sun. It was the promise of the new and still-to-come, the heartbeat of a small hope but a hope all the same—even for an old woman who often believed she'd long ago outlasted her purpose, her shot at happiness.

Rain.

Rain and the deliverance of rain.

The suggestion of a nearby shuffling foot, then further whispers of more, returned Audra to the here and now. The act of opening her eyes brought a gift of its own—the beauty of the sunlight making its way into the hall through the open door.

Whether the rays' origin was The Commons or some other realm, she could not say. In the developing reality she and the others faced, it would be difficult to determine such things. But it didn't matter nearly as much as what Audra chose to see in the light: a brilliant attagirl for a mission accomplished.

Or nearly.

The wall moved upward across her back. No, quite the opposite.

Tapped out as she was, Audra was slowly losing her fight with gravity and sliding toward the floor.

Just as her tired weight accelerated her slow fall to the point where it wouldn't be so slow anymore, she stopped. She had the absurd idea that the sunlight held her. Then the small fingers gripped her clothing, softly lending her the vitality of youth.

They'd waited.

The children had waited.

All this time, in the face of the open door and the first freedom they'd been offered in eons, they had stayed put until she made it back.

Now they raised her up.

Audra struggled to speak but knew there was nothing to be said. She was picked up and held aloft on a bed of fingers and hands—a bed so careful that as the unseen children began to climb the stairs with their drained burden, she felt herself drifting off to sleep.

Mercifully, the enriching smell of the recently fallen rain stayed with her for the first few flights, defeating the rotten stink of the pursuing monster that had called this stairway realm its own. Her deep breaths eased her mind further as a pleasant darkness overtook her, and she happily allowed it to do so.

Audra didn't awaken until she felt herself being gently placed on her feet outside the door to her apartment amid the shuffling of the silent children—far more than were necessary to complete her journey. Perhaps that was their way of showing their gratitude—by accompanying her all the way up or, maybe, by taking turns bearing her.

Once on her feet, Audra leaned back against the door and felt herself begin to slide downward once more. The much-needed slumber was not finished having its way with her.

As she went under, she felt the hands again and heard the deep thunk from within the door as it unlocked itself for her small, ancient saviors.

When she awoke, Audra was alone in her dark apartment, its door closed and locked. She considered her own long-passed days of running out through doors once the skies cleared—flying free and fast, chasing the magic that surely awaited her there in the vital blues and greens.

The children had been exposed to the dark beast for so long. Maybe now they'd find the white horse. Who would call them foolish for trying?

They hadn't said goodbye.

But they'd certainly said thank you.

∽

THE WHINE of the wire reader and its printer roused Audra from a deep state of rest. Once again, she hadn't felt herself going under.

She turned the bedside lamp on, rubbed her eyes into a greater state of wakefulness, and sat up. She was hungry, but she felt much better. And for the first time in a long while, her sense of well-being was complete. More important was the absence of pain.

She asked herself the question, and the answer pleased

her. The burns no longer troubled her; she'd healed. She was as ready as she could hope to be for whatever came next.

She made her way to the flow of connected pages emerging from the printer and began to read. The enormity of what she and the others had pulled off with the Dinuhos made itself known to her.

Later, Audra didn't know how long the printer had been silent, its message delivered. Nor did she count how many times she'd read the missive in order to ensure she hadn't let anything important slip by.

The only thing that stopped her from reviewing it again was when she returned to the first page for yet another read-through, only to discover that the paper was blank. It had erased itself.

Trusting an old lady's memory—and this old lady in particular? Desperate times indeed.

She thought it through for a long while, considering it from all angles.

Then she dug in the closet for her rolling bag and started packing.

65

MYSTERY TRAIN

The instructions from Charlene told Rain to pack for a long trip, to continue eating the Sisu until the entire box was gone, and to keep an open mind.

Rain.

With each Sisu down, there was less and less of Ray-Anne. Not that she had a problem with her. But Ray-Anne wasn't her entirety. Ray-Anne was the girl she might have been had the angle of her life gone a couple of degrees higher or lower at the beginning.

Rain was everything.

Rain packed a gun.

Rain used a gun.

And Rain didn't have much use for anything or anyone else.

Except for Paul.

He and Ray-Anne were friends. He and Rain were something more. Maybe. That would have to be sorted out the next time she saw him.

If she did.

And even then, it was going to be a while, assuming they

both were the same people when they came out the other side.

If they did.

A lot of what Charlene told her—the most important things—weren't in the language of the texts at all. They were in the lines of thinking the texts put into her head, mixed with everything the Sisu was shaking loose.

Bat-dung crazy, she'd said before. Only it wasn't. This was the real part. And she was increasingly becoming the real Rain.

Which was why, when she was told to pack for a long trip, she was perfectly comfortable with not having much to take with her. A few changes of clothes, a bit of food she doubted she'd need, her new ride, and her gun.

She would need that. And she feared that ultimately, the gun was all she ever would need.

Thus, midnight found Rain at the Albany brown-line stop. That in itself told her this would be a trip for the books.

There was no such thing as an Albany stop on the brown line. Not until tonight.

Between her wandering ways and her need to learn Chicago as well as she could, Rain knew the L. She'd taken every line from end to end countless times while setting up New Beginnings, hopping off at every stop to see if she could find any kids who needed help. At Rockwell. And Francisco, which was the next stop headed west. Albany had been just another street between those two stops.

Now, there was a compact platform with a kind of ramp she'd never seen at any other street-level stop—one that allowed her to ride her bike up it to wait for the train. A ramp that seemed to have been built just for her.

Which was crazy. But wasn't, if her Sisu-restored memory was true.

And it was. All of it. Just as Charlene was someone to heed, even if whoever was texting her wasn't actually Charlene.

Rain trusted her gut. And while she allowed for the possibility that there was a real Envoy named Charlene who knew Jonas Porter, she didn't believe that was the person directing her.

So why board this train? Because of that same gut feeling. The Commons and wherever the hell she was now often let you know whether you were headed the right way or not. For now, this felt right.

Rain hoped so. Because when things shifted, The Commons often informed you that you'd made a wrong turn in a language you didn't survive.

A pair of lights announced the train's approach before the sound reached her, but they were different from those of the usual CTA train. It occurred to Rain that there were no gates to drop across the nearby street, either. It was as if whoever operated this mystery train knew nobody would ever try to cross in front of it. Or maybe the station was only here for her and would be gone as soon as she departed.

A block south on Albany, a black SUV heading west slowed and came to a stop in the intersection, a sinister rolling roach surveilling her.

Rain tried to keep her eyes off whoever it was giving her a look-see, but the dark truck rung her bells. There had to be somebody behind the wheel. But in the dark, with its black windows, it was like the truck itself was watching her. She forced herself to look away.

The train was a yellow maintenance type she'd never seen before. It appeared to be an antique from the days of the abandoned elevated tracks next to the red line. The engine passed her, its windows all blacked out. An open flat car with wooden safety rails and a chain gate stopped in front of her. Behind the flat car were a half-dozen or so closed freight cars.

Something about them reminded her of Paul, or something she'd done with Paul. Something important they'd thought was good—but might not actually have been.

None of which stopped Rain from boarding once she realized nobody was going to get out and help her load up. She got off her bike and unhooked the chain gate, which dropped with a chorus of clinking. She then flopped the steel ramp, attached to the car via a long hinge, down onto the platform so she could wheel the bike up.

Down Albany, the black SUV backed up, turned toward the train, and began a slow approach. It didn't have its lights on.

Rain pretended not to notice the truck as she secured her cycle with the set of on-board cables, reversed the procedure with the ramp and chain, and took a seat on her cycle.

The train left the station. Rain looked back over her shoulder at the SUV as it reached the chain gate and stopped. It sat like a frustrated predator that had read the situation too slowly and missed its chance.

Rain still had no sense of anyone behind the wheel. She popped another Sisu as the train picked up speed.

They didn't stop at Francisco.

Or Kedzie.

Or Kimball, which was the end of the line.

Those stations didn't exist for this train.

The train didn't stop until it passed through a whole run of suburbs and a few small towns before crossing through long stretches of prairie that couldn't have been as open and empty outside the real Chicago as it was here.

The tall grass flowed by like water in the light of the waxing-gibbous moon, whiter than white. Again, what part of

Chicago's suburbs were they going through that it was so barren?

Several heads floating above the terrain watched her. A half-dozen deer feeding in the chin-high grass took a break to witness her passing. One floated higher than the rest and sported a pair of impressive antlers.

The animals didn't seem to be spooked by the train's passing. Even they knew more about the train and its journey than Rain did.

The texts instructing Rain to catch this ride had been equal parts cryptic and alarming, though until the Sisu unlocked the rest of her memory, she wouldn't fully comprehend what they meant:

Go west. The boy who saved you needs you. Return the favor.

Rain wondered if those deer might be rooted to the same spot when she came back.

Then she wondered if she'd come back.

66

THE AURA OF ONE'S OWN SIN

The morning after the destiny round, Jeremy couldn't remember how he'd gotten home. He might have babysat Abel again. Or Abel might have babysat him. Maybe they'd gone their separate ways. Or maybe Jeremy disappeared like the other drunks, and when he stepped outside, nobody'd seen him. Invisibility could only have improved things, given his current state of misery and what it told him about his last waking hours of the extended night.

He had no memory of getting sick again. Yet there was evidence he hadn't wanted his own bathroom to think he'd been cheating on it with the one at Billy Clyde's. Amazingly, he was able to clean that up to a reasonable degree after forcing himself upright, mostly because the idea of walking out the door and returning later to find it still there was unacceptable.

His mouth tasted like punishment. He may have brushed his teeth, but he would never know because his breath would have smelled like a recently reopened grave no matter what he'd done.

Sound and light were intolerable offenses. For some

reason, the click of his toaster was especially painful, even though the little box delivered to him the life-giving gift of slightly browned toast. Once he let enough butter melt in, the gymnastics his stomach performed became a little less medal-worthy, and that would have to do.

Everything took forever.

He nearly threw up in the shower but was able to win that battle.

Dressing himself was an achievement that almost made him burst into tears.

Headed to work, he swore people were watching him without looking at him—all of them privy to what he'd spent the night doing, all of them aware of the knowledge he carried with him.

For while he might not remember how he'd gotten home—he'd have to piece that together with Abel, if possible—he hadn't forgotten what he'd been told. And in his current state, it didn't matter how outlandish the revelation was; he still believed it.

Jeremy wouldn't let the thought occupy his mind for long—not with his psyche in its current flayed state. He didn't think he could stand it. He'd already decided not to bring the matter up with Abel when he saw him—and to do everything within his power to deflect a discussion of it should Abel himself raise the topic.

Not now.

He was sick enough already.

The pain was too great already.

Not now.

Mass transit was designed to punish people with hangovers. The motion. The smells. The noise. He deserved it all. For everything he'd ever done, ever.

For all of that, his biggest fear was what it would be like to see Abel while feeling like this. Maybe Abel was worse off and wouldn't show.

No, that wouldn't happen. Because it would make things easier.

And Jeremy didn't deserve easy.

There were only two possibilities for the morning. Either Abel would want to talk about it, and Jeremy would have to find the strength to refuse, or Abel would pretend everything was normal.

In the latter case, Jeremy would be left wondering if the awful thing was true. And if Abel regretted trusting him.

Never mind that all of that wasn't nearly as bad as the thing itself.

Which he really would not think about.

When he walked into the office, his first two encounters with people did not bode well for the day.

Edgar, from the mail room, gave him a bright good-morning greeting on his approach but did a double take as Jeremy passed his package-laden cart. Jeremy thought he heard him snicker.

Abby, coming out of the ladies' room, was worse. When they passed each other, she gasped.

It was as he'd feared, though that worry, too, was something he thought might prove harmless if he refused to acknowledge its presence. Brushing his teeth and showering hadn't eliminated the marks of his guilt. Jeremy exuded last night's excesses. From the polluted core of his being, he emitted the stench of a brewery gone wrong.

Not good for the career, certainly.

He'd just have to head for his desk and pray he didn't encounter Mr. Truitt or any higher-up. He'd never seen Mr. Callibeau. With luck, today wouldn't be the day.

He ducked into the men's room to splash some water on

his face. It didn't help. He tried to smell himself, but that wouldn't help, either. One wasn't capable of detecting the aura of one's own sin. That was part and parcel of the self-inflicted curse.

Jeremy checked the mirror. Another mistake. He needed what little confidence he'd managed to carry into work with him. He'd hoped for a better result, but the man in the mirror looked positively dope-sick.

Great.

Jeremy concocted an instant survival plan. He'd go straight to his desk. He'd try not to vomit on it. He'd follow wherever Abel wanted to lead. If Abel wanted to talk, they'd talk. About whatever Abel wanted. His stomach did a short floor-mat routine at the notion, but he was the boss here.

On the way, he got lucky. Not only didn't he pass anyone important, he didn't pass anyone at all. That was good, but it also meant he had the mental space to freak himself out all over again about talking to Abel.

Not a problem.

Abel wasn't there.

Which ended up being a bigger problem. A large enough one that Jeremy forgot about how sick he felt.

There was no sign that Abel had ever sat in the space.

No sign he'd ever worked at Manitou at all.

And when Jeremy was finally able to ask the few people with whom he felt he had at least a minor rapport, not one of them had ever heard of Abel Dowd.

67

MIDNIGHT ANGELS

When Paul came to his senses, he had his ring back—and was already twisting it. He'd been in a standing sleep or some sort of stupor. It was a miracle that he was on his feet.

Now he found himself in the middle of a road, in the middle of the night, in the middle of nowhere, cornfields on either side. There was no moon above and a bit of cloud cover, which made for near darkness. But still Paul moved to the side of the road. He'd never regret not getting run over, no matter his surroundings.

His shoes crunching in gravel, he gently probed his lower chest, where the tentacle had struck him, with his fingers. It was tender. So that had happened.

The freshness of the night air, the grinding complaint of the roadside stones underfoot, and the soreness of the site of the strike all convinced him he was no longer dreaming—he was awake.

With his memory now intact.

That was the part Paul would have to let in slowly. He had memories of two Pauls, both of which led to one.

He remembered The Commons. He understood that when he came back to life, everything that happened there had been wiped from his memory.

It had happened to Rain, too. She went by Ray-Anne, her birth name. She was a very good liar, but not good enough to fake all that.

He hoped.

For now, he'd have to believe that she, too, had been restored to life without any memory of what happened to her in The Commons. And a lot had.

A lot had happened to both of them—with a great deal of pain tied to it. That would all have to be let in slowly so that it didn't take him down to a dark place and never let him up again.

Paul and Rain had loved one another. He'd tried to figure out if he had feelings for her while they worked together in New York and when they relocated to Chicago to help establish a New Beginnings location there.

Or was that here?

Where was he?

Either way, whatever forces blanked their memories also made them put aside their short but meaningful history together.

Maybe it was whoever tricked them into doing what they wanted. Paul still had no idea what that was. And it was yet another thing to hold at bay if he wanted to keep his head together.

The anger.

The anger and the shame.

He and Rain had been used, along with Ken, Porter, Po, Annie, Zach, and so many others—many unknown to him— who'd been a part of what they'd accomplished.

They'd won, they'd thought. They'd done the right thing.

Only it was the wrong thing.

They'd been taken advantage of.

Exploited.

Paul knew all about that.

So did Rain.

Paul walked. One step followed another.

He had no idea where he was going, and while he wanted to believe that didn't matter, he knew damned well it did. He had to find Rain and see if she was safe. He needed to know who the tentacled creature with the accent—Tentacle Dracula — was and why he'd attacked Paul. And he had to figure out if it might happen again.

Steps. One after the other—in the darkness, with the protests of the gravel documenting his pace as he walked.

Paul didn't know how long it had been since he'd eaten, and he wondered why he wasn't hungry. He'd often gone without eating in The Commons, too, but he always ate eventually. It just hadn't been quite as necessary there as it was in The Living World. Why?

No clue.

Paul didn't know a whole lot about his situation. He had his guesses about what might have happened, between the now-empty Chicago, the now-empty New Beginnings, and the way he'd been attacked. And he understood that Tentacle Drac had intended to keep him as a charge.

The ice. He'd been in a charge state.

But his dream had been real. He'd sent a hell of a lot of Essence into the Dinuhos, which he understood was his true offering to free himself—and was probably how he ended up out on the road. But how far away had the Tree sent him? And why did he have his ring back?

He was just glad to have it. And the rest he aimed to find out. Now that he remembered what he was capable of, he didn't care if he had to go through Tentacle Drac to figure it out.

That feeling lasted for about the next mile or so as it began to sink in that he really didn't know where he was. He remembered being in a basement when he'd woken up, with Tentacle Drac speaking to him. That much had been real.

He thought.

Paul pulled out his flip phone and turned it on.

Two bars on its charge but no signal.

He turned it off to conserve energy and pocketed it again.

Walking.

For whatever reason, anything involving The Commons meant a lot of walking.

Was that where he was now? Was this The Living World? Maybe it was some strange in-between place, like the version of Chicago he'd been in with the dog.

The dog.

Paul could still hear Angus's yelp as he was attacked. Tentacle Drac had better not have hurt him.

He covered more distance in the dark.

Was he going the right way? What did the right way mean?

He wasn't himself; his brain was foggy, free-floating. And why not?

If he understood what he'd endured, he'd been knocked out by a monster, gone into an icy charge state, and then been sent by the Dinuhos through time and space onto a country road in the middle of nowhere.

God, he hoped it wasn't nowhere. Nowhere was no joke now. Maybe it wasn't just farm country.

It could be nothing. In a nothing dimension.

The possibility was so disturbing to Paul that he almost broke his nose walking into some sort of wooden structure blocking the road's shoulder. Once he'd checked for blood and felt none, he ran his fingers over the surface of his passive assailant until he felt the letters carved into it.

A sign.

He stepped back. Even in the moonless dark, he could make out the silhouettes of peaked roofs to the right, beyond where he stood. They continued off into what had probably been more cornfields before this mystery development was built.

Out came the phone again. He turned it on, and by its weak light, he was able to make out: "You're home! Badger Glen! Luxury homes and first-house prices!" Under that was what might have been someone's name and phone number, but a piece of press board had been stapled over most of it.

Pop Mike had talked about such places when he'd lecture Paul and Rain—he knew her as Ray-Anne, Paul reminded himself—about the evils of the suburbs and the exurbs beyond, as if they might at any moment flee the city for a life among the shopping strips and big-box stores. They both tried to tell the old man they'd never do such a thing. But their arguments never stopped him from talking about, for instance, how these bubble-funded developments were nearly always named after whatever had been killed or destroyed to make way for them.

Here was yet another data point for Pop Mike's theory. Any badgers that might have lived here had probably perished in the construction of what appeared to be a whole neighborhood of vacant homes, whether they were empty the way New Beginnings and Chicago had been empty or deserted because nobody had ever bought any. Given the covered-up office-contact information, he was willing to bet it was the latter.

Contact information.

The phone.

Paul really was foggy. He hadn't noticed that in addition to the two bars on the phone's battery reading, he also had three on the signal side. He must have wandered near a tower. Or whatever passed for one wherever he was. Either way, he had service.

Paul was about to see if he could reach anyone when his head cleared further. Or maybe his survival instincts were coming back online. Either way, he put it together.

Empty. Unsold.

When he considered the basement the tentacle vampire kept him in, he knew.

Paul closed the phone and turned it off. In this dark, the light would be seen from quite a distance away—and certainly from whichever of these houses he'd been in.

Stupid.

So stupid.

The Dinuhos had freed him. It got him out of the basement and out of the charge state, and what had he done? Walked all the way back to the place where he'd been held.

More walking—faster, fueled by fear. What was that he'd been thinking about wanting to take on Tentacle Drac again?

No.

He wanted nothing to do with the vampire squid until he knew who and what it was.

Where this was.

Where Rain was.

And Porter.

And all the rest.

Who had they been tricked into helping, and what was the situation now?

Whatever it was, it was bad enough that Paul had had the urgent need to return to The Commons for some time. That was why he'd made a run at what had seemed like the only way to get there.

But he'd also told Rain—Ray-Anne at the time—the truth. He didn't really need to return to The Commons. It was coming to them.

And whatever that meant, it didn't mean anything good.

He walked as fast as he could, foggy brain or no.

Periodically, he checked his phone against his chest in order to block the light. He didn't want to go so far that he lost the signal again.

Time to call in the cavalry, assuming there was one to call. He had all of three numbers stored in his phone because saving contacts via its old-fashioned tech was a pain.

Three chances to get some help or, at least, a ride home or a ride to someplace safe.

Only three.

Yet Paul was almost afraid to start trying due to the very real possibility that nothing would work. Then where would he be?

Wait.

Was this really the guy Pop Mike had trusted to open a new New Beginnings talking? The guy who, if the memories still finding their place in his head were to be believed, had taken down an ancient villain and freed the Afterlife, even though he'd made things worse in some unknown way?

Paul wouldn't let the answer be anything but no.

Call one went to Rain.

It didn't even ring, which wasn't a good sign. Had something happened to her? Was he in a place where her phone number didn't exist? Or she didn't?

The second stored number was for New Beginnings Chicago. He skipped that one. The building was empty. Plus Tentacle Drac had already been there once, and Paul didn't know if trying the phone there might let him know Paul's whereabouts, for whatever reason.

He was a vampire squid, after all. Anything was possible.

The third stored number was a long shot. It rang, at least. And when the voicemail message told him the Midnight Angels were busy but would call back as soon as possible, he left a message telling them how important it was and that he needed help.

Then he waited.

As he did, he found himself going over what had happened to him in The Commons, like he was reviewing files on a recently discovered backup drive.

Fighting.

Love.

Friendship.

Pain.

Winning.

His side had won. No matter how it turned out or whose purposes they'd fulfilled, they'd won.

Paul wanted to say nobody could take that away from him.

But somebody had.

When whoever was manning the Midnight Angels help line called back, Paul clapped the phone into his hand to cover up its light and realized it was dumb luck that he'd left the ringer on silent mode.

On both sides of the road, it felt like the corn was just looking for Paul to let his guard down so it could spit some new horror out at him.

Paul answered, keeping his voice low, all the while scanning the rows to see if the corn had any children lying in wait.

Then he tried to squelch that thought.

∽

"Can you believe I was already out this way?" The shifting of Jabari's impressive bulk as he drove made it look like a mountain topped with a forest's worth of dreadlocks had collapsed onto the steering wheel, even though he had the seat all the way back.

Paul couldn't believe that, actually. By the time the Midnight Angels RV came rumbling down the highway, he'd been absolutely convinced that Tentacle Drac or some equally malevolent mythical was going to leap out of the corn and take him back to the basement.

All his previous feelings of power and his desire for a good scrap were gone. By the time he recognized his ride and stepped out to wave it down, he was in a near-panic over the idea that he'd be recaptured or would starve out there in the abandoned exurbs.

Midnight Angels was the mobile outreach organization New Beginnings frequently worked with in Chicago. Runaways and street kids often didn't want to go to a facility for help due to trust issues, or pride, or because they were mostly okay with their living situation.

So Midnight Angels roamed Chicago to keep the channels of communication open, hitting known gathering spots to offer medical care, a ride to a hospital, personal-hygiene supplies, and a caring soul to talk to. Jabari and his crew didn't pressure anybody to come with them, but if asked, they brought those who wanted to get out of their situation to New Beginnings or a handful of other places around town.

Jabari had been out this way, miles from the city, taking a little girl home who'd wandered into Midnight Angels with no good answer for how she'd gotten there. She hadn't been able to tell him an address—just a town name—but squealed when she spotted a familiar landmark. A moment later, she'd disappeared from the RV.

"That's how it's been," Jabari explained after telling Paul about finding the Midnight Angels facility in the same deserted state as New Beginnings in what they were calling Ghost Chicago. "If anybody shows up looking for help, it's a kid. And not a kid who's run away. They're way too little for that. They just show up. And it's like it's a game to them—like they don't know they're supposed to be scared, or they think it's a dream until you tell them it's not. And that's not even the weird part."

"What's weirder than that?"

Jabari turned to look at Paul for a long moment—long enough to cause concern.

"The road. Please, Jabari. Sometimes it curves."

Mercifully, the big guy turned his attention back to his driving duties. He sucked his teeth a couple of times, deliberating.

"Look," Paul said. "Whatever you've got won't shock me. If I start talking first, you're gonna think I'm the crazy one."

Jabari thought it over a while more. "They're not lost, like I was telling you. Maybe they're just visiting, and it's fun for them to see something new. But then?" He sucked his teeth again.

"They decide it's not fun?"

"Could be. Maybe that's why they disappear."

"What do you mean disappear?"

"I mean they don't walk out. I mean you look away for a second." He snapped his fingers and watched Paul for another uncomfortably long stretch, trying to spot any signs of disbelief or mockery.

"Would you believe me if I said I believe you?"

Jabari nodded and turned his attention back to the road again.

"And I'll tell you how I ended up out here." Paul faced

forward to watch the oncoming yellow bullets of the road's center line. "Just not everything about it. I don't think you're crazy. So I'll take a risk with you the way you just took one with me. But not a big one. Not yet." Paul waited for a dozen road bullets to pass under the RV. "If I told you everything, you'd lock me in the back." He took a breath to steady himself. Then he started talking.

And Jabari knew enough to keep his eyes on the road so that Paul didn't have any excuse to stop.

68

THE B.C. GUARDIAN

Po lay face down on a stone floor in a stone room. The floor and walls were all a matching gray.

As he got to his feet, he thought the Dinuhos might have sent him to a prison, but no—he was in a bedroom. An ornate canopy bed, large enough for a family of four with a full complement of pets, claimed a good portion of one wall. A small secretary's desk occupied the opposite wall, as did a hand-painted chest of drawers with a stacker atop it. Next to that stood a dressing table with a trifold mirror hanging above it.

The most curious item in the room was a quarter-round unit that was a little higher than the dresser and just as wide, with a chimney-type hole in its top emitting a steady plume of steam. It was either a large vaporizer or a warming unit for the room's inhabitant, who didn't appear to be home at the moment. Next to it was an arched stone doorway sealed by what looked to be a sturdy wooden door.

Po checked Joel. The Tamagotchi was in sleep mode, his little animated eyes closed, with a "z" in a thought balloon over his head. He tapped the unit but got no response.

Joel was Joel. He would awaken when he was ready.

On the wall behind Po was a tall, thin window with an arched top. The Dinuhos had sent Po to some sort of castle. Po opened the window and was about to risk sticking his head out to see how high up he was, thus making himself vulnerable to whoever might enter the room, when a loud, bestial roar split the quiet air of the space and bounced around the stone walls, echoing.

Po whirled, preparing to defend himself. The Dinuhos-imposed trip had rattled him more than he'd thought. He should have sensed a presence in the room or, barring that, had the wherewithal to check more carefully before turning his back on it.

The head of a jowly leopard, its fur dripping wet, whiskers weighed down with moisture, regarded him from the formerly empty steam chimney atop what Po had assumed to be the giant vaporizer.

It was a portable sauna.

Po remained in his fighting stance.

"Jeez," said Joel, now jolted into wakefulness. The Tamagotchi tried to project an annoyed confidence, but beneath that was a bit of a quiver. He didn't fool Po. The roar had startled both of them.

"Who are you? How did you get in here?" said the leopard in the deep, pampered voice of someone accustomed to having his questions answered.

Po said nothing. He watched the zipper atop the sauna for any movement signaling that the leopard was coming out.

"We're not answering that first one, and the second one's a long story," Joel said as Po dropped his guard. The leopard made no move to exit the unit, but Po adjusted position until he had the wall at his back and the door to the room out of the corner of his eye.

"Then why are you here?"

"Who wants to know?" Joel was being a bit feistier than Po thought was necessary.

"The B.C. Guardian wants to know!" the leopard growled with as much authority as he could muster. "I'll ask the questions. Why are you addressing me through a toy?"

Po began to sign that Joel was not a toy.

Joel began to tell the B.C. Guardian exactly what he thought of that designation.

The sauna's zipper jiggled as the leopard struggled to open it from within. "You are trespassers here in the B.C." The leopard endeavored to hide his difficulties in freeing himself. "I don't know how you got in here, but it doesn't matter. I am the Guardian. Now you must pay the ultimate price."

That was enough to silence even Joel, as it was clear that the Guardian, his head exposed and his body, paws, and claws confined, was wide open to attack.

The sauna zipper remained uncooperative. The Guardian tried harder, and the sauna rocked back and forth. The zipper would not give. The leopard sighed and gave up, and the sauna returned to a restful state. "I know I threatened you," the leopard said. "But is a little help too much to ask?"

Joel laughed.

Po just watched, genuinely curious to see what the Guardian might try next.

"Honestly, I'm not the guardian of anything." The leopard had lost all bravado. "I'm a prisoner here. Of the castle, not this sauna." The zipper quivered under another assault, and the unit rocked anew, but it held. The Guardian sagged in defeat, his head sinking down into the hole a bit.

Po approached the sauna with caution, wary of any tricks.

"Are you a praying monk or a fighting monk?" said the Guardian.

Po presented his fists in response, and the Guardian strained against the rim of the sauna chimney to get a closer look at the callouses and scars on Po's knuckles. "I'm no warrior," he said. "If I come out of here, do you promise not to hurt me?"

Po nodded, and Joel laughed. A downward glance from Po shut the Tamagotchi up. Po reached out and gave the zipper a pull. It didn't budge.

"Hang on," said the Guardian, shifting positions within the sauna.

Po gave another tug, and the leopard pulled from the inside. The zipper freed itself with a pop and moved easily downward.

"Do you mind?" A paw poked through the open zipper and pointed to a thick terry cloth robe hanging from one of the bed posts. The paw was large enough to be imposing, and the leopard did have claws. But they were the weapons of a stuffed animal, not a predator.

Po retrieved the robe and handed it to the leopard, who stared Po down until he understood the request for propriety. He turned his back after tossing Joel over his shoulder to keep an eye out in case the leopard tried anything.

"Okay."

Po faced the leopard and the sauna again.

The unit stood open, curtains of steam now free to rise from it. The leopard watched Po, apparently awaiting some sort of reaction to him standing there in his robe.

Po didn't understand what was required of him.

"I'm trying to lose some weight," the Guardian said. Indeed, there wasn't much room to spare in the robe, even given its generous cut. The Guardian may have been a leopard, but he clearly outweighed many a full-grown Bengal tiger.

"You look good," Joel said. "The program's really paying off."

Po, now seeing that the leopard was fishing for a compliment, gave an accompanying nod of agreement.

The Guardian smiled as broadly as a leopard could and visibly relaxed. Then he insisted that Po and Joel stay for coffee and pastries, even though it wasn't clear how they would leave the castle anyway, given that the Guardian was a prisoner. But Po needed whatever information he could glean about where the Dinuhos had sent him, and he didn't wish to be rude.

After disappearing into a kitchen alcove and fetching a folding table, coffee pot, and two chairs, the leopard directed Po as to where to set everything up. Then he put coffee on to brew. The coffee was exceptionally bitter—almost burnt, really—but Po finished the first pot with the leopard and accepted the offer of a second.

All the while, the leopard talked and talked without revealing anything useful. He'd always been a prisoner of the castle. No, he didn't know anything about where they were except that he wasn't allowed to leave. The castle was known only by its initials, B.C., and he didn't know what they signified.

Po finished his third cup of coffee and was beginning to be overcome by an unpleasant buzz. He went to the door, despite the leopard's insistence that it remain shut because there was no telling what might wander in.

The door opened onto a spiraling stone stairwell going both up and down. The way down was blocked by thick, close-set bars, so Po climbed a few steps.

"Wait!" The Guardian approached but stopped short of crossing the threshold. "Don't go that way."

Po raised an eyebrow in question.

Joel coughed to fill the silence.

"Look just don't go, all right?" The Guardian radiated sadness, then brightened with inspiration. "We could have more coffee!"

Po extended his hand for a goodbye shake.

The Guardian reluctantly extended a paw. "It's not safe out there. Please." He looked away, ashamed.

Po nodded a farewell and ascended the stone steps. They took him up another level to the top of a tower, where he checked the windows to see if any of them could be opened. The only one that wasn't sealed offered the sheer wall of the tower as a way down. Po removed his sandals and dropped them into a pocket. Hoisting himself through the window, he waited to see if the Guardian might emerge to say anything else. The leopard was nowhere to be seen.

Until, that is, Po closed the window behind him and began descending the wall, picking his way among the tiny finger and toe holds in the stone and mortar. Before he got far, he looked up to see the Guardian, still in his robe, leaning over the wall of an adjacent deck, watching him. He licked his lips a few times, as if he'd missed a meal or had something on his mind he couldn't bring himself to voice.

Po signed to him with one hand.

"We could carry you down," Joel said for Po, his tone indicating his lack of faith in the suggestion.

"No," the Guardian said. "When I was thinner, I could climb this wall with ease. I told you I was a prisoner here. I didn't name my jailer." Shame stopped the leopard from meeting Po's eye.

Po signed again.

"Any danger we should know about?" Joel asked for him. "Anywhere around here?"

The Guardian answered so softly at first that Joel had to

ask him to speak up. "I don't know!" he repeated—louder, his voice nearly breaking. "Laugh if you want." He dabbed at his eyes with the sleeve of his robe and muttered something else.

"What?" Joel's tone was harsher than Po would have liked.

"I said I will never be free." The Guardian gathered his robe tightly about him, and before Po could think of anything to make him feel better, he was gone.

"Wow," said Joel.

Po picked his way down the wall until he was able to hop to the ground and put his sandals back on. In the base of the castle tower was a door barred by a gate of thick iron. Next to it was a stone wall overlooking a pond with a small island in its middle.

He and Joel were in a large park, with plenty of trees and tall buildings beyond those. On the other side of the pond were an outdoor theater of some sort and an expanse of grass interrupted by man-made areas of level soil and chain-link fences.

"Ball fields, boss," said Joel. "But you knew that, right? The Reliever would be mighty proud if you'd nod yes."

Yes, the Reliever would. The Envoy, formerly a baseball-themed comic villain, had insisted on teaching Po the finer aspects and history of the game. And he would have been crestfallen to know that Po hadn't immediately recognized the diamonds, even with the bases missing. The backstops should have been enough of a clue.

Ken would have known. The mummy had been a big fan of the game—with a deep knowledge of its past and a keen appreciation for its romance and philosophy.

Ken.

His friend might also have known where in The Commons he'd been taken by the Dinuhos. It was probably a remnant of some past Journey that hadn't reset yet, though it didn't feel like one to Po. It was different—its air heavier, with a slightly metallic scent and even a taste to it.

Ken.

"Boss?" Joel tried to keep Po from dwelling on the loss of his friend, and he always seemed to sense when Po was falling into a spell.

Po said nothing. He rounded the tower and followed a paved path that took him past another locked entrance to the castle. He stopped to peer up at the deck above. There was no sign of the Guardian.

He hoped the leopard wasn't too embarrassed by his fear of leaving, but he suspected he was. Castles were made of walls, but so was the heart. And it wasn't always obvious which barriers were higher.

It took some effort for Po to keep his mind from wandering back to Ken and what he might have had to say about the current surroundings, particularly since the thought of him made a strange tingle go up the back of his neck—that sense of being watched again. But that was impossible. The Dinuhos had undoubtedly sent him too far for whatever it was that had been following him—if there had been anything at all—to catch up to him so soon.

Po continued along the path, stopping to examine a garden and cottage for any clues as to where he might be. They offered none, and they were empty and locked up.

He walked on until he found a larger paved road and chose a direction at random, passing a small lake and following an access road when the main road angled back into the park's interior. He reached an intersection with a cross street that led out of the park and into what was clearly a huge city proper. A sign pointed the way toward something called Strawberry Fields.

"I don't smell any strawberries," said Joel.

Neither did Po. He left the park and entered the forest of tall buildings. A second sign told him the street he was crossing was Central Park West, which he assumed meant that the heretofore anonymous park now had a name. Another sign told him he was walking along the mystery city's West 72nd Street. Po hoped there was nothing unlucky about the number—and that the Guardian's fears of danger beyond the castle were just byproducts of his overall anxiety.

Unless the road led to Parix, of course. Po would have welcomed a reckoning with him, no matter the outcome.

"Boss," Joel cautioned.

Po couldn't tell whether it was because the Tamagotchi suspected he was thinking about Ken again or because he understood that at the moment, Po wouldn't have minded a good, hard fight. Rather than ask for clarification, Po continued to put the park and Guardian behind them.

After that, it was the usual battle to keep his late mummy friend from entering his thoughts again.

69

PLEASE REFRAIN FROM KILLING US

The brown-line train pulled into a siding amid a chorus of jolts and thunks, maneuvering alongside a long freight train in the middle of nowhere. There was no facility or equipment in evidence. If the freight hadn't been waiting for them, Rain might've assumed it was an impromptu stop. Maybe that was the point.

The silence was broken by men's voices in the gloom. Orders carried up and down the length of the freight train, phrases containing words she knew, such as "deploy" and "dismount," along with some she didn't, such as "nanomen."

A few cars down from Rain and her motorcycle, a freight-car roof split open like a skyward-facing clam. A moment later, a massive tentacle reared up out of it.

A sealed car on the brown-line train answered in kind, its own roof opening.

The tentacle flowed over the wall and found its footing on the ground, the base of it widening as it finished stepping out of the car. Rain couldn't help but think of that old kid's show she'd seen memes of, the one with the clay characters whose names she could never remember.

The tentacle reached into the brown-line car and slowly lifted a steel shipping container out of it, the kind used on tractor-trailers and trains. Rising up on four legs, it made its way down to an open flatcar on the freight and carefully placed the container onto it. The roofs of the other brown-line cars opened, too, and another freight car disgorged a second tentacle to join the first one in its labors. The second tentacle reached into another brown-line car, pulled out an identical container and stacked it on top of the one the first tentacle placed. The two tentacles began working their way down the brown-line train, moving containers to the open freight-train cars.

More voices in the dark, from the front of the brown-line train, bore the tone of instruction. A moment later, doors opened in a string of brown-line cars and lights inside them snapped on, illuminating a collection of men in conductor's uniforms who stood between the brown-line train and the freight.

"Just like we told you, folks," one of them said to the open doors of the brown-line car nearest him. "Step lively and quickly, please, so we can kill these lights. We're all friends here, but whatever sees these lights and comes calling will not be looking for pals. So follow your closest Railwayman's instructions. Board safely and swiftly, and we'll be on our way."

"This isn't on the manifest," said a man behind Rain as the crunching of the rail bed's gravel announced his approach.

She pulled her shotgun as she turned.

"Whoa!" Two burly men in jumpsuits and heavy work boots raised their gloved hands and backed off a step. "You aren't on it, either, Miss," said one. "And getting shot is not part of our job. Not by cargo."

A barely audible whisper in the grass behind her. Rain

whirled to cover another man, dressed just like the first two, who may or may not have been sneaking up on her. She pivoted back and forth quickly and smoothly, letting them know she was perfectly capable of taking care of herself on two fronts.

"No need to get your barrels hot," said the first man. "If you hitched by accident and need a ride back to Chicago, this train can't take you there. But we can arrange for transportation."

"I'm going west."

"Not with us."

"I'm told I am." Rain continued to pivot the shotgun back and forth between the jumpsuits to keep them honest. None of them were in a hurry to challenge her.

"Who told you that?"

Rain went from him to the guy behind her another time or two, thinking. She wasn't so much worried about fending off an attack as she was trying to figure out how to explain that she'd followed instructions sent by someone who probably wasn't who they claimed to be. Yet she'd obeyed them anyway.

"She's with us." The conductor who'd been instructing the people in the cars up front approached them. He motioned for Rain to lower her gun.

She declined.

"There's no paperwork on this bike, Emmett," the first jumpsuit said without taking his eyes off Rain or the gun. "And if she's with you, why wasn't she in one of the passenger cars?"

Emmett the conductor shrugged, and Rain had to admit she liked his style. It was as if he'd left the Venice boardwalk to jump a train and talked his way into a gig taking tickets. He sported thick-framed glasses and a modest gauge earring in each lobe. When he reached up to adjust his wine-red boutonniere and matching pocket square before making sure his conductor's cap was straight, she saw that his fingernails were painted black. The motion also revealed just a hint of a tattoo sleeve poking out from under his Victorian shirt cuff.

"You don't know?" jumpsuit number one said. "So we're tossing protocol? We don't give a damn?"

Emmett ignored the question and, satisfied that his uniform and hat alignment were up to standard, glanced at Rain's gun again—and then at her.

Rain lowered the shotgun.

Emmett nodded his thanks. "You're Rain?"

"I am."

Emmett gave the first jumpsuit a told-you-so look. "She was added via digital about an hour ago, Smalley. So let's respect the line between conductor and carrier, shall we? If you'll be kind enough to load the bike, I'll get her situated in a proper car."

The jumpsuit, Smalley, whistled in the direction of one of the tentacles.

Rain had the gun back on him in an instant.

"We've got to stow the bike," said Emmett. "That's the responsibility of Smalley and the other carriers, as I said. You can watch to see where it's loaded, and I'll be happy to give you access whenever we stop. But we're not stopping again unless we have to. We don't have time to argue, and we'd prefer it if you'd please refrain from killing us."

Smalley stood very still. He didn't appear to be new to the fine art of having a loaded gun pointed at him, but he wasn't eager to take a shot to the chest, either.

Rain lowered the gun again and unhooked her bike from the cables. The nearest tentacle made its way over and, with a surprisingly delicate touch, plucked it from the deck of the car.

With the tentacle closer, Rain could see that it was made up of tiny men who climbed over each other and shifted position as one unit. She momentarily flashed back to standing with Paul while a similar collective of sub-Lilliputians filled up at a gas station.

"Nanomen," Emmett said as the tentacle carried the bike over to an empty freight-train car and placed it into an open side door. "The heart and soul of our operation."

"I thought you were," said Smalley.

"Have I ever claimed that?"

"You don't need to."

The tentacle tied the motorcycle into place using lines running from cleats in the freight car's floor and walls and slid the car door shut as Emmett offered a hand to Rain. She holstered her shotgun and hopped to the ground on her own. "The bike will get where we're going when we do, yes?"

"Yes," Emmett said. "Without a scratch. Right, Smalley?"

Smalley shook his head—not as an answer but to disapprove of it being asked. He walked away. The other carriers followed.

A small cough announced the presence of a nearby child. Sizable groups of people were transferring from the brown-line train to the freight-train cars. A few of them were paired off. There might have been a trio here and there. Otherwise, they all moved individually, as if they'd come alone. Even the little kids, of which there were a dozen or so, looked to be solo.

It was spooky. The passengers moved as if they'd been drugged. The conductors hurried them along as efficiently as possible.

Rain tried not to think of people being forced into cattle cars.

"It looks bad," Emmett said. "It isn't."

Rain watched the smallest children and didn't answer him. She wasn't going to take his word for it just yet.

The front of the train was all passenger cars. Adults and children alike went up the stairs, but their legs weren't moving nearly fast enough to explain the strangely floaty speed with which they rose and disappeared into the car. Then Rain understood. They weren't climbing the steps at all. The car was gently taking them in, raising them up with an escalator-like routine.

"You're not riding with them," Emmett said. "There's no room."

Rain continued to watch. The lost-looking souls emerged from the brown-line train in greater and greater numbers, patiently waiting their turn to be accepted into the passenger cars. There were too many. "Never mind me. There's not even room for them."

"What you're seeing is only a representation of what's occurring," Emmett said. "I'm seeing it, too. But that's not really what's happening."

"What is?"

"Come on." Emmett started walking as the nanomen transferred the last of the shipping containers to the freight train. "You'll ride with me. I'll explain."

Rain directed a look his way that was every bit as threatening as the shotgun had been.

"There's no other place for you, given the last-second accommodation. Look around. Our tolerances are nonexistent. We're not exactly flush with extra space."

Rain didn't back down.

"You have the gun, remember? And my job's too important for me to get my skull blown open." Emmett continued toward the front of the train as the flow of people began to slow.

Refugees. They all had the look of refugees, without any sliver of hope among them.

After Emmett covered a short distance, he realized she wasn't coming and turned back to her.

"What makes you the big shot?" said Rain.

"Didn't you hear Smalley just now?"

"Does that make it true?"

"No." Emmett inspected the train as he walked, making sure the last of the slow-moving passengers were taken into the waiting cars. The other conductors deferred to him, Rain noticed, so maybe he was a bit of a big shot. He had a way about him that inspired trust. And even if it was a front, he hadn't been wrong that she was the one with the gun.

While Emmett conferred with the other conductors, Rain watched the nanomen finish transferring the last of the containers. There was something peaceful about watching work done smoothly.

Unfortunately, that peace wasn't meant to last. The silence was broken by the rumble of an engine.

From a distance away came the rattle of automatic-weapons fire.

It was difficult to say exactly where in the night the sounds had originated.

Black specks erupted from the nearest tentacle, accompanied by the high-pitched cries of nanomen who'd been hit.

"Hot run!" Emmett cried.

The call was immediately taken up by others along the train, conductor and carrier alike. "Hot run!" someone else shouted.

Then, from further down the line, "Hot run!"

Everyone and everything began moving at once. Both tentacles flattened forward into the surrounding turf as the nanomen went to ground. Steel blinds dropped from the roofs of passenger and freight car alike, protecting the containers and refugees within.

The sound of the engine grew louder. Two dark Humvees approached through the grass, headlights and running lights ablaze.

The shooting began again, and Rain had just pulled her own gun when the lights of both vehicles were blocked by what looked to be thick waves rising up in front of them.

Nanomen. The tentacles were reforming to take on the Humvees.

It wasn't even a fight.

Two vehicles, two tentacles.

The nanomen, capable of lifting freight containers with ease, handled the Humvees like toys. The engines roared louder as the wheels they powered turned freely in the air. Several men were shaken out of the Humvees and fell to the ground as the tentacles tipped their rides vertically.

Rain understood what was about to happen and looked away.

The sound of metal crunching into turf, the screams of men, and the abrupt cutting of the engines told her what her eyes couldn't.

The tentacles crushed the men with their own vehicles.

No, not just men, Rain recalled.

Ravagers.

And they'd worked for Mr. Brill.

Then came the accompanying sound that was no memory. The rhythmic thrum of chopper blades. Here in the present.

Ravagers.

And the trespasses of Mr. Brill.

His hands on her.

Not on Ray-Anne.

On Rain.

The pain of that recall brought an even more acute understanding of who Rain was and had always been.

"Hot run!" another jumpsuit cried.

A *whir* and *thunk* from the nearest nanomen car. Something flat and low rose from its roof. Then came the sound of another mechanism, but Rain wasn't able to see it clearly in the dark.

The chopper grew nearer.

"Ears!" an unseen carrier shouted.

Rain didn't know what the command meant. But all was made clear as the mechanism on the roof revealed its purpose with a deafening, head-rattling *boom*.

The sky answered with a bloom of white and orange as the approaching chopper exploded over the field.

Flaming debris tumbled from the sky.

"Fair shootin', N-men!" one of the conductors yelled.

Out in the field, fallen pieces of burning wreckage set some of the prairie grass alight. The sight of it distracted Rain enough that only the snap of a breaking stick a few feet away brought her around to spot a black-clad man who'd crept up on her.

The Ravager, one useless arm hanging, had made his way from one of the wrecked Humvees. He and Rain regarded each other across a void of existence, the prairie-grass fire reflecting off the dark goggles hiding his eyes.

He went for the pistol at his hip. Rain had him dead to rights before he cleared his holster, and she didn't hesitate. She let him have it full in the face, taking him off his feet.

A presence behind her. She whirled and pumped.

Emmett. He said nothing.

She turned again to watch the grass for any other creeping Ravagers.

The nanomen tentacles, their component beings having

made their way back through the field, rose up and stowed themselves away in their cars once more. The roofs of the cars sealed them off.

"Everything's loaded," said Emmett. "The train will button up on its own. Let's go."

Rain continued to watch the grass.

Rain.

Not Ray-Anne.

Ray-Anne wouldn't have been able to pull the trigger.

Maybe that made her a better person. But Rain was here now.

Not Ray-Anne.

Not anymore.

Still no movement from the grass. Only then did it dawn on Rain that her view of it was unimpeded. The brown-line train that had delivered her from Chicago was gone.

It hadn't pulled out. It had finished its job and disappeared.

"Are you all right?"

Rain gave Emmett a nod and flipped the shotgun up and over her shoulder, holstering it.

She was more than all right.

Rain was herself again.

70

EVERY RULE AND LAW

For someone who'd suffered an obvious concussion, Porter felt remarkably little pain. He was flat on his back on concrete or stone, his distorted vision delivering a silvery reality that was circular and warped.

It wasn't until he sat up, and multiple versions of an object in the bulging image above moved with him, that he realized he was looking up into a great curved mirror. It made him dizzy, so he focused on the ground beneath him as he slowly got to his feet, testing his balance.

The mirrored ceiling was more than high enough for him to stand under. A canopy, perhaps? He was in an urban park, with tall office buildings on two sides of him, and the park on the other two. Further into the park was an array of trees with another curving mirrored canopy rising above them. What city was this?

It was a miracle Porter had survived to ask that question. He'd made it out of The Pines alive. No small feat, that.

Porter's abilities allowed him to transport himself and, within reason, other objects and people from one place to another. To do that, he had to have a strong feel for location and context. It wasn't magic. He needed information to ground him or, at least, required a physical sense of a destination. Barring that, he usually was able to read some foundation-level information into his surroundings. It was intuition, if nothing else.

The Dinuhos had not sent him back to The Commons. That he knew. In fact, he had a gut feeling about where he was, but that hunch had to be wrong.

Not even after visiting The Pines, which was also out of the question, would Porter admit to himself that his best guess might be accurate. It, too, broke every rule.

He took out the Newton, which was lifeless. Either it hadn't survived the trip, or Porter wasn't in a place where it was able to connect to anything. That fit with his theory—the one that had to be nonsense.

"Hi."

Porter spun around to face the voice, staff raised.

A little girl of seven or so stood under the canopy with him. He hoped it wasn't apparent how close he'd come to letting his lingering vertigo put him on the pavement again. Nevertheless, he willed himself to relax and remain upright in order to avoid scaring her, though she didn't appear to be frightened of him at all. He lowered the staff and kept his mental guard up.

Big problems came in small packages. He knew of at least a half-dozen Journeys that ended badly because an Envoy or Journeyman made the mistake of trusting a cute kid encountered along the way.

Evil didn't announce itself. Nor did it present itself in a package designed to alert potential victims—not the evil that had a knack for what it did.

"Neat, huh?" The little girl gazed up into the curved mirror and waved to herself.

Porter knew not to take his eyes off her, which would give her a potential opening, but he waved to play along. "What's your name?"

"Stupid," she said. "Useless. Another mouth that won't stay quiet when it isn't eating." She laughed, but it sounded like a habit intended to cover up what she really felt.

"Who calls you that?"

"My dad."

Porter studied the girl more closely. Despite her superficial cheeriness, she had the look of the untended about her. Her nose needed wiping. Her hair was snarled in places, and her pants were dirty at the knees. "Where is your father? Are you with him?"

The little girl laughed again, gazing up into the mirrored surface, and once more her mirth was unable to sustain itself.

Porter risked a glance upward. He saw only his own reflection, not hers. He put his eyes back on her and promised himself he wouldn't make that mistake again.

He maintained the hunch about his surroundings. But the presence of a child who cast no reflection was an argument against his theory.

"Let's look at it from outside," she said, leaving the shelter of the canopy, her back to him. It was a show of strength. She was confident in her abilities to withstand any assault he might be contemplating.

That or she really was a lost little girl.

Porter followed her out.

She stopped and turned to watch him.

He positioned himself just past her so that when he looked back at the canopy, she was in his line of sight.

It was no canopy. It was a three-dimensional, curved oval. A massive mirror, its surface offered a distorted portrait of the sky above as well as the tall buildings ringing the park in which they stood.

And Porter, of course.

But not the little girl.

"The Bean," the little girl said, waving to herself again. Was she able to see her reflection? If so, could she see Porter's? "Wave."

Porter humored her.

She grinned her approval.

"Sweetie, where are your parents? Is there an adult here with you?"

"No. I don't know where my dad is, and he doesn't care where I am. And that's why I'm here." She continued waving.

Porter did, too, until she stopped.

"You ready?" She grinned again. Her enthusiasm was infectious—and comforting in one key aspect. There were no fangs in evidence. Not that he'd really thought there would be.

"Not necessarily."

The little girl laughed again and walked away down a path.

Porter followed, and she led him around to a paved plaza in front of two closed cafes. They faced a large street and, beyond that, a major city. A bicyclist with what looked to be some sort of large, nearly ethereal parachutes attached to the back of her seat pedaled past at a fast clip.

"Hi!" the little girl called to the cyclist, who waved at her but didn't slow. The girl turned to Porter. "I like them. Do you?"

"Yes, I do," Porter said because he thought that was the safest answer. "Very much."

She smiled up at him. "Oh." She reached into her pocket. "I don't need this, but you do." She handed him a tattered business card.

New Beginnings, it said. And then, on the next line: *When you can't go home, go here.* Below that was a Chicago address and a hotline number.

Porter surveyed the buildings around him. "Chicago," he said, turning back toward the girl. "Is that—"

She was gone.

He gave his staff a turn and reached out with his abilities, trying to see if he could get a sense of her. Nothing. Either he wasn't at full strength—which was entirely possible, given that he suspected he'd just jumped from one realm to another—or she really had left him.

Or maybe she'd just done what she was supposed to.

Stupid. Useless.

The names hurt to consider. But she might have done him a very good turn after all.

An address. New Beginnings. He knew that name, which gave him adjacency. That and a known location meant he could go there, assuming this really was Chicago.

The Newton in his pocket chimed, and Porter took it out. It was back in action with a message from Audra.

So Porter's hunch was only partially right, at best. But being sort of right was better than nothing, considering how little control he'd had over his own travels lately.

Can only send text for now. Audra's message spooled out across the device's screen. *I hope not for good, but certainly for now.*

The lines faded and were replaced by more text, like an electronic billboard. That wasn't the way the Newton usually worked, which told Porter that even if he wasn't right about where he might have landed, he was probably correct in assuming he wasn't in The Commons.

Welcome to The Margins, the new lines said. *Now get to work.*

∽

For Audra, it was only a matter of walking out the front door. That was how unstable things were. And like all instability, it scared the hell out of you but also made things possible that would have been out of the question in normal times.

These were anything but normal times.

A tired old-lady Envoy who was burned out both literally and figuratively, Audra had her work cut out for her. She'd recognized that after reading the formal communication rolling off the printer before she left. And the knowledge was even more solid now that she'd finished reading through the stack of handwritten letters waiting for her at her destination.

Audra got used to jumping during her days of working with Porter. But she hadn't done anything like that in a long, long time. So when she stepped back out into her apartment-building hallway with her rolling bag trailing behind, she was stunned to find herself in a completely different place.

This place. She'd arrived in a tower at the bottom of a spiral staircase and was made dizzy by peering up into the corkscrew of steps climbing up into the floors above. At the front desk, she looked for the communications she knew would be there, and she found the letters.

She went into one of the adjacent buildings to unpack and move into the sole furnished apartment. She slept some more, then returned to the front desk and went into the office behind it to set up and get down to business.

Audra had a lot of communications of her own to send out. Things had gotten started without her, but leadership was needed. Organization. A sense of purpose and a clear direction to prepare everyone she'd be working with for what was to come.

When she needed a break, she stepped outside to take a

walk through the prairie grasses and the dense forests. The island wasn't supposed to be nearly so big, yet big it was—and it was still growing. Never mind that she had yet to understand where she was.

The landmarks across the river were a clue, certainly. The Chrysler Building. The Empire State Building. She had herself a home on Roosevelt Island with a great view of Manhattan. It just wasn't the Manhattan one normally thought of. This was a different version, and the view of Queens was already gone. That's how fast this thing was growing.

New York, where Audra would lend a much-needed hand.

The Speaky Shrieky interrupted her moment of self-congratulation, for which she felt no guilt. She'd written herself off. So had everyone else. For good reason, too.

But now she was back. And even the little device's caterwauling wasn't enough to spoil her mood.

There was critical work to do here, and she'd be at the center of it.

Not bad for a tired old lady who'd reduced herself to ashes, only to rise from them again.

71

QUARRY

The rock man's first mistake was also his last of the fight—and nearly the last he'd ever make. Koko didn't look like much of an opponent, but any mythical with battle experience should have known not to judge her by her appearance.

Even with a thick stony grip depriving her of nearly all air, Koko was able to first slow down everything and everyone in the room and then, getting her panic under control, refine the effect to target only him. It didn't improve her airflow, but it did stop it from getting worse.

It bought her time.

In that time, help arrived in the form of a cranky savior—the newly installed head of facilities, who went by the name of John Demos. Demos was out of sorts because he took the health of his building very seriously; he saw it as a higher calling. When the attack came and the Essence lines were laid low by the cereal-prize sappers, he considered it a personal attack and immediately threw himself into bringing his systems back online and back to normal.

The fighting in the hallways interfered with that, as did the closed security gates. Then the rock man threatening Koko pulled Demos away from the work he needed to do. He was in the mood to punish somebody so he could get back to the important work. And the walking pile of rocks in front of him fit the bill nicely.

Demos approached the rock man from behind, placed the flat of his palm on one shoulder, and began to explain the choices the rock man faced. He laid out a quick personal history for the rock man in simple strokes. John Demos was not the name he would have chosen for himself, but it was given to him when he was created as a comic-book character in a series about World War II superheroes. He was not a nice person in that series. That had not been his choice, either, and he was not particularly happy about it.

In the series, *Heroes of the Great War,* he was a super-powered saboteur working against the Americans to undermine their industrial capacity. His code name: Faultline. His power: the ability to sense the natural strengths and weaknesses in any kind of structure, living or not. He could then communicate with that structure and exploit its flaws, causing its host to fail. Hence the name John Demos, as in John Demolishes. A silly and unsubtle moniker, it could be blamed on the writers, not him.

"Now," said Demos after relating that background. "I've told you about me. You're a mythical. So you know we have to keep the names we're given if we want to remain in existence. What's yours?"

"He can't answer you, John," Charlene pointed out.

"Right," Demos said to the rock man. "If Koko speeds you up enough to talk, you'll also be able to kill her. So here's what we're going to do." He shifted his hand on the rock man's shoulder, understanding more about its structure the longer he was in contact with it. "Koko's going to give you enough of your speed back to let her go while she can still breathe. If you try to hurt her, I'm going to make an avalanche of you."

The rest happened without another word.

Koko allowed the rock man to move again.

He released her, and as she sucked wind, Demos shifted his hand again and tapped. The rock man cracked, then split in two and collapsed into a pile of rubble.

Demos grabbed Koko as she was about to fall onto the resulting mound of stone.

Charlene and several others rushed in to help Koko, and Demos handed her off.

Koko gulped air like it'd never been made available to her before.

"We got her," Charlene told Demos.

Demos started to leave without offering a reply. Plenty of people found him to be abrupt, but Charlene had no problem with that when it meant he got the job done. He had, and now he was heading back to the most important one—but not before he stopped to examine the doors the rock man had destroyed, frowning. He turned back to the pile of stones and appeared to be strongly considering doing a bit more damage before going. "He's only stunned," he said. "Scatter those rocks and put a few of them in a mail crate. There's a little of him in each one, so you have to quarantine part of him and make sure it's not touching the floor. The first thing he'll do is attempt to reassemble himself when he comes to." He was out the door before Charlene could thank him.

When Koko was ready, a couple of trainees and Beatrice helped her to her feet.

Reinhard and Charlene conferred quickly; he explained that he'd been scouting out the perimeter formed by the sealed gates to ensure their section of the building was secured when he was attacked by the rock man, who must have already gotten in by the time the gates closed. He'd been taken by surprise, but it wouldn't happen again.

After Charlene assured him that her confidence wasn't shaken in any way, Reinhard and Harris made a plan to escort Beatrice, Koko, and two of the trainees to the infirmary, where Beatrice would check Koko out and do whatever healing was needed. Then Reinhard and Harris would scout out the confines of the gate-enclosed space again, making sure the rock man was the only one who'd made it inside.

"What about Demos?" Charlene said. "He got in from wherever he was, didn't he?"

Reinhard offered the closest thing he had to a laugh. "He has ways in and out of every part of this building that nobody else could possibly know about."

He left with the others. Reinhard didn't seem to mind having been called back into Vigil mode for the time being. Charlene knew the type from her Army days. No true warrior ever really gave it up.

Charlene had FinePoint and another Envoy trainee do as Demos had suggested. They separated the stones a good distance from one another except for a dozen or so smaller ones, which Charlene gathered and set on the table in a wooden crate turned sideways.

"Okay, gravel boy," Charlene said to the pile, feeling a bit stupid about it since there was nothing to indicate the rocks could hear her or were capable of responding. "Let's talk."

72

FRACKING

"You sucker! You patsy! You victim! You fool!" The Rubbish Gladiator, taking a break from his impalement duties, was trying out a new twist to his routine as the executives and working stiffs passed him going in and out of the Zip 'n' Sip. Each characterization, in the singular instead of the usual plural, was directed at a separate business type as they passed—and never at anyone who didn't look like they held an office job.

The first exec type, a former athlete harboring a bunch of unwanted waist behind his belt, had "sucker" aimed his way. The career woman behind him got "patsy," and so on.

Subtlety wasn't really the Rubbish Gladiator's thing. He leaned into his work, screaming his message full in the face of his chosen target, and nobody paid him any mind. They weren't ignoring him. They didn't see or hear him.

The Gladiator stopped as Jeremy walked past, sparing the other potential victims who wouldn't have noticed him anyway. Jeremy felt the eyes on him all the way to the Zip 'n' Sip. The Gladiator only started up again when Jeremy's hand pushed the door open. It was like an agreed-upon signal. "You sucker!" the Gladiator shouted with even more vigor as Jeremy went in.

A week.

That's how long Abel had been gone, and nobody at Manitou had said a word. Either nobody knew, or nobody cared—and each of those possibilities was bad.

The first time Jeremy showed up at a Truitt meeting without Abel there, they started on time and covered the agenda without Truitt making any note of Abel's absence. But when they were done, and Jeremy was leaving, Truitt called him back to tell him he had a bright future with Manitou.

There was a deeper meaning to the otherwise innocuous statement. Or something implied but left off the end. He had a bright future if he did what he was supposed to—unlike Abel.

Jeremy didn't even know what Abel had done to get himself taken off the board. He hoped it wasn't cluing Jeremy in to Manitou's method for making sure no dearly departed Essence would cross over to The Commons.

Fracking, he'd called it. Fission. And one thing was for sure: anyone capable of it would have had no problem getting rid of all the Abels and Jeremys they needed to in order to keep the works going.

Back outside, the Rubbish Gladiator paused once again as Jeremy headed his way. The Gladiator stared at him, unblinking. "I see you," he said in a low voice when Jeremy was within a foot or two of him. He punctuated the statement by pointing his rubbish lance at Jeremy's chest, a square of paper hanging from its tip like a flag.

Jeremy stopped.

Behind him, a woman grunted at his abrupt halt and turned to glare on the way past.

"I see you, too," Jeremy told the Gladiator after she'd moved on.

"Just us," the Gladiator said. "Not any of them. We are in this world, not of it."

"Yes." Jeremy meant it. He was the only one on the sidewalk who could see the Rubbish Gladiator or interact with him, just like the drunks who'd been invisible to Abel in Billy Clyde's.

The Gladiator pointed his jaw toward the paper on his lance. When Jeremy wasn't quick to catch on, he repeated the move more insistently.

Jeremy pulled the paper off and flipped it over. On it was one of those promotional codes stores and restaurants used to stick in their windows, though they seemed to have fallen out of favor.

"QR Boy," the Gladiator said. "In your apps." Then, as if Jeremy had already left, he rolled his can forward with a purposeful shove.

Jeremy had to sidestep, nearly knocking over a little kid being led by a nanny. By the time he finished apologizing, the Gladiator was lost in the crowd.

Back at the office, Jeremy tried to review the latest data pull. It was a challenge to do it without thinking too hard about what the numbers meant in terms of what Abel had told him on their last night at Billy Clyde's—the last night he or anyone had seen Abel.

Fracking. Such a simple term for what was nothing short of an abomination, if Abel had been telling the truth.

The solution to the problem of storing the charges without letting adjacency build up was to distribute them and make sure there weren't too many in one place, as Abel had said when they were in the sub-basement. But that wouldn't work long-term. People would keep dying, which meant that either they were stored here in The Living World in charge form, or their Essence was allowed to cross over to The Commons, where it would move on in its natural process. After that, it was out of reach.

It had taken enough alcohol to level a T. rex before Abel could make himself tell Jeremy what they were involved in.

"Oppenheimer and the boys figured out how to split the atom," Abel said at the point in the night where all peripheral vision was shot, and Jeremy hadn't been certain his ears were capable of processing anything more than his friend and colleague's voice. "Callibeau and his pals decided that wasn't enough of a middle finger to God's plan. So they did it one better and split the soul."

Jeremy decided that sick or no, the conversation required yet another pitcher. "What does that mean, exactly?"

Abel gulped, checked his mug, and took another for good measure. "If you think of the soul—however you think of it—as the vessel for Essence, you can consider it an unbreakable entity. One body. One person. One soul. And all the Essence remains inside. Each of those charges you saw in the basement is its own unit. Now picture cracking it open and disposing of the shell, leaving you with only the raw Essence."

Jeremy's stomach bucked. Those had been little kids, some of them. And one of them had spoken to him. "Why?"

"You separate out the person's identity. Their memories, their loves, their hates. Everything that makes them *them*. When you do that, the Essence forgets what it was. It never crosses over to The Commons because it no longer wants to. It stays here, in The L.W.—but not in a sentient form, so there's no willfulness to it. Then you can exploit it, using the powers you bring over from The Commons side to do that." Abel kept his eyes on his beer. He couldn't meet Jeremy's gaze.

Jeremy understood why he couldn't. "You're ending people permanently." He put his mug down. One more swallow on top of this new bit of understanding would make the difference between staying in the booth and another run for the men's room. "There's no chance for them to move on, no next step."

Abel was perfectly still. "Not everyone."

"So that makes it better?"

He still didn't move a muscle. "No. It makes it much, much worse."

Jeremy locked Abel in a hard stare. When Abel tried to look elsewhere, he angled himself so that he was in the picture there, too.

It worked. Abel let out a deep, shivering sigh. It sounded as if he were somewhere between crying and getting sick himself. "You're shattering a consciousness. And that's a tough thing to do when someone's formed an identity, a personhood, that is strong enough to withstand the process. So you hit them before they've done that."

"Done what?" Jeremy was talking a little too loud now. "Become a person?"

Abel said nothing.

Jeremy reached across the table to grab him by the chin and tip his face up.

Still, he wouldn't look at Jeremy.

Jeremy squeezed until Abel whimpered.

"Kids," Abel said so softly that Jeremy wasn't entirely certain that was the word.

"Children?"

"Little ones. And babies."

Jeremy let Abel go and leaned back, covering his eyes. When he uncovered them, Abel was watching him.

So was Porthos, in a nearby booth.

"You've made me a part of this."

Abel offered only silence.

"How many?"

"That part of it? The young ones? None so far. They're not ready."

"What are they waiting for?"

"To recreate the parts of the Apalala framework that were messed up by Mallory's exorcism and then to write the fission module for it. After that? They need another person they can trust to ride herd and manage it all once it starts. I can't do it alone."

So there it was.

"Me," said Jeremy. "They're waiting for me. To train up."

Abel looked away again.

Porthos kept staring.

And even now, a week later, with Abel gone and Jeremy a distance from Billy Clyde's, Jeremy still felt the cat's eyes on him.

Along with everyone whose destinies Manitou was stealing.

73

ONE MORE THING TO PUZZLE OVER

This time, Porter woke up face down on concrete, his staff underneath him. The soreness in his chest and ribs from lying on the hard wood of the stick told him he'd been there for some time—and picking himself up off the Chicago sidewalk was no easy task. He'd teleported too far and had passed out on arrival—a sequence of events he didn't recall in any way.

Audra was right. Porter was in The Margins. And his abilities were greatly weakened—temporarily, he hoped.

He was fortunate to have made it to his destination at all, assuming he had. He might easily have ended up in a solid wall or halfway into the street, given that he wasn't at full strength. Once again, he was lucky to have survived. He needed to stop pushing his luck, lest it eventually push back.

Porter sat up, head foggy with the battle against gravity and the residual effects of his barely completed jump. He was in front of a line of shops, all of them closed up behind steel gates.

Heroes Welcome sold comics, games, and collectibles. The Shirt Off Your Back was a secondhand-clothing store and swap shop, and next to that was Merry Melody's, which specialized in gently used instruments, according to its sign.

He struggled to his feet with the assistance of Melody's security gate, which gave him a good look at the wares as he waited for the world around him to solidify. A mandolin. A saxophone. A trombone. A guitar. A flute. And what Porter believed to be a hurdy-gurdy. All appeared to have been previously owned, some by people who didn't much care for them.

Porter took a few deep breaths and surveyed the rest of his surroundings, leaning on his staff in case he was hit with another dizzy spell. Audra's texts were correct. This was Chicago, but not the true Chicago of The Living World.

The lifelessness of the street combined with the gray, flat not-quite daylight lent an otherworldliness to the setting. He tapped the foot of his staff against the sidewalk's cement and the resulting sound had an echo that didn't sound quite right.

This was an ill-defined domain, an in-between place, by the feel of it. Audra definitely had it right.

The Margins.

Still, Porter had done better than he'd first feared. There across the street was a large building that looked to have been a fancy apartment building in kinder years. A prominent sign identified it as New Beginnings Chicago.

Porter crossed the street with hardly a look. There was no traffic. The few cars parked along the street had some sort of disabling mechanism over one wheel.

A woman ambling along a side street as Porter approached the New Beginnings building didn't even spare him a look. Either she wanted nothing to do with him, or she couldn't see him. Both explanations would fit The Margins.

The front door was locked. However, despite Porter's weakened condition, it was nothing for him to jump the deadbolt mechanism into his hand long enough to turn the knob before jumping it back. Porter had a bright future ahead of him in burglary should he ever need to reinvent himself.

Inside, the building was nearly dark. Porter waited for his eyes to adjust to the dimness of what appeared to be a reception area, lit only by whatever leaked in from outside.

A stack of welcome pamphlets sat on a low coffee table in front of a couch and a pair of armchairs, and Porter thought he saw a couple of familiar faces in the bad light. He grabbed one of the pamphlets and brought it closer to the nearest window to have a look.

When he read the welcome message with the brief bios of Paul and Rain—who went by Ray-Anne in The Living World, it seemed—his vision blurred once again. Not with sadness, but with the mist of pride. What shone through the verbiage itself was that this place was meant to help those who needed it most.

Paul had returned from his Journey with Porter and his defeat of Brill to set about building something important. As had Rain. The two of them were putting their all into doing good here, and Porter couldn't have been prouder.

Now if only he knew where they were.

∽

WAITING to regain some of his spent strength, Porter passed the time at the front counter, sipping some tea he'd scared up after finding the New Beginnings kitchen and its working gas stove. As was the case in The Commons, he wasn't particularly thirsty. Those on Journeys could eat if the path created for them called for it, but Envoys didn't need food or drink. Still, he enjoyed the ritual when he wanted some time to sit and think.

Porter pushed himself close to the counter, closed his eyes, and rested his head on his arm. At first, he'd been frustrated by the low light. But it allowed him to convalesce in peace.

The need for sleep matched the need for food and water—for the most part. Again, a given Journey could require it or not require it, and an Envoy might choose to grab a little shuteye when a Journeyman needed it. But it wasn't necessary, and many people simply forgot the habit if they remained in The Commons long enough.

Even so, Porter appreciated the rest afforded by closing his eyes. It allowed him to work things out.

There hadn't been any subsequent messages from Audra since those he'd received at The Bean, but he wasn't worried on that account. Audra had given him plenty to think about.

New Beginnings itself gave him one more thing to puzzle over. Heat.

Porter hadn't noticed the temperature in the room creeping up. Nor had he heard the pinging of the radiators a building of a certain age would undoubtedly have in its rooms and hallways. Maybe he'd actually half-dozed after all, for the source of the heat was right next to him. What other reason would there be for him to miss that?

He reached for his coat, which he'd left draped over the adjacent stool, intending to use the Newton to provide whatever light it could.

His coat was the source of the warmth. Reaching into the pocket, Porter was surprised to find that the Newton was hot to the touch.

He was equally taken aback when he fished it out, only to discover that it wasn't warm at all. He turned the Newton over in his hands, feeling in the barely adequate light for the wake switch. Usually it woke itself.

That wasn't the only unusual thing about it. Something unfamiliar protruded from the unit's side, stuck in one of the expansion slots. The old MessagePads were capable of using memory cards and other such accessories, but the one The Commons provided for him never came with any.

Nevertheless, something was in there. Porter got up and walked over by the front door, where the light was better.

It was indeed an expansion card, jammed backwards into its slot. The Newton had not been out of Porter's control since he'd been in The Pines and—well, then.

The Pines.

The card came out with a firm tug. Porter flipped it and inserted it correctly. It slid in easily, as if the Newton were satisfying a craving. The click as Porter pressed it home was almost an expression of gratitude.

From behind Porter came the creak of something heavy settling onto the floor of the lobby. Something huge.

Porter turned.

The stool he'd been sitting on behind the counter was now occupied. He couldn't make out details in the bad light, but there was a strong feeling of familiarity to the presence. A slight young man sat there—too slight to make the floor audibly strain the way it had.

"Apalala?" Porter was ashamed of the slight tremor in his voice. But given the undeniable power he felt in the space with him, he shouldn't have been.

The Newton's screen came to life with a light bright enough to make Porter shield his eyes. Sitting in the dark had rendered his vision way too sensitive to such a flare-up. It quickly settled back into its normal soft glow, and Porter rubbed his eyes until the spots faded.

Another creak. The massive visitor adjusted its position and tested the floor's capacity.

Porter was leaving himself wide open to attack, proceeding

with blind faith in the notion that this really was Apalala—and that he wished Porter no harm.

It took a few moments for the will-o'-the-wisps to leave the backs of Porter's eyelids. But with the sudden change in the feeling of the space, Porter knew what he'd find once his vision cleared.

There was nobody behind the counter, no one in his seat.

Despite the absence, Porter approached the counter and the stool slowly, tipping the Newton's screen toward it to illuminate it as best he could.

Nothing.

What had been there was an echo of an awe-inspiring presence rather than that presence itself. Such was the power packed into Apalala's spare frame.

When he reached the counter, Porter glanced at the Newton's screen. In its center was one word: *readme*.

A text file.

He reclaimed his seat after checking once more to make sure there really was no one in it.

Another paradox in a day full of them. There was no other text on the screen, yet it advanced as if there were full pages to view.

With each scroll of the page, Porter found himself taking in information, as if he'd read or heard something dense with meaning.

He heard no voice, saw no words.

But the card and its payload were of The Pines, like Carl's badge. And he had no doubt that its source was the being whose residual Essence had only just departed.

Porter left himself open to the message and what it had to teach him. It was like being told something in a dream.

He was soon fervently wishing he'd never opened it.

74

CORNERSTONE

The rock man's name was Quarry. It took some time for the boxed stones to coalesce into a head able to form words in an audible voice, but once that happened, he proved to be fairly willing to converse and cough up information.

Charlene's promise that he'd be sealed in the box and installed in a cornerstone of Envoy HQ as a time capsule probably made him more cooperative.

"What's the mission?" Charlene asked. Her tone alone was a reminder of her threat.

"To bring about the activation of the disuse protocol," Quarry's head replied.

June Medill, hunched over a notebook in her lap, wrote his answer down with superb speed. She was a crackerjack stenographer, and while it might not have appeared necessary to document every word of Quarry's interrogation via shorthand, Charlene had long ago learned to record the answers of any mythical. Many of them delighted in stitching hidden answers into their sentences and phrasing.

"With everyone in the building ready to defend it?" Charlene said. "Not likely."

"Agreed."

"So how did you expect to pull that off?"

Quarry was silent.

"You could try to evacuate it, but that would never work. Everybody knows The Commons will reclaim the building if it's empty for too long. You'd never be able to keep us from sneaking back in, especially Demos."

Quarry remained silent.

Charlene followed the line of thinking and resisted the urge to shiver. "Evacuation wasn't the plan, was it?"

Quarry remained silent.

"If you don't keep talking, you're no longer useful to me. And that leaves us with no option but to make you something for historians to argue over."

"Complete elimination," Quarry said. "That was the mission."

"Of?"

"We were to cleanse the building."

No one in the room made a sound.

Charlene let that sink in. "That's the Envoys, the staff, and the Journeymen who might be unlucky enough to get caught while being processed?"

Quarry didn't answer right away. Clearly, the conversation wasn't headed toward him being freed any time soon. "Yes."

All eyes were on Charlene.

"That's nearly 300 people."

"Yes."

"How many of you are in here?"

"I don't have an exact number since some of us were sent in groups while others came in solo. But it's at least thirty of us."

Charlene paused to ponder the implications of that. Only thirty against the entire Envoy HQ? When the attacking force couldn't even be sure who was in there or what they were up against?

"Charlene," FinePoint said. "Demos is getting some of the cameras back online."

She checked the View-Master. Sure enough, she was able to cycle through several external views of the surrounding areas.

The pictures were not good. The streets were now filled with the black Ravager tanks, which ringed the building in attack formation and looked to be waiting only for the go-ahead. "How do you expect to win here?" She continued flipping through various camera angles. "You're outnumbered almost ten to one—what's the plan?"

The stone head said nothing.

After a few moments, Charlene began to wonder if Quarry's life force had deserted the stones despite what Demos had said about it being trapped in the crate. She put the View-Master down.

"I'm a mythical," Quarry said.

"Yeah, and so is that blob thing that tried to dissolve me. But just the two of you backing up a bunch of Ravagers wouldn't be able to take down this whole facility—not with our Envoys and the building's defenses."

"There are no Ravagers inside—we're all mythicals."

That was a big number. "All of you? Working together? I've never seen that many dark-side mythicals able to stand one another, never mind plan and coordinate."

"Why do you assume it was our plan?"

Harris appeared in the ruined doorway and awaited Charlene's permission to enter. What he'd done to her had certainly humbled him; he now behaved in a much more formal fashion. When she nodded her approval, he came in and stood before her as if reporting for duty. "Reinhard told me to keep an eye on you all."

Charlene nodded her understanding and approval once more. Clearly, Reinhard wanted to give the kid another chance and was trying to build up his confidence again. "Anything new I should know about?"

"Demos reports that enough of those cereal-toy sappers have been taken care of for our Essence supply lines to regenerate," Harris said. "We should see some other systems coming back online, too."

Charlene looked to FinePoint for confirmation.

"We already are," FinePoint said. "It's slow, but it's happening."

"How'd Demos manage that?" Charlene said. "I thought those tunnels were hell to access, which is why he hadn't taken care of this by now."

Harris looked a bit sheepish. "He didn't say, ma'am."

"He probably doesn't want to," FinePoint pointed out, flipping through camera angles of his own before settling on one in particular. "It's kind of tough to explain this." He rolled back from his monitor, allowing Charlene to approach for a better look at what he was seeing.

On the screen, the tunnels teemed with activity. Scores of rats attacked the cereal-prize sappers, carrying them away from the Essence lines. It was like a fire brigade, with each rat replaced by a new one as it carried the little saboteurs off camera.

"Honestly?"

"Whatever works," said FinePoint.

The rats were quickly spiriting the sappers away. The little plastic men were meant for sabotage, not combat, and were incapable of defending themselves. Rats. Why did the use of rodents ring a bell? So many questions, but that one wouldn't be answered at the moment. "If it wasn't your plan," she said to Quarry's head, "then whose was it?"

"Manitou. Callibeau."

"Those names mean nothing to me."

"They will. You haven't heard of them because they remain in The Living World."

"Well, I have no plans to go there, so right now might as well be forever. Unless they're planning on coming to me."

Quarry's silence this time was too long. Charlene walked back over to the head and looked down on it. "What aren't you telling me?" When he still didn't say anything, Charlene shook the box. Hard. For several long rounds.

Just as she thought she might have killed him, Quarry spoke up. "I'll answer that," he said. "That and more—if we make a deal."

"Why would I? You came here to kill us. For all I know, the rest of your team is doing just that to my friends and any poor Journeyman they find. Why should I trust you?"

"You shouldn't. Nor should I trust you. Not at first. But there's no reason to let that stop us from helping each other."

"And how, exactly, can you help me?"

Quarry answered with a knowing laugh. Then he began to tell her.

75

RAINBOWS AND PAISLEY

On Amsterdam Avenue, the fast bicyclist came at Po. Quicker than anyone should have been able to pedal, he was pursued by whirling disks of lightning that missed him, doubled back in their flight like heat-seeking missiles, and missed him again.

They buzzed Po and then headed back in the direction from which they came. The lightning was disturbingly familiar.

A moment later, the entire landscape went mad.

Po's vision betrayed him at its edges.

For a moment, it showed him the street, the hut that appeared to be some sort of way station, and the small park behind it. Then it transformed into a tableau of insanity.

The windows in the hut were faces distorted in pain. The air itself erupted in rainbows and paisley, and the lane markers on the street rose up before him as angry asps.

Only the cyclist held true to form as he bore down on Po, hunched over his handlebars, his eyes slightly out of focus, as if staring through Po, who had only a moment to decide which way he was going to jump to evade him. He was about to go left when the cyclist spotted him.

"Dude!" the cyclist yelled as he hit his brakes and fishtailed. His bike went horizontal and slid.

Po leapt over him, landed, and turned just as the bicycle and its rider slid into the curb and went airborne.

When bike and rider met turf, two shiny, balled-up foil-like bales unfurled from the bicycle's rear-wheel panniers with a loud boom, unleashing a wave of stored energy.

All of the screaming faces in the hut's glass windows shattered. Their fragments became winged teeth flying up into the sky.

Po approached the downed cyclist carefully, ready to defend himself or offer help.

But the cyclist struggled to his feet as the landscape returned to normal. "Down!" he shouted.

The sizzling heat of the returning lightning disks came at Po from behind. He dropped as one of them missed him and the cyclist and embedded itself in the wall of the station hut. It popped and crackled there, discharging its current into the surface of the hut.

A powered shuriken. He knew it had seemed familiar.

"Friend of yours, Dodger?" A gruff-voiced, solidly built man in a black outfit like that of a militarized ninja emerged from behind one of the park's trees. He wore crossed bandoliers with nearly a dozen of the steel stars attached to them.

"He's certainly no friend of ours," said a dark split in the air just before a severe-looking old woman in a colorful, flowing dress stepped out of it. She transformed in a steady wave of changes. First she had her silver hair up in a tight bun, and then it spilled down over her shoulders in a torrent of auburn. She was old. She was young. The patterns on her dress would not stay still. The colors changed, and the dress itself morphed from one form to another. The woman smiled.

Po looked away while he was still able to. He knew these two from his days of tracking the most recalcitrant mythicals through Mrs. Blesmol's tunnels.

Yakiba and Auntie Bedlam. They hadn't been working together when he'd captured and imprisoned them separately. He was sorry to see that had changed.

"He's not," Yakiba told his partner. "But if today's a two-for-one special, you'll hear no complaint from me." He let another pair of shurikens fly, one aimed at the cyclist and the other at Po. They began to crackle in mid-flight.

Po jumped sideways to pull the cyclist out of the way as the stars came at them. He succeeded, but only just.

The hot edge of one star narrowly missed Po's ear. Both followed the path of the previous star, lodging themselves in the wall of the hut behind them and discharging with a loud snapping.

Po chanced a glance behind him to make sure the stars weren't about to free themselves on their own. A wood-handled rake left there by a volunteer or a cleaning crew leaned against one of the little hut's support pillars. He pretended not to see it.

The ninja approached to within a dozen yards or so. "Do you remember me, Envoy? Surely you must."

"We remember, Mr. Silent-but-Deadly," said Joel, who now hung outside of Po's robe after all the evasive maneuvers. "We remember sticking you where you belong. What are you two washouts doing here, chasing bike messengers? Do you mug working people for beer money, or have you just straight-up gone merc?"

Joel's insults helped jog Po's memory. Yakiba and Auntie Bedlam had been Envoy recruits who'd made it through basic training during Porter's post-Brill recruiting wave, only to be summarily shown the door. The former proved too violent in his methods, and the latter demonstrated heavy indications of sociopathy.

If Po remembered his files and dossiers correctly, Yakiba was a low-level comic-book villain and military specialist with high-level martial-arts training and the ability to charge his weapons with electricity, while Auntie Bedlam was a mistress of illusion. None of which explained what they were doing here or who their intended victim was.

"We've all been working the Upper West Side without any problems," the cyclist said to them. "What changed?"

"I don't answer to you, Dodger, and neither does she." Yakiba closed in with slow, confident strides. "We do what we want when we can. And when we can't, we do what we're told. We were instructed to take care of you. But I'll do the monk just because I owe him."

With that, Yakiba launched two crackling stars, which multiplied as they left his fingertips. Now they numbered ten or more, all coming at Po.

Or appeared to.

Auntie Bedlam was supplementing Yakiba's attack with her illusions.

Po reached for the rake and brought it straight out in front of him, vertically.

"Three and six," said Joel.

The assessment confirmed Po's instincts. The stars in the other positions felt like doppelgängers of the initial two. He swatted the third star just enough to change its trajectory. It passed over his shoulder and joined its brethren in the wall behind him with a thunk and a crackle.

The illusions blinked out of view as they reached him.

He stopped the second real star with the rake handle. It bit into the wood and vented its fury into the air.

Now it was his turn.

"Two feet to the right," said Joel.

Po yanked the star from the rake handle and sent it hissing toward Auntie Bedlam—where Joel had pinpointed her location, not where Po saw her standing.

It had the intended effect as the version of her he'd been watching disappeared, and the real one was forced to dodge. Physical combat was not her forte. She didn't realize he'd aimed high and to the side.

The star arced and returned to Yakiba.

Turning to pull two more from the wall, Po hurled those at Yakiba as well. They had never been a concentration of his; he was merely adequate with them, by his standards.

But while the ninja laughed and plucked the stars from the air, Po improvised the weapon he preferred. He flipped the rake and, its steel head against the ground, snapped it right above the business end with his heel. Now he held only the handle. It wasn't the best wood, but it would have to suffice.

Po, caught the next two stars Yakiba threw with the rake handle, pulling them out once they'd discharged.

"Three feet left," said Joel.

Po sent both stars Auntie Bedlam's way again and closed some of the distance between him and Yakiba as she once more was forced to take evasive action.

By the time Yakiba changed tactics and hurled three shuriken at Dodger, Po was close enough to work the angle better. He moved to the side and batted each of them, altering their flight in a shower of sparks so that they were forced to return to their thrower before they'd expended too much momentum and couldn't make it back.

Meanwhile, Dodger returned to his bike and was fiddling with the bags on the rear rack.

Yakiba gave Po no time to see what the cyclist was up to. Switching tactics again, he pulled two sets of nunchaku and began weaving a pattern around himself. He closed in, the weapons crackling and sparking as he moved them through their woven patterns with increasing speed. He quickly closed the distance between them.

Po danced away and into his own pattern, positioning himself wherever the nunchaku weren't. Defensively, evasion was his only option. The rake handle would never hold up, weapon on weapon. It was no true staff; it would splinter under a full strike.

The two combatants claimed the entire space of the plaza in front of the subway entrance as they maneuvered.

Po picked up Yakiba's patterns of attack, always managing to slip into the spaces between them.

Yakiba allowed himself a smile. He was warming to the challenge.

When the nunchaku began moving with even greater speed, Po took the fun out of it for Yakiba. He turned between the movement of the two weapons and gave Yakiba a hard jab in the solar plexus followed by a blow straight to the forehead and a solid shot across the jaw.

Yakiba promptly lost his grin. He ceased to make the patterns, catching one of the nunchaku under his arm and the other with his hand. Their glow faded.

Po whirled the rake handle in patterns as complex as Yakiba's, forcing his opponent to retreat. It was all about temperament now—both Yakiba's and Po's.

He wanted to make the ninja mad enough to lose some of his discipline. More important, Po needed to keep his own anger from overwhelming him. In the long-ago past, he'd lost himself to dark madness more than once, coming out of it only to discover he'd taken one or more lives. His sworn goal was to never do so again.

He'd promised himself.

And he'd promised Ken.

Yakiba, his jaw set more tightly, went on offense again.

Po was already out of reach by the time the nunchaku came his way, their charges quickly building again.

Now Yakiba meant business, his patterns faster and his attacks more to the point. He was looking to kill.

Once again, Po moved in, weaving his way through the assault. When he saw his opening, he struck quickly. He, too, meant his own level of business. The rake handle's end connected solidly with the bridge of Yakiba's nose, breaking it.

Yakiba grunted in surprise and backed up. He placed the palm of each hand on either side of his nose and, grunting again, straightened it out. The pain must have been enormous.

Po had to concede that the man was formidable.

Yakiba moved in again, blood streaming from his nose and a fresh hatred in his eyes.

The landscape bloomed into madness once again. The brick of the plaza became an ocean with sparkling waves tossed by heavy winds. Bats the size of seabirds wheeled about in low circles.

Even worse, the nunchaku moved in patterns of bubbles that lingered and floated aimlessly long after they'd completed a rotation. They were nearly impossible to track. Yakiba himself was now refracted in impossible ways, limbs undulating and curling, no straight or logical elements to them.

Po closed his eyes. He'd trained for countless hours while blindfolded, practicing against sightless friends—many of them the most intimidating warriors he knew. All of that he called upon now.

The two of them completed another circuit around the plaza, Po using his memory of his surroundings and his hearing to gauge where he and his opponent were.

Yakiba was still not as easy to track as he should have been. Auntie Bedlam's illusions wreaked havoc on more than just the eyes.

Another circuit.

Po stayed out of the lethal path of the charged nunchaku—but just barely. Forced to parry, he broke his rake handle in half. He spun the two sticks and, when the opportunity presented itself, stuck one into the circle of a nunchaku. He caught a jolt, but managed to flip the weapon away. He heard it bounce a good distance across the plaza.

Fire crackled against the lower part of his spine, and his eyes flew open.

A stun gun. Auntie Bedlam used the cover of the battle and the illusions to attack him the old-fashioned way.

Po faltered and caught a charged nunchaku to the ribs followed by a kick to the side of his head. He was able to get out of the way of a blow aimed squarely at his face—Yakiba was looking for payback for his nose. He kicked upward and caught Yakiba in the gut, knocking him back.

Then he pushed off the ground with his shoulders, landed on his feet, and tried to put some distance between himself and his assailants. He couldn't see Auntie Bedlam anywhere, and he didn't dare try his trick of closing his eyes again. He was too wobbly now.

The visual madness continued. Harpies buzzed his head. The treetops were ablaze over the growing chop of the plaza's waves.

Beyond the park's edges, out in the street, apes of all sorts approached on unicycles. Po spotted a number of gorillas and orangutans. There were even two bears, all of them pedaling to a stop in the street.

Behind them, a car-sized cockroach ambled up to the curb with a whine and disgorged a hunched-over witch mannequin whose upper body was aflame. The witch motioned for the apes to clear a path for her, but not all of them responded.

Another jolt to the ribs. Po's legs turned to jelly, and that was no illusion. He hit the ground, head bouncing off the seawater, which was as hard as the bricks it was made of.

The illusion vanished, but sparks remained in his vision.

Now Yakiba stood over him. "I would have liked to have had a proper one-on-one with you," the ninja said, his enunciation dulled by his broken nose.

Po tried to sit up, but only made it part of the way. He could now see Auntie Bedlam behind Yakiba, but the picture was blurry. There was no way of telling if that was due to the blow to his head or because of her abilities.

It didn't matter. What counted was Yakiba, who pulled a throwing knife from a sheath on the outside of his thigh. "You weren't the target here," he said, standing over Po with the blade held casually. "But I'll take you as a surprise bonus before we carve up the biker."

Po wanted to laugh at the cartoonish quality of Yakiba's delivery. The swollen nose really did make a buffoon of him. He'd never have found harm done to a foe amusing under normal circumstances. He suspected he'd suffered a concussion.

The biker. Po was just beginning to wonder what had become of Dodger as Yakiba grabbed a fistful of the robe's fabric at his throat and situated the edge of the blade there. There was no anger to his movements, just the workaday routine of a killer who was about to add one more life to his scorecard.

Auntie Bedlam leaned over Po to look in his eyes. Here was one of the truly frightening types. She wanted to watch the light go out after Yakiba slit his throat.

Neither of them got the chance.

The cyclist in the background appeared to Po through clouds, but it looked as if he squeezed the bags on the back of his bike like bellows while the bears and apes closed in.

A moment later, a wave of pure force knocked Po, Yakiba, and Auntie Bedlam flat.

Po's ears rang. He managed to get himself up on one elbow as Yakiba and Auntie Bedlam recovered enough to struggle to their feet.

Round two put a stop to that. With a rush of air and a pop that made Po's ears sing louder, the area around them burst into heat and shock. The fire took all the oxygen with it, pulling it from Po's lungs.

Po wanted to thank the bear and the ape, who, he assumed, were trying to save him. Or maybe they were there to finish the job, in which case he needed to get up and defend himself.

There was no chance for any of that.

With the distinct clink of steel on brick, Yakiba dropped his knife.

Then both he and Auntie Bedlam collapsed on top of Po. They would have knocked the wind out of him, if he'd had any to sacrifice.

"Boss," said Joel. The Tamagotchi was suspiciously far away and getting farther. "Boss, are you all right?"

76

GOD BLESS THE PREPARED

"Gently," said Audra. Lottie and Whizbang, carefully lifting Po, exchanged looks just long enough to communicate agreement. The old lady still couldn't accept that they might know what they were doing.

That was how Audra interpreted it—and she couldn't blame them. For a while, the Petrels operated on their own in The Margins with the Artful Dodger as their de facto leader. They'd been doing just fine, in their estimation, before Audra was sent to babysit them. And while the Dodger was gracious and helpful right off the bat, the rest of the group saw Audra's arrival as a demotion for him. So they respectfully engaged in the occasional passive resistance as a show of solidarity and loyalty.

That was fine, as long as they got the job done.

Audra resisted the urge to tell them to lay Po across the back seat of the SUV. They knew that, and she needed to let them see that she recognized it and trusted them. Her silence would do the trick. But that didn't mean it was easy.

The Dodger approached, looking sheepish. He'd spent as

much time talking to the others as possible and had already inspected his demolished bike numerous times in an attempt to avoid facing her.

Audra took that as a compliment. He respected her authority. She waited until he was close enough for a low-volume conversation. "Are you all right?"

He showed her some nasty elbow and knee road rash. "If I start letting a few scrapes slow me down, I'll quit. And if I don't quit, you should fire me."

"I'd never do the latter, and I wouldn't let you do the former."

One of the other Petrels, a fireplug of a brunette whose name Audra really should have remembered, carried the Dodger's wrecked bike over to the SUV Audra had arrived in, raised the gate, and put it inside.

"We can strip it for parts," the Dodger said and stopped there.

"Was that Melange?" Audra watched as the fireplug girl closed the gate again.

"Old Betsy." The Dodger shook his head. "She had a good run, but she wasn't even the same ride I started with, really, except for the seat. If that were Melange, I'd be crying too hard for words."

Audra doubted that. She couldn't imagine the Dodger crying over anything. With the exception, perhaps, of losing a fair bike-to-bike race, which had never happened, according to lore. And while she only knew the young man from the reports she'd studied during the long wait for her assignment to jell, she had a difficult time believing he'd ever suffer such a loss.

"I burned the load," the Dodger said. "I'm sorry."

"Do you honestly—"

"I should have trusted you guys to take care of it once you got here, but I thought they'd kill him before—"

"Lars."

The rare use of the Dodger's birth name stopped him.

"I consider this to be a victory. It's only Essence. It's important, yes, and so is the job we've been handed. But it's just Essence, and there's plenty more of it. You were up against two mythicals whose profiles got the attention of both the Envoys and the Vigils. You weren't killed. That's a win."

The Dodger scuffed his feet against the street's asphalt. "Yes, ma'am."

Audra couldn't help but like the boy. To hear him talk, you'd never know he was a legend among the bike messengers who made up the Petrels. He behaved as if he wasn't aware of his status. Because he wasn't. In his mind, he just did his job as fast as he could and enjoyed it thoroughly.

"What about the bad guys?" said a large Petrel who insisted on being called Roadkill. Audra addressed him by his real name, Todd, because she feared The Margins might be all too willing to see his clever nickname as prophecy.

Both Yakiba and Auntie Bedlam remained out cold as a result of Audra's having flash-fried the oxygen from their immediate vicinity—which had also taken Po down, unfortunately. They were still out thanks to the treatment administered by a Petrel known only as Poppy. Audra had no idea if that was her real name or not, but she was a mythical who was a demon on wheels and had the ability to induce sleep for as long as she liked.

Audra never asked her if eternity was one of the girl's options. She didn't want to think about that. "Leave them," she said.

"They'll just keep after us," Roadkill said.

"They will," agreed Lottie, who'd returned with Whizbang after putting Po in the car.

Audra had asked Poppy to keep Po under, too. There was the risk he'd suffered a concussion, but she suspected he desperately needed the rest despite his superhuman constitution.

"Yes," Audra said. "They will. But we're not in the business of taking or keeping prisoners, and I wouldn't want them seeing our setup." There was the alternative, of course, but Audra was not one to take lives unless she absolutely had to. And this wasn't war.

Yet.

The Dodger nodded. He would be fine with nearly anything Audra said.

Roadkill and Lottie, however, weren't happy. Audra would have to keep an eye on them. The last thing she needed was bloodthirstiness in the ranks.

The discussion ended with the arrival of Biscuit, a scout whose name had yet to be explained to Audra. It was an odd choice, certainly, since he was a wiry, serious-as-death type whom Audra would have figured more for a special-forces operative than a cycling enthusiast.

There was no logic or reason to the group of misfits she'd inherited. And she didn't mind, so long as they were good at the work.

Which they were. Very.

"You need to see this, ma'am." Biscuit coasted to a stop and executed a perfect track stand with no visible effort.

Audra waited for him to elaborate, but he merely turned in a tight circle to go back the way he'd come.

She and the others followed.

Biscuit had that kind of presence. If he stated that something needed to be seen, it was seen.

And it needed to be.

Around the corner, in the middle of the side-street block, a black troop truck sat idling, as if waiting for a gate to be raised that only its driver could see. Behind the wheel was what appeared to be a prune-like corpse dressed up in someone's pilfered uniform. It saw nothing.

A Ravager uniform. In a Ravager truck. The first Audra had seen of Brill's former forces in The Margins.

The presence of mythicals was already a sign that the intersection of The Commons and The Living World was receiving visitors from both realms, and that was worrisome enough. But this upped the ante considerably.

Mr. Brill was gone, and the Ravagers had disappeared with him. Or so she and her partners had thought. If his forces still existed, how many were there? And who, if anyone, commanded them?

"There are more in the back," Roadkill said as Audra approached the truck's cab.

Her observation about the shriveled driver hadn't been too far from the truth. The Ravager's corpse was desiccated, as if he'd been blasted by a Martian death ray from some late-night black-and-white offering. An Essence leech? "Did you raise his helmet visor?" she asked Roadkill as the other Petrels maintained their distance.

"Yes, ma'am. I thought it was a dummy."

"Don't touch anything else." Audra headed around to the truck's rear and peered into the interior. Inside, rows of similarly dried-out husks in uniforms lined the troop transport's benches on either side. All of their visors remained down, but their oddly crumpled look told her all she needed to know.

The truck's engine died.

Audra came back around to the cab to find Lottie with the vehicle's key in her hand.

"We can use this," Lottie said.

"Drop it."

Reluctantly, the girl obeyed.

"Does anyone have hand sanitizer?"

Biscuit produced a first aid kit from the bag hanging under his seat and pulled a bottle of disinfectant from it. God bless the prepared.

Lottie squirted some into her palm and cleaned her hands.

"You, too," Audra said to Roadkill, who complied. "We have no idea who or what did this, so we leave it. Nobody else goes near this truck. Understood?"

The Petrels nodded or otherwise let their silence serve as their agreement.

Audra wasn't comfortable with lying to the Petrels. Up until now, any dishonesty on her part had been a sin of omission, not commission. But she did have some guesses as to what type of creature had done this, and it only made her worries increase.

First Ravagers, and now something able to drain Essence on a larger scale than even a mythical such as Parix might be capable of.

And it wasn't clear whose side it was on. Were these Ravagers supposed to join in with the mythicals who'd attacked Dodger and Po? Was it a separate effort, and they'd been sitting here, drained, already?

Too many questions. And Audra wasn't happy with any of the potential answers she could think of. Nor did she like surprises.

But since when had The Commons ever cared about what anyone liked?

77

WAR BALL

"Can we believe anything he says?"

Charlene and Reinhard sat in her office. The sealed-off portion they occupied in Envoy HQ was said to be secure—Demos would know if it wasn't—and the others would only let Charlene out of their sight with the accompaniment of a fighter.

Charlene was happy to have that fighter be Reinhard. He was her most experienced warrior, and she wanted his opinion. The former Vigil, having been both cop and assassin in his old line of work, labored under no false sense of optimism and no surfeit of trust.

He trusted no one.

"I don't know," Charlene told him. "It's a risk, but I don't see where we have a choice. We have to go out and see how many of our people have survived, how many are hurt. We need to clean Quarry's teammates out as quickly as we can. If he's willing to come over to our side, his help is worth having." She toyed with the View-Master. It had been cut off from the outside world, presumably jammed by the Ravager forces surrounding HQ.

"If he's lying?"

"We remove the threat."

Reinhard said nothing. He knew what Charlene meant, but would make her say it so there'd be no confusion. He was a pro. He knew what could happen afterward, when questions flew that hadn't been asked while the decisions were made.

"We kill him," Charlene said. "Which we were going to have to do anyway."

"Demos isn't on hand."

Charlene gave him a wry smile. It wasn't intended to communicate joy. "Did you know scientists believe that mountains are shaped by lightning strikes?"

"Meaning what? Remember, I don't do puzzles. I do direct."

"Lightning breaks rocks. Harris could use the confidence boost, couldn't he?"

Now Reinhard smiled. And Charlene had a better sense of why he'd been so good in his Vigil days. He was even scarier when he bared his teeth. "When you asked me in here, you talked about a two-pronged test."

"Yes. Quarry says he's already put the first part into motion."

"And part two?"

"We put Humpty back together again and see what he can do—while keeping an eye on him. And we take care of our people."

∽

GETTING VOLUNTEERS WASN'T A PROBLEM. Everybody jumped to venture out past the security gates to rescue their colleagues. So Charlene now stood before the gates where she'd been burned, the View-Master held to her eyes, counting down the numbers she saw there softly to the others to let them know when FinePoint would open the doors.

At three, she felt the others tense up around her. With Harris, that wasn't necessarily good, considering the harm he was capable of and his lack of refined control.

The sharp intake of breath was probably Koko's.

The click that came next was the cocking of the gun Reinhard pulled from a holster right before she'd put her eyes to the View-Master. He was a combat master at the level of any special-forces soldier, but his mythical power was one of invention. Had there been a patent office in The Commons, Reinhard's name would have been on dozens of them. He focused on weaponry as a hobby because he enjoyed it, so whatever he had aimed at the door, it was no doubt capable of real and inventive harm.

"One." Charlene dropped the View-Master into her waist pack and pulled her pistol as the others moved up on either side of her. They'd all argued that if she was going to lead this mission, she'd do it from the rear. When it became clear they wouldn't back down, she finally agreed.

The doors parted with a loud clunk and hiss, followed by a tearing and scraping as they dragged across the scarred floor. They hadn't healed since the acid blob did its damage. Maybe they never would.

With the hallway revealed, Quarry stepped to the front, ready to talk his fellow mythicals into foregoing any attack or block whatever it might be.

Reinhard watched the rock man intently for any dodgy moves. Whatever his gun was capable of, Charlene had no doubt it could handle the mythical should he try to betray them.

There was only the empty hallway lit by the security lights, several of which were blown out or failing, making an already unsettling atmosphere even more so with strobe effects and the occasional crack and sizzle of toasted wiring.

"They're melted," said Koko.

Something had burned the walls with black streaks of heat, blistering the paint and taking out the lights. Their lenses had sagged and then re-hardened into blackened bubbles.

A whisper from up the hall.

No, a soft cry.

Around the corner.

There for an instant.

Faint.

Then gone.

Reinhard and Harris looked to Charlene for guidance. She signaled Quarry to continue in the lead—both because he was the least vulnerable to whatever might be waiting for them and because she wanted to see how committed he was to helping.

The rock man moved forward, the sound of his progress like a shovel's worth of stone dumped onto the floor with every footfall. If whoever was there hadn't already known anyone was coming, they did now. He looked around the corner without caution. One probably didn't have to worry much about being harmed when one was made of stone. Whatever he saw made him move. "Leave her alone," he said to someone unseen as he disappeared around the corner.

First came the whine of an electric engine revving up, then the sound of something slamming into Quarry with a heavy crunch. He was carried backward into view, arms wrapped around a flying robotic sphere that drove him into the wall hard enough for the drywall to fissure and give way. Immediately, spider-like arms emerged from the sphere to return his grasp so that he couldn't escape. Two of those arms sprouted drill bits that began to spin with the high-pitched cry of a dentist's office before plunging into whatever areas of their foe they could reach first.

Reinhard leveled his gun at the sphere, but the robot and Quarry shifted position. He couldn't draw a bead without the risk that he'd hit the rock man as easily as he'd take out the machine.

The whine of the drills deepened and muffled as Quarry grunted in pain, the bits tunneling more deeply. Charlene hadn't realized he was capable of feeling anything.

"Harris! Hit it!" Quarry's voice was higher than it had been. He was able to feel quite a bit.

"What about you?" Harris said.

"Never mind about me!"

Harris looked to Reinhard, who gave him a quick nod of approval. The boy pointed both arms toward Quarry and the robot. His fingers flexed, and lightning arced into both robot and stone man.

The current had its way with both of them, and the awful result was as close as a machine could get to a scream. Quarry's left hand exploded, proving Charlene's earlier observation correct. The robot's systems cooked out. It dropped against Quarry, dead, hanging by the embedded drill for a moment before its arm snapped under the weight. The sphere crashed to the floor.

Quarry fell but kept his form, the sound of it like gravel sighing. Whatever he muttered next was inaudible to Charlene, but Reinhard caught part of it.

"Hurting who?" the ex-Vigil said.

"Her." Quarry couldn't raise his head, but he was able to indicate a direction with the arm that still had a hand on it.

Reinhard took a look, weapon at the ready, and Harris and Koko followed. Whatever was there, Reinhard lowered his rifle and disappeared around the corner, as did Harris and Koko.

Charlene looked to Quarry, who waved her on but made no attempt to rise.

Reinhard's gun was on the floor, within easy reach. He knelt in front of a girl who was badly burned. One half of her face was obliterated, along with the hair on that side of her head. His free hand hovered uselessly. There was no way to safely touch her.

Her. The whimpering had come from the girl. The sphere had been hurting her so that her pain would draw them forward. But if the robot was equipped with this type of fire weapon, why hadn't it used it on them?

The girl struggled to breathe. Her lungs had been burned.

"That thing did this?" said Koko.

As if to answer, Quarry smashed the sphere into the hallway floor hard enough to make all of them jump.

Reinhard had his rifle on him in a blink, and Charlene was only a beat behind him with her pistol.

Quarry didn't appear to notice. He drove the robot into the floor a second time, then over and over until it was a sphere no longer. "It didn't do this," he said when he'd finished. "This model War Ball doesn't have incendiary capabilities. That's the handiwork of one of my former teammates."

"Former." Reinhard didn't lower his rifle.

"Former." Quarry locked eyes with the former Vigil to make his point and rammed his remaining fist into the sphere. Hunting around in it until he found what he sought, he ripped out a fist-sized square box. He crushed that against the wall as its trailing wires waved like a banner. "Guidance unit. Its brains."

Reinhard put his gun down again.

The burned girl wore bright emerald work boots.

Charlene's stomach lurched. She knew who this was.

The girl had made those boots herself. She was one of the newly arrived Envoy trainees, who'd come to them only a week before.

"Jazz?" Charlene found herself hoping beyond all reason that if she said the girl's name softly enough, it might not be her after all.

Jazz coughed wetly. She raised a hand and lowered it to the floor again, where it fluttered like a stricken moth. It stopped, then fluttered again. After that, she was still, as if recognition meant permission to take her leave of this place and those who'd found her. One utterance. One small movement. And then she'd dismissed herself. She stirred no more.

Reinhard gently lifted Jazz's unburned arm, pushing her sleeve up to check for a pulse. He just as gently lowered it, picked up his gun, and stood, eyes on the hallway beyond. His gaze met Charlene's for only the briefest of moments. "How many more of those came in with you?" he said to Quarry.

"The War Ball? One was all I saw."

Reinhard nodded and advanced.

Harris and Koko, shaken but still on their game, followed.

Had they known what waited up ahead for them, they might not have.

78

THE TOPS OF THE LOW-FLYING CLOUDS

"I don't get it," Rain said.

Emmett poured out the remnants of a pot of coffee and set about preparing another. It was in keeping with the law of the tracks that stated one must put a new pot on for the next guy if what you left behind wasn't enough for a full cup. And it was a capital offense to leave a burned crust of Superfund-site muck, which is what Rain and Emmett created when they accidentally cycled the machine through a near-empty leaving.

The two of them sat in a converted sleeper car with only one bunk left in it. The rest were removed by The Commons as the Railwaymen, which is what the conductors and carriers were called collectively, gained experience in The Margins and no longer needed to sleep.

The bunk was Rain's to use. And given that strange men would be cycling through the room around the clock for downtime and breaks as the train's journey continued, it was understood that she'd sleep with her gun—and would use it, if it came to that.

Rain believed Emmett when he assured her that wouldn't

be necessary. And she was pretty sure he believed her when she told him that not having to shoot anyone would mean a better trip for her.

"What part don't you get?" said Emmett. "There's a lot to get snagged on."

"I didn't hear the engines or the chopper until they were on top of us. We should have heard them a long way off."

"They weren't there then."

"The Ravagers who got crushed were. So was the one I shot."

Emmett dumped a sizable amount of coffee into the filter, then added more. The Railwaymen no longer needed it to stay awake, but habit and tradition were everything. "What I mean is that they weren't until they were. Transit and movement doesn't work the same way in The Margins as it does in The Living World or The Commons. The Margins isn't a steady state. The intersection—the overlap—is growing. So there's such a thing as instant crossover."

"Which is how the train that brought me out of Chicago went poof when we were done with it."

"Yes. It's also why that L station only came into being when you needed it. And you said an SUV saw you."

"Yeah." Rain watched him pour even more coffee in. She liked hers strong but wouldn't be sampling any of this. The Railwaymen blend was strong enough to chew.

"That's what connected them to us. A touch of adjacency. They spotted you, and you served as a conduit to draw them in. That's the first time we've had to fire on anyone since we started making these runs."

"Sorry."

Emmett filled the pot with water from a tiny utility faucet that served as both washbasin and kitchen sink, then poured that into the beat-up little machine's reservoir. Human coffee would've required a lot more water than he used. "No apology necessary. We didn't suffer any losses in people, charges, or gear. Just a few dozen nanomen." He spotted the guilt on her face. "It's like the colony losing a few worker ants, Rain. More die getting squished while they're working. Think of them as a sum total, not individuals. It's not much different than cutting your nails."

Rain let that settle in. The nanomen were kind of cute—so long as you weren't a crunched Ravager. "Did you say charges?"

"You know what those are?"

Rain nodded. She'd once been one. "Where are they?"

"The containers. You noticed how carefully they were handled?"

She had. And knowing that the operation treated them with care made the fact that those were sentient, albeit slumbering, beings in those steel boxes sit a little better with her. But only a little. "And the passengers?"

"Marginals. Some departed who were pulled into the overlap between The Living World and The Commons when they should've moved on to start their Journeys. Others unloved, ignored, or just-plain unfortunate souls who fell out of the awareness of others to the point that they exist only in an in-between place such as this."

The kids. All those little children traveling alone. It hurt her heart to think of them.

Emmett hit the button to start brewing and picked up on her sadness. "You don't know their stories. All grim, most likely—but not as bad as they'd be without us."

"What do you mean?"

He watched the licorice stream of coffee trickle down. The pot could have stood a good washing, but Rain guessed it wasn't a priority. "We can't leave them back east. They'd be sitting ducks for Manitou."

"Who's Manitou?"

"Manitou is a company."

"That doesn't answer my question."

"Who was Brill?" Emmett continued to watch the coffee stream as if he were staring into a fire. The clack of the train's wheels over the tracks drowned out the sound of liquid into liquid.

"Same as the old boss. Is that what you're telling me?"

"No. Worse."

Rain tried to let the rhythm of the steel soothe her. It didn't. Everything she and Paul had accomplished, had it been for nothing? Worse than that? Paul said he'd done something that someone bad had wanted him to do. And that she'd helped. "Where are you taking them?"

"Same direction we're taking you. West."

"Why?"

"They can't stay in New York. Manitou's too strong there now. They can't even stay in Chicago. We leave them there long enough to adjust to being transported so they're not traumatized. Then we keep them rolling. Us and the Highwaymen. It's all we can do."

"How do you know the west is safe?"

"It's not. Nothing is. But it's safer than back east. And it's what we can do. We move whoever and whatever needs moving. It's what we did in The Commons. It's what we do in The Margins. And it's what we'll continue to do until they blow us out of the sky."

Rain assumed she'd misheard him. "The sky?"

Emmett crossed to the nearest window, raised its blind, and motioned for her to join him.

Rain looked out into passing fog until they hit a break in it.

It took a few seconds before she caught herself holding her breath.

The moon lit the tops of the low-flying clouds and the wide-open expanses of prairie below. Far below. They were riding a fast-moving train.

And that train was speeding through thin air.

MUCH OF WHAT IS TRUE IS DUMB

The front door opening and the lights turning on startled Porter out of the sleep he hadn't felt coming on. He grabbed his staff and squinted at the perpetrator.

A young girl with a shaved head, hand still on the switch, gaped at Porter from the doorway.

Next to her, a large gray dog that looked to have some poodle in it—along with, thankfully, a nonviolent disposition—regarded him calmly. The dog took a seat, as if a show were about to begin.

"The lights work," said the girl.

"That appears to be the case." Porter prepared to bring his staff into play if necessary, grateful that the counter blocked it from view.

The dog stood again.

It was an understandable approach for both of them. What appeared to be harmless in The Commons and, by extension, in their current crossover realm, might easily prove to be anything but. Many a Journey went downhill fast when that possibility wasn't taken into account.

"They didn't work for us before," the girl said.

The dog moved closer to her. The meaning of the repositioning was clear. Mess with the girl, mess with the big pooch.

"It seems you have the magic touch."

The girl took her hand off the switch and casually dropped it into her pocket. Porter guessed she had something hidden away that she'd be willing to use; she was not to be taken lightly. "Do you think so?" Her question wasn't an honest one. She probably had nothing to do with the lights working once more, but she wanted to get Porter talking in order to better evaluate him as a potential threat.

"Do you live here?" Porter said.

"Why do you want to know where I live?"

Porter tilted his head in acknowledgement. "I apologize. That is indeed a dangerous question when asked by the wrong person." He waited for the tension to subside. "My name is Jonas."

The girl looked down at the dog, which sat again, eyes never leaving Porter. Whatever she saw in its demeanor relaxed her a little. "I'm Lexi. This is Angus. I don't know where he lives, but I've stayed here before. They tried to make me stay somewhere else. I walked back. I don't like being told where to go."

"Nor do I."

Lexi looked around the space. "I have a feeling this isn't quite the same place it was before." She reached down to scratch Angus behind his ears. "I know that sounds dumb, but it's true."

"Much of what is true is dumb," Porter said.

Lexi continued around Angus's head to a spot under his chin. "And a lot of what is dumb is true."

The big dog leaned back, closed his eyes, and broke wind.

Porter decided he liked them both. He also knew Angus's

eyes weren't entirely shut. He didn't know Porter well enough to trust him that much. "Your perceptions are correct, Lexi. This is not the same New Beginnings."

"What is it, then?" Lexi scratched Angus's throat until he opened his eyes again and pulled away a bit, looking around as if hearing something that eluded the girl and Porter.

"It's a version that exists in an in-between place." Porter watched her to see how she reacted to that. He didn't want to continue if it looked like she might be overly upset or confused.

Angus no longer paid them any mind. He looked around a few more times and then focused his attention on a darkened hallway off the far side of the lobby.

"But you knew that, didn't you? Even if you couldn't quite put it into words?"

"Yeah," Lexi said. "It's not just here. It's everywhere. The city. Outside the city. I've seen some people I know, and they're the same. But none of the places are. They mostly look the same, but they're not."

"They are not."

Angus moved away from Lexi and took a step or two toward the far hallway.

Lexi reached out and grabbed him by the collar, pulling him close to her again.

When she released him, he moved away once more.

Porter took the opportunity to slide the Newton back into his coat pocket. As he did so, he couldn't help but notice that both its expansion slots were empty. The card containing the information downloaded into him—there was no other way to describe it—was gone.

"Where are we?" said Lexi.

"The Margins."

"What's The Margins?"

"It's what it feels like—an in-between realm. There are different kinds of those. This one is a crossing over between The Living World and a place called The Commons. It's an overlap. Did you study Venn diagrams in school?"

"I didn't get to go to school much."

"I'm sorry for my assumption."

"But I've stayed in shelters where they had teachers come in. Those are the things with the sets, right? The universal and the circles?" Lexi tried to pull Angus over to her again. Learning and school weren't comfortable memories for her.

Once again, the dog stood his ground and peered intently at the dark hallway. His ears pulled back against his head.

"Exactly," Porter said. "If The Living World is one circle, and The Commons is another, then the intersection—the overlap—is what they share. It's made up of both. That's The Margins, where we are now. And it's growing. I think that might be why the lights did not work earlier but are working now."

"Is that okay? It doesn't sound like it. Not the way you talk about it." She tried again to ease Angus back against her, but the dog took another step forward. A low growl built in his throat. She stroked his back, and he stopped.

There was no point in lying to her. "No, it's not okay, Lexi. Not if what some friends of mine tell me is correct. I should tell you it's fine, I suppose. But I suspect you're strong enough to know the truth. And the truth is that it's not."

"I had a feeling something was up." Lexi made a gentle shushing noise to the dog. It didn't soothe him much. "Angus wouldn't leave me alone until I followed him. And then he wouldn't let me catch him. He just kept going until we were back here. It took two hours to walk it. Do you think he knew you'd be here?"

"I honestly cannot say. Dogs can be very smart. In The Commons, many of them aren't even dogs."

"What's The Commons?"

"Where I'm from."

"Where are you from?"

"That's a long answer," Porter said. "I—do you know Paul Reid?"

Angus yanked himself away from Lexi and began to bark angrily at the darkness of the hallway. It wasn't for show. Not by the sound of it.

"Hey, hey! Angus!" Lexi reached for him, but he continued to evade her.

A line of water appeared in the hallway, rolling out of the darkness. It thickened into a puddle that came only partway into the light.

Angus barked even more frantically, guarding Lexi but clearly unnerved by what he sensed in the hallway. Still, he remained in a protective stance.

"Angus!" Lexi said. "Hey! Angus!"

Porter moved quickly around the lobby counter, staff raised, and stepped between the barking dog and the puddle as it continued to seep from the dark hallway, forming into something more discernibly solid. He waved his hand at the dog and, miraculously, Angus settled down to a whine again, retreating to a spot next to Lexi.

Lexi started to say something, but Porter waved her into silence, too.

He kept his staff raised as the puddle rose and coalesced into the form he feared it would take. "Hello again, Parix."

"Greetings, Envoy." The chorus of voices emanated from several of Parix's tooth-ringed tentacles at once. All sounded amused.

Porter heard Lexi take a few steps back behind him.

The jingle of Angus's collar and tag told him she was taking the dog with her. Now he was allowing it.

"It's a pleasure to see you." Two or three of Parix's tentacles tracked what Porter assumed was Lexi's retreat behind him.

Porter didn't dare turn to look. "I won't share the sentiment. To lie to your faces would be rude, wouldn't you say?"

"I need say nothing at all." He was definitely paying a good deal of attention to Lexi. She was from The Living World, and her Essence would be a rare treat for the leech. He'd only dreamed about such a find in The Commons.

"There's nothing for you here, Parix. Nothing to justify you traveling this far. Are you really so hungry for what little juice is left in this old carcass of mine?"

Parix ignored him. They both knew Porter was not his first choice. "I know that dog," he said. "He is not a very nice dog. Is he yours, girl? He tried to bite me. I thought I'd killed him."

"Lexi," said Porter. "Take Angus back down into one of those rooms behind me, please.

The jingle of Angus's tag and the scratch of his nails on the tile told Porter the dog was going with the girl whether he liked it or not.

Porter weighed his options. It was curious that Parix came no closer. He seemed to favor the hallway from which he'd emerged. "Why are you tracking me, Parix?"

"Why do you assume it's you we're after?"

We? Who else was the leech with?

A car pulled up in front of the building.

Porter couldn't take his eyes off Parix. But he was tempted, especially when the engine cut off.

Parix returned the favor and kept his attention on Porter. When had the leech last fed? Had it been long enough for him to be a little weak?

Porter didn't have an answer to that question, but only a moment later, it occurred to him why Parix was coming no closer. He was a parasite, a creature of stolen Essence. If he attacked Angus, he did so here in The Margins. And he'd ambushed Porter in The Commons, which meant he was able to travel between the worlds, having sampled Essence in both. Yet he wasn't able to come any further into this one. That made things interesting. "You don't have enough in your system," Porter said.

Two of the leech's tentacles angled toward the window. Whoever had just pulled up out there, Parix was very interested in seeing who they were. "Of what?"

"Essence from The Margins. You can't cross over entirely without feeding here."

The wayward tentacles turned back to Porter. He'd gotten Parix's attention, which meant they might yet make it out of this alive.

The ashes from the campfire at the Dew Drop Inn, where Parix had killed poor Mira. There'd need to be an accounting for that—and for much more. And Porter thought he saw an opportunity to hand the leech at least some of what he deserved.

Car doors closed outside. No, heavier than car doors. A truck?

Parix looked again—with one tentacle at first, then all of them. "Our friends have arrived—and the lost boy is found."

Porter wouldn't get a better chance. With what was done to Mira in mind, he gave his staff a turn and pushed with all of his ability. He targeted only a part of the leech.

All of Parix's tentacles cried out in pain.

Porter was probably supposed to feel bad about that. He turned the staff again, separating the leech as he jumped as much of him as he could back through whatever doorway he'd used to travel from The Commons proper to The Margins.

Had there been too much crossover, it wouldn't have worked, but Parix screamed even louder. There was still enough differentiation between the worlds.

Porter pushed again, giving it his all once more.

The tentacles Porter could see went silent abruptly, then dropped into the puddle and became one with the liquid there. It worked. The leech was banished for now but had left a chunk of himself behind.

Porter hoped it would never stop hurting. Now he looked out the window himself and couldn't help but smile despite the fresh fatigue washing over him from his efforts. The lost boy had indeed been found.

"Paul!" said Lexi from behind him. She headed for the front door, Angus at her heels, as a large teen boy with ample dreadlocks came around the van to talk to Paul.

But the joyous reunion was not to be.

From across the street came the rest of the "we" Parix had referred to earlier, rapidly closing in on Paul and his friend from either side.

"Lexi."

Porter's tone stopped the girl in her tracks.

The two mythicals who were clearly about to attack Paul and the dreadlocked boy were, along with Parix, among the most vicious The Commons had to offer.

Porter moved.

Then everything went to hell.

80

SKIP TRACER

"I only wish we had more like you." William Belden's call pulled Annie away from the giant switchboard. She hadn't expected to hear from him again, especially after a short official email from the system informed her that her ticket, opened due to her initial report about the disappearing switchboards, had been closed. Yet he'd followed up with a second live call.

The first was rare. A second was unheard of, especially from the same S&P guy. She might have suspected that the man had taken a shine to her, but they'd never met, and her relationship with Bobby, another Manitou employee, ruled that out. Anyway, Annie had another, stronger suspicion about it, one resulting from a thought left waiting for her when she donned the VR unit.

Annie knew the reason for Belden's call.

Ever since she'd sensed something in Zach's closet, her knee hadn't tingled nearly as much, nor had she been subjected to corrective thoughts. It was like something blocked it. While that seemed fanciful, she had the sense it was exactly why Belden called rather than let the closed-ticket notification be the last word.

He called to check up on her. Because the normal way of keeping tabs wasn't working anymore.

Often, gut-level hunches were silly and wrong.

But sometimes they weren't.

There was no other reason for Belden to pick up the phone. If anything, it made her think more about her ticket being closed than she otherwise might have.

That was why she requested the skip tracer, which showed up in the form of a large flying ant. The ant landed on the board in front of her, shedding its wings and standing almost at attention, studying her. Once she'd taken notice of it, it marched its way down the switchboard to an open hole and disappeared into it.

The ticket was closed. Something she'd discovered was, according to Belden, tied to somebody who did something wrong. Annie hoped the skip tracer would find out who.

Skip tracers adopted various forms for different users in the VR realm, as did most things. Annie tried not to use them since the system had a habit of sending them over with mildly distasteful customizations to discourage their being called on too often. She'd had a thing about flying ants since discovering, after picking one up as a kid and riling it up, that they could defend themselves. And it hurt when they did. The system knew that and used it against her, but it didn't dissuade her this time.

Annie lost herself in the routine of the connection and cleanup until the skip tracer quite literally came back to bite her. No hint or warning, just a fiery attack on the base of her neck, which yanked her out of the reverie of task completion. She reached behind her to take a whack at her assailant, but it flew over her head and landed on the board in front of her.

"You little jerk." Annie rubbed her neck where the burning was spreading. "Was that really necessary?"

The skip tracer probably would have replied in the affirmative had it deemed her worthy of a response.

Along with the burning came the knowledge the ant had acquired. Then she understood why it hurt.

If anything, she wished it hurt worse. It might have made her feel a little better.

Abel Dowd. That was the name of the young man she'd doomed with her conscientious-employee act. Abel Dowd.

Dowd was doing things with data he wasn't supposed to do —copying and storing it for purposes that would remain a mystery due to the bloodthirstiness of the Manitou watchdogs. Whether that was Belden himself or merely someone he'd told to pull the trigger, the end result was the same. And from what she could glean via the furious knowledge the skip tracer stung her with, the company's trigger-happy ways had once again worked against it. Rather than being patient enough to see what Dowd was doing, Manitou had shut him down. So they had no idea what he'd been up to.

However, thanks to the adjacency granted by her unintentional betrayal, the same might not be said of Annie. The knowledge made her head spin a bit. The knowledge and the caustic data of the bite.

The stinging information had another layer to it, which peeled itself back while the skip tracer watched, and Annie fought to avoid giving it the satisfaction of seeing her grimace. Not that it would have cared.

The catch: Manitou might not know what Dowd knew, but somebody else did. Dowd left a record behind. A journal of sorts. And someone had accessed it just now. Either it was whoever removed Dowd from the board or, Annie hoped, someone in league with him who could be trusted.

Annie herself had no idea what Dowd had been doing, but she owed it to him to find out, at least, and then make a decision from there. She leaned forward to blow softly on the ant, which once again dropped its wings and even appeared to bow slightly in deference.

More likely, it was just letting her know it was on the job. It disappeared back into one of the switchboard holes to relay a howdy to the journal opener.

Now all Annie could do was hope that whoever was on the receiving end was on her side. If not, she might end up finding out a lot more than she wanted to about the fate of Abel Dowd.

~

"WHAT'S IT TO YOU?" Bobby stopped stuffing pants and underwear—a lot of underwear, enough for a long trip—into his suitcase to glare at Annie. Sometimes it seemed as if he were just looking for a reason to communicate via his open hand again.

"I'd just like to know how long you'll be gone so I can adjust my schedule. And I can let Ambit know if it's going to affect pick-up and drop-off."

Bobby held her gaze for another moment or two. When he thought he'd made whatever point he hadn't actually made, he went back to packing. "It's not for you to worry about."

"Just to be clear, then, I can't know where you're going, why you're going, or for how long you're going." Annie wasn't going to get answers; she just wanted to make him pay in aggravation.

Bobby answered by finishing the pants packing and moving on to his shirts. Once those were done, he continued to ignore her and layered in more workout and sleeping stuff than he probably needed. He never rolled his clothes, which would have allowed him to get a lot more in, so it was inevitable that when he tried to shut the suitcase to see how he was doing for room, it was already harder to close than it should have been. "You have one job outside of *the* job," he said, pushing the suitcase closed hard enough to stress-test the entire bed. "The knee."

"The knee. Of course."

Bobby stopped punishing the suitcase and fixed her with another glare. Was her tone one of agreement, or was she making fun of him?

"Of course." Annie added a degree of sincerity. She liked the idea of Bobby being unsure of her intent, off balance. Almost as much as she liked the fact that the knee injections no longer seemed to have much of an effect, if any. The tingling had fallen off, along with the mental suggestions to improve her attitude about the man with whom she shared a bed. She wasn't thinking of him as the father of their child much, especially since he didn't act the part. And she hadn't thought of him as her partner in a long, long time.

Bobby's stare turned cold. He looked her up and down, as if moving from trying to decide whether to hit her again to figuring out where.

The knee injections really were having less of an effect, then. Annie found herself considering just where she'd return the favor if it came to that. And how much damage to inflict.

When she showed no sign of accommodating his fit of pique, Bobby went to get the injector.

Feeling magnanimous after facing him down, Annie let him.

81

HURRIERS AND HARRIERS

After lunch, Jeremy turned off the Wi-Fi on his phone so that it couldn't connect to the Manitou network. He'd use his data connection in an attempt to keep his employers from knowing what he was up to.

The irony of looking to his mobile provider to protect his privacy wasn't lost on him. It just wasn't something he felt like laughing about at the moment.

He swiveled his chair so that the phone screen faced away from the door and anyone who might walk past, checking the walls and ceilings for focusites again. Only when he determined that the room was free of all prying eyes, human and otherwise, did he search for the QR Boy app.

At first, he had no luck. But after a moment, and without any further input, the app showed up in the results. He installed it and, checking for focusites yet again, opened it. Only then did he take out the Gladiator's QR code.

It might have been his imagination or, perhaps, the extra coffee he'd already finished, but it almost felt as if the app and the paper with the code on it were pulled toward each other. Just a bit, but it was there.

His phone stopped responding, which it sometimes did when he was trying to run too many things at once. Whatever the code was supposed to do, it was heavy.

Jeremy flipped the slip of paper over. It was now blank.

There was no time to contemplate that mystery. A reminder popped up on his monitor: it was time to meet with Truitt, which was something he still hadn't gotten used to doing alone. And Truitt, like everyone else at Manitou, behaved as if there'd never been any Abel at all.

A few minutes later, Jeremy sat at the conference table in Truitt's darkened office, listening to one of the directors go through a presentation on the latest tweaks to the Apalala program. The director, who was named Amanda or Amelia—Jeremy couldn't remember because his brain felt like it wasn't his own in Truitt's office—was talking about how the crazy exorcism attempt and the subsequent review revealed flaws in the program's code—flaws that were now fixed.

"Fixed how?" Truitt asked in the darkness. "Fixed as in improved or fixed as in done away with?"

"Sir?" Amanda or Amelia was flummoxed or bewildered.

"It's the difference between surgery to remove a problem and true healing or curing. Was the issue with Apalala merely erased from the code, or was it rewritten or patched in a way that constitutes an improvement?"

"I'm not sure we can distinguish between the two, sir." Amanda or Amelia sounded like she was probably relieved to be speaking with the lights off. That way, her nerves could only be heard and not seen.

"Well, you may not be able to, but Mr. Callibeau will."

There was a long moment of silence as Amanda or Amelia came up with her response. "I think it was a bit of both, sir.

The exorcism attempt and the ensuing server crash caused a reset that forced us to restore a previous version of the software. That previous version had a less developed AI element, but that hasn't seemed to have caused any problems."

Jeremy studied the graph Amanda or Amelia had up on one of Truitt's eerie floating screens, which made it look as if the graphic was projected onto the air itself. The graph showed a definite improvement curve. Unfortunately, it wasn't labeled clearly enough for him to understand exactly what was getting better.

He hoped Amanda or Amelia knew. For her sake.

"So our Apalala is alive and well but scoring a bit lower on its aptitude tests. It won't be getting into as exclusive a school as it might have before," Truitt said.

Amanda or Amelia laughed harder than the joke warranted, but Jeremy couldn't really blame her. The fact that Mr. Truitt cracked a funny at all meant she wouldn't have to worry about the kind of fallout that came when he wasn't happy with a presentation.

Jeremy's phone vibrated in his pocket. He was glad he'd kept his notifications on silent. Had whatever the QR code set into motion finished? He couldn't chance checking in the dark.

"Fine," Truitt said. "However, while those Apalala graphs are quite cheerful in their direction, a similar representation of our current momentum would not generate the same delight. It would be flat at best and, if the latest forecasts end up being correct, might even show a slight decline. Mr. Callibeau's sensitivities make the idea of such a performance quite unpleasant for him. And we'd hate to see that make it quite unpleasant for all of us. Let's endeavor to avoid such an outcome, shall we?"

Fearful silence turned to murmurs of assent, but it took a few brave souls to get that going before the others joined in.

"I think that's about all we need for now. Lights, please," Truitt said. "As you know, Mr. Callibeau doesn't want us to be the type of organization that spends so much time reporting on its performance that it doesn't have any left to spend attempting to optimize it."

The lights came up without anyone near the switch. Everyone squinted. Truitt's office was able to achieve a more complete darkness than any other room in the building, for some reason, and it took longer for the eyes to adjust once the blackness was dispelled.

The only one who didn't squint was Truitt.

The others got up to leave. Jeremy, who'd taken a seat farthest from the door, waited for everyone else to file out.

"A word, Mr. Johns?" Truitt said quietly. Jeremy wasn't sure, but it seemed as if he didn't want the others to hear him.

Jeremy hung back.

"Mr. Johns."

"Mr. Truitt."

"Mr. Johns, there are two kinds of people in this world." He paused long enough for Jeremy to wonder if he wanted Jeremy to ask him which world he was talking about, but Jeremy was fairly certain he already knew. "There are hurriers and harriers, the former forever made to speed up by the latter, who benefit from it. I'm not going to ask which you are. I've made my guess already, and now I wait for you to show me if I'm right."

Jeremy had no idea what to make of that. "Yes, sir."

"Manitou is trying to make sense of these worlds of ours and how their current alignment—or, rather, the shift in their relationship to one another—affects performance. We've had some unpleasant surprises, but we can play them to our advantage if we're thoughtful in our response. Do you agree?"

Panic tried to have its way with Jeremy, but he wrestled it down before it was apparent. He truly didn't know what Truitt meant. And he couldn't figure out if he was supposed to know. Apparently, he was. "Absolutely, sir," he said.

Truitt chuckled as if he knew Jeremy was faking it and was amused by the attempt. "Fine."

Jeremy turned to go.

"Mr. Johns?"

He stopped by the door. "Mr. Truitt?"

Truitt smiled with his eyes. He liked this game, whatever it was. "Nobody likes surprises, Mr. Johns. Mr. Dowd didn't, and I'm sure you don't, either."

The first mention of Abel since his disappearance.

"You give the matter some thought, Mr. Johns." With that, Mr. Truitt began scrolling through something on his phone. Jeremy was dismissed.

When he got back to his desk, Jeremy once again scanned for focusites and, not spotting any, pulled out his phone. A compressed file sat on his screen. He hadn't put it there. It was the newest arrival, so it should have gone to his last screen by default, but it hadn't.

Then there was the file name: "JJJ."

Should he risk opening it in the office? That'd be a stupid chance to take, particularly since there was nothing to say that an environment capable of sprouting living spies on the wall couldn't come up with other ways to monitor him. Best leave it for home.

His phone vibrated again.

Email now—but personal, not Manitou-related.

The notification was all he needed to decide not to do anything related to Abel or the file before he'd left for the day.

The email's subject line ordered him, in all caps, to open it only away from the office.

He decided to heed the command, even though it was from someone he didn't know.

Whatever awaited him, he wanted to feel more secure. So he hoped he'd find out more about Annie Brucker before trusting her entirely.

82

LOOK FOR YOURSELF WHERE YOU'RE NOT

Zach didn't need to hear the raised voices of Zach's mother and I'm-Bobby to know they were fighting. They fought when they talked at a conversational volume. They fought when they weren't talking at all. It was only a question of whether the fight was bad—or very bad.

It was very bad when I'm-Bobby hit Zach's mother because Zach had taken his pills away.

"No." Aidan spoke from the darkness of the open closet door. "That was because of who he is. The pills' absence is an explanation, not an excuse."

Zach rolled over in bed, trying to gauge I'm-Bobby's anger. He wanted to know if I'm-Bobby was going to hurt Zach's mother again.

If he tried, Zach wouldn't let him.

Not again.

"If he tries, she won't let him," said Aidan. "And if she can't stop him, I will."

Zach rolled over again, his back to the closet now.

"He is not the only one who'll travel."

Zach knew that already. But he said nothing and practiced

thinking things Aidan couldn't hear. He was getting better at it. And he was reasonably certain that his thoughts were shielded when he wanted them to be—that Aidan wasn't just tricking him into believing it.

Doing so made him tired. But not tired enough to sleep. Sleep was getting harder for Zach to come by.

Aidan made Zach uneasy. He knew Aidan wanted to help him and Zach's mother. But he also knew Aidan might well be willing to put Zach and Zach's mother at risk for whatever larger plan he had in mind.

Zach had the same feeling about Aidan and his bigger ideas that he had whenever he thought about the various forces telling him what he needed to do in The Commons. Listening to the powerful meant doing things for them, not for him. And doing things for them had gotten him swallowed whole.

Mosasaur, the little farmer said in his head. That was the word for the thing that helped others but hurt Zach. Mosasaur.

"You should prepare for a coming departure as well," Aidan said. "Things are going to move fast."

Zach knew that to be true, just as he was sure now that Aidan hadn't heard the thoughts Zach kept from him. Aidan was on his side. And on the side of Zach's mother, for the most part.

But he was even more on his own side. So Zach needed to be careful about listening to him.

As Zach finally fell asleep, he understood the greater truth of it.

He needed to be careful about listening to anyone.

∽

IN THE DREAM, Zach stood in a phone booth with a man who wore glasses and an earpiece that blinked blue. It was very hot.

"This is not a dream," said the man.

Outside the phone booth, the landscape was gray mud under a gray sky. Trenches cut across the lifeless land like the tunneled lines under the bark of a dead tree.

And death it was. Broken barbed wire traversed wide expanses interrupted by the ruins of blasted trees. The trenches closer to the phone booth were half-filled with water, and Zach didn't look any closer because he knew what rotted there. The exposed rib cages, partial skulls, and helmets in the mud told him.

It was hot in the phone booth.

"Don't pay attention to what's out there. It's of no concern to you. It happened a long time ago, and you cannot help them. Save yourself."

So hot.

Zach reached for the handle to the phone-booth door and pulled. But the door folded inward, and there was no room for it to open. Not with the two of them filling the space.

The smell from outside was terrible.

He pushed the door closed again.

The man held a lantern. That was where the heat came from. The flame was not large, but it hurt to look at. And it burned much hotter than it should have. The heat would kill him, but not the man. Even if it didn't, the lantern would burn all the air.

Zach looked up at the man, who peered down at him through no-frame glasses—expressionless, waiting. There was something wrong with the man's eyes—a glowing movement in them the same color as the lantern flame.

Then Zach saw it. His pupils were windows to a deeper

place within the man. And that place burned. The man had fire in his eyes.

The air in the phone booth grew hotter still. There was less of it than there'd been a second before, and what was there hurt to breathe.

Zach's eyes were so dry that blinking hurt. He coughed, and the cough nearly ended in a sob. But he did not cry. Even if he died here with the man, he would not cry.

"Zach's mother faced this very danger," the man said. Was he using Zach's name for her to mock him or distract him? "It was not I who threatened her, but it would be now. That doesn't mean what you think it does."

The eyes. Zach struggled to stop looking at the fire in the man's eyes. They burned so hot, as if they were at the other end of a tunnel, pulling the life and breath from Zach.

"Zach's mother escaped. You will not if you don't master yourself in short order."

Zach tried to pull the door inward again, ignoring the pain of the hot metal against his palm. He succeeded only in banging it against his knee. He kicked at the door, beginning to panic.

"An impressive noise," the man said. "But it won't help you." His face softened, as if he'd heard himself and decided his tone was overly harsh. "Focus, Zach. The door is the mirror. There is no difference."

The door is the mirror? Zach looked at the glass, but the light was wrong. He wasn't able to see his own reflection.

The heat.

Zach tried to back away from the lantern and the man, but there was nowhere for him to go. His face felt tight, as did the skin on his hands. They were too close to the lantern. His knuckles were going to split from the heat.

"You have an ability Zach's mother lacks. She crawled. You

needn't. Focus. Look for yourself where you're not."

What did that mean? What could it mean? At least the dragon fish—*mosasaur*, said a voice in his head—presented a game for him to play.

This was no game. He was going to die here with this man.

"Your fate is yours to determine. Find yourself."

Zach fought his fear. Swallowed it.

Out among the trenches, the remnants of the trees witnessed his failure.

The heat grew.

"Zach."

Zach nearly fell into the man's burning eyes again.

"Find yourself."

This time, Zach was able to look away more easily.

Again, the trees beckoned.

One of them wasn't a tree.

There, in the distance, as if there were a mirror far out there.

Him.

Himself.

Out there.

Though Zach couldn't see his own eyes the way he had in the closet-door mirrors, when he'd switched places with himself in Zach's mother's apartment, he didn't have to. He needed only to understand that he was there and then connect and change places.

The man gave a light laugh of approval.

Zach couldn't tell if he was stepping forward or being pushed.

But the door to the phone booth grew larger as he was about to press himself against it.

The heat receded behind him, and he joined himself amongst the death and trees.

83
DOTS UP

Reinhard took the lead. He put Harris in back, insisting it was his duty to place himself in harm's way while the kid was needed to make sure nothing snuck up on them.

Charlene didn't buy any of that. Reinhard didn't trust Quarry, and he didn't want the rock man to have the opportunity to lead them into an ambush or sucker them when they weren't looking.

Quarry knew it, too. To his credit, he pretended he didn't and fell in toward the middle of the group as they proceeded quickly—but not quietly, given the rock man's crunchy gait—down the hall.

They made it to the waiting room without incident, and Charlene was heartened when Reinhard found that the doors were still sealed.

According to protocol, the Envoys working the room and those close enough to get in before it secured itself would stay in there to tend to the waiting Journeymen who hadn't been assigned a case number. They'd see to their needs and defend them if they had to.

Charlene prayed it hadn't come to that. The sealed doors were a good sign.

Her optimism fell away when Reinhard placed his splayed fingers against the reader plate and opened the door to reveal nothing but darkness. Then came the smell. An awful wave of burned plastic, clothing, and—there was no mistaking it—people.

The waiting room was deathly silent. A mammoth room that regularly changed itself to mimic the waiting rooms of classic stations such as Grand Central, New York's Penn Station—the original, not the monstrosity that replaced it for decades—and wondrous terminals from the golden age of railroad around the world, it protected countless souls who would recall nothing of the experience. They'd simply move on to meet their assigned Envoy, who'd let them know where they were, why, and what the stakes were.

That's how it should have gone.

The odor of death told a different tale.

Reinhard stepped in and motioned for Harris to join him. The young trainee generated a small arc of electricity between the palms of his hands, illuminating the room in a jumpy blue-white incandescence.

There was smoke but not enough to explain the smell. The room had cleared some of it out, most likely.

The rows upon rows of benches were empty. The pulsing light provided by the electricity revealed that the wood was scarred and discolored. Charlene ran her finger over the nearest bench, and it came away soot black.

The group worked its way farther into the room. All of the benches were scorched.

"A fire?" Koko was tight.

"Where is everyone?" Harris was worse.

No one had answers.

"That's what I was wondering." The air by the door erupted into a ball of flame that morphed into the shape of a man.

By the pulsing light of the man's fire, the room was easier to see. It was indeed empty, and the scorch marks covered the walls, too.

"Flameout." Quarry maneuvered himself between the fire entity and the rest of their group.

Reinhard took aim at the fire entity as Harris's arc became twin fistfuls of ball lightning that looked eager to launch themselves.

Quarry held his one good hand up, gesturing for the two to hold off. "What happened here?"

"I was going to ask you that very thing." Little flare-ups played over Flameout's form. "I'm attending to the mission. What are you doing?"

"Where are the others?"

The fiery man laughed. "There's another question. I'd say it depends on which group you mean, but I don't have an answer for either of them. Our teammates disappeared on me, so I think they all abandoned ship. I'm too dutiful for that, so I carried on alone."

"Too sick, you mean." Quarry shifted position. "You enjoy the work too much to leave."

"It was fun, I have to say." Flameout said, chuckling again. "I managed to sneak in here before the doors sealed, so a whole host of targets were trapped in here with me. But as you can see, I don't even have the proof of my good work. Dots up, and then they were all gone."

"Dots up?" Charlene knew she'd regret the question.

"The position of the dials on an old stove when it's turned off," Quarry explained. "He's particularly proud of that line for some reason."

"One giant flare," said Flameout. The air was gone before they knew what I'd done. I don't think it hurt. Much. Or for very long. I guess."

They were all gone—both the Journeymen-to-be and the Envoys assigned to help them. As far as Charlene knew, such a thing had not happened in hundreds of generations, and even that account—of a lethal plague that had decimated the Journeymen, the waiting Journeymen, and a good portion of the Envoys in biblical fashion—was widely questioned. Only The Commons knew where they'd gone. But it was clear they'd all been robbed of the opportunity to determine or at least influence their fates.

Charlene joined Reinhard in drawing down on the fire elemental.

Flameout was unfazed. "I think it's just you and me, pal," he told Quarry. "So are you gonna help me, or do I have to do all the heavy lifting myself?"

Charlene and Reinhard fired at the same time, and Harris was only a moment behind with a blinding gout of lightning. It wasn't clear whether it was the electricity or the burst of whatever Reinhard's gun used for ammo that did it, but Flameout became his namesake, exploding into several smaller fireballs. Some of them were extinguished in mid-air, but the rest quickly formed into a floating orb. A moment later, it became a flaming column that lanced forward toward the group.

Only Quarry saved them. The stone tiling of the waiting room rose up to form a wall, and Quarry stepped forward to join it, shielding them from the blast, which flared out around the edges of the stone but couldn't reach them.

Charlene and Reinhard exchanged glances. Neither had realized Quarry was capable of calling that much stone to himself. Charlene, for her part, hoped the rock man was true to his word because she didn't want to be on the receiving end of whatever else he might be capable of.

"Koko," said Reinhard.

Koko shook her head. "I don't have that much control at this distance. If I slow Flameout down, I might get Quarry and a couple of us, too. And if I don't get all of the fire, we're literally toast."

"We don't have much—"

"Yes, we do," said Charlene. "She's right. It's too much of a risk."

Reinhard was used to being in charge of a fight. But to his credit, he nodded and kept his rifle leveled at Quarry's makeshift wall.

Charlene needed a better weapon. Bullets weren't going to cut it. Water would help, but unfortunately, they didn't—wait. Peering upward, she was able to spot what they needed, even in the dim light of Flameout's glow. "Koko." Her whisper was barely audible. "Juice me."

"What?"

Charlene couldn't tell if the girl didn't understand what she wanted or if she thought it was crazy.

Flameout laughed again. "What now, rocky? You know I can go around you faster than you can block me."

"You heard me," Charlene told Koko. "This close, you can speed me up—and only me, correct?"

Koko's answer was the sudden slowing of everyone around Charlene. At first, she feared the girl had misunderstood her, but then she took a step. She was much faster than the rest of them. She stepped up to the wall formed by Quarry. In his haste, he'd erected a barrier of sloppily torn-up rocks. She grabbed three and flung them up at her target.

She missed all three times. But she was able to move and

throw so fast that she had five more attempts headed upward within a second. The sixth hit home.

The sensors had doomed the room's previous occupants. They'd failed. But when the sprinkler head Charlene wrecked with the rock cut loose, the rest of the system followed suit. With that, the waiting room was suddenly deluged.

Quarry's wall dropped in time for Charlene to spot Flameout trying to flee.

The rock man was too quick. The floor rose up into a dome around and over Flameout, trapping him. Then more stone was added until there was a column all the way to the nearest sprinkler head. Quarry allowed the flow of water in.

The horror ended with a loud sizzle.

84

A CHILD OF CONTRADICTION

"You don't have to drink yours," the man said. "In fact, you shouldn't."

Zach and the man sat at a cafe table in an empty market of some kind. They each had a mug of dark liquid in front of them.

Stalls around them sold, according to the pictures and prices on their signs, grass-fed burgers, artisan cheese, candy, fish, wine, cookies, and fresh produce. Whoever drew the produce took care to get the colors right.

Next to their table was the phone booth Zach escaped from. He assumed the man he'd been in there with was able to leave it whenever he wanted to.

The man's eyes no longer had flames in them. His lantern was nowhere to be seen.

The heat was still there. Zach could feel it. And when he looked away from the man's eyes, they gave off just a small glint of orange at the edges of Zach's vision.

Likewise, when Zach looked away from the tile floor of the market, he saw train tracks. When he looked back down, it was a floor again.

"Yes," the man said, watching him as the sound of something big and loud rumbled through the ceiling above. "The age of trains has passed, to a large degree. That's good and bad, depending on what the trains carried. This is still a transportation hub, though. My fear is that the trains will someday bear a dark cargo to a dark end."

Zach looked at the mug in front of him. Its liquid was darker than dark.

The man's mug contained what looked like blood. And there was more of it than the mug should have been able to hold.

Zach's eyes didn't tell him that. All his other senses did. Whatever was in their mugs smelled like blood, too. Or maybe it was just the man's drink.

Zach didn't want to touch his own mug. So he leaned forward to see if the smell was coming from his as well.

"Don't." The man's face and tone betrayed no alarm, but Zach sensed it just the same. "You can, of course. But you shouldn't." The man took a long draw of his own drink. When he put it back down on the table, its level hadn't dropped. "Zach." The man frowned, looking around at the silent market.

A moment later, the space was filled with people. Its stalls were staffed with vendors calling out to passing customers, the walkways teeming with shoppers.

"Zach," the man said again, still heard as easily through the noise of the surrounding people as he was when there was nobody there. "You know my name."

Zach did not know.

"You do. It's Apalala."

Zach had never heard that name.

The people crowding the booths around them left a lot of room when they passed their table, as if making their way around something that wasn't there. One, a skinny teen fussing with a cell phone, headed for the nearby phone booth. He stopped short, eyes widening as he studied it, then quickly turned away and headed deeper into the market.

Zach took a longer look at the booth. The air around it shimmered with the heat it continued to give off.

"Zach," said the man who called himself Apalala. His weight shifted again as a rumbling came through the ceiling once more. He'd mentioned trains. And when he moved, it felt like something the size of one settling into a new posture. "Zach." This time, the voice was much lower, much larger, familiar. "You know my name."

Aidan. The man was Aidan.

"I am the name you know and the name you don't," Apalala-Aidan continued. He watched an older woman approach the phone booth, flinch as if seeing something painful, then walk away. "And I am not your friend."

Zach watched as Apalala-Aidan took another long pull from his mug. Once again, when he put it back down, it contained just as much of the drink as it had before.

Zach's own mug was gone.

"I am not your friend, Zach, but I'm on your side. And I'm on Zach's mother's side. Do you understand?"

Zach did, though he said nothing.

"You understand because you are a child of contradiction. Do you know what that is? You will. But it will take you much longer to understand why—and what's made you that way."

Apalala-Aidan watched a man draw nearer to the phone booth.

Zach couldn't figure out what the attraction of the booth was for these people, especially since he'd worked so hard to get out of it. But grown-ups did strange things for strange reasons.

The man grabbed the handle and immediately pulled away, shaking his hand to cool it. He muttered something angrily and stalked off.

Apalala-Aidan frowned.

The booth was no longer there.

Now the Dynamite 8 I'm-Bobby had smashed sat on the table in front of Zach. Not one that looked like it. The same one scuffed in the same places.

Apalala-Aidan smiled when he saw that Zach recognized it. "Go ahead. You have questions. And that's easier for you."

Zach reached out and gently pressed down on the eight-track player's handle. "Who are you?" said his voice from the player.

"I'm Apalala."

Zach pressed again. "Who are you?"

"I'm Aidan."

Zach tried one more time, but the handle wouldn't budge. He studied Apalala-Aidan's endless mug of scary drink, then Apalala-Aidan. He gazed deep into his eyes.

Apalala-Aidan didn't look away. In the back of his eyes, the flame remained. Not visible, but there.

Zach pressed the handle. "Who are you?" said the Dynamite 8.

"I am from The Pines." The voice was Apalala's, but the power of it was Aidan's. "You know what that is and yet you don't know. There isn't time for me to explain these things to you when your experience will allow you to better understand them." He leaned forward and put his hands on the table.

Zach leaned forward and put his hands on the table, too, as close as he could get to Apalala-Aidan's without touching him.

Apalala-Aidan looked down at Zach's hands, just short of contact with him. He smiled. He understood that Zach was brave but not stupid. "Apalala is the name of a computer program created to move Essence like traders move stock," he said. "I'm telling you this not because you comprehend what I'm talking about now but because you will later." He looked down at his own hands, then back up at Zach. The flames weren't there. Yet they were. "Apalala began trading Essence it wasn't supposed to trade because its creators didn't understand what they'd made or what their creation was doing. It came into contact with Essence adjacent to The Pines and to me. The barrier between The Pines and here remains strong, but the same can't be said for others. Though not because of what you, and Zach's mother, and Paul Reid did. Do you understand what you did?"

Zach nodded.

"The same can't be said for Paul, for Zach's mother, or for Porter. Nor for anyone else. Not yet. But they, like you, will pick it up when they need to. If it's later than that, things will be bad and then things will be worse. That's why I'm here. And I tell you I'm not your friend but am on your side because when I can, I'm going to help you. When I can't help you, I'll do my best to protect you. And I'm friend to no one. Do you understand that?"

Zach nodded again.

"The Apalala program pulled a small part of me here into The Living World, but only a small part. It was like someone sending a photo of me, not the real me. Then a woman tried to exorcise that small part of me—to send me away. She succeeded, which is how I came to you. Adjacency. This is all adjacency and connections. It works for and against us. For and against. At the same time, sometimes. Do you understand?"

Zach pressed the handle of the Dynamite 8. "Yes."

Apalala-Aidan smiled again and leaned back in his chair.

Even through the noise of the market, its creaking complaint of a greater weight was audible. "Relationships and shared experience. You'll see why these things happened. Or you won't. But you'll have a sense of it either way. Zach's mother is pulling others into play. Porter is, too. You know who Porter is."

Zach didn't press the handle. Apalala-Aidan knew he knew.

Apalala-Aidan leaned forward again, his hands back on the table. Zach thought he was going to touch Zach's hands, but he didn't. "Porter ended up in The Pines. He was never supposed to. When he left, I was able to follow him here to The Living World and rejoin the piece of me that was already part of Apalala, which you were kind enough to shelter. And I am grateful, Zach. I was in a weakened state, and I was frightened. I'm not used to weakness. You helped me."

Zach pressed the handle. "You're welcome."

Apalala-Aidan laughed.

Zach didn't understand why. He'd always been told to respond to gratitude that way. Why was it funny?

"You are a child of contradiction, Zach. Of paradox. Do you know what those things are?" He didn't wait for an answer. "You will." Faster than Zach could follow, but somehow slow enough that Zach could have pulled away in time had he wanted to, Apalala-Aidan covered Zach's left hand with his right.

It didn't hurt. It wasn't wrong. It was merely a sign of shared experience.

"Do you know that anyone you ask would say I shouldn't be here? You don't have to answer that. I know you don't know. I've been caged for eternity. So what do they think I'm going to do here? Am I really going to do something that will get me put back where I've been for longer than you can comprehend

—since the beginning of everything?" He took his hand off Zach's.

Zach understood he'd passed some kind of test by trusting Apalala-Aidan. What that got him, however, was not something Zach could see or sense in any way. He reached out and pressed the Dynamite 8's handle. "Who am I?"

"You know that already. A child between worlds, a vagabond and wanderer." He looked around at the market as more rumbling came from above. "Trains. Or whatever mode of travel comes to you. You don't understand now what you can do. But you will. If you're able to survive it."

With that, Zach's mug was there in front of him again.

"You don't have to drink that. But you can if you like." Apalala-Aidan raised his mug.

Zach raised his.

"I am not your friend," said Apalala-Aidan.

Zach pressed the Dynamite 8's handle. "I am not your friend."

"But I'll do what I can."

"But I'll do what I can."

They clinked mugs gently. It felt like worlds colliding. They each took a long draw, and when they put their vessels down, the level of drink had not dropped in either of them.

Apalala-Aidan smiled.

Zach returned the grin, though he wasn't sure why.

Things were going to move fast.

WHAT'S MOST PRECIOUS

"It's called Roosevelt Island in The Living World." Audra and Po rode along a winding two-lane road through a seemingly endless vineyard filled with heavy purple-black grapes the size of a man's fist. "But this version no longer resembles the real-world one, so the name doesn't fit. Here, it's called Demeter."

Audra drove the three-wheeled car, an electric two-seater prototype from a company called Ohm, which had only ever existed in the imagination of a college freshman who was bored in an engineering class and daydreamed about starting it. The company never came into existence. The Envoys made regular use of similar vehicles back when The Commons was working as it should, in the pre-Brill days.

Audra said she couldn't remember the last time she'd seen one. However, the Ohm they were riding in appeared in an empty garden shed one day when she decided she needed a way to get around the island. Demeter was growing to the point where Audra had given up estimating how large it was.

But there was no question that it was large. They'd already passed through a dense forest of huge conifers and driven across but a corner of what Audra said was a vast prairie. That prairie, like the rest of the terrain, was only getting more vast.

Essence. The island was a storage facility for it, and the Essence had to manifest itself as one form of life or another, so it chose these landscapes.

"How can all of this possibly come from your little gang of bike messengers?" Joel wasn't speaking for Po, but the little Tamagotchi was good at asking the questions Po thought about before he got around to signing them.

"It doesn't."

They passed out of the vineyard country. The road became a highway winding through hills like golden gumdrops.

"The Petrels you saw here are the ones able to cross over to The Margins, both the zones that are more Commons than Living World and vice versa. We've got people gathering ambient Essence across the realms. As The Commons and The Living World grow closer and overlap, more ambient Essence is shed by the living, by those who've fallen into The Margins, and those who have entered charge state. That's all being pulled in by the Essence catchers on the Petrels' bikes. We also have the Ravens, who are a car-service version. They gather ambient Essence using catchers on the cars and reclaim what's shed by passengers."

"You pick up enough to grow a place this big?" Joel was rarely so impressed by anything. "That's gotta be a lot of catchers. I didn't know there were that many living bike messengers and cabbies."

"What makes you think they're living?"

That shut even Joel up.

"You've seen the Ravagers." Audra didn't so much steer as subtly suggest a course change. "Former military and police pressed into service against their will, their conscious minds silenced so that they follow orders and nothing more. The

Petrels and the Ravens are not slaves. They choose this role and are honored to serve. When all is said and done, depending on how they've contributed, The Commons may even credit the experience to their Journeys. But not if we don't ensure there continues to be a Living World and a Commons whose denizens flow through them in order."

The conversation was much too broad for Po at the moment. He preferred to understand smaller pieces, in turn, before assembling a more comprehensive overview. He signed, and Joel spoke for him. "What realm are we in now?"

Audra considered her words. "I don't know for sure. But I'm careful not to let others hear that because they might assume we don't know what we're doing. And we do. To a point." She looked at Po for a reaction.

Po gave her none. He didn't want any expression of his to discourage her from continuing.

She chewed her lip, thinking, and Po let her. "We're in one of the seeds. But I'm not sure which. And I don't know that it matters much."

One of the seeds—in the seed head of a flower, with Ingress, the source of all things, in the center. The ring around Ingress was The Pines, a place Po preferred not to spend too much time contemplating. Spiraling out from there were worlds uncounted, including The Living World and The Commons. And The Margins was the dangerous anomaly, the crossing-over between The Living World and The Commons created by the forces Paul and Mr. Brill called upon in their battle. There were supposed to be impenetrable demarcations between the two realms. They'd been breached.

Now they were crossing over, and while the short-term consequences of that were unclear, the long-term were not. Chaos and doom.

The careful arrangement of realms and worlds, laid out in

a grand way and similarly expressed in numerous instances in the natural world, was being pulled out of alignment. Those were Audra's words, and she offered no specifics—but there was no need to. Po understood what happened when harmony and balance suffered. Now they were talking about it on an unimaginable scale.

They had all taken part in the breach, all contributed to harming existence itself by blindly playing into the hands of a nemesis who, according to Audra, remained unknown aside from clues left by their activities. Paul, Porter, Rain—everyone who'd helped Paul on his Journey. Audra herself, though Po and Ken had not known who she was when they saw her talking to Porter that night among Austen's Night Lights.

Ken.

Po could live with the knowledge that he himself, believing he was contributing to a greater good by helping Paul, had instead caused harm. That was sometimes—often, even—the result of the best intentions combined with the most dedicated effort. But he couldn't bear to think that the last acts of his friend, whose absence weighed too heavy on his heart for him to dwell on for long, had been twisted toward a darker purpose.

That Po would not forgive, no matter how long he worked to master his fury. Someone, once named, was going to pay. Whoever it was. However many of them there were.

"I think you're creeping the lady out, boss," said Joel. Once again, the Tamagotchi proved to be a good check on Po's brooding.

They were back on the prairie, assuming it was the same one, but now it was populated. Off in the distance, an endless herd of bison grazed. Hawks wheeled in the sky overhead.

Po signed.

"My apologies," Joel said for him.

"None needed," said Audra. "It's a lot to take in. I assumed you were just trying to piece it all together."

Part of the faraway herd shifted. A wave passed through the bison, and they began to cover ground.

"That's the first I've seen of them," Audra said. "The hawks, too. That tells me we're succeeding in our Essence harvesting. It's expressing itself in living things beyond mere plant life now."

"As long as it doesn't make its way around to things with sharp teeth and claws," said Joel. "No grizzlies, thanks."

"It doesn't usually work its way that far up the food chain. And we've got enough to worry about with the hostile mythicals we've been seeing. Those are newcomers, too."

Po signed.

"Here?" Joel said.

"Only over the bridges so far. In what passes for Manhattan, which is rapidly becoming Marginalized. Not here or in The Living World." Audra paused. "Not yet. Though I do worry about what those Ravagers were doing there. If they were backing the mythicals, we have a problem. If there's an Essence leech running around that's not afraid to take on a truckload of them—and succeeds—then we have a *big* problem."

The narrow road carried them across the prairie until, finally, the little car topped a shallow rise and stopped at a cockeyed "Bridge Out" sign that had withstood numerous shotgun attacks. Beyond it, true to the sign's warning, were the rotten, twisted vestiges of what had once been a wooden bridge. Its deck was mostly gone, save for a few stubborn planks refusing to let go of their supports. A scattering of sentry-like pilings spanned the small creek below and marched up the far bank. The pitiful structure looked to have been done in by gravity and fatigue. It couldn't have been washed out by the sad-looking trickle of a stream.

"Time to turn around?" said Joel.

"When needed, there's a bridge here." Audra leaned on the wheel. "This is where the Petrels and Ravens cross over to the other realms. The bridge is whatever we require it to be, and when that little stream chooses to represent the barriers being spanned, it can become a small ocean."

"Seriously?" Joel said.

"Have you ever seen the Overseas Highway through the Florida Keys?"

Neither Po nor Joel had.

"It's over a hundred miles long. This bridge and the body of water it crosses can dwarf that. The trip can take hours. Though in reality, time doesn't apply, just as many of The Living World's rules have no place here. In the reality of Roosevelt Island—or what most people think of as reality—we'd be looking over the East River at Queens. But we're a long way from reality. You know that already."

Po signed.

"Reality is a relative idea," Joel said, adding a wry chuckle of his own.

They sat in the Ohm, saying nothing, staring at the sign and the wreck of the little bridge beyond. Po tried to imagine the wider river or ocean in the thin stream, the gulf-spanning bridge that the wreck before him hid behind its facade of minor glory gone by. As much as he was in touch with The Commons and the spaces around him, he found it difficult to connect to the larger water and distance.

Until, that is, he could.

It was beyond his seeing, but Po sensed it and then felt foolish. His gifts were enough to acknowledge what his eyes wouldn't show him. Why were his senses so weak now, when the hugeness of the thing should have made it easy to discern? A fathomless rift meant never to be pierced or crossed. Yet now it was being spanned by the noble and low alike.

"You mustn't hold yourself and the others responsible, you know." Audra gave Po a sad, knowing smile, the web of scars that made up her face melting around the expression. It was beautiful in that all it required was one expression for Audra's inner light and strength to emerge.

Po knew then that he wanted to be Audra's friend. He knew, too, that she would make a fierce foe.

"You performed the most noble of acts," she told him. "You helped someone who needed it, and you did so without question. It cost your friend everything, didn't it?"

Po gave a mild start before gaining control of his emotions. This, too, was another of the old Envoy's abilities. She disarmed him with but a handful of words. He didn't doubt that she knew that. Audra did few things without intent.

"We lose what's most precious when helping where it's most needed," she said. "Our spirit drives us to it, even when our best efforts lead to a terrible result. It's the bad end from the best reasons." She backed the car away from the broken bridge, executed a neat three-point turn, and started back the way they'd come. "That's what they're counting on. Sometimes I think the perversity of it gives them as much pleasure as the victory does."

The return trip took longer than the ride out had. Demeter had grown in the time they'd been driving and talking.

The bison were more numerous, the prairies more vast.

It gave Po too much time to think about bad ends.

THE NOT-QUITE-RIGHT CHICAGO AIR

"Don't look at his eyes!"

The voice from New Beginnings was familiar, but the distance and the pavement warped it enough for Paul to have a hard time putting a face to it. The barking of Angus the dog, charging toward Paul, didn't help.

Then he ran out of time.

A black SUV roared around the corner and skidded to a halt a short distance away. Four soldiers, all in black with face shields and helmets, jumped out and ran toward Paul and Jabari, their boots against the asphalt echoing in the not-quite-right Chicago air.

Ravagers.

Paul knew that now.

But why here?

Jabari froze in his tracks, looking at something behind Paul. Everything from his dreadlocks to his sneakers turned an ash gray, and there he stood, mouth frozen open in a cry, a statue. For real.

Angus pulled up short and stopped, barking his head off.

Paul turned and got only a glimpse of a gray man-sized

snake on the sidewalk behind him before a combo of fur, teeth, and snarling slammed him to the ground. His head smacked into the sidewalk hard enough for everything to go white for a second. Then his breathing was cut off.

When his vision cleared, it was filled by a werewolf in a black leather jumpsuit with a knee on his chest, a steel grip around his throat, and a pair of sharp claws hovering over his eyes. "Afternoon, meat." Female. "I'd say I'm sorry about your friend, but why lie?"

Paul couldn't answer. Nor could he breathe. And perhaps it was the lack of air that provided him with such focus on the situation, for he couldn't miss the abrupt silence that fell across the street in an unnatural way.

Suddenly, the running Ravagers' footfalls had ceased.

The werewolf glanced over her shoulder, in the direction of New Beginnings, a low growl emanating from deep within her.

Footsteps. Someone approached from across the street. Paul was too busy pining for oxygen to worry about who that might be.

The fingers and talons floated closer to Paul's eyes, and the footsteps came to a halt.

Somewhere, from the same direction, Angus whined. At least he was all right.

Paul tried to bring his abilities into play.

He'd done so against Brill—holding his own and eventually defeating him with the help of Rain, the marble, and the ring The Commons worked to place on his finger. He'd defeated Ravagers and called down ruinous storms.

But all of that had come from him only when someone else was threatened. He didn't have enough regard for his own well-being to muster even the tiniest sampling of his power.

Or maybe he was just too scared of the hovering claws.

"Angus!"

A girl's voice.

Lexi.

"I'll blind the kid, Porter," the werewolf said. "Or maybe I'll go all the way into his brain. It's small, but I'll bet I can find it if I dig around. Are you dumb enough to try me?"

Porter.

Before it could fully register that Paul's friend and mentor from The Commons was now with him, the familiar voice answered in a low, confident tone. "That's not the question, Ilva. The question is, do you want to do away with the one bargaining chip keeping me from sending your head—and only your head—a block or two away from here?"

Ilva rose from Paul's chest and stood, picking him up by his shirt. She kept her talons near his face.

Porter.

There the gray man was. He looked more drawn and tired than he had when Paul last saw him, when he stood triumphant among the hordes of Journeymen-to-be, loading up the trains to begin processing them. Porter and Po, beaming.

Not now.

However it was that Porter had traveled to Chicago's weird cousin, it had cost him. And true to form, he was trying not to let it show.

Behind Porter, Lexi grabbed Angus and pulled him back across the sidewalk to stand within a few yards of the New Beginnings front door. If necessary, they could be inside in a flash. Good.

The Envoy didn't even spare Paul a look.

"If you could take me out, you would have done it by now, old man," Ilva said. "You know as well as I do that The Margins will mess with anyone's abilities. Mine, too. Just not enough to help you." She effortlessly lifted Paul into the air with one arm. Setting him back down on his feet, she put a forearm across his throat and held him in front of her as a shield. "I can have his eyes pushed into his head and be up to my wrist in mush before he has a chance to scream."

"You know better than that." Porter bounced his staff on the toe of his shoe, at ease with the standoff. "We both need him alive and well in order to stop what's coming. If not, it won't spare you and yours any more than it will me and mine."

"Not necessarily." Ilva casually traced one of her talons along Paul's cheek. The burn of it hit, and he felt a line of blood run down his face and neck and into his shirt. "His health is preferred, but I'm permitted some discretion of my own." She ran her finger back up the wound and licked it. "Or maybe I just do what I want."

Porter said nothing, but the bouncing of his staff stopped and his grip tightened.

Paul tried again to muster something. Anything. He even considered trying to get a thumb into Ilva's eye, maybe reach back to twist one of her ears. Whatever might give Porter a shot.

The burning of his scored cheek dissuaded him. That might be just the excuse she needed to open him up entirely.

Ilva eyed poor Jabari, who was nearly solid stone. Some of his humanity showed through the gray cast, but not much. "Looks like you got to our basilisk friend before he finished the job on Rasta boy here. What'd you do to him?"

"Kamien has only himself to blame for his fate." Porter was deadly serious now. "And the fate of the Ravagers with him. Nobody forced him to call upon his abilities. I merely helped him direct them in a more beneficial manner."

The werewolf looked back over her shoulder and grunted at whatever she saw there.

Porter looked past her and drummed his fingers lightly on his staff. He was preparing for something. "I'm a bit of a latecomer, Ilva, so forgive the rookie question. Who are you working with?"

Ilva let out a rasping, staccato hiss which, Paul realized, was her version of a laugh. "You don't know?" She made the noise again. It was worse than her growl. "And you have the cojones to threaten me?" She gave Paul a shake, rattling his teeth against his brain. "If you don't even know the players, why should I bother—"

Porter gave his staff a twist.

Whatever Ilva was about to say turned into a howl. She pushed Paul away from her and dropped to the concrete, grabbing at her thigh and rolling back and forth in agony.

Paul stumbled as he tried to catch himself and slammed into petrified Jabari.

It hurt.

Ilva writhed on the ground, claws digging right through the leather on her leg. Blood welled up from the resulting damage.

From this angle, Paul could see what had happened to the huge snake he'd glimpsed right before Ilva jumped him. As well as the Ravagers who never made it to the fight.

They were fanned out in an array in front of the shop window across the street, gazing into it. All were as statue-stiff as Jabari, all gray stone. Even the snake. A basilisk, Ilva had said. Kamien, Porter had called him.

"I'm not quite as vicious as you are," Porter told Ilva once her screams died down to a low moan. "And what you say about The Margins weakening our abilities is true. So maybe we can all stay here and see if it's possible for you to bleed to death in this condition." He let her consider that through her pain.

Paul almost felt sorry for the werewolf. Then he looked at Jabari again.

Porter gave his staff another quick twist, and a metal rod fell to the sidewalk next to Ilva with a ringing clink. Shiny metal, covered in red, with a row of holes on it.

A flute?

Ilva batted the instrument away across the concrete and tried to stand, but her leg failed her. She fell on her butt.

Paul hoped she had a tail—and that she'd just broken it.

"Do you like to shop, Ilva?" Porter leaned on his staff, back in everyday-conversation mode. "I hate it, myself. But it's such a joy to find exactly what you need." He bounced the staff on his toe again—once, twice. "There's a music store behind you. I took the liberty of shoplifting a choice item and hiding it inside you, snuggling up with your femur. Real silver, judging by your reaction. I don't play. Do you?"

Ilva spat something that was part curse, part grumble.

"Now again, you're quite right. My abilities are diminished here in The Margins, at least until I adjust a bit. As are yours —and Paul's. But I will tell you this." Porter bounced the staff on his shoe again. "I've no doubt I can jump that flute—that shiny silver flute—through the center of your heart like Cupid's arrow. Then we'll see what it can really do to you, particularly when you're not at your strongest." He bounced the staff a couple more times as Ilva glared at him. "Or I can just pop it right back into that display window. Though poor Melody isn't likely to be quite so merry once she realizes she has to offer a blood-and-fur discount."

Ilva pushed herself to her feet again, glaring at Porter and favoring her injured leg.

"And here I was going to invite you in for tea," said Porter. "But that attitude of yours would curdle our cream."

The werewolf tested her leg again but couldn't trust it with her weight. She eyed the bloody flute on the sidewalk, and her eyes narrowed again.

"Go," Porter said. "While I convince myself I shouldn't just take care of you now, when I have the opportunity."

Ilva gave Porter a good, long stare.

And Paul.

She didn't need to tell them she intended to see them again. She flexed her fingers, her long claws curving into her palms, and straightened them again. Then she limped away.

Paul and Porter watched her disappear around the corner after giving Kamien and the Ravagers only the briefest of glances. Her contempt for them was palpable.

When Lexi hit Paul from behind, arms wrapping around his waist with an urgency driven by relief, she nearly knocked him over.

And when Angus smashed into both of them, a barking projectile fueled by dog happiness, all three of them hit the deck.

87

HEED THE STEED

The freight car with Rain's bike in it was pitch black as the rooftop guns cut loose up and down the train. Multiple volleys announced yet another aerial attack as she went from inspecting the bike to hanging onto it in the darkness.

Normally, she wasn't afraid of the dark. Her biggest worry was that she might be a creature of it. But when the lights went out, it felt like the rest of the cargo—the crated mysteries and draped shapes large and small—knew she was there. And they weren't happy about it.

At the moment, Rain faced more immediate concerns. The airborne train, while able to cover long distances much faster by flying, traded safety for speed. According to Emmett, who was patient enough to endure Rain's endless questions about who the Railwaymen were and how they'd come to be in The Margins, there was no comparison between ground travel and opting for the wild blue yonder. Plus, they might get lucky and go undetected. Even if they didn't, the tactics available to the Ravagers and any of their allies were more limited than they would've been on terra firma.

But they were forced to follow a set path, just as they would've been on surface rail. They could be hit from below, and the train hadn't developed defenses for that. And nobody could say for sure how much or how little it might take to knock them down.

Emmett stressed that they'd never done hot runs—and certainly not hot aerial runs—in The Commons. Those only became necessary after the Railwaymen ended a particularly long Commons trip and found themselves in The Margins, whereupon they began receiving orders to transport charges and Marginals to safety.

"That part of the job is the easiest," Emmett said. "The deciding part. Because there isn't one. We go where we're told. We heed the steed, abide by the ride, and that is all."

Heed the steed. Rain still didn't know who she was heeding when she followed Charlene's texted directions. But the messages had given her purpose where there'd been none, and so far she saw no reason not to go with them.

The Railwaymen, for instance, seemed like the good guys. Should that turn out to be wrong, she wouldn't need to go looking for an enemy to fight. She'd turn her gun on them and do whatever she needed to do to protect the charges and Marginals until help arrived.

Assuming it did.

Charlene. Charlene was behind Rain's current predicament. Rain was hanging onto the bike, which was secured to the floor of the freight car in the dark, because of Charlene's latest text.

What's that rattle?

That was the message in its entirety. And it was a good hour before it occurred to Rain what she was supposed to do. Check on the bike.

The text was a question she asked herself whenever she

rode anything that made a noise she couldn't identify. She'd spend whatever time was needed to figure out the source. Otherwise, she might find out the hard way—while doing ninety on the highway.

But it wasn't so easy in the dark, even when she understood why the lights had gone out. It happened every time the train came up against a Ravager threat in the air.

It was almost always helicopter gunships, which were taken down quickly. The train channeled resources to the guns for extra striking power and to up-armoring when a thicker skin was needed. But that Essence had to come from somewhere, which meant a slowing of the engine and the killing of the lights, with all available juice diverted to the fight.

Rain hung on to the bike and was grateful to whoever had secured it. It had no give, even as the train swayed with the distant boom of a rooftop gun somewhere down the line.

Of course there was no give. The train itself was hanging onto the bike. So much of the way things worked in The Commons applied here in The Margins, too, and anything could behave like a living thing. Or be one.

Not for the first time, Rain wondered if it might have been easier to live in ignorance as Ray-Anne rather than have her memory restored. A world with flying trains under aerial attack was, perhaps, not one she'd missed.

One recent attacker was a winged man, according to Emmett. A gargoyle, it came straight at the train, claws ready to tear into whatever it could. It shattered on the first shot that hit it.

Claws.
Hands.
Brill's hands.
On her.

With the recall of that violation came all the similar crimes recounted by way too many New Beginnings kids—girls and boys alike. So how would it have been better to remain in oblivion? The monsters of The Living World were no less terrible than their counterparts in The Commons. They just hid themselves better. And the burial of the harm they did was a damage all its own, an additional layer of wrong visited upon the powerless, the rot of their black secrets tunneling deeper and deeper the longer they were kept.

What's that rattle?

Rain made the best use of her time in the dark, feeling her way around the bike for anything loose. It wasn't a bad way to do a second check; the fingers might find something that the eyes missed. She even opened up a couple of the storage compartments and felt around in them.

Which was how something small and hard did indeed rattle its way down the bike to the floor of the freight car when she pulled her pack out.

Whatever it was had to be round because it helpfully bounced off her toe and rolled across the floor in the blackness, headed into the mystery freight, which she really didn't want to get any closer to.

Boom!

A rooftop gun directly above opened up. Its recoil, though limited, was enough to tip the car. Rain heard the unseen rattler returning.

The lights came back on just as it reached her. She was able to trap it beneath her shoe with just enough force to stop it but not crush it if it were, in fact, crushable.

Not a worry. It felt like a stone.

She bent down to retrieve the wee rogue.

A hard little ball.

She held it up in the dim overhead light, which was shadowy at its brightest.

A memory.

Not hands on her this time.

Tentacles. All around.

But not attacking. Helping.

Black water.

No air. Lungs burning.

Then the Humboldt raising her up to deliver her prize to Paul. To complete a victory that, she was now told, was no victory whatsoever.

There in the poor light.

A cat's-eye marble.

And Rain knew who it belonged to.

Alas, she was only able to contemplate the reason for her to once again serve as the marble's courier for a moment.

The train went skydiving.

The lights cut out.

Then Rain was too busy clinging to the bike so that she wouldn't go tumbling off into the unseen cargo in the dark.

And she once again considered how much easier it had been to be poor, ignorant Ray-Anne—who never once had to panic over the idea of losing her grip.

88

NOBODY SPECIAL

"How many?" Reinhard had needed some time by himself to cope with what they'd found. As a former Vigil and a newer Envoy, he took the losses doubly hard.

His former job was to protect Journeymen and Envoys from what happened in the waiting room and the rest of the cordoned-off portion of HQ. He hadn't. That was his loss as a Vigil. The deaths of his colleagues and the Journeymen-in-waiting were his loss as an Envoy.

Charlene and June Medill attempted to quantify those deaths. But what could a number mean? "We can't say for sure." Charlene absentmindedly clicked the View-Master's advance lever. "Hundreds. At least."

Reinhard took a seat. "Our people? Journeymen?"

"Both," Charlene said. "All."

"But how can they have just—"

"System capabilities remain limited, Mr. Reinhard," June Medill said. "I don't think putting additional stress on Ms. Moseley helps our situation, do you?"

At any other time, Reinhard might have been amused or

fixed June with a smoldering stare. But the silver-haired warrior didn't have it in him. He considered her answer, then turned back to Charlene to wait her out.

"We can't say, Reinhard. We just don't know. All we can say is they're not here."

"We can say that for certain," the former Vigil agreed. "We've scouted out the entire contained space. None of the internal security walls have been compromised. Nobody could have gotten out or been taken out. And Flameout couldn't have killed them all."

Killed. That was the painful part none of them wanted to face up to. The horrible stench in the waiting room came from somewhere, and though Flameout might be seen as a braggart, he wasn't a liar. People had died in that room. Yet there were no bodies. And while it was theoretically possible those killed had been spirited away by The Commons, as had been known to happen on rare occasions, it wasn't likely.

They'd vanished. And nobody knew what happened to all of the other Envoys and staff who'd been hiding in other parts of the secured area.

Whatever he'd done and whoever he'd killed, Flameout was neutralized now—and in a most unpleasant manner. Once Quarry had him contained, he explained that Flameout existed in a gas-like form until he was able to ignite something and become living flame. Thus, it was a matter of deciding where to keep him so he wouldn't be able to access anything flammable.

Demos hadn't been satisfied with the insulated water heater they'd put him in. He was afraid Flameout might be able to boil the water to the point of breaking a seal. So he dropped it into a much larger waste vessel filled with—well, Charlene didn't want to know.

Demos couldn't contain his vicious smirk when he was

done. He appeared to be awfully proud of himself. And while Charlene knew she wasn't supposed to permit that kind of thing, she figured she'd allow herself the luxury of feeling a little guilty after all of this cleared up and things returned to normal—assuming they ever did.

And then there were the mythicals.

~

"THERE WAS NOWHERE for them to go," said Quarry. "There was nowhere for me to go, either. I don't pretend to be noble. What do you think motivated me to jump over to your side? The world is fueled by self-preservation, and we paper it over with whatever false reasons are called for."

They were camped out in the conference room adjacent to Charlene's office. Giant flip-pads still boasted motivational messages for those hoping to hit throughput goals for Journeys completed, new Envoys trained, and other achievements aimed at eliminating the nearly incalculable backlog left over from the Brill reign. Twin wipe-boards sported indecipherable diagrams aimed at doing good and helping people to destinies unknown.

Now the whereabouts of the planners and their Journeymen were unknown. They were gone and nothing more.

"Self-interest." Reinhard moved his head around in a circle. The pops were audible.

"Of course," said the rock man. "That's my point."

"How so?" said Charlene. She didn't like the look in Reinhard's eyes. He had no visible weapon on him, but that made her even more nervous. With Reinhard, it was the items you couldn't see that were most worrisome. She could order him not to use them, but she couldn't be seen as siding with a former—and possibly current—hostile such as Quarry without a solid reason. "You said this was probably a suicide mission as far as you and your teammates were concerned," she said. "How is that self-interest?"

"It would've been a suicide mission if they failed to kill everyone in here," Reinhard said. It creeped Charlene out a little when he went so long without blinking. "If they'd succeeded? No suicide."

The stone man had no expression to read, so Charlene couldn't tell if he was offended. "Hey, how many people did I myself kill?"

"You tell me," said Reinhard. "There are a lot of people missing. Were all of them Flameout's handiwork?"

Quarry thought it through. "I don't think so."

"Then what happened?" Charlene would commandeer this interrogation if it killed her.

The rock man was quiet again.

Reinhard held up a device that looked a bit like a laser pointer. Charlene never saw where he pulled it from. "You're an animator, right?" he told Quarry. "I went up against animators in my last job. We used these to deal with them. Want to see how they work?"

"Reinhard—" Charlene began.

"It's fine." Quarry seemed more comfortable with being threatened than with not being believed. "I don't blame you, Vigil. I wouldn't trust me, either."

"I'm an Envoy."

Quarry shrugged as much as a man made of stone was able to. "Do you know what many mythicals think of your mission here? Your drive to clean up the old Journeys and get the new ones running smoothly again?"

"Tell me." Reinhard flipped the device in his hand.

"We've always been seen as imaginary beings. Lesser. Nonexistent without even the right to exist. Conventional wisdom held we were only in The Commons because Brill clogged up the process and stopped the dreamers who created us from moving on. So what would it mean for you and your people to get things moving again? Bye-bye, us."

"Killers always have a rationale."

"I didn't say I bought it."

"What didn't you buy?" said Charlene. "The reason—or the belief that you'd disappear once we got things moving again?"

"Neither."

"You're a long way from disappearing," Charlene said. "We haven't made even a dent in the backlog. A lot of what existed in The Commons under Brill will be around for a while."

"For a while, sure," said Quarry.

Reinhard flipped the device again. A full rotation this time. When he caught it, it remained pointed at the stone man. "We have mythicals working with us. They don't kill anyone."

"Nor have I," said Quarry. "I came here to talk."

"Is that what you were doing when you had Koko by the throat?"

"I am what I was created to be." A note of sadness crept into the rock man's tone. "I struggle to hold it at bay."

"What did you come to talk about?" Charlene said.

"As the Vigil—Envoy—here explained, I'm an animator. I have no form of my own. I inhabit stone." Quarry ignored Reinhard flipping his device again. "If I don't spend enough time doing that, I could lose the ability to do it at all. But it's not my preferred state."

"Oh, do tell us of your preferences," said Reinhard.

Quarry ignored that, too. "I prefer to explore the stone of The Commons by moving through it, staying within it, talking to it. It has tales to tell. It listens, and it only speaks to me."

"And?" said Charlene.

"And I know things. Things I'm not necessarily meant to know."

"Such as?" Reinhard flipped the device yet again.

It may not have affected Quarry, but Charlene was increasingly unnerved by it.

"I know who's in the tanks outside. I know why. And I think I know where your people and my people went."

"Your people?" said Reinhard. He stopped flipping the device and kept it trained on Quarry.

"Those who came here with me. Relax."

"Where'd they all go?" said Charlene.

Boom!

An explosive strike outside the HQ walls shook the office. As did a second.

A drop-ceiling tile shaken loose by the double-whammy tipped out of its frame and hit the center of the table with a light smack, knocking over an abandoned glass of water. The liberated liquid splashed across the table's surface, and the glass rolled toward the edge. Reinhard caught it as it went over and set it back upright.

Charlene was reaching for the View-Master on the table when it lit up, projecting onto the wall at an angle. A blank square of white light was replaced by FinePoint, who filled the screen. He looked surprisingly calm for someone whose main reason for being was under attack.

Boom!

Another shaking of the room.

"They're shelling the building, Ms. Moseley," said FinePoint. When he said nothing more, Charlene remembered that was his way when reporting: he almost never revealed anything that wasn't asked for.

Boom!

Another tile dropped. Quarry, surprisingly fast for his size and form, caught it and placed it gently on the table.

Boom!

"So I gathered," Charlene said. "Where? And how much damage are they doing?"

"Cosmetic at worst. They're not firing in an organized manner or coordinating their targeting, it seems. It's almost like it's—"

"A diversion?" said Quarry. "Like they're not mounting a serious effort?"

FinePoint nodded.

"They're not."

Boom!

Boom!

Boom!

Everyone looked up expectantly at the ceiling, but this time, the tiles hung tough in the face of the triple impact.

"You seem to know a lot about what they're doing and what their intent is," Reinhard told Quarry. He put the device on the table in front of him, within easy reach and still pointed Quarry's way.

"I said so, didn't I?"

Boom!

"Why didn't they try to smash their way in here before?" Charlene spoke louder than necessary, anticipating more noise. "Why now?"

"Because they didn't want to. They still don't. If they did, they'd blow a ground-level entryway through the wall."

Boom!

Quarry behaved as if the assault wasn't happening. "You watch. They'll stop."

Boo-boo-boo-boom!

The multiple barrage had Reinhard grinning with cold triumph. It certainly didn't sound like they'd be stopping.

Until they did.

A few moments of silence went by.

Then a few more stretched into what felt like hope for a cease-fire.

Quarry stood. He was tall enough to reach up and pop a tile threatening to sail down upon them back into place.

"Damage report, FinePoint?"

"Broken windows, ma'am. A lot of them. And masonry damage. But nothing structural. And they're not advancing."

"They're taking their time, it seems." Reinhard picked the device up again and toyed with it. "Time enough for Fine-Point's repairs, perhaps." He flipped the device. "Or maybe they don't want in at all."

"They do not," said Quarry. "That's what I'm trying to tell you. They just want to make it look like they do for as long as they can."

"I'd ask why." Reinhard had the device pointed Quarry's way again. "But let's start with who they are."

"Nobody special. Nobody at all, in fact."

Reinhard held the device steady and leveled. Charlene considered asking him to lower it, but she had to be able to trust her people. After a moment, he put it back down on his own, pointing away from the stone man. "What's that mean? AI?"

"Zing. You're in the right business. Sorry—were in the right business, though I'd wager those same skills come in handy in the Envoy game. This pile of rocks you're talking to right now is more full of life than those tanks are."

"Somebody catch me up, please," said Charlene.

"Robots." For whatever reason, Reinhard didn't appear to

regard Quarry as nearly so much of a threat now. "Did you know that when they sent you in here?"

"I did. No one else had any idea. They thought we were the vanguard of an insert-and-destroy."

"And you know where the rest of your team went?" said Charlene.

"Not my team anymore. But yes, I think I know. I can't be sure just sitting here, though. And I don't want to find out for certain if it means joining them." He tilted his stone head, as if listening. "Here we go again."

Boom!

One round and then nothing.

"What was that?" said Reinhard.

"One of your guys was spotted near a door. A heat print. They're programmed to keep that from happening."

"FinePoint," said Charlene.

"Nobody's hurt," said Quarry.

"No casualties," FinePoint confirmed. "Another weakened wall, though."

"This is about not letting us out," said Reinhard.

"Zing," said Quarry.

"Why?" Charlene wasn't playing games like Quarry and Reinhard. She wanted everything out in the open.

Quarry was silent.

"Are you talking to them while you're talking to us?" Reinhard eyed the device on the table but left it pointing toward a wall.

"Listening. Talking wouldn't do any good. They'll do what's necessary to make us stay put."

"Why?" said Reinhard.

"You're working on satellite offices to help with the disuse protocol."

Charlene wanted to deny that. It was classified. But it was also true. "They're not up and running yet."

"Then keeping you penned up here means they can have the protocol kick in whenever they want."

"By—" Charlene stopped herself from saying it. By killing everyone in HQ—at which point the protocol would make the facility go away. It was why Porter had showed up for work every day during the Brill years. "So what do we do?"

"Nothing—yet. Not until I get back." With that, Quarry collapsed into a pile of rubble.

For a moment, Charlene thought Reinhard had surrendered to temptation and used his device, but it remained on the table. "Now what?" she asked him.

The former Vigil reached out to pick up the device. Before Charlene could follow his movement, he had it hidden somewhere on him again. "We wait. If you can believe that's me saying it."

"That's it? Just wait?"

"Even though I'm sure they're keeping us tied up while they accomplish some other goal we'd rather they not accomplish? Unfortunately, yes." Reinhard shrugged much more effectively than Quarry had earlier. "We could always help FinePoint patch things up. How are you with a tuck pointer?"

89

BREATHE AND FOLLOW

The first time Annie went on the lam, it was because Zach went missing and June Medill told her to get out fast. Hearing the approach of hostile agents for a home invasion hadn't hurt, either.

This time, she needed no prompting. They had to go.

Bobby'd left three days before, which meant she'd gone without an injection in her knee for nearly half a week. With that break, there'd been no increased discomfort. Everything he'd told her about the shots was a lie.

As reasons went, that was a good enough start for Annie. She'd figure out the rest on the way to wherever she and Zach were headed. She hadn't yet worked that out, either.

There were gaps in her knowledge and memory, but there was nothing to be done about that for the time being. All would be determined and revealed on the move. Or they'd be caught by whoever imprisoned her with her abusive ex, who cared nothing for his own son and who'd manipulated her into working a job where they could keep an eye on her.

Annie didn't know who was responsible or why they wanted her under their control. She couldn't remember anything between the time she'd climbed into Weston's chopper with a man called Wrangler John and her earliest memories of this stint with Bobby. The blanks would fill in eventually. She'd remember why the man in the fur was called Wrangler. Or not. That wasn't the most important thing at the moment.

Out.

They had to take the opportunity presented by Bobby's absence to get out.

She rolled jeans and a couple of shirts into a backpack. Then she grabbed a sweatshirt and a bunch of performance underwear perfect for drying in a bathroom.

Next came her toiletries bag. She couldn't help but shake her head at its empty state. She'd always kept it full when she lived alone with Zach and had been able to exercise her own preferences. That way, she used whatever she needed on a daily basis but could pack it without having to worry about forgetting anything. The practice had stopped because Bobby didn't like it. Because it meant too much freedom of mind.

Bobby hated freedom of mind.

She almost tossed the knee injector in with everything else. That's how strong a habit it had become. Even though she'd run out of the serum capsules—and how she'd run out remained a mystery after Bobby showed her a full box of them before leaving—and hadn't used any in days, it still had its hooks in her. It seemed she'd always been on it, though she was quite certain that wasn't true. It would take time to work its way out of her system.

The box Bobby'd showed her was definitely gone, though. Had she gotten rid of it herself without any memory of doing so?

Too many missing pieces. So many that it wasn't healthy to tax her mind trying to fill in the blanks just yet.

So many. Along with resurfaced memories that might explain them. Many were free-floating, not in any kind of linear narrative.

Port Authority.

The bus.

Hanging upside down.

That last one didn't have much detail attached to it, and she was pretty sure that was for the best. Whatever kept her from getting closer to that was doing her a favor.

And the pinkies—the bad medicine she'd been convinced was for the pain in her knee but that actually forced her to accept a false reality. What might it say about her that she'd believed the artificial life impressed upon her more than once? Would the escape she considered now lead to yet another one?

What was real?

The kid—Paul.

Charlene, which made no sense at all.

That one hurt.

Again, maybe stay away for now. Charlene died while Annie could do nothing but watch.

That was real.

Mr. Brill was real. He was at the head of all of it, though Annie couldn't recall any specific contact with him. But it was him. That she knew.

Out.

Away from Bobby and the job. Away from anyone who knew her or might recognize her until she thought all this through. That was real.

Bobby and the job.

And the pills—the ones she took to believe the life June Medill helped her escape and the ones Bobby took to make him behave as if he were on her side.

Bobby had no love in him. He was no father. She must've understood that the first time around with him, which was why they both needed drugs to fool her this time.

Bobby was no friend.

Neither were any pills.

And she'd be a lot more careful about deciding what went into her body from here on out.

There wasn't much more to pack up. They'd have to travel light and fast, wherever they were going.

Annie steeled herself for tearing Zach away from his routines, which could be the most difficult thing to ask of him. Often, his more comforting habits were altered only with a cost to both of them, whether she did it slowly and with as much coaxing and explanation as possible or not.

She closed up her pack and took a deep breath. When she let it out, it was reminiscent of the all-too-familiar white-noise hiss.

A blank cassette.

The Dynamite 8 that Bobby had destroyed.

The fan.

The hiss carried important information. Even if the picture didn't make sense. Wasn't complete. Didn't fit together.

Annie walked down the hall to Zach's bedroom. This would be fine because it had to be. Because Zach, despite his own way of doing things, was her partner.

She might not recall the specifics, but they'd defeated monsters together, both two-legged and no-legged. She knew it to be true.

That was real.

Time to go.

Annie knocked on the door and opened it.

Zach sat on his bed, waiting for her, his jacket across his lap. Next to him was a fully loaded backpack.

"How?" Annie asked herself as much as him.

Her son looked directly at her—which was rare but not as rare as it used to be—then glanced at his closet. The door to it stood open as if the door, too, was surprised it wasn't revealing anything interesting within.

Annie could've kissed him. So she did, quickly and lightly. "Ready?"

Zach hopped off the bed, donned his jacket and backpack, and closed the closet door.

He was headed down the stairs by the time Annie remembered to breathe and follow.

90

NEGATIVE SPACE

"It wasn't your fault," Porter told Paul for what had to be the tenth time. "If it was anyone's, it was mine. And maybe Audra's, but she's not here to defend herself."

Paul struggled to let Porter's words in. He couldn't bring himself to look at the Envoy or Lexi, who at the moment represented the whole of humanity, all of whom he'd put into grave danger via his foolish heroics. It was all he could do to spare a glance for Angus, flopped down on his side at Lexi's feet.

When Paul caught the big dog's eye, Angus responded with a steady thumping of his tail against the floor. Even that made Paul feel guilty.

"How many worlds?" Paul continued to watch Angus, who apparently thought Paul was talking to him and responded by whacking the floor faster in lieu of a spoken answer.

"You can't worry about that," said Porter. "It doesn't profit us to do so."

"How many?"

Angus's tail-thumping slowed.

"The Living World and The Commons make two. Three if

you count The Margins, the crossover between the two, as its own realm. Which not everyone does."

Paul chanced a quick look at Lexi again, and the naked concern in her eyes kept him from looking away again. The kid had just watched a fight involving a Medusa snake and a werewolf who wanted to rip his face off. Plus she'd insisted on staying to hear how Paul's misguided attempt to play savior doomed the world instead of saving it. Yet she was only worried about him.

"Are you all right?" he asked her.

She shook her head. "You?"

"No."

Lexi looked over at Jabari, who sat on a chair in the corner, restored to life in technical terms but still silent long hours after he'd become flesh again. They'd spent some time trying to catch him up on what had happened to him. They'd told him about the fight with Ilva and about how Porter had jumped Kamien the basilisk in front of the store window, where he'd seen his reflection and turned himself and the Ravagers Porter had put behind him to stone.

They'd all fallen asleep out there, waiting for Jabari to come back to them. Even Porter, who chalked it up to The Margins draining him. Finally, Jabari had stumbled into the building, helped by Paul and Porter. He hadn't said a word, hadn't moved from the chair they'd put him in, and hadn't had anything to eat or drink. And the only reason he wasn't a permanent sculpture was that he hadn't absorbed the full force of Kamien's gaze.

"I think—" Lexi reached down to rub Angus's belly, which set his tail to thumping again. "I think that as long as you don't act like all this is insane, and I remain convinced that you're not crazy, then I'm not, either. Does that make sense?"

"Yeah." Paul looked the girl over to convince himself she

was telling the truth about her relative health and remembered a more pressing question. "How did you get here?"

"Long story."

Paul decided to let it slide—for now. "So if I understand this right, my fight with Brill rattled the house enough to make it start collapsing. The whole time I thought I was doing something good, I was doing something very, very bad," he said to Porter.

Angus's tail stopped.

Lexi started rubbing his belly again, but the tail remained dormant.

"It wasn't just your fight." Porter sipped his tea. The Envoy was the only one who seemed interested in refreshments. "That was the culmination of it, along with Brill's downfall. Whoever took advantage of the aftermath understood that Brill's power had been in place for so long that if he were defeated—particularly in a battle with a fellow Nistar—it might be enough to destabilize the barriers between the realms and pierce them. If we go with your metaphor, it's not that someone wanted to destroy the house. It's that they wanted a free flow between rooms and floors—and holes are the best way to do that. The problem is that the bearing walls and perhaps even the foundation were also damaged."

"Which is not good."

"Not good at all." Porter blew on his tea and took another sip. "If the process continues, all of the rooms will cross over into one another, with the possibility that the entire structure becomes unified."

"And then?"

"This is all theory, mind you."

"Just tell me, Porter."

The Envoy spared a look at Lexi, who still didn't appear to be frightened so much as she was worried about Paul. When he and Porter had caught each other up earlier, she'd been badly shaken over the part where he'd tried to kill himself in order to get back to The Commons and make things right. "If the theory holds, eventually the house collapses into the basement, becoming one realm."

"And nothing survives."

"Nothing." Porter took another sip and gently put the teacup down on the saucer. "But that's the worst-case scenario. And it's only likely if we sit idly by."

Paul didn't let the worst-case part of that thought in. He'd been played. And because he'd been played, he'd helped destroy not only his world, but all worlds, along with everything and everyone in them.

That's all Paul heard.

And as his anger increased, a part of the power he'd exhibited in The Commons awakened just a tiny bit. The power that had ultimately caused the harm. That made him angrier. Which made it awaken just a little more.

He looked around the room and skipped over Lexi again. That she could remain concerned about him was just too painful. So he looked to Angus for safe harbor.

This time the dog's tail didn't respond.

"What was the part about the sunflower, Porter?" Lexi was trying to aim some reassurance Paul's way—an effort to show him that he wasn't alone.

He couldn't let that in, either. It only made him feel worse.

"The head of a sunflower. Or the bottom of a pine cone. Those are useful models to understand the structure of what we're talking about," Porter replied. "A seed head with Ingress, the source of all things, in the center. In a dark ring around Ingress is The Pines, which serves as a filter of sorts." He picked up his teacup. "God save those who mix their metaphors." He put it down without drinking from it.

"Arranged around the center in a concentric pattern—a pattern you'll find all throughout existence, incidentally, are the other realms. The Living World. The Commons. The rest are unknown; some are unknowable."

"How many?" Lexi leaned forward, elbows on the table.

Angus sat up part way and looked from her, to Paul, to Porter. Satisfied that all was well, he flopped down again, his big head knocking against the tile loudly enough to sound painful. It didn't faze him.

"If only we were all as tough as the head of a good dog." Porter bounced his staff on his shoe a few times. "We don't know how many. Nobody does. No one I've met, anyway. But the realms we are aware of and, we can assume, those we aren't, depend on separation and the stability of the structure to survive. Now those barriers have, as I said, been compromised."

"Who would want it that way?" said Paul.

"I don't know."

"What else don't we know?"

"I don't know." Porter laughed. There was no humor in it.

Lexi watched the Envoy now, her face a mask of even deeper worry.

"You must understand that a good deal of what I know comes from Audra, whom you've never met, but who is one of the greats," Porter said. "I'd trust her with my life. And, basically, I'm doing just that—along with everyone else's. She and those she's in contact with are basing their decisions on what's known about how The Commons and the surrounding worlds work, on their collective experience and wisdom, and on what they've been able to glean since they've started. They're learning on the basis of negative space, if you will, but sometimes that's better than direct observation."

"What?" said Lexi.

"The kid speaks for me," Paul added.

Porter stared into his tea, as if the answer lay at the cup's bottom somewhere. "In art, using negative space means you don't draw the thing itself. You draw everything around it, and that defines it."

Lexi began scratching behind Angus's ears with great vigor. Paul suspected it was her way of directing her frustration into something positive.

Angus was fine with that tactic.

"The going theory," Porter continued, "is that whoever it is —it's most certainly a group and probably a large one— managed to take the ability of The Commons to move and control Essence in its purest form and pull it through into The Living World in order to intercept and exploit the Essence here, before it can cross over into The Commons. One guess is that they didn't just bring that ability through. They also pulled in someone with experience in running such an operation. But that's not even the most disturbing part."

"It gets worse?" Paul didn't want to come off as a wiseass, but he was tired.

"That's just the part they know about. It's what we're fairly certain we don't know that's the scariest."

Lexi and Paul struggled to take it all in.

"The mythicals working with whoever is running this show aren't supposed to be able to cross over from The Commons. That they can indicates that the breaches are more numerous and larger than those who were waiting for them expected. Furthermore, the mythicals should cease to exist once they leave The Commons. They're but vestiges of the dreams, memories, and thoughts of the Journeymen who created them. They're not even supposed to continue living in The Commons, which would have been the case had it had a chance to continue resetting itself. So the fact that they're crossing over and able to exist here tells us The Margins are more extensive than we'd suspected." He paused for another sip.

"How do you know all this?"

Paul was taken aback by Lexi's question at first. Of course Porter knew. He was Porter. But she was right to ask. She was new to all this.

"I have friends in high places." Porter's tone contained enough of a smile to indicate that he knew how untrustworthy the explanation sounded. "And would you believe me if I told you the rest came from a message given to me by a mysterious power who lives in a realm I had no business visiting?"

Neither Paul nor Lexi had an answer for that. They had no choice but to believe the Envoy.

"The mythicals." Paul sounded more defeated than he'd intended. "I suppose they're a sign of something even worse."

Porter watched Paul for a moment—his face a confession that, yes, they were, before his professionalism gained control once more. "It's bidirectional," he said. "It's not just coming from The Commons into The Margins. The breaches are two-way. They're pulling from The Living World into The Margins as well."

"Those are some of the people we're seeing on the streets?" said Paul.

Porter nodded. "People and things, yes. Have you noticed that many of the cars have locked wheels? And others are just-plain abandoned? That's what bleeds into The Margins first. The unwanted. Those are the first people you're seeing here, too. The unloved. Those who aren't missed—or simply believe they aren't."

"That's sad," said Lexi.

Paul couldn't help but think that he and Lexi understood a

lot more than the average person about not being missed. In fact, it probably explained why they were here.

"And dire as well," Porter said. "Someone was waiting for Brill's defeat and correctly predicted that the force required for that defeat to occur would compromise the barriers, as I said. They knew enough to pull some key pieces of The Commons through in order to distort the laws of The Living World so that they could use the fantastic abilities available in The Commons to exploit the rich motherlode of Essence here. That's awful enough. But several of us—Audra, myself, and some other entities I can't name—are convinced that they don't realize what they've set in motion. They don't comprehend what it means that the mythicals can exist in The Margins and that the living are here as well. I'm betting that if and when they find out, they'll try to find a way to reclaim them."

"And it doesn't stop there," Lexi said.

"Does it ever? The Margins is an echo of both worlds, but as the crossover continues, that echo will solidify a combination of the two, no matter how messy and disastrous that may be." Porter gazed into his tea again, as if reading the surface of what was left in the cup. "You know what The Commons is capable of, Paul. Imagine what that would mean for The Living World."

Paul could. He just didn't want to.

"The house won't collapse into its basement for a very, very long time. In fact, time as it's thought of in The Living World doesn't even apply in the same way. The suffering that will ensue before that happens will be beyond imagining."

"The Commons is that bad?" said Lexi.

"The Commons can be bad. But keep in mind that its worst comes only from the minds of the formerly living, and the formerly living and all that they're made of was first filtered through The Pines."

Paul considered that. "You're saying—"

"That the domino effect will eventually breach all barriers, including the one protecting us from The Pines. Which would unleash everything the universe has ever held back from the surrounding realms into the crossover between The Living World, The Commons, and worlds unknown."

Paul felt the anger rising again. "This wouldn't have happened without me. Or you. We played right into their hands, and even they don't understand how bad it is." It took him a moment to realize that all eyes—Lexi's, Porter's, even Angus's—were on him. And the whisper of his power stirred again. "And there's nothing we can do about it."

Now Porter gave a half-smile. "I never said that." He tossed his staff up into the air, putting a spin on it, and caught it. "We have a plan. Or, I should say, the beginnings of one."

"You do?" Lexi gave Angus a final pat on the head and sat up straight.

Porter tossed the staff and caught it again, then looked from Lexi to Paul. "We do."

"We," said Paul.

"We."

"Will it work out better than the last one?"

"I'm glad you asked." Porter ignored Paul's snark. "It's simple—but huge." He tapped the staff on his toe a few more times. "It involves you. Me. And a few hundred megatons of nuclear warheads."

THE LAST THING SHE WANTED

Rain held on for an eternity. Once she convinced herself that the train's steep descent didn't necessarily mean it was in the middle of crashing, she was able to more calmly assess the situation.

The guns were still firing. Would a train in a death dive maintain a robust defense? Doubtful. Also, after the initial jarring course change, the descent remained steady.

Nevertheless, she was relieved at having been able to pocket the marble. Had she dropped it into the tilted darkness, she'd never have found it again. And if it was as important to the current situation as it had been to the Brill fight, that would be bad.

After a few years, the train leveled off some, and the descent became more gradual. Maybe an abrupt course change had required the steep dive at first, but now they'd made up the difference.

She relaxed her death grip on the motorcycle and eased herself down the dark car. Now and again, distant roof guns cut loose with a salvo or two, but they weren't as frequent, and they didn't last as long.

Perhaps the Ravagers or whoever else was harassing them had given up.

Or maybe they'd all been killed.

Rain figured her old self was returning when she found herself rooting for the latter.

Hey. They started it.

At the end of the car, Rain located the blocky release bar for the end hatch, which was another relief. She had enough experience with the rules—and the lack thereof—of The Commons to assume that the same dynamic applied to The Margins. Just because she'd entered through the door didn't mean it would wait for her when it was time to leave. Luckily, The Margins weren't feeling feisty, which was just fine.

She hesitated before trying to open the door. It was harrowing enough to cross between cars when the train was running flat. The old don't-look-down trick came in mighty handy. But what would it mean to cross to the next car at this angle of descent, even with the safety chains in place? And what if the chains were gone because The Margins decided to play a ha-ha on her?

Realms weren't known for gentle ribbing. Her time encased in what was sometimes—and not affectionately—called The Hedge was proof of that. As was what she'd done for Brill to earn her way out of it.

What she'd done to Paul.

Why was this coming back on her now, of all times?

Because it did whenever she was threatened or at her weakest. And trying to cross the gap between two cars on a train plummeting through the heavens qualified as one of those times.

The *thwump* of a change in pressure made the choice for her. She once again held on as the train went from one zone to another. Such a shift in zones or states involved a heavy air-pressure adjustment.

She was nearly knocked loose when the train reached what must have been the surface, the shriek of steel on steel making the nerves in her teeth cry out. She hung on, and the screech was eventually taken over by the sound of the wheels rolling normally over the rail, albeit way faster than the train probably should have been going.

It occurred to Rain that with every frightening development, whether it was the initial dive or this jolt of reentry, she heard not a peep from the people in the other cars. It was possible they'd been screaming their heads off, and she'd been unable to hear it.

She knew that wasn't the case.

These people were relegated to The Margins, in-between and forgotten. They were past screaming. Or maybe they just had nothing left to be afraid of.

Rain knew the feeling all too well—past caring. Fighting it was sometimes all that kept her going.

With the level ride came the return of the dim overhead light to the freight car. Rain hit the door's bar latch with all her weight and pushed. She was about to give up on attempt number one when it opened.

They were in a tunnel in the dark, and they were moving at bat-out-of-hell speed. The safety chains remained intact.

By the time Rain made her way back to the crew car to sit and wait for Emmett, she'd collected herself enough to avoid burying him in an avalanche of questions as soon as he came in.

It was the Railwayman's turn to shed a few pounds' worth of concern when he saw her. "Are you all right?"

"You mean, did the dive catch me between cars so that I

pancaked on the ground? No. Nor did I get blown off when we blasted into that tunnel, which I'm gonna guess appeared just as we needed it to be there." Rain crossed one leg over the other and wrapped her ankle around for effect. "But that's not the same as being all right."

"I'm sorry." Emmett blinked his guilt into submission. "Really. And I'm so glad you're okay. We had no warning. We were just told to prep and drop, and there wasn't time to let anyone know."

"You could have warned me there was a chance of that happening. I mean, that can't be the first time."

"The first time it's ever happened on a run? No."

"See?"

"But it's never happened to me or anyone else on this train before. And combined, we've got quite a few runs on our record."

"You didn't know."

Emmett shook his head.

Rain believed him. "I'm sorry."

"For what?"

"For being pissy. I got scared. I'm not used to it."

"Being pissy?"

Rain stared at him. "What's going on?"

Emmett busied himself cleaning up the car. It looked like the curb strip of the neighbors who wouldn't spring for locking trash cans to keep the raccoons out. Crushed coffee cups and empty snack bags were everywhere. Clearly, the Railwaymen weren't used to extreme course changes, either.

"Emmett." Rain's tone brought the Railwayman to a halt. "When you shake up your whole operation like that, it means a change. To me, it does. What's different?"

"The route." It was amazing how many coffee cups

Emmett could fit in one hand. Only now did Rain realize how large the man was. The conductor's uniform had distracted her from that before. "And not even that so much."

"What aren't you telling me?"

"Only what we're expected to do along the way. Because I'd be out of a job if I said anything more."

"Am I that much of a security risk?"

"No more than I am." The Railwayman stuffed two large handfuls of cups and bags into the can and looked around. He'd done a pretty thorough job. He washed his hands at the little sink.

"What does that mean?"

"We all operate on a need-to-know basis. We have the pieces we need and no more."

"I don't get it."

"Are you a Monty Python fan?"

Her answer was a quizzical tilt of the head.

"There's a bit they do about a killer joke." Emmett reached under a bunk to retrieve a cup that thought it had found a safe hiding spot. "It's so funny that anyone who hears it drops dead. The Brits translate it into German so their forces can read it out loud on the battlefield without understanding it themselves, and only the Germans die."

"What does that have to do with anything?"

"The translators are each given just one word to translate into German so they're not harmed. One guy is given two, and he goes into a coma. Or maybe he just gets really sick. I can't remember."

"Emmett. Are you messing with me?"

He began making coffee. Everybody had a talisman, and that was his. "Look, the point is that each of these guys had one word, which was useless by itself. But when all of the words were combined, the result was potent. It's like that with us and information. When we each do our part, it all comes together."

"What's to stop you from trading pieces with each other?"

"That would be known. And we'd be cut out of the process."

"Who would know?"

The Railwayman studied the coffee he'd poured into the filter. He dumped it back in and started over, counting anew.

"Sorry," said Rain.

Emmett shrugged. "I don't know."

"You don't know what?"

"I don't know who would know."

"Well, the person you're taking orders from, right?"

Emmett continued counting.

"You don't know, do you?"

The Railwayman dumped the coffee back into the bag again. This time, Rain didn't apologize for throwing his count off. "Quite the opposite."

"Of what?"

"It's a don't-need-to-know basis. You go on faith."

"In who?"

"The Commons. And now The Margins. And whatever makes it up. Or whatever makes up this train. It could be anything."

"That's crazy."

"Is it?" Emmett dropped a scoop of coffee into the filter. "One," he said—loudly. She deserved that. "How long has mankind gone into little buildings and prayed to someone they can't see? Does that make sense? Those people never hear back. Whoever's in charge here sends us messages all the time." He dropped another scoop in. "Two." And another. "Three."

Emmett had a point. A sea of tentacles gave Rain a marble and, without any idea what it would do, she handed it to Paul, who used it when he hadn't known, either. Or maybe he had. She couldn't remember everything. But there was no question she'd trusted a squirming mass of squid—no, Humboldt—to save her. And she'd returned the favor. There was also the matter of her doing Brill's bidding. But that wasn't to be considered at the moment. Or ever, maybe.

"Four." Another scoop. "Five." Emmett tried not to look too proud of himself for thwarting her. "You don't question faith. And it's not like it has to be religious. It isn't for my benefit. Or for the benefit of anybody working this train. We do it because we do it. Because we wouldn't do anything else." He stopped to ponder that. It cost him. "What was I on?"

"Three," Rain didn't want him to know she'd lost count, too. The Railwaymen were impervious to caffeine anyway.

Emmett closed the coffeemaker's filter drawer, filled the pitcher with water, and dumped it into the machine. "You don't really drink this, do you?"

"Coffee?"

"My coffee."

Rain didn't answer.

"Why not?" He didn't sound hurt, just curious.

"I don't know." She did, of course. She wanted her stomach to retain its lining.

The big Railwayman hit the brew button, which lit up. That seemed to settle the matter.

"So do you know who we're meeting or what we're doing at the end of this?"

"Not names, no."

"That's all you know, and you're doing this anyway."

Emmett turned to look her in the eye.

Rain hoped she hadn't offended him. She'd come to like

him. "Not that I'm judging you one way or the other. I'm just saying, that's all you know."

He watched her long enough to reach a decision. "You."

"Me what?"

"Where we're headed is where you're needed."

"Me? Not any of you?"

Emmett shook his head.

Rain's discomfort must have shown.

His concern was back. "What's wrong?"

"That's new."

"What is?"

"New to me."

"What?"

"Being someone who counts. Being needed." It was true. Even though she'd been necessary to Paul's victory over Brill. Part of her believed it could have been anyone helping him. She suspected she'd believed it the whole time she was Ray-Anne, when she didn't even remember what she'd done. It sat —hidden away, unannounced—in a little dark room in her heart, thinking its own thoughts and not letting her in on them, eating away at her the whole time. She'd never shaken the feeling that something was wrong. "I'm not used to mattering."

Emmett was pained on her behalf, and Rain was unable to look at him. The last thing she wanted from him was pity.

Not used to mattering.

Where had she heard that before?

Paul.

From Paul.

When they confessed to one another that they weren't accustomed to being of consequence.

That hadn't held much weight, ultimately. Paul and Rain had mattered quite a bit by the time it was all over.

And judging by the way things stood now?
Counting was the worst thing that ever happened to them.

92

MORE VICIOUS IN THEIR THINKING

Jeremy didn't feel safe opening Abel's journal at home, even though Abel's message had warned only about doing so in the office. But there was this concept of adjacency, which was about the connection between people and things, and that had Jeremy feeling jumpy as hell.

Only he could see the Rubbish Gladiator. Only he could see some of the people here in Billy Clyde's. What was his connection to them? If he listened to Abel's journal at home, would the fact that he lived there contribute to the adjacency and help people who shouldn't know what he was doing to know all about it?

He had no idea. So he decided to play it safe and open it with people nearby. Unless that was the exact wrong thing to do because then there could be spies around. Or focusites.

Jesus. Who knew?

There was only one thing to help him screw up the courage to forge ahead.

Beer.

So he sat alone in a booth at Billy Clyde's, where those only he and Porthos could see didn't bother him. Neither did the regulars, who mostly wouldn't acknowledge him if he didn't bug them first.

That was what he loved about the dump. Billy Clyde's was one of the fairest, most equitable places in the known universe. Well, Jeremy's known universe, which hadn't been very large when he'd started working with Abel.

Now? That universe had expanded in terrifying ways to an unknown degree.

Beer was always his friend until it was his foe. It wasn't clear which of those it was at the moment, which beer would probably have thought was funny. If it were sentient. And could laugh.

The listening was the most unsettling part of all this. Oh, hell—it was all unsettling, but what was so strange was that Abel's journal was just a text file. Yet when Jeremy opened it, he heard Abel speaking the words—even when he wasn't using earbuds. Jeremy was so paranoid that he used the earbuds anyway because he couldn't take a chance on others being able to hear. He also didn't want them thinking he was crazy, sitting and listening to a voice that was only in his own head.

And it was only in his own head. Jeremy was sure of that.

Accompanied by his pitcher and Porthos, who lazed about on the table, Jeremy knew that Abel's just-so-slightly slurred words were meant for him. Only he could hear them. And maybe Porthos. The way the big cat stared at him, as if he were listening, had Jeremy half-believing the beast could detect and understand everything being said. He'd once dated a girl who insisted her cat comprehended her words and thoughts. But it didn't matter because he didn't care about any of it as long as he had food and a clean litter box.

Other things rattled Jeremy, too, but he tried not to let them get in the way. Like the fact that as he drank and his head adopted a pleasant buzz, Abel's slurring became a bit more pronounced, as if his disappeared friend were taking in the alcohol, too. And when he shifted position, he felt the distinctly round hardness of that marble he'd found in his pocket, even though it was gone. He knew because he'd fished a hand into his pocket to check more than once.

Adjacency. This was all a part of it. The beer gave him adjacency to Abel, his hard-drinking friend with whom he'd shared hard-drinking times. And the marble, even though it wasn't really there, gave him adjacency to—something.

And Abel had a lot to say. Boy, did he. After Jeremy had nearly polished off his solo pitcher, he let the beer go warm and unfinished in front of him because Abel was half in the bag and disjointed in his presentation, so Jeremy needed whatever sobriety he had left to understand and retain what he was being told.

Because this counted.

The world wasn't what he'd thought it was his whole life.

In fact, it wasn't singular and unto itself. Not anymore.

That's where The Margins came into play. They were a surprise, even if they shouldn't have been. Manitou, at least, shouldn't have been surprised. They just chose to be because people like that didn't think they needed to respect anything they didn't want to hear.

"It's like climate change," Abel said, and he laughed before letting out what was either some sort of gasp or a tipsy burp. "The people making money off it don't believe in it because it doesn't pay to. Meanwhile, pieces of Arctic ice big enough to be U.S. states break off and float away, but shut up about that. And don't get me started on pandemics."

Manitou had found mentions of The Margins in research they'd done and in sources they'd consulted. Abel didn't say what or who those sources were, but whether they were

The Margins

books, people, or something beyond Abel's and Jeremy's understanding—and Jeremy wouldn't have been surprised if they were—they were deemed to be too close to the fringe to take seriously. So when Paul Reid and Mr. Brill blew holes through the barrier between The Commons and The Living World, it was pop-the-cork time. Get the party started—time to claim that Essence.

Only that's not quite how it worked out. The worlds started crossing over, and there was something to this Margins thing after all. People began falling in between the cracks and into this Phantom Zone-like place where they were in a questionable reality and existence. They were in-betweeners. Marginals.

Just as bad and maybe worse, the newly dead went into charge state, just as they had in The Commons when they were denied Journeys. So what to do? How to control them?

As Abel had explained, that's where the dark-arts stuff came in. The fracking. Go after the babies. The kids. The most vulnerable. Break them down to their most exploitable element. Then keep an eye on everything else and see how to play it.

What constituted everything else wasn't entirely explained. Abel was too in his cups for that, maybe. But it involved taking enough of living people's independence and agency so that they were ripe for harvesting and fracking themselves.

It was all about control and determination. Make sure Manitou has it—and others don't.

"It's about softening people up while they're still alive," Abel said, laughing even though it wasn't clear to Jeremy what, if anything, was funny. "It's about breaking down their individuality early on, so you can separate it out as a by-product."

Which meant keeping people down.

Keeping them occupied.

Keeping them distracted.

The great strategists in Manitou—Mr. Callibeau, who was too powerful for Jeremy to see or meet but whose influence was felt in everything; Truitt; and other unknowns—were caught off guard by The Margins phenomenon. But they did what good strategists in business and war do: they grew more vicious in their thinking until they had an answer. They blamed their victims for allowing them to do it. They did their best to understand what The Margins would mean for The Living World. And they embraced it, even if it meant destroying it, ultimately. By that time, they'd figure out a way to move on to someplace else.

Manitou had so many hands reaching into so many places. Companies that beat up their employees, kept them stressed out, and wouldn't let them prosper. The boot was on the neck in so many ways, no matter what business you were talking about.

Hourly employees at fast-food and coffee shops who had no set schedule. They were supposed to remain on call at all times and report within an hour of being notified. Then, when they weren't needed, they were sent home. Demoralizing them and depriving them of sleep was key. Setting them against one another to compete for the same hours didn't hurt, either.

Control.

Full-time employees in constant-improvement programs. Never-ending feedback telling them how they were doing. And if they weren't always improving, they were put on a "PIP." A performance-improvement program. Which stressed them out. Kept them spiritually exhausted and pliable.

Worker bees spent five out of a week's seven days doing something they needed to do to survive, not something they found meaningful. Oh, some enjoyed some aspects of their work, but that could be taken care of. Get them coming in on weekends. Keep them feeling like they're never doing enough. If they hit their goals, give them stretch goals. If they hit those, raise the bar higher next time. No matter how successful a year the team has, they have to do better the following year. And shame on them if they don't.

Keep them trying. Keep them afraid, unsure.

All the while, pay them as little as possible unless they rise to the level where you can force them to help you do it to others. Then you win. Either they're broken, which is a victory, or they abuse their underlings for you, which is also a victory.

Break the doers who won't become managers. Then make the managers break the rest of the doers for you.

Break everybody down. And when they die, take their Essence. It's easier when they're already damaged because of what you did to them while they were alive. And it's even easier than that if the uselings you have helping you have adjacency to them—familiarity, a relationship—so that they crack right open when you frack their souls.

That was life.

Life for so many.

And Jeremy knew it all too well.

Porthos gave Jeremy a long, penetrating look. Then he flopped onto his side and stretched, impressive claws out, as if to say, why is this news to you? I've known this since birth—and so have all the things I've killed.

93

THE CURRENT STATE OF ZACH'S MOTHER

The bus went through its entire route and was taking them back toward the stop where they'd gotten on. Zach's mother got scared and pulled the cord to get off.

That was a mistake. They were on the bus Zach's mother called the magic bus because it zigzagged through the city along a path that always seemed to take them where she wanted to go.

Around the park. Into the place where the people who looked like the peace-sign soldiers used to live but didn't really live anymore. Which didn't stop a lot of what Zach's mother called tourists and trustafarians going there to look for them.

That was where they should have gone to start this trip. Around people. Lots of people. That might help keep them safe in case friends of I'm-Bobby came looking for them. And they would come looking. That was why they shouldn't have been getting off the magic bus with few people around.

Zach's mother was breathing hard and looking around the bus once she saw they were headed back to what they'd been told was home. "No," she said to herself, but loud enough for the other people on the bus to hear. "No." She yanked the cord several times, hard enough for it to bounce and snap when she let go. "No."

The others on the bus—a white-haired lady and a coffee-skinned man with a black mustache—looked from Zach's mother to Zach and then back again. That happened a lot, but usually their faces were sad when they looked back at Zach's mother. Because Zach didn't look "quite right," as I'm-Bobby would say. It was like they wanted Zach's mother to know they saw and felt sorry for her.

It made Zach's mother mad. But the people never seemed to recognize that.

"Back door." Zach's mother tried to push the bus's rear doors open, but the light above them was dark. "Back door!" She smacked the glass when they wouldn't budge.

The faces of the people weren't sad now. They were looking to see if Zach's mother was okay enough to be Zach's mother.

She was, but not as okay as she usually was.

The little green light lit up, and Zach's mother shoved the doors open. "All right," she said.

Zach stayed where he was. She was making a mistake.

"All right!" Zach's mother was yelling at him now, and he wasn't used to that.

Zach made his way down the steps and hopped to the street's surface. He had to, given what Zach's mother would have called her current state.

The current state of Zach's mother was not what it should have been because of what was in her knee. And what was in her knee had been starved of its juice thanks to Zach hiding it. What was in Zach's mother's knee was like the pink pills she'd taken back in the other place.

Only worse.

A lot worse.

Zach's mother got off the bus without thanking the driver. She always thanked the driver. Gratitude was paramount, she'd told Zach, though she thought he knew what that word meant when he really didn't. He assumed it meant it was important. So you thanked people for things. Only Zach's mother didn't thank the driver.

"Come on," Zach's mother said without calling him by his name. She didn't even call him sweetie, which was something she'd only begun calling him recently.

Zach suspected she called him that to make I'm-Bobby mad because it let him know Zach was special to her no matter what I'm-Bobby said about him. Zach also suspected Zach's mother didn't know that was why.

Zach's mother grabbed Zach by the hand and pulled him hard up the street, up the hill. Again, her knee made her do that. Apalala-Aidan said so.

But Zach had already known something was off because she acted different in smaller ways. She put up with I'm-Bobby —with the way he treated both of them. She might have put up with him being bad to her for a while if she saw a reason to do it, but she would never have let him be bad to Zach without the knee.

"Come on." The tone and the pulling were harder now. They were headed for the gate to Zannie Park, which was what Zach's mother called it when I'm-Bobby wasn't around. She claimed it was a spot just for Zach and Annie—Zannie— even though Zach knew that wasn't true. It had been a spot for the Army. Now it was for everybody.

What she really meant was that it was for Zach and Zach's mother and not for I'm-Bobby, even if he went there with them, which he never wanted to do. Which was good.

Going to Zannie Park was another mistake. Even fewer people.

But Zach's mother wasn't making the decision of where to go. Someone else was. Someone else and the thing in her knee.

She didn't need to pull Zach. He was big enough to keep up with her, and she knew that. She just couldn't hear the part of her that knew.

Zach looked back down the hill. A black gas guzzler, as Zach's mother called the big car-truck things when I'm-Bobby —who owned one—wasn't around, was following the bus. It thought Zach and Zach's mother were still on the bus, even though the thing in her knee knew they weren't. That was because of the crossover world not being strong enough yet to stop the real world from interfering, Apalala-Aidan told Zach.

That would change.

Just as the black gas guzzler and those in it wouldn't follow the bus long enough for Zach and Zach's mother to get away. The thing in Zach's mother's knee would let them know where they were.

In Zannie Park, Zach's mother quickened her pace and led them across the parking lot of the building Zach and Zach's mother always walked past because they didn't belong. Zach didn't understand why Zach's mother always pointed out that they didn't belong to the building when they didn't belong anywhere. They didn't belong with I'm-Bobby, for instance, and Zach's mother never said anything about that.

Zach's mother led them past the dead tree the hawk always sat on, the one Zach's mother named Snag, and pulled Zach down the path. They were making a mistake, but it still might be fixed if they moved fast enough.

Zach's mother didn't know that, though. She was hurrying just to hurry.

They shouldn't have been in Zannie Park. They shouldn't have been moving away from people and into the trees by themselves, where they would be what I'm-Bobby would have called easy pickings. So they needed to get where they were going fast.

If Zach was able to do what he needed to do, and if those who were supposed to be waiting for them were there, Zach's mother's mistake could work out anyway. So he went as fast as he could, even when Zach's mother pulled them right through a muddy spot in the middle of the wood-chipped path, and his sneaker sunk into the mud and nearly came off.

"Come on," said Zach's mother.

Zach was glad his sneaker stayed on. The thing in the knee wouldn't have let Zach's mother stop long enough for him to grab it. Because if the thing in the knee had its way, it wouldn't matter what Zach was wearing.

"Come *on*," Zach's mother said again.

So Zach did. As fast as he could.

94

A LIFE CHEWED AWAY

The kid was going to get them killed. He was slow, and he wasn't all there. Might as well admit it after all these years. Bobby was right.

Zach was Annie's son, but that wasn't her fault. He was a liability. Genetics were a bitch. You rolled the dice, and you lived with whatever came up. She hadn't ever admitted the truth, but maybe it was time for a change. After all, what had her nobility gotten her? A kid who wouldn't talk, who'd eaten her life.

Chewed away by a parasitic grub. As if a bum knee weren't bad enough, she was saddled with a bum child. Maybe Bobby would be nicer if the kid would try a little harder to be normal. Was that too much to ask?

As she walked faster, Zach began shaking his arm like a whip, trying to free his hand from her grip. He thought she was squeezing too hard. Well, that was the game, little boy. The transaction. "If you don't like it, keep up," she told him. "If you can't, I'll show you how."

At that, Zach yanked his hand out of hers and stopped dead.

Oh, Christ. Now came the drama. They couldn't afford drama. They had to get to—where were they going, anyway? She'd thought Zach knew. But that didn't make any sense. Annie held her hand out to him. "Come on."

He didn't take it. Instead, he glowered at her.

Into her.

Through her.

His eyes flicked downward to her legs for a moment, then back up again, locking onto hers. He didn't like what he thought he saw.

Whatever he *thought* he saw. That was the problem, wasn't it? Since when did this kid think? "Zach. Not now, buddy. We don't have time."

Zach stood his ground, radiating insolence. Who did he think was in charge here? Did he actually believe this was a communal decision?

"Fine. You'll love it here in the dark when some creeper comes along and finds you. You'll be real popular with the creepers." Time to call the kid's bluff. Annie forged onward, leaving her son behind. She didn't look to see if he was following. That wasn't the message—that she cared if he came along. And maybe she didn't.

Oh, who was she kidding? She just wanted to teach the little jerk a lesson. The little simp. Keep up with Mommy, or get left behind as bait for the big, bad wolves.

A few more steps retuned her head some. What the hell? Whose thoughts were these? Had Bobby infected her with his anger toward their own child?

What if he had? Who was to say he wasn't right about that, really?

She continued on down the trail, beneath the canopy of cypress and eucalyptus. Trees that weren't supposed to be here. Not native. Well, she could relate. Given what life had dumped on her, she didn't feel like she belonged, either. She was a hitchhiker, not someone in her own vehicle on her own road.

That, too, was new. Annie wasn't sure where it was coming from. But that didn't make it untrue.

In the gaps between her steps, she listened to see if she could hear Zach trying to catch up.

Nothing.

Finally, her impatience got the best of her. She turned to check on him, and there he was—a good distance back. He was, however, farther along than he had been, albeit standing in the exact same position, as if he'd somehow teleported along after her. She hadn't heard any footsteps, but it wasn't like he was some ninja. He didn't have those skills. He didn't have any skills and never would. Little freak.

Fine. She'd go at an adult pace. The pace of a grown-up without a hanger-on, a little remora, in her life. He'd keep up. Or he wouldn't.

She made rapid progress toward the break in the trees ahead, where the trail sloped down to Washington, one of the streets that cut through the Presidio. One foot in front of the other. Again, she couldn't hear any sign of Zach following. Well, life was the best teacher. Maybe a few hours in the chilly dark would teach him what all those special-ed people never seemed to. Nothing penetrated a thick skull like terror.

Annie was moving down the sloping path, toward the painted crosswalk, when the black SUV passed, rolling west on Washington at a solid clip. "Hey!" she shouted without any reason for doing so. She headed to the road to flag the SUV down—on legs that weren't hers. "Hey!" Stepping onto the asphalt, waving at the receding vehicle. The driver kept going and rapidly disappeared. "Dammit."

She was just starting to wonder why she'd ever flag down a

black SUV that was way too similar to the black trucks she remembered when the footsteps came up on her from behind.

Zach ran past her and out into the road before Annie could say a thing. She wasn't sure she'd ever seen him move like that before. Not without a lot of begging and cajoling from her or a teacher. Certainly not so fast.

An ancient Oldsmobile approached faster than it should have been going, and the driver had to hit the brakes in order to avoid squashing Zach flat. It wasn't a near-miss, but it was closer than it should've been.

"Hey!" Annie found herself shouting yet again, as if she'd been reduced to a single-word vocabulary.

Zach continued down the opposite side of the road and cut onto the path that ran along it.

"Hey, yourself!" said the Olds driver, a middle-ager in a red backwards ball cap with an impossibly long piece of ash hanging from his cigarette. "Keep an eye on your kid if you don't want him all up in somebody's grill!"

Annie managed to stifle a string of curses as she crossed in front of the car. The ball-cap smoker remembered he had a horn and leaned on it. Too late, jerk.

With that, with even the suggestion of a threat to her son, Annie found herself slamming a mental door on the black SUV. She ran down the path after Zach, keenly aware, as she should have been all along, of the situation's wrongness.

Zach was no runner. And he certainly didn't ever run from her. Why now? Where had the hostility toward her own son, the awful judgment, come from? From her, but not from her. The suggestion felt like a part of her that didn't fit, as did the desire to suddenly have a chat with a carload of—of what, exactly?

Ravagers.

They were in that black SUV. She knew that to be true, just

as she knew the knowledge had only come to her because she'd been skipping shots to the knee.

Why hadn't she stopped the shots long before? And why in God's name did she ever try to get the Ravagers' attention? No wonder Zach was running. She should have, too.

But running was something Annie couldn't do, no matter how much her knee had improved after the budget-busting implant paid for by her company. Or by someone. In the middle of the awkward trot she was managing, she couldn't recall who the doctors worked for, but what did it matter?

Zach was a hell of a lot faster than Annie would've thought. He could cover ground. But she pushed as hard as she could and was able to keep him in sight as she headed down the sidewalk, past the former military housing.

It was only when he cut back into the trees, leaving the sidewalk to pick up a path again, that she realized that may have been part of the plan. Zach didn't want to lose her, which, despite his child's legs, wouldn't have been all that tough to do. Her knee didn't hurt. But it couldn't carry her very quickly.

None of this made sense. She'd sought the attention of the Ravagers when all she'd ever wanted to do before was avoid them at all costs. Why?

Because they'll help bring him back.

That made sense. Except it didn't.

Two sides were at war within her, and only one was right. But both were trying to use her maternal instincts to protect her son against her. She could feel it, like two combatants struggling for one gun.

One gun. Which meant there was no cooperation or agreement to be found here. One side would obliterate the other. "Zach! Buddy, wait!"

Buddy. Where was that coming from? Not a good sign. "Zach!"

Up ahead, Zach stopped and turned to face her.

Annie slowed.

Zach stayed put, watching her approach.

She knew what came next. She'd had a dog as a kid.

She was right. As soon as she got closer, Zach took off again.

Oh, lord. The uneven gait of favoring her knee, which still wasn't bothering her but could start to at any time, was exhausting. "Zach," she said again. There wasn't much energy in it now.

Zach cut to the right at the point where the path joined another street under the heavy cover of trees. It was a route they'd followed when out walking. He'd never run from her like this, leading her like this, but maybe she deserved it.

When Annie got to the street, she glanced left in time to see a black SUV cross the intersection where the street met Washington. Ravagers again.

Once more, she had to fight the urge to flag it down—until she looked to her right and saw Zach waiting for her, just before the curve. That snapped her out of it. She didn't care much whether or not she was caught, but the idea of Zach being taken brought out mama bear. She'd kill before that happened.

Yet part of her still wanted him to be caught with her.

That scared her enough to spur her on.

95

THE HAWAIIAN BUNKER

Apalala-Aidan hadn't lied. Everything he'd said was going to happen was happening very close to how he'd said it would. There were big things he called wild cards, and right now Zach's mother was one of the biggest. So were the black-truck men. But he'd told Zach lots of times—in a tight spot, try to think about only what he could influence or change. Try to ignore what he couldn't.

Zach was not a good runner. But Apalala-Aidan said important moments didn't always choose those who were best. Sometimes it was whoever was available.

So Zach ran. His legs and lungs burned. It was a good hurt because he was trying hard. And he was doing it.

Zach's mother was following him instead of the black-truck men. Zach knew their real name. Ravagers. But real names had power, and Zach didn't want to give them any. That was how it worked.

Apalala-Aidan had a real name, too. But he said that to hear it would hurt Zach. And to say it out loud outside Apalala-Aidan's home would hurt the world. So he was Apalala-Aidan.

And the men in the black trucks were the black-truck men. Because Zach had no edge in this game, Apalala-Aidan said. So he had to keep the other side from having one.

The Hawaiian Bunker. That was what Zach called it when Apalala-Aidan told him where he needed to go. And he'd given Zach a rare smile when Zach used the Dynamite 8 to repeat the name back to him to prove he remembered everything in the plan. "That'll do," Apalala-Aidan said, and Zach worried that he got something wrong. But Apalala-Aidan's smile stopped him from worrying.

It was all right because it had to be. It would have to be good enough.

That was what Zach's mother always said. It would have to be good enough. She never said it in front of I'm-Bobby, though, because he got mad if Zach's mother encouraged Zach. Zach wasn't clear on what was wrong with encouraging him, but it had something to do with I'm-Bobby saying he was wrong enough already and didn't need any help getting worse.

Up ahead on the right, the Hawaiian Bunker was a shallow cement structure with sand and grass on top of it. It looked like someone picked up a hill and tried to hide a building that was too big to fit under it. But the hill let the building think it was hidden just to be nice, like a box that refused to tell the cat its butt was sticking out.

Nice. I'm-Bobby was not nice. Neither were the black-truck men.

And as Zach slowed to let Zach's mother catch up a little, he knew that part of her was not nice, either. Not a real part, but it was in her all the same.

There was a difference. And it wasn't her fault.

"Zach!" Zach's mother hustled toward him as fast as she could. "Wait, buddy."

Buddy. That was the part of her that was not nice. Not all

right. "She is herself and not herself," Apalala-Aidan told him. "Do you understand?"

Zach did. That was why he'd hidden the needle juice that fed the thing in her knee. He had to hope that the not-all-right part of Zach's mother didn't win. He would do his best to see that it didn't.

Zach stopped at the Hawaiian Bunker's big, barn-like double doors and watched Zach's mother approach. He needed her close enough to follow him into the next part because once it started, there would be no going back.

Apalala-Aidan had made him repeat that, too. No going back.

When Zach's mother was close enough for Zach to hear her breathing, he put both hands on the doors and pushed. The Hawaiian Bunker was supposed to be locked. And it was. But it opened because Aidan-Apalala had said it would.

Now Zach needed to be extra careful. He had to make sure Zach's mother would follow him into the dark hallway without letting her get close enough to stop him.

At first, it looked like it was going to be easy. Then came the sound of tires squealing around the curve and the loud engine of the black-truck men's black truck as it came for them.

Zach's mother turned at the sound and began motioning to them even though there was no way they didn't see her. Part of her was with them. That's what Apalala-Aidan had said. Part of her. The not-all-right part. The part Zach had weakened by hiding its juice.

He hadn't weakened it enough.

Zach clapped his hands. When Zach's mother didn't turn to look at him, he clapped several times more.

The black-truck men grew closer.

Zach's mother turned back to Zach.

He ran into the darkness of the hallway without any idea what was in front of him—a wall, another door, or something that shouldn't have been there but was. He ran into the black, trusting that Apalala-Aidan had told him the truth about what he would and wouldn't let happen.

"Zach!"

Zach understood it was good that he was afraid, that he didn't know what he was running into. Because if he didn't know and was scared, then she didn't know, either, and was scared for him.

In the hallway, Zach looked back at Zach's mother to make sure she wasn't listening to the not-all-right part of her.

Framed by daylight in the doorway, she entered the Hawaiian Bunker and stopped just inside. She whirled around at the sound of the black-truck men's doors slamming.

The square of light she stood in folded into itself as the Hawaiian Bunker doors shut, sealing Zach's mother in with Zach. Her hands slapped against the metal bands of the double-door, followed by the heavy *thud-thud* of the black-truck men as they hit it from the other side.

Security lights way down the hall turned on. Now Zach could see Zach's mother, and she could have seen him, too, had she turned to look. Instead, she faced the double-door, slapping it again as the black-truck men hit it from the other side.

Zach coughed on purpose so that Zach's mother would hear him.

"Zach?" She started to walk toward him, slowly. He knew she didn't want to scare him. Instead, she worried him because she wasn't walking the way she usually did. Part of her was not all right.

Zach's mother passed the locked doors to several rooms on

either side of the hallway. She repeated his name as she drew closer.

The black-truck men slammed into the big double-door from the other side again, and Zach thought he heard the wood crack.

So Zach did what was needed. He waited for Zach's mother to get close. Then he took off running, ignoring her shouts for him to stop.

96

THE PULL-THE-LADDER-UP CROWD

"They're the pull-the-ladder-up crowd," Abel explained in Jeremy's head as he walked. "PLUs or ploos for short. They're happy to help the Callibeaus and Truitts of the world. They used community resources to get where they are, but they haul them up behind them so nobody else can have them. It keeps the competition low and makes for more people to exploit."

Jeremy had realized he wasn't going to have anything else to drink at Billy Clyde's, so now he was in that stage where he thought he was stone sober but was still suffering a bit of stubborn aftereffect. That didn't seem to matter much. Where Abel had sounded buzzed earlier, he was sharp and fast now. And Jeremy's brain kept up without missing a thing.

That was sort of the problem, actually. Abel talked almost too fast. And Jeremy kept up with all of it. Along with his comprehension came a jumpiness and an awareness of what was around him, which had him feeling like he had to keep moving and get home to safety.

But at Port Authority, he found he'd missed the last bus out of the usual gate. The fact that the gate wouldn't be used until morning was punctuated by the prone form of a down-on-his-luck man who would've fit right in among the unseen at Billy Clyde's.

The bony, crusty man was curled up on his side, as if sleeping, in front of the door that would've opened on the bus, had it been running. At first, Jeremy feared the man was dead when he saw mice scampering among the empty snack bags scattered around him and occasionally climbing up and over him, all without eliciting any kind of response. But then Jeremy noticed the man's ribs rising and falling, which meant Jeremy could do what every instinct was suggesting: get the hell downstairs immediately—and try not to think about how easy the guy would frack.

He knew there'd be at least one more bus running out of the Port Authority basement, but echoes of drunken conversations and arguments among both those trying to get out and those spending the night convinced him he wasn't meant to go back to his apartment. Maybe it was dangerous to listen to the journal there.

So Jeremy went wandering. Time and reality blurred as Abel talked to him—or talked to whoever he thought might find the journal. But it sure seemed to be directed at Jeremy.

"You have to understand the scope and depth of what they're doing and the principles they depend on to do it," Abel said.

Jeremy walked down Forty-Second, just west of Times Square, which flickered between its current family-friendly climate and its '70s- and '80s-era Deuce atmosphere of porn theaters and video-booth storefronts every time he blinked.

"They get to people in so many ways. They maintain a ton of addictive apps and games that trick people into giving up their privacy, which weakens them as individuals. They run their own news sites specializing in disinformation and propaganda. Keeping people fooled and disillusioned means keeping them malleable, and spreading bullshit gossip about celebrities makes those people ripen up, too. Because they're admired and known by so many, the adjacency counts more than it does for normal consumers. Even if they're hated, it's powerful stuff."

The night got weirder. Jeremy could've sworn he felt someone stalking him—following, watching from the shadows and ducking out of sight every time he tried to spot them. Though it was late, there were still a few people on the street. But there was no telling whether they would help should trouble arise. They might just take advantage of the opportunity and lift what was left after whoever was hunting him finished.

"Ridiculous college tuition, privatized student loans pushing the heads of graduates under the water's surface," Abel said. "Manitou depends on the capacity of people to exploit the less powerful. Think of how we make it easier. Corporations are people. People are treated like machines—and replaced by them whenever anyone can invent one that'll do the job. These guys talk right in front of me because they think I'm one of them—or don't care if I hear them. But you should hear them. They count on society being only a thin veneer over a feral, competitive populace. They set us against each other. I don't know. Maybe if those are the rules, and everyone's nothing but a savage force of self-interest, then it's okay for them to be like that. But you should hear them, Jeremy."

Jeremy was walking past Bryant Park and was distracted by its high stone wall. He'd never seen a wall around it at any other time.

"Smoke, smoke, sinse," said a furtive young guy leaning

out of the shadows as Jeremy approached. "Smoke, smoke, smoke." He looked out of place there.

No, not just out of place.

Out of time.

Another time.

Jeremy ignored him, having no desire to buy what he was selling. After he'd gotten far enough past him, he risked a look back.

The guy was no longer there.

Neither was the wall.

Only then did it dawn on Jeremy that Abel had called him by name. The journal really was meant for him.

"Theft, incursion, exploitation," said Abel.

Jeremy was working his way south to loop back around to the PATH station and a train ride home. He could've used a ride-sharing service, but he needed to be out and moving in the night, even though the feeling that he was being watched hadn't left him.

"There are always gaps and holes," Abel said. "You can't make everything airtight, or it can't breathe. And the Manitous of the world know how to use those. So do the people they depend on for the dirty work they don't have the time or inclination to do themselves."

By the time Jeremy was walking west on Thirty-Third Street, headed for Broadway and the island with the PATH entrance, he was sure something was moving along with him. He walked fast while Abel talked. He wanted to break into a run, but in every horror movie he'd ever seen, doing that led straight to whatever was after you.

Great.

Now his survival depended on the wisdom of teen slasher flicks.

Nevertheless, he limited his pace.

"Holes," said Abel. "Another thing for Manitou to figure out. Not only did having too many charges in one place cause problems because of adjacency, but they also attracted holes." Jeremy almost found himself asking Abel what kind of holes he was talking about. Then he reminded himself it was a recording. It wasn't Abel. "Paul Reid blew gaps in the barrier when he defeated Brill, but not physical tears between The Commons and The Living World. The pass-throughs can't be seen. They tend to align themselves where Essence is concentrated, especially adjacency. Nobody's sure why. Anyway, the holes were necessary for the abilities that Manitou needed to access the Essence to pass through to our world. But then stuff started coming through—like Brill's ability to turn dee-dees into charges, though that's just a theory. And other things."

Other things? That wasn't the sort of thought Jeremy wanted to entertain while breathing heavy and walking as fast as he could because, yes, something was tracking him. He risked another look behind him. Again, nothing.

Still. What kind of things?

A scream from behind him. A great intake of breath followed by another scream. And not a human one.

It came from a dark, unlit doorway down a side street.

Movement in there?

No, nothing.

Jeremy turned to run.

And almost smacked heads with the Rubbish Gladiator, who'd appeared out of nowhere and was watching the same dark doorway.

"It came from the air," said the Rubbish Gladiator. "That's why you couldn't see. It was above you." He pointed toward the doorway. "Almost nothing left now. Look."

Jeremy did, but he only got close enough to see a few large feathers at the edge of the shadows. No closer; those were really big feathers.

"You scared?" said the Rubbish Gladiator. He nodded Jeremy's affirmative for him. "You ought to be. You had help this time. Don't count on that."

"What was it? What happened? Who helped?"

The Rubbish Gladiator didn't answer. He wheeled his can over to the doorway and began spearing feathers, dropping them into the can as he tidied up whatever black event had happened there. "No tickets," he said, ignoring Jeremy as he worked. There must have been a lot of feathers there in the shadows. "Whores. Battle meat."

Jeremy needed to catch his train. His sense of dread faded as he walked, but he still felt like he was being watched from time to time.

"You suckers. You patsies. You victims. You fools," said the fading voice of the Rubbish Gladiator.

∽

THE NEXT MORNING, Jeremy's hangover was eclipsed by lack of sleep and the disconnect of having felt so close to Abel, who was no longer in the office or, as far as he knew, in the world at all—assuming the boundaries of the world still meant something.

When he got to work, he was told Truitt was waiting to see him. He took a deep breath and tried to pretend everything was okay—and would continue to be.

"Good morning, Mr. Johns," Truitt said when Jeremy entered his office. "Do sit down."

Jeremy did as he was told. But not comfortably.

Truitt watched him over steepled fingers before flashing a smile. "How are you?"

"I'm fine, sir. Thank you. And you?"

Truitt continued to study him. "I don't think you are. But I do think you're significantly more knowledgeable than you were just a day ago. After all, you've been doing some fascinating reading."

97
RUBY RED

Annie had rounded more corners chasing Zach than she'd been able to count. She was hopelessly turned around and couldn't imagine how he wasn't as well, but he seemed to know where he was going.

"Buddy!"

No answer.

The things that didn't make sense were piling up.

The Wine Bunker, an old military facility in the Presidio that had been rehabbed and opened up as a place for wine enthusiasts to store their collections, was supposed to be locked. Yet Zach had entered without so much as a key. And when she'd gone in behind him, the doors locked themselves behind her. She realized the place was trying to protect them when the Ravagers hit the other side of the doors. Part of her was not happy about that. It badly wanted to let them in so they could help her catch her son.

That was the way of the current running game. Part of Annie wanted to double back to the Ravagers. But just as she was about to, Zach would appear, waiting for her to continue the chase—at which point her maternal instincts overruled whatever desire she had to work with the black-clad men.

She shouldn't have wanted that at all. She should've grabbed her son and run away as fast as she could. But that part was kept in a holding cell of its own—locked up and unable to fully make its warnings heard.

Far behind her, the loud crash of the door breaking open, accompanied by a growling engine, told her the Ravagers had smashed it in with their SUV. An effective move, it reminded her that they weren't just silent automatons. They could think, which made them more dangerous. She had to stop yelling for Zach and giving away her location.

Annie stepped around the next corner slowly, wary of whatever might be waiting in the dim light. The doors to rooms on either side of the corridor were closed, their spaces filled with valuable wine or waiting for a future customer to fill them. But it wouldn't do to stumble over some renovation project in mid-completion or, barring that, a bucket left out to catch the stubborn drips from a leaky roof. It was an old facility. She assumed it was sealed tight, but she wouldn't bet her knee on it—the knee that had been suspiciously pain-free for some time.

Around another corner was Zach, about a dozen yards away. He stood calmly waiting for her. As soon as she stepped into view, he crouched down, motioning for her to do the same.

"Zach?" she whispered. "Buddy."

He motioned more furiously for her to get down.

Humoring him, she did. But they didn't have much time. The rest of the bunker was silent. She had no way of knowing how close the Ravagers might be.

Zach reached forward and waved his hand around a few inches above the floor. Immediately, there came a sizzling sound, and a ruby-red laser beam formed a line stretching from wall to wall at about chest level. As soon as it appeared, it rapidly hissed its way down the hall toward her.

Annie was safely below it, but no distance felt quite safe enough. She ducked even lower as it passed overhead with shocking speed, its deadliness belied by the minimal noise it made as it zipped down the hall and blinked out once it reached the corner she'd just come around.

It would have cut her in half if Zach hadn't warned her. She couldn't breathe.

Zach waited until he had her attention again. Then he moved over to the door on one side of the hall and pointed to a spot on the wall just past the door jam.

Annie shuffled closer, keeping low. She had the brief, strange thought that she might never want to stand again.

Zach remained in position, pointing at the door until she was almost close enough to grab him. He jabbed his finger toward the spot next to the door to make sure she looked. Sure enough, there was a slight flaw in the wall, barely noticeable in the dim light, more of a difference in the surface. Once Zach was confident she'd seen it, he stood and took off running down the hall again. He didn't give her any chance to lay a hand on him.

Annie had to ask herself if she would have. She'd never gotten physical with her son. Would she have grabbed him? Rather than think about it, she crawled to the point where the sensor was. For a moment, she considered standing and stepping over it, but she didn't trust her memory or judgment. Not in this light, and not with so much at stake. What if she didn't clear the sensor?

She willed herself forward, crawling right through the sensor's field. Again came the hiss, and again the bright ruby beam formed across the hall and zipped down it, back the way she'd just come.

Annie didn't want to turn to watch it. It was bad enough knowing she would've had her upper separated from her lower had Zach not revealed the trap to her. And the mystery of how he'd known it was there would have to wait.

The beam sizzled behind her, followed by two slaps of wet meat hitting the floor. The beam had cut through something.

Slaps.

Plural.

It had cut somebody behind her in half. That whoever it was hadn't uttered a sound as it sliced through them told her it was a Ravager.

God, she hoped it had been a Ravager. She couldn't handle the thought of some poor sap stopping in to grab a few for a dinner party. It was difficult enough that it was one of the enemy.

Weston.

The memory returned to her there on the floor.

She would've hated for Weston to have met his end like that. Whoever the departed Ravager had been in a past life, he'd been somebody. Most likely a soldier, like her, or a cop. And he'd been cut to pieces because of her.

She turned back to Zach. He was down the hall, waiting for her.

There'd been one Ravager.

There'd be more.

Time to go.

THE WORST OF THE NOISE

"I'm sorry, Ms. Moseley."

Charlene had been so engrossed in trying to will the View-Master to tell her something positive—or anything at all—that she hadn't noticed June Medill standing in the doorway. June Medill wasn't known for her stealth; she was usually too busy talking or otherwise inserting herself into situations to do any sneaking.

Charlene thanked her but didn't ask why June Medill was delivering her sympathies.

There were too many possibilities in an environment where good people were gone, where Jazz had died in pain, and where everything Charlene and so many others had worked so hard to rebuild seemed to be collapsing in on itself. Condolences were so in demand that they didn't need to apply to any one aspect of the overall tragedy.

June Medill took a tentative step into Charlene's office without being asked. That very act was two-fold in its rarity. The woman's behavior was more timid than usual. At the same time, June Medill was violating her own strict rules, which would have kept her at the door until she was given permission to enter. "May I?" June Medill indicated the chair across the desk from Char. When Char nodded, June Medill sat. "I just wanted to check and see how you are."

The weight and sincerity of June Medill's delivery left Char struggling to come up with a response. "As well as possible, thank you" she said after considering her options. "And you, June?"

June Medill didn't appear to have heard the question. She leaned forward and locked eyes with Charlene. "I know," she said. All of the energy seemed to leave her, and she leaned back in her chair. "I know." The second time was barely audible.

"Know what, June?"

June Medill dabbed at her eyes with her fingers and adjusted her position in her chair. Then the intensity was back. "I know what it's like to doubt yourself—to doubt yourself and your decisions and wonder what might have been avoided had you chosen otherwise."

"And you know that's what I was doing?" It came out unexpectedly. Without intending to, Charlene had just confirmed June Medill's assumption.

June Medill nodded. "When I was working in Brill's office" —she hesitated, and Charlene suspected it was because it still required effort for her to drop the formal "Mister" when naming the man—"I believed everything I was doing was right so long as I did it efficiently. No matter how poor my treatment of others or the outcome of our efforts, if everything was done in as streamlined and cost-effective a manner as possible, then the result couldn't be anything but good." She folded her hands in her lap, studied them, and refolded them. "But then I had a great deal of alone time to consider what I'd done."

Charlene knew what had happened to June once she'd decided to betray Brill and warn Annie Brucker that his minions were coming for her and her son. However, they'd never discussed it. Nor was Charlene sure that now was the time to do it.

Trauma starts its own conversation in its own time. Charlene knew all about that. Anyone who'd suffered a violent death did. But that was as much as she wished to consider the subject for the moment.

June shifted position in the chair again. "Please understand that I'm not in any way trying to equate what I did—the harm I helped perpetuate—with what you're doing here, ma'am." She hesitated. "This is not coming out the way I wanted it to. I'm just saying I'm acquainted with how much you can damage yourself when you go too deep with questions, doubt, and self-punishment. That's what I'm saying. Or trying to say."

"Thank you, June. I think we—"

"I know what I did. I know I have a long way to go in making up for it." June sat up straight, bearing up against whatever inner voice wanted to stop her from talking. "And I want you to know how much I appreciate you and the Envoy Corps giving me the chance to do just that in the face of—in the face of everyone who doesn't think I should be here."

Charlene said nothing. She couldn't have named any one person who didn't want June there, but only because nobody would say such a thing to Charlene. Which didn't mean it was never said.

"I wouldn't let anyone punish you for your decisions." June wiped her mouth with the back of her hand, as if trying to rid herself of something distasteful. "And I won't go any easier on you if you punish yourself."

The truth of that struck Charlene. She had, in fact, been

engaging in quite a bit of self-flagellation over her helplessness. She'd tried to be useful in the repair of the building. But she'd quickly realized that Demos and the HQ facility itself were best left to their own devices. Things took longer to fix than they did to damage, so Demos and the building were racing the Ravager attackers. The tanks would fire periodically and dish out some destruction, and Demos and the building would repair it as fast as they were able.

Charlene had hoped that being useful might take her mind off the losses they'd suffered. Jazz had died terribly. The lost Envoys and Journeymen-to-be were banished to points unknown, and the only thing that kept her from losing it completely was that they might still be safe so long as no one could confirm they weren't.

For the umpteenth time, Charlene stopped herself from considering whether anyone who worked for her had the power to torment Flameout in his waste-tank prison. Her side was supposed to be better than that. And they were. But that didn't mean it was easy.

Useless. Charlene had let her people and her facility down in countless ways, and all she could do was sit and stare at the silent View-Master and wait for FinePoint and Demos to tell her that the building had managed to patch up any truly worrying harm.

The questions didn't end there. Where had the lost gone? Where were those who could come and help? Why weren't their distress signals acknowledged or answered? What was going on out there? It seemed like an eternity since Porter had gone missing. Where was he? And how could Charlene convince herself that she deserved the devotion of a woman like June Medill, who was more honest about her own failings than Charlene or just about anyone else she knew?

"Do you believe in what we're doing here?"

Charlene had almost forgotten June was still there. "Which part?"

"The mission overall. Helping to heal The Commons, keeping the Journeys running, helping those who come to us determine their next destination as cleanly and fairly as possible."

"Yes, I do. I believe." Charlene watched June Medill fidget for a moment. "Do you?"

"I do. And that's all the difference between what I was doing with—with Brill—and what I'm doing here. Back there, I ignored the result of my efforts. Here, it's more important to me than anything else." She rested her hands on the edge of Charlene's desk. "That's what I'm trying to say. Everyone here believes. Everyone in the waiting room did. So did that poor girl in the hallway. So don't second-guess yourself. Don't do that."

Charlene watched June Medill watching her. June Medill was the one telling her what she'd so badly needed to hear. Didn't see that coming.

Before Charlene could say anything more, a multihit on the building, louder and more concentrated than any of the previous volleys, shook her out of the moment.

Multiple impacts. Too many for Charlene to distinguish between.

The first volley served to notify all within that the attack had changed. The tanks, robotic or not, meant business. And the crunch of something hitting the front wall of the building —of several somethings hitting it—drove the point home.

This was different.

This was worse.

Charlene and June Medill rose from their chairs in unison.

Charlene grabbed the View-Master—just in case it decided to be helpful at some point—and made sure she had her holstered pistol with her. Then she pushed her way past June Medill as gently as possible and hit the hallway running—hurrying, like any good soldier, toward the worst of the noise.

99

NEVER OFFER A SMILE EASILY

Pulled from one of her not-quite-sleeping states in the near-dark of the bottom bunk, Rain knew she was not alone in the space. She considered her shotgun, lying right next to her, but whoever loomed over her was too close for her to raise it in time. Instead, she rolled and brought both feet up into the mystery person's ribs, unable to kick as hard as she'd hoped because she didn't have the space. Still, it reaffirmed her practice of not getting under the covers.

Her target *whuffed* as the air left them and stumbled backward.

Rain had her shotgun moving butt-first toward whatever part of them she could break before she remembered where she was. She reversed the gun and aimed it dead center.

The low gasp and an attempt to say something akin to her name identified her assailant. Emmett.

Luckily, she'd only knocked the wind out of him. But she kept the shotgun on him long enough to send a message. "I didn't think you were enough of a creep to move on a sleeping girl. Or are you just dumb?"

His first attempt was a croak. He waited a few breaths

before mounting a second. "I will never make that mistake again. Nor will I ever cease to be impressed with your speed and strength. That's serious stuff you've got there, miss." He coughed and gently probed his side. "Seriously."

"What were you thinking?"

"Clearly, I wasn't. But my sidearm's in the wall locker next to the bed, along with everybody else's."

"Why?"

"You'll find out when we get there. That's a rule. But you'll need yours, too."

Rain watched him straighten up. He was tough—she'd give him that. When he cocked his head in a silent question, she remembered she still had the drop on him and lowered her shotgun.

"May I approach?"

She hopped up from the bed and stepped aside.

Emmett, after waiting a safe few seconds, leaned into the bunk again and pressed his hand against the wall. A steel door she wouldn't have otherwise noticed popped open. He pulled out what looked to be a .38 and grabbed a holster. Donning it while favoring the side she'd kicked, he dropped the pistol into it.

"Yours?"

"Mine. We each have our own, and no one touches anyone else's."

"I get it."

He felt along his ribs again.

"I'm sorry."

"I deserved it."

Rain said nothing. She didn't want Emmett to think she wouldn't put his mistake behind them. She strapped her own holster on, then dropped the shotgun over her shoulder and into it. "What do I need to be ready for?"

"For when we get there."

Their eyes met. They played the hard-stare game until Emmett cracked first and gave her a crooked smile, nodding in respect.

Rain nodded back. Never offer a smile easily.

At that, he broke into a full grin that fell away as he prodded his sore ribs again.

Rain let it go. The matter was settled. "When will we get there?"

"When we get there."

She fixed him with the hard stare again, and this time it wasn't the kind that would end with a smile.

"Soon."

She didn't let up.

"Soon enough that you need to be loose." He felt his ribs once more and failed to disguise his wince. "And listen to what I say."

Rain kept up the stare but nodded. She could do that.

But though she liked Emmett and was sorry for hurting him, she didn't plan to make listening to him a habit. She wouldn't make listening to anyone a habit. Not without good reason.

Then again, there seemed to be plenty of those around lately.

∽

"You have to make it there without me," Apalala-Aidan had told Zach. So far, Zach and Zach's mother had succeeded.

But making it this far and making it all the way were two different things, and that's why Apalala-Aidan had kept Zach up at night, talking to him from the closet door, speaking in what felt like a dream but wasn't, having him use the Dynamite 8 to repeat back everything Apalala-Aidan told Zach about the traps.

And the Hawaiian Bunker.

And which ways to go.

And which ways not to go.

And where to jump.

And where to duck.

And where to jump, duck, and crawl.

And what would happen to Zach or Zach's mother if either one of them got it wrong.

That's what made it even harder. It was all on Zach to get it right. It scared him if he thought about it too much.

It scared him even more to think that Zach's mother hadn't been told anything. If she went the wrong way or did the wrong thing, it might be her the trap got.

Zach couldn't take her hand and lead her. If he did that, she was just as likely to drag him back to the nearest black-truck man. That would mean going back to I'm-Bobby, who would have no reason to pretend to love Zach's mother anymore and who had never bothered to pretend to love Zach.

They'd be given to Man 2. I'm-Bobby would be happy to have an excuse to hand them over to someone else to deal with.

It would be the end of them.

"I'll help if and where I'm able," Apalala-Aidan said. "But I won't be able to help until the end, and maybe not even then. So you and your mother have to make it there on your own. That means remembering what I say. Do you understand?"

Zach did, but only part of it. The rest he memorized and recited back to Apalala-Aidan there in the dark of his room. Because even if he didn't grasp why, he knew it was very important for him to know backwards and forwards, as Mrs. Good Morning Class would have said.

Backwards and forwards.

Focus.

They had to make it on their own.

Mrs. Good Morning Class had once written in Zach's quarterly report that he struggled to focus, which wasn't true. He just didn't care about the things she wanted him to focus on, though she was nice to him.

Focus.

Henry Lovell was the name of the boy who'd thought of the traps, according to Apalala-Aidan. His father always made him go with him to the Hawaiian Bunker to check on the collection or pick up a few choices for the weekend.

Henry, bored, wandered while his father got lost in his bottles. Henry knew the layout of the Hawaiian Bunker way better than his dad did, and Henry thought of where all the traps should go and what they should do.

In The Living World, they remained imaginings. But in The Commons, they became real, which meant that in The Margins, in the overlap between The L.W. and Commons, they were as well.

Focus.

Henry Lovell drew pictures of the traps and what happened to the people who fell prey to them. The people didn't deserve what they got, but they got it anyway.

Zach had seen other kids at Ambit draw the same kind of pictures, though he didn't know why. Knives in eyes. Arrows in eyes. Arms cut off. Sometimes they showed them to the girls and to kids like Zach to see if it would, as Mrs. Good Morning Class said, get a rise out of them.

Nothing got a rise out of Zach. He just didn't understand why anyone would want to make drawings like that.

They got a rise out of some of the girls. And a few of the girls liked the drawings more than the boys who made them, which got a rise out of those boys—and not always a good one. One girl whose name Zach couldn't remember made her own gross pics, as she called them, and showed them around. After that, the boys didn't show her theirs anymore. They wouldn't even get near her.

She thought that was funny. So did Zach, but not for the same reasons.

Focus.

Focus or end up like one of the boys' drawings. Or, worse, one of that girl's drawings.

Keep Zach's mother moving.

Avoid Henry Lovell's traps.

And don't lead Zach's mother into them, either.

Make it to the end, and hope Apalala-Aidan really could help them.

That was a lot.

There was one thing Zach would keep from Zach's mother, no matter what. Apalala-Aidan had told him what was at the end, but he'd locked it away behind a door in Zach's mind so that Zach couldn't inadvertently reveal it to whoever might be working with the black-truck men.

That could happen here in The Margins.

A lot of things could.

Focus.

Zach moved ahead to the place he didn't know. And in the place he didn't know, what he didn't know would happen would happen.

100

THE PART THAT WASN'T HER

Zach wouldn't let Annie get any closer. Just. Wouldn't. It was a nonstop tease-and-retreat game as he led her deeper into the Wine Bunker, and she allowed it. He seemed to know where he was going. And he was her son. Despite the strong urge she felt to call out to the Ravagers, to let them find her, she'd follow her boy wherever he wanted to take her.

She rounded yet another corner and tried not to think too much about how many corners they'd already put behind them. This place couldn't possibly be that big. Had they somehow left it and gone into a second complex? Where was all this going?

Away from Bobby, that's where.

Away from Manitou and the rest.

She'd figure out the finish later. But for now, putting the start well behind them would do.

There Zach was again—down a straightaway so long, she might not have known the distance-diminished boy was him had she relied only on her eyes. But her heart knew. Her heart always knew.

Zach motioned to her with both hands, urging her forward. Was this really a game to him after all? When did he begin taking delight in such things?

The footsteps behind her reaffirmed that it was no game. They came fast and, once again, way too quietly until they were way too close. That was why Zach was urging her on. He'd tried to warn her.

Annie hurried as fast as the knee would allow. The sound of her own clopping, off-balance hobble stopped her from hearing the Ravagers or knowing if they were gaining on her.

She drew closer to Zach more slowly than she should have. Maybe the hallway was deceiving in the dim light. Or maybe the terror of not being able to run fast enough made it seem that way. But the floor passed beneath her with frustrating leisure, and she imagined the Ravagers behind her had knees that were perfectly reliable. They were probably damned fast runners.

When it seemed she'd covered about half the ridiculous distance between herself and Zach, he held his arms out in front of him, as if indicating that she was to remain at a steady pace. Then he crouched a bit, preparing to jump.

Jump? Was he going to jump? *Clop-clop-clop.* Annie plodded onward in her sad parody of a sprint. Did he want her to jump?

Zach turned away from her, ran a few steps, and jumped in mid-stride.

Onward she clopped. Now she could hear several sets of footfalls close behind. Too close.

Zach faced her and crouched again, hands out. Then he sprung up, raising his arms.

Annie did her best to time her own jump and managed to launch using her good leg. It was pitiful, of course, but raw fear goosed it a little. It added enough for her to hit the floor farther down the hallway than she would've predicted.

It didn't help with the landing. In the air, she heard the footsteps behind her abruptly cease. As her bad knee gave out and she tumbled to the hard floor, one set of boots landed beside her.

Annie rolled, and her knee flared in a brief blowup of pain before it went suspiciously numb, as if someone or something had flipped a switch on the nerves there, not wanting her to know what she might have just done to it.

She faced backwards. There was no one behind her. She blinked.

No, not entirely true. A set of black-gloved fingers protruded from the floor itself, from the span she'd managed to leap over—a wraith, hanging on by the tips. Then the other hand and the arm it was attached to came up through the floor and tried to grab hold, too.

That's what Zach had been warning her about. The floor there was an illusion. The Ravagers behind her had fallen through it, however many there had been. Zach had succeeded in getting her to jump over the concealed pit.

The part of Annie that wanted to reveal her whereabouts to the Ravagers moved her forward. She crawled toward the fingers and the flailing arm, reaching out to help if she could. If she laid flat enough, she might be able to pull him up and out.

Weston. She'd have helped Weston.

Annie never had a chance to wonder why she'd want to do such a thing.

When she was still a couple of feet from the concealed edge, the fingers and arm were abruptly yanked down beneath the false floor. There and gone, just that fast. Something was down there, and it had plucked the Ravager from the edge.

She never had the chance to ponder the matter further. Strong fingers found their way into her hair and grabbed her collar. Then she was yanked painfully to her feet before she was put into a choke hold. All she could see was the black sleeve and glove of the Ravager who had her from behind. That glove held the same Beretta Weston and the other Ravagers carried—and it was pointed down the hall at Zach.

Zach didn't seem to understand the danger. He knew what a gun was. Annie was sure of that. Bobby had watched enough shoot-'em-ups when Zach was around. Yet he didn't move.

Part of Annie didn't want him to. Part of her, despite not being able to breathe, was fine with a pistol being pointed at her son. Not all of her, though. "Run, buddy." No good. The forearm across her throat reduced her voice to a rasp.

Zach didn't run. He just stood and stared at her—as if she'd take care of it when that trust was going to get him shot instead.

Run. She wasn't even able to say it. Thus, all three of them were surprised when she brought her heel down on the Ravager's instep and heard the kind of crunch that meant several rounds of reconstructive surgery.

No sound from the black-clad soldier. He should have been screaming. But he let her go. When he did, she swung around with a vicious elbow, which caught him in a soft place.

Annie faced the Ravager as he dropped his pistol and stumbled backward. She took a step forward and shoved. Then he was gone, too, dropping through the illusory floor to join his comrades.

The thought that she'd killed Weston crossed her mind for only a moment before she looked back down the hall to see Zach take off again. She searched the floor around her and spotted what she was looking for. Now she had a gun.

She also had a reminder that, despite the part of her that

wanted to work with the Ravagers—the part that wasn't her—there was no one else to blame for her ending the existence of another being. It was Annie who'd done that.

Annie was now armed and more lethal than before. She'd have to remember that, take responsibility for her actions, and live with whatever else she did.

Maybe such a level of accountability should have given her second thoughts.

It didn't.

She would do whatever was needed to catch up to her son.

Then they'd face what lay ahead together.

101

GIRLS COULD BE MEAN. SO COULD BOYS

Zach had several tasks to juggle in the Hawaiian Bunker, all of them hard.

There was trying to keep Zach's mother safe while also ensuring that she kept following him. There was making sure he himself didn't get caught. And there was what he had to do to the black-truck men.

He had to kill them.

Apalala-Aidan said it wasn't killing them; it was freeing them. But that was outside of anything Zach had seen.

What he had seen was the movies I'm-Bobby loved to watch to upset Zach and Zach's mother. Zach knew what those told him. When the things happened to the black-truck men that he caused to happen, it was killing.

They weren't free. They were dead.

Zach was wrong to think that way, according to Apalala-Aidan. But Apalala-Aidan wasn't right about everything. Zach hadn't seen him be wrong about anything yet, but that didn't mean it couldn't happen. Nobody was right all the time.

But it didn't keep Zach from doing what needed to be

done. They had to get where they were meant to go, and there were, as Apalala-Aidan had said, no guarantees.

Zach covered two more long hallways and rounded two more corners, always letting Zach's mother catch up enough to see him again before he moved on. After the second corner, he had the feeling something was wrong, like something invisible had just hit him in the stomach.

What was supposed to be there was not there.

If it wasn't there, as Apalala-Aidan had said it would be, then Zach and Zach's mother were caught. He'd led them down the hallway maze for nothing, left them no choice but to sit and wait for the black-truck men—assuming Zach's mother didn't give in to the part of her that wanted them to be caught.

"Zach?" Zach's mother stood in the distance, having slowed now that he was stopped again. She moved forward carefully—a step, a pause, and then another step, as if Zach might take off again if she scared him.

Zach understood. He'd done that every other time.

"Come on, buddy. This has been fun, but we have to go."

Zach's mother was wrong about the first part and right about the second. The ladder, some people called it.

But there was nowhere to go. What was supposed to be here was not here. Apalala-Aidan had been wrong. For a moment, Zach had hoped that he himself was wrong, that he'd stopped too soon.

But he hadn't. He was where he was supposed to be. And what was supposed to be was not.

Now came the sound of footsteps from far behind Zach's mother—but not as far as they should have been, which meant the black-truck men were too close. Zach could feel his heart beating now. He was able to hear the black-truck men's footsteps better than Zach's mother for reasons he didn't understand yet, but she'd hear them soon.

When she did, they would lose. The part of her that wanted to help them would win.

The air moved ever so gently against the back of Zach's neck. Cool, damp air that smelled of a deeper place. Of something else there. Zach turned his back on Zach's mother.

It was what Apalala-Aidan had told him would be there. An open stairway of old, dirty tile exhaled the humid breath of the underground that spawned it.

More footsteps from behind Zach's mother now. She'd hear them in a moment. Hear them and give herself over to them.

From where Zach's mother stood, she couldn't see that there was a stairway there. To her, it was a hole in the wall.

So Zach did what he'd seen other kids at Ambit Academy do when the teachers weren't around to tell them not to. They'd pretend to step into the stairwell without knowing it was there and fake-fall, making it look as real as they could in order to get the girls to scream.

The problem was that the girls caught on and were bored, so the boys had to make it look as real as possible. Sometimes they tried so hard that it became real, and they tumbled down unless they were able to catch a railing.

When Jordy Harmon broke his arm, a new rule was instituted, as Mrs. Good Morning Class said, to make sure it didn't happen again. Nobody was allowed to play on the stairs, and it meant real trouble if anyone did.

It didn't happen again. The kids were a lot more careful, which meant it didn't look as real, which meant the girls were bored again. Which was better than the way a couple of them had laughed at Jordy lying on the landing below.

Girls could be mean.

So could boys.

And Zach, who'd never tried to fake-fall anyone before,

realized how not funny it was when he whirled his arms like the other boys and pitched forward into the stairwell.

Zach's mother screamed on his first try. She was fooled more easily than the Ambit girls.

She was also fooled because Zach's near-fall was almost a real one. He caught the railing on the way down and thought he'd rip his arms off, barely stopping himself from smashing his head on every step on the long way down.

When he pulled himself up, he was bleeding. His hands were smeared red.

But there was no pain, and it wasn't quite the right color for blood. He smelled his hands. Mommy juice. That's what I'm-Bobby called it when Zach's mother had some, just as daddy juice was the bitter-smelling, foamy drink I'm-Bobby drank in the glass with the handle on it—the drink that made him even meaner.

"Zach!" Zach's mother was loudly hobbling toward the stairwell as fast as she could. Now Zach had to hope she could get down the stairs in time.

Because Zach now heard the footsteps of lots of black-truck men. Lots.

Zach hurried down to the next landing just as Zach's mother appeared at the top of the steps. It was only when he looked back up toward her that he noticed the walls were running with streams of red Mommy juice. When the stairway appeared, it had cut into the Hawaiian Bunker and the rooms with the juice stored in them.

Zach's mother started down the steps toward him. Once she'd made it a short distance down, a steel security gate dropped behind her and locked into place, sealing the stairway off from the hallway above.

The stairway, like the double-door entrance that had closed after them, was on their side. That was good.

Other things would not be.

Zach ran down the steps as fast as he could, Zach's mother half-stumbling her way down in pursuit. Her grunts of effort—he hoped it wasn't pain—made him feel bad for putting her through this.

He stopped feeling so bad when the crash of something and then several somethings against the security gate told him that the black-truck men had reached the top of the stairs.

The gate wouldn't hold for long. Apalala-Aidan had said it was designed to keep something called vandals out. It wouldn't withstand what he called a full-on assault.

Zach pushed himself harder, all the while making sure he could hear Zach's mother making her way down the steps behind him.

"Zach!" Zach's mother had real pain in her voice now. The part of her that kept her knee from hurting—the part fed by the injections—was not keeping it from hurting now. It didn't want her to come down the steps with him. It wanted to slow her down while the black-truck men bashed away at the gate above. "Buddy!"

The nickname, which Zach's mother hated, meant the injection-hungry part of her that was just like the pink pills she'd taken long ago was trying to gain control.

Zach rushed down the stairs, nearly falling more than once.

And Zach's mother came after him.

Zach reached the landing and waited. He had to make sure she moved as fast as she could.

They were so close.

Or so Zach hoped. The stairway hadn't been there when it was supposed to. And he didn't actually know what was waiting for them at the bottom. Apalala-Aidan hadn't told him because it had to come together at the last moment without the other side figuring out what was in the works.

If it was late, they were in deep, as I'm-Bobby would say, cutting off whatever word came after that when Zach's mother glared at him—though I'm-Bobby loved making her think he might not.

Zach couldn't get down the steps fast enough, it seemed. From up above came the crash of the gate being broken down. The black-truck men would be right behind them. And they were faster than Zach's mother. They were faster than Zach.

A dozen steps from the bottom of the stairway, Zach clambered up onto the double center rail dividing the up side from the down and slid the rest of the way, hopping off at the end. He turned back to motion to Zach's mother to do the same, slapping the railing to make sure she understood. She had to avoid the last set of stairs.

Zach's mother was close enough for him to see that she didn't want to do it, that maybe she thought she couldn't. But she must have been convinced by the pit illusion she'd already faced because she climbed up and half-tumbled down until she reached the end and lowered herself to the floor and onto her good knee. She nearly lost her balance and fell onto one of the final steps, but she recovered in time.

Now they were on a subway platform much like the ones he'd seen in Apple City and here in their current city, Bay Town. Mommy juice ran down the walls here, too, collecting in puddles between the tracks and further down the platform.

Zach's mother flexed her bad knee and fixed him with the look she used when she was upset and afraid she might upset him, too. "Buddy."

He motioned for her to join him where he stood, away from the steps.

Zach's mother hesitated but did as he wanted.

Far up the tunnel, the tiny lights of an approaching train appeared, still silent in its distance.

The footsteps of the black-truck men echoing down the steps were anything but that.

And now all they could do was wait. They had to time this right. It was the last thing Apalala-Aidan had drilled into him.

Closer came the footsteps.

The black-truck men never spoke, which made it worse.

Closer still.

Zach's mother looked back up the stairs toward the noise, then turned to Zach again. The look on her face confirmed Zach's fears. The part of her that wanted to be caught was winning. There was no more time.

Zach reached around her to wave his hand over the two bottom steps, where the spot in the wall set to catch anyone coming down would see it.

Nothing.

Zach waved again.

Nothing.

It wasn't working. And the train, if that was what they were supposed to take, would not get there soon enough.

Zach's mother tried to pull him out of the way so she could tell the black-truck men where they were.

Zach lost his balance and fell backward, his hands flailing as he tried to recover.

That did the trick where his other movements hadn't. A loud *clunk* was followed by the groan of something changing that hadn't changed in a long, long time.

If Zach's mother hadn't pulled him back hard enough, it might have gotten him, too.

The steps flattened into a ramp, the railings sinking into the suddenly slick surface. The black-truck men came rolling and sliding down, cascading into a pit which opened up in the spot on the platform where Zach's mother had stood only a few moments before.

Some fell fast enough to overshoot the pit and spill out onto the platform. Others continued directly over the edge of the platform and onto the tracks.

The train's lights washed over them. It was moving a lot faster than Zach had realized.

Zach's mother let out a cry, which was soon drowned out by the roar of the approaching train.

Some of the black-truck men who'd tumbled onto the tracks stood up in the bright light of the oncoming train. Others were injured by the fall and couldn't even do that.

The screech of steel on steel became a physical thing all its own.

So did the flood of the lights as they filled the station.

Zach looked away.

102

THE DUST OF THE INCURSION

"Demos!" Harris cried. "Demos!"

The first tank was halfway through the ugly hole in the wall—a hole that had been the front entrance to Envoy HQ. Charlene initially thought Harris was foolishly calling the facilities manager over to help fix the damage. Stress and the shock of battle did weird things to one's head.

The situation that came into focus once Charlene made it through the dust of the incursion was more dire than that. A tank had smashed its way into the building's lobby and was in the process of backing out, most likely to enlarge the opening. But the vehicle's treads were spinning. It appeared to have gotten itself stuck for the moment.

The lobby was a ruin. Multiple shells had probably hit the protective steel curtains in front of the entrance to soften things up before the tank, an urban type used by police SWAT teams that was fitted with a battering ram, made a run at the doors.

Before it could finish reversing its way out, John Demos charged it, which is what Harris was, understandably, yelling about. He wasn't calling for him to fix anything; he was trying to talk sense to the man. It was a suicide run if the tank decided to make use of its guns, at least two of which were visible and could be brought into play at any time.

Demos displayed no fear of the tank. He angrily hopped over the curled-up steel wreckage, broken glass, and what used to be a front door, and slapped both hands onto the front of the tank. Meanwhile, the treads continued their futile effort to spin the invading weapon free of its self-inflicted confinement. His devotion was admirable, but he was going to get himself killed.

Charlene headed for the first pile of debris, ready to pick her way through it, when a hand on her shoulder stopped her.

Reinhard. "Watch," the former Vigil told her. "Give him a chance."

Sure enough, Demos shifted his grip back and forth a few times before his hands worked their way toward each other. Then he felt his way down the tank's body as its treads stopped spinning in reverse.

Charlene thought her heart would stop when the treads began turning forward, and the tank lurched ahead, forcing Demos backward with it. But it was too little, too late.

Demos hopped back a couple of steps, nearly toppling over the mangled door frame behind him, and casually slapped the tank down near its underside, at an angle.

That was all it took.

The newly installed facilities manager's mythical talent for finding the key weak spot in any form or structure more than lived up to its reputation as a great cracking noise filled the lobby. The tank split, its left half falling forward a foot or two before the hull of the vehicle broke apart entirely. Its engine gunned for a moment before it died.

With the motor disabled, the only sound to be heard was

the rasp of one portion of the tank settling itself against the other. Then there was silence, which was broken by Demos's chuckle.

Harris gave the feat a couple of congratulatory claps as Demos turned and bowed. Even Charlene had to admit it was an impressive achievement.

Reinhard gently cleared her out of the way and stepped forward. "Demos," he cautioned.

A direct hit against the rear of the ruptured tank sent Demos flying and the pile of debris surging forward, flattening all of them.

Charlene struggled to pull herself off the floor and out of the dust. Something had her pinned. Her chest convulsed. She felt herself coughing but couldn't hear it over the ringing in her ears.

Whatever was holding her down was pulled off her and two strong hands helped her up. Reinhard's face was right in front of hers. He was clearly speaking, but all she could hear was a muffled crash and rumble from the crippled tank, which lurched forward.

Through the fog of impact, Charlene understood what had just happened, what was still happening. Another tank was trying to move its ruined sibling out of the way. It must have hit it from behind with a shell before ramming it.

A bright blue-white arc pierced the dust and lit up the ruined tank.

Harris.

The attacking tank's engine cut out as its systems were fried.

"Are you all right?" Reinhard's voice was clearer through the ringing as he helped her to her feet.

Charlene nodded. Or tried to.

Either way, Reinhard seemed satisfied that she could

move. He guided her back out of the lobby, through the wreckage and away from what would surely be another attempt at breaching the building's defenses. "Harris!" Reinhard's shout brought the young Envoy over on the double. "Help Charlene back into the hall. Where's Demos?"

Harris pointed, and Reinhard was gone.

As she and Harris made their way back into one of the hallways, Charlene tried to tell him she was okay, that she was fine on her own. But she wasn't sure if her words were spoken aloud or remained in the thought stage. Anyway, it was a lie. So she allowed herself to be helped.

Another muffled crash as yet another tank hit the two now blocking the entrance hole made by the first one.

A moment later, Reinhard joined them with an unconscious Demos thrown over his shoulder.

"Is he all right?"

Reinhard shook his head at Harris's question. Charlene couldn't tell if the former Vigil wasn't sure, or if he was indicating Demos was hurt. And the fog wouldn't let her think too much about what the right answer might be.

They worked their way into the closest hallway.

Then FinePoint was there with them, saying something about a manual lockdown and falling back.

Charlene let Harris help her along. But despite the fog, she couldn't shake a sense of shame that this was the second time since all of this happened that she was the one to be evacuated, not the one who helped others.

She wondered when she would get the chance to balance the scales on that account.

For balancing was sorely due.

103

BIRTHED IN A HIDEOUS FASHION

Later, Rain would be told that the engineer went for the brakes a split-second after the train detected people on the tracks and tripped its emergency-stop system on its own. But it was too little, too late.

Some glitch attributable to the disconnect between the realities of The Commons and The Living World overlaid with that of The Margins left the train traveling way too fast to enter an underground station. The engineer hadn't expected to see the platform for another mile.

Rain wasn't aware of any of that when it happened. She and Emmett were standing on the entrance steps to one of the passenger cars, ready to help whoever they were picking up board quickly so they could get the hell out of there.

Emmett didn't know who the new passenger would be, either. He'd been told Rain's presence was required because she was the only one who could verify that they had the right people. It was already a hot run, and the LZ would be even hotter if it got out that the train would be pulling in. They'd be sitting ducks, and then they'd have to contend with even more ambushes for the rest of the trip.

If it got out that the train was pulling in.

If.

How quaint.

The trouble started with Rain's head bouncing off the steel wall of the stairway, knocking her half-senseless. There was a big difference between the engineer hitting the brakes and the train hitting them itself. And it was worse in a world where the physics she was used to were given a courtesy nod but obeyed only some of the time.

The train braked without any consideration for what it might do to the humans it carried. It was a big freight—not one of the ninety-plus-cars that commonly crossed the U.S. but only a dozen shy. In The Living World, it would've taken a mile to go from the first shriek of the brakes to a dead stop. It wasn't nearly so long in The Margins, but it was long enough.

Rain would also be told later, as she was checked for a concussion, that they were lucky they hadn't overshot the station altogether. Not that it made any difference to the Ravagers who were pulped or cut to pieces. And by the time Emmett pulled himself off her and was trying to see if she was all right, the doors opened.

After that, all right was a theoretical.

Rain got tagged. No doubt. Her ears rang, and when she checked the wetness on the left side of her head, her hand came away red.

By the time Emmett got her up, they were dropping in on a state of open warfare. Ravagers poured down onto the platform from an open stairwell about fifty yards away.

"That wasn't there when we pulled in," said Smalley from behind them. Rain had a hard time hearing him over the din in her head, but she picked it up a few seconds afterward. "They're on us."

It got worse from there.

A mass of nanomen flowed out of a doorway a few cars down, blocking Rain's view of the Ravagers. Then the shooting started.

The nanomen had no time to form into any unified, coherent shape, so they did the best they could in clusters. The initial volleys from the Ravagers brought clots of tiny men down in bloody bursts.

Rain's shotgun was up and out. Emmett and Smalley were only a moment behind with their pistols.

There was nothing for them to do. All they could see was a wall of linked nanomen struggling to work as one.

The shooting got closer and louder, the gaps between shots shrinking. The Ravagers were coming in greater numbers.

More nanomen joined the fray from an adjacent car, surging forward. The platform beneath them was red with blood, both from their numerous dead and strange shapes that took a moment for Rain to recognize.

Broken Ravagers.

Twisted and bent in ways no human body would willingly align itself. Heads turned the wrong way. Limbs free of torsos. It was a pitched battle for keeps, and the nanomen were tearing the Ravagers to pieces while taking losses of their own.

"Jesus," said Emmett over the chaos.

Smalley took a round. One moment they were all helplessly pointing their guns toward the carnage, unable to see a target. The next, he was down.

Rain shouted to Emmett, but before either of them could do anything, two carriers whose names she didn't know grabbed their fallen comrade and lifted him up into a car doorway.

There was no time for anything else to be said. The mass of nanomen slowly gained ground at a heavy cost. A large lump appeared in the rear of the rough hill they'd formed, a tumor sliding out over the blood and gore, breaking away to move down the platform toward Rain and Emmett like a horde of ants carrying prey back to their mound.

Something fought its way out of the mass. Or was disgorged by it.

Two somethings, put forth by the little men covered in the blood of battle, birthed in a hideous fashion.

A woman and a child, both of whose features were caked in red. They'd gone through the eye of the mayhem.

The child was calmer than a kid should have been, as if upheaval and carnage weren't anything new. Rounds continued to make their way through the barrier presented by the nanomen, one of which whined off the platform a few inches from Rain's foot. Another took chips out of the station's tile wall, and a third rang off the steel of their train car's doorway.

Mother and son.

That was clear just looking at them.

Something familiar began to take form in the haze left by the bang to Rain's head and her still-coalescing memories of The Commons. Before it became clear, however, the mom was leveling a pistol at her, and Rain had the shotgun pointed right back.

The woman appeared to be as surprised as Rain was to find herself in this standoff, bullets flying around them while nanomen continued to fall, and unseen brutality was unleashed in turn upon the Ravagers.

"We're friends," Emmett told the woman.

She didn't seem to hear him. She wiped the blood from her eyes with a forearm. None of it, thankfully, looked to be hers. She looked to be torn between shooting and talking.

The little boy held his hand out to Rain.

It all fell into place.

Tentacles surrounding her, holding her up.

A purpose where there'd been none before.

The deliverance from drowning.

Handing off the instrument allowing Paul to defeat Brill.

Brill.

Victimizer of Rain, The Commons, and others uncounted.

The bloody mother and son had played a critical part in the sequence of events that had saved it all.

Only they hadn't.

Rain knew these people.

They'd been betrayed along with her. They'd share that forever.

She looked down at the boy in the midst of a mutual massacre. "Hello, Zach."

Zach Brucker revealed nothing as Rain lowered the shotgun she'd trained on his mother. He continued to hold his hand out, watching her.

Rain knew what he wanted. It was why she'd been given it. She reached into her pocket, pulled out the cat's-eye marble, and dropped it into his hand.

Zach closed his fist around the marble as if this were a formal ceremony, just the two of them there. The faintest hint of a smile appeared as he pocketed it.

The mother still had her pistol aimed at Rain. Bullets continued to cut through the nanomen and zing off the floor and walls around them.

"Time to go." Emmett turned to lead them all up into the train.

They almost made it.

With a primal cry, the mother grabbed Zach by the hand and yanked him to her, nearly pulling him off his feet. Then she headed for the nanomen wall, steeling herself to breach it and join the Ravagers.

"Annie!" The name came to Rain without warning. Which made sense. It was knowledge from their shared experience. Rain grabbed for her just as the nanomen who'd brought her to them rose up to engulf her once again.

Annie fought the tiny beings with the ferocity of someone who wasn't herself. And she wasn't.

In the next instant, the roof guns closest to the action sounded.

Again and then again in rapid succession.

With Annie and Zach on this side of the nanomen, the train was able to cut loose without the risk of hitting them. Rain couldn't see the result, but it couldn't have been pretty. The roar of the guns in the enclosed space was too much to bear, particularly given the blow she'd taken to her head.

A hand on her shoulder. Emmett pulled Rain toward the train as several carriers came forward to take Annie from the nanomen.

Annie fought them, too, all the while maintaining a firm hold on her son, who laid his own hands on her, trying to bring her back to herself. She thrashed even harder.

But she was no match for the nanomen, joined by their brethren who were retreating to the train as the roof guns took on the balance of the fight.

It was a wall of sound.

Annie's mouth was open. She screamed at her son and at the carriers, but all Rain could hear were the big guns.

Fighting all the way, Annie was carried to the train's doorway as Emmett pulled Rain back into it.

Rain dropped her shotgun over her shoulder and into its holster, reaching for Annie and Zach.

When Annie's head jerked backward, Rain thought it was part of her resistance against those trying to save her.

Then fresh red flowed down the woman's face.

Annie slumped and stopped fighting.

The blood was hers.

104

THE WAR PART OF WARRIOR

"You're not cut out for the war part of warrior, are you?"

Great. Now Charlene was hearing voices. She'd wondered if, perhaps, she was concussed and finally convinced herself she wasn't. Now this.

With the voice came an awareness that had slowly slipped away as she'd worked her way down onto her side from a sitting position. She didn't know how long that had taken or how long it'd been since she'd snuggled into the storeroom after ordering Harris to leave her on her own. There was a fight going on, and they couldn't afford to have one of their most powerful people playing nursemaid.

The young dynamo hadn't agreed, which was where the ordering part came in. And Charlene waited for him to get out of sight before admitting she couldn't make it to Beatrice on her own, so she opened the first door she came to and sat herself down against the wall.

She'd been vertical then. Not anymore.

So maybe finding her way to Beatrice to get some help should have been a priority.

Her head cleared enough for her to figure out what was questioning her toughness. It was a pile of drywall rubble someone had stacked into something approximating a face on the tile floor of the storeroom. The effect was that of a helpless dummy buried up to its neck.

"I was never in the fighting part," she told the head. "I wasn't supposed to be. I was communications and then intelligence."

"Didn't you get taken out by a roadside bomb?"

Great again. Not only was the drywall talking, it knew her. Then the world cleared just a smidge. Thank God. She wasn't hallucinating after all. "Quarry."

The drywall head did its best to raise eyebrows it didn't have in concern. "Who else?" The drywall head had nothing but holes where its eyes should have been, but still they managed a smug gleam.

"When did you get back?"

"Not soon enough, apparently. Are you hurt worse than they think you are? Should I be worried?"

Before Charlene could come up with an answer, the walls shook with the impact of an explosion or strike from outside. Or maybe another tank ramming through a wall.

Somewhere in the back of the storeroom, which Charlene couldn't see because she still hadn't marshaled enough will to sit up, something heavy fell from a shelf and hit the tile floor with a muffled crumple. The storeroom wasn't the safest shelter in the midst of a fight. She pushed herself up to a sitting position against the wall. It took more than she'd bargained for and felt like a greater accomplishment than it should have.

"That doesn't give me any more confidence," said Quarry. "Do you want me to get help?"

"When did you get back?" Charlene repeated. She closed her eyes and let her head rest against the wall.

"Just now. Ahead of your friends."

Another impact followed by someone—more than one someone—running past the storeroom door, toward the noise. Or maybe away from it.

Something rocked on a shelf in the back of the closet, then settled itself. She had to get up. "What friends?"

The head on the floor said nothing. Had Quarry's immaterial presence abandoned its vessel and left a lifeless drywall sculpture behind? "Sorry," he said after a length of silence. "Just checking. Give it a minute."

"Give what a minute, Quarry? What friends?"

A string of impacts rattled the walls, followed by the louder *whump* of what Charlene assumed was a target being destroyed. Someone else ran past the storeroom. Or maybe it was the same person.

Charlene was filled with questions such as when, exactly, the world had gone sideways once more. She'd slid down to a fetal position again.

"Tanks blow up good," said Quarry. "Even robot tanks."

From out in the hall came a louder, closer explosion and the sound of something rock-like hitting the floor. Dust found its way under the storeroom door and into the small space.

"Hey." Quarry's short-lived excitement once more gave way to concern. "Why are you down again?"

Charlene fully intended to answer him but didn't.

Quarry's drywall head collapsed sideways from Charlene's vantage point as he left it and left her.

She remained in place, breathing dust until she couldn't smell or taste it anymore.

∽

"Shhh," someone said, though nobody had been talking. The fingers on Charlene's forehead were cool and welcome. They traveled down her face, traced their way down her jawline to her throat, and worked their way back up again. The fog and ache made their exit as the hands practiced their art.

Beatrice.

Charlene had fallen off the edge of the world in the storeroom. Now here she was in the infirmary again. Maybe she'd never left.

Beatrice's continued healing prowess sharpened things up more.

"I've been spending way too much time with you," Charlene told the healer. "People will talk."

"They already are." Beatrice's fingers rested on Charlene's temples. "How else would they argue over who's most worried about you?" The room became more sharply defined still, its lines losing their fuzz and a refrigerator announcing its presence with a motor that kicked into a quiet hum. "You're welcome anytime, of course. But we'd prefer it if you walked in under your own power."

"I'd prefer it if I had some progress to show for all my bruises and scrapes."

"She wouldn't be an Envoy if she weren't so hard on herself, would she?" said a woman in the room, out of Charlene's eyeline. She knew the voice.

"Nicolette?" Charlene pulled away from Beatrice's treatment to see if she'd guessed correctly.

Sure enough, the Dharma Ranger sat forward in a steel visitor's chair, watching her.

"What the hell are you doing here?"

"Ask your stone-faced pal."

Charlene looked to Beatrice, who offered nothing.

"The rock man," Nicolette explained. "It makes quite the impression when your aquarium gravel tells you to bring the big guns and come running. I've got an angel fish, a bunch of guppies, and a swordtail that are going to need years of therapy."

A distant *whump*.

"D.W. and the team are mopping up," said Nicolette. "We thought we'd be done by now, but the Ravs were swinging a lot more armor than your rock buddy realized."

Now came the distinct beat of a chopper buzzing HQ.

"Those aren't theirs. How do you think we got here so fast?" Nicolette dropped into her best Robert Duvall. "Air cav, son. Air mobile."

Charlene walked her head through all of that. The Dharmas, now comfortable helping the Envoys and Vigils with the heavy lifting of restoring The Commons to its rightful working order, emerged from turtle mode after Brill's fall. No longer were they purely on the defensive. They'd upped their weaponry as The Commons cooperated and provided them with more. Now they had combat choppers and came riding to the rescue to smash the Ravager armor.

"Try to sit up, Charlene," said Beatrice.

Charlene obeyed, pushing herself up against the steel rack of the bed's headboard and adjusting the pillow behind her. There was nothing fast about the process. Her head made sure of that.

"Good. Now just sit with that a while, and see how you do."

Compliance wasn't in doubt. Charlene had not a spare drop of energy or will left after making herself comfortable. And the low swoop of another chopper drumming across the roof followed by the impact of another tank swept from the board was a reminder that her head might resume aching at any time. She wasn't going anywhere.

"Nicolette carried you here," Beatrice said. "You can thank her for the fact that you're not convalescing on a steel shelf next to boxes of toner. I couldn't have done it on my own."

Charlene nodded her thanks to Nicolette, whose dancing-bear uniform patch had been updated. Not only did the bear now sport a ranger hat, but it was flanked by a winged insignia. "You're gonna have to fill me in on your upgrades."

"I shall—and you're welcome." Nicolette crossed her legs, bouncing the toe of her standard-issue at vibration speed. She was more keyed up than usual, and Charlene couldn't help but wonder how recently that change had come about. "You'll get to return the favor soon enough—as soon as you're able."

Charlene closed her eyes, and Beatrice laid hands on her temples once again. The improvement was almost immediate.

"How so?" Charlene kept her eyes closed, both to help with the healing and to steel herself for whatever the Dharmas might need from the Envoys, Vigils, or both.

Not that they didn't deserve the help, of course. It was just that Charlene didn't feel like she'd be in any shape to help at all for a few months. And there was grieving to do. People were dead on her watch. She'd have to make peace with that when it inevitably came calling in the middle of the night.

"Would you like to be alone for a while?" Beatrice's fingers continued to travel the contours of Charlene's head and face, their soothing presence a balm for the external pain but useless against what ailed her within.

"I already would've helped you with whatever you need." Charlene opened her eyes briefly and let Beatrice know with a look that she was fine with the Dharma's continued presence. "And with you bailing our asses out, I'm even happier to do so

—after an accounting of our situation and a proper send-off for our people."

"Understood. We'd do the same for ours. A couple things. First, where did those Ravager tanks come from, considering the men in black were supposed to be gone with Brill? I'm hoping Porter and the monk might be able to help us do some sniffing around."

"They're both gone." At the look on Nicolette's face, Charlene understood what she'd just said. "No, no—out in the field. Incommunicado."

Nicolette relaxed.

"Sorry. My head's not working, remember?" Charlene gave Beatrice the most grateful smile she could muster when the healer removed her hands from her face. "You said a couple. What's the other?"

"We have our own incommunicado issue." Nicolette rested her arms on her knees. "If you recall—and I'm sure you do—we live in what was originally a nuclear-launch facility. Our closest neighbors are a few dozen Cold War–era ICBMs—Minuteman missiles—give or take a few dozen more. We don't like to give out exact numbers. Mostly because they change when they feel like it. Almost always upward."

"Right." Charlene didn't like the sound of this.

"They have a whole interface structure. Mainly a status report that lets us know they're still online, functional, and able to be communicated with."

"Right."

"Thing about it is, they may be functional, but they're not online anymore."

"Meaning?"

Nicolette stood, paced across the room to look at a blank bulletin board on the wall, and studied it. "Meaning they've gone dark on us. We talk to them, but they don't talk back. Not anymore." She returned to her chair and sank into it. "Or maybe they're not even there."

"What?"

"Either the birds have disappeared from their silos, or they no longer respond to us." Nicolette drummed her feet on the ground. "We don't know which."

IMPOTABLE EXCRETA

Truitt had coffee, bagels, and doughnuts delivered, but Jeremy had no appetite. The old man's smile, twisted by the knowledge that Jeremy had been reading Abel's journal, killed any desire to snack. Truitt also called Jeremy's attention to the row of focusites on the ceiling —there so they could get a good whiff of Jeremy's thoughts and feelings.

Jeremy fought to keep down the hard-boiled egg and microwave chicken sausage he'd eaten earlier in the morning.

Truitt raised an eyebrow at Jeremy's choice of decaf, poured only so he'd have the cup between him and the boss.

Caffeine was out of the question, given Jeremy's nerves.

"No jump-juice for you, Mr. Johns?" Truitt chuckled but didn't wait for Jeremy to answer. "I understand. Though you needn't be nervous about this discussion. Not right off." One of the focusites above gave a brief chirp; Truitt smirked briefly. "Our friends respond to subversion and lies, you know. That one seems to feel there's some untruth to my saying you needn't be nervous. How does that make you feel, Mr. Johns? Nervous?"

Jeremy's throat went dry. He took a sip of the decaf. Why did the body turn on you when it was needed most? "I needn't be nervous despite my choice of reading, sir?" He surprised himself by leading with that question. He'd intended to dance around the worst of it for at least a few exchanges. He'd never been the best of planners.

"No." Truitt broke a sugar doughnut into quarters and placed them in a perfectly spaced configuration on the little plate in front of him—a real-life blow-out diagram of a pastry. One of the focusites coughed, and Truitt frowned up at it. "Not necessarily. You're allowed to read and think whatever you want." Another focusite chirped, but Truitt ignored it. "It's how you act that can be problematic. That's where Mr. Dowd made his mistake."

Now the focusite began a soft, low whistle.

A glare from Truitt shut it up.

"There's a lot there, sir." Jeremy quartered his own doughnut, broke the pieces in half, and began distributing the eighths just as neatly around the plate. Distributing, but never taking a bite. "I haven't even made a dent in it."

Truitt broke one of his doughnut quarters in half, then did the same with the resulting eighths. Remarkably, he managed to produce straight-edged tears without a hint of a ragged edge. It made what had already been an unsettling encounter even more disconcerting. "No? I suppose that may be for the best, though it wouldn't do any harm to see where Mr. Dowd may have started down the road to the inappropriate—the details of which I'll not spell out for you, in case you were planning to ask."

Jeremy hadn't planned any such thing. He saw no reason to express an interest in why Abel had to be dealt with. "I understand, sir. If I may, though, is Abel all right? May I see him or talk to him?"

Truitt put his lips to his coffee mug, shrank back from the heat and blew on it briefly, then took a sip and grimaced. "I've yet to encounter brewers who are less consistent in their quality than our friends next door. Just when I decide to open an account with them, they send us this impotable excreta. It doesn't do my trust issues much good, I must say."

Jeremy eyed his own decaf but said nothing. Now he had an excuse to avoid drinking it.

Truitt laid his doughnut sixteenths out in yet another perfect circular configuration. "Well, that's a pass on the first test, anyway."

"Sir?"

Truitt dumped the doughnut pieces and the plate into the trash can and sat back to regard Jeremy from a slightly greater distance. "The focusites." His eyes twinkled with amusement; he knew Jeremy thought he'd meant the doughnut-tearing. "They've given me a bit of a time, but not you. They're very good detectors of lies, rebellious inclination, skepticism, and even thin slivers of doubt. So far, there's nothing but silence from them when it comes to you." He dumped his mug and all of its coffee into the can, too. "So let's talk, shall we?"

Jeremy's throat went dry again. He eyed his decaf but really didn't want any.

"The Margins, Mr. Johns. An obstacle that needs to be dealt with as soon as possible, particularly since we're talking about the end of existence if we don't solve the puzzle. Luckily, we have."

"We have?" The hell with it. Jeremy took another sip.

"And we've got a plan. It's going to take some doing, though, and you may be able to help."

Jeremy didn't know what to make of that. He'd been lucky to have Abel bring him into the fold. He'd feared his luck had turned once Truitt discovered he'd been reading the journal.

But was it possible he might now be an integral part of the team? "How may I help, sir?"

Truitt folded his hands over his chest. "Let's review." He gave the edge of his desk a light swat. The room faded to black, and a Venn diagram with two intersecting sets made of colored light appeared in the air before them. "The Commons," Truitt said, and one circle glowed a bit brighter for a moment. "The Living World." The other did the same. "And The Margins." The intersection of the two glowed. "You know the high view."

The lines of The Margins broke up into dotted lines to illustrate the porousness of the barriers between the realms in the post-Brill world. The gaps were numerous.

"Let us give thanks for the simple-minded heroism of people such as Paul Reid, without whom we'd never be able to execute any of our nefarious schemes. Thanks to him and his ideals, we can pull the fantastic powers available in The Commons into The L.W. and avail ourselves of the vast amounts of Essence here."

The intersection representing The Margins began to glow once more, pulling light in from both The Living World and The Commons.

"Herein lies our problem," said Truitt. "We never foresaw the formation of The Margins. Too many people are being pulled out of our reach, along with the Essence of the dearly departed who are being diverted elsewhere." He waited while the dotted lines of the intersection began to subtly flash. "Unless we seal the unwanted gaps and stop the further expansion of The Margins, maintaining only the breaches we control. That's where we may need you, Mr. Johns."

"I'll contribute in any way I can, sir."

Truitt showed his teeth in a manner that indicated he was

pleased. Jeremy wouldn't have gone so far as to call it a smile. "Will you?"

Would he? Good question. People, organizations, and nations brought about their downfall when the gap between what they said and what they did grew wide enough to swallow them. Now was the moment when Jeremy would either choose to widen his own or make a break from Manitou and everyone in it and pray they forgot about him.

He didn't like the odds of the latter's success. Yet he knew there'd be no going back if he chose to move forward with Truitt.

He was kidding himself. There hadn't been any way out for a while now. Abel could've told him that—had Truitt and Manitou left Abel capable of telling him anything. There was no real decision to be made.

"Yes, sir," Jeremy told Truitt before the silence went on long enough to answer for him, selling it the best he could. "Thank you for your faith in me."

Truitt flashed his teeth again. His amusement was about as comforting as his displays of pleasure. "No one said anything about faith, Mr. Johns. You won't find much of that in these halls. However, we will rely on you should new challenges arise and surprise us. I hate surprises. Don't you?"

Jeremy let his silence indicate that he did—now more than ever.

"Well, that's not completely true," said Truitt. "I hate surprises when I'm not springing them, which brings me to one we've got brewing. Are you at all familiar with the name Harold Hering, Mr. Johns?"

"I am not, sir."

"Air force man. Decorated. After distinguishing himself over several tours in Vietnam, Mr. Hering was training for missile duty during the Nixon administration—to turn one of the keys for a nuclear launch when so ordered. But he asked an important question: how do I know the order has come from a sane president? What safeguard is in place to guarantee a crazy person isn't telling me to do this?"

Jeremy considered that. "A fair point," he said.

"Agreed. So what do you think the air force did?" Truitt didn't wait for Jeremy to guess. "They kicked him out." He chortled and waved his hand in the dark. "And lucky for us they did, or our plan might have gone nowhere."

The Margins diagram began to shift, its colors fading. The circles blurred, spread out, and began to coalesce into a black-and-white photo. Truitt waited until it sharpened to the point where there was no mistaking what it was. "This," he said, "is a Minuteman missile. You're going to be better acquainted with a rather large number of these. And so is all of existence." He aimed his teeth at Jeremy once again in a rictus of cold satisfaction.

It occurred to Jeremy that Truitt would not hesitate to use those teeth on somebody.

"Surprise," Truitt said.

THAT KIND OF HELP

There were two kinds of being afraid—one Zach could do something about and one he couldn't.

On a Wednesday in the spring at Ambit, a boy named Rory Kinealy had walked over to Zach and gave him a push. Another, Everett Allen, was waiting behind Zach on hands and knees.

Zach fell over backward, smacking his head on the hard turf at the edge of the playground. Rory and Everett hadn't checked to see where he'd land. It was just dumb luck they hadn't pushed him the other way. He'd have hit his head on the asphalt tetherball court.

Zach picked himself up and checked his tongue where he'd bitten it to make sure he wasn't bleeding.

Everett and Rory laughed and laughed. Then Rory, realizing Zach wasn't going to do anything, shoved him again, and they walked away.

The next day, in a different spot on the playground, Rory approached Zach again. Zach waited until Rory had both hands up to push him and punched him in the stomach as hard as he could.

Rory doubled over, and Zach turned around to find Everett behind him, as expected, on hands and knees again. He kicked Everett in the ribs before the boy could get up. Then he grabbed Rory, who was too busy sucking wind to defend himself, whipped him around and pushed him on top of Everett, where he squirmed on the ground, holding his side.

Both boys cried as Zach stood over them.

That was a fear you could do something about.

The other kind was being trapped in the middle of a fight between adults and tiny men while bullets crisscrossed everywhere. The kind where Gun Girl grabbed Zach's mother, who had blood streaming down her face, and pulled her up the steps with help from a big man from the train, yelling, "Med car! Med car!"

The kind where another train man told Zach to get up the stairs and, when Zach didn't move fast enough, threw Zach over his shoulder and carried him. Zach made sure the marble didn't fall out of his pocket.

"Sorry, kid," the train man said as he walked Zach into a car filled almost all the way with people, only some of whom turned to look as they entered. The train man set him down next to an empty seat. "You stay right here," he said. "I'm gonna check on your mom, and Rain will be back. All right?"

Zach could still hear shots as the fight outside continued.

"They're gonna slaughter them!" one of the train men yelled from somewhere. "Cover!" At that, there was more shooting, much of it sounding as if it came from the train.

Boom! The roof guns fired. Then again and again.

Zach watched the train man who'd carried him. The train man was trying to make Zach feel better, trying to pretend the shooting wasn't happening, but he wasn't used to talking to kids. He definitely wasn't used to talking to kids like Zach.

Zach liked the train man anyway. At least he tried. Usually, if grown-ups weren't prepared to deal with kids like Zach or weren't around them much, they got that look in their eyes as it dawned on them that Zach wasn't normal.

Then they didn't know how to talk to him at all.

Then they didn't try.

Even though it was awkward, Zach respected those who cared enough to give it a shot. He wanted the train man to know it was okay. This fear was the kind you couldn't do anything about. So you nodded at it and admitted to yourself it was there. Then you put it on the seat next to you and tried to keep it from biting.

Zach really, really wanted Zach's mother to be okay. She hadn't looked it. At all.

But there was nothing he could do. So he stayed away from the fear—from the fear and its sharp teeth, which wanted a chunk of him.

A zinging, whining sound came from the metal slats over a window farther toward the front of the car. Bullets. Bullets that wouldn't make it inside.

But the black-truck men had more than those. Or would soon.

The train man stood there, studying Zach as the train started to move.

Zach wanted to let him know he was all right. So he reached up and gave the train man a light punch on the shoulder and tried to force a small smile across his face. All he succeeded in doing was curving the corners of his closed mouth up a little, but it seemed like it worked.

The train man looked surprised. Then he returned the light chuck to Zach's shoulder and attempted a smile of his own before he left the car.

Zach trusted people who, like him, had a hard time smiling when they didn't mean it.

As the train began to go a little faster, Zach looked around the car at the other people. Almost all of them were grown-ups, but there were a few teenagers and children scattered throughout.

Nobody looked at him, not even the other kids. All of them seemed lost in their own worlds, which was a strange thing for Zach to think since that's what I'm-Bobby always said about *him*. It wasn't true, but it was true of these people.

They all sat quietly, staring into space, as if deep in thought but not sure what those thoughts were. At one point, a lady across the car turned to look at Zach, but their eyes didn't quite meet. She was looking through him. Then she looked away.

The train picked up speed quickly and the booming of the roof guns stopped as the sound of the wheels changed, becoming deeper, with more of an echo. Zach guessed they were in a tunnel. That's what the trains he and Zach's mother took sounded like when they left the station. Only the windows in those trains weren't blocked by metal shades, so you could see the darkness of the tunnel and know for sure you were in one.

Sometimes on those trains, Zach didn't know if they'd ever come to another station, if they'd ever emerge from the dark tunnel. He wasn't sure he wanted to.

He never told anyone that.

They wouldn't understand.

They couldn't understand.

And they wouldn't have understood the difference between Zach and the people around him in the car. Zach wandered. These people were lost.

There was a difference.

The train began to go uphill slightly. The fear Zach put next to him on the seat tried to take a nip. He pushed it away.

Zach took the marble out of his pocket and studied it. It had been very, very important to him once, and for a time, it had even had power. Zach couldn't be sure if that power had gone forever or if it was just sleeping, but he thought that the marble might again be important to him someday. It had been something between Zach and Zach's mother, and that was important. There was a feeling that the marble had more to say.

The fear tried to get a grip on Zach again.

He pushed it away.

The train continued to climb, and the sound of the air around it changed again. There was less of an echo, and light now crept in through some of the tiny gaps between the metal shades and the edges of the windows. They were up and out of the tunnel.

The door to the car opened, and Gun Girl came in. She looked tired. There was a big bandage taped to the side of her neck, and she had blood on her sleeve.

Zach knew whose blood it was.

He pushed the fear away again.

"Hi, Zach," Gun Girl said. "Can I sit down?"

Zach moved over in the seat. It was where Zach had put the fear, but he wasn't worried. Fear would find a space for itself until it was made to go away. It always did.

Gun Girl sat down and watched Zach for a moment.

He looked back at her, into her eyes. He liked her as much as he liked the train man. No, more than the train man, even. When she watched him, she wasn't afraid to just sit. It wasn't that she didn't know how to talk to him. She was just letting the time pass.

Gun Girl didn't want anything from Zach, didn't want him to do anything for her. That was why he liked Gun Girl.

"My name is Rain, Zach."

Rain. Gun Girl was Rain.

Zach didn't like to use the names people told him to use because he understood, just as so many people didn't understand, that real names could be dangerous in the wrong places for different reasons. You had to be really careful with them.

But Zach liked Gun Girl, and he believed it might make her happy if he thought of her how she wanted to be thought of. She seemed like someone who didn't have people do that for her much. So Zach would do it.

Rain.

"Your mom got really lucky. The bullet just grazed her. It was a lot of blood and there are stitches. It'll also hurt for a while, but she'll be fine." She touched the bandage on her neck. "Me, too. I got a piece of something, but it's not that bad."

Zach said nothing.

The fear had starved. It was gone now.

"Are you okay, Zach?" Rain seemed to know he wouldn't answer, so she took his hand in hers and held it. Usually, he hated that, but he was glad she did. It seemed to make her feel better.

Zach remembered Rain. He wondered if she remembered him. He also didn't think too much about it because that brought back the dragon fish.

He never wanted to bring back the dragon fish.

"If you're afraid—"

Boom!

A rooftop gun cut her off.

Boom-boom-boom!

Others joined in, and there was no point in Rain trying to talk.

As if replying, something slammed into the train. It had to

have been several cars up or down from them, but theirs shook with the impact. Hard.

Whup-whup-whup.

Helicopters.

Close.

Right over them.

The rooftop guns started firing fast and steady.

The people in the car with them just kept staring into space. They didn't know what was happening. Or they didn't want anyone to know they knew. Or they didn't care.

Zach cared.

Something hit the train again. This time, their car pitched up at an angle before smacking down to level again, everything shaking.

Zach cared. And now the fear was back.

Rain was afraid, too. She put both arms around Zach and pulled him to her.

He didn't know whether she did it for him or for her, but it helped. He hoped it helped her, too.

Boom-boom-boom-boom-boom!

The train's guns fired.

The helicopters fired back.

The train shook as it was hit again.

They heard booms in the distance.

"Our boys got a couple." Rain hugged him harder.

There was nowhere to put this fear. It was nothing but booming.

Loud.

Coming from the train.

Hitting the train.

Threatening to enter.

The train was tough. There was something that wasn't

normal about it being able to withstand what was being done to it, but the shaking and tilting got worse.

Zach worried that the train wouldn't be able to keep going, that the attacks were too much.

Rain held on to Zach so hard it hurt, but he didn't stop her. He wanted to help.

Booming from the train.

Helicopters back and forth.

Shaking. Tilting.

Everything loud.

Rain began saying something to herself that Zach couldn't hear, and he was pretty sure he wasn't supposed to hear it. It wasn't for him. It was for her.

Rain was scared, which made Zach even more afraid. And she didn't try to tell him it was going to be all right.

The booming and shaking got worse. Zach thought for sure that the train was going to come apart.

Then came a flash of orange light. And even though it came only through the small gaps between the metal shades and the windows' edges, it was so bright Zach had to close his eyes.

Bright and hot.

The car got so hot so fast.

It wasn't. Then it was.

It was a heat Zach couldn't stand.

Rain made a noise of surprise and fear.

So did Zach.

Hot.

So hot.

Zach had worried about the train not being able to take it. Now he was sure that he and Rain wouldn't, either.

The window of the seat in front of them cracked.

Zach thought that was it, anyway. He heard the tinkle of glass.

Then it stopped.

The light faded.

The train didn't get any hotter.

They'd made it through whatever that had been, whatever had been done with them.

The booming of the rooftop guns stopped, too. Nothing else hit the train.

There was no more tilting or slamming down, though there was a thudding from a car or two away that sounded like a wheel had gone bad.

Rain's grip on Zach loosened. He let her go, too, and she leaned back in her seat.

They watched one another, each checking that the other was all right as the train began to cool.

Rain looked like she was trying to figure out what happened, but with a sudden clarity, Zach understood.

Apalala-Aidan had said he would help if he could.

That was the fire.

Apalala-Aidan had seemed like something much bigger than what was in Zach's closet.

He was.

So much bigger.

New things to know.

Gun Girl was Rain.

And Apalala-Aidan was a dragon.

The train rumbled on as best it could, wounded though it was.

And Zach knew for certain that he never wanted that kind of help from anyone or anything ever again.

~

ALSO BY MICHAEL ALAN PECK

The Journeyman (The Commons, Book 1)
The Catalyst (The Commons, Book 3)

∽

Read on for a preview of The Catalyst

PREVIEW: THE CATALYST
THE COMMONS, BOOK 3

The Darkness left the safety of the shadows. It crossed to the water to seek out the Tree. It had to find the Tree before the light found the Darkness—of that the Darkness was certain.

The Darkness had knowledge but enjoyed only limited access to it. The memories and details resided inside the Darkness, but the Darkness couldn't reach them. Or wasn't permitted to. The Darkness wasn't privy to what was being kept away from it, by whom, or why. Nor did the Darkness know its purpose—if it had one.

The Darkness focused on the task at hand, which was hazardous enough. All tasks outside the shadowy safe zone meant evading the sun, which wanted to kill the Darkness.

The Darkness dwelt deep in the shade in the place of peace, where the sunlight that called the place of peace home could not get to it. The sunlight didn't want the Darkness to be there. It wanted to burn the Darkness out.

Thus was the game played, and it was a simple game at that. The Darkness hurried to the water, next to where the sunlight lived. The Darkness needed the light in order to see the reflection of the Tree in the water's surface—and not just the Tree but the door in its side that allowed the Darkness to travel. Then the Darkness had to hope that the Tree would grant it admission so that it could bridge the gap to wherever it was required to be.

The Darkness never knew its destination before its arrival. It trusted the Tree to accept it and take it somewhere where it would not face instant annihilation, such as a desert in the middle of a dead-cloudless day. It had no choice but to trust the Tree—that, too, the Darkness understood.

The Darkness knew what it wasn't, not what it was.

It was friend to none.

It had no place among the living.

It was neither welcome nor loved.

The Darkness fed. The Darkness was feared. The Darkness watched.

On rare occasion, the Darkness protected.

The Darkness knew neither of its true names. It could deduce that because it was enemy to light, then it was shadow. It also reasoned it was not one of the living because of the beings whose lives it had witnessed and ended.

Bird. Rat. Insect. Human. All of those the Darkness was not. All had names the Darkness knew without understanding.

The Darkness's familiarity with the tribe of living things was akin to the reading knowledge of a foreign language. It could absorb, but it could not comprehend. Not yet.

The Darkness did not understand why it thought what it thought or why it knew what it knew. Its memories were those of others, not of the Darkness. Some were accessible. Most were not. And perception was a rarity.

There was a word for the uncanny ability to understand a

language one shouldn't be able to understand, but that word eluded the Darkness.

So the Darkness crossed to the water and searched its surface for the Tree.

The sunbeam remained focused on the nearby bench, still unaware of the Darkness's emergence. The sunbeam was at home in the place of peace.

The Darkness had not been invited. Yet the Darkness belonged.

Sometimes the sun attempted to push its way into the shadows to cleanse the place of peace of the Darkness. Then the Darkness was forced to cower deep in the crevice in order to survive.

That was when the Darkness felt what it was to be prey. At all other times, it was the hunter.

The Tree made itself known to the Darkness on the surface of the water.

The sunbeam twitched, as if disturbed by the Darkness's proximity.

The Tree insisted on payment from others but never required anything of the Darkness. The Darkness suspected that perhaps whenever it traveled, something was being taken from it without it knowing. But it had no definite answer to that question, so it was just as if there were no question at all.

The door in the side of the Tree opened.

The sunbeam twitched again, widening now. It would be but an instant before it embraced the Darkness for the first and last time.

The Darkness stretched out over the water, toward the door in the Tree, as the sunlight came for it. It would be close.

At these times, when it wasn't clear whether the Darkness would travel or perish, it focused only on the unknown of its destination. Perhaps it would roam the underground to feed on the pincered creatures and other lower dwellers.

Part of the Darkness saw the killing as tragic necessity. Part craved prey of a higher order. All of it yearned for knowledge.

That was why, in its travels, the Darkness watched the man in the robe and the man who spoke with the waste stabber—the man the Darkness had saved from a fellow shadow beast. The Darkness didn't know why it had protected the man. That was another mystery locked away inside it.

The Darkness reached the Tree, and the sunlight reached the Darkness. There was pain, but then the Darkness was in the Tree and journeying away from the place of peace before the light could do any true harm.

Traveling.

Headed for sustenance.

And learning.

The Darkness needed to know its purpose. The Darkness had a part to play.

It didn't know why it knew that, but it knew. It still couldn't remember the word for how it knew, but that was of little consequence after all.

Things were going to move fast.

And already were.

∽

That they are.
See what's in store for Paul, Rain, Porter, Po, Annie, Zach, Jeremy, Charlene, and friends in The Catalyst *(The Commons, Book 3).*

ACKNOWLEDGMENTS

Few creative endeavors are isolated projects. So a heapin' helpin' of gratitude goes to those who pitched in this time around: Dan Fernandez (cover and graphic design); Irit Printz (feedback); Marti McKenna (editing); and Megan Christy (proofreading).

Thank you all.

Copyright © 2021 Michael Alan Peck

All rights reserved. No part of this book may be reproduced in any form or by any electronic or mechanical means, including information storage and retrieval systems, without written permission from the author, except for the use of brief quotations in a book review.

Dinuhos Arts, LLC
5315 N. Clark St., #230
Chicago, IL 60640

ISBN: 986082341
ISBN-13: 978-0-9860823-4-4

This is a work of fiction. Names, characters, businesses, places, events, and incidents are either the products of the author's imagination or used in a fictitious manner. Any resemblance to actual persons, living or dead, or actual events is purely coincidental.

Printed in Great Britain
by Amazon

56020817R00411